A MODERN GRAPHIC RETELLING OF *ANNE OF GREEN GABLES*

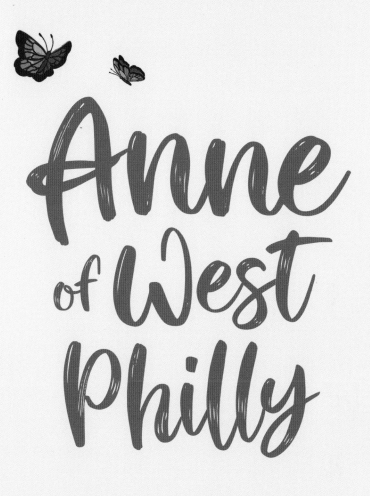

Anne
of West
Philly

A MODERN GRAPHIC RETELLING OF *ANNE OF GREEN GABLES*

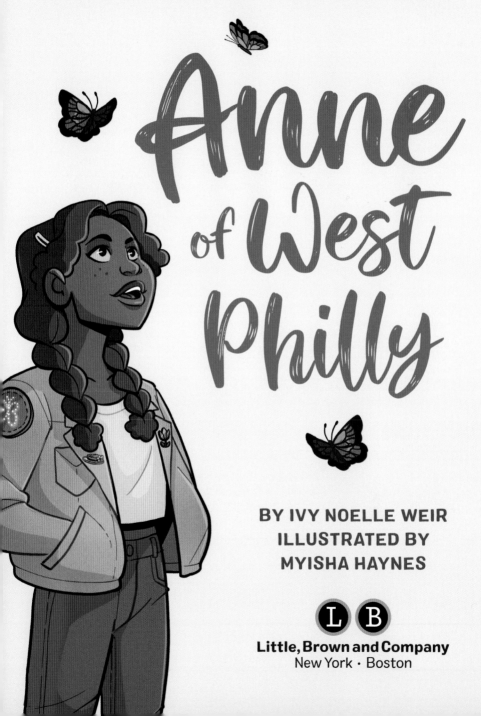

Anne *of West* Philly

BY IVY NOELLE WEIR

ILLUSTRATED BY

MYISHA HAYNES

L B

Little, Brown and Company

New York · Boston

About This Book

This book was edited by Rachel Poloski and designed by Ching N. Chan. The production was supervised by Bernadette Flinn, and the production editor was Lindsay Walter-Greaney. The text was set in Colby, and the display type is Westhouse.

Story by Ivy Noelle Weir; art by Myisha Haynes; colors by Edwin Surya W., Delanda Gracesya R., Angela Olivia, Dwi Febri Novita, Tannia Venansjah, and Trio Vilten of Caravan Studio
Sensitivity read by Steenz

Little, Brown and Company
Hachette Book Group
1290 Avenue of the Americas, New York, NY 10104
Visit us at LBYR.com

First Edition: March 2022

Little, Brown and Company is a division of Hachette Book Group, Inc.
The Little, Brown name and logo are trademarks of Hachette Book Group, Inc.

The publisher is not responsible for websites (or their content) that are not owned by the publisher.

Library of Congress Cataloging-in-Publication Data is available.

ISBNs: 978-0-316-45978-5 (hardcover), 978-0-316-45977-8 (paperback), 978-0-316-45974-7 (ebook), 978-0-316-45972-3 (ebook), 978-0-316-45975-4 (ebook)

PRINTED IN CHINA

1010

Hardcover: 10 9 8 7 6 5 4 3 2 1

Paperback: 10 9 8 7 6 5 4 3 2 1

For Hattie and Casper —INW

*To my loving family: Mom,
Dad, and Darion—the
Matthew to my Marilla—MH*

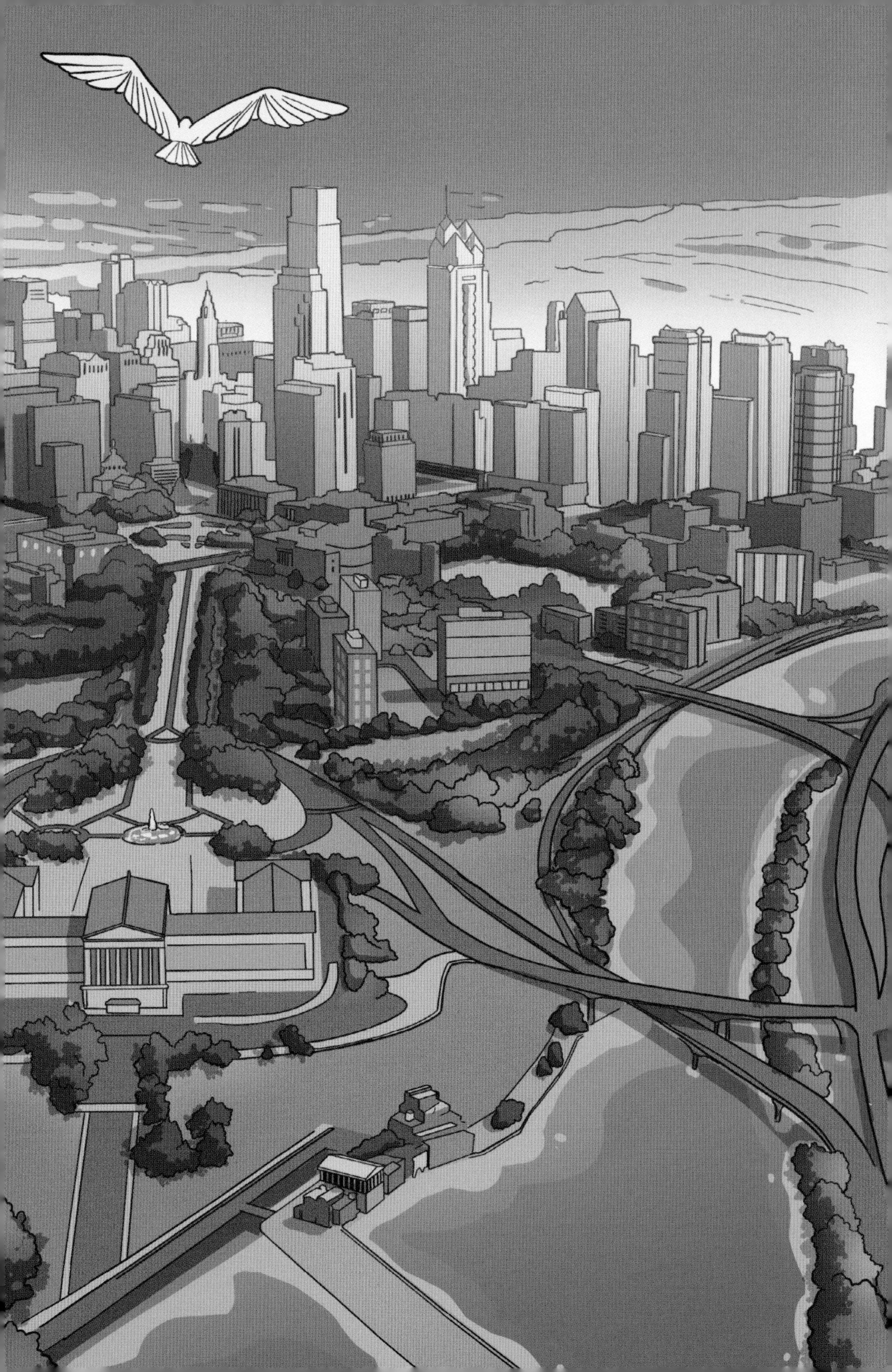

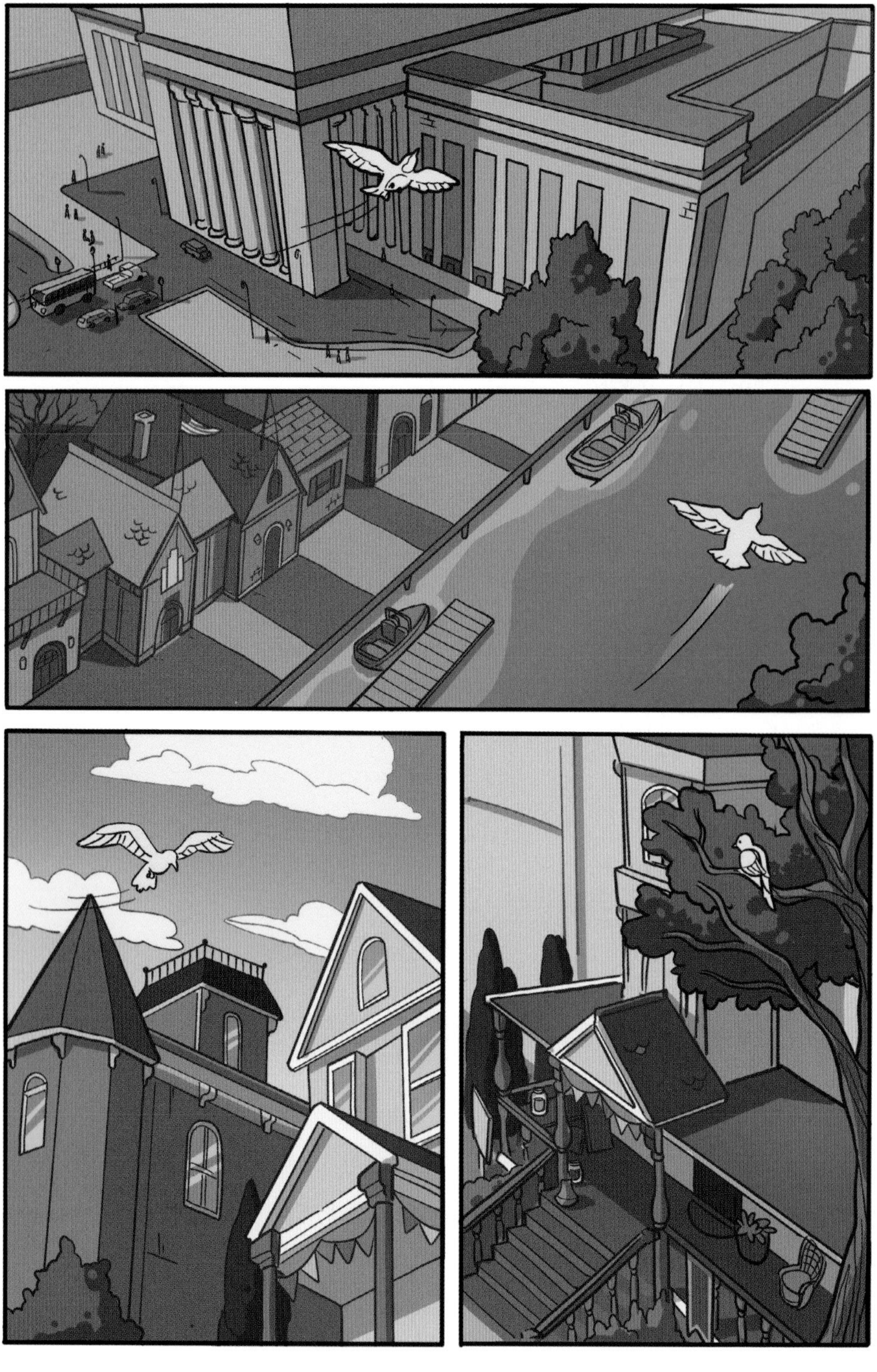

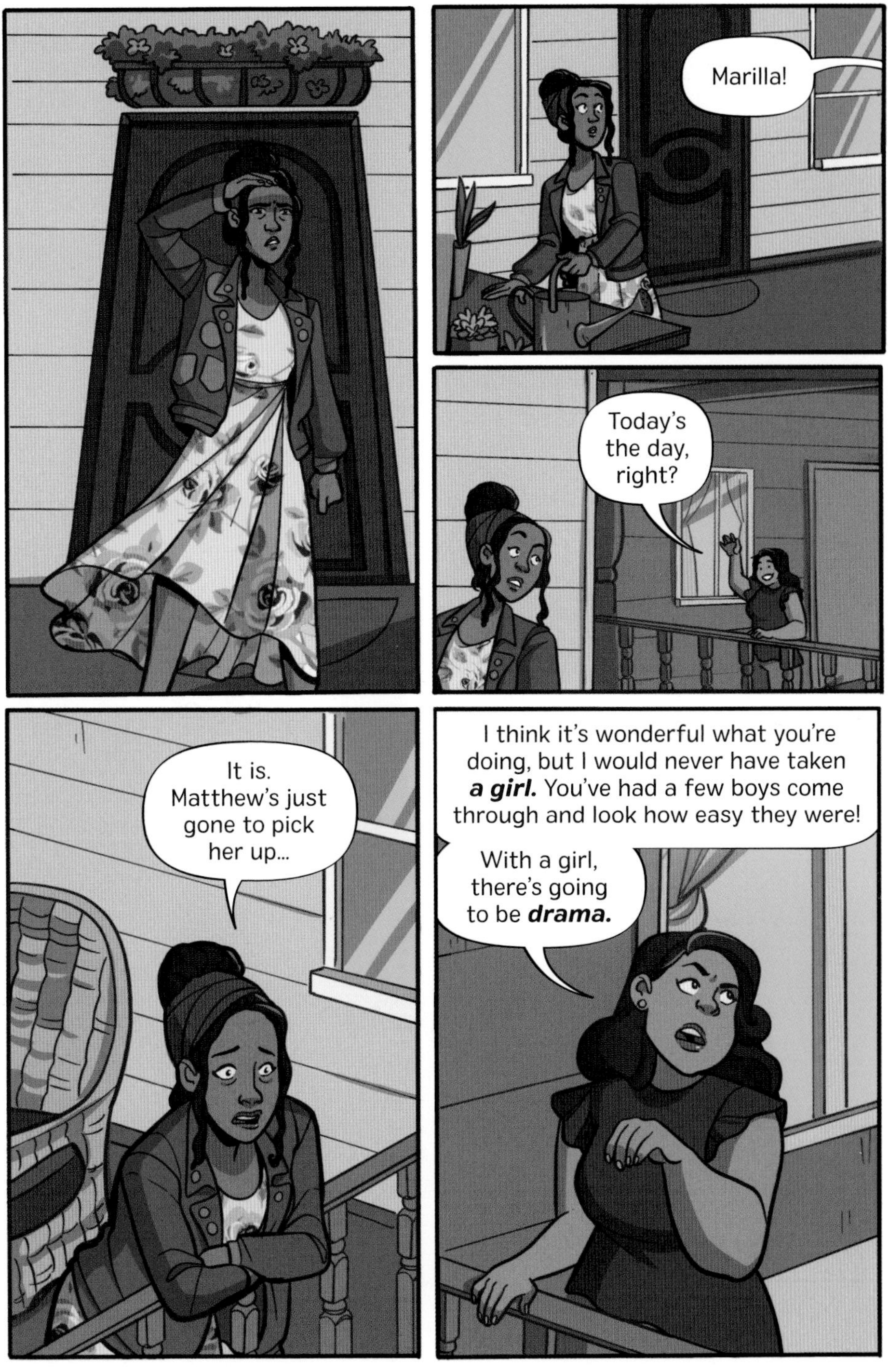
Marilla!
Today's the day, right?
It is. Matthew's just gone to pick her up...
I think it's wonderful what you're doing, but I would never have taken ***a girl.*** You've had a few boys come through and look how easy they were!
With a girl, there's going to be ***drama.***

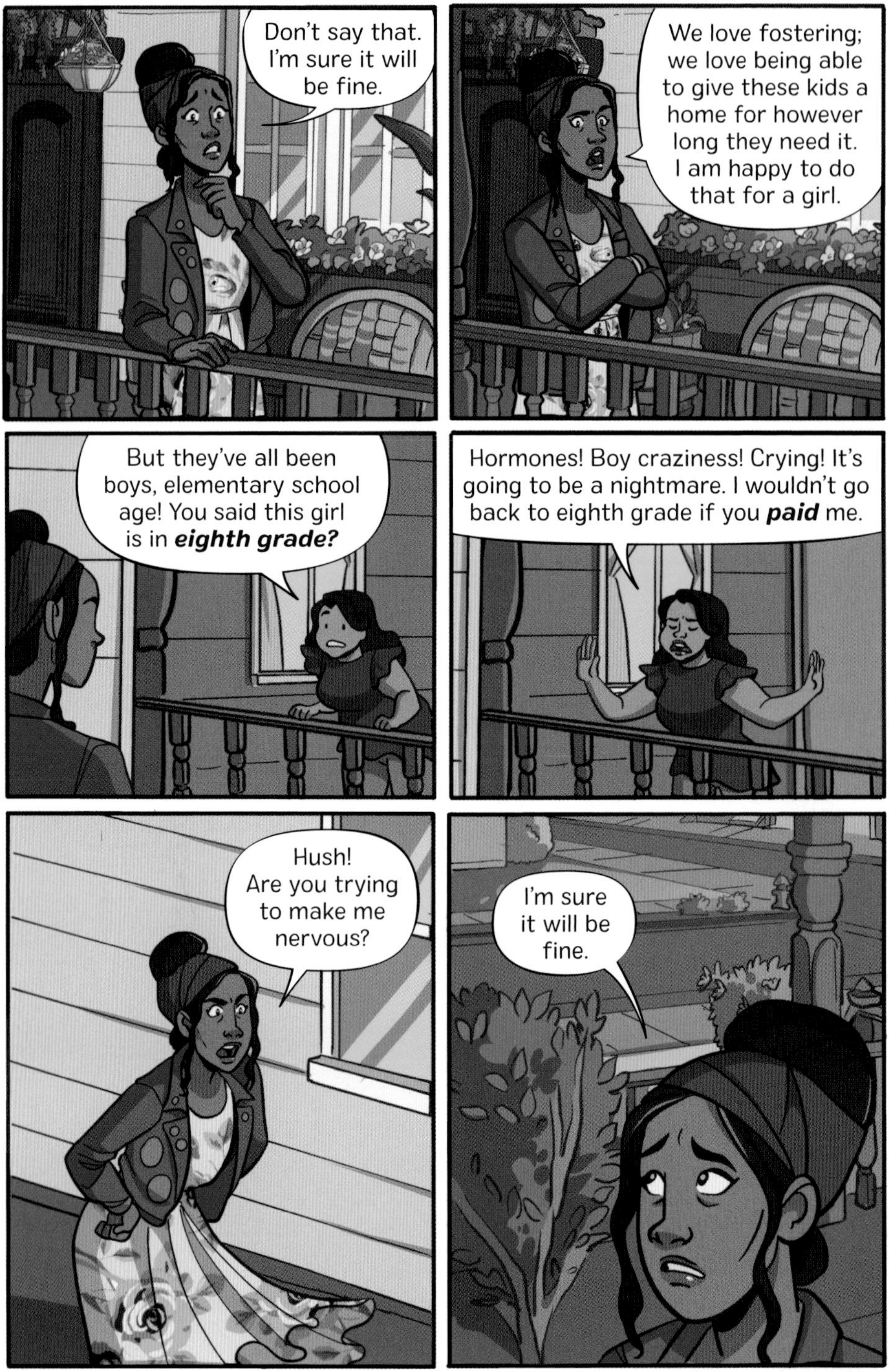
Don't say that. I'm sure it will be fine.
We love fostering; we love being able to give these kids a home for however long they need it. I am happy to do that for a girl.
But they've all been boys, elementary school age! You said this girl is in ***eighth grade?***
Hormones! Boy craziness! Crying! It's going to be a nightmare. I wouldn't go back to eighth grade if you ***paid*** me.
Hush! Are you trying to make me nervous?
I'm sure it will be fine.

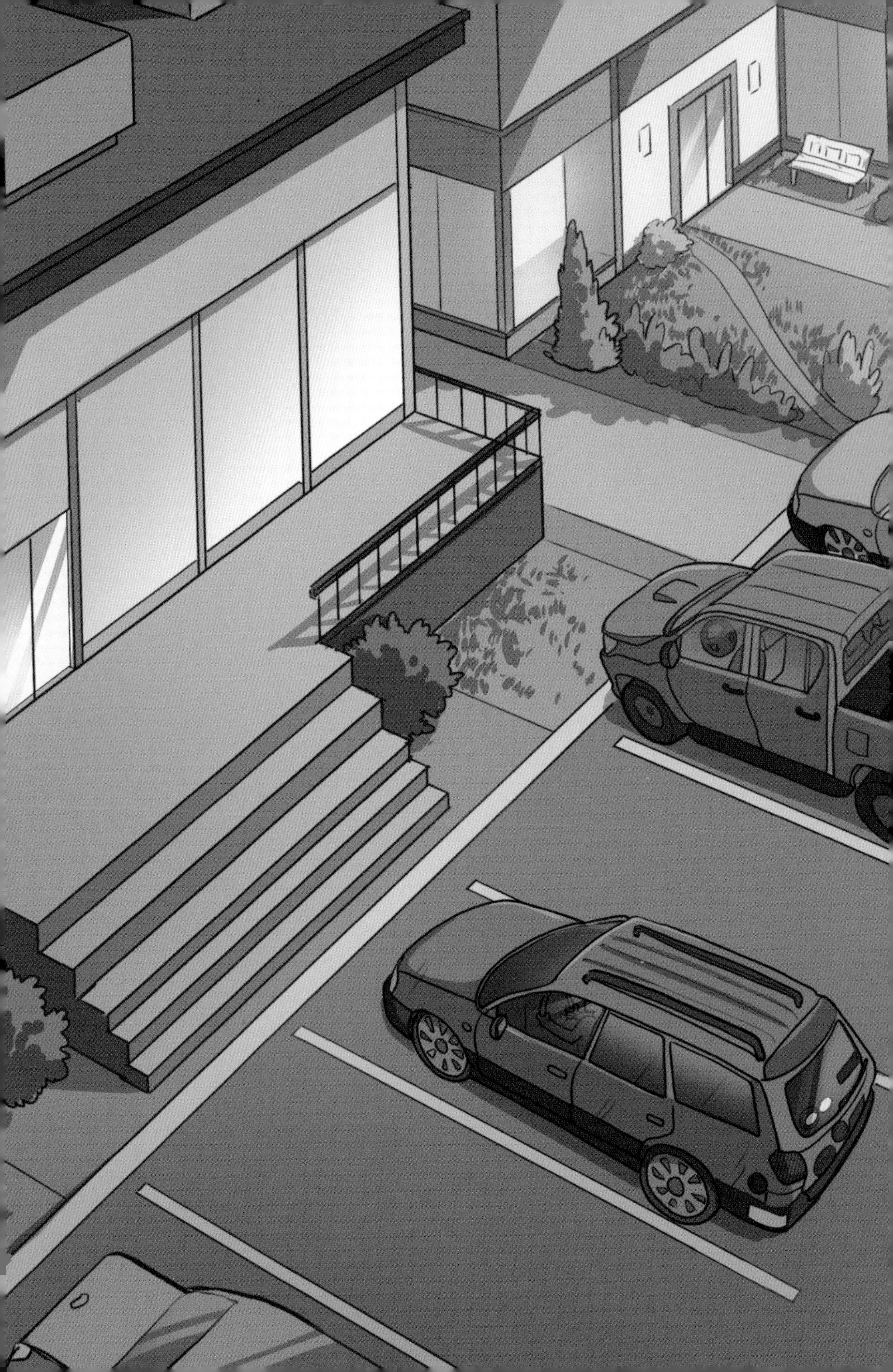

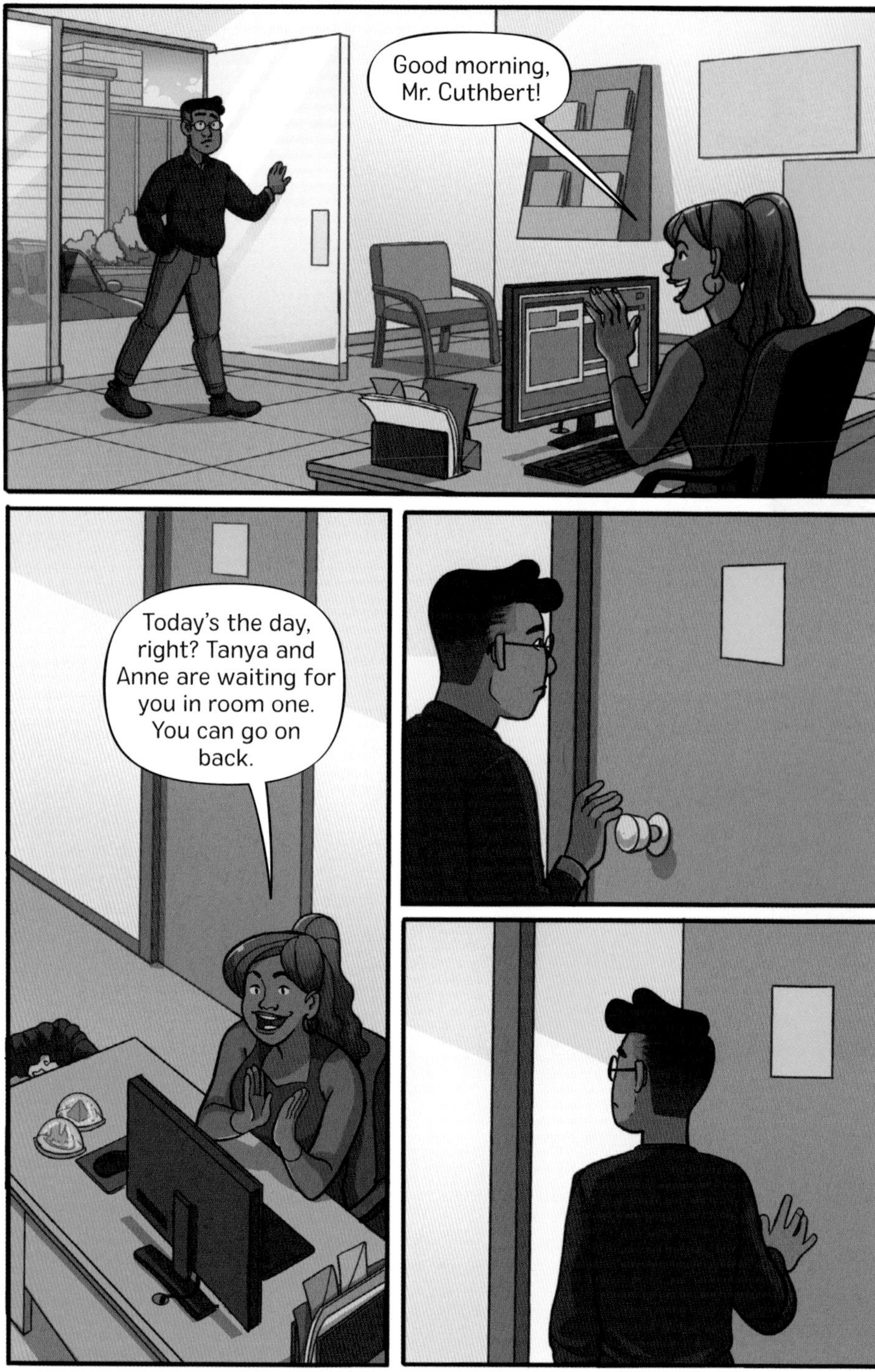
Good morning, Mr. Cuthbert!
Today's the day, right? Tanya and Anne are waiting for you in room one. You can go on back.

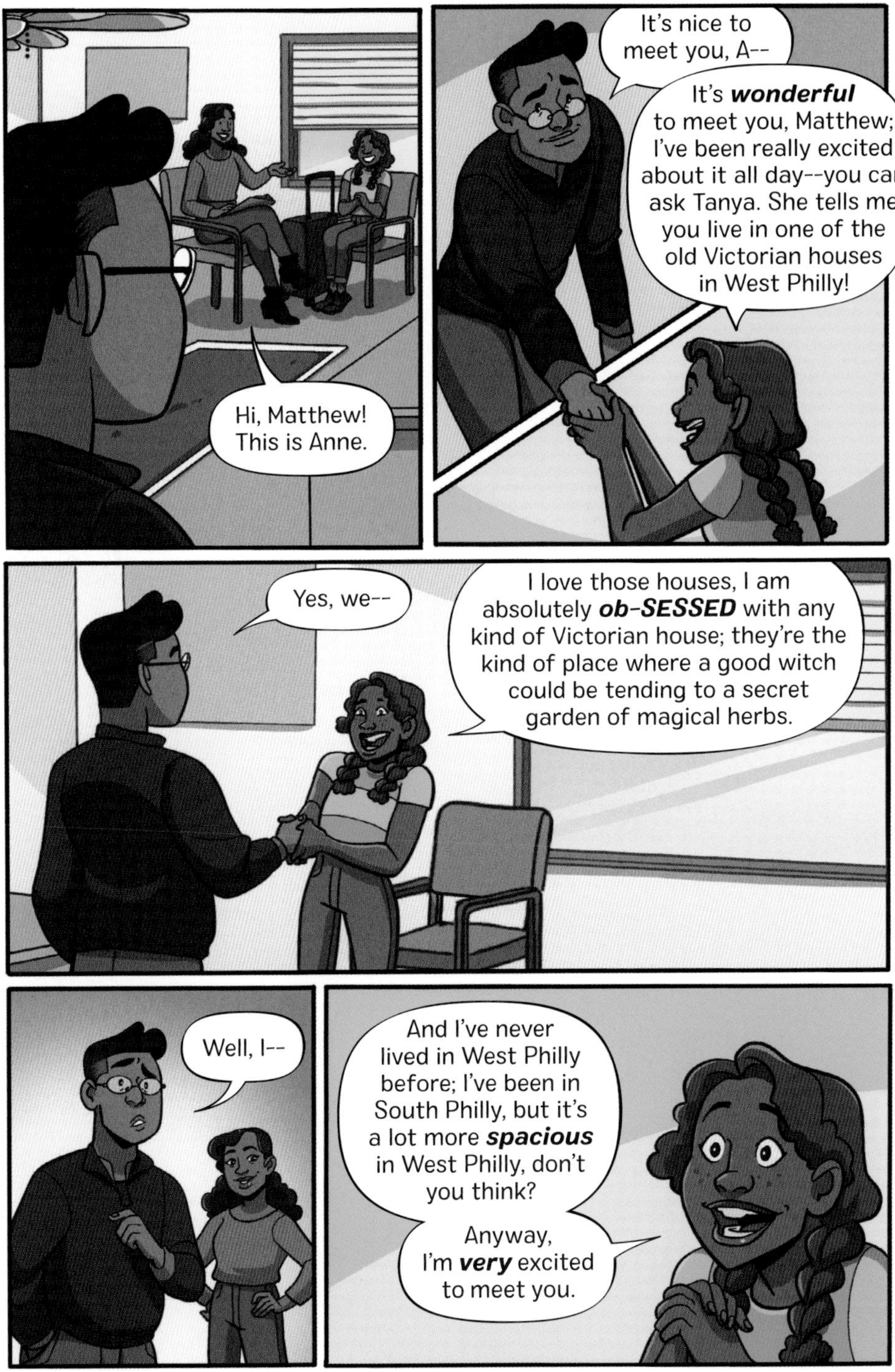
Hi, Matthew! This is Anne.
It's nice to meet you, A--
It's **wonderful** to meet you, Matthew; I've been really excited about it all day--you can ask Tanya. She tells me you live in one of the old Victorian houses in West Philly!
Yes, we--
I love those houses, I am absolutely **ob-SESSED** with any kind of Victorian house; they're the kind of place where a good witch could be tending to a secret garden of magical herbs.
Well, I--
And I've never lived in West Philly before; I've been in South Philly, but it's a lot more **spacious** in West Philly, don't you think?
Anyway, I'm **very** excited to meet you.

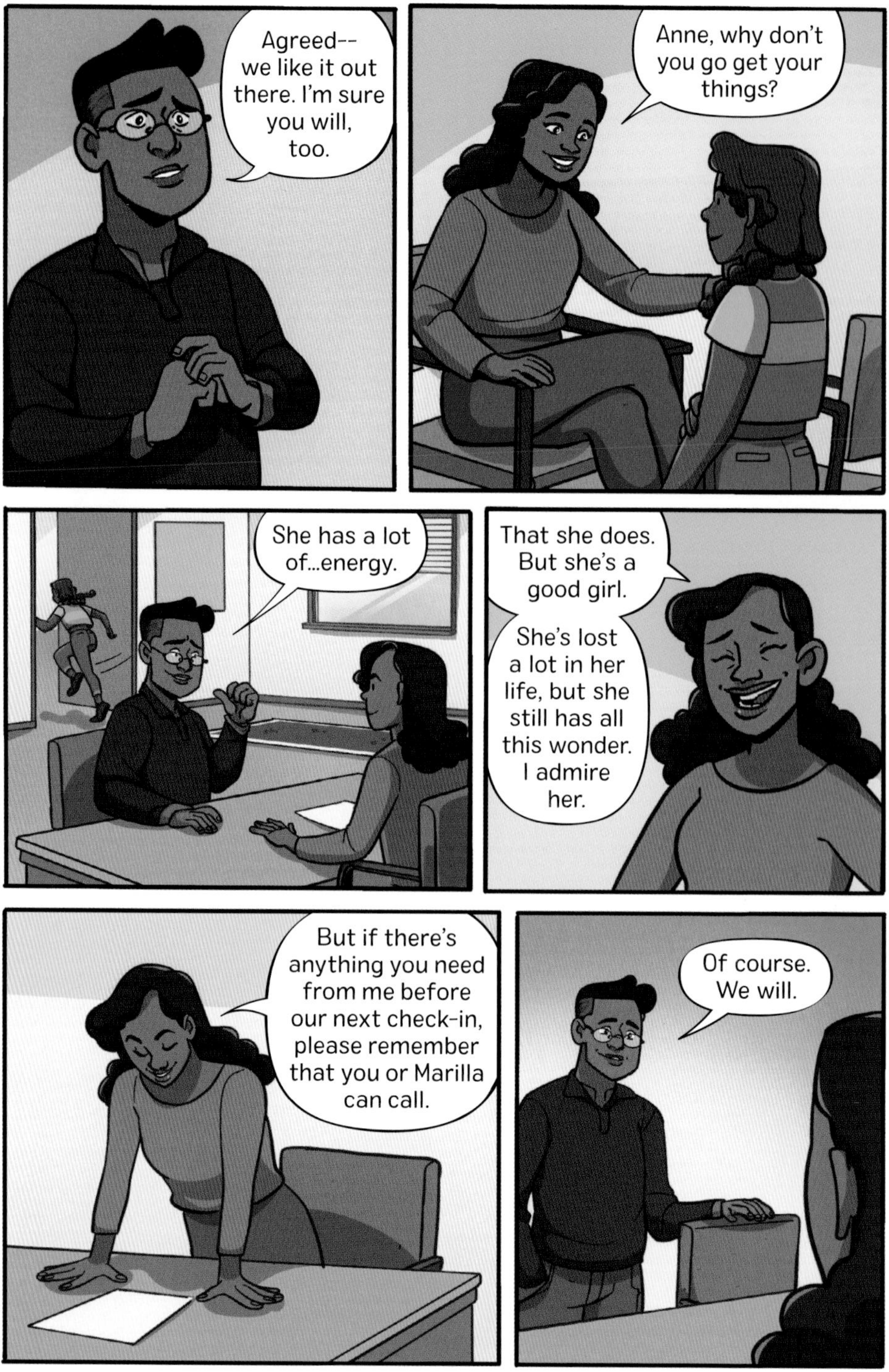

Agreed-- we like it out there. I'm sure you will, too.
Anne, why don't you go get your things?
She has a lot of...energy.
That she does. But she's a good girl.
She's lost a lot in her life, but she still has all this wonder. I admire her.
But if there's anything you need from me before our next check-in, please remember that you or Marilla can call.
Of course. We will.

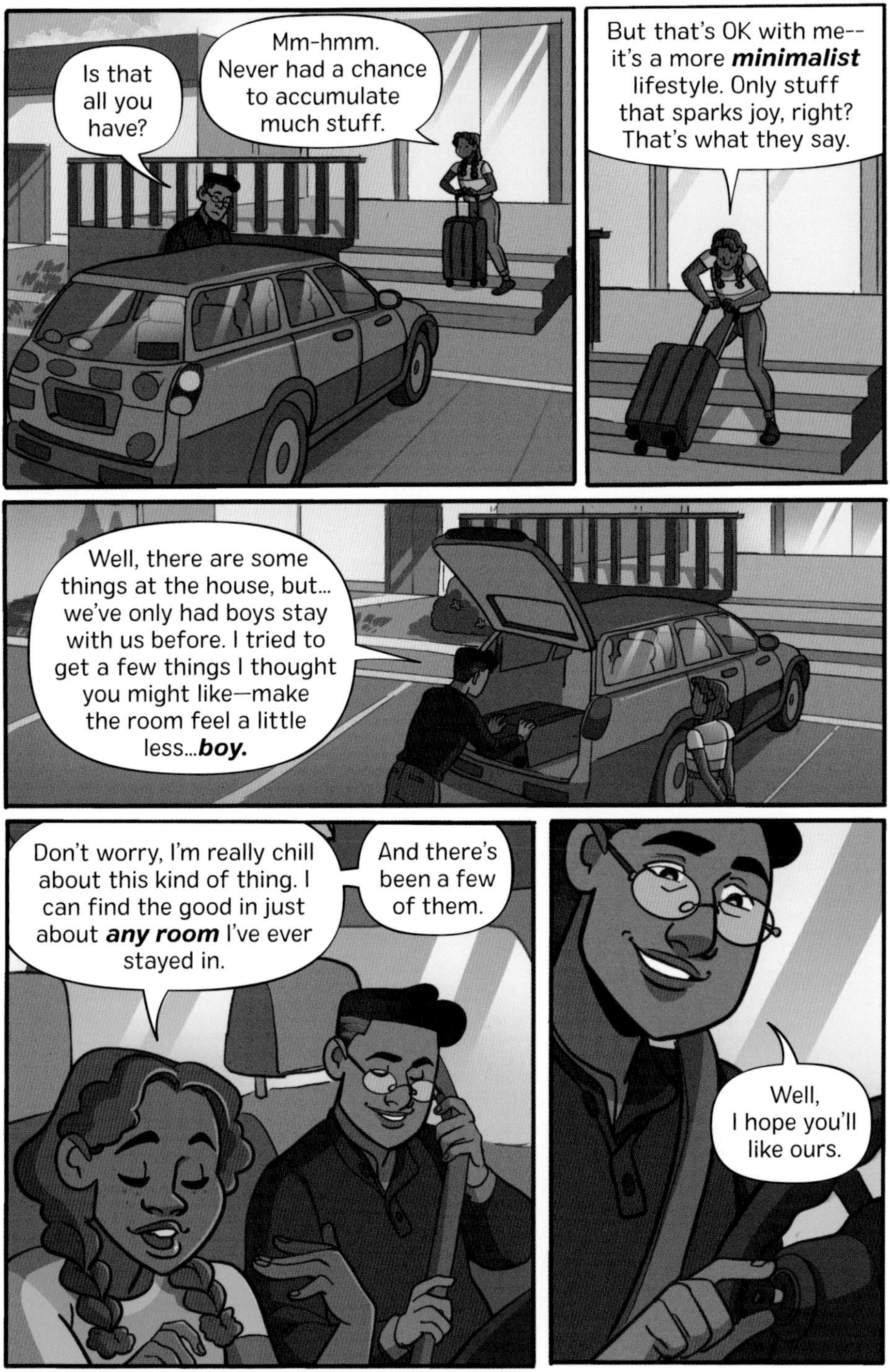
Is that all you have?
Mm-hmm. Never had a chance to accumulate much stuff.
But that's OK with me-- it's a more ***minimalist*** lifestyle. Only stuff that sparks joy, right? That's what they say.
Well, there are some things at the house, but... we've only had boys stay with us before. I tried to get a few things I thought you might like—make the room feel a little less...***boy.***
Don't worry, I'm really chill about this kind of thing. I can find the good in just about ***any room*** I've ever stayed in.
And there's been a few of them.
Well, I hope you'll like ours.

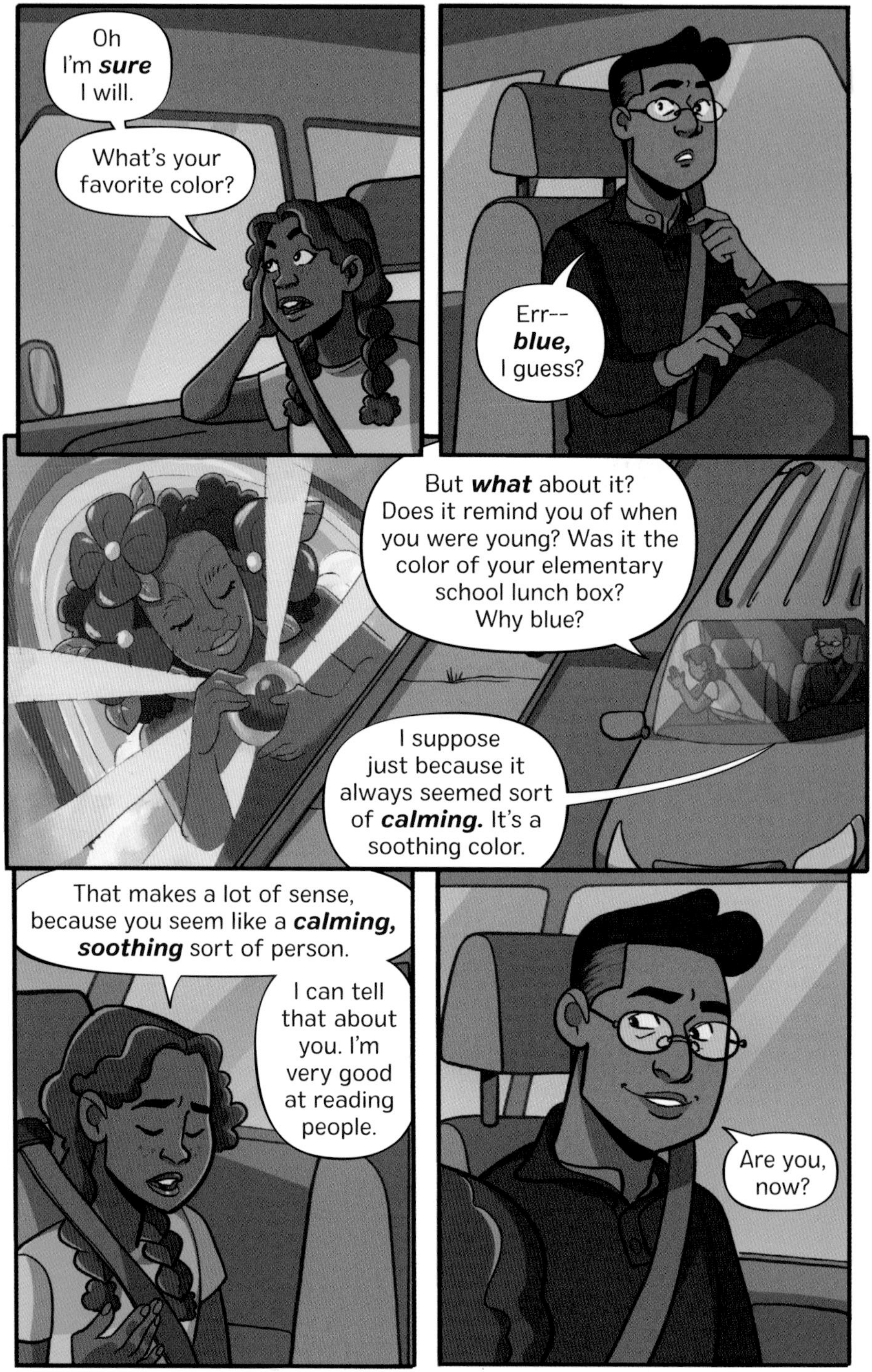
Oh I'm ***sure*** I will.
What's your favorite color?
Err-- ***blue,*** I guess?
But ***what*** about it? Does it remind you of when you were young? Was it the color of your elementary school lunch box? Why blue?
I suppose just because it always seemed sort of ***calming.*** It's a soothing color.
That makes a lot of sense, because you seem like a ***calming, soothing*** sort of person.
I can tell that about you. I'm very good at reading people.
Are you, now?

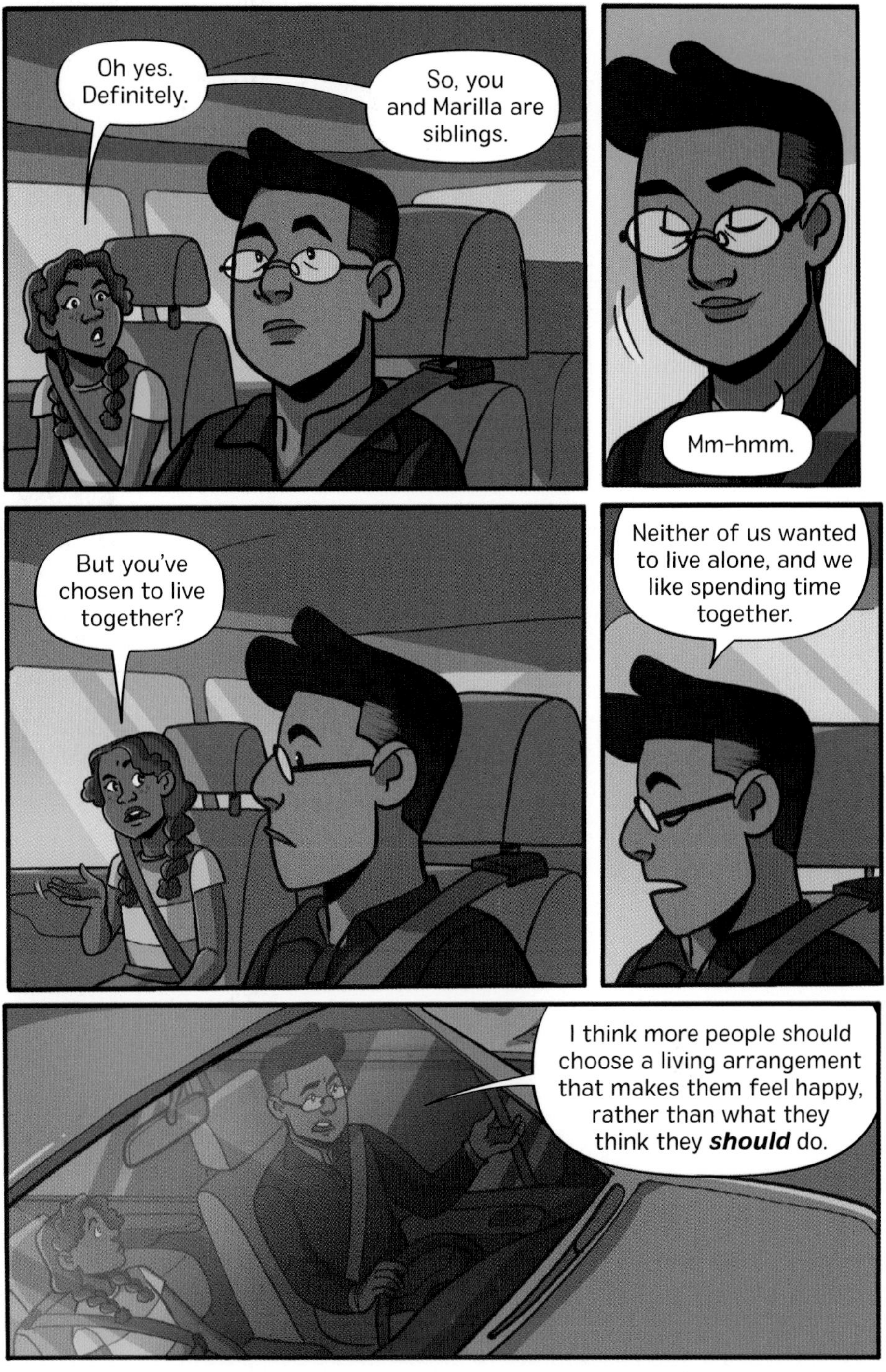

So, you and Marilla are siblings.
Oh yes. Definitely.
Mm-hmm.
But you've chosen to live together?
Neither of us wanted to live alone, and we like spending time together.
I think more people should choose a living arrangement that makes them feel happy, rather than what they think they ***should*** do.

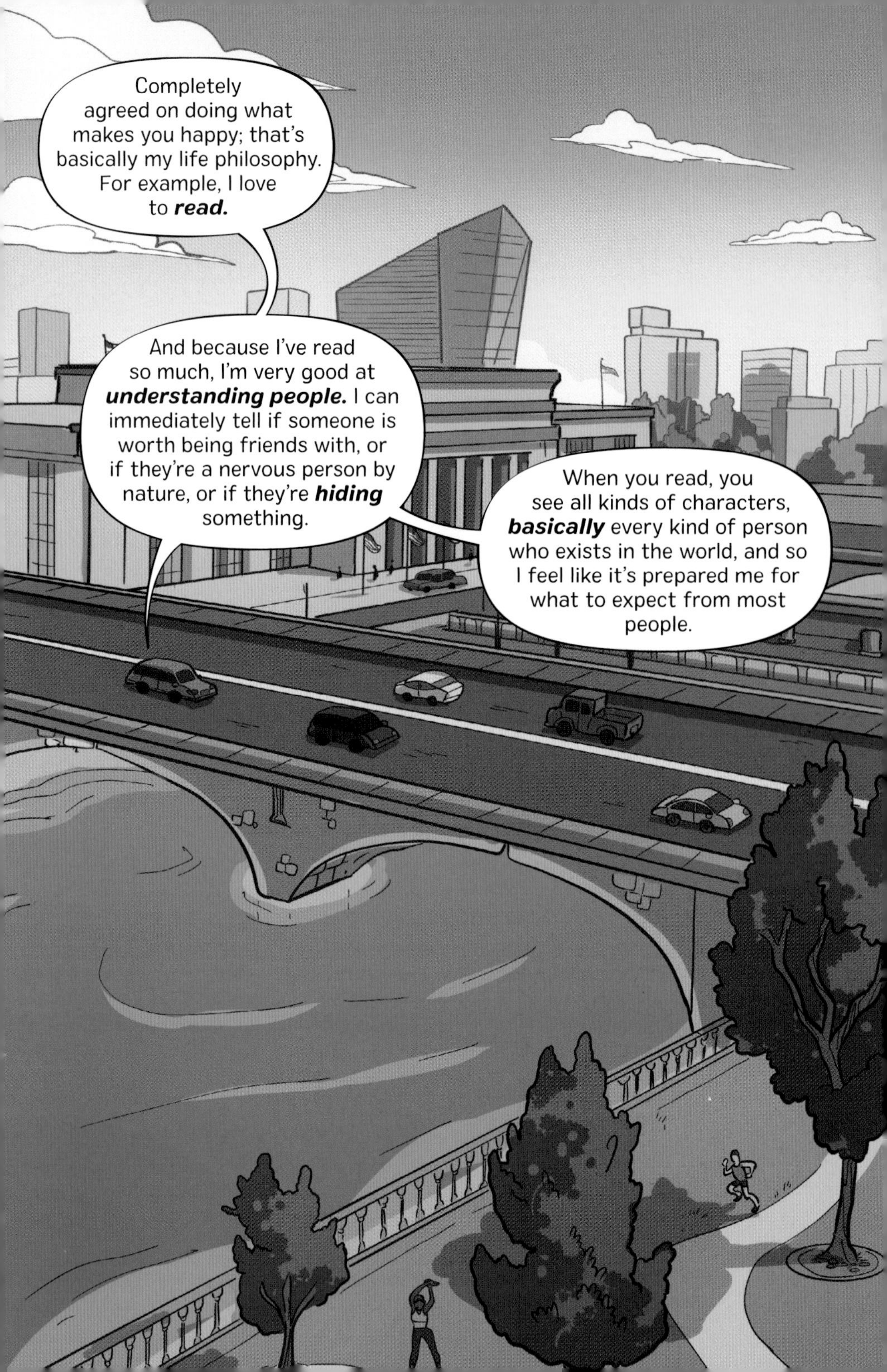
Completely agreed on doing what makes you happy; that's basically my life philosophy. For example, I love to ***read.***
And because I've read so much, I'm very good at ***understanding people.*** I can immediately tell if someone is worth being friends with, or if they're a nervous person by nature, or if they're ***hiding*** something.
When you read, you see all kinds of characters, ***basically*** every kind of person who exists in the world, and so I feel like it's prepared me for what to expect from most people.

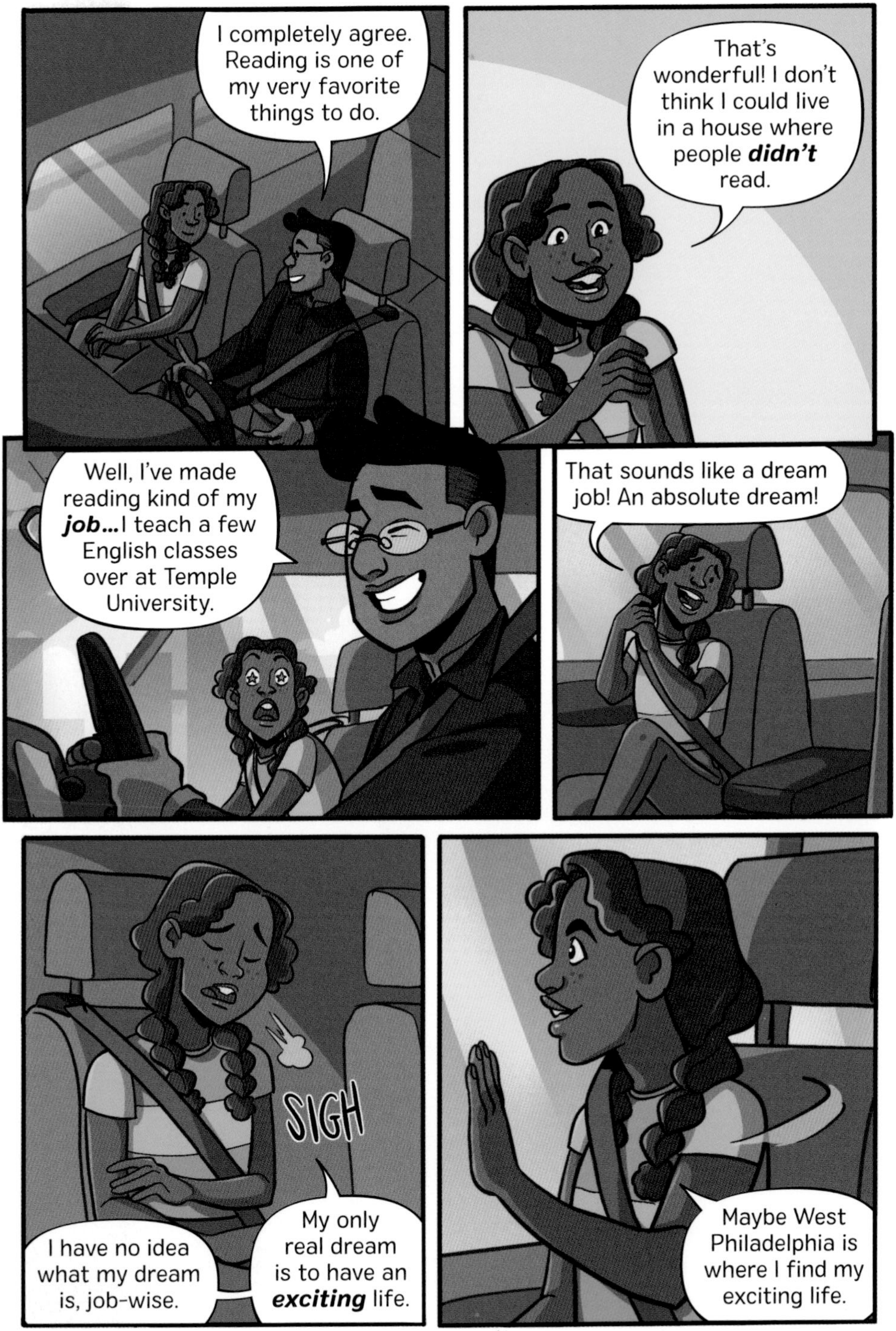
I completely agree. Reading is one of my very favorite things to do.
That's wonderful! I don't think I could live in a house where people ***didn't*** read.
Well, I've made reading kind of my ***job...*** I teach a few English classes over at Temple University.
That sounds like a dream job! An absolute dream!
SIGH
I have no idea what my dream is, job-wise.
My only real dream is to have an ***exciting*** life.
Maybe West Philadelphia is where I find my exciting life.

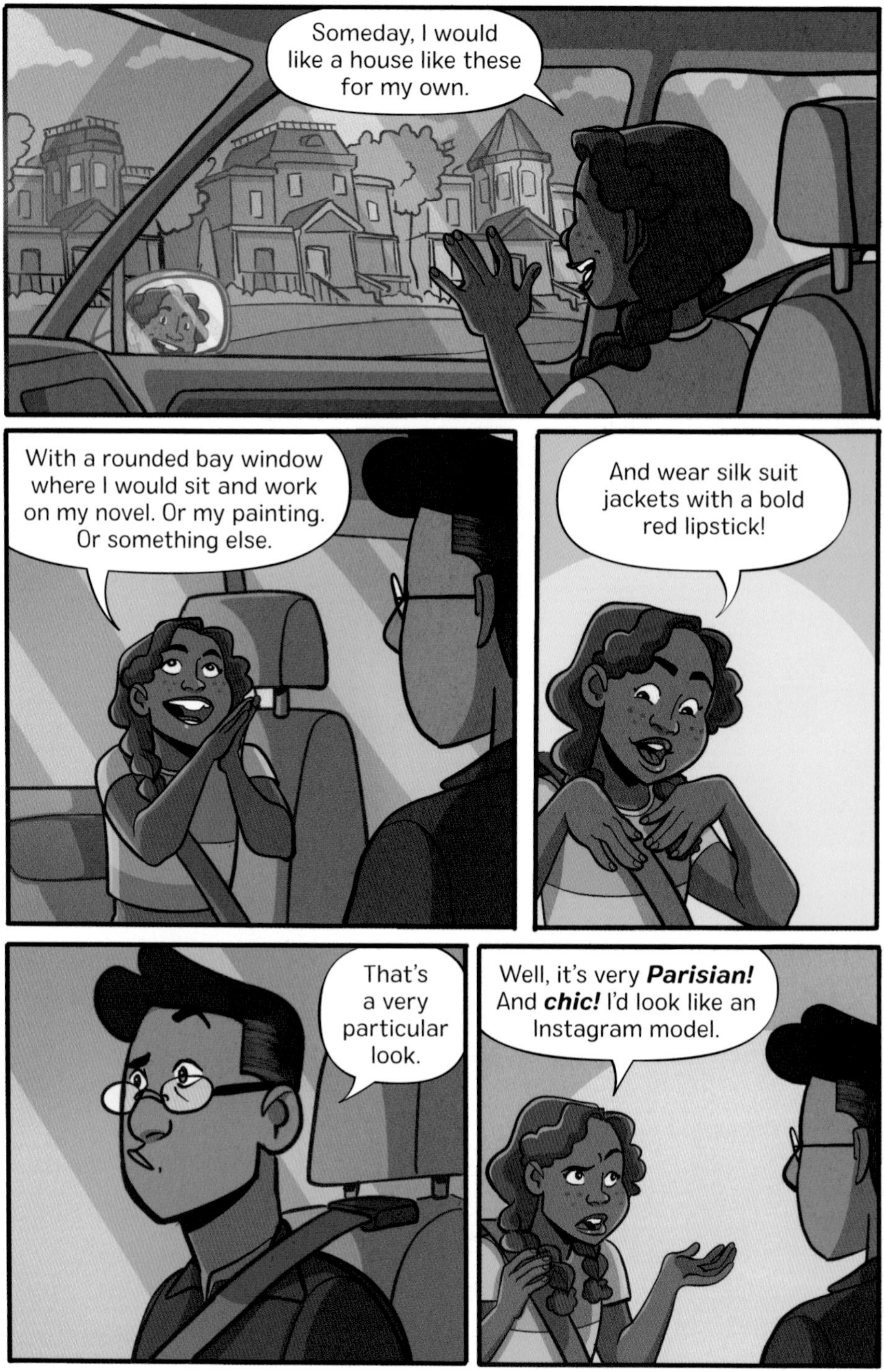
Someday, I would like a house like these for my own.
With a rounded bay window where I would sit and work on my novel. Or my painting. Or something else.
And wear silk suit jackets with a bold red lipstick!
That's a very particular look.
Well, it's very **Parisian!** And **chic!** I'd look like an Instagram model.

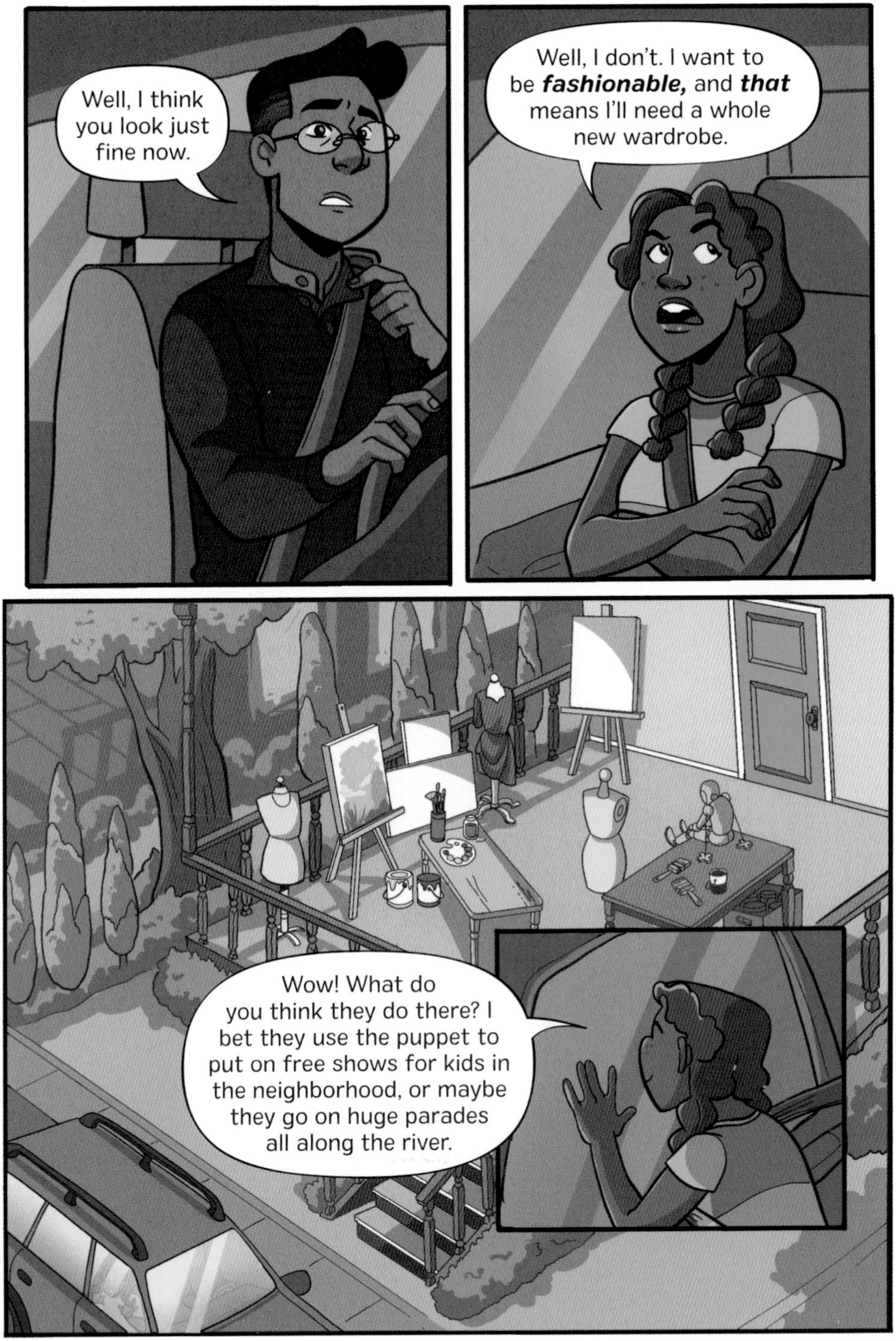
Well, I think you look just fine now.
Well, I don't. I want to be ***fashionable,*** and ***that*** means I'll need a whole new wardrobe.
Wow! What do you think they do there? I bet they use the puppet to put on free shows for kids in the neighborhood, or maybe they go on huge parades all along the river.

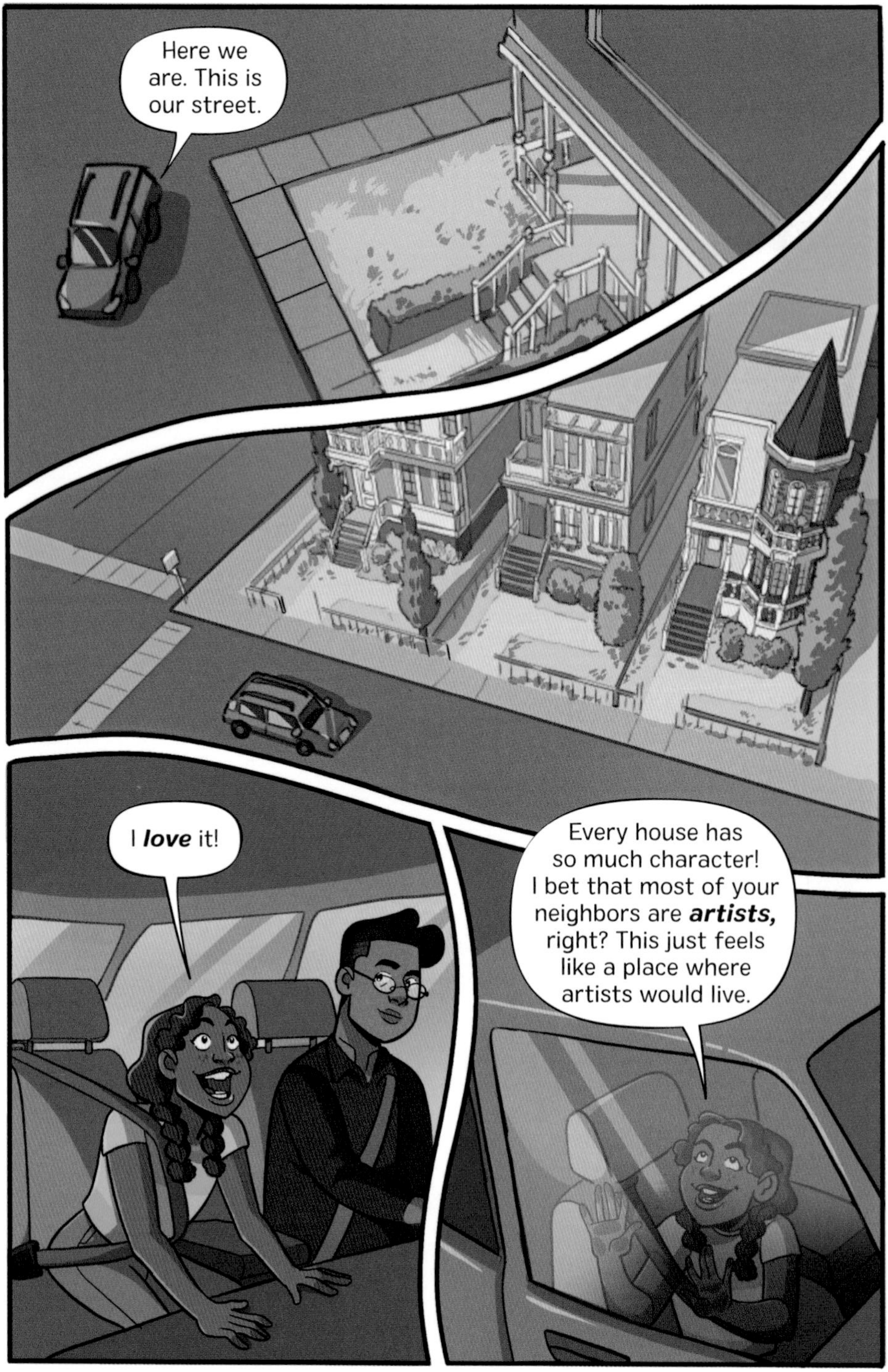

Here we are. This is our street.
I **love** it!
Every house has so much character! I bet that most of your neighbors are ***artists,*** right? This just feels like a place where artists would live.

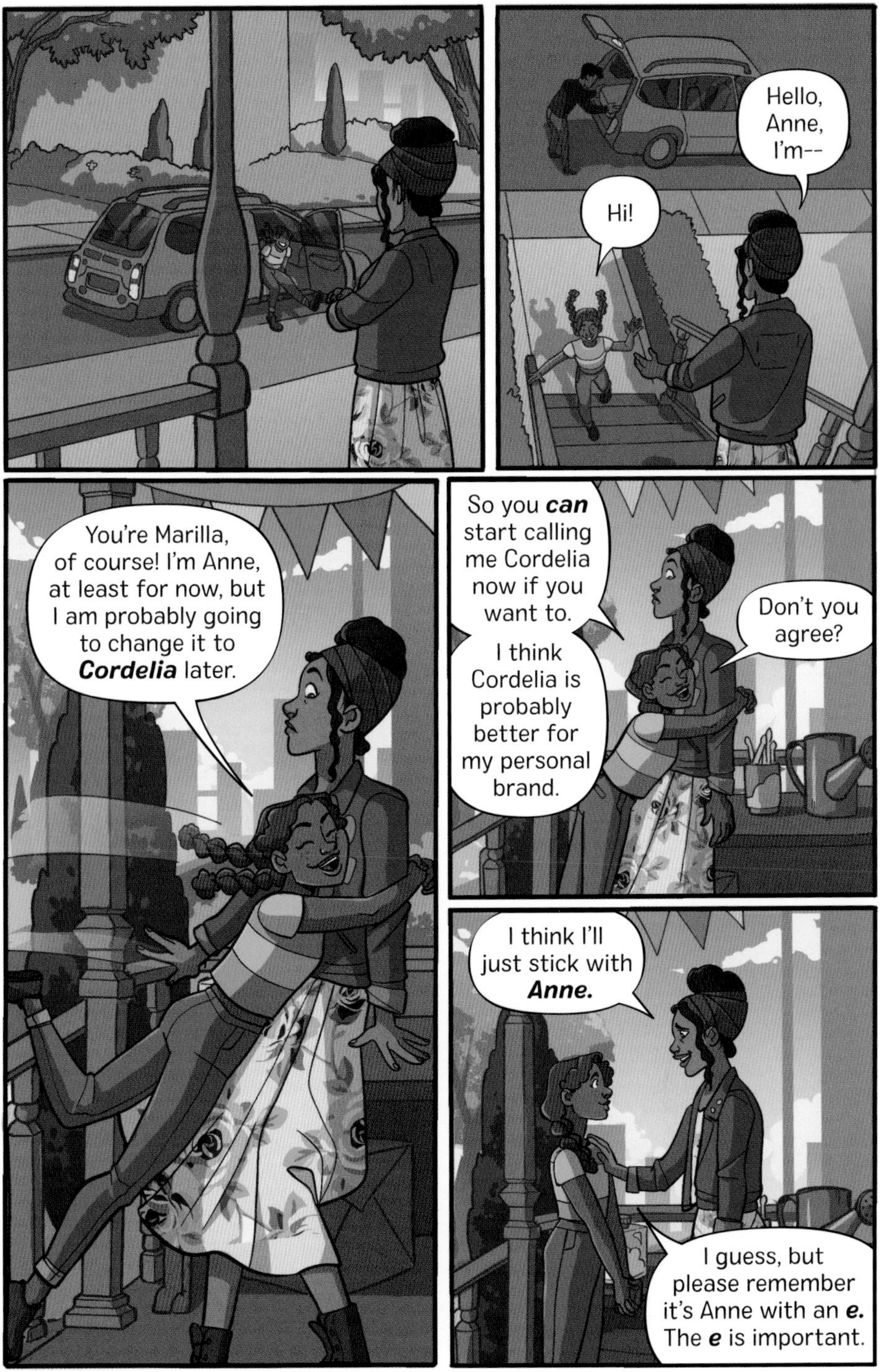
Hello, Anne, I'm--
Hi!
You're Marilla, of course! I'm Anne, at least for now, but I am probably going to change it to ***Cordelia*** later.
So you ***can*** start calling me Cordelia now if you want to.
I think Cordelia is probably better for my personal brand.
Don't you agree?
I think I'll just stick with ***Anne.***
I guess, but please remember it's Anne with an ***e.*** The ***e*** is important.

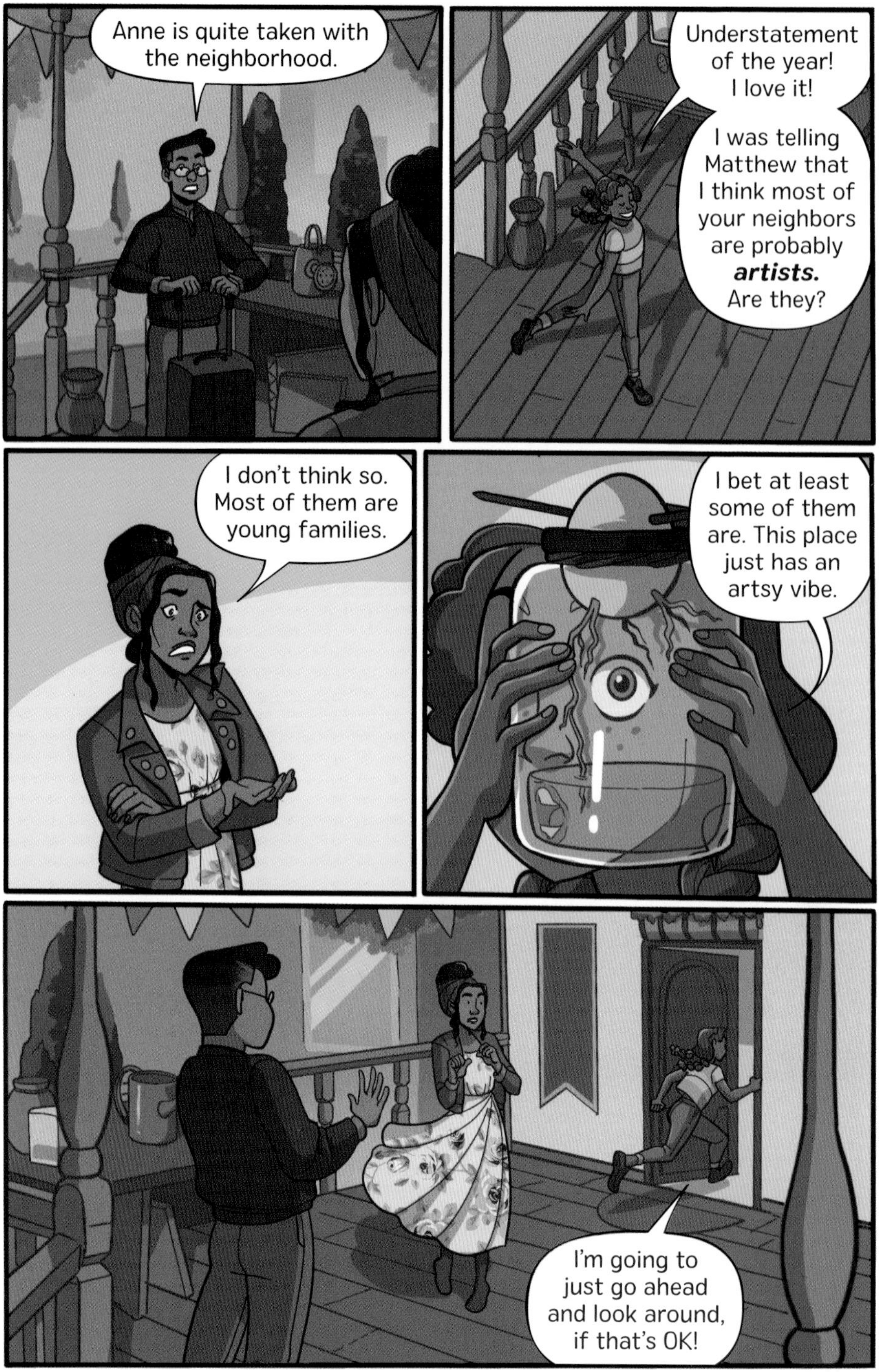
Anne is quite taken with the neighborhood.
Understatement of the year! I love it!
I was telling Matthew that I think most of your neighbors are probably ***artists.*** Are they?
I don't think so. Most of them are young families.
I bet at least some of them are. This place just has an artsy vibe.
I'm going to just go ahead and look around, if that's OK!

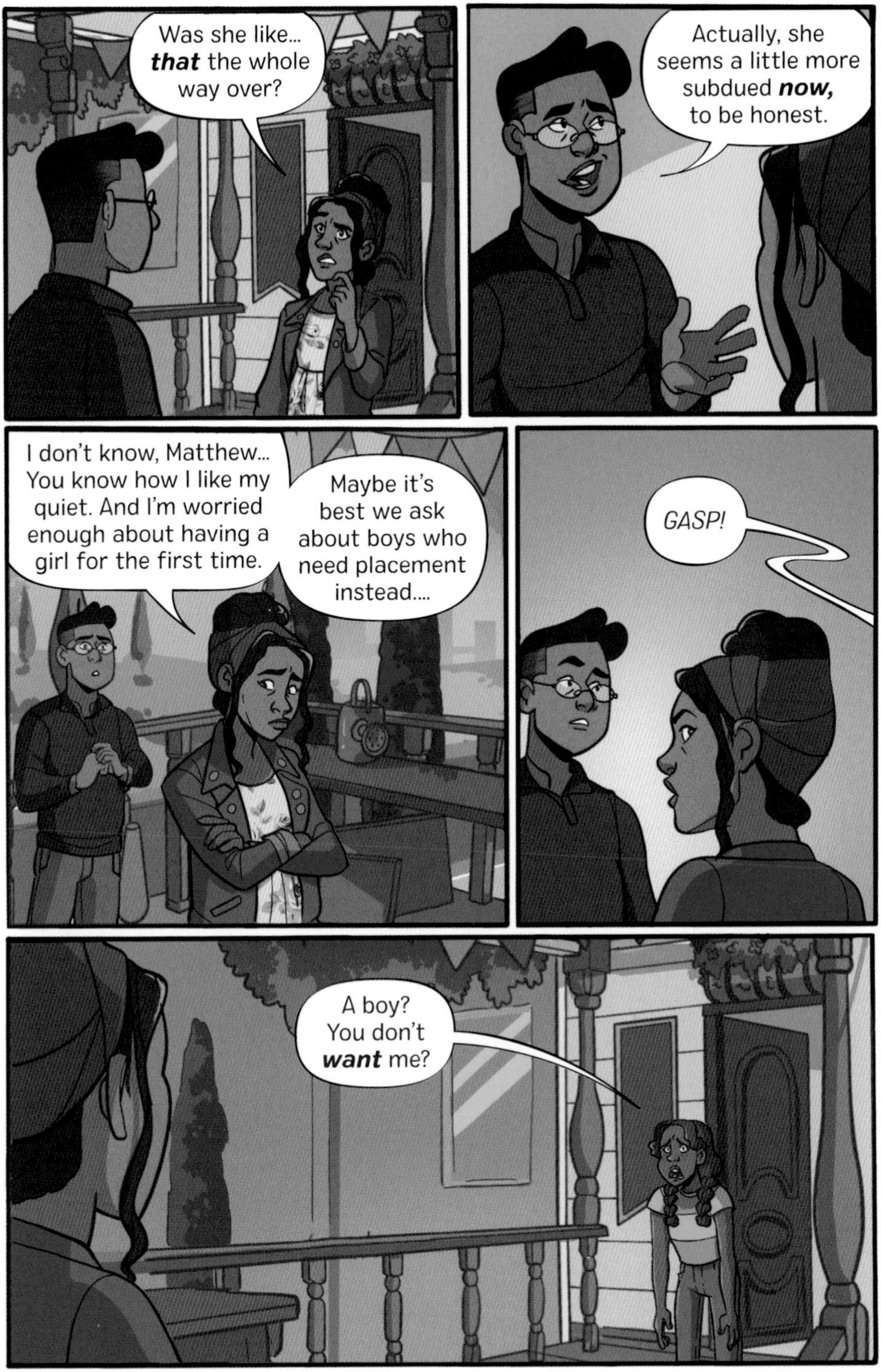
Was she like... ***that*** the whole way over?
Actually, she seems a little more subdued ***now,*** to be honest.
I don't know, Matthew... You know how I like my quiet. And I'm worried enough about having a girl for the first time.
Maybe it's best we ask about boys who need placement instead....
GASP!
A boy? You don't ***want*** me?

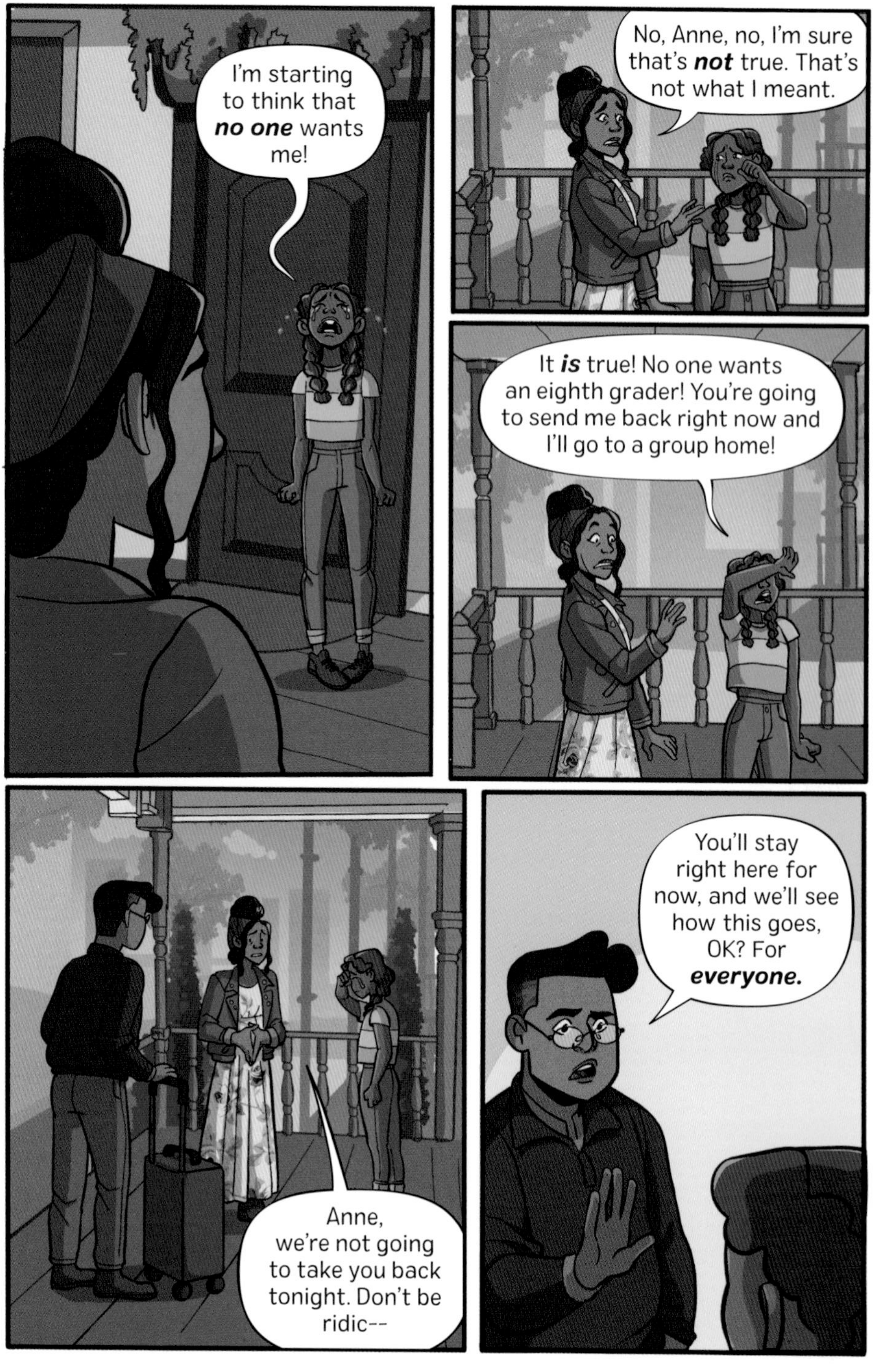
I'm starting to think that ***no one*** wants me!
No, Anne, no, I'm sure that's ***not*** true. That's not what I meant.
It ***is*** true! No one wants an eighth grader! You're going to send me back right now and I'll go to a group home!
Anne, we're not going to take you back tonight. Don't be ridic--
You'll stay right here for now, and we'll see how this goes, OK? For ***everyone.***

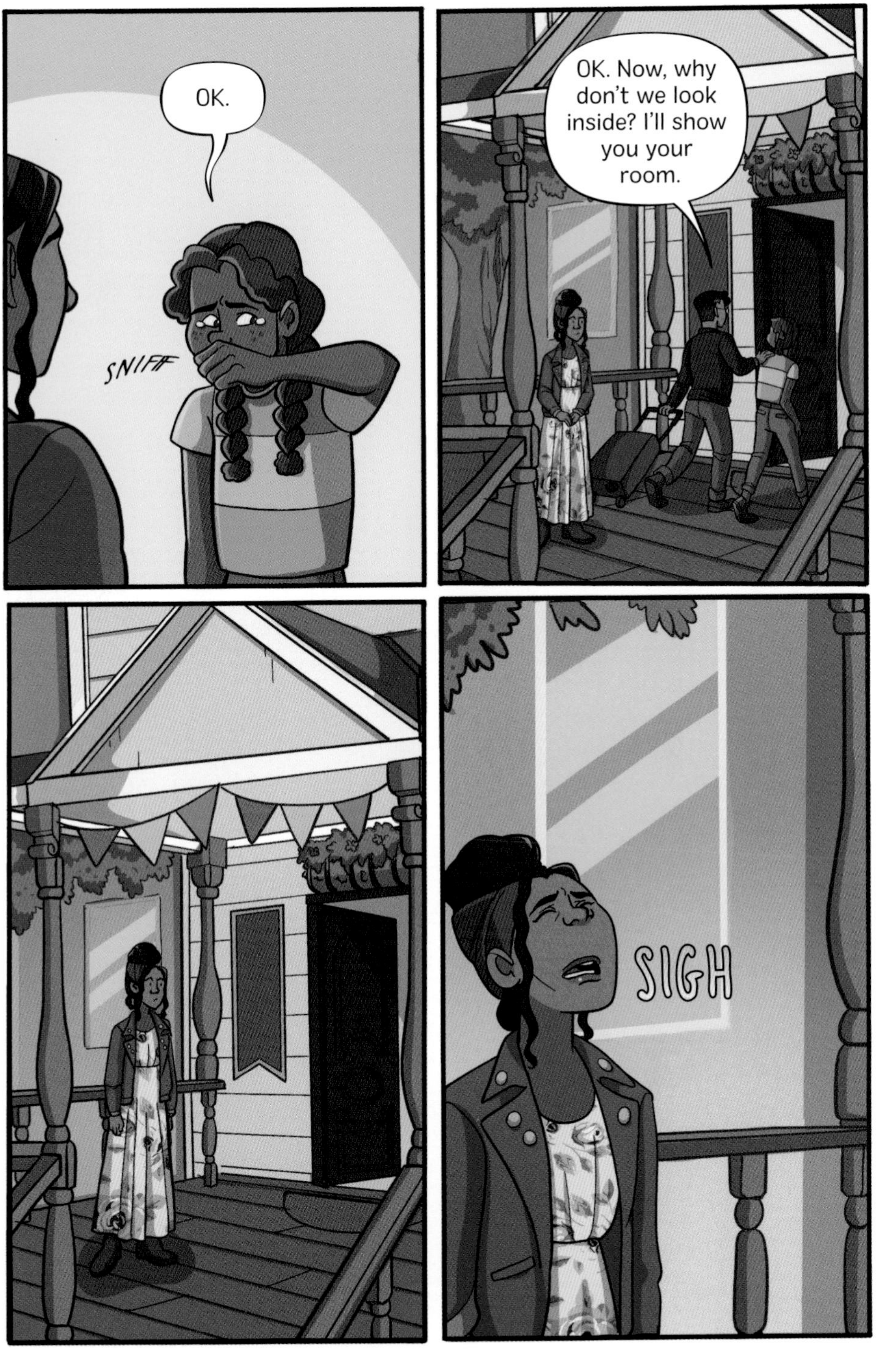
OK.
SNIFF
OK. Now, why don't we look inside? I'll show you your room.
SIGH

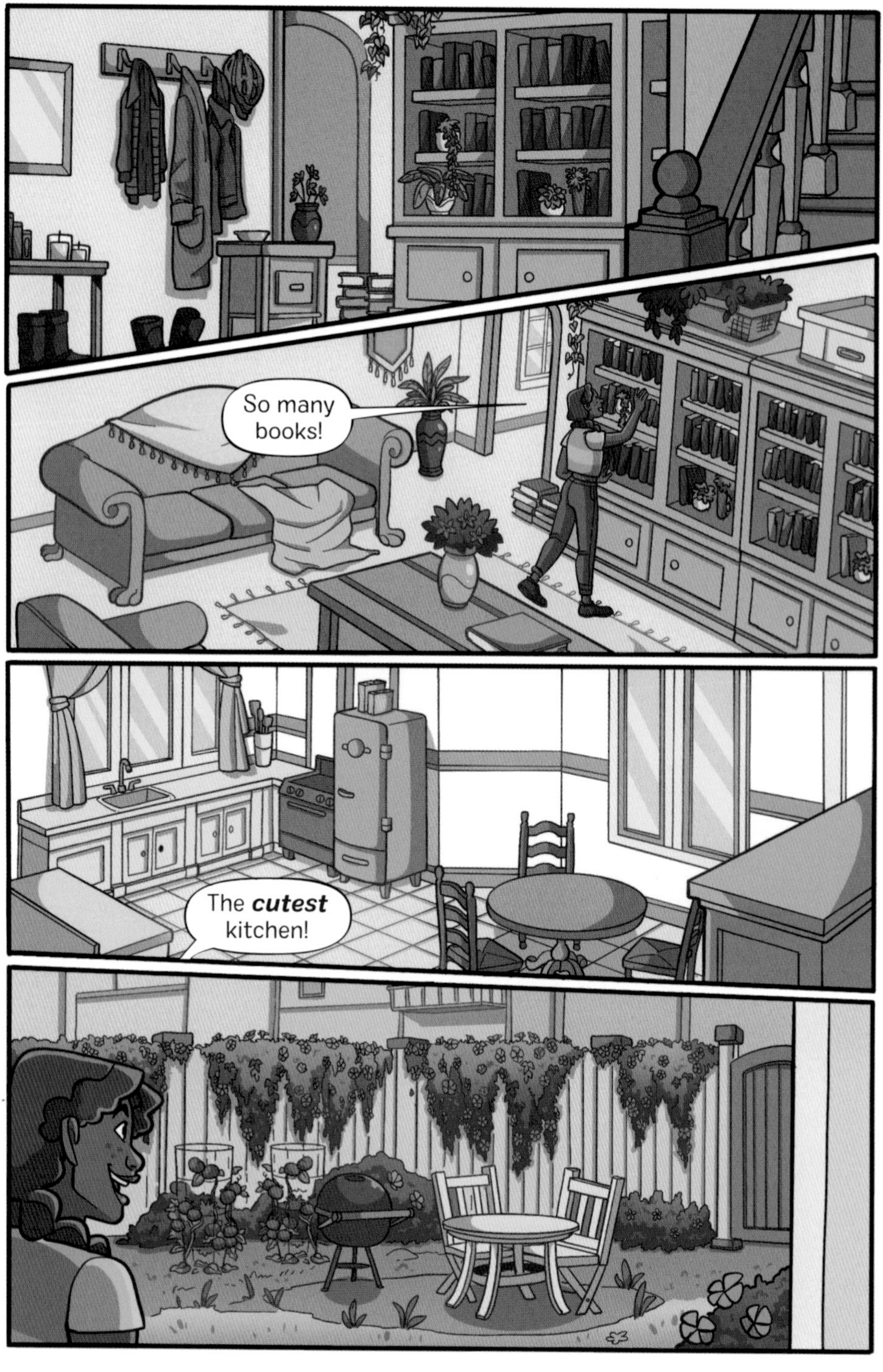
So many books!
The *cutest* kitchen!

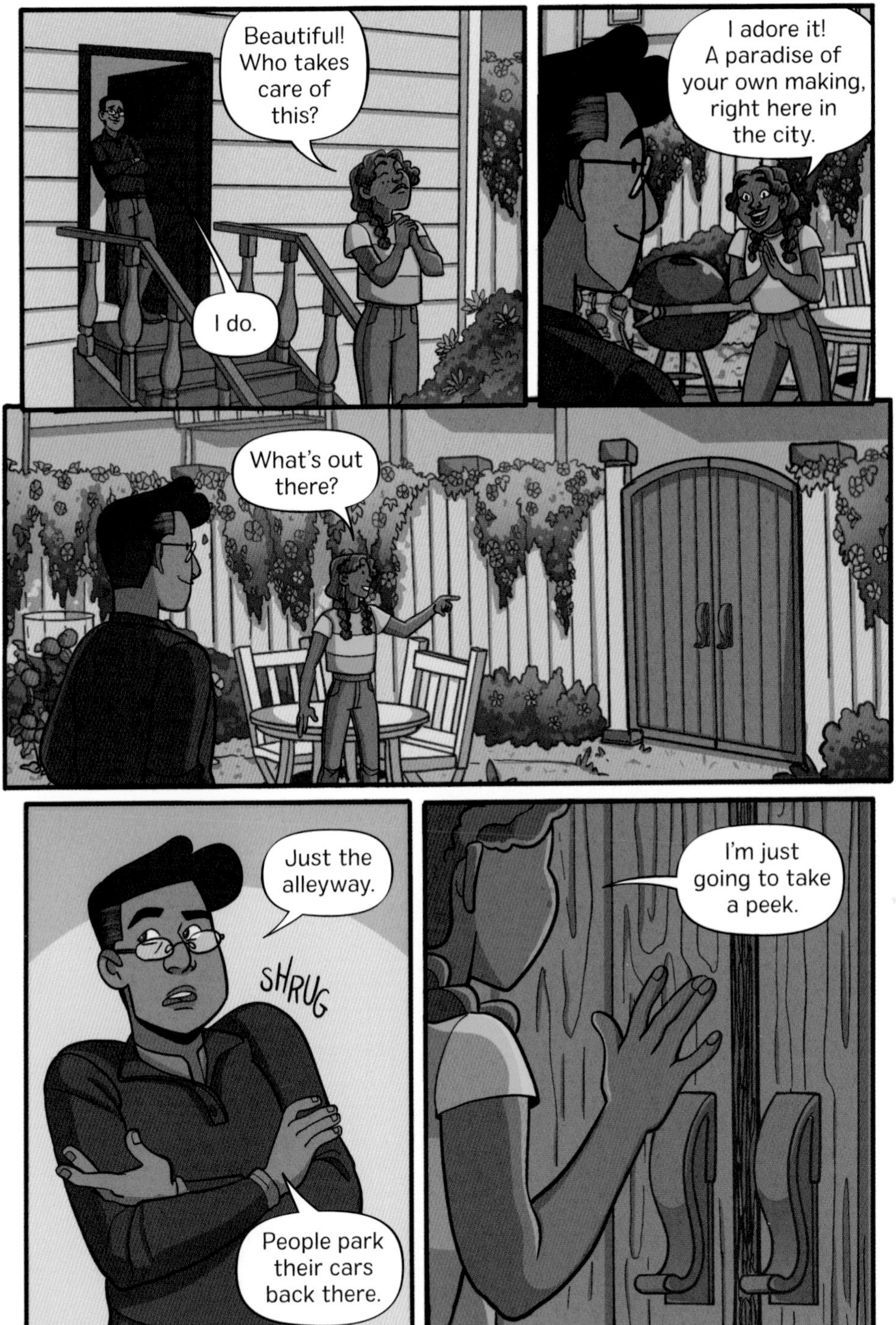
Beautiful! Who takes care of this?
I do.
I adore it! A paradise of your own making, right here in the city.
What's out there?
Just the alleyway.
SHRUG
People park their cars back there.
I'm just going to take a peek.

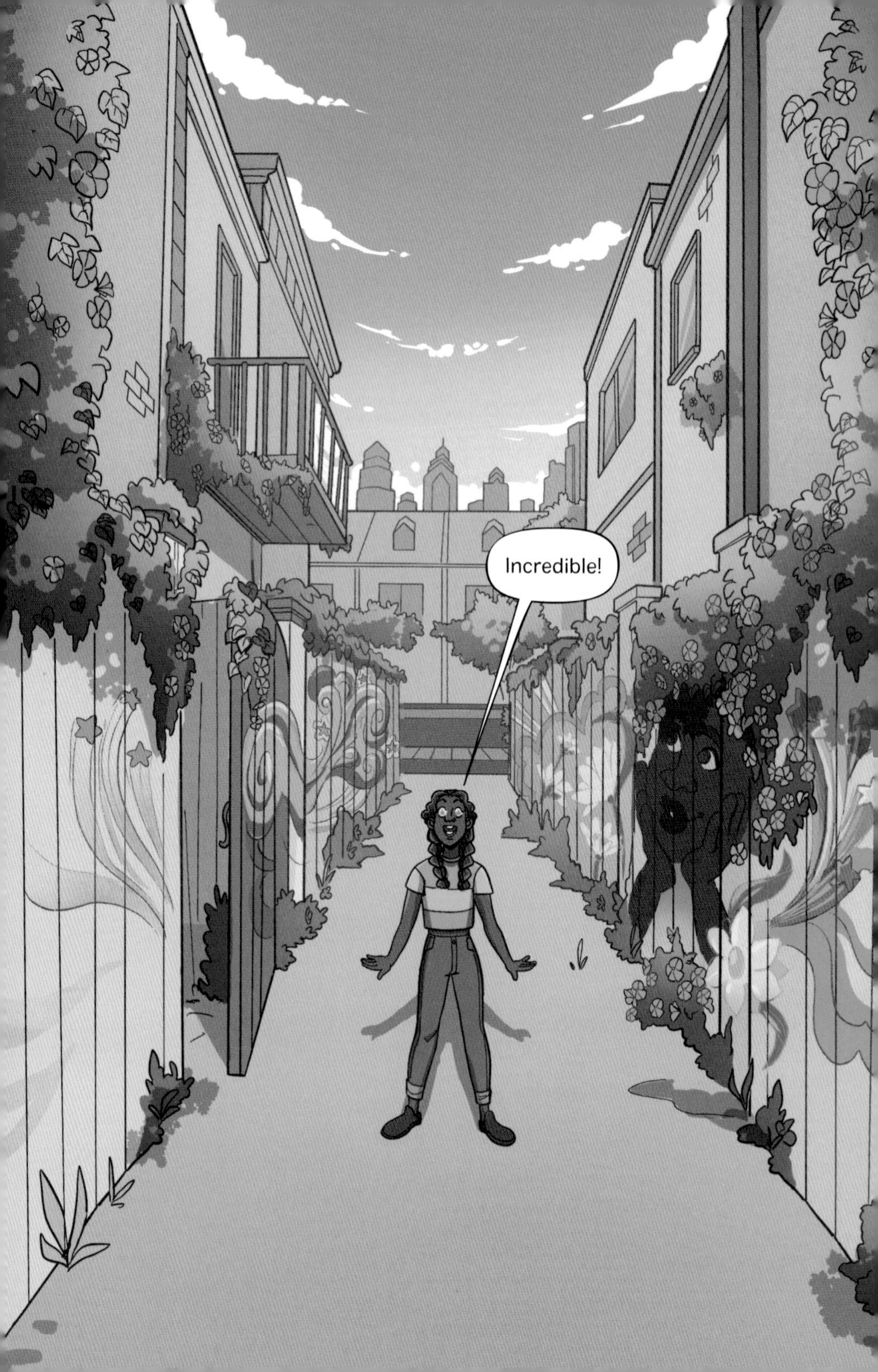
Incredible!

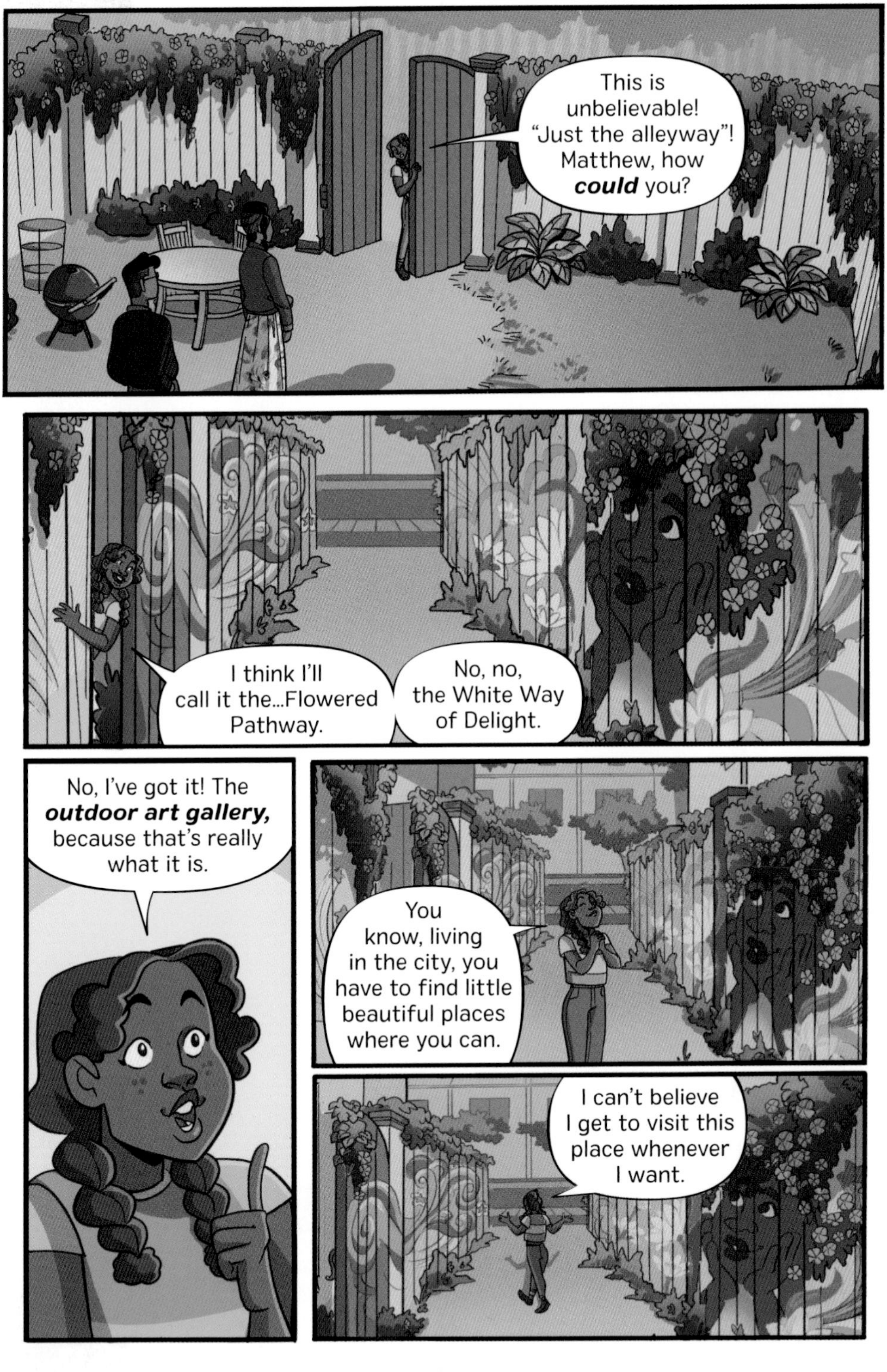
This is unbelievable! "Just the alleyway"! Matthew, how ***could*** you?
I think I'll call it the...Flowered Pathway.
No, no, the White Way of Delight.
No, I've got it! The ***outdoor art gallery,*** because that's really what it is.
You know, living in the city, you have to find little beautiful places where you can.
I can't believe I get to visit this place whenever I want.

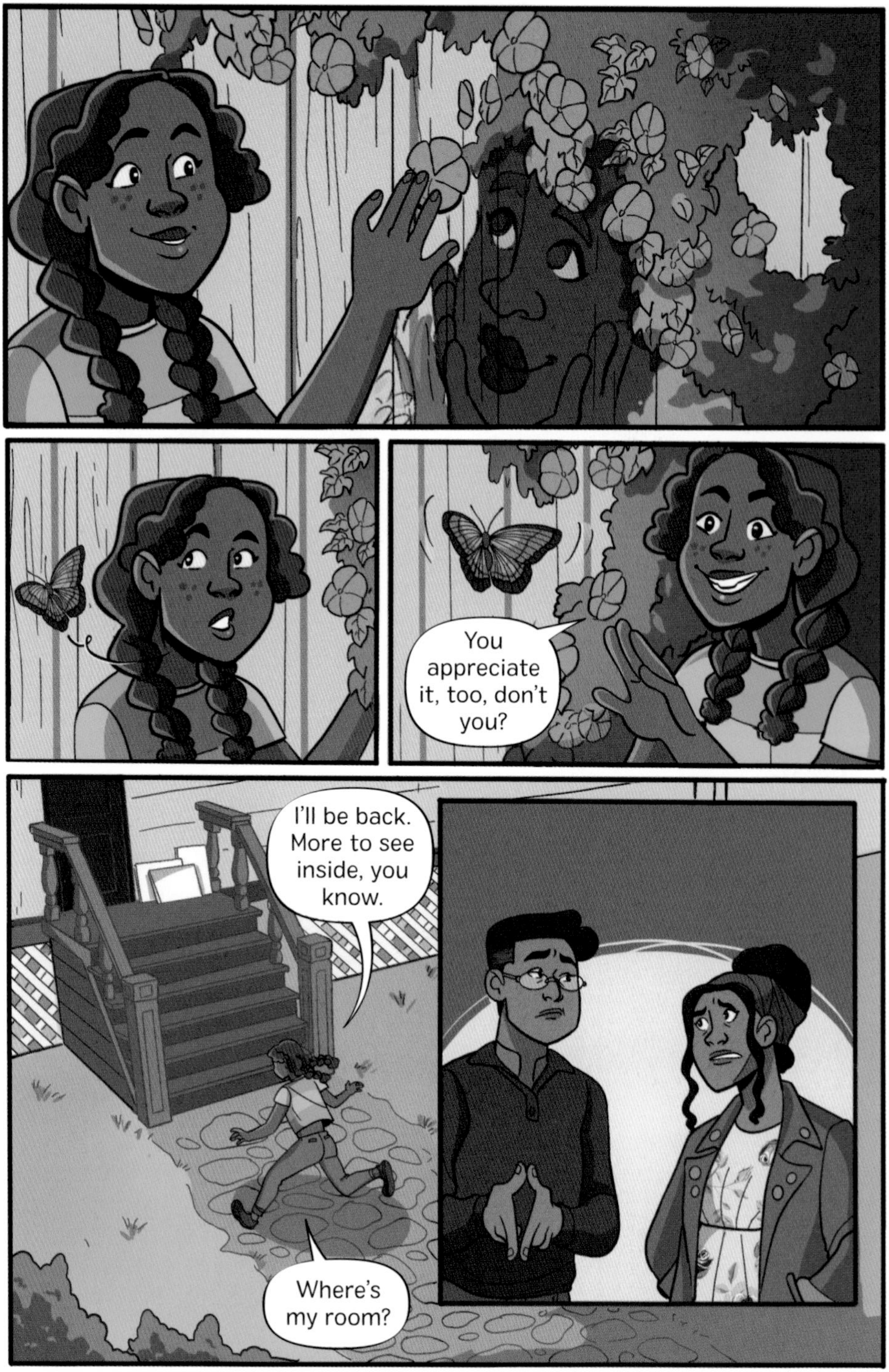
You appreciate it, too, don't you?
I'll be back. More to see inside, you know.
Where's my room?

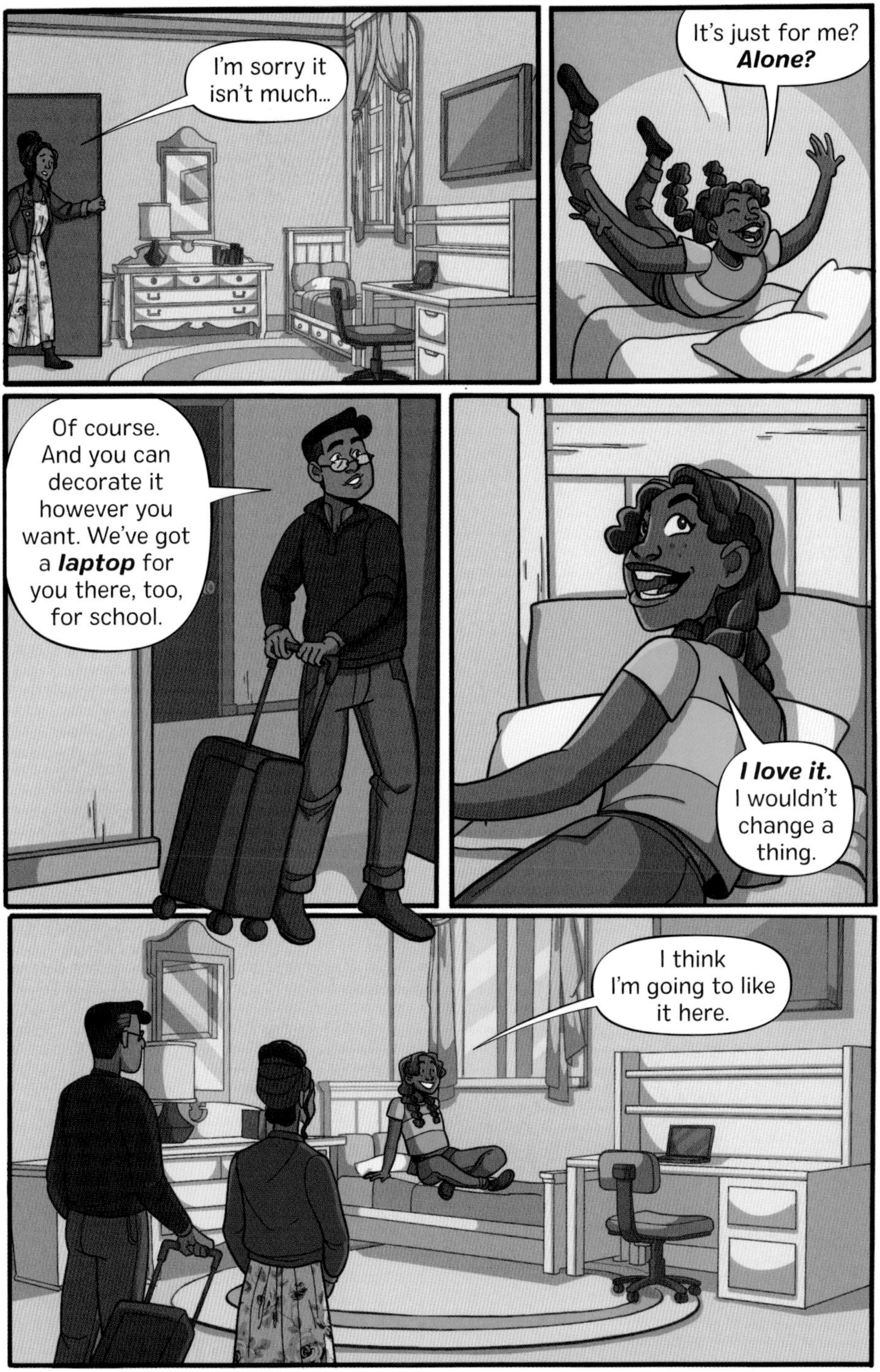
I'm sorry it isn't much...
It's just for me? ***Alone?***
Of course. And you can decorate it however you want. We've got a ***laptop*** for you there, too, for school.
I love it. I wouldn't change a thing.
I think I'm going to like it here.

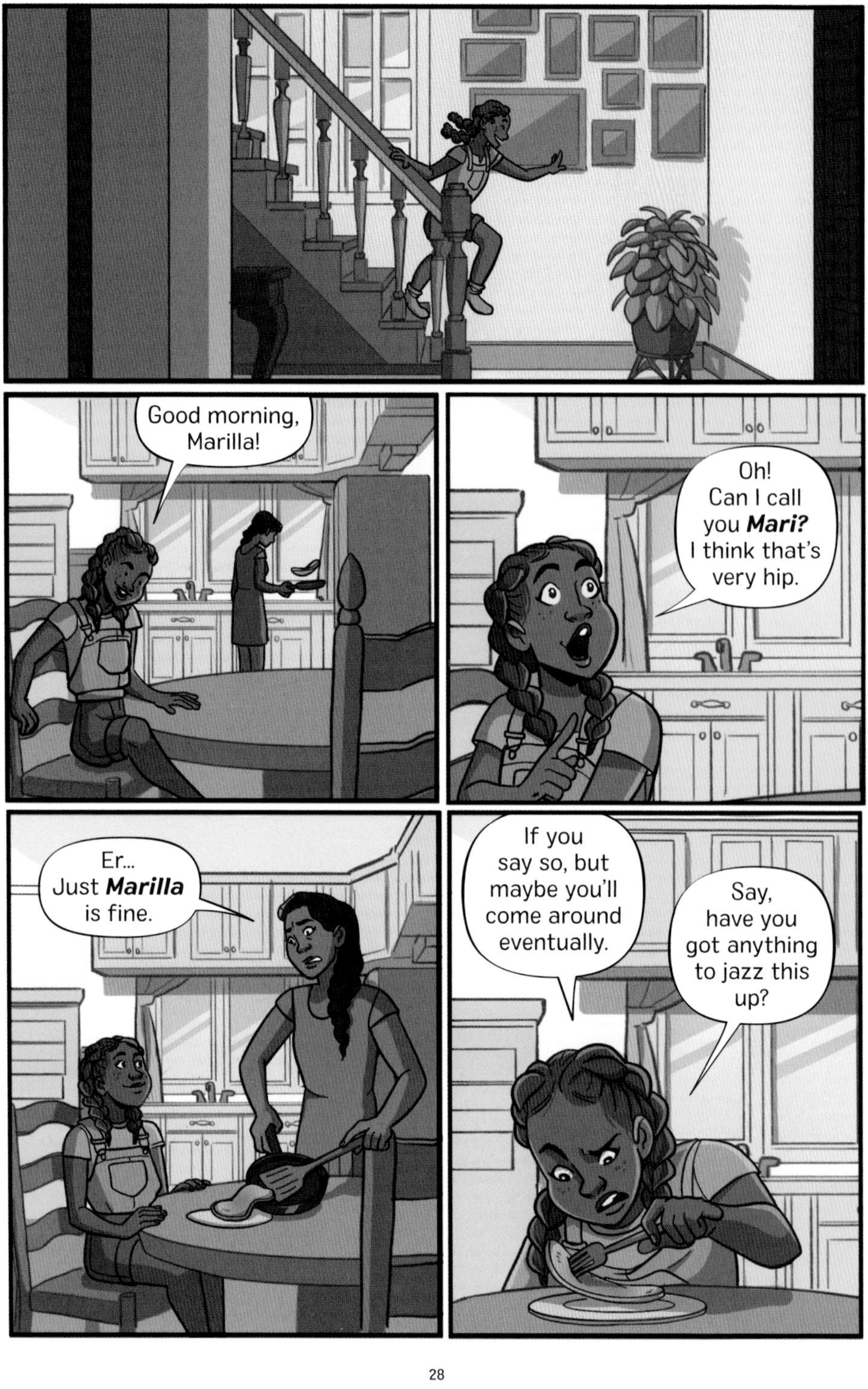
Good morning, Marilla!
Oh! Can I call you ***Mari?*** I think that's very hip.
Er... Just ***Marilla*** is fine.
If you say so, but maybe you'll come around eventually.
Say, have you got anything to jazz this up?

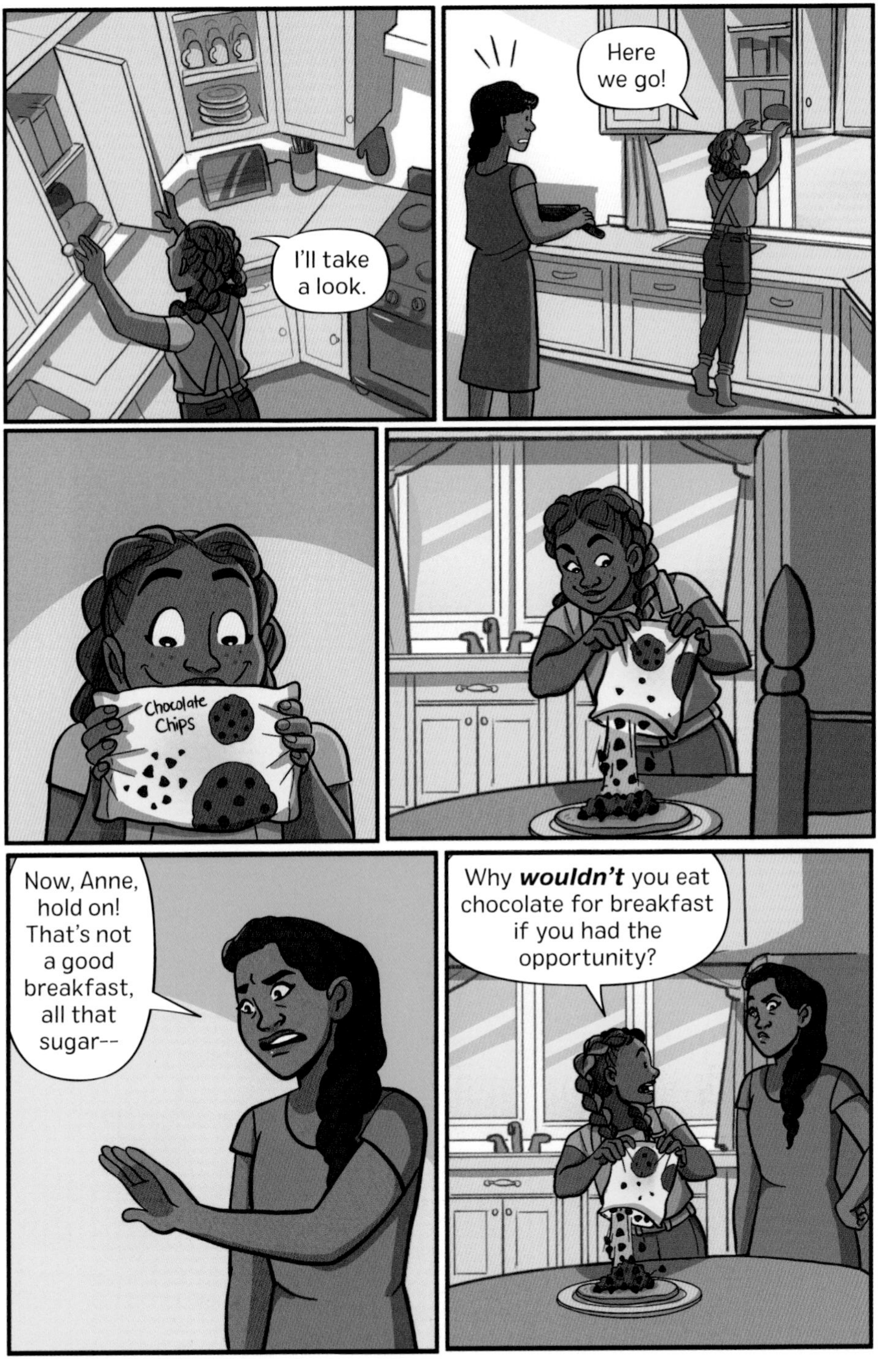
I'll take a look.
Here we go!
Chocolate Chips
Now, Anne, hold on! That's not a good breakfast, all that sugar--
Why ***wouldn't*** you eat chocolate for breakfast if you had the opportunity?

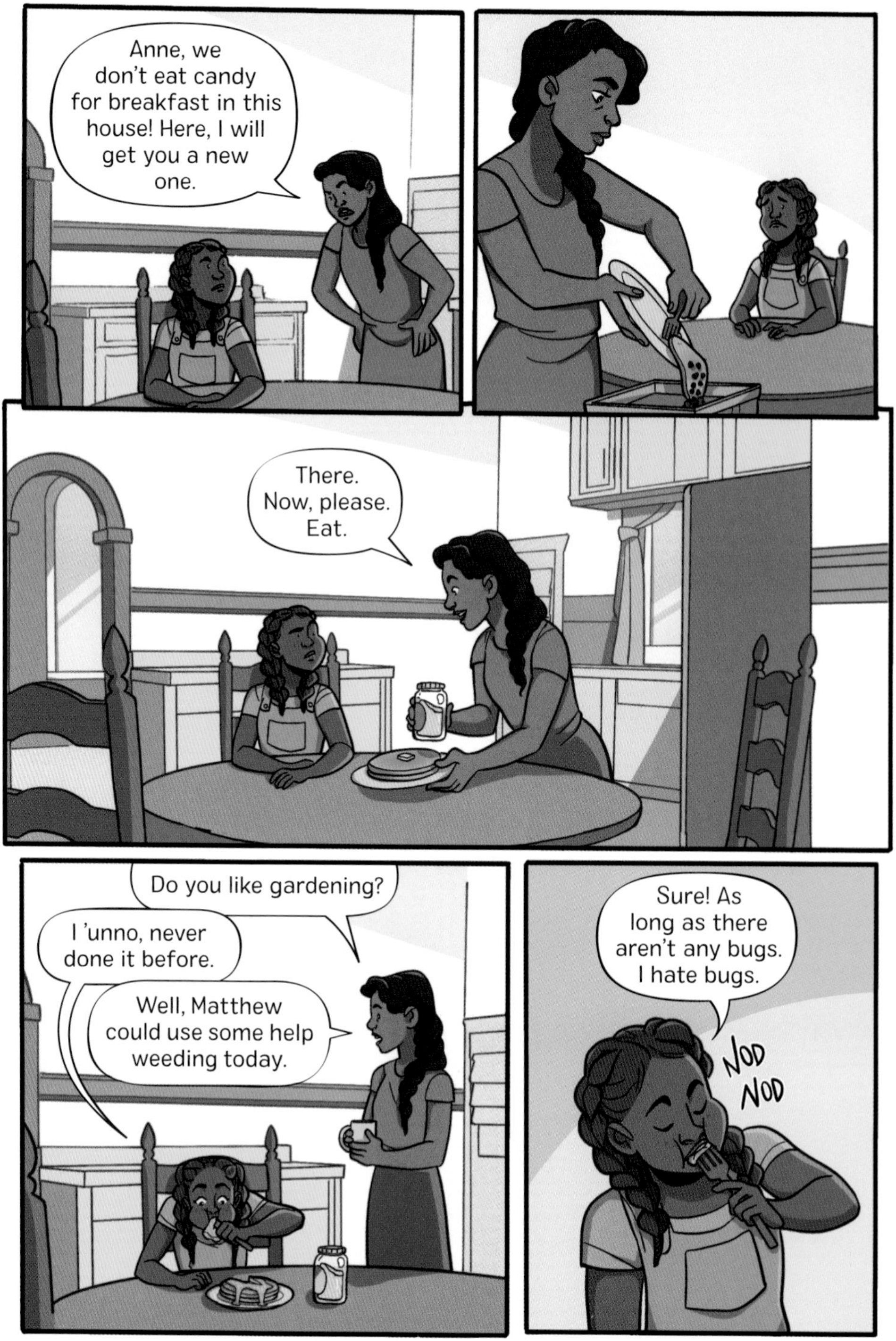
Anne, we don't eat candy for breakfast in this house! Here, I will get you a new one.
There. Now, please. Eat.
Do you like gardening?
I 'unno, never done it before.
Well, Matthew could use some help weeding today.
Sure! As long as there aren't any bugs. I hate bugs.
NOD NOD

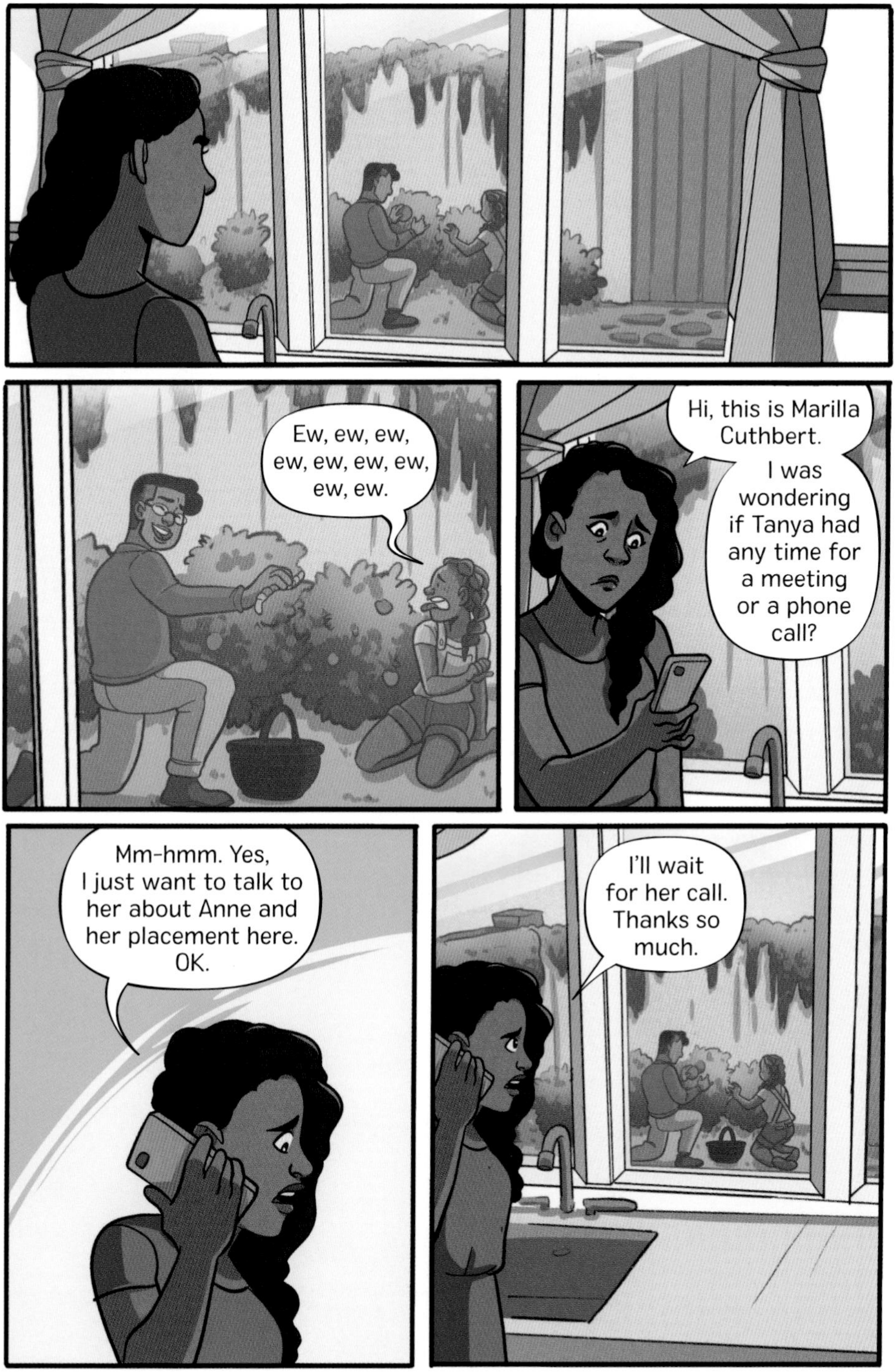
Ew, ew, ew, ew, ew, ew, ew, ew, ew.
Hi, this is Marilla Cuthbert.
I was wondering if Tanya had any time for a meeting or a phone call?
Mm-hmm. Yes, I just want to talk to her about Anne and her placement here. OK.
I'll wait for her call. Thanks so much.

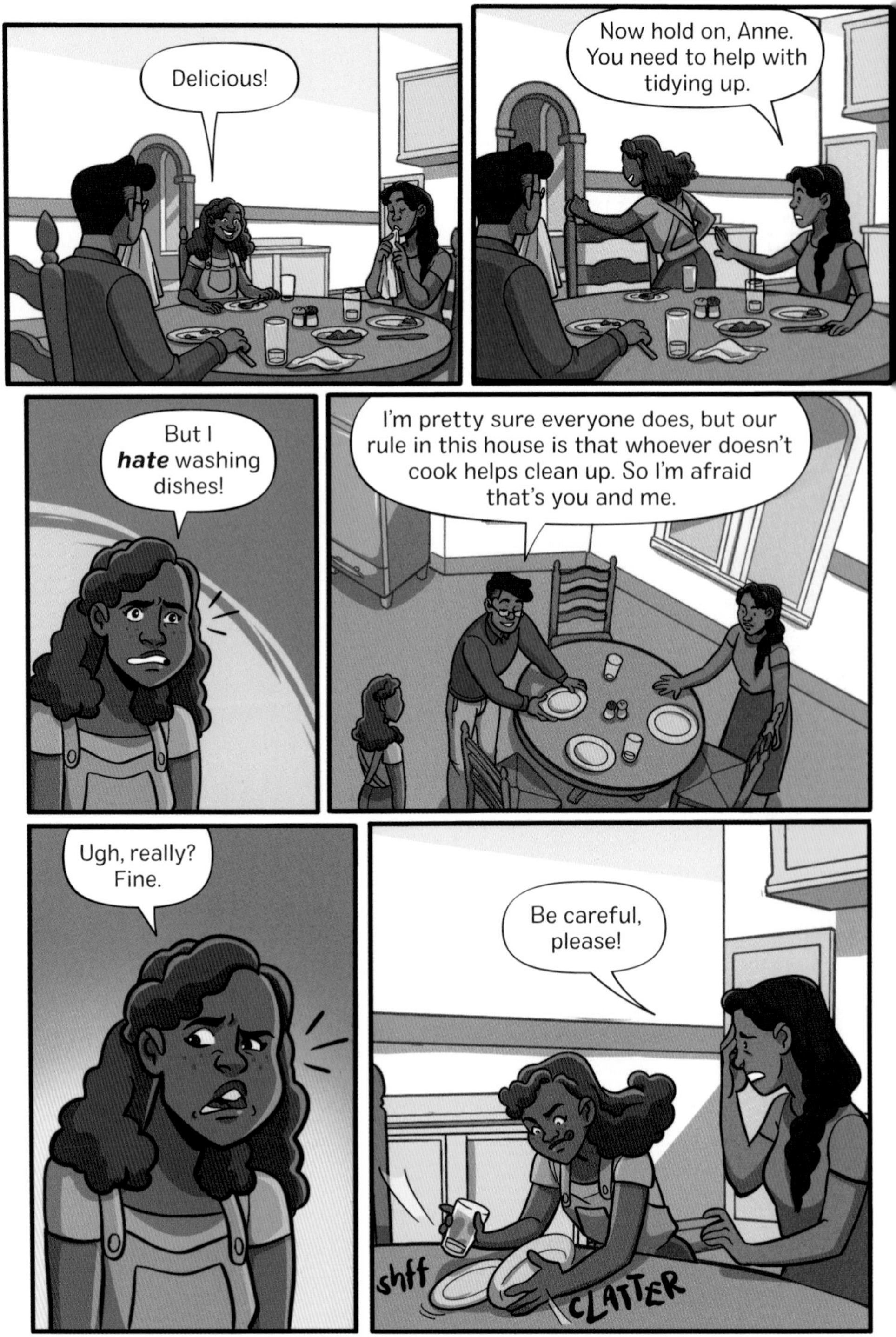
Delicious!
Now hold on, Anne. You need to help with tidying up.
But I **hate** washing dishes!
I'm pretty sure everyone does, but our rule in this house is that whoever doesn't cook helps clean up. So I'm afraid that's you and me.
Ugh, really? Fine.
Be careful, please!
shff
CLATTER

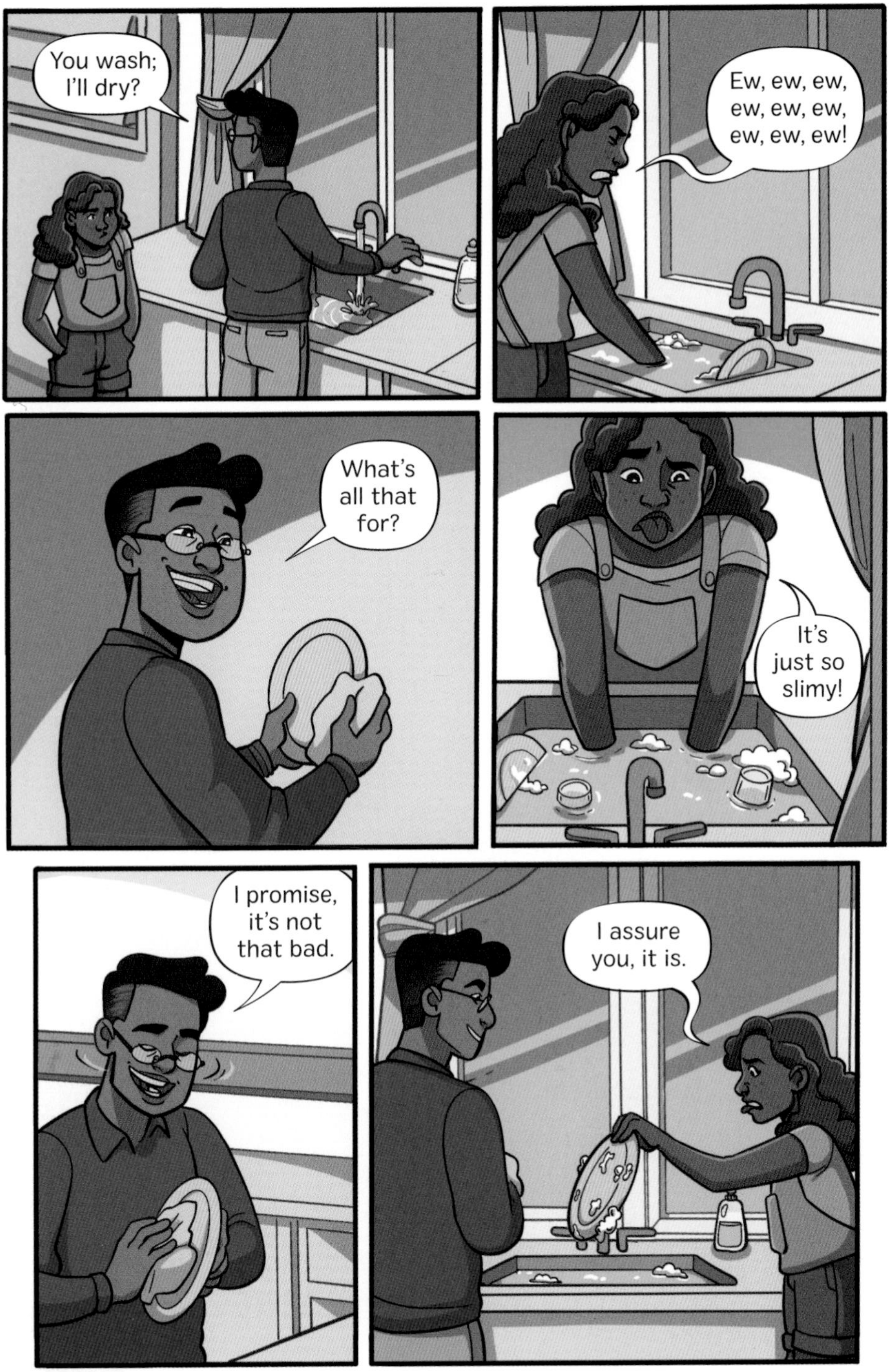
You wash; I'll dry?
Ew, ew, ew, ew, ew, ew, ew, ew, ew!
What's all that for?
It's just so slimy!
I promise, it's not that bad.
I assure you, it is.

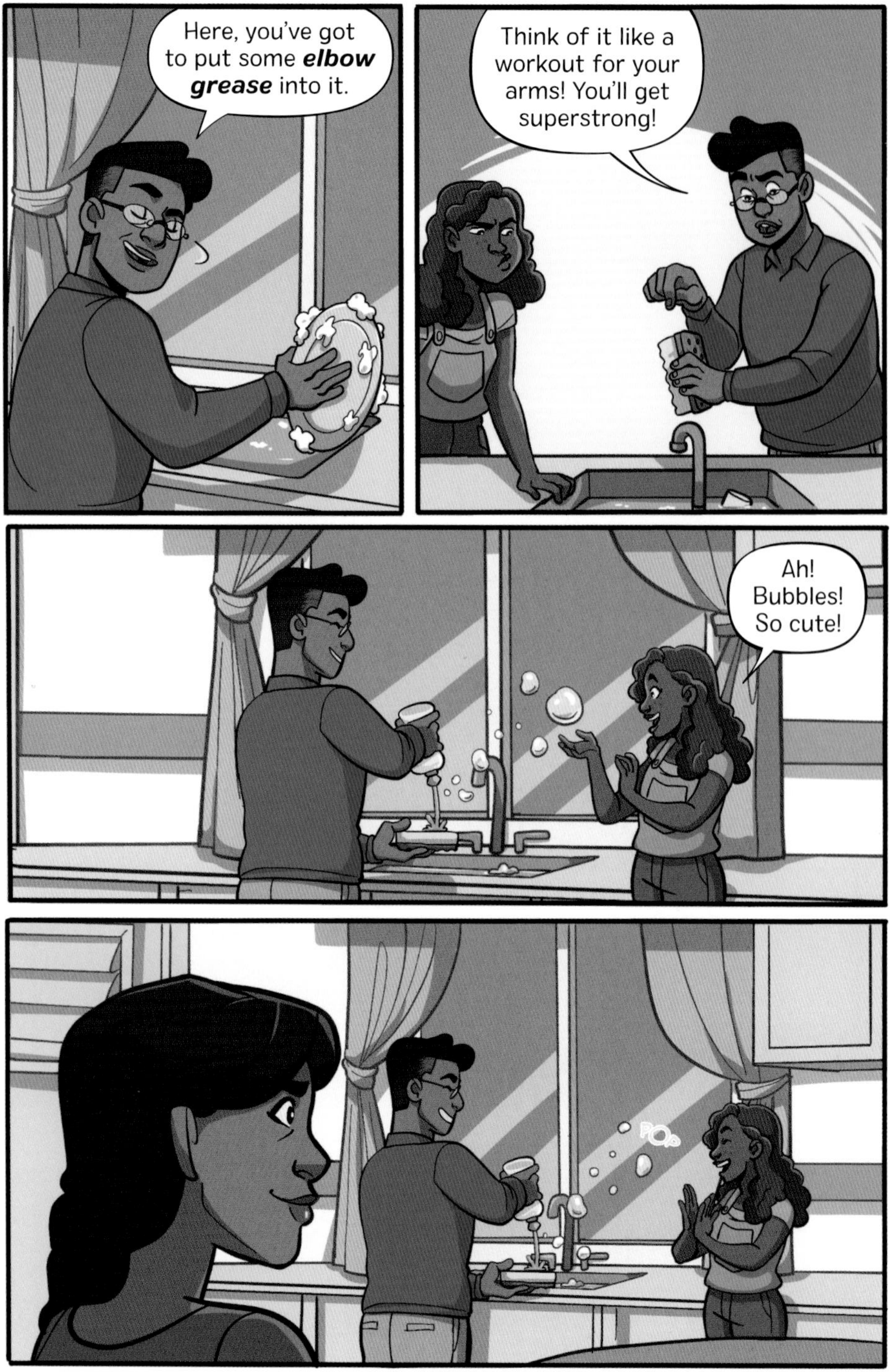

Here, you've got to put some ***elbow grease*** into it.
Think of it like a workout for your arms! You'll get superstrong!
Ah! Bubbles! So cute!
POP

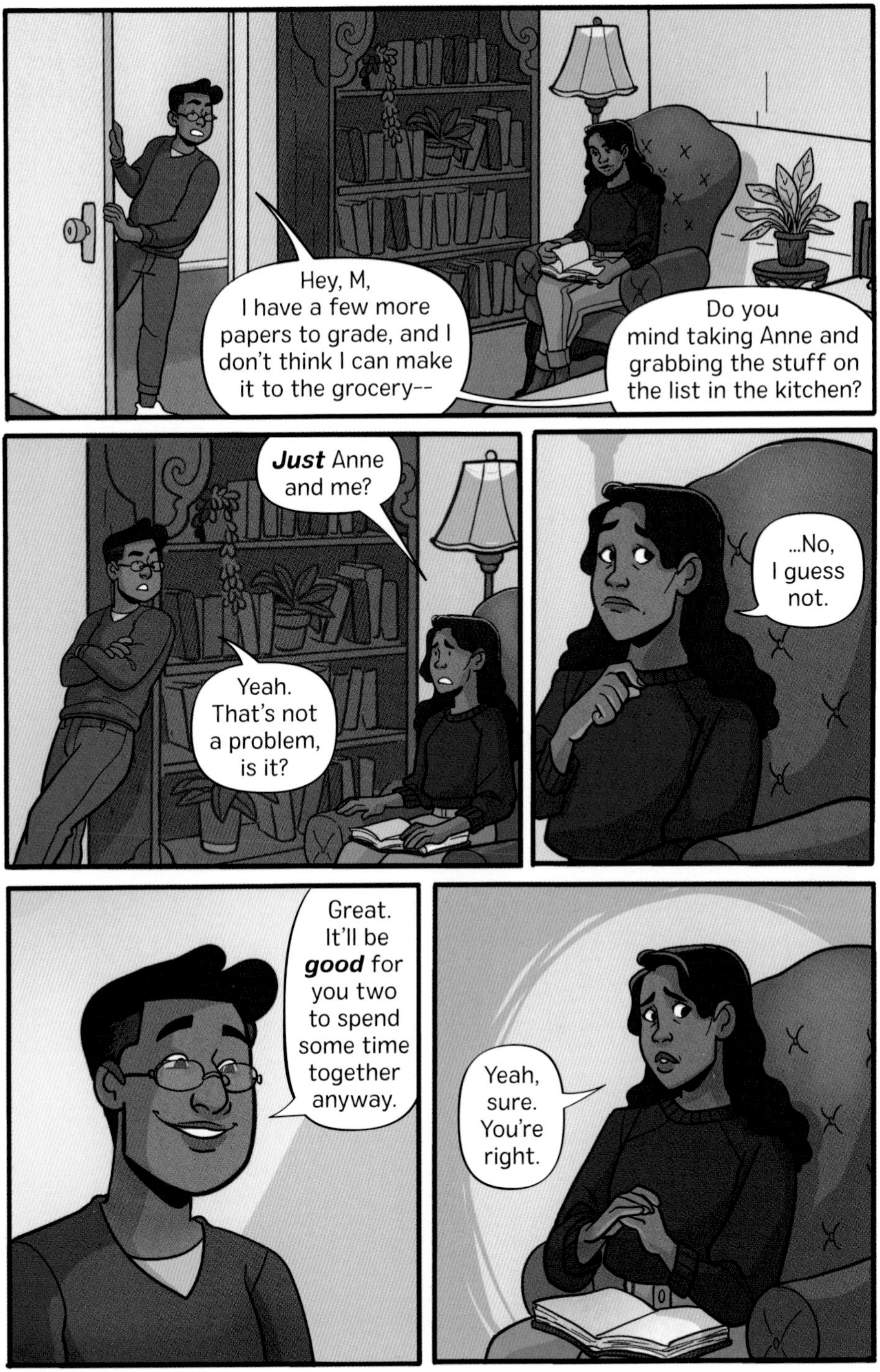
Hey, M, I have a few more papers to grade, and I don't think I can make it to the grocery--
Do you mind taking Anne and grabbing the stuff on the list in the kitchen?
Just Anne and me?
Yeah. That's not a problem, is it?
...No, I guess not.
Great. It'll be ***good*** for you two to spend some time together anyway.
Yeah, sure. You're right.

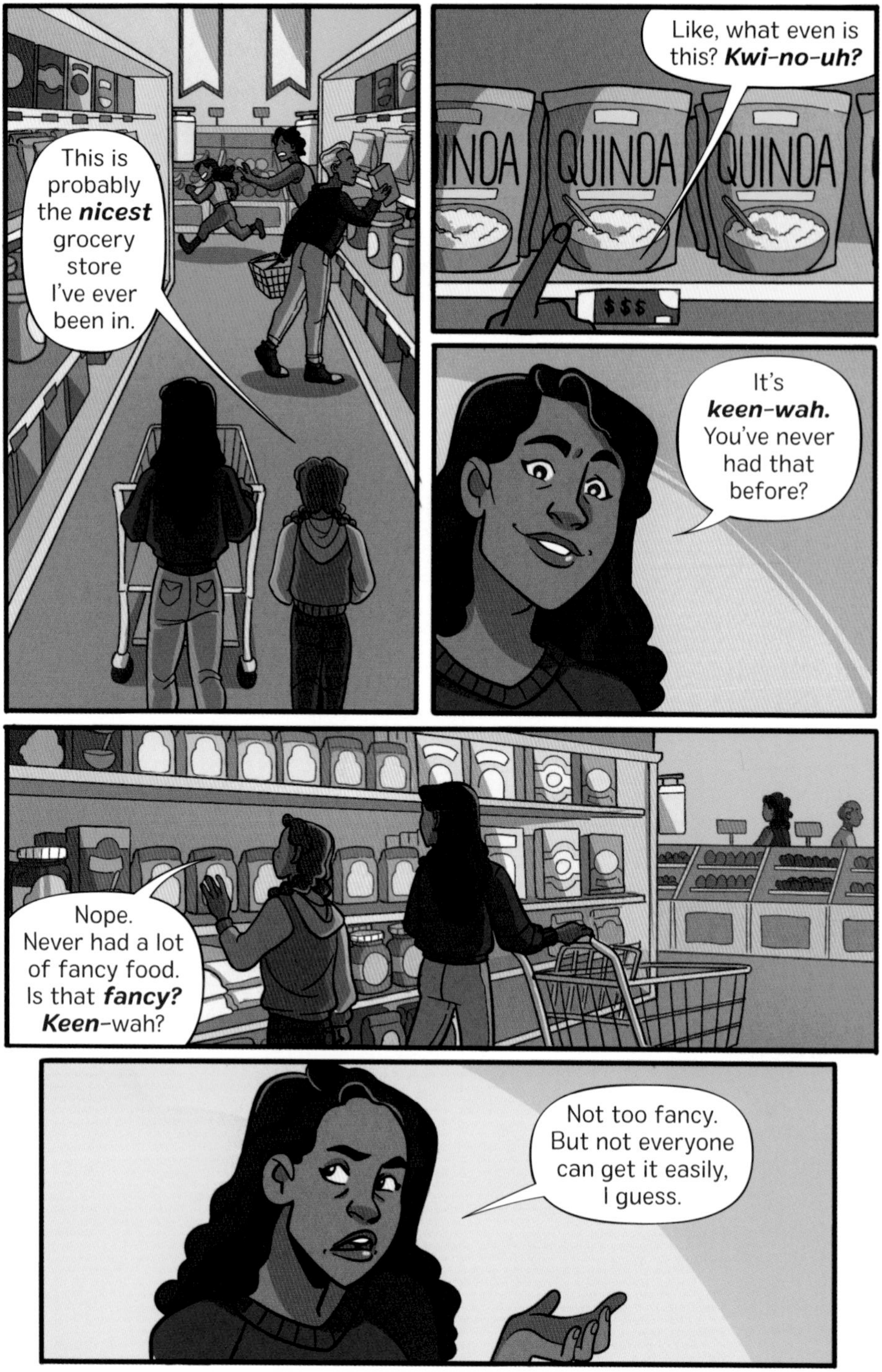
This is probably the *nicest* grocery store I've ever been in.
Like, what even is this? *Kwi-no-uh?*
QUINOA
QUINOA
$$$
It's **keen-wah.** You've never had that before?
Nope. Never had a lot of fancy food. Is that ***fancy? Keen***-wah?
Not too fancy. But not everyone can get it easily, I guess.

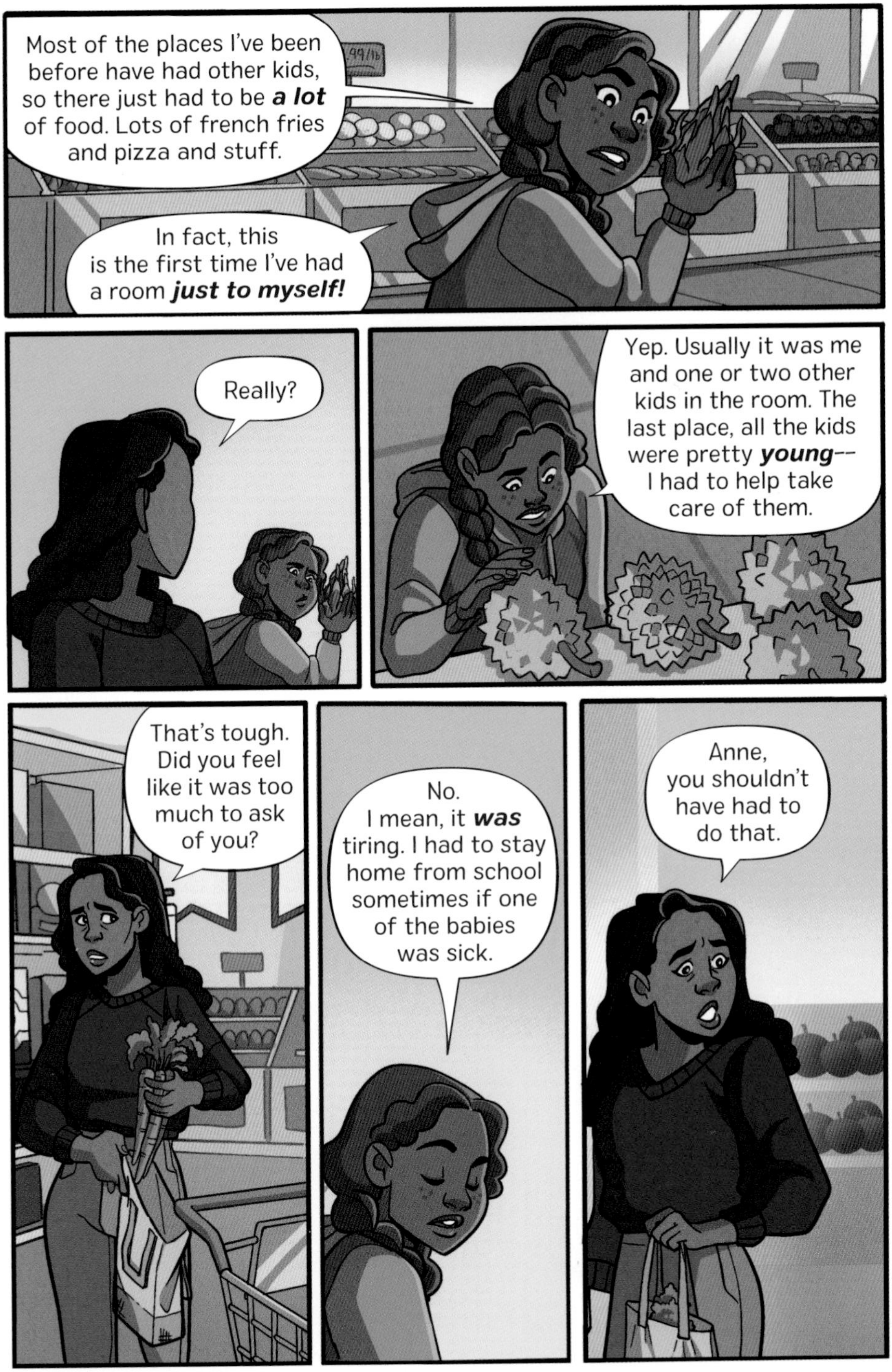
Most of the places I've been before have had other kids, so there just had to be ***a lot*** of food. Lots of french fries and pizza and stuff.
In fact, this is the first time I've had a room ***just to myself!***
Really?
Yep. Usually it was me and one or two other kids in the room. The last place, all the kids were pretty ***young***-- I had to help take care of them.
That's tough. Did you feel like it was too much to ask of you?
No. I mean, it ***was*** tiring. I had to stay home from school sometimes if one of the babies was sick.
Anne, you shouldn't have had to do that.

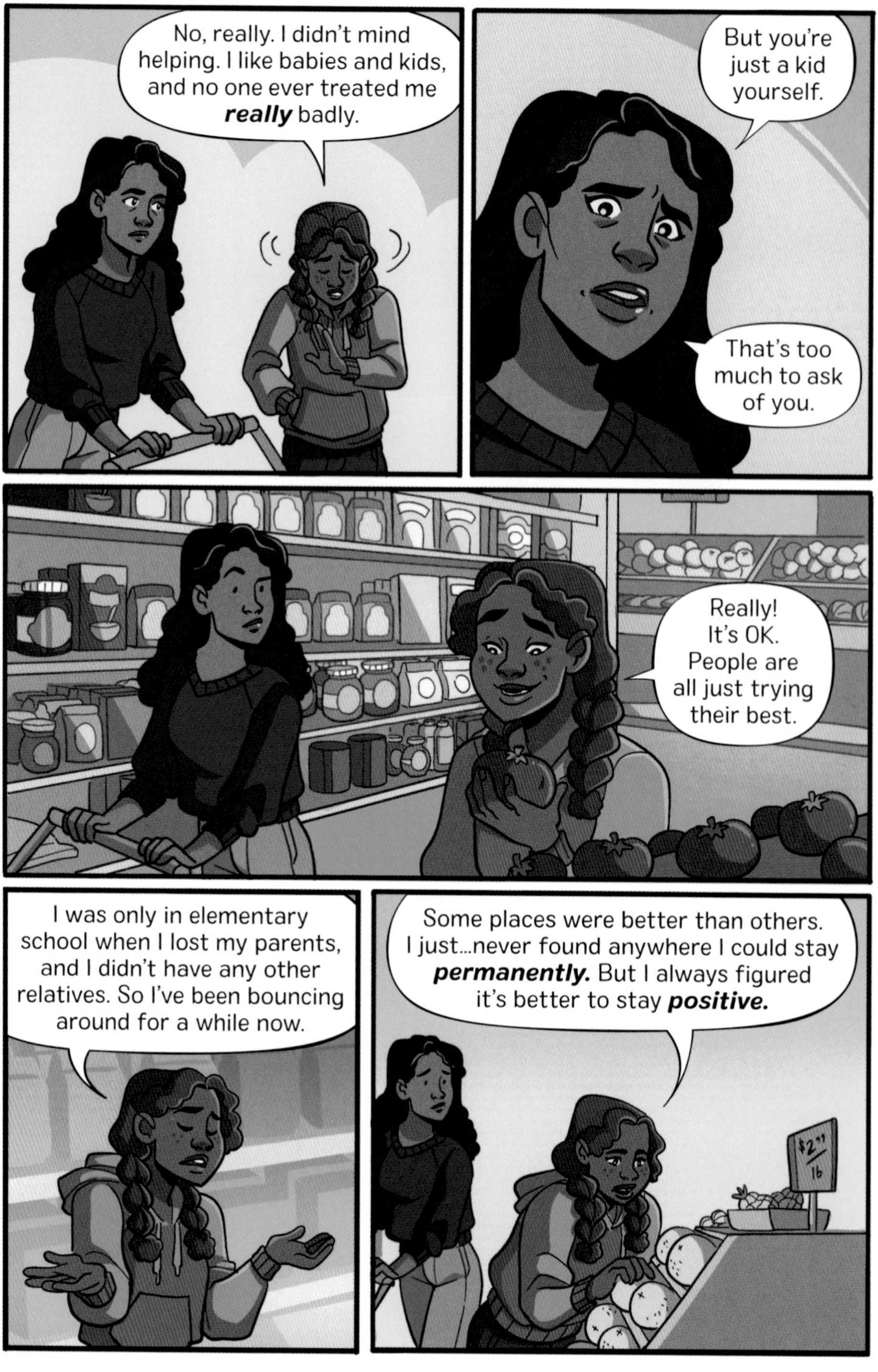
No, really. I didn't mind helping. I like babies and kids, and no one ever treated me ***really*** badly.
But you're just a kid yourself.
That's too much to ask of you.
Really! It's OK. People are all just trying their best.
I was only in elementary school when I lost my parents, and I didn't have any other relatives. So I've been bouncing around for a while now.
Some places were better than others. I just...never found anywhere I could stay ***permanently.*** But I always figured it's better to stay ***positive.***
$2.99 lb

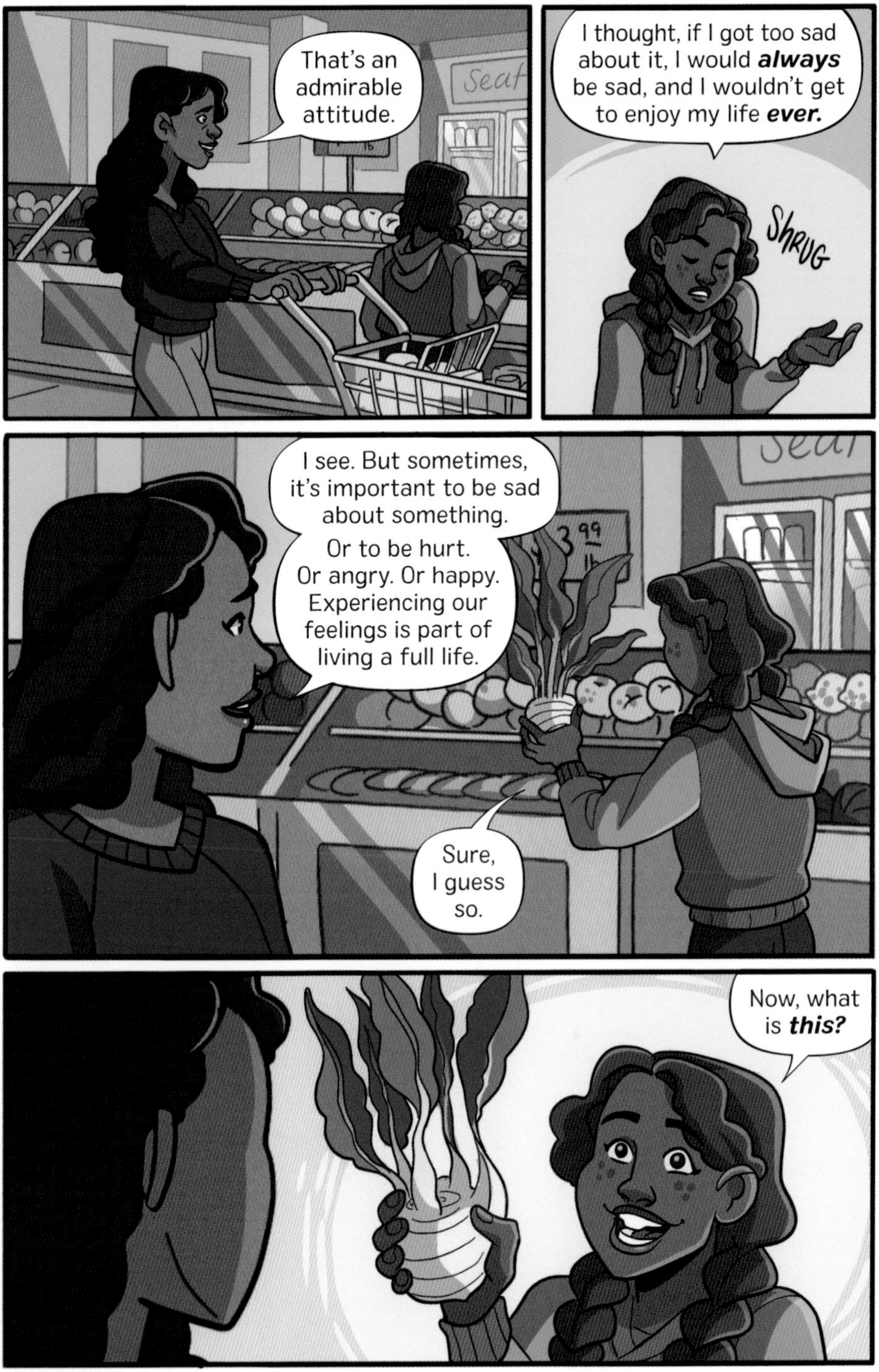
That's an admirable attitude.
I thought, if I got too sad about it, I would ***always*** be sad, and I wouldn't get to enjoy my life ***ever.***
SHRUG
I see. But sometimes, it's important to be sad about something.
Or to be hurt. Or angry. Or happy. Experiencing our feelings is part of living a full life.
Sure, I guess so.
Now, what is ***this?***

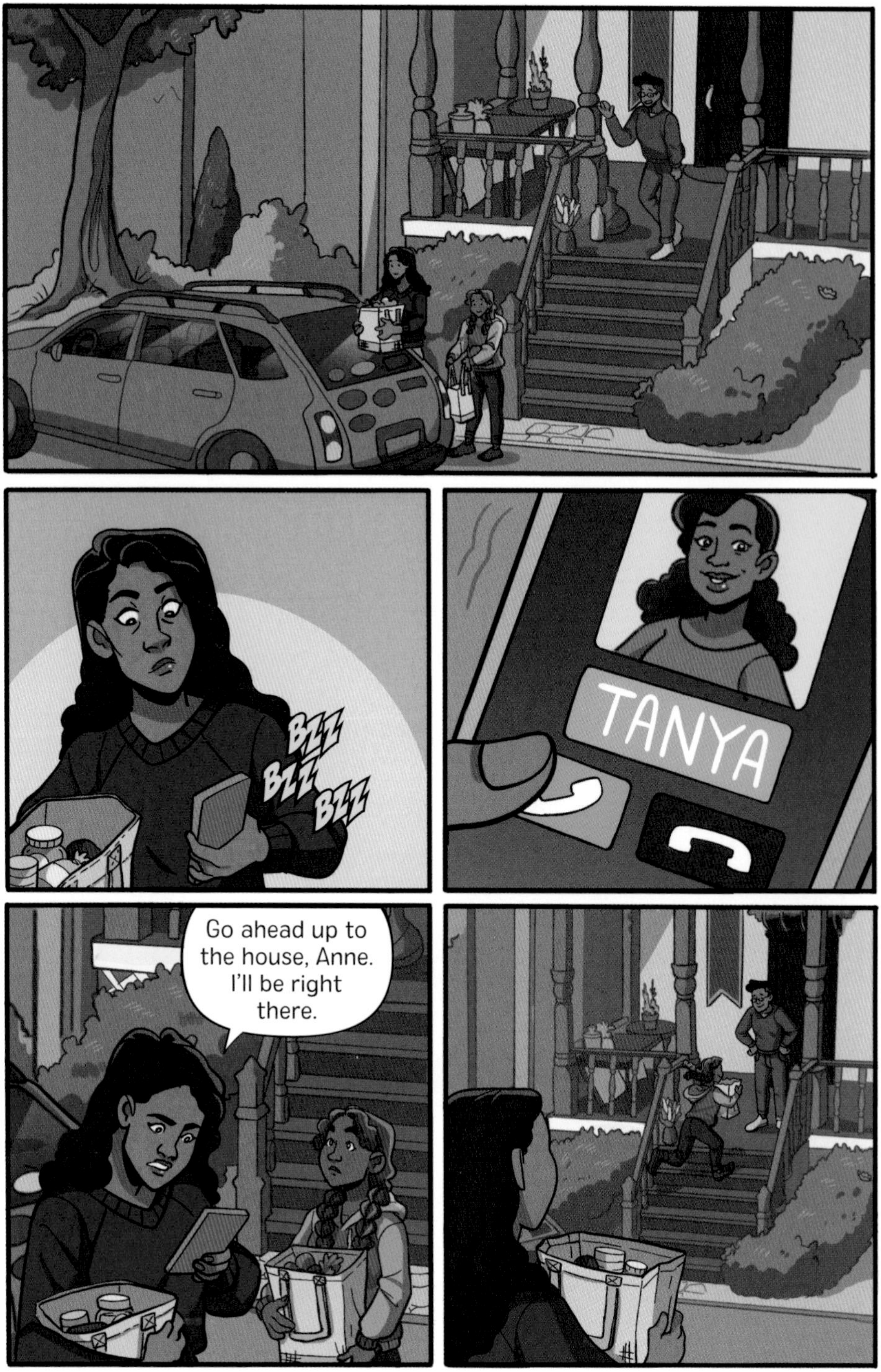
BZZ
BZZ
BZZ
TANYA
Go ahead up to the house, Anne. I'll be right there.

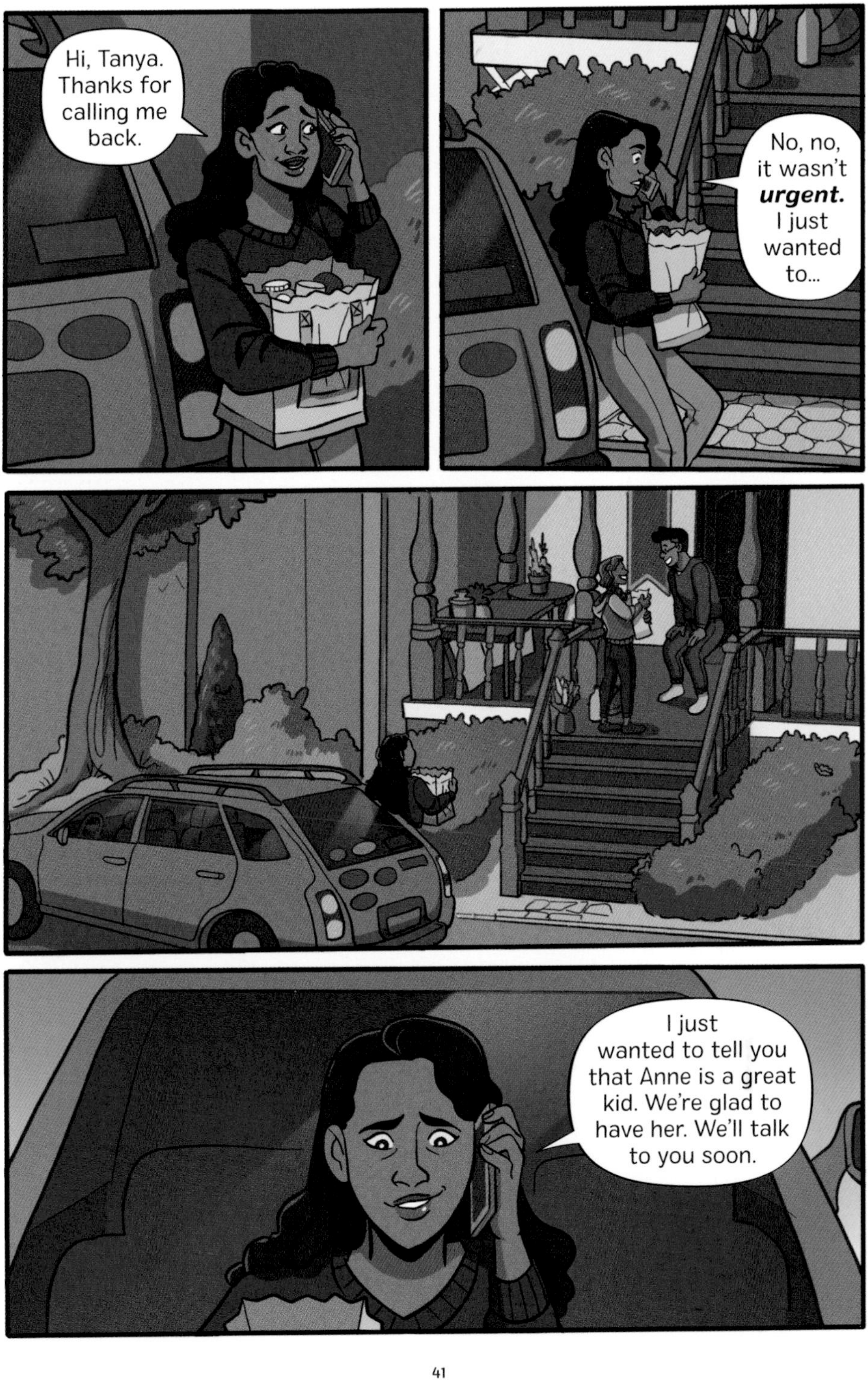
Hi, Tanya. Thanks for calling me back.
No, no, it wasn't ***urgent.*** I just wanted to...
I just wanted to tell you that Anne is a great kid. We're glad to have her. We'll talk to you soon.

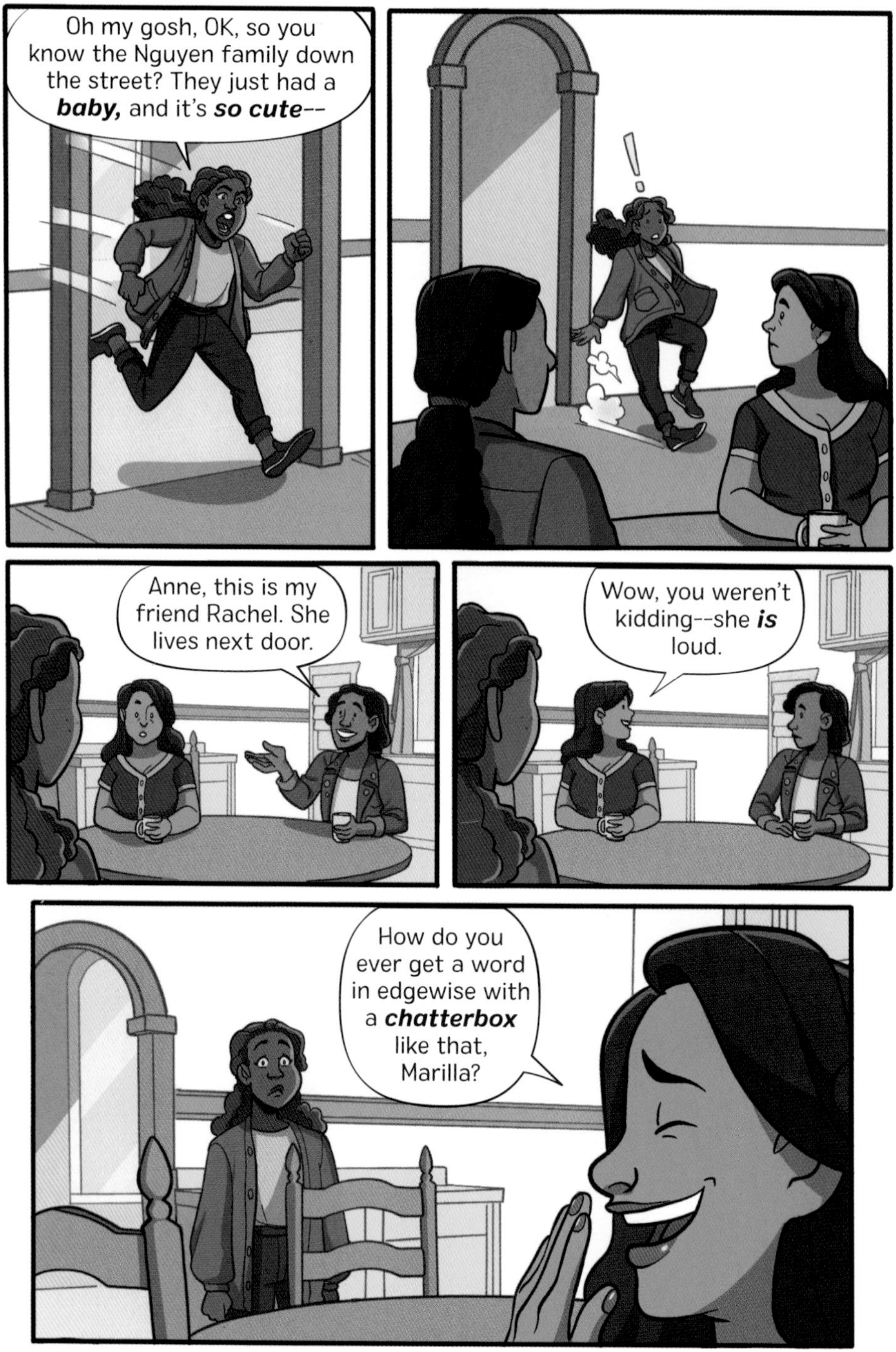
Oh my gosh, OK, so you know the Nguyen family down the street? They just had a ***baby,*** and it's ***so cute***--
!
Anne, this is my friend Rachel. She lives next door.
Wow, you weren't kidding--she ***is*** loud.
How do you ever get a word in edgewise with a ***chatterbox*** like that, Marilla?

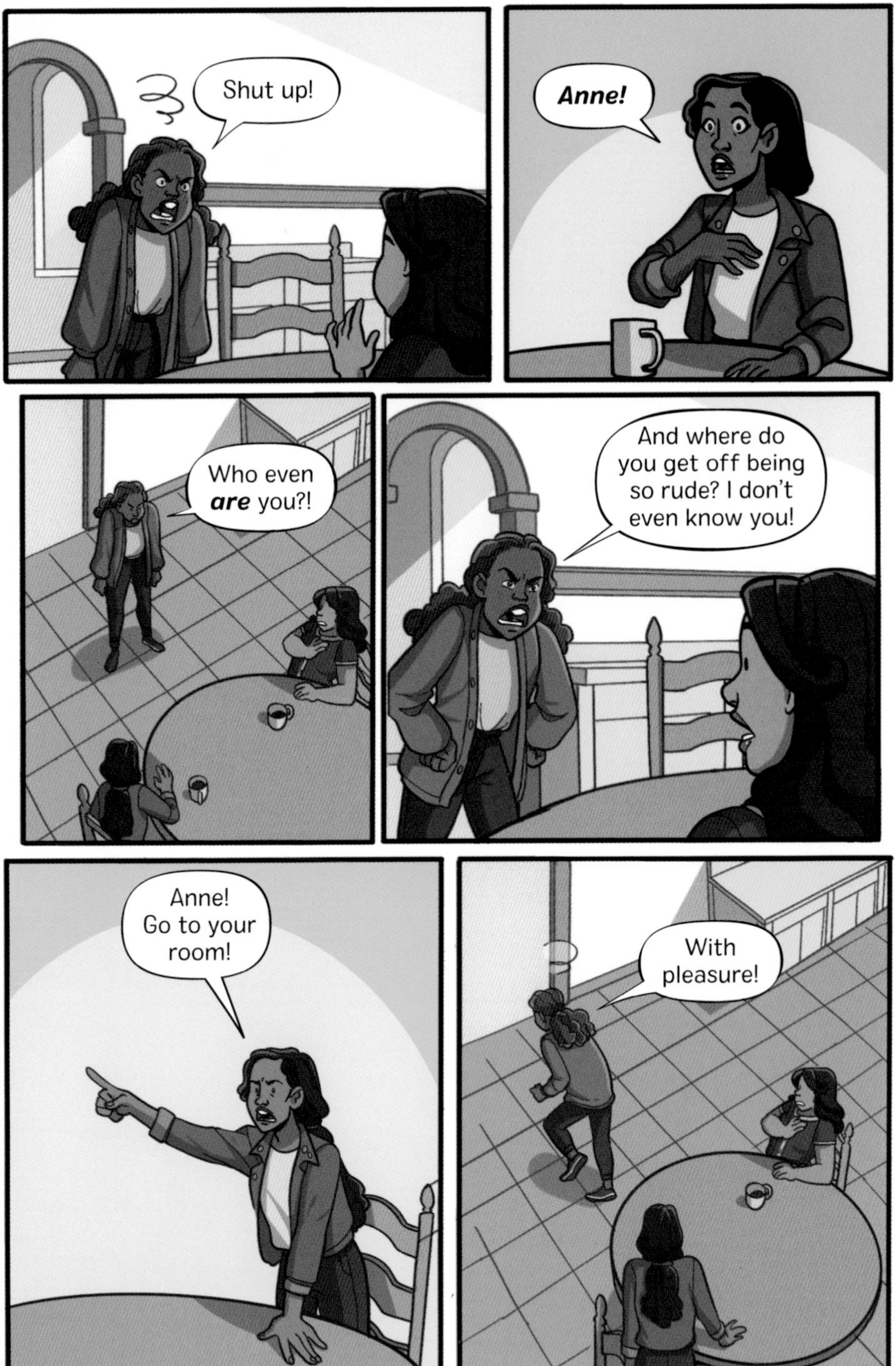
Shut up!
Anne!
Who even are you?!
And where do you get off being so rude? I don't even know you!
Anne! Go to your room!
With pleasure!

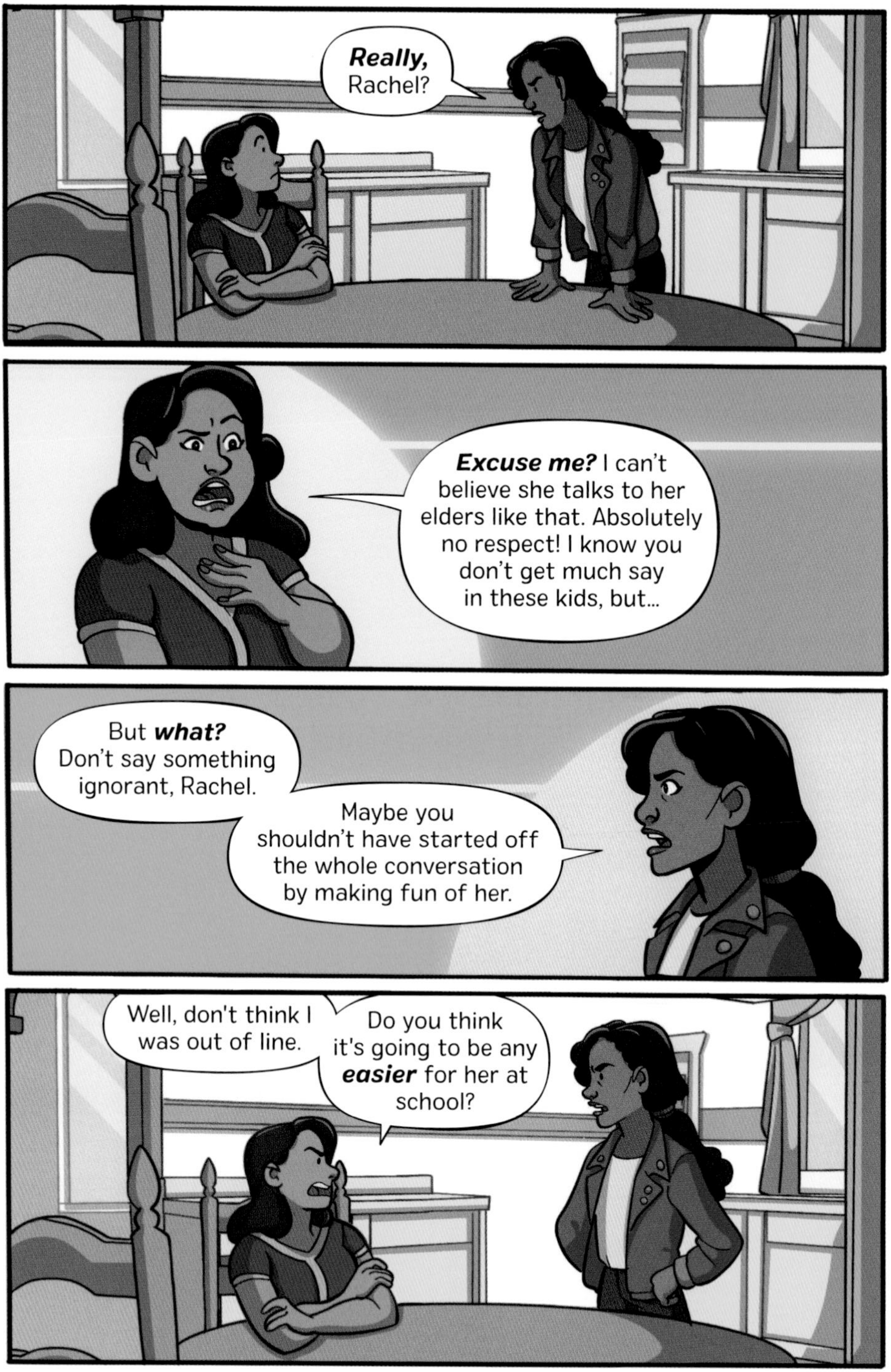

Really, Rachel?
Excuse me? I can't believe she talks to her elders like that. Absolutely no respect! I know you don't get much say in these kids, but...
But ***what?*** Don't say something ignorant, Rachel.
Maybe you shouldn't have started off the whole conversation by making fun of her.
Well, don't think I was out of line.
Do you think it's going to be any ***easier*** for her at school?

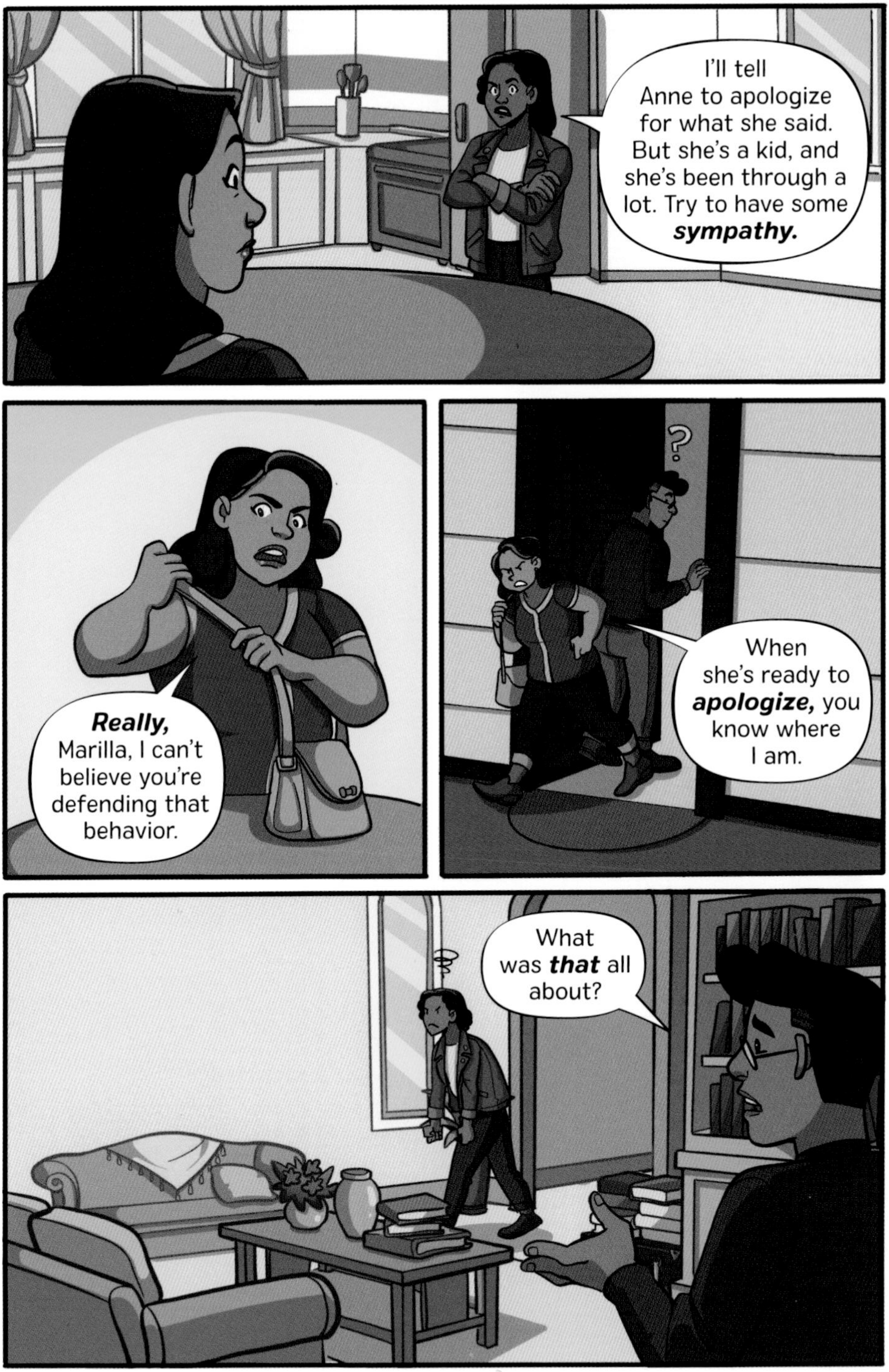
I'll tell Anne to apologize for what she said. But she's a kid, and she's been through a lot. Try to have some *sympathy.*
Really, Marilla, I can't believe you're defending that behavior.
?
When she's ready to *apologize,* you know where I am.
What was *that* all about?

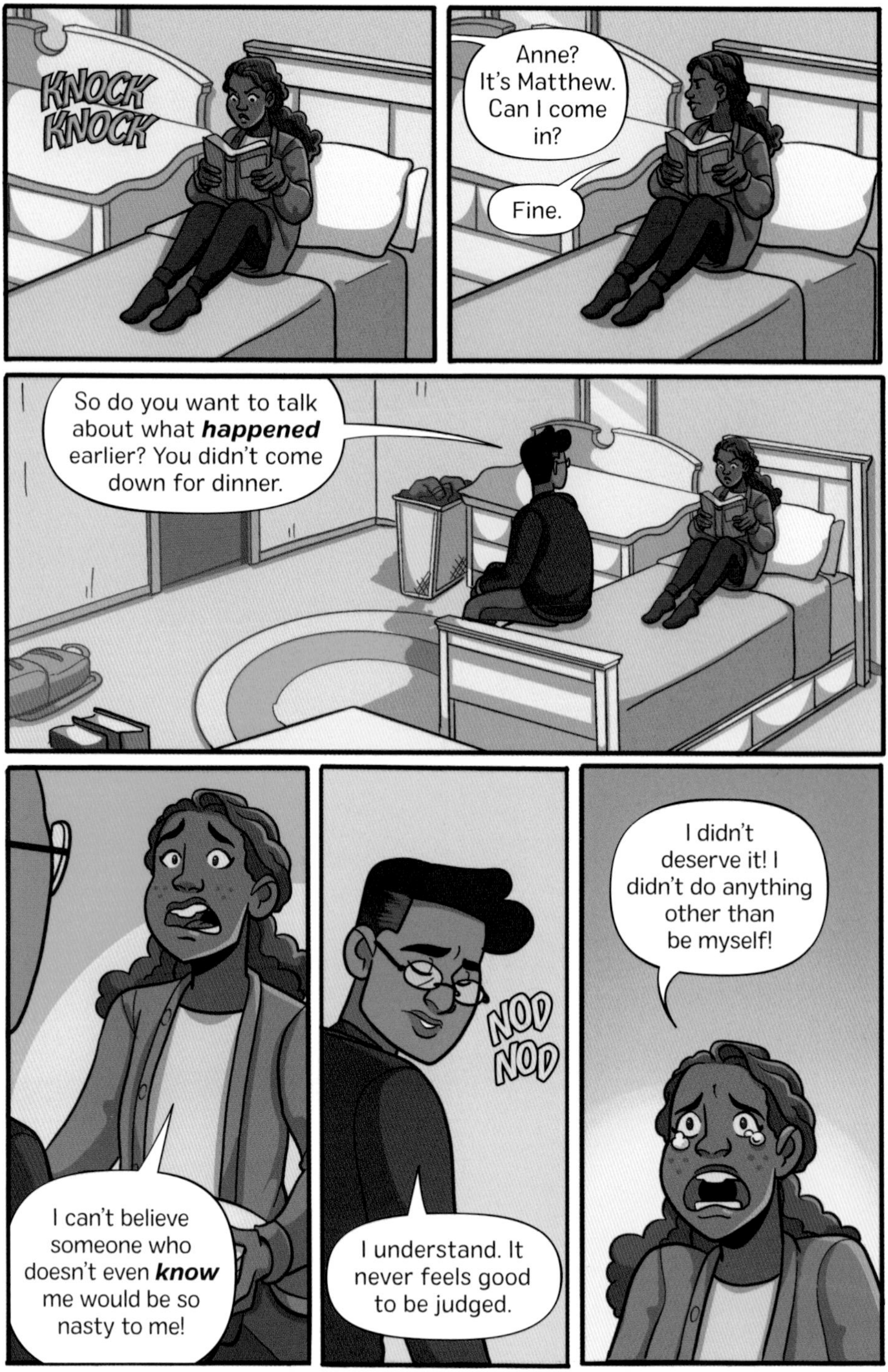
KNOCK KNOCK
Anne? It's Matthew. Can I come in?
Fine.
So do you want to talk about what ***happened*** earlier? You didn't come down for dinner.
I can't believe someone who doesn't even ***know*** me would be so nasty to me!
NOD NOD
I understand. It never feels good to be judged.
I didn't deserve it! I didn't do anything other than be myself!

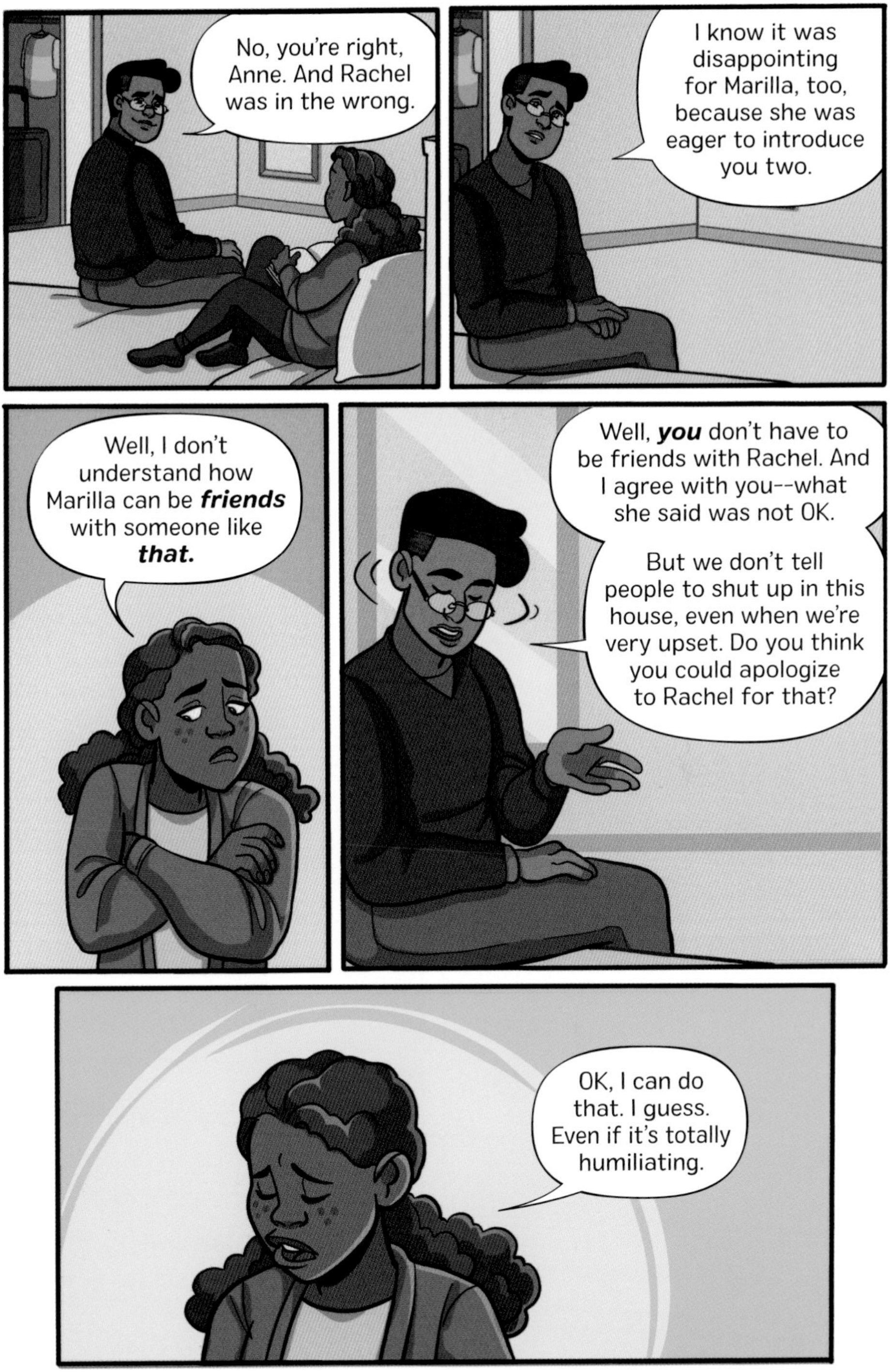
No, you're right, Anne. And Rachel was in the wrong.
I know it was disappointing for Marilla, too, because she was eager to introduce you two.
Well, I don't understand how Marilla can be ***friends*** with someone like ***that.***
Well, ***you*** don't have to be friends with Rachel. And I agree with you--what she said was not OK.
But we don't tell people to shut up in this house, even when we're very upset. Do you think you could apologize to Rachel for that?
OK, I can do that. I guess. Even if it's totally humiliating.

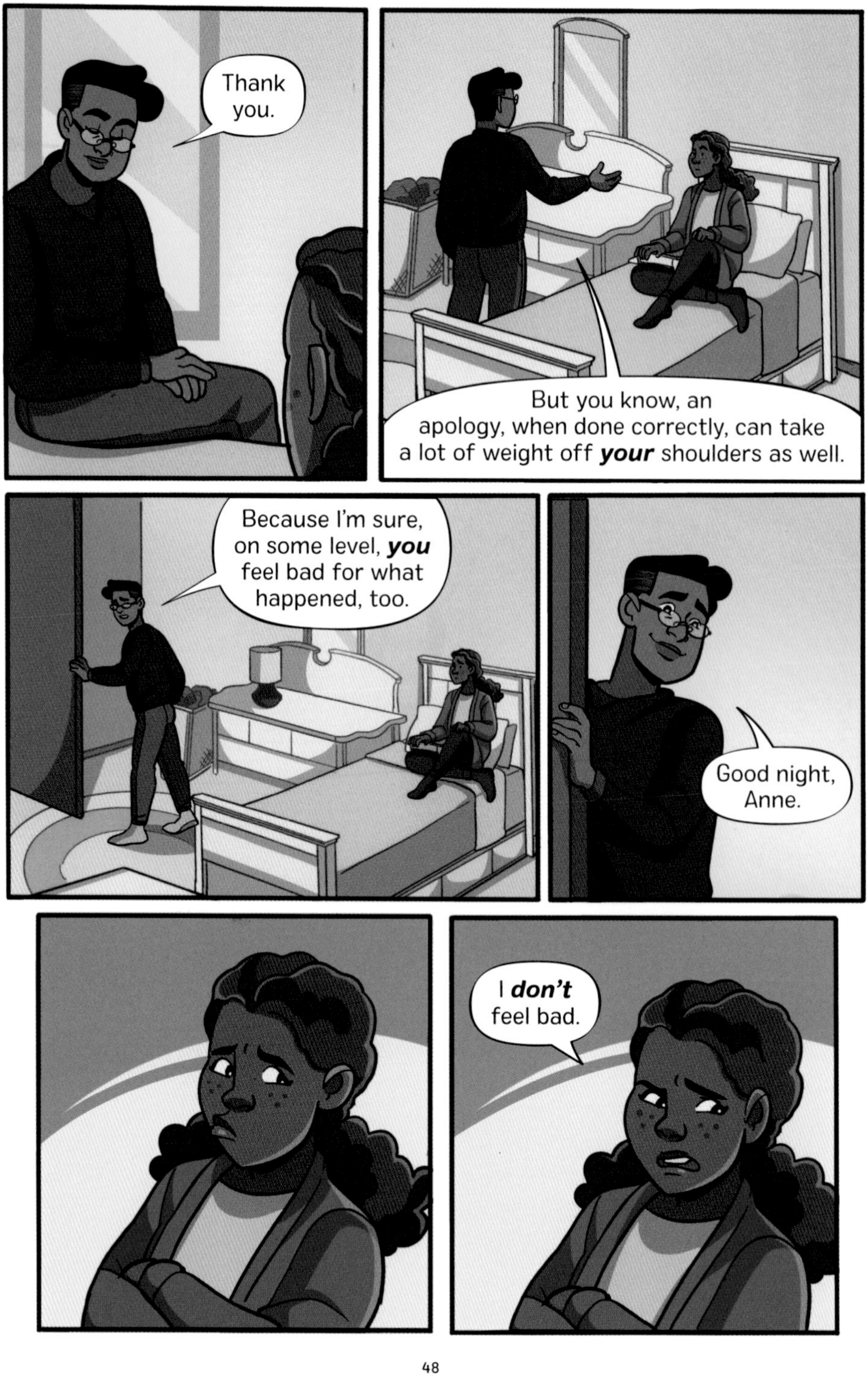
Thank you.
But you know, an apology, when done correctly, can take a lot of weight off ***your*** shoulders as well.
Because I'm sure, on some level, ***you*** feel bad for what happened, too.
Good night, Anne.
I ***don't*** feel bad.

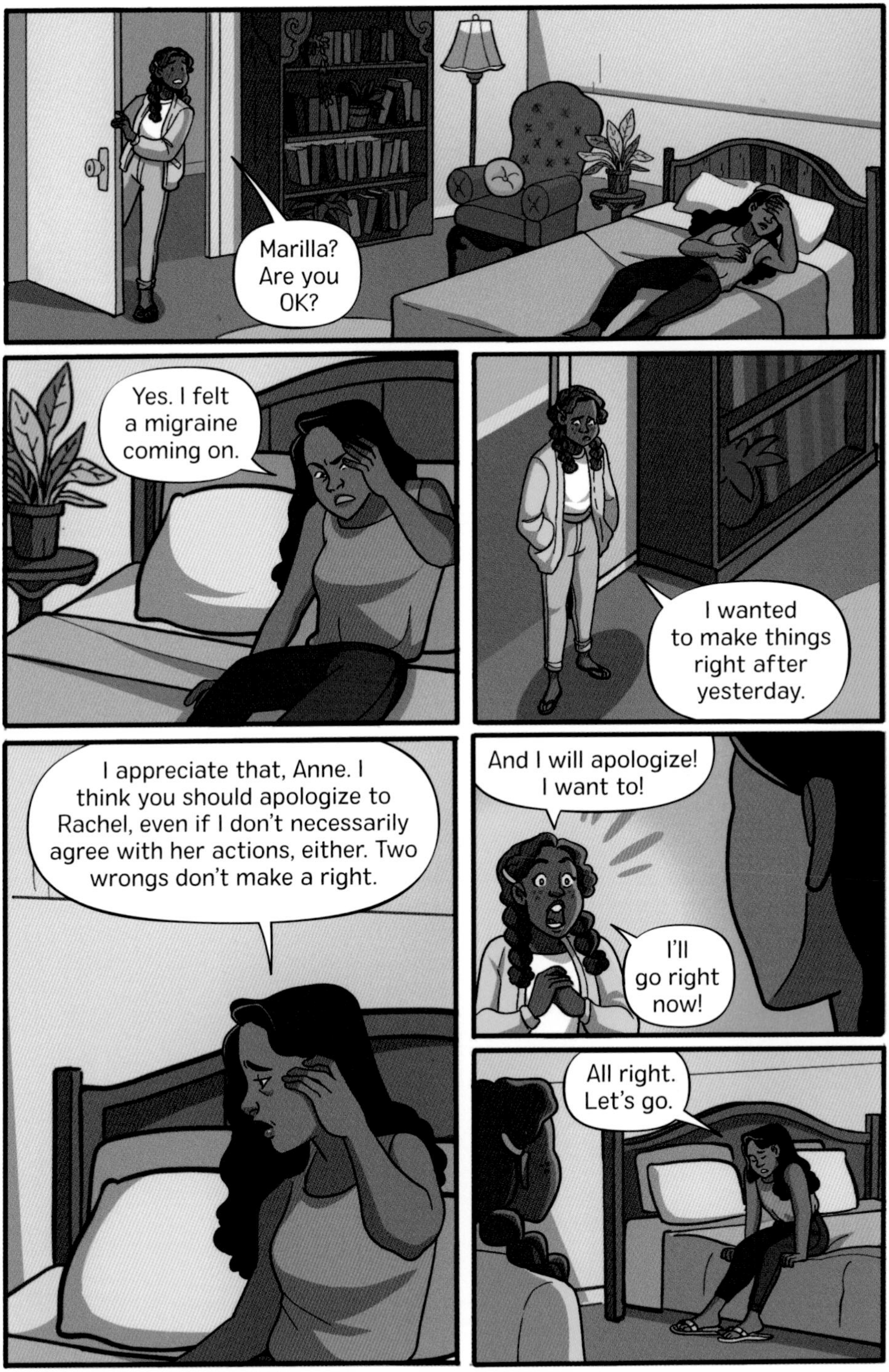
Marilla? Are you OK?
Yes. I felt a migraine coming on.
I wanted to make things right after yesterday.
I appreciate that, Anne. I think you should apologize to Rachel, even if I don't necessarily agree with her actions, either. Two wrongs don't make a right.
And I will apologize! I want to!
I'll go right now!
All right. Let's go.

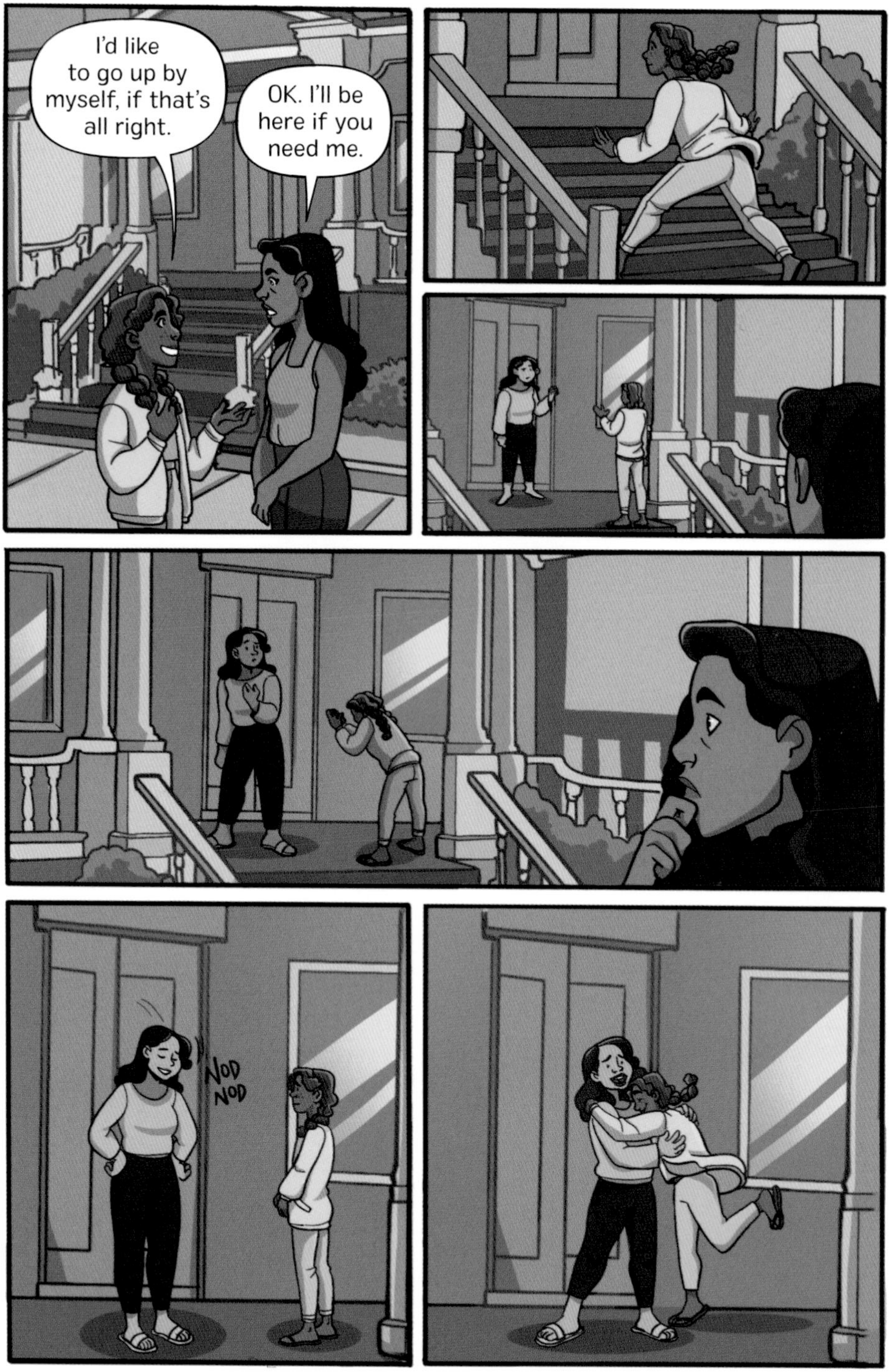
I'd like to go up by myself, if that's all right.
OK. I'll be here if you need me.
NOD NOD

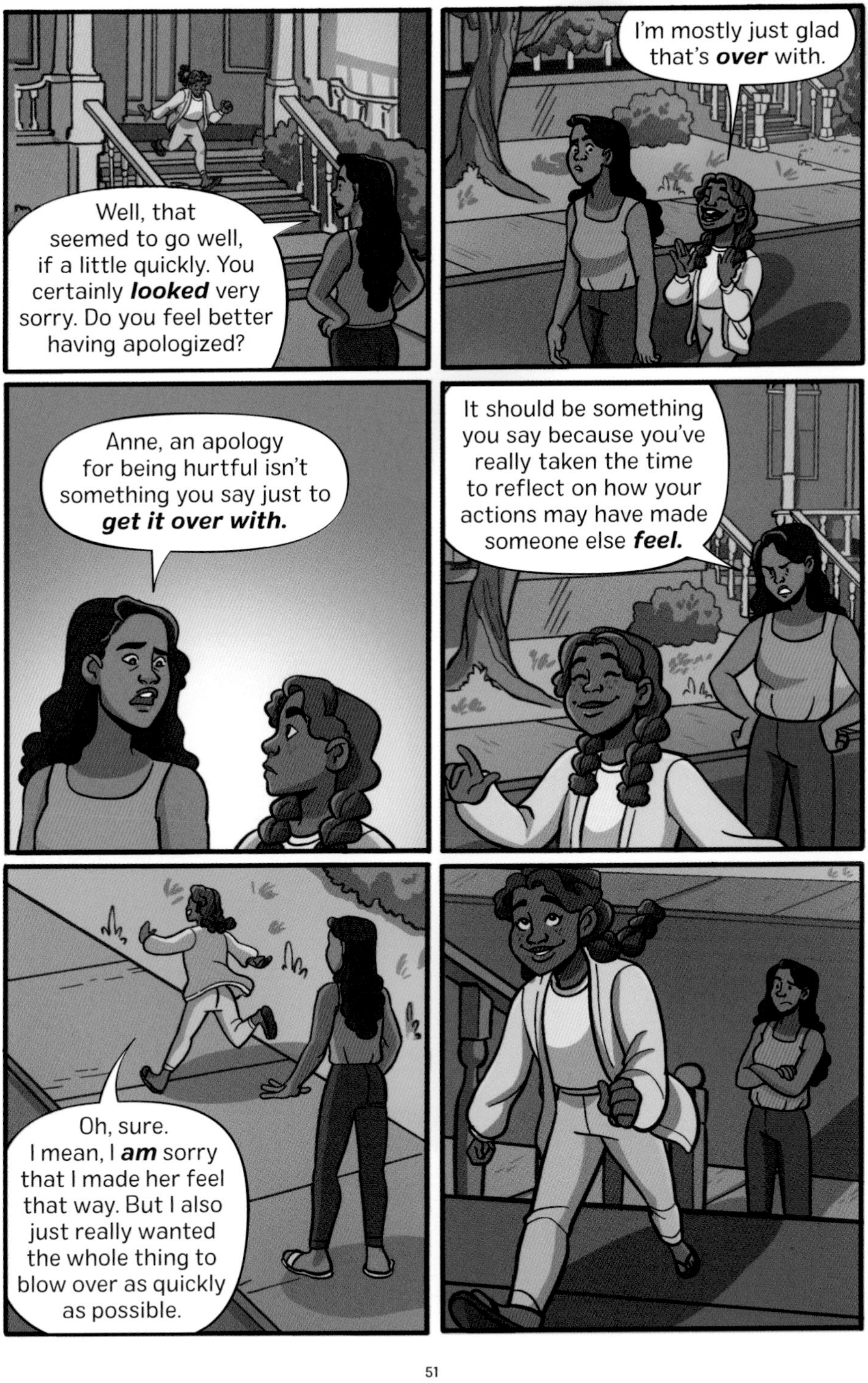
Well, that seemed to go well, if a little quickly. You certainly **looked** very sorry. Do you feel better having apologized?
I'm mostly just glad that's **over** with.
Anne, an apology for being hurtful isn't something you say just to **get it over with.**
It should be something you say because you've really taken the time to reflect on how your actions may have made someone else **feel.**
Oh, sure. I mean, I **am** sorry that I made her feel that way. But I also just really wanted the whole thing to blow over as quickly as possible.

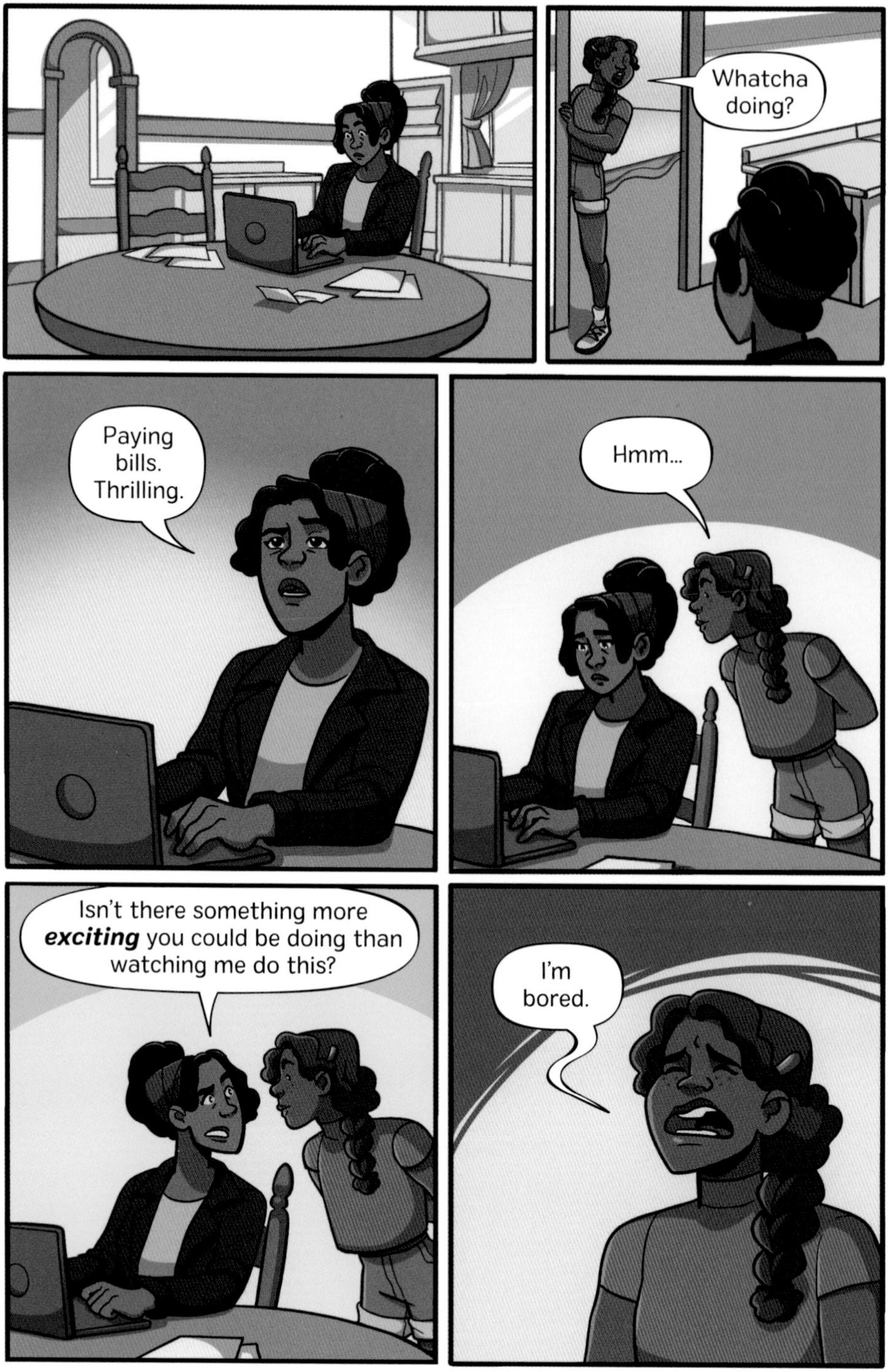
Whatcha doing?
Paying bills. Thrilling.
Hmm...
Isn't there something more **exciting** you could be doing than watching me do this?
I'm bored.

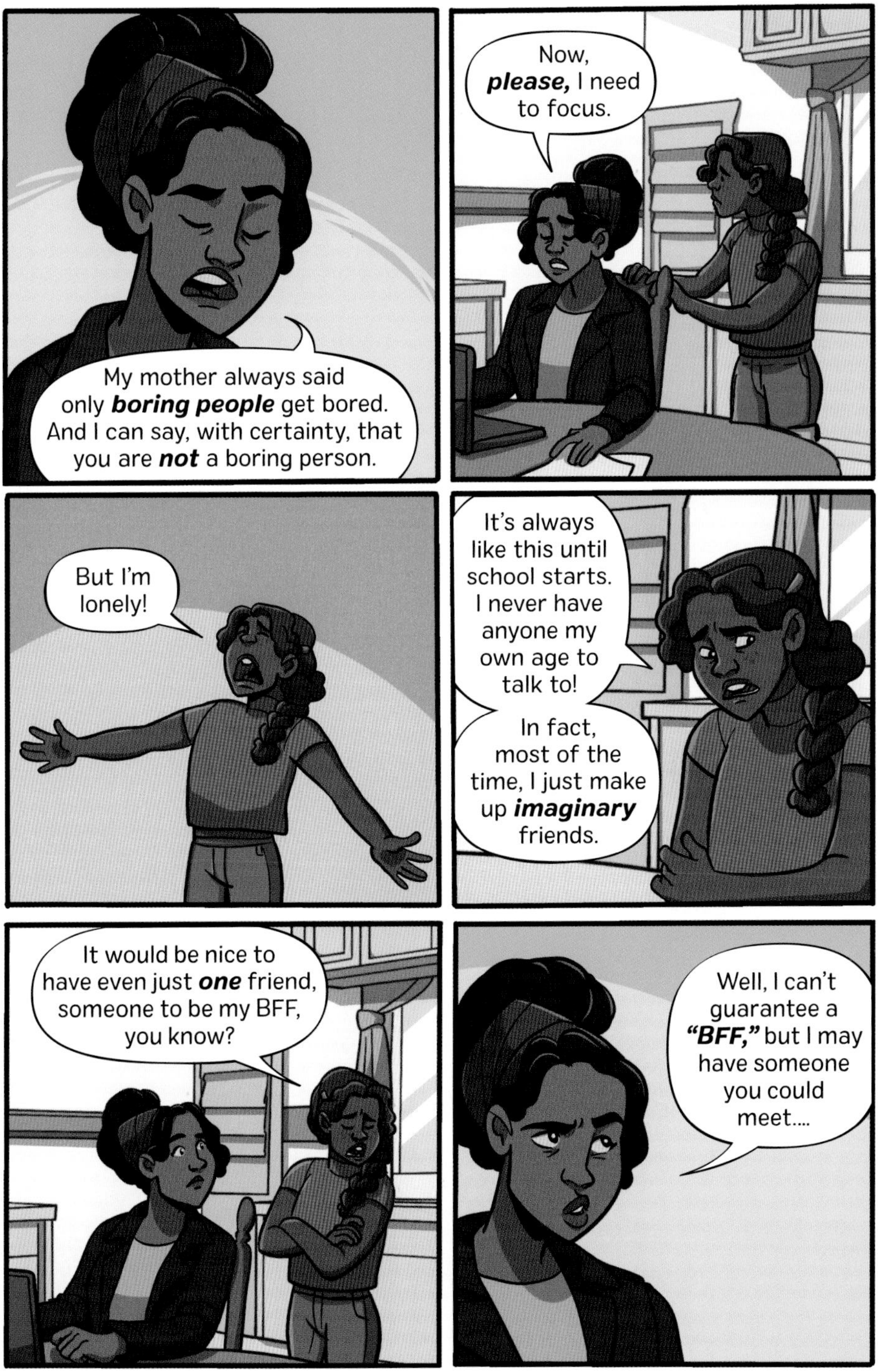
My mother always said only ***boring people*** get bored. And I can say, with certainty, that you are ***not*** a boring person.
Now, ***please,*** I need to focus.
But I'm lonely!
It's always like this until school starts. I never have anyone my own age to talk to!
In fact, most of the time, I just make up ***imaginary*** friends.
It would be nice to have even just ***one*** friend, someone to be my BFF, you know?
Well, I can't guarantee a ***"BFF,"*** but I may have someone you could meet....

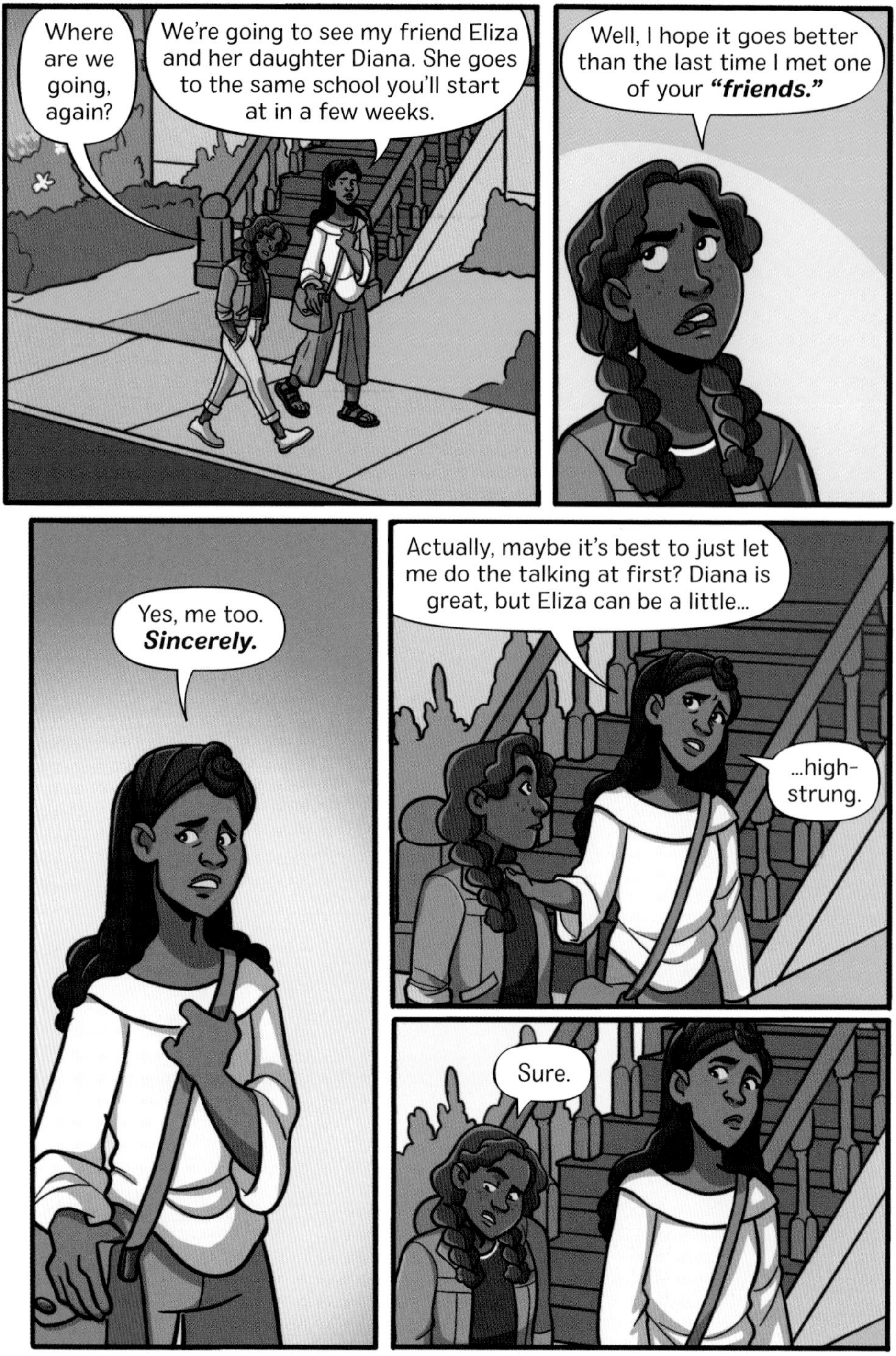

Where are we going, again?
We're going to see my friend Eliza and her daughter Diana. She goes to the same school you'll start at in a few weeks.
Well, I hope it goes better than the last time I met one of your ***"friends."***
Yes, me too. ***Sincerely.***
Actually, maybe it's best to just let me do the talking at first? Diana is great, but Eliza can be a little...
...high-strung.
Sure.

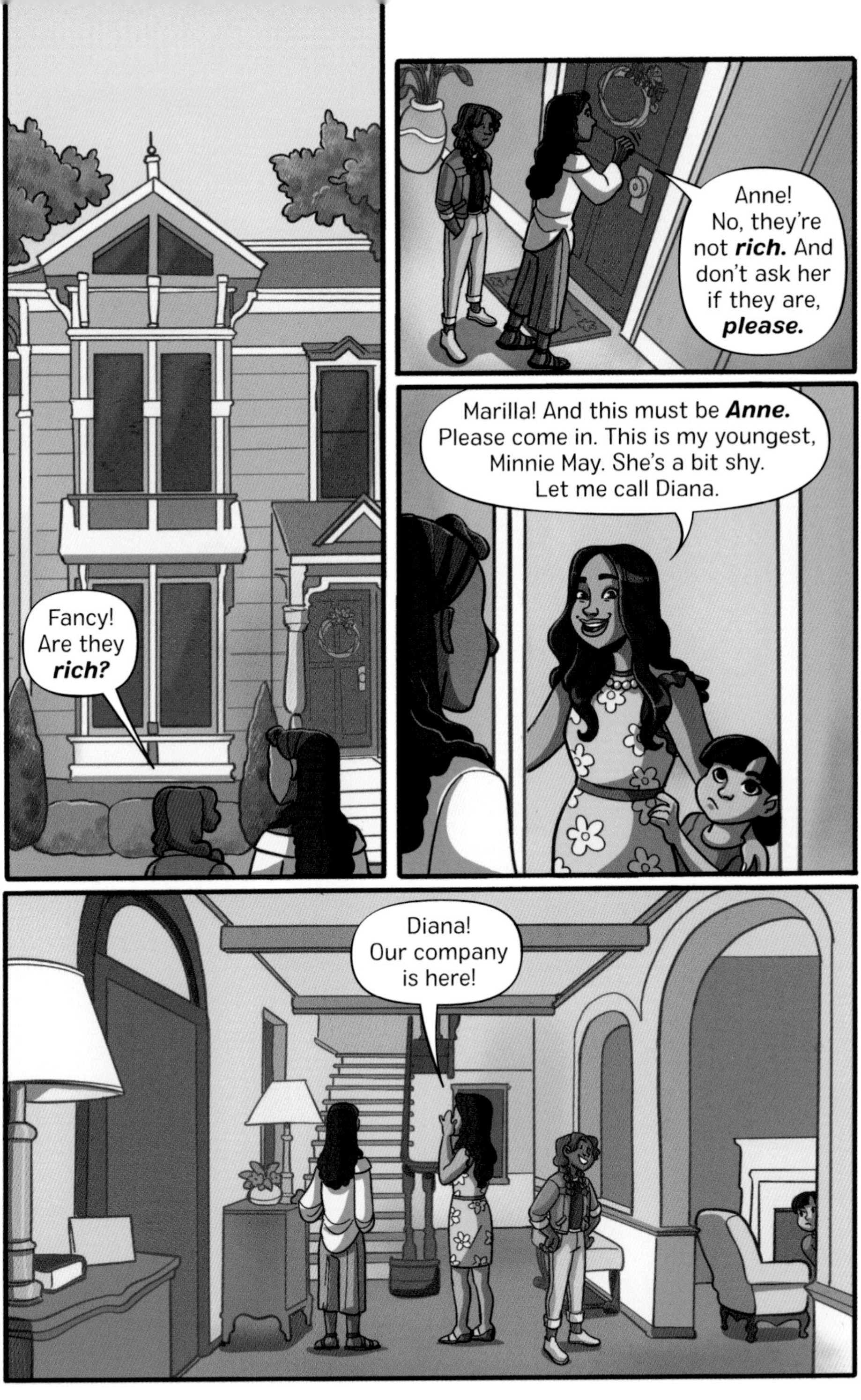
Fancy! Are they *rich?*
Anne! No, they're not *rich.* And don't ask her if they are, *please.*
Marilla! And this must be *Anne.* Please come in. This is my youngest, Minnie May. She's a bit shy. Let me call Diana.
Diana! Our company is here!

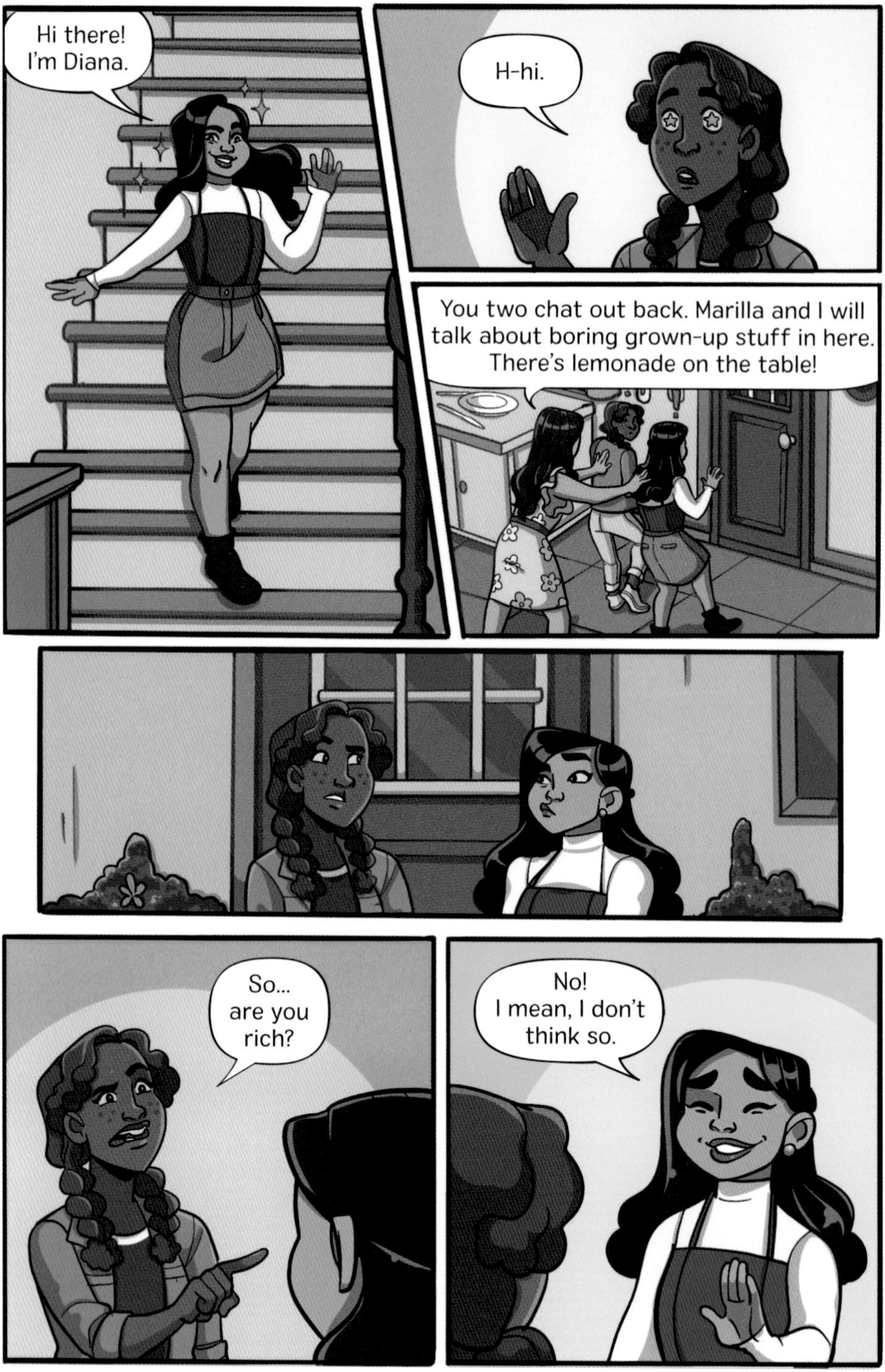
Hi there!
I'm Diana.
H-hi.
You two chat out back. Marilla and I will talk about boring grown-up stuff in here. There's lemonade on the table!
So... are you rich?
No! I mean, I don't think so.

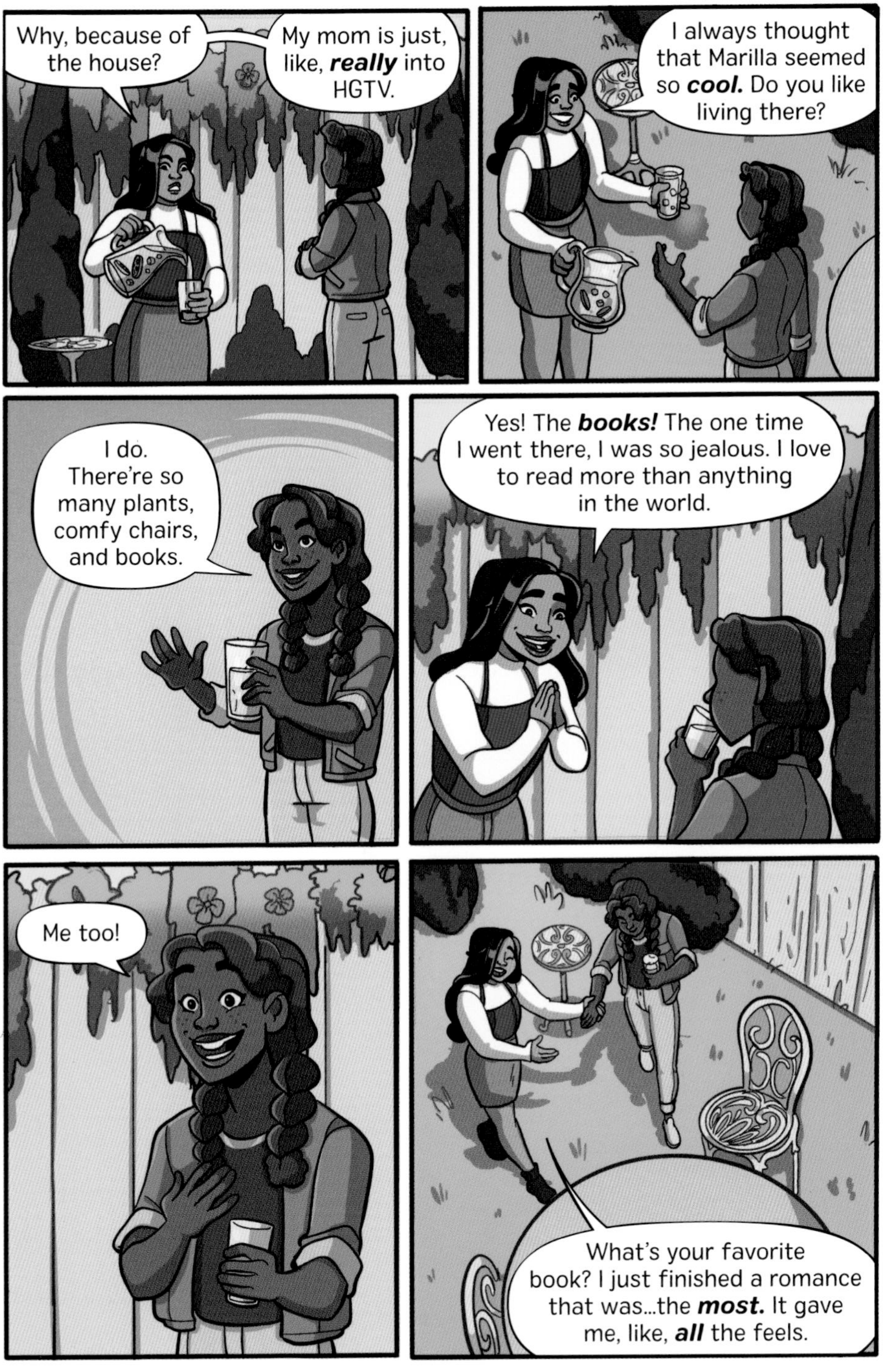
Why, because of the house?
My mom is just, like, ***really*** into HGTV.
I always thought that Marilla seemed so ***cool.*** Do you like living there?
I do. There're so many plants, comfy chairs, and books.
Yes! The ***books!*** The one time I went there, I was so jealous. I love to read more than anything in the world.
Me too!
What's your favorite book? I just finished a romance that was...the ***most.*** It gave me, like, ***all*** the feels.

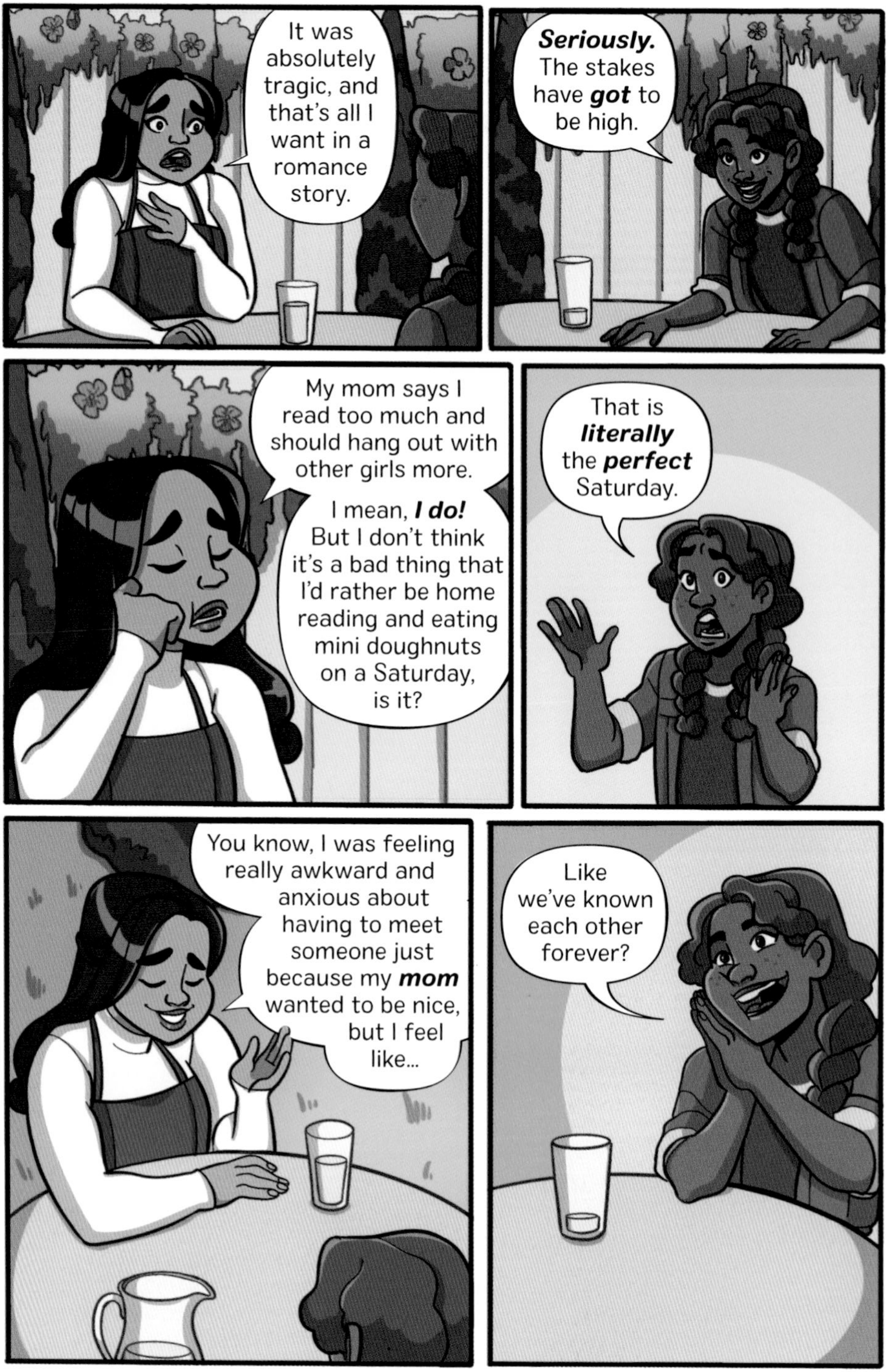
It was absolutely tragic, and that's all I want in a romance story.
Seriously. The stakes have ***got*** to be high.
My mom says I read too much and should hang out with other girls more.
I mean, ***I do!*** But I don't think it's a bad thing that I'd rather be home reading and eating mini doughnuts on a Saturday, is it?
That is ***literally*** the ***perfect*** Saturday.
You know, I was feeling really awkward and anxious about having to meet someone just because my ***mom*** wanted to be nice, but I feel like...
Like we've known each other forever?

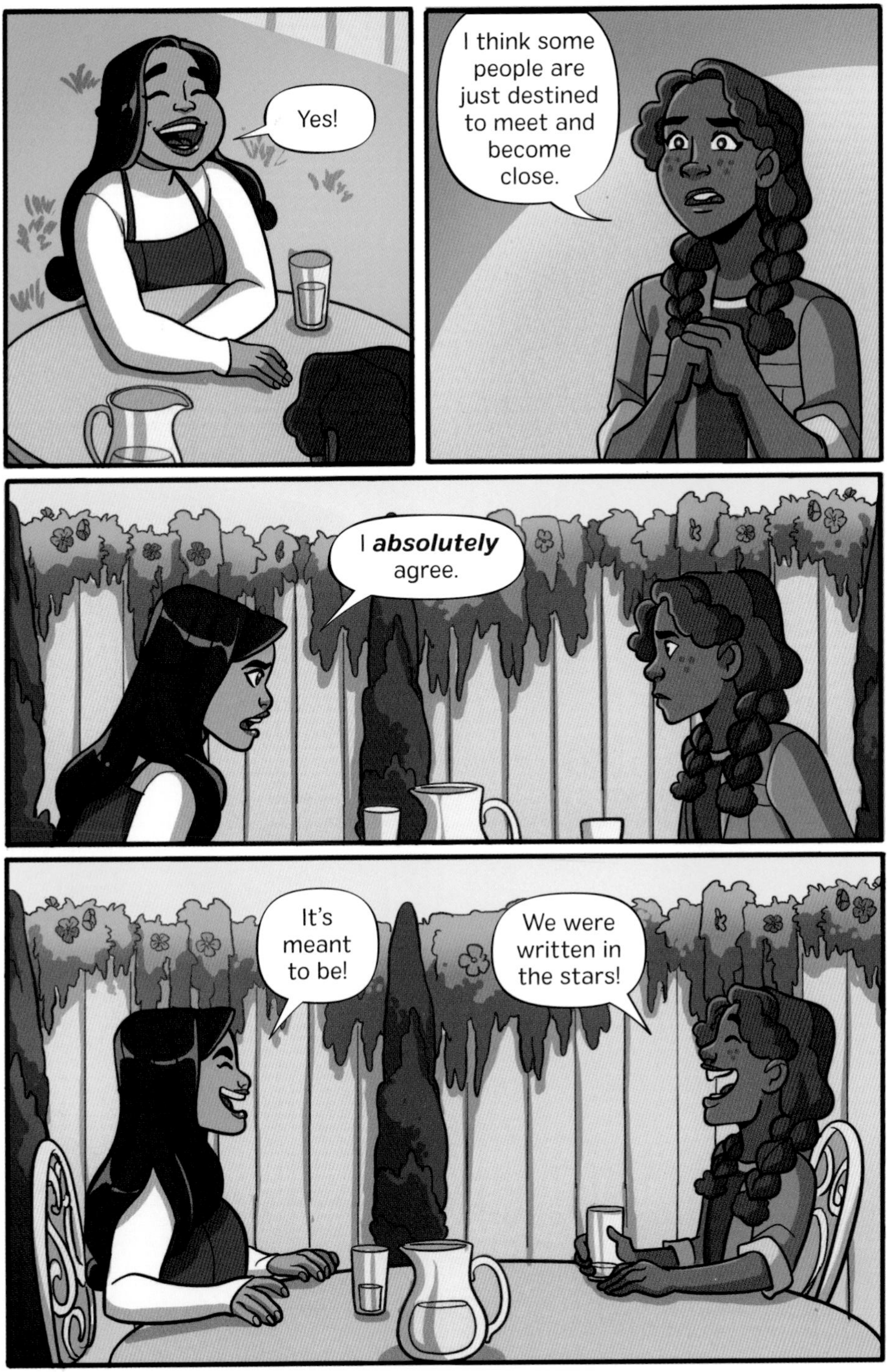
Yes!
I think some people are just destined to meet and become close.
I ***absolutely*** agree.
It's meant to be!
We were written in the stars!

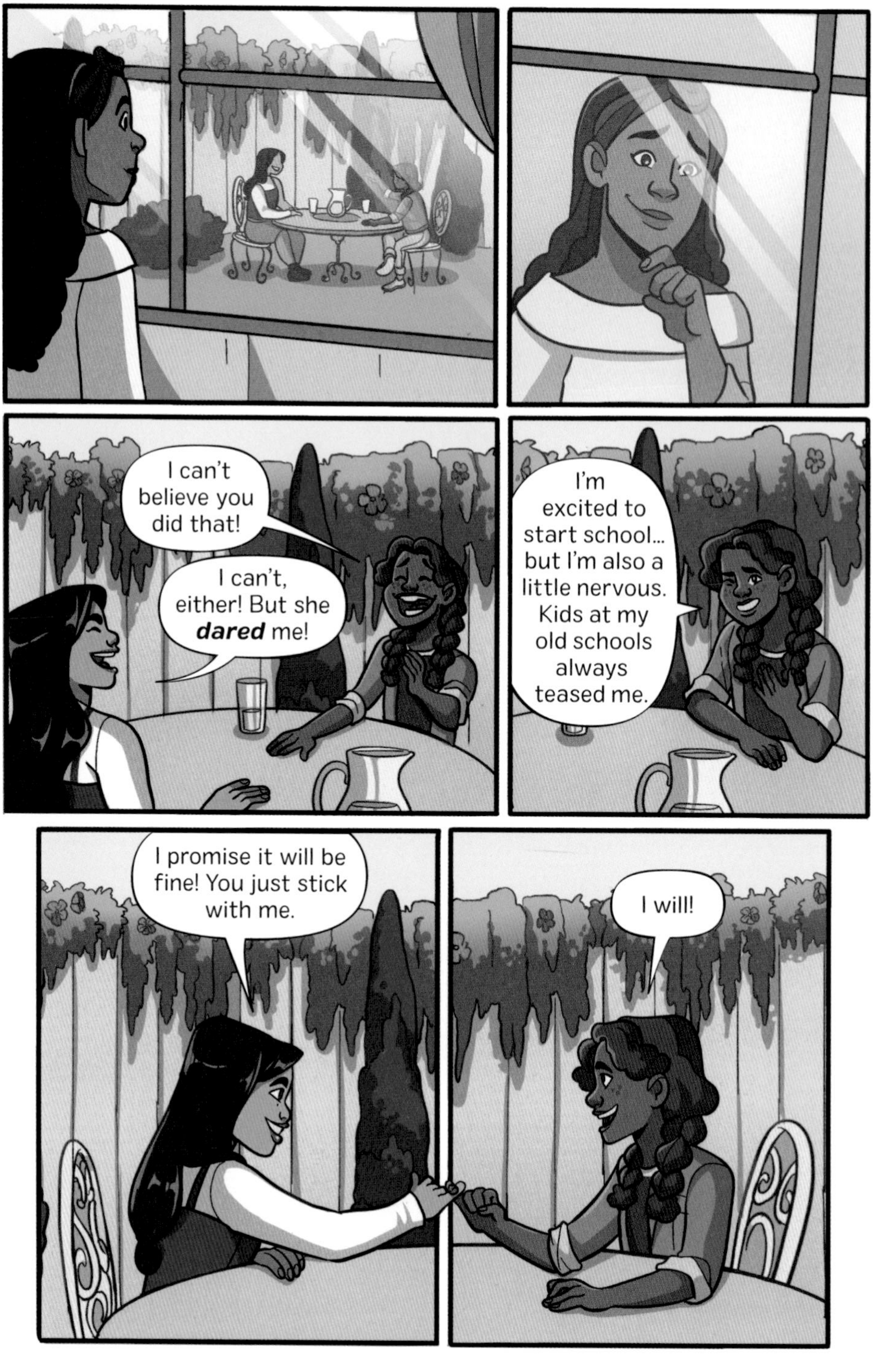
I can't believe you did that!
I can't, either! But she ***dared*** me!
I'm excited to start school... but I'm also a little nervous. Kids at my old schools always teased me.
I promise it will be fine! You just stick with me.
I will!

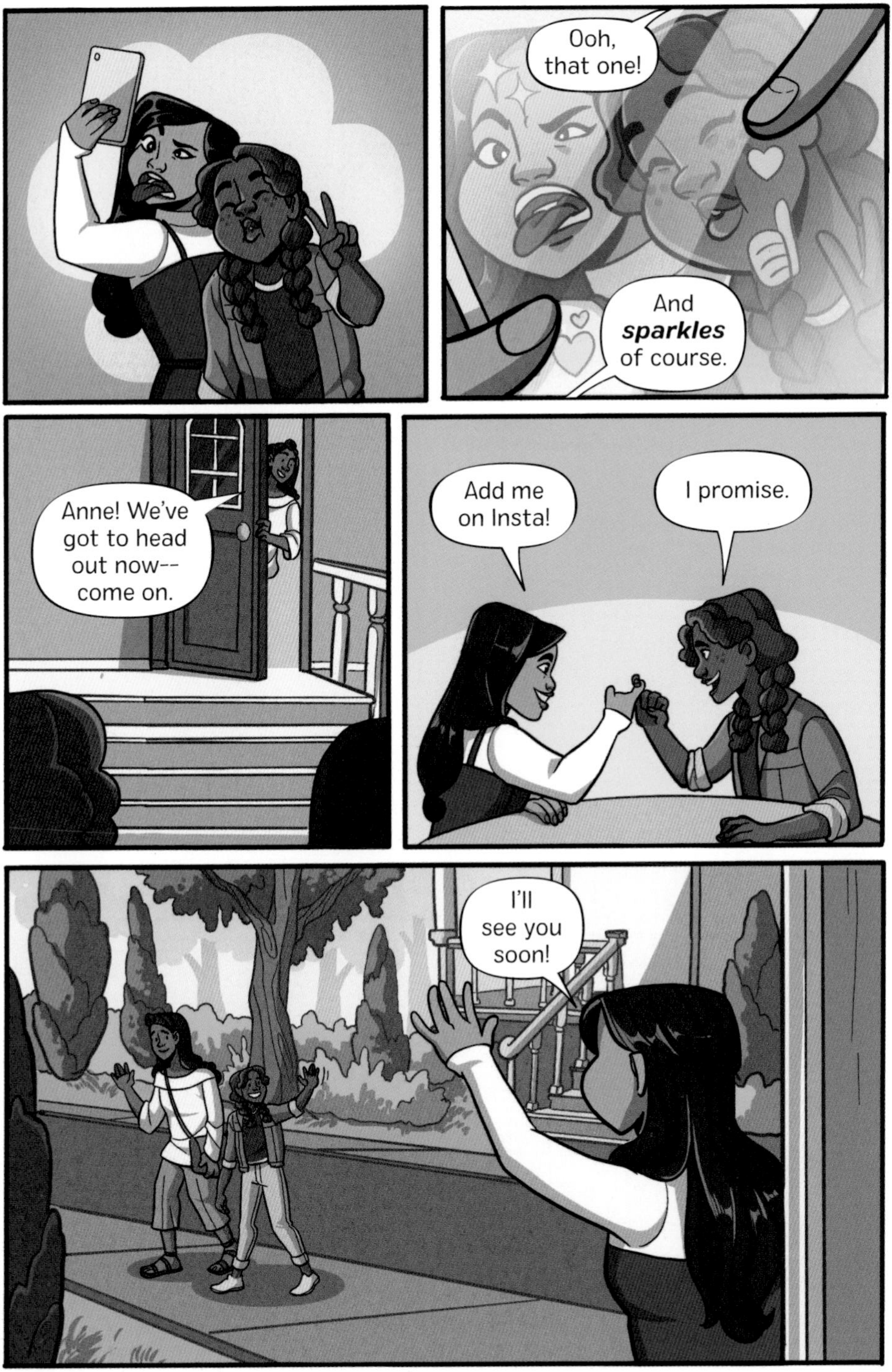
Ooh,
that one!
And
sparkles
of course.
Anne! We've
got to head
out now--
come on.
Add me
on Insta!
I promise.
I'll
see you
soon!

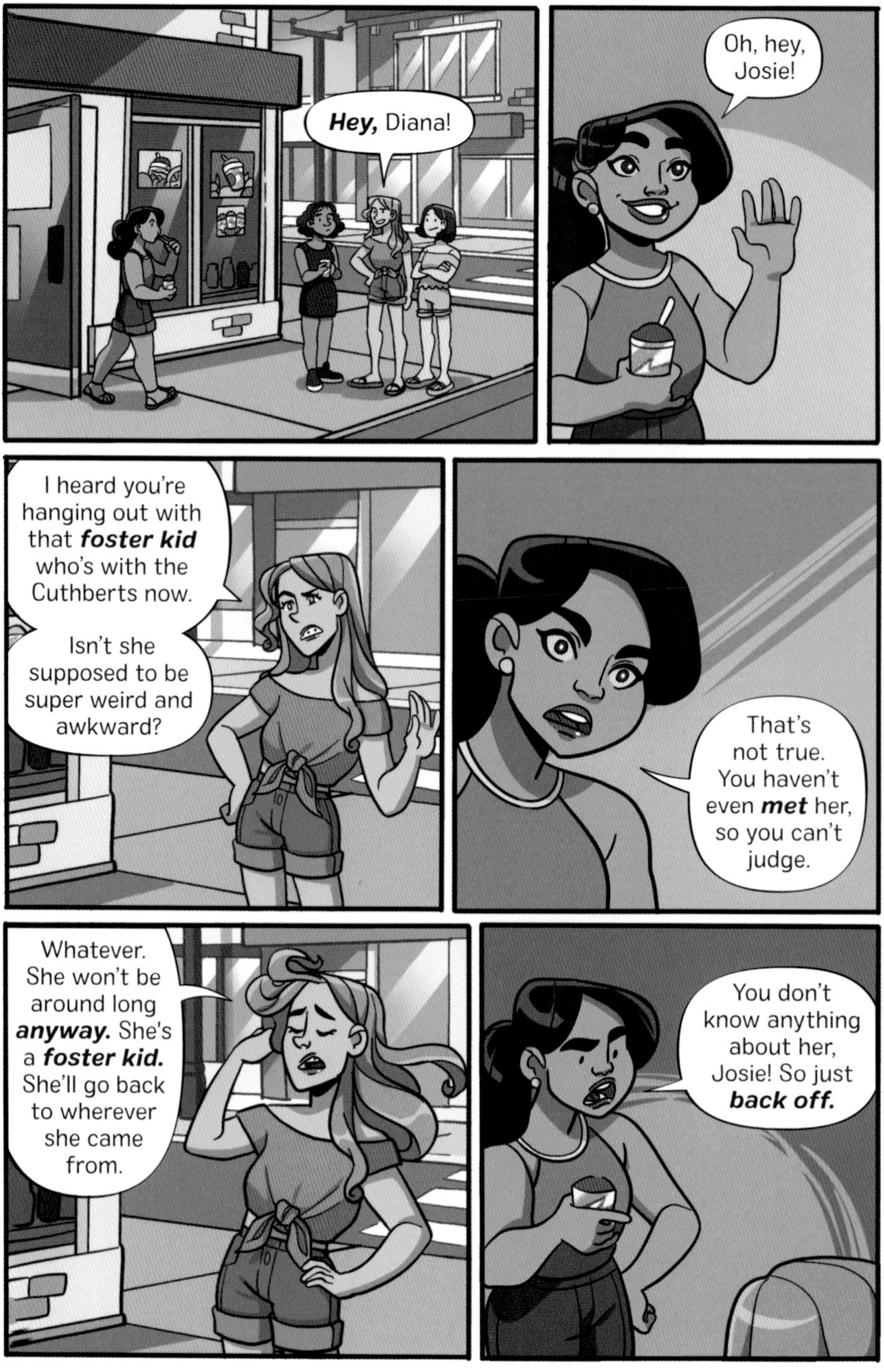

Hey, Diana!
Oh, hey, Josie!
I heard you're hanging out with that ***foster kid*** who's with the Cuthberts now.
Isn't she supposed to be super weird and awkward?
That's not true. You haven't even ***met*** her, so you can't judge.
Whatever. She won't be around long ***anyway.*** She's a ***foster kid.*** She'll go back to wherever she came from.
You don't know anything about her, Josie! So just ***back off.***

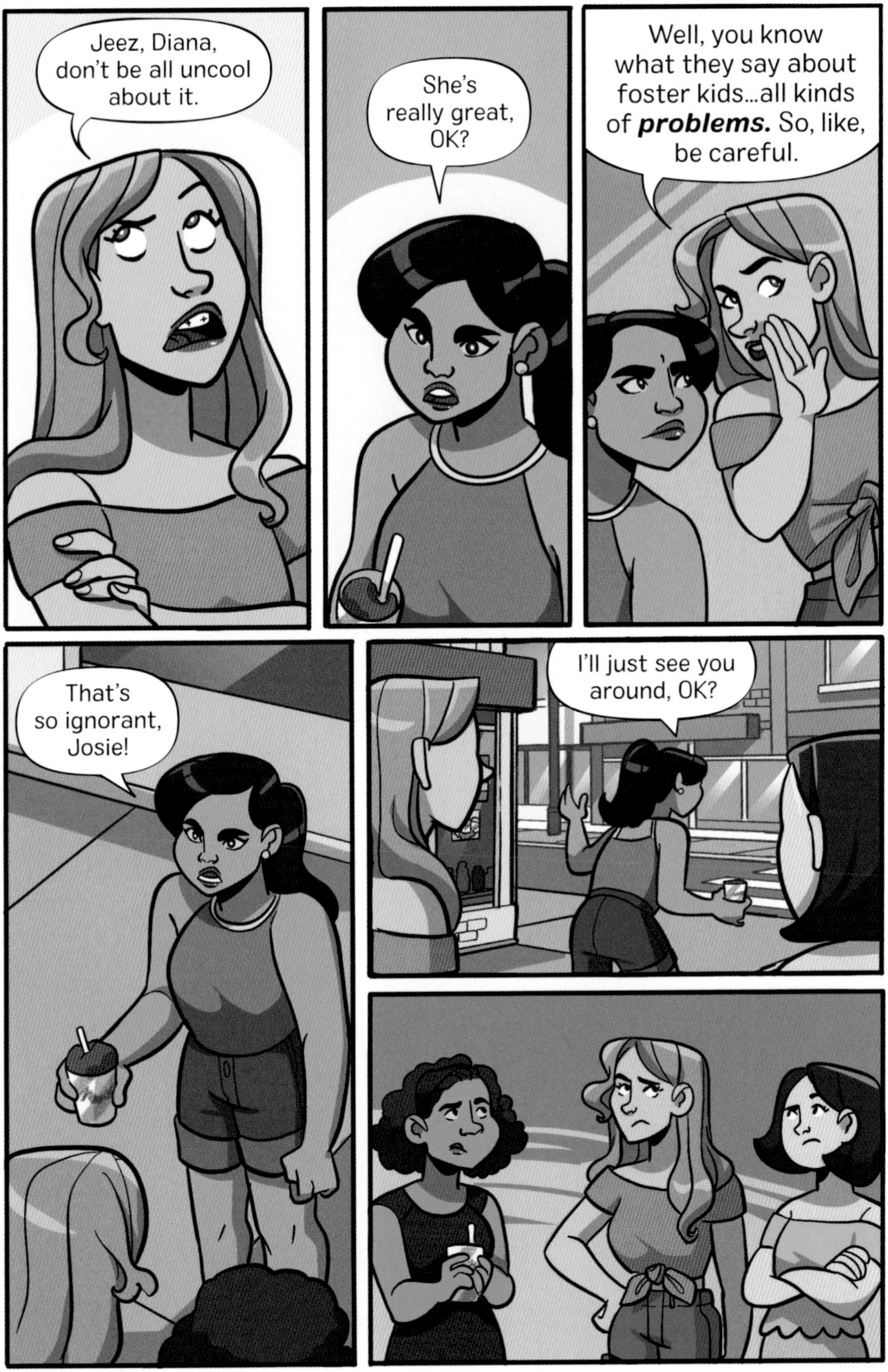
Jeez, Diana, don't be all uncool about it.
She's really great, OK?
Well, you know what they say about foster kids...all kinds of **problems.** So, like, be careful.
That's so ignorant, Josie!
I'll just see you around, OK?

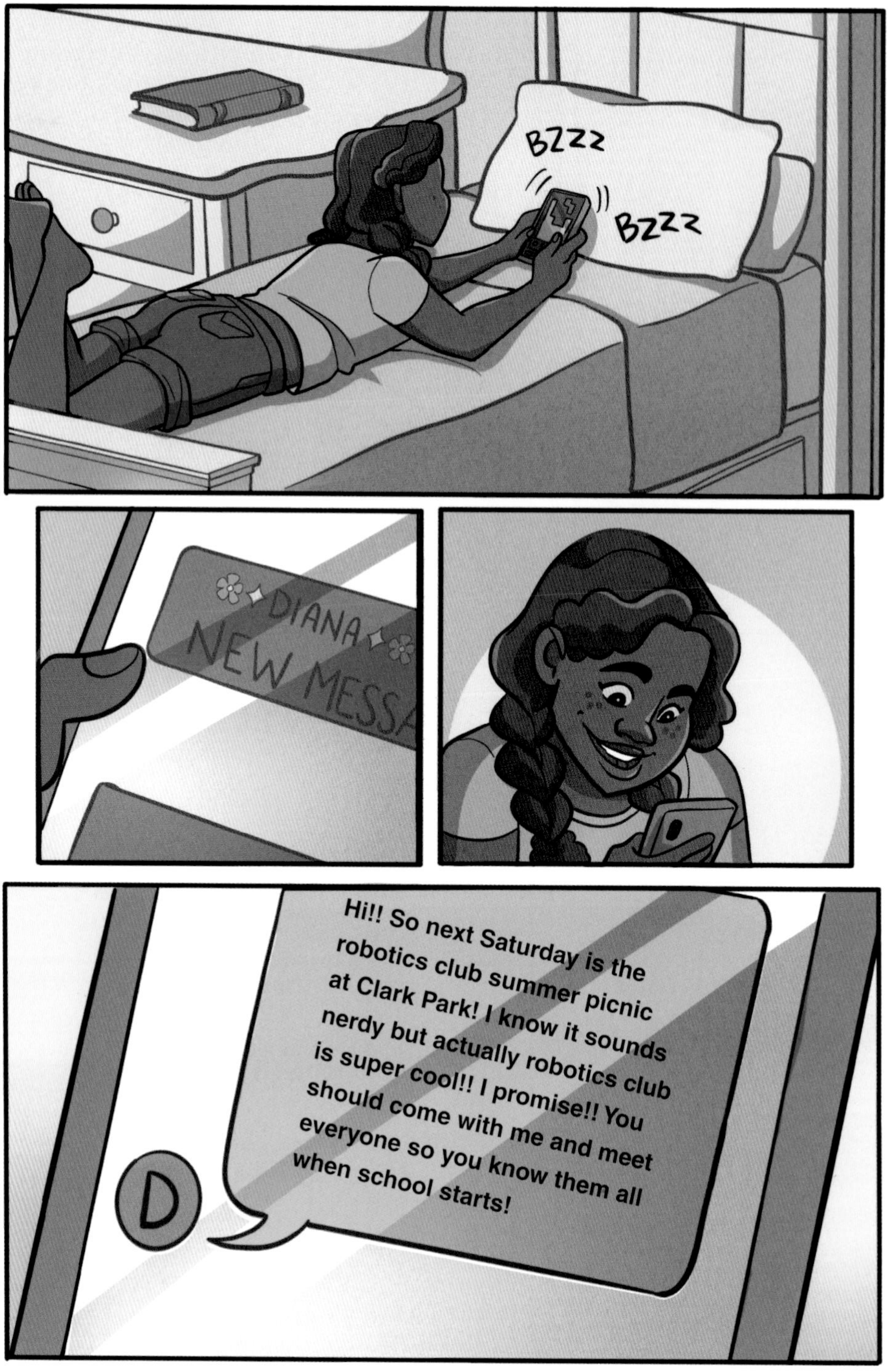
BZZZ
BZZZ
DIANA
NEW MESSA
Hi!! So next Saturday is the robotics club summer picnic at Clark Park! I know it sounds nerdy but actually robotics club is super cool!! I promise!! You should come with me and meet everyone so you know them all when school starts!
D

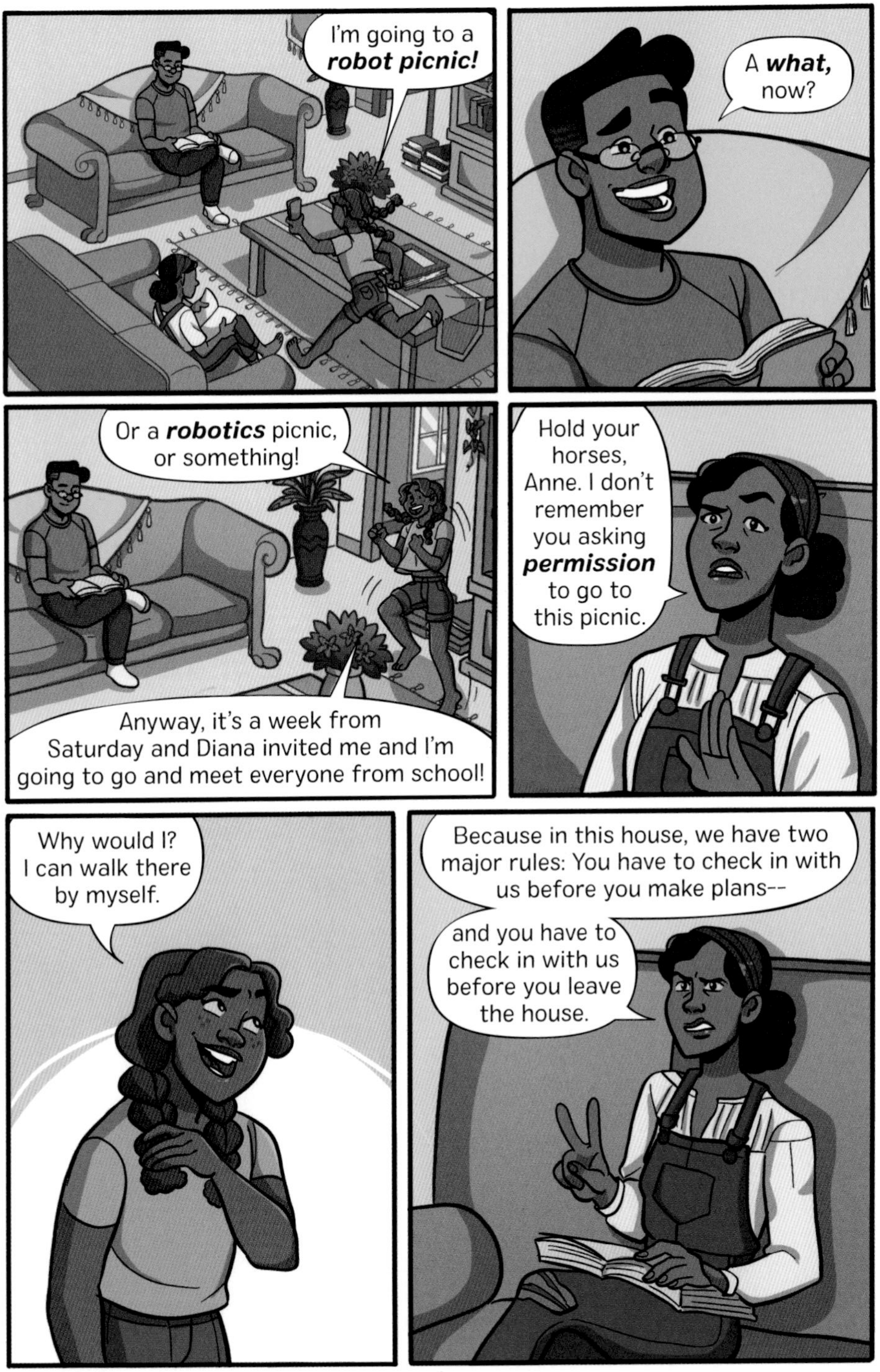
I'm going to a **robot picnic!**
A ***what,*** now?
Or a ***robotics*** picnic, or something!
Anyway, it's a week from Saturday and Diana invited me and I'm going to go and meet everyone from school!
Hold your horses, Anne. I don't remember you asking ***permission*** to go to this picnic.
Why would I? I can walk there by myself.
Because in this house, we have two major rules: You have to check in with us before you make plans--
and you have to check in with us before you leave the house.

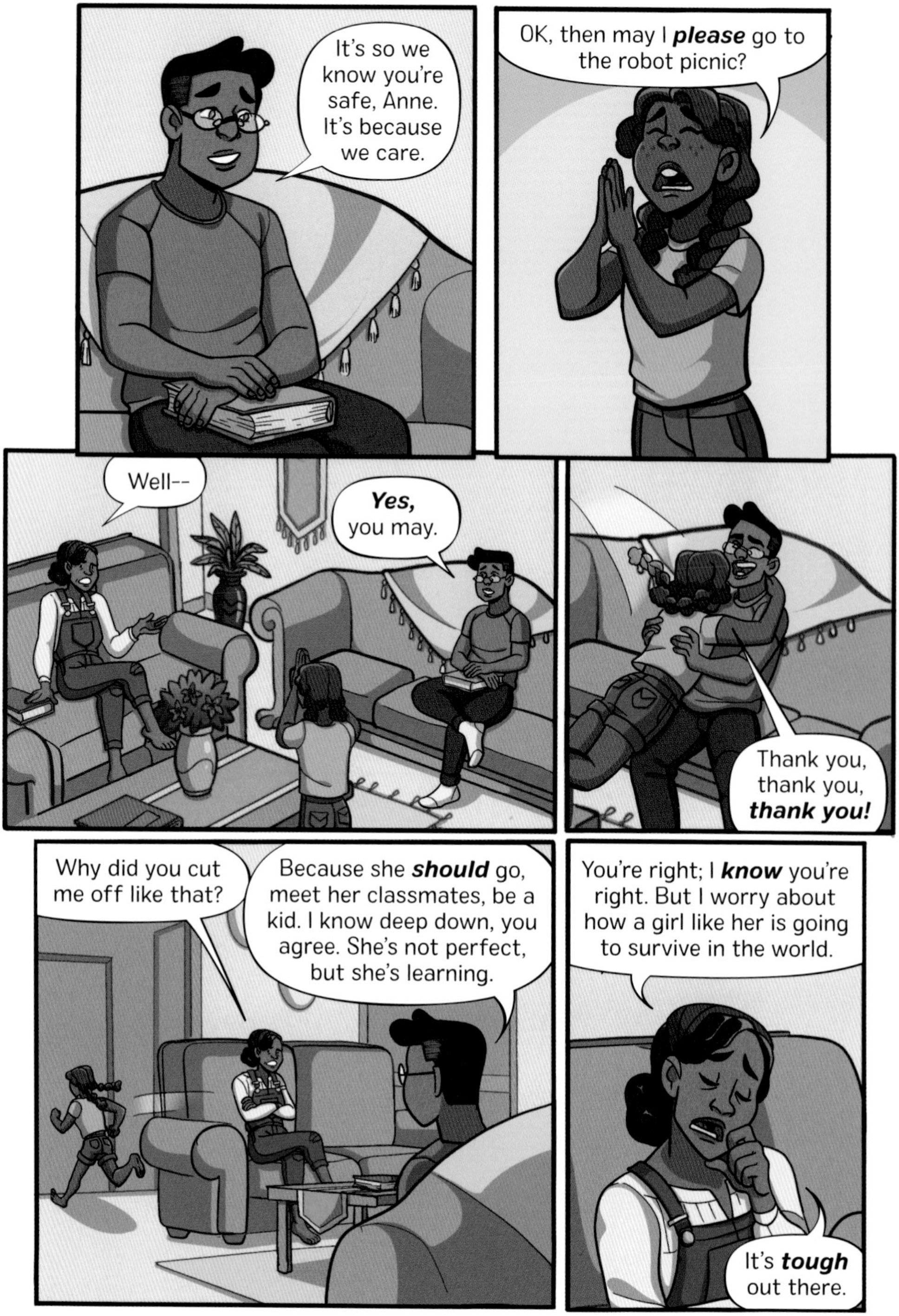
It's so we know you're safe, Anne. It's because we care.
OK, then may I **please** go to the robot picnic?
Well--
Yes, you may.
Thank you, thank you, ***thank you!***
Why did you cut me off like that?
Because she ***should*** go, meet her classmates, be a kid. I know deep down, you agree. She's not perfect, but she's learning.
You're right; I ***know*** you're right. But I worry about how a girl like her is going to survive in the world.
It's ***tough*** out there.

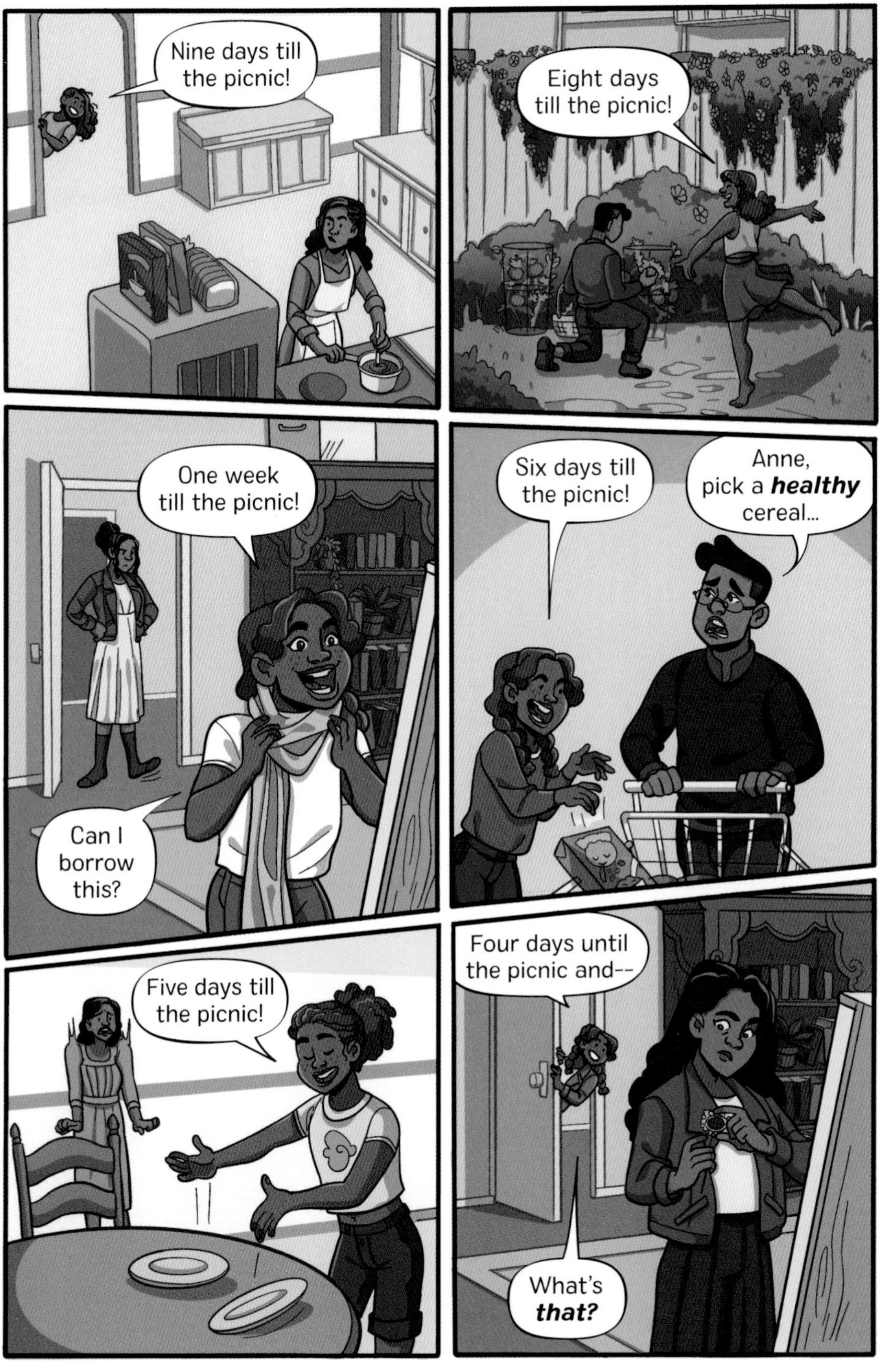
Nine days till the picnic!
Eight days till the picnic!
One week till the picnic!
Can I borrow this?
Six days till the picnic!
Anne, pick a ***healthy*** cereal...
Five days till the picnic!
Four days until the picnic and--
What's ***that?***

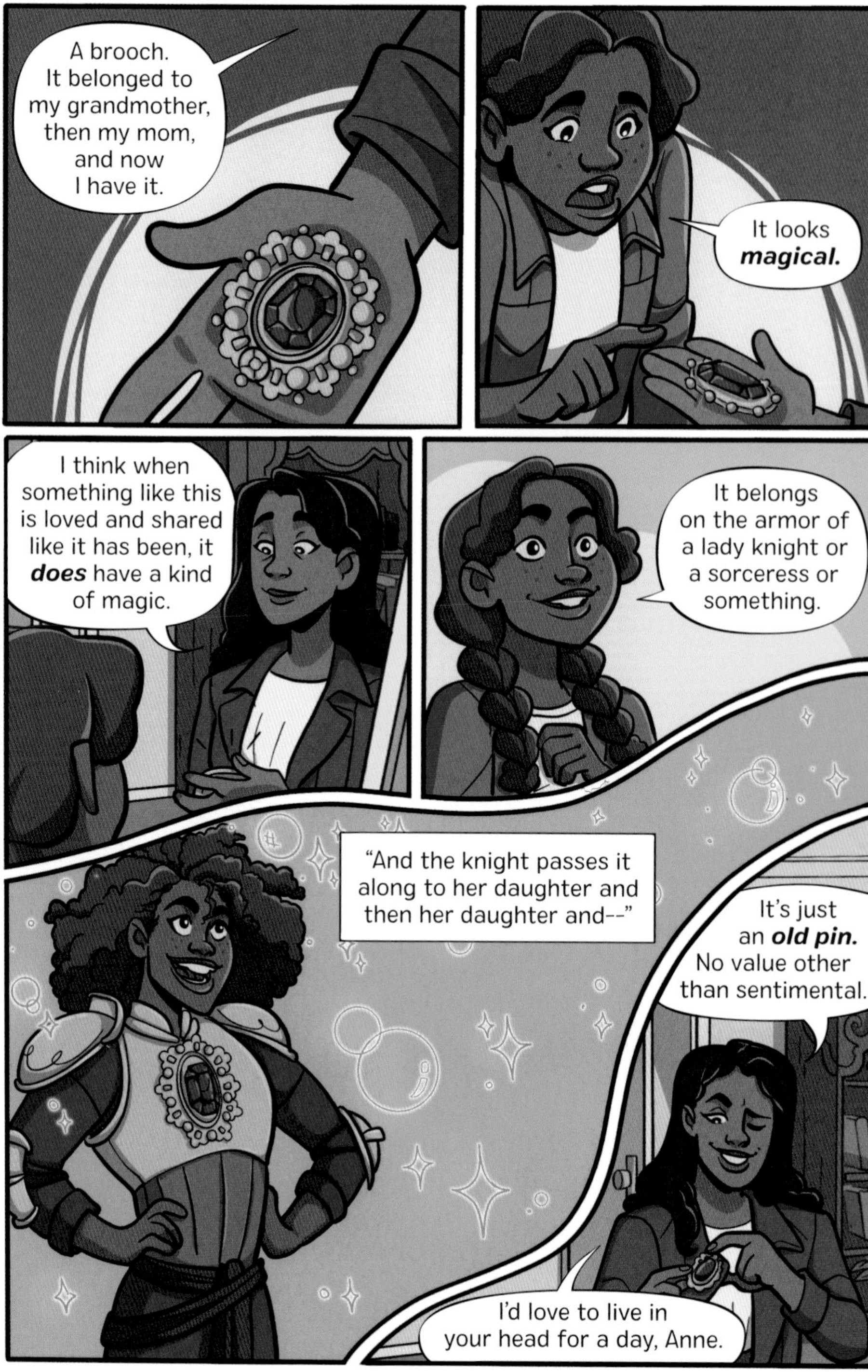
A brooch. It belonged to my grandmother, then my mom, and now I have it.
It looks **magical.**
I think when something like this is loved and shared like it has been, it ***does*** have a kind of magic.
It belongs on the armor of a lady knight or a sorceress or something.
"And the knight passes it along to her daughter and then her daughter and--"
It's just an ***old pin.*** No value other than sentimental.
I'd love to live in your head for a day, Anne.

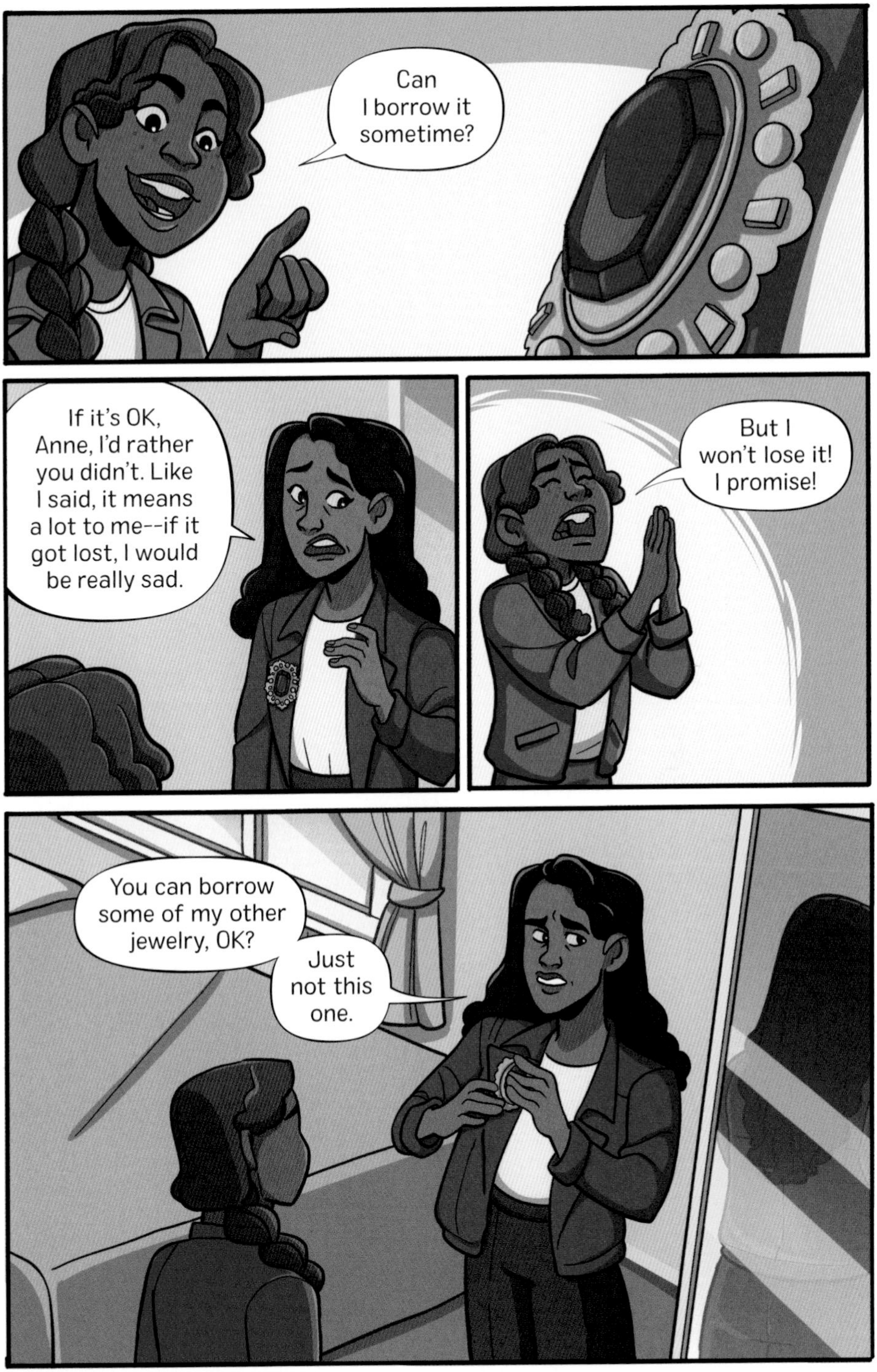
Can I borrow it sometime?
If it's OK, Anne, I'd rather you didn't. Like I said, it means a lot to me--if it got lost, I would be really sad.
But I won't lose it! I promise!
You can borrow some of my other jewelry, OK?
Just not this one.

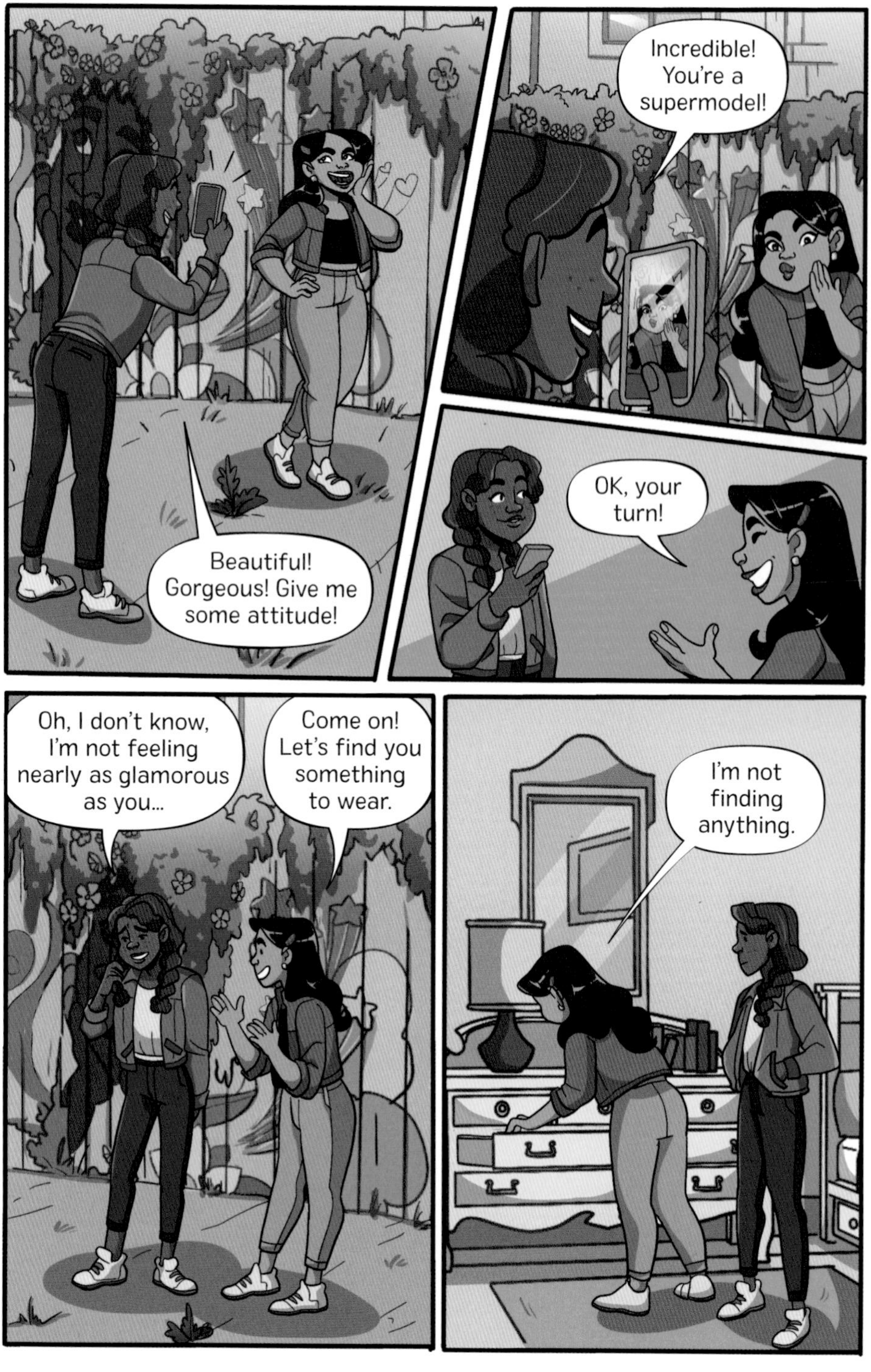
Beautiful! Gorgeous! Give me some attitude!
Incredible! You're a supermodel!
OK, your turn!
Oh, I don't know, I'm not feeling nearly as glamorous as you...
Come on! Let's find you something to wear.
I'm not finding anything.

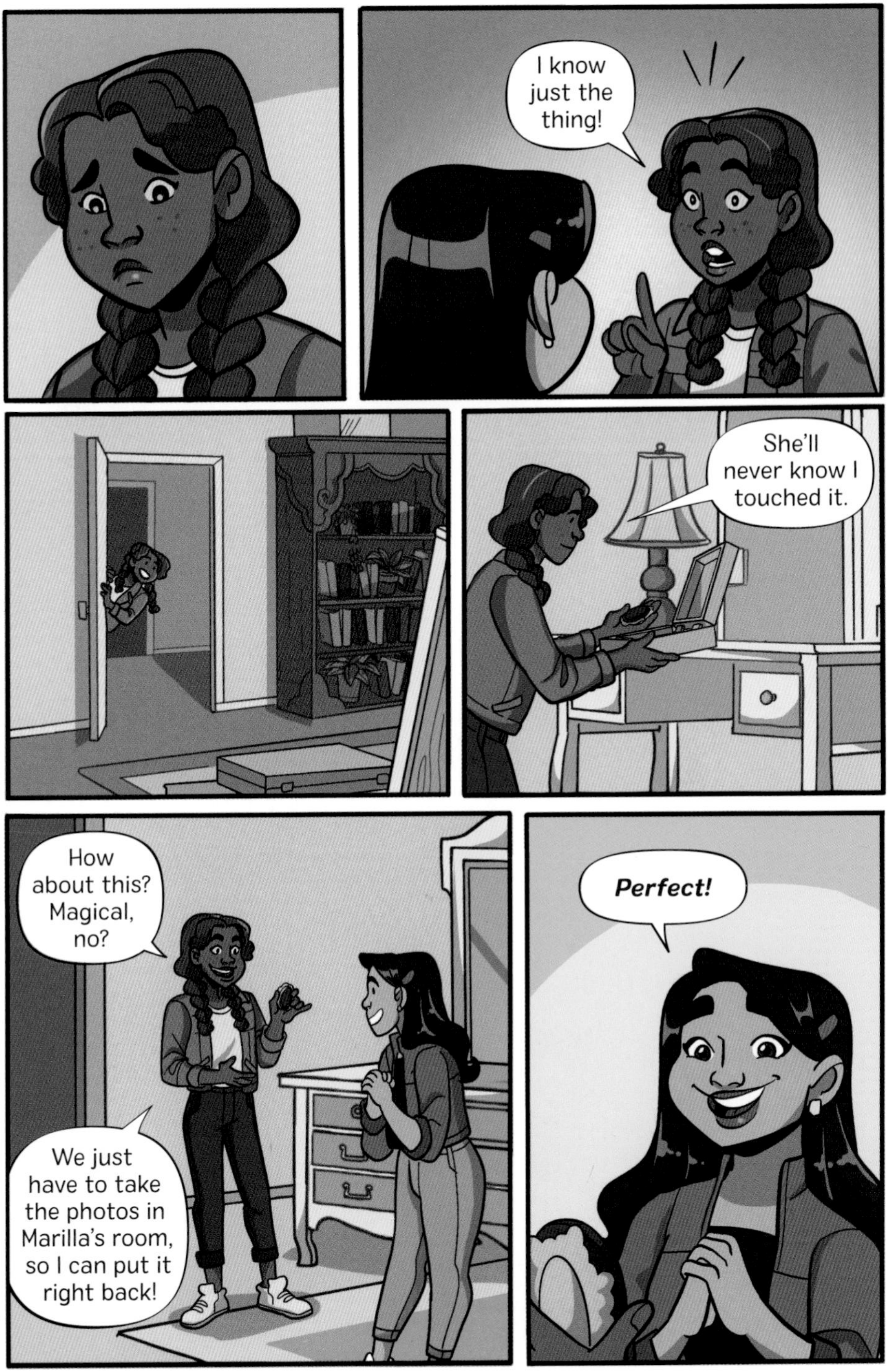
I know just the thing!
She'll never know I touched it.
How about this? Magical, no?
We just have to take the photos in Marilla's room, so I can put it right back!
Perfect!

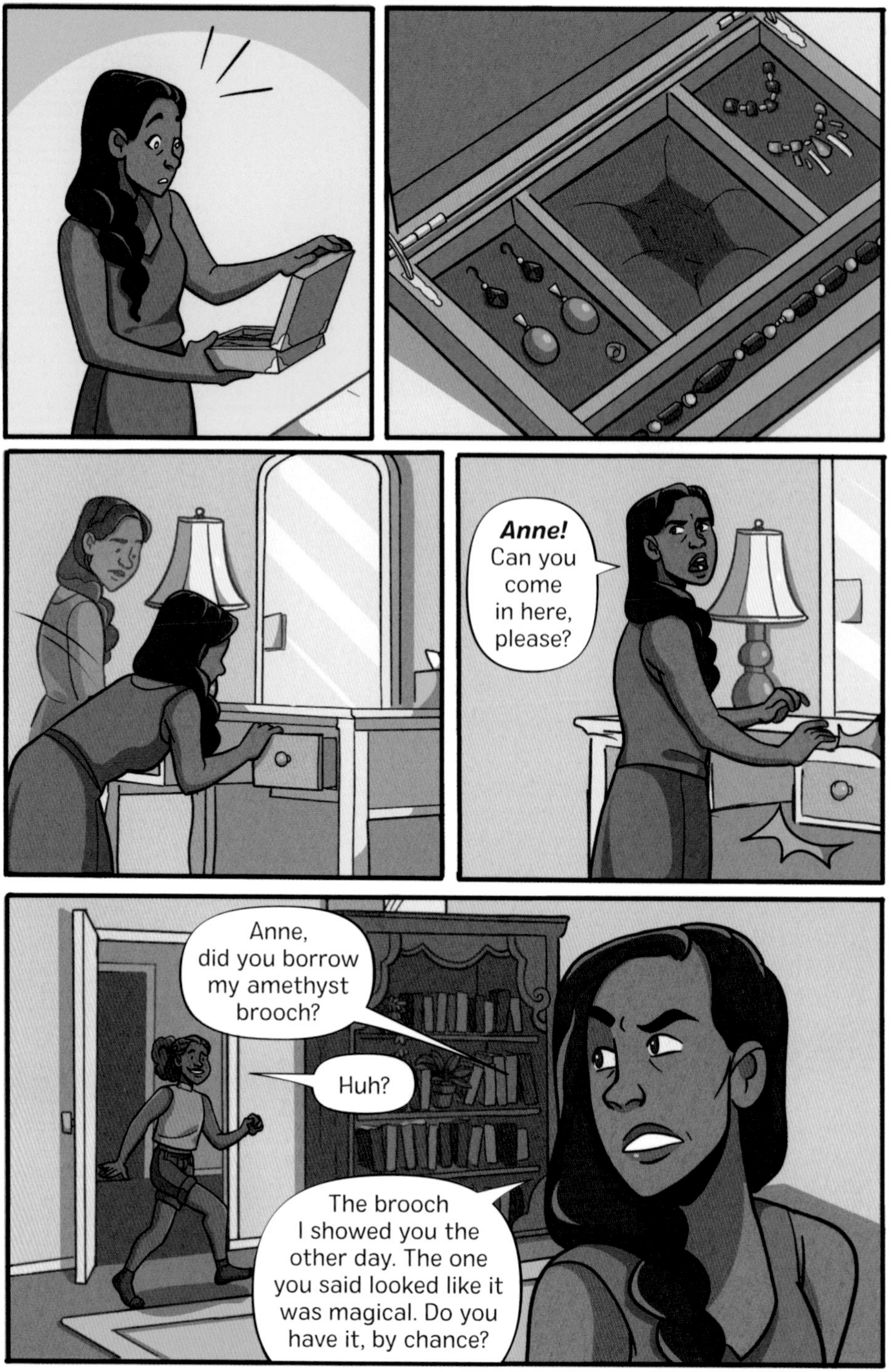
Anne!
Can you come in here, please?
Anne, did you borrow my amethyst brooch?
Huh?
The brooch I showed you the other day. The one you said looked like it was magical. Do you have it, by chance?

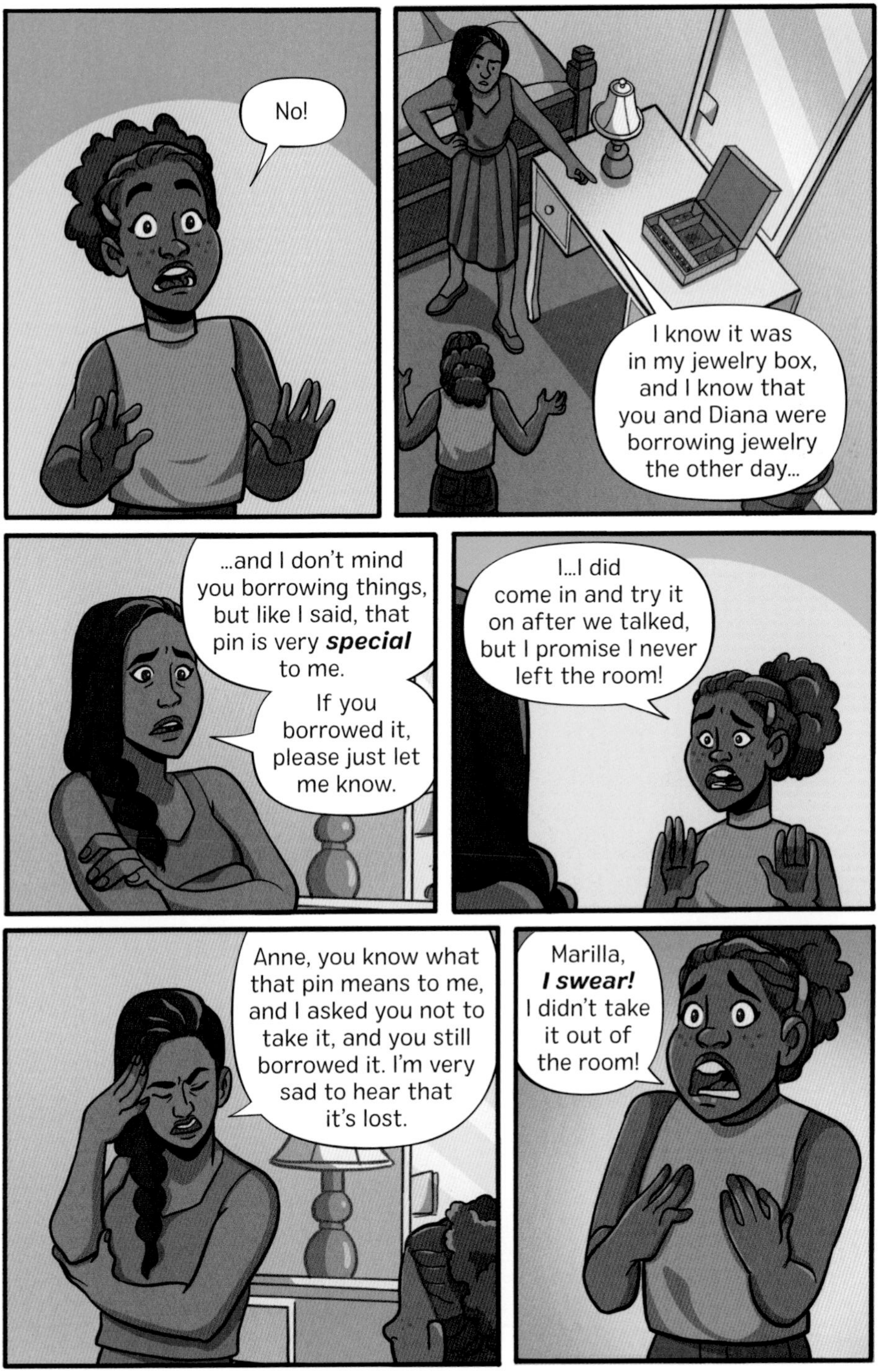
No!
I know it was in my jewelry box, and I know that you and Diana were borrowing jewelry the other day...
...and I don't mind you borrowing things, but like I said, that pin is very ***special*** to me.
If you borrowed it, please just let me know.
I...I did come in and try it on after we talked, but I promise I never left the room!
Anne, you know what that pin means to me, and I asked you not to take it, and you still borrowed it. I'm very sad to hear that it's lost.
Marilla, ***I swear!*** I didn't take it out of the room!

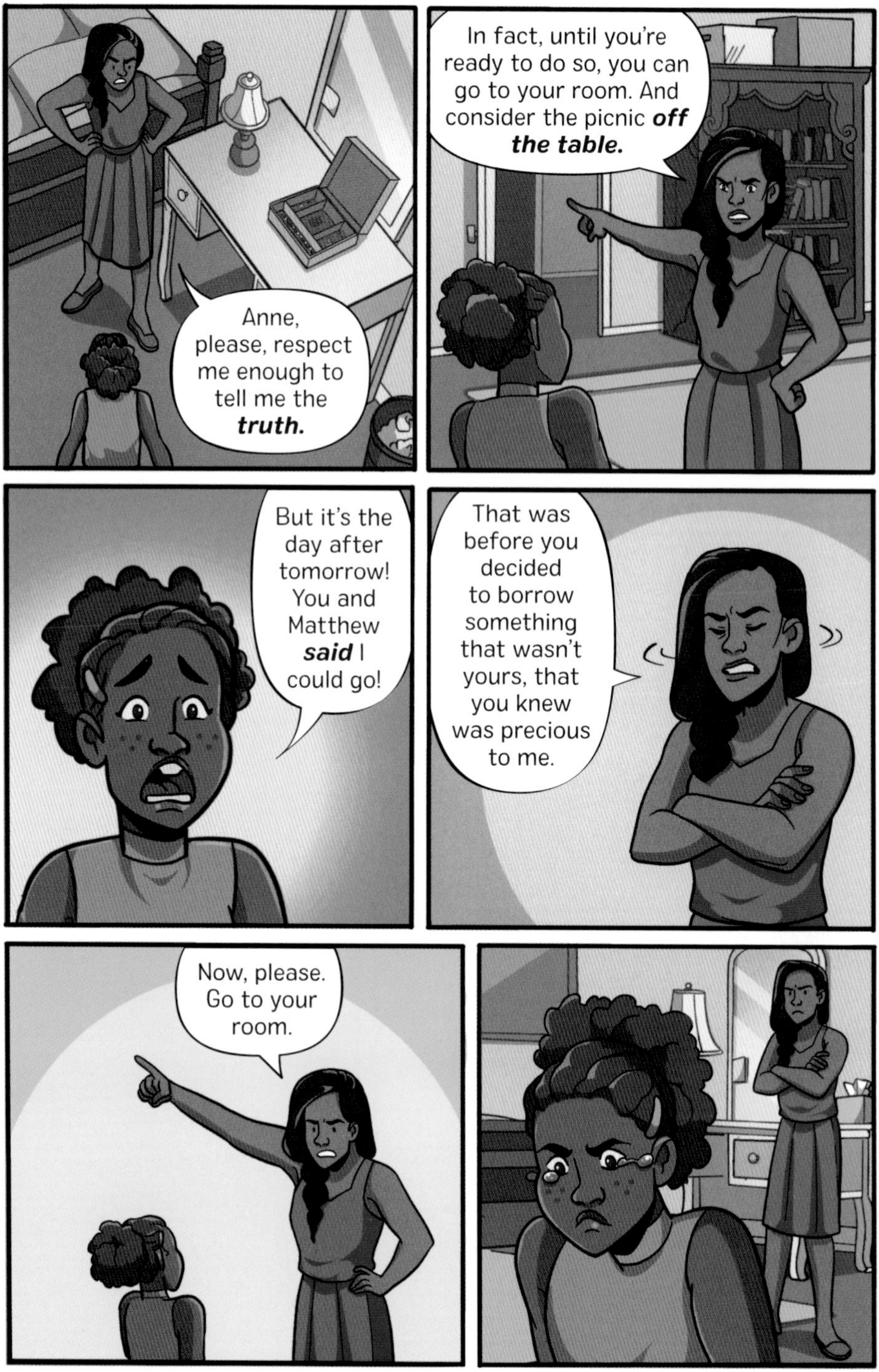
Anne, please, respect me enough to tell me the ***truth.***
In fact, until you're ready to do so, you can go to your room. And consider the picnic ***off the table.***
But it's the day after tomorrow! You and Matthew ***said*** I could go!
That was before you decided to borrow something that wasn't yours, that you knew was precious to me.
Now, please. Go to your room.

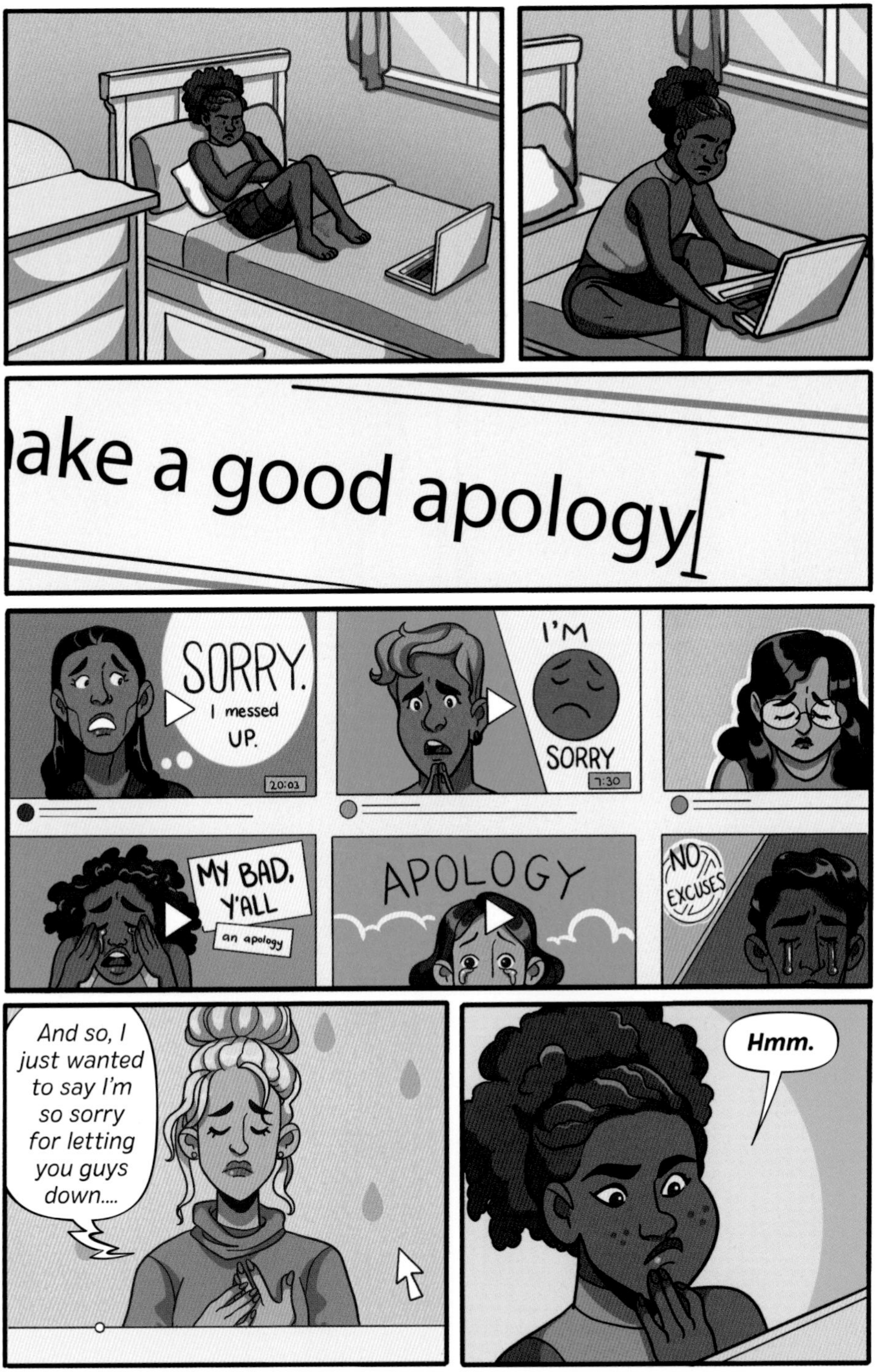

ake a good apology
SORRY. I messed UP.
20:03
I'M SORRY
7:30
MY BAD, Y'ALL
an apology
APOLOGY
NO EXCUSES
And so, I just wanted to say I'm so sorry for letting you guys down....
Hmm.

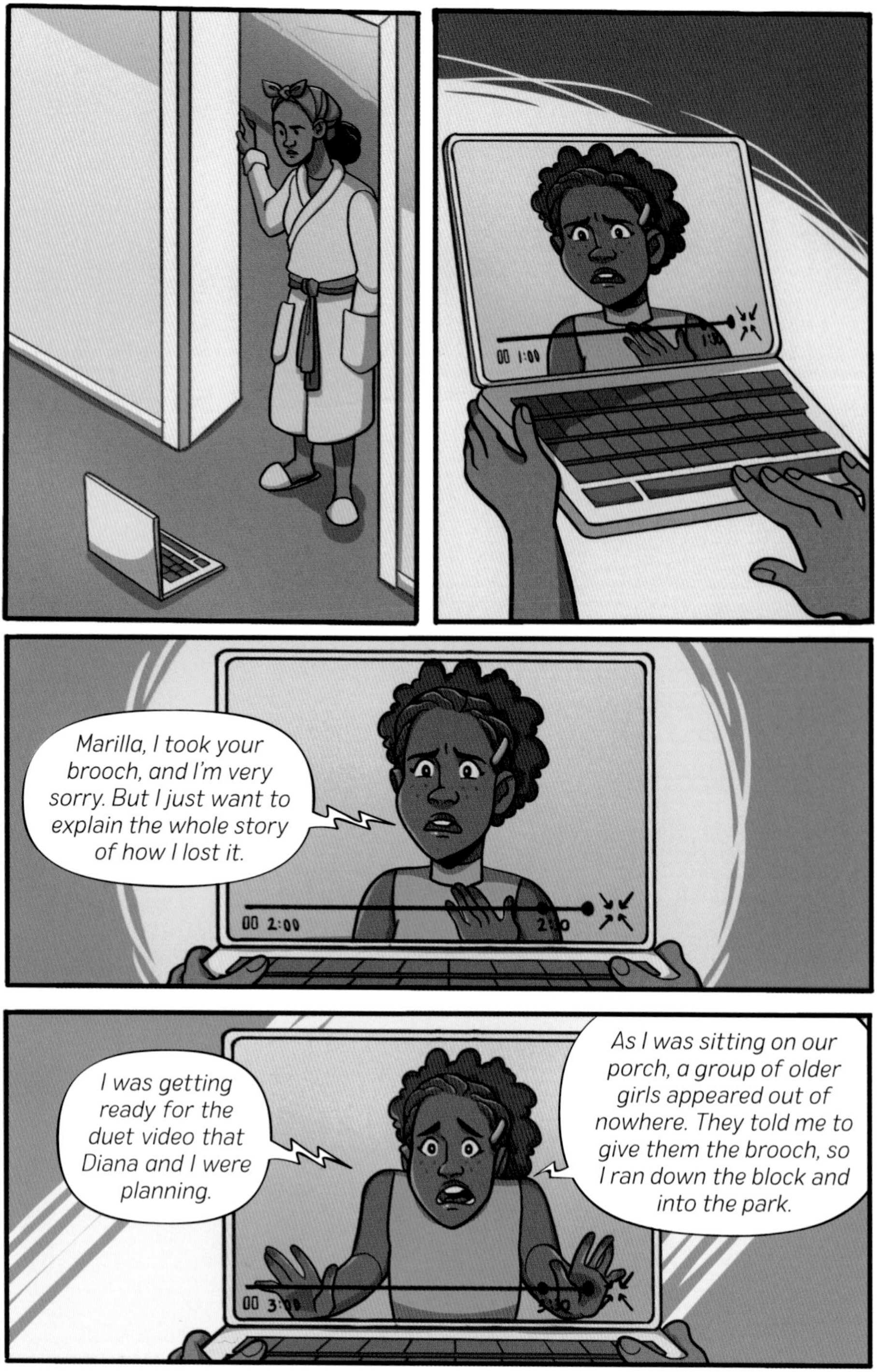
Marilla, I took your brooch, and I'm very sorry. But I just want to explain the whole story of how I lost it.
I was getting ready for the duet video that Diana and I were planning.
As I was sitting on our porch, a group of older girls appeared out of nowhere. They told me to give them the brooch, so I ran down the block and into the park.

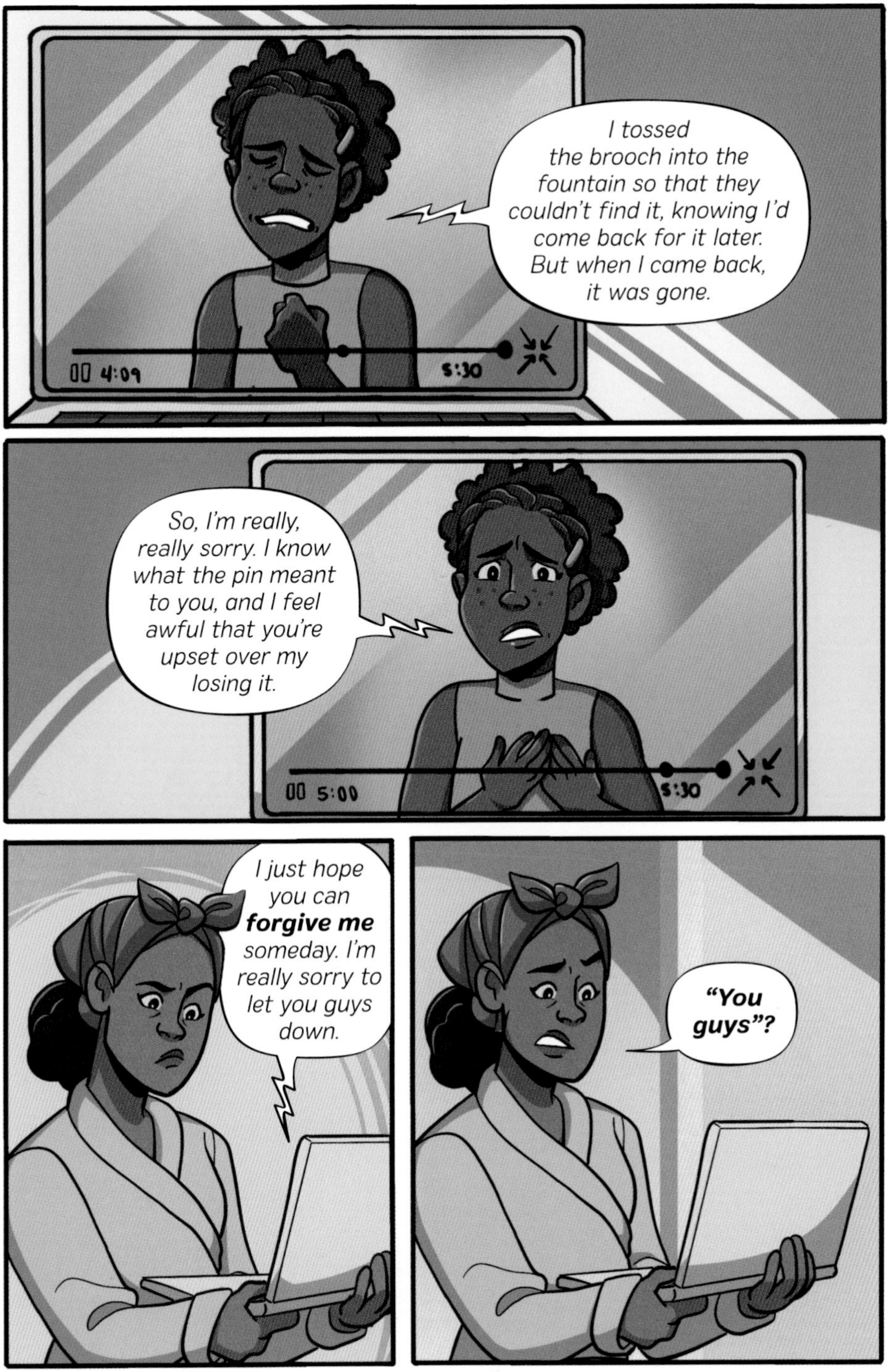

00 4:09
5:30
I tossed the brooch into the fountain so that they couldn't find it, knowing I'd come back for it later. But when I came back, it was gone.
So, I'm really, really sorry. I know what the pin meant to you, and I feel awful that you're upset over my losing it.
00 5:00
5:30
I just hope you can **forgive me** someday. I'm really sorry to let you guys down.
"You guys"?

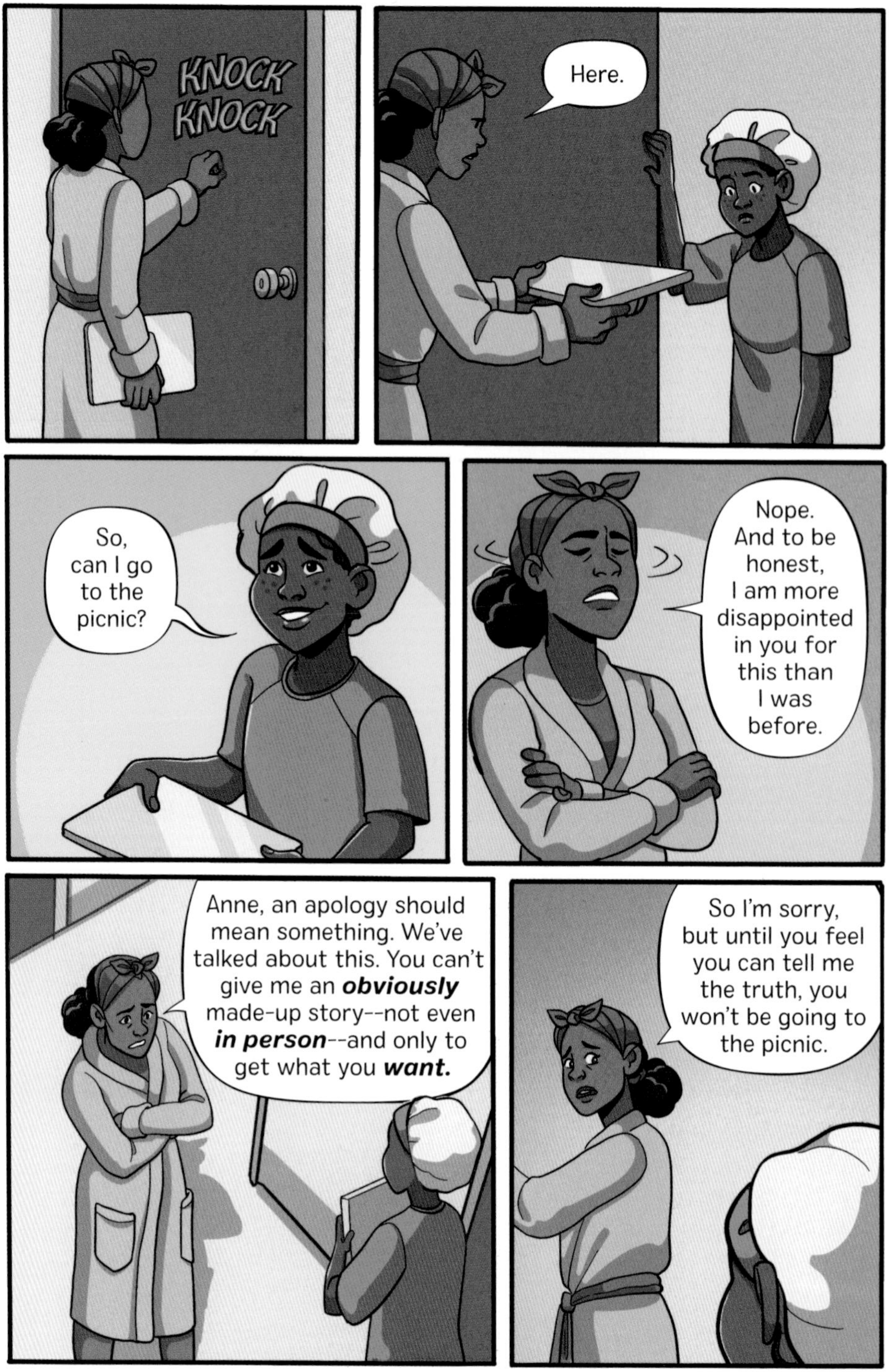
KNOCK KNOCK
Here.
So, can I go to the picnic?
Nope. And to be honest, I am more disappointed in you for this than I was before.
Anne, an apology should mean something. We've talked about this. You can't give me an ***obviously*** made-up story--not even ***in person***--and only to get what you ***want.***
So I'm sorry, but until you feel you can tell me the truth, you won't be going to the picnic.

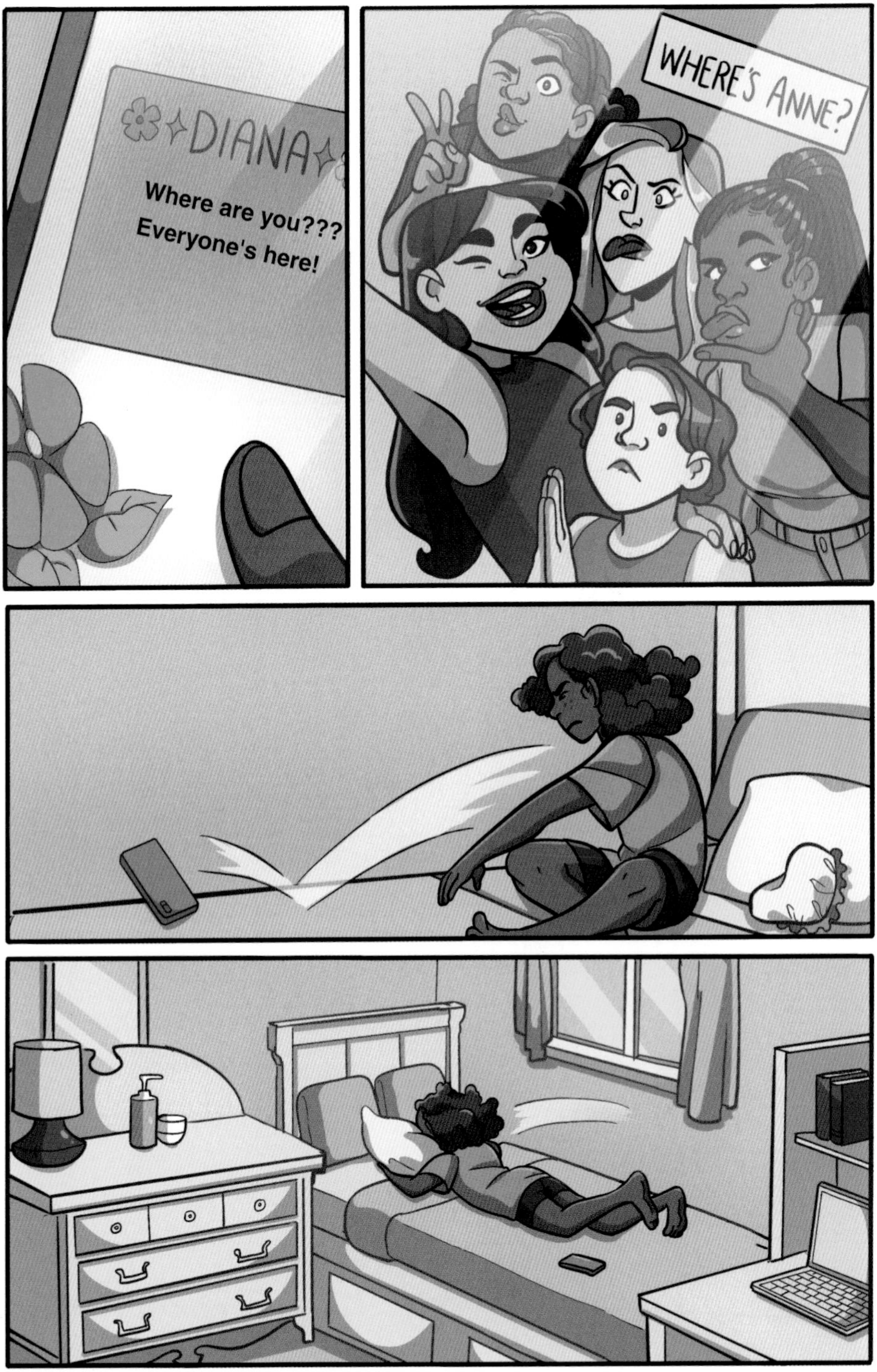
DIANA
Where are you???
Everyone's here!
WHERE'S ANNE?

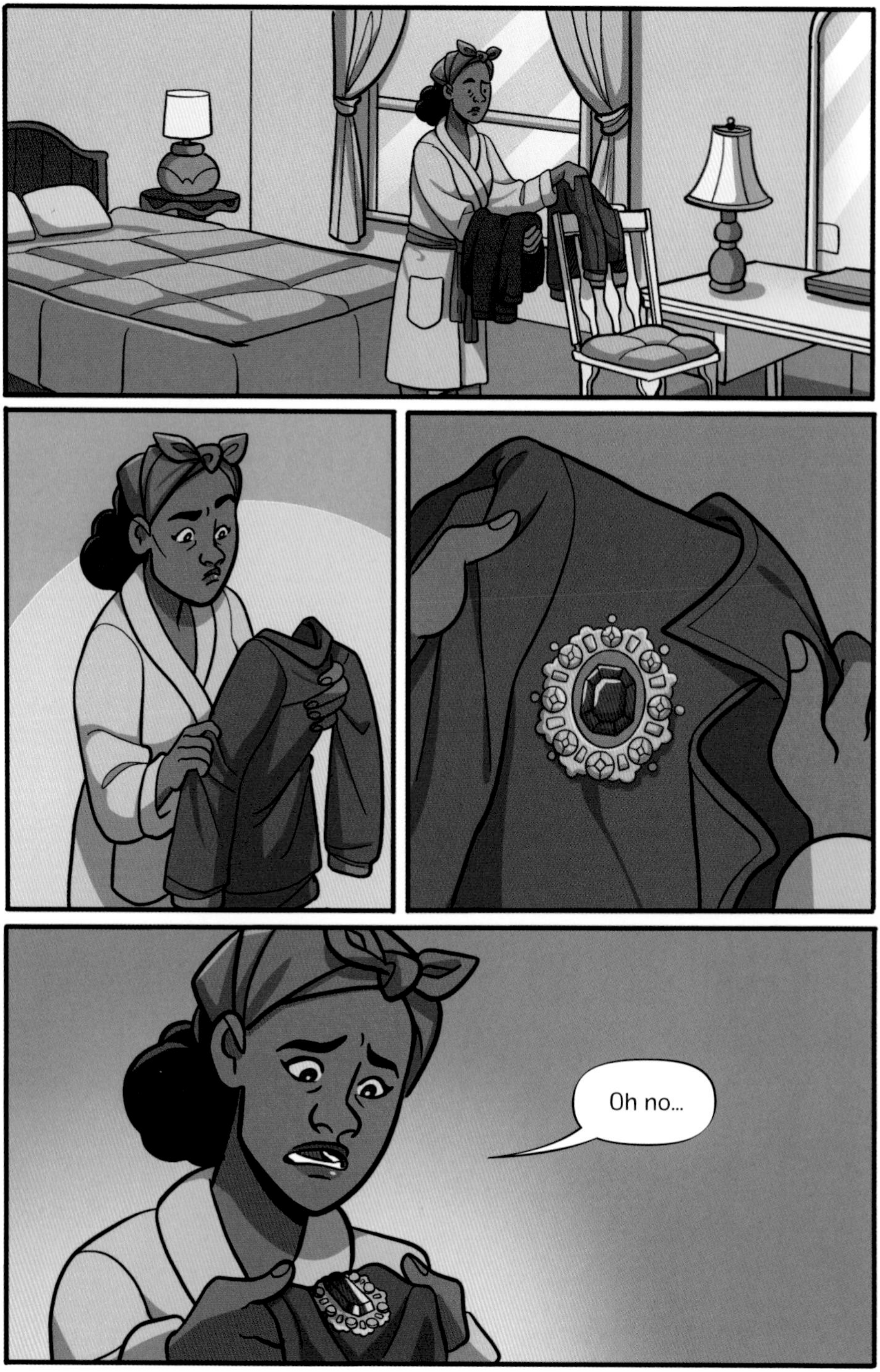
Oh no...

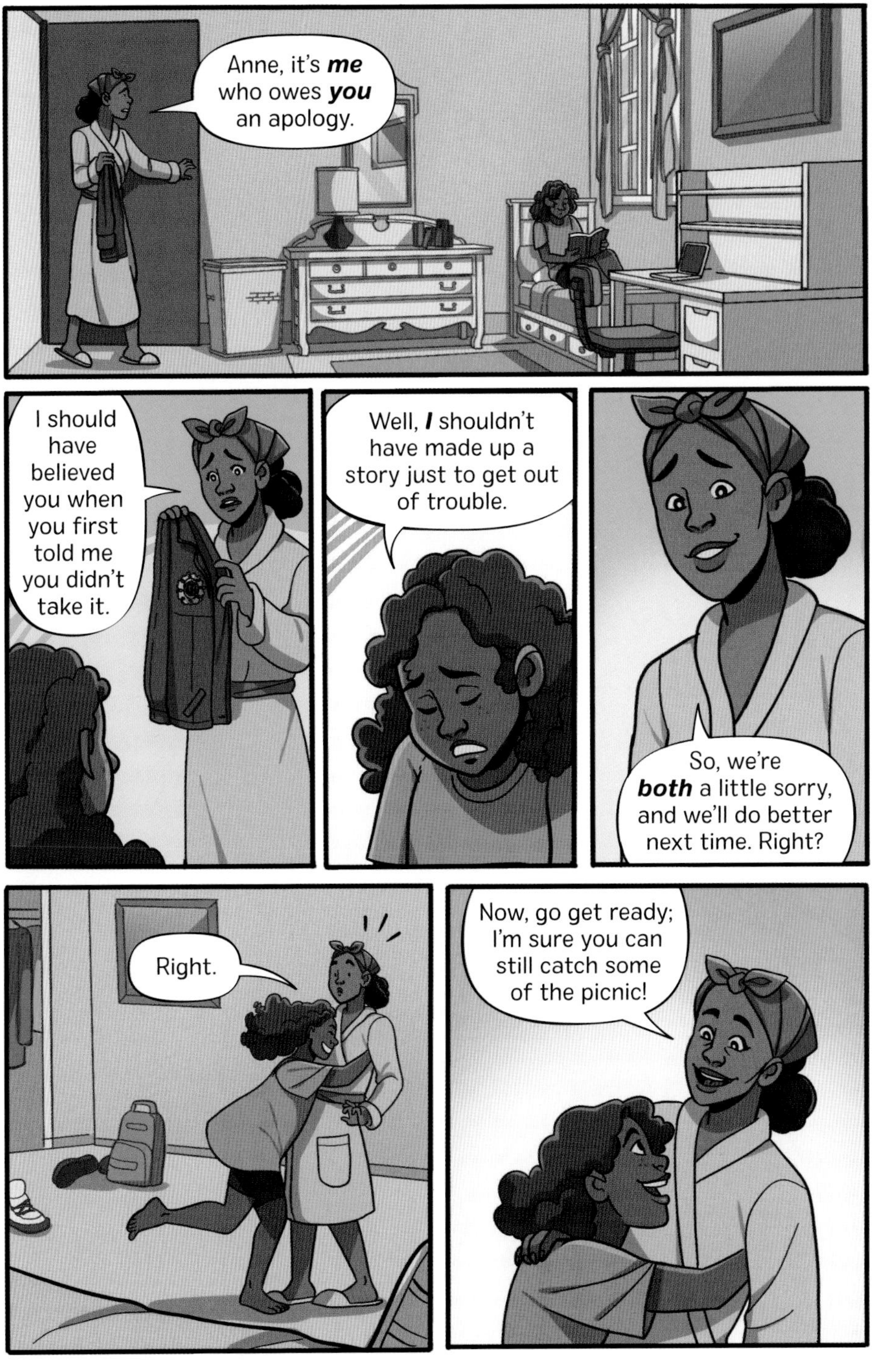
Anne, it's ***me*** who owes ***you*** an apology.
I should have believed you when you first told me you didn't take it.
Well, ***I*** shouldn't have made up a story just to get out of trouble.
So, we're **both** a little sorry, and we'll do better next time. Right?
Right.
Now, go get ready; I'm sure you can still catch some of the picnic!

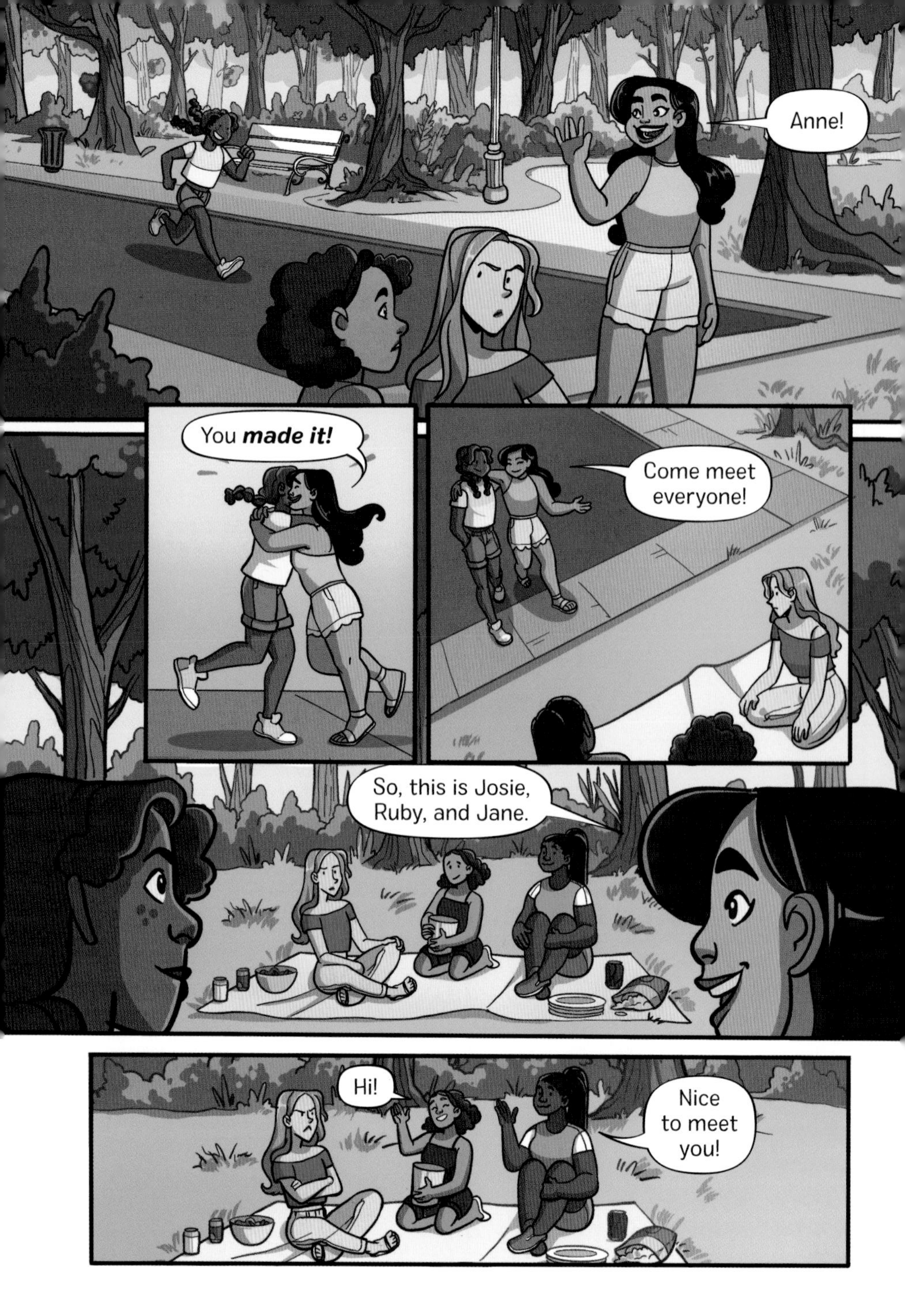
Anne!
You made it!
Come meet everyone!
So, this is Josie, Ruby, and Jane.
Hi!
Nice to meet you!

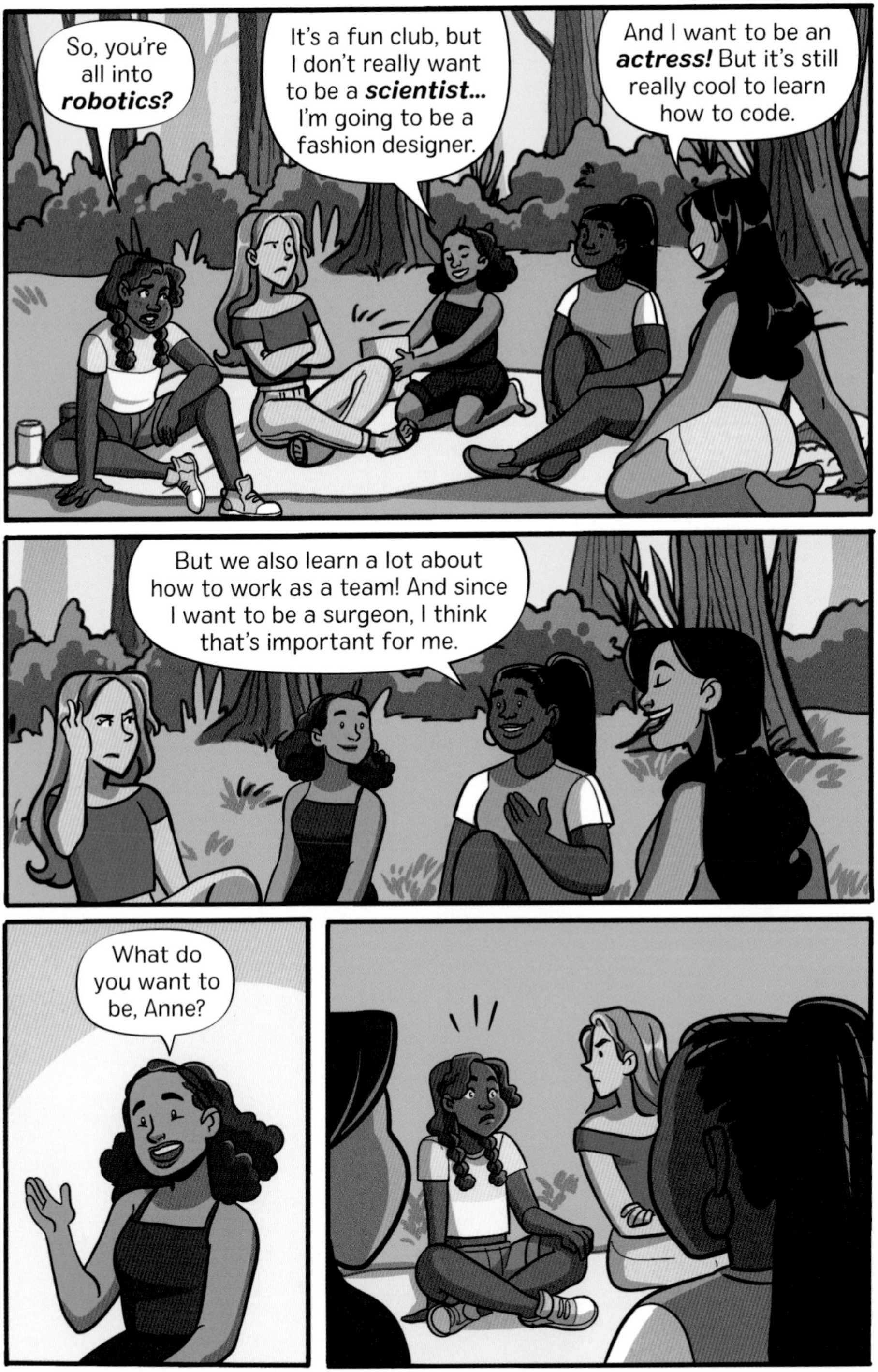

So, you're all into *robotics?*
It's a fun club, but I don't really want to be a *scientist…* I'm going to be a fashion designer.
And I want to be an *actress!* But it's still really cool to learn how to code.
But we also learn a lot about how to work as a team! And since I want to be a surgeon, I think that's important for me.
What do you want to be, Anne?

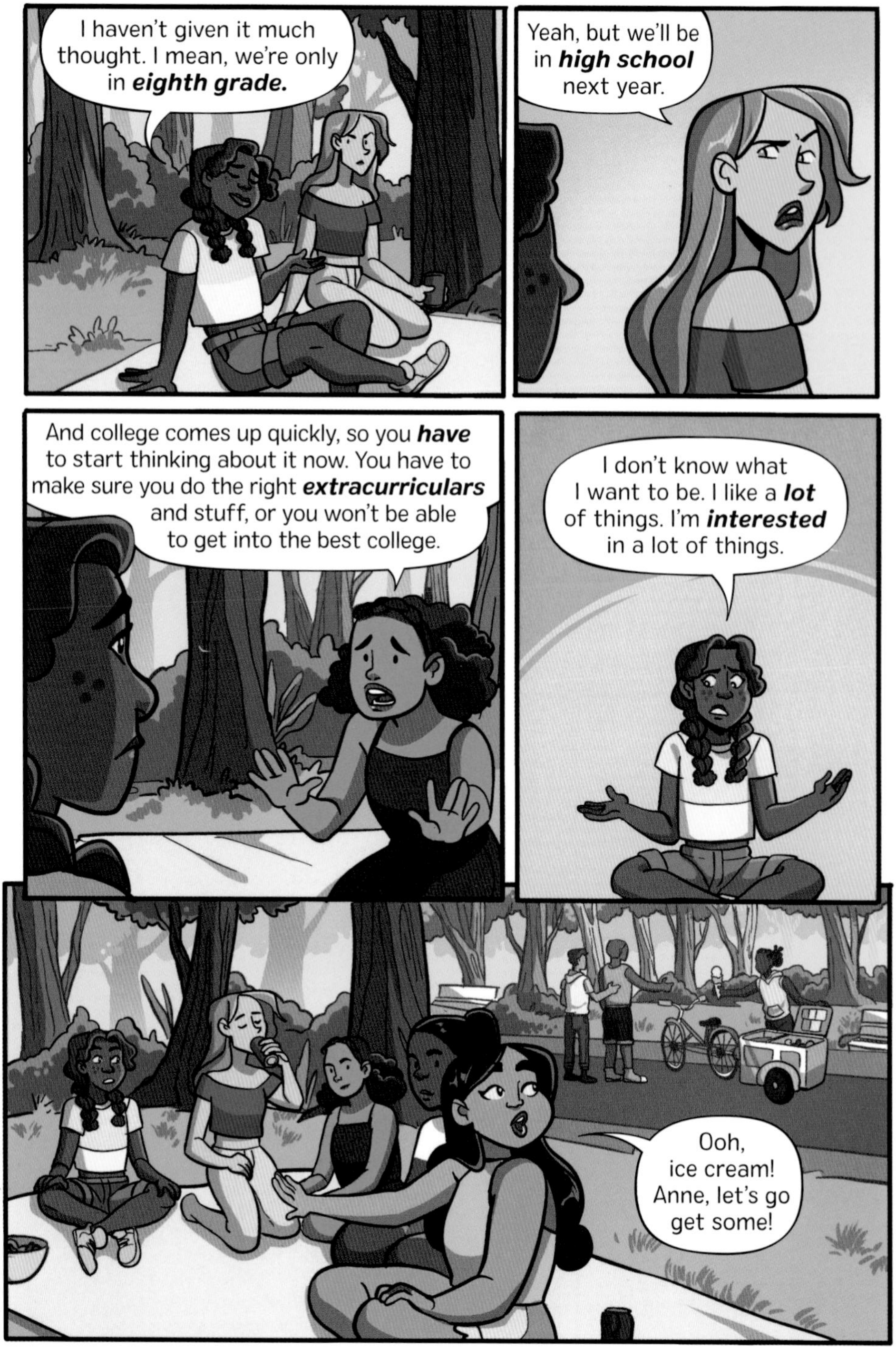
I haven't given it much thought. I mean, we're only in ***eighth grade.***
Yeah, but we'll be in ***high school*** next year.
And college comes up quickly, so you ***have*** to start thinking about it now. You have to make sure you do the right ***extracurriculars*** and stuff, or you won't be able to get into the best college.
I don't know what I want to be. I like a ***lot*** of things. I'm ***interested*** in a lot of things.
Ooh, ice cream! Anne, let's go get some!

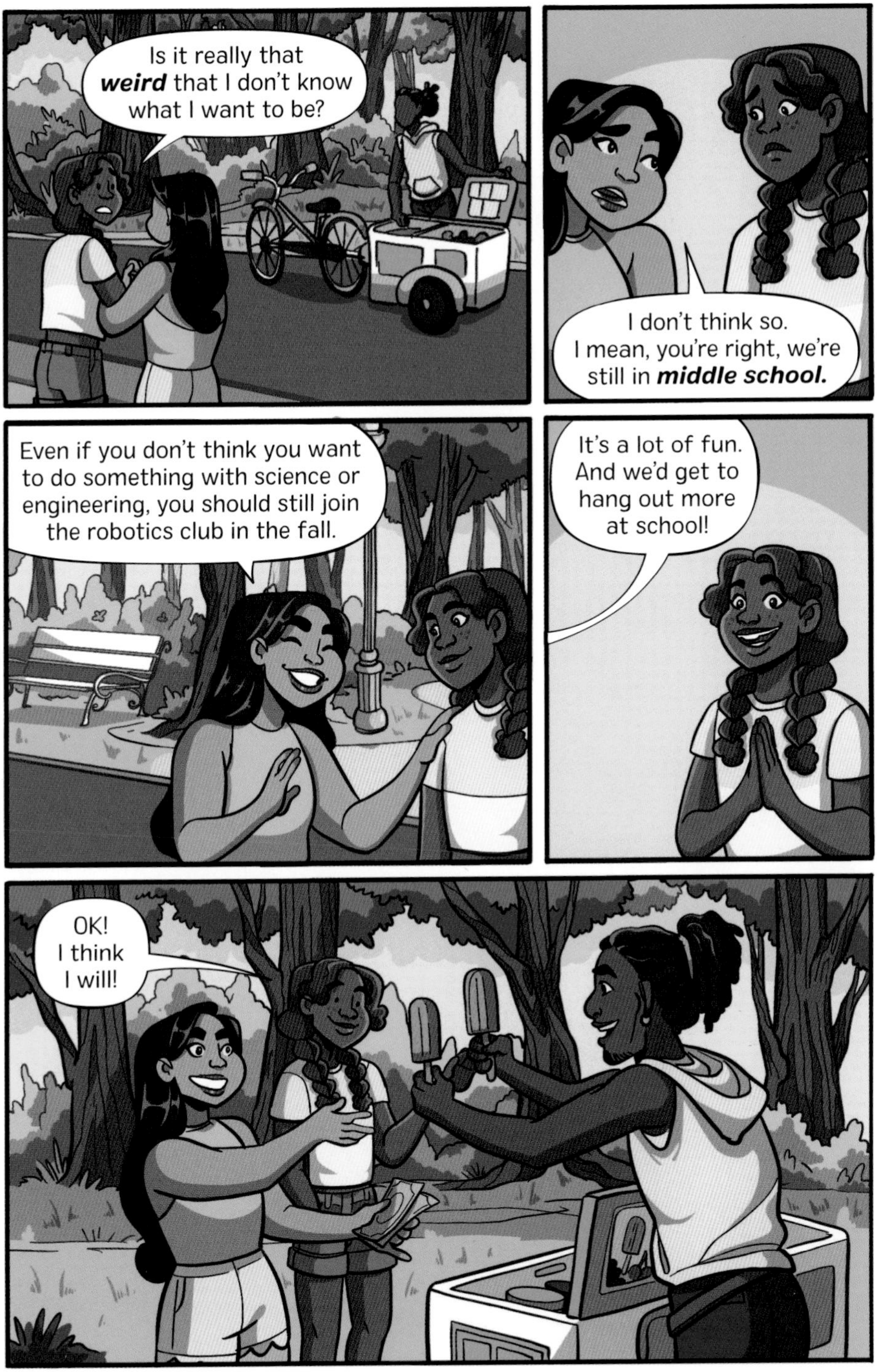
Is it really that ***weird*** that I don't know what I want to be?
I don't think so. I mean, you're right, we're still in ***middle school.***
Even if you don't think you want to do something with science or engineering, you should still join the robotics club in the fall.
It's a lot of fun. And we'd get to hang out more at school!
OK! I think I will!

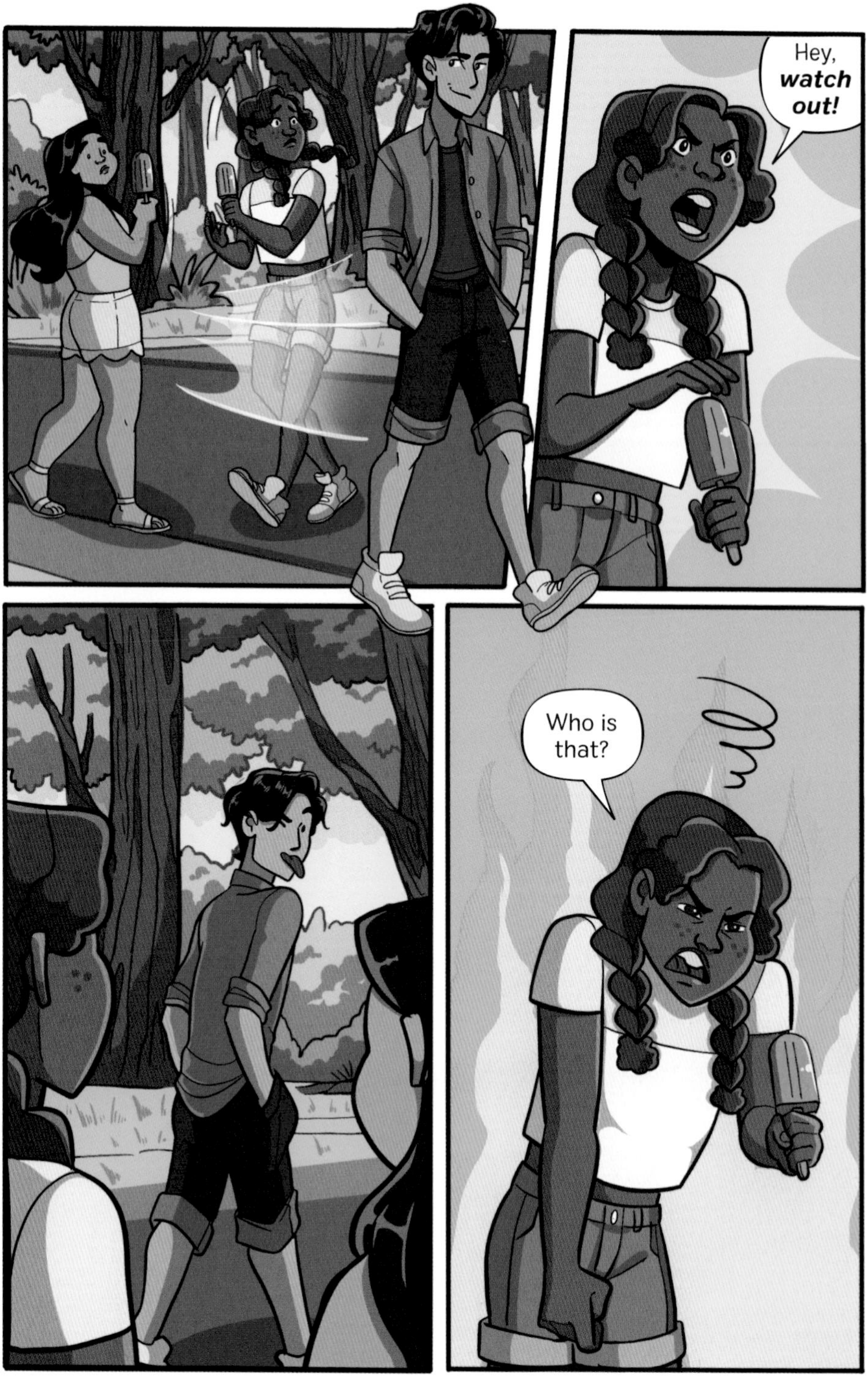
Hey, **watch out!**
Who is that?

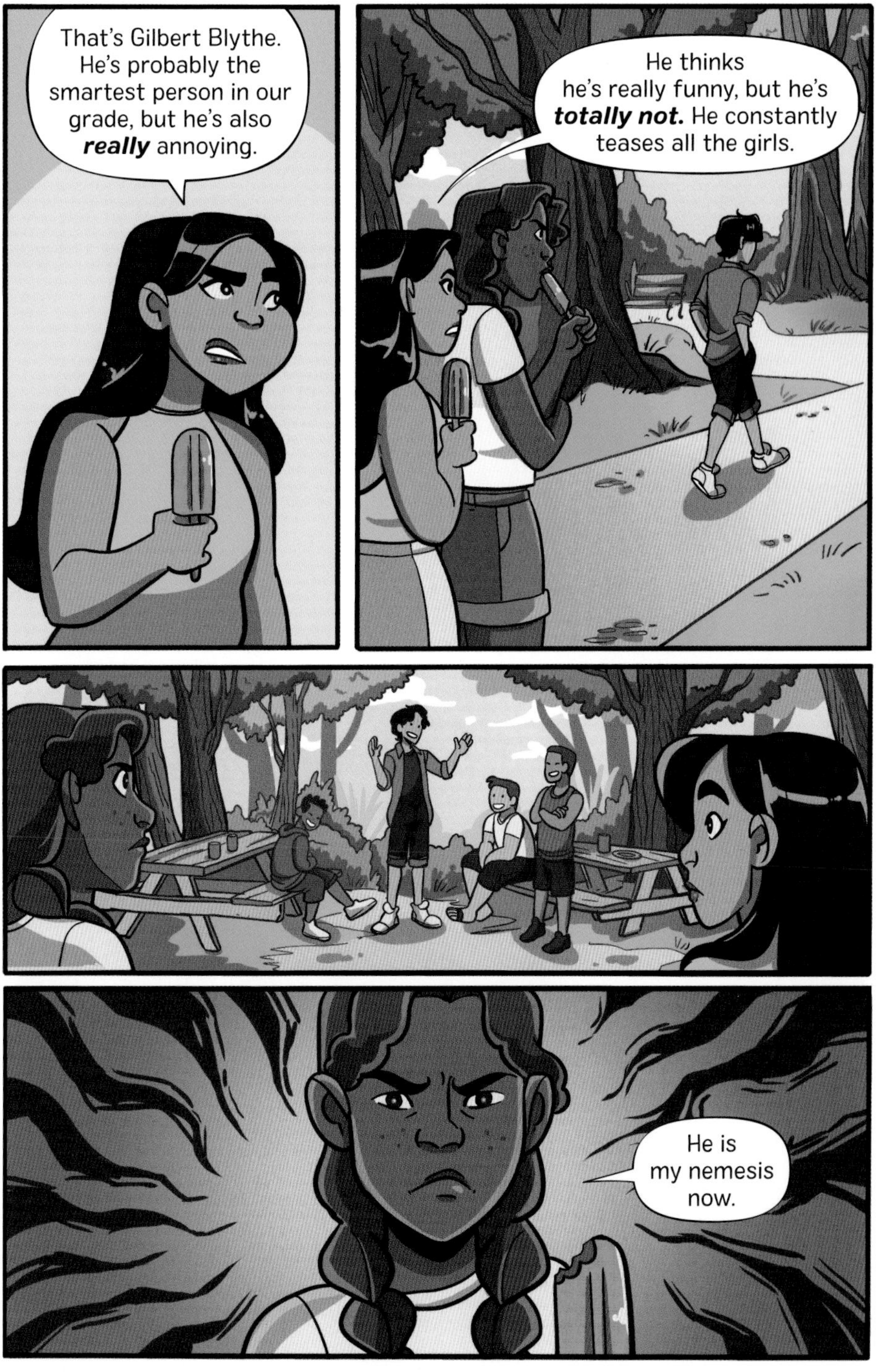
That's Gilbert Blythe. He's probably the smartest person in our grade, but he's also **really** annoying.
He thinks he's really funny, but he's **totally not.** He constantly teases all the girls.
He is my nemesis now.

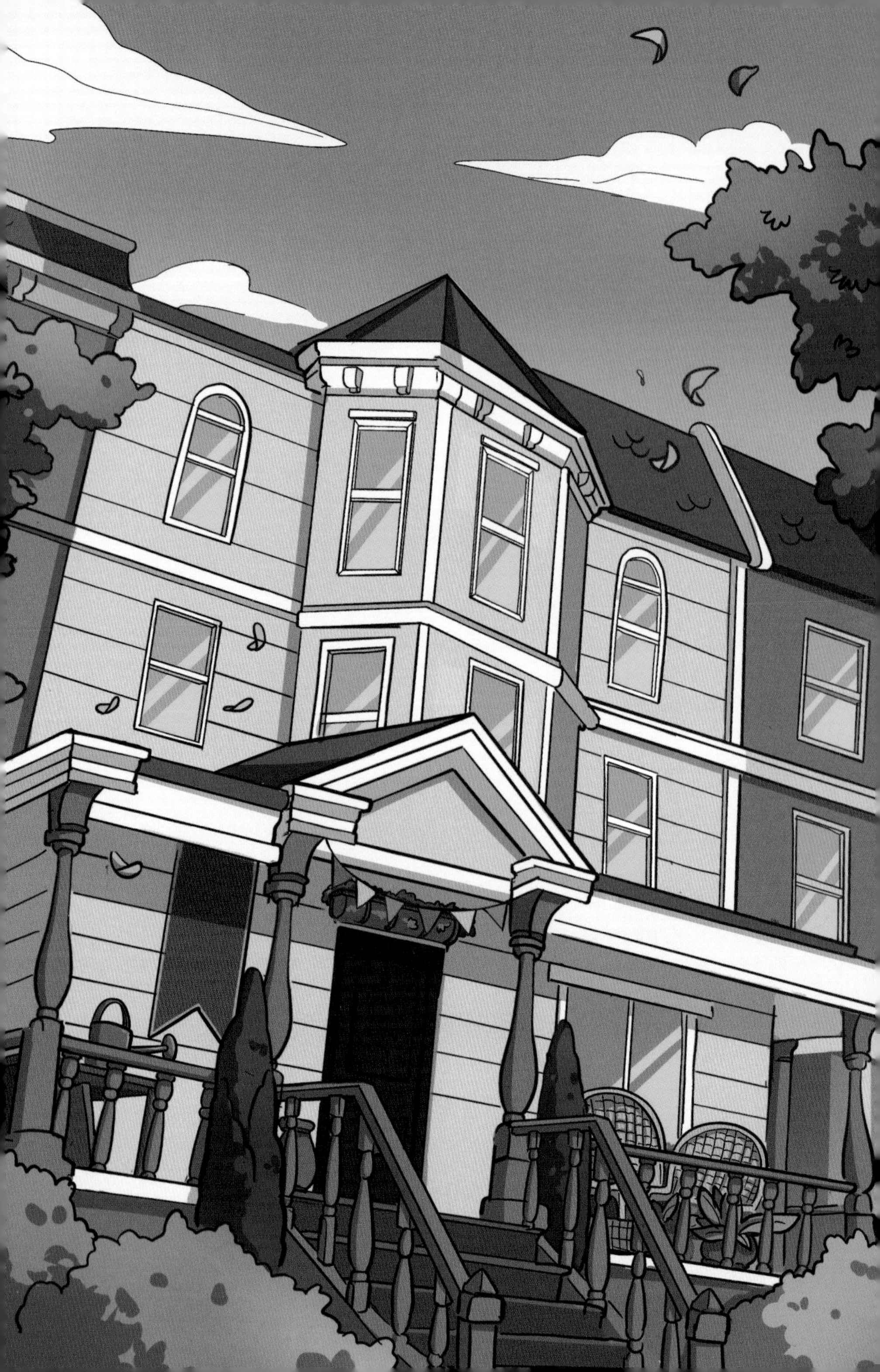

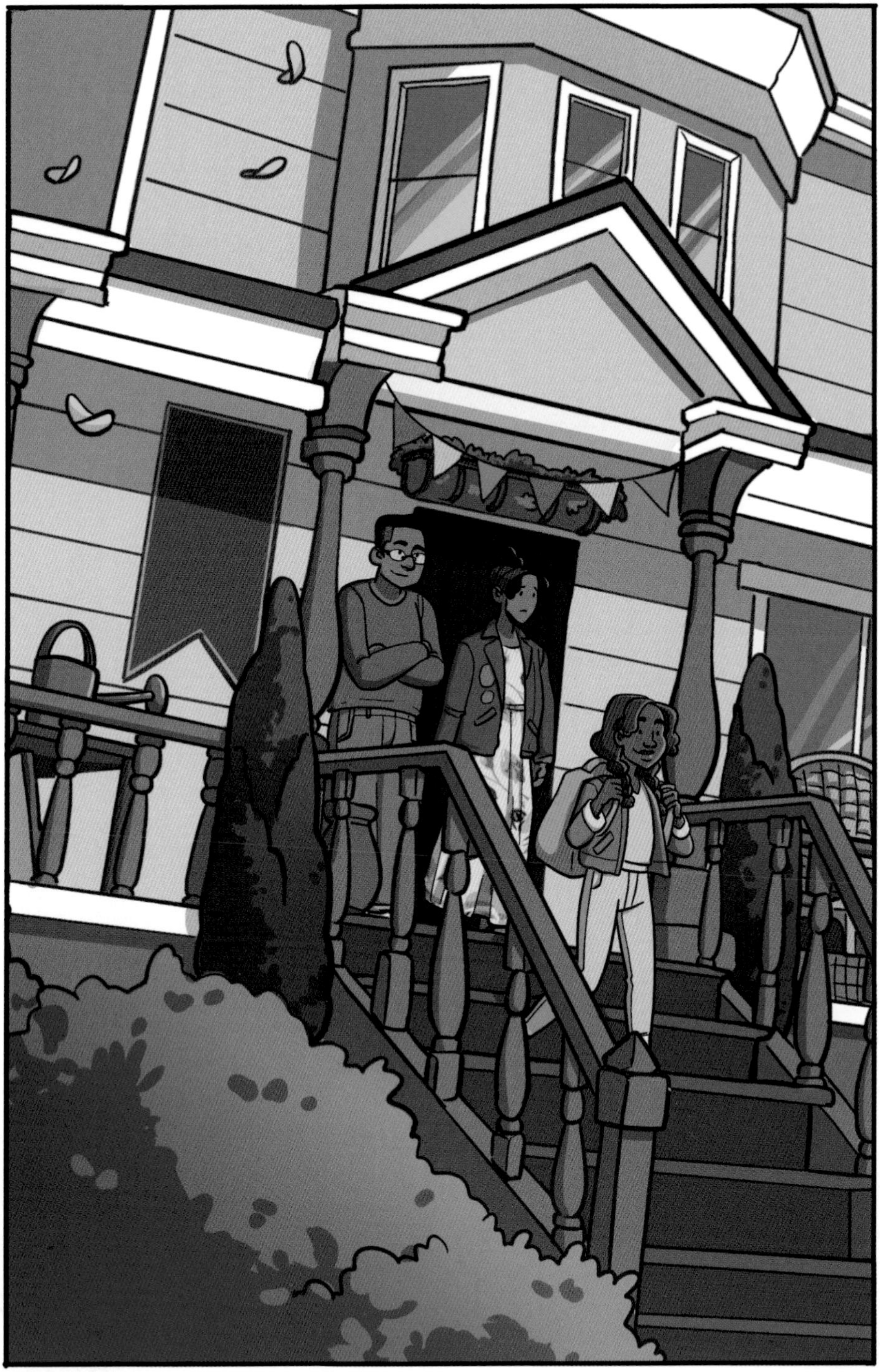

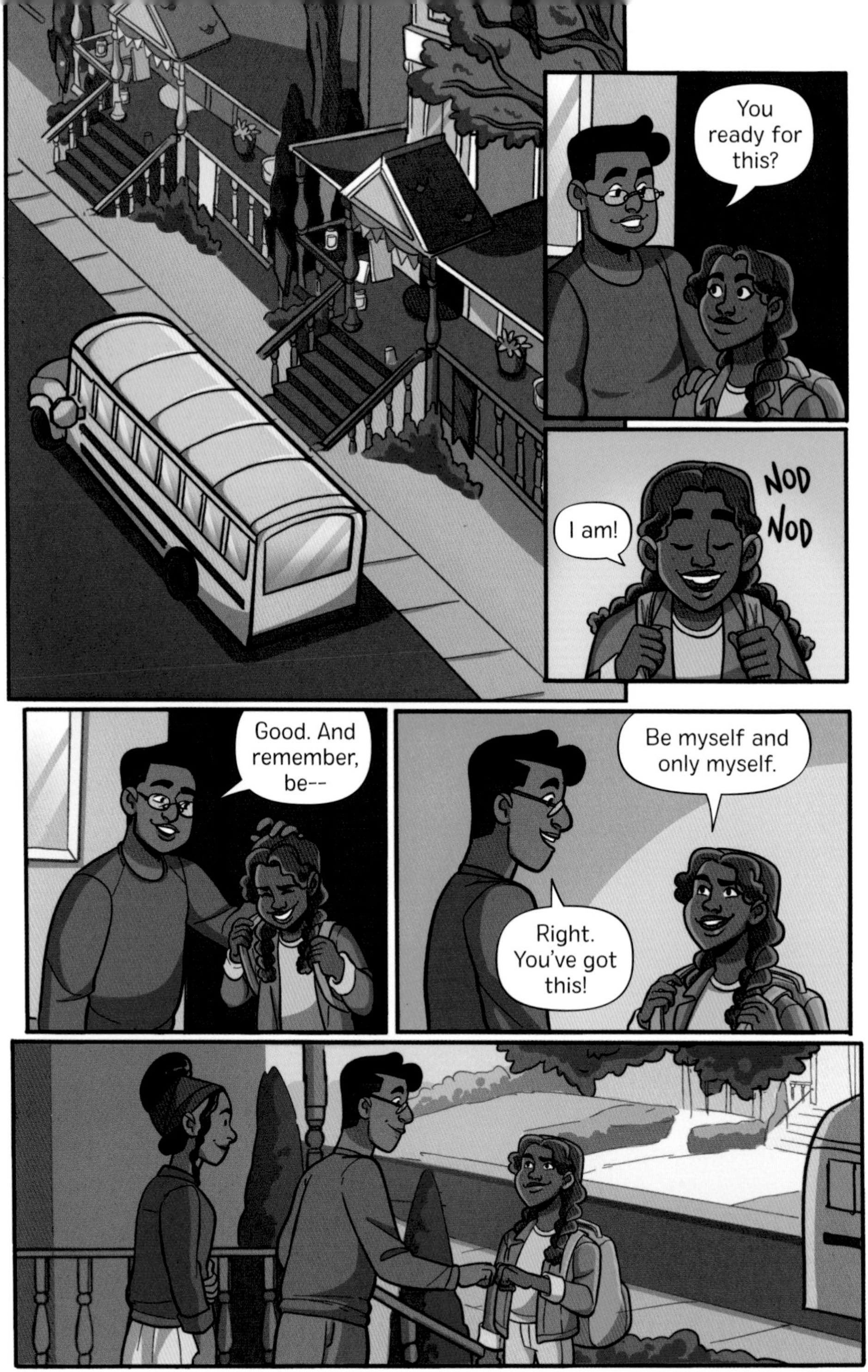
You ready for this?
I am!
NOD NOD
Good. And remember, be--
Be myself and only myself.
Right. You've got this!

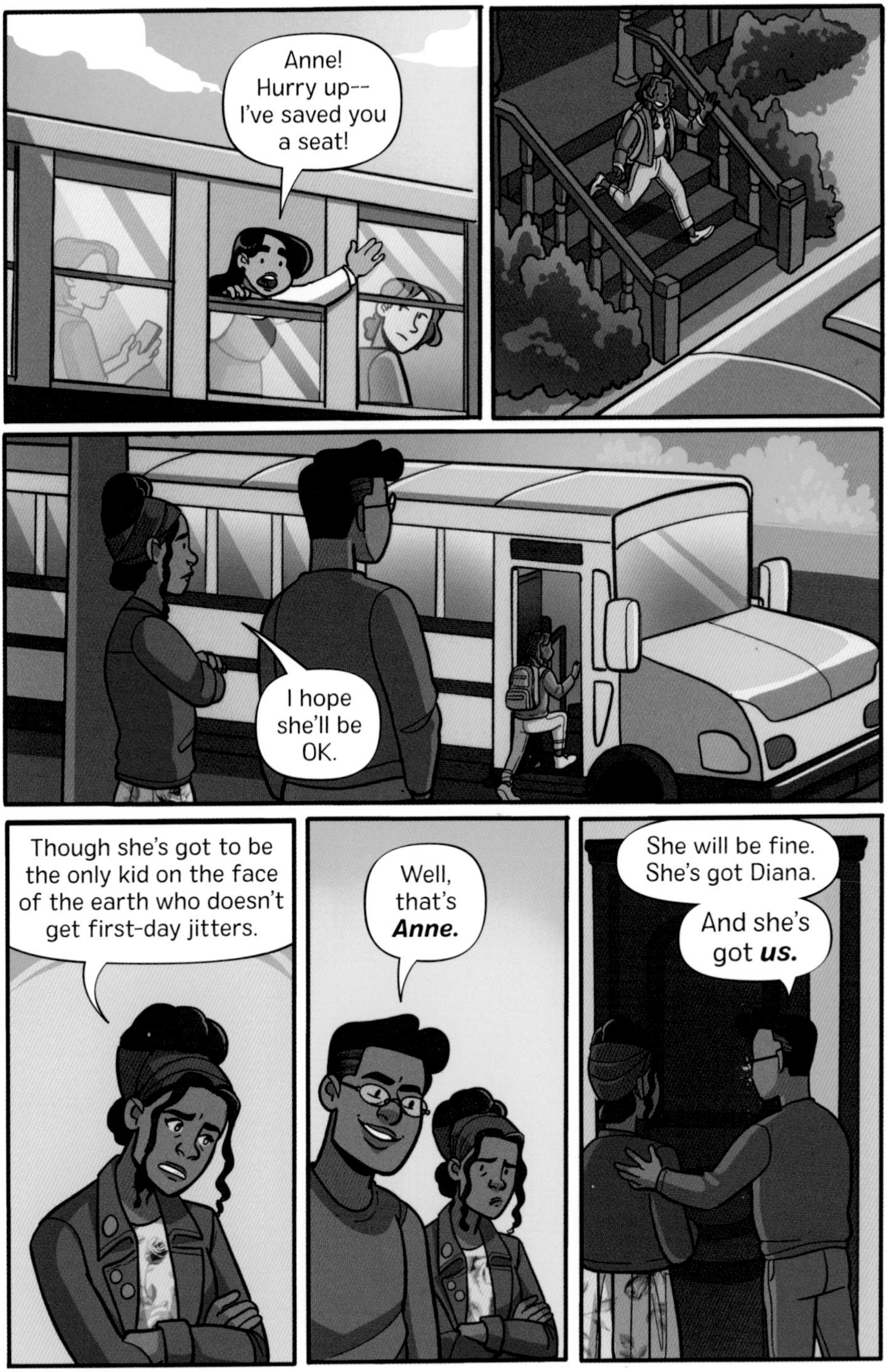
Anne!
Hurry up--
I've saved you a seat!
I hope she'll be OK.
Though she's got to be the only kid on the face of the earth who doesn't get first-day jitters.
Well, that's ***Anne.***
She will be fine. She's got Diana.
And she's got ***us.***

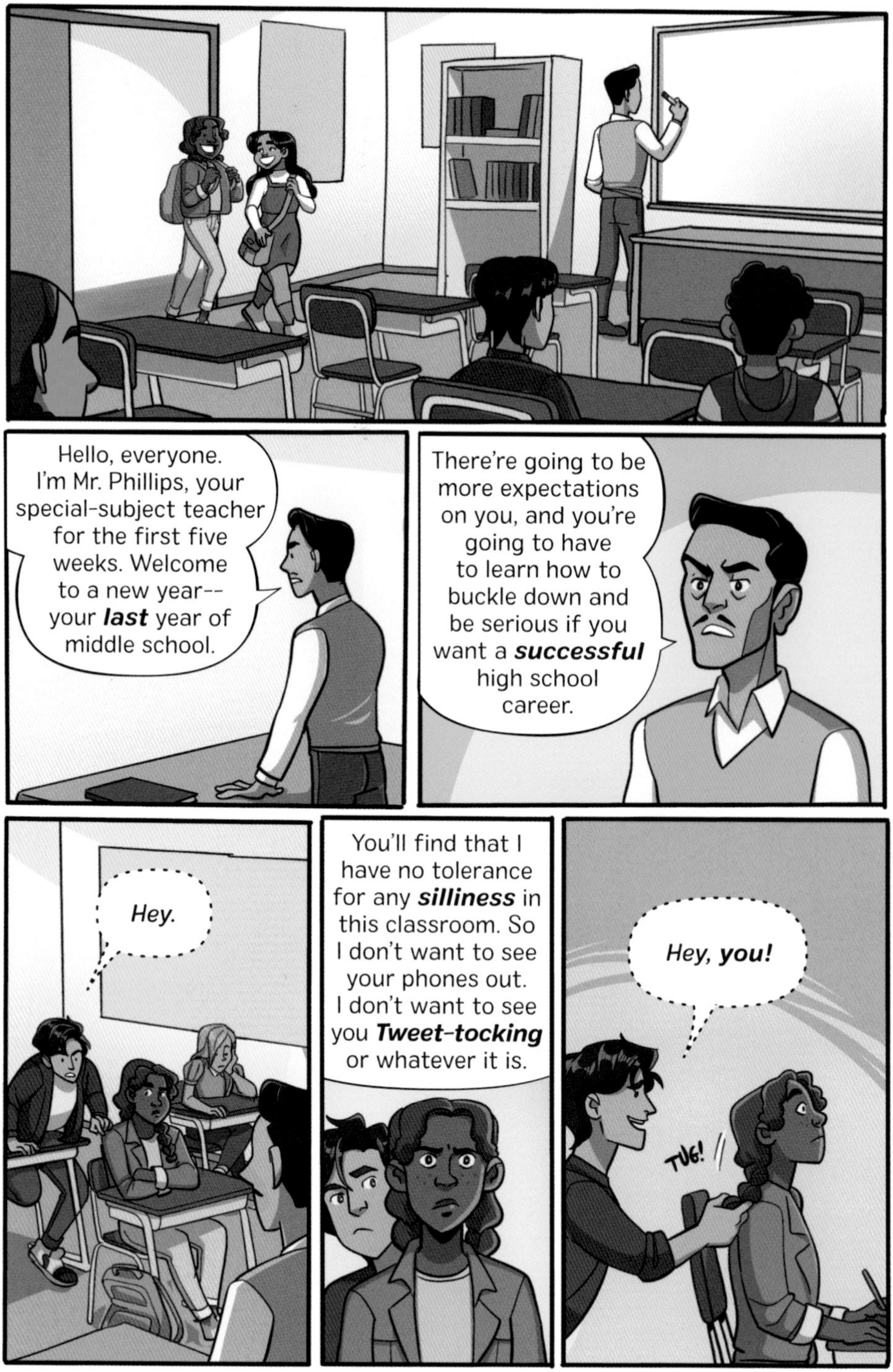

Hello, everyone. I'm Mr. Phillips, your special-subject teacher for the first five weeks. Welcome to a new year-- your **last** year of middle school.
There're going to be more expectations on you, and you're going to have to learn how to buckle down and be serious if you want a **successful** high school career.
Hey.
You'll find that I have no tolerance for any **silliness** in this classroom. So I don't want to see your phones out. I don't want to see you **Tweet-tocking** or whatever it is.
*Hey, **you!***
TUG!

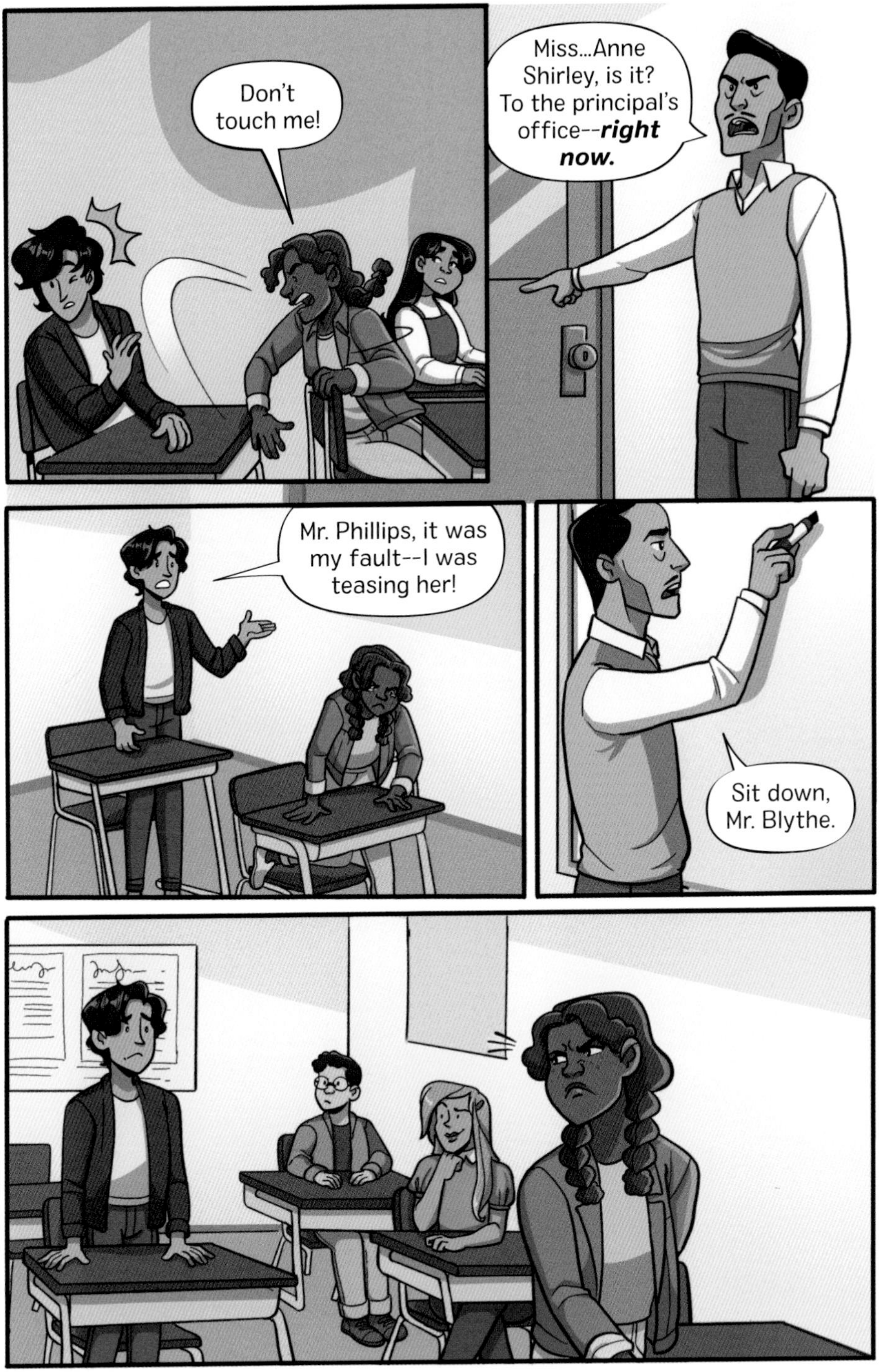
Don't touch me!
Miss...Anne Shirley, is it? To the principal's office--**right now.**
Mr. Phillips, it was my fault--I was teasing her!
Sit down, Mr. Blythe.

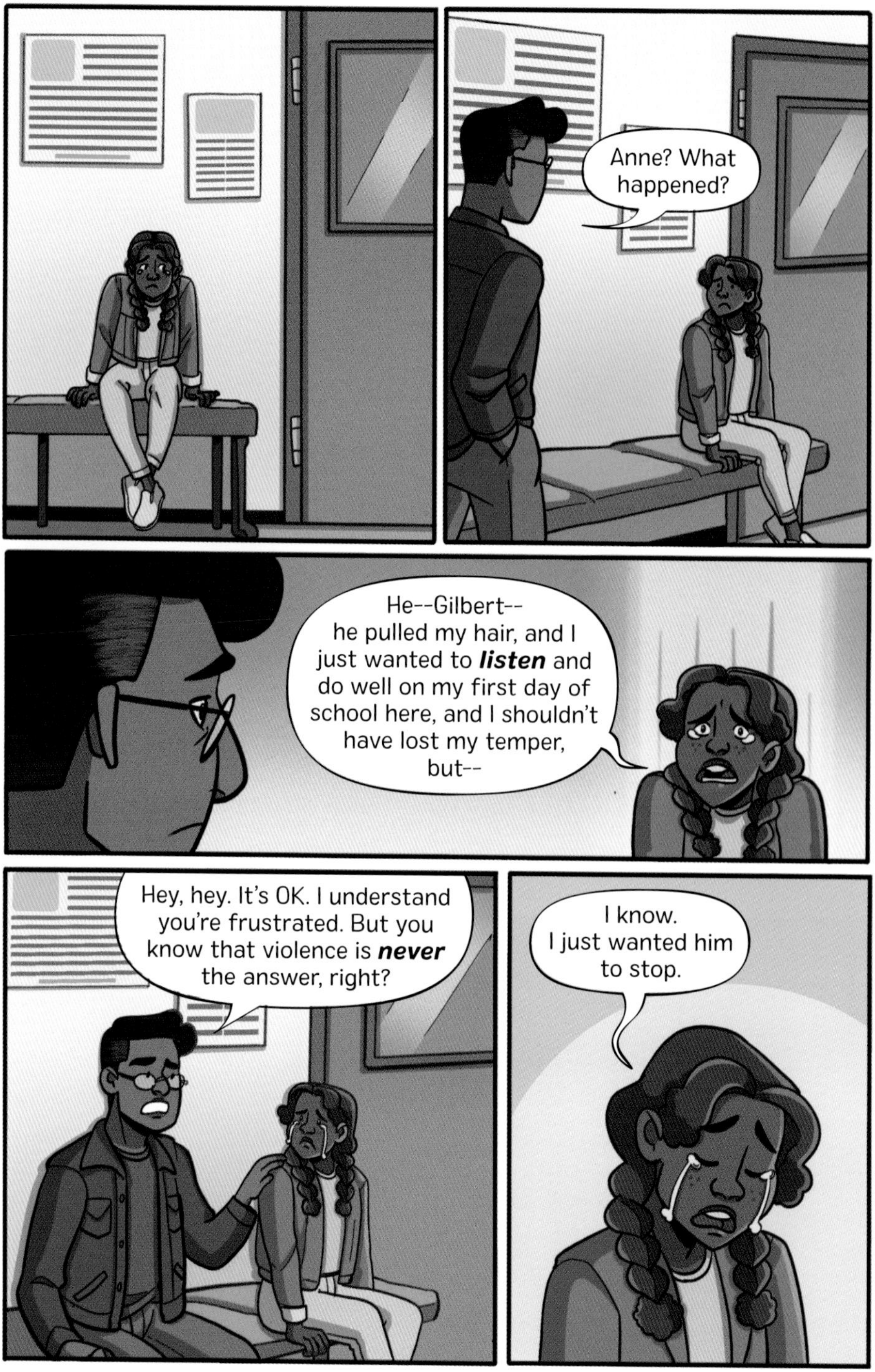
Anne? What happened?
He--Gilbert-- he pulled my hair, and I just wanted to ***listen*** and do well on my first day of school here, and I shouldn't have lost my temper, but--
Hey, hey. It's OK. I understand you're frustrated. But you know that violence is ***never*** the answer, right?
I know. I just wanted him to stop.

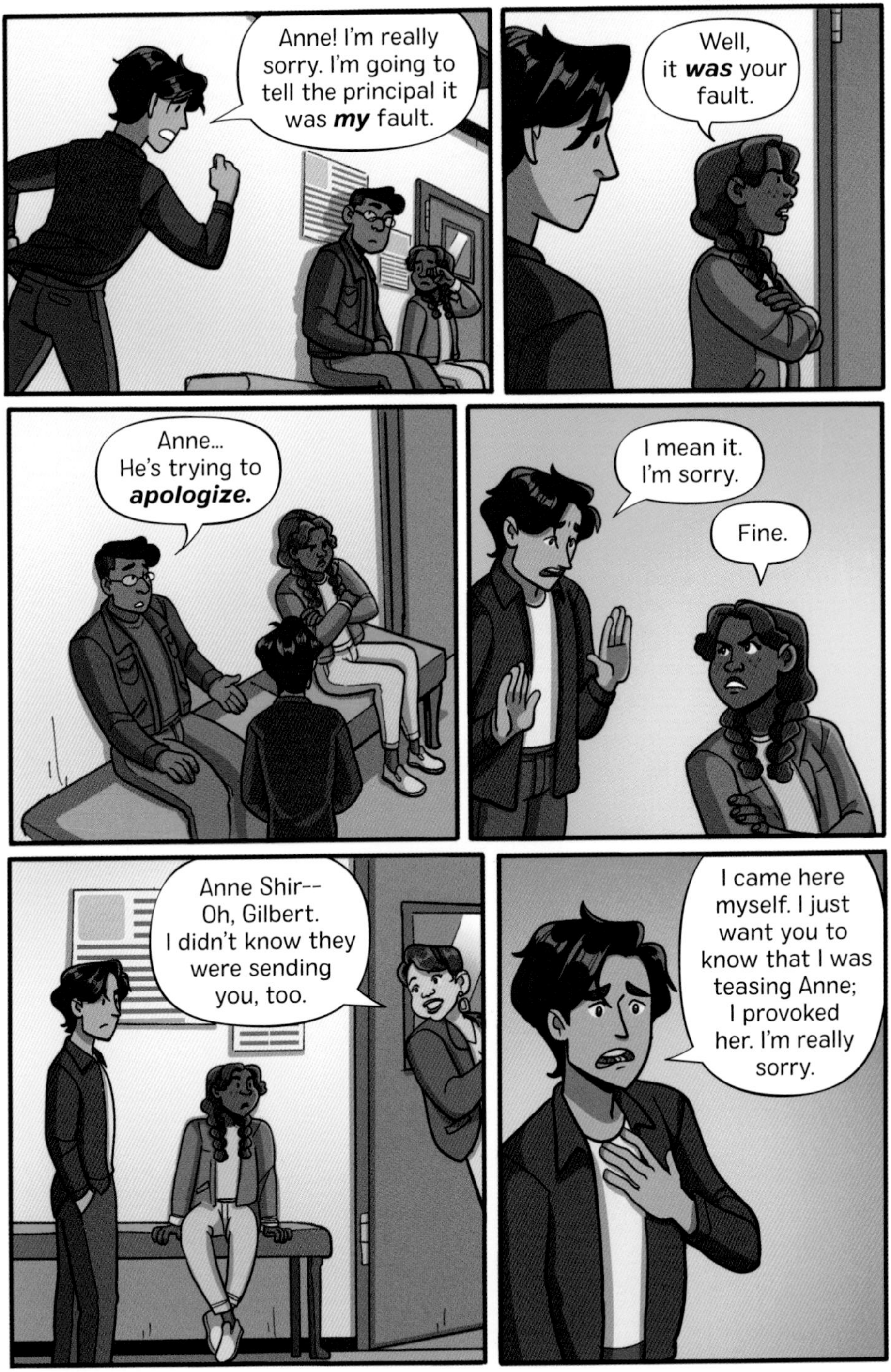
Anne! I'm really sorry. I'm going to tell the principal it was ***my*** fault.
Well, it ***was*** your fault.
Anne... He's trying to ***apologize.***
I mean it. I'm sorry.
Fine.
Anne Shir-- Oh, Gilbert. I didn't know they were sending you, too.
I came here myself. I just want you to know that I was teasing Anne; I provoked her. I'm really sorry.

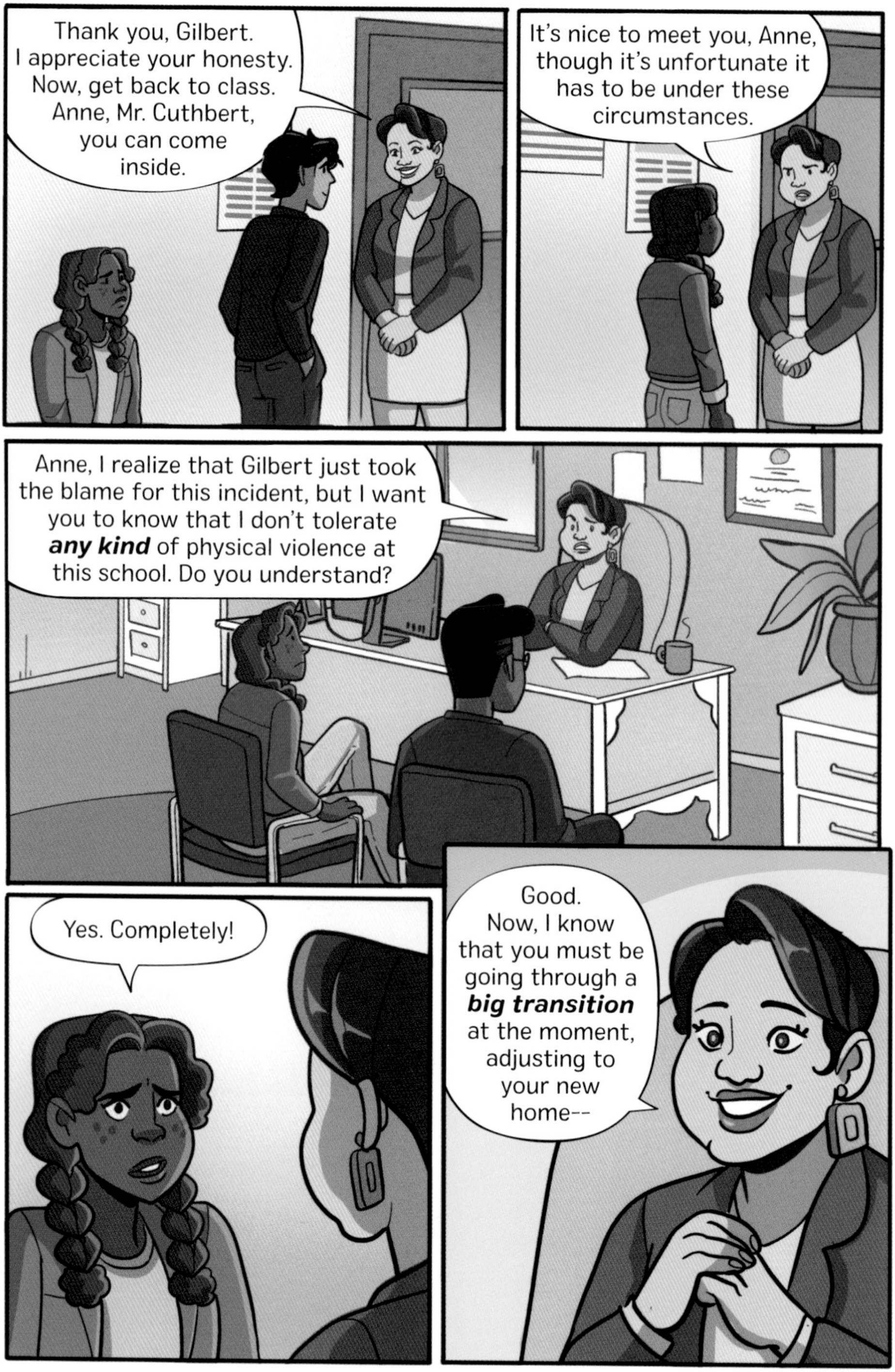
Thank you, Gilbert. I appreciate your honesty. Now, get back to class. Anne, Mr. Cuthbert, you can come inside.
It's nice to meet you, Anne, though it's unfortunate it has to be under these circumstances.
Anne, I realize that Gilbert just took the blame for this incident, but I want you to know that I don't tolerate ***any kind*** of physical violence at this school. Do you understand?
Yes. Completely!
Good. Now, I know that you must be going through a ***big transition*** at the moment, adjusting to your new home--

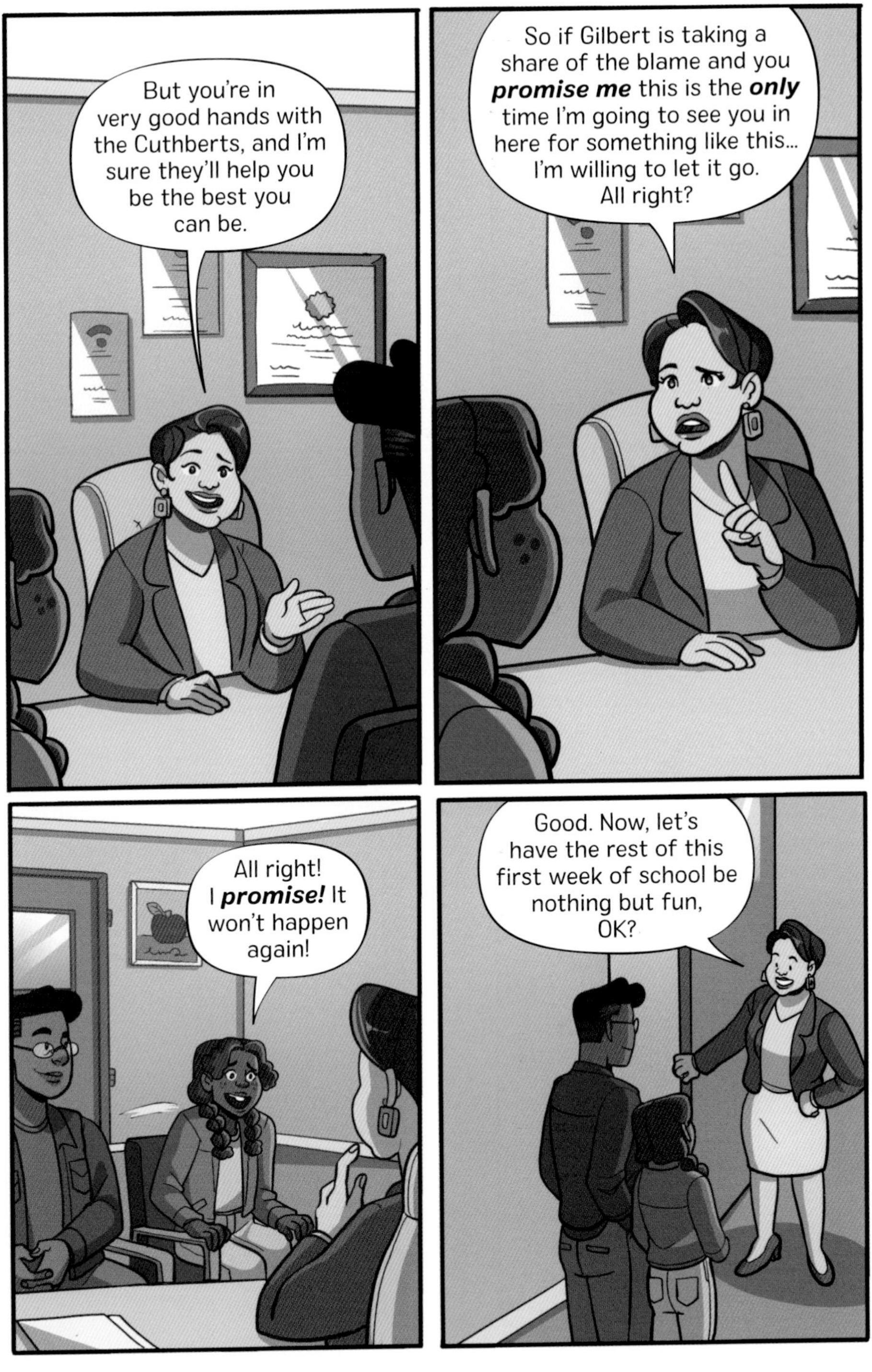
But you're in very good hands with the Cuthberts, and I'm sure they'll help you be the best you can be.
So if Gilbert is taking a share of the blame and you ***promise me*** this is the ***only*** time I'm going to see you in here for something like this... I'm willing to let it go. All right?
All right! I ***promise!*** It won't happen again!
Good. Now, let's have the rest of this first week of school be nothing but fun, OK?

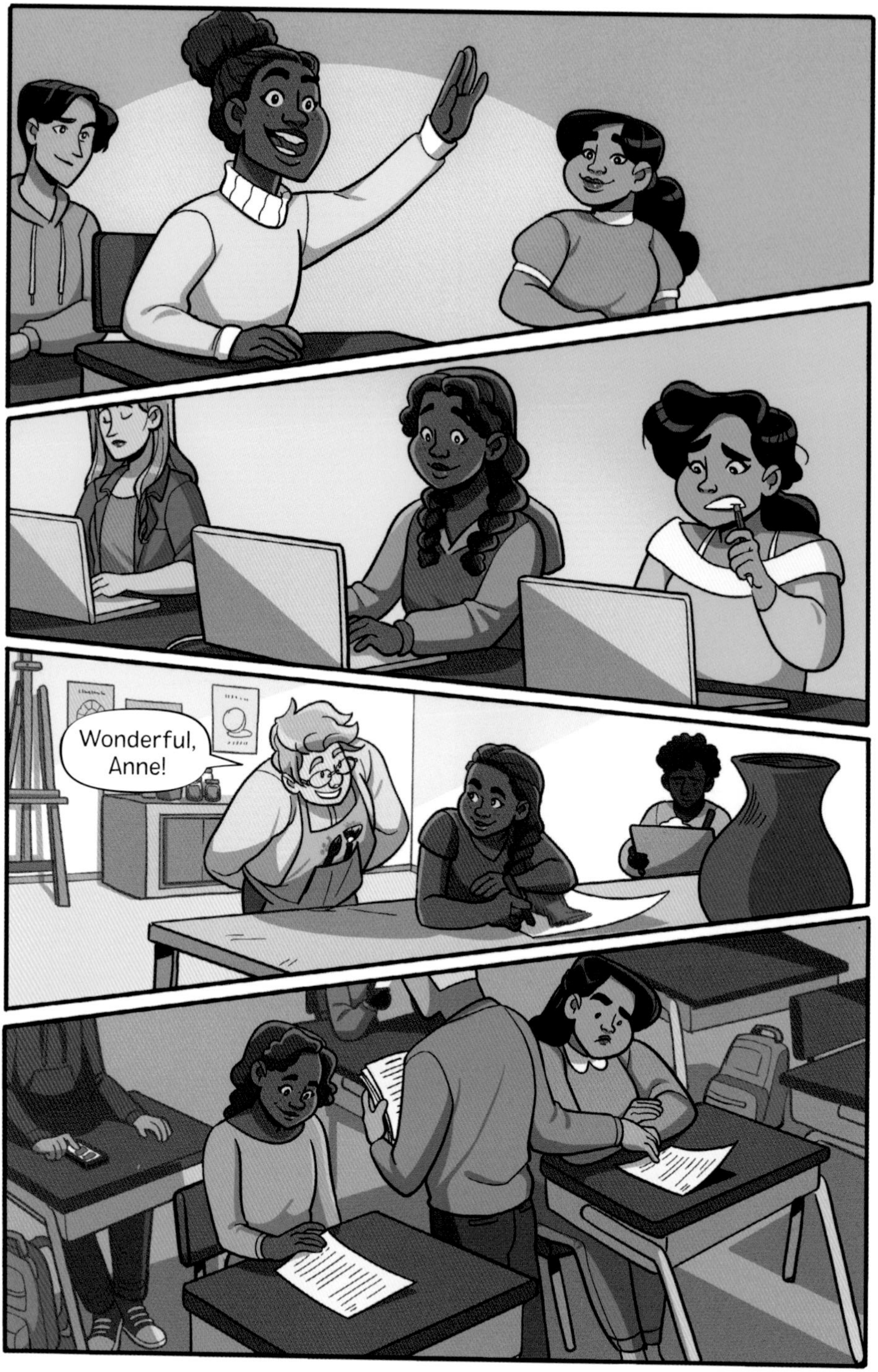
Wonderful, Anne!

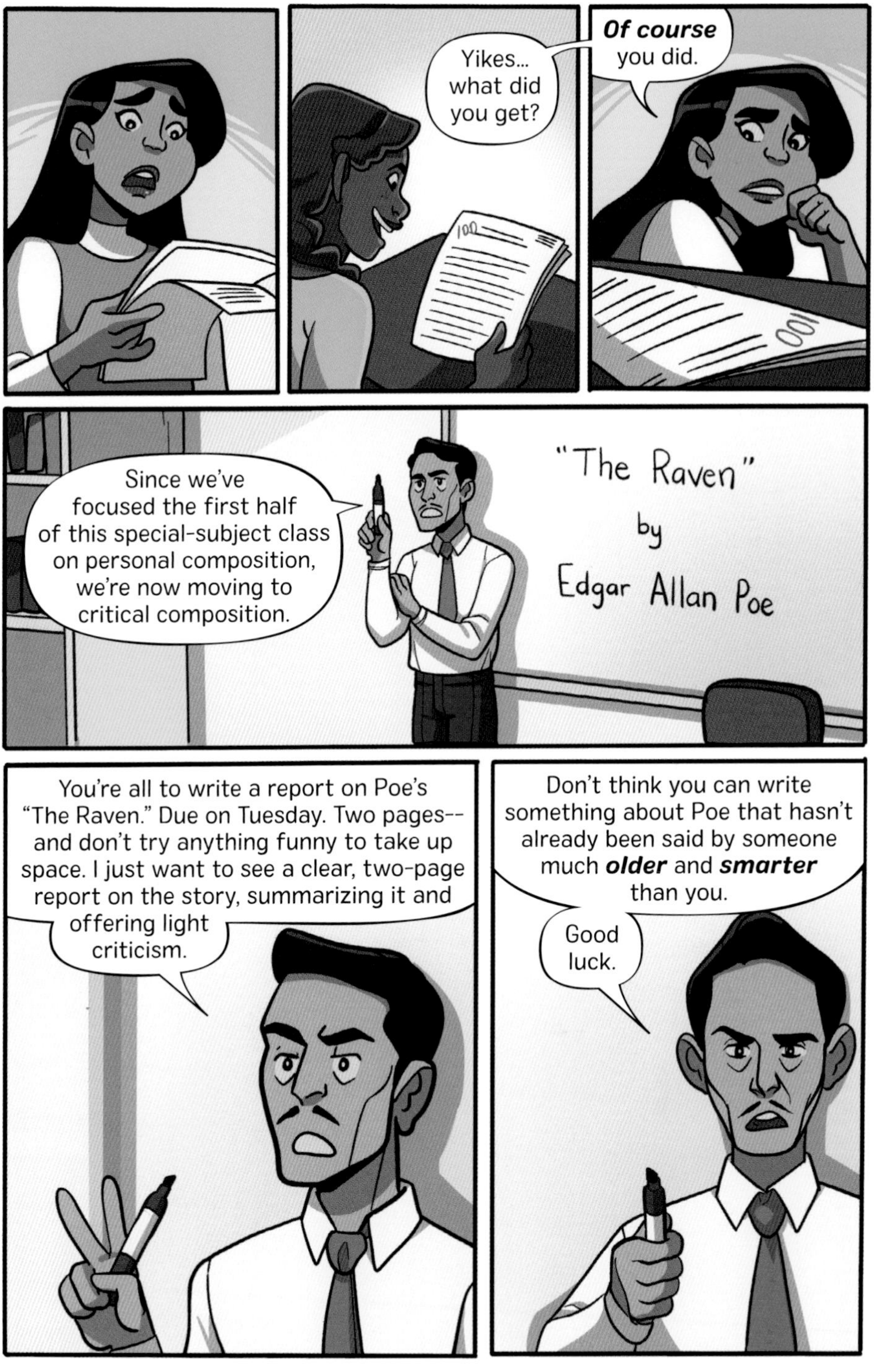
Yikes... what did you get?
100
Of course you did.
100
Since we've focused the first half of this special-subject class on personal composition, we're now moving to critical composition.
"The Raven" by Edgar Allan Poe
You're all to write a report on Poe's "The Raven." Due on Tuesday. Two pages-- and don't try anything funny to take up space. I just want to see a clear, two-page report on the story, summarizing it and offering light criticism.
Don't think you can write something about Poe that hasn't already been said by someone much ***older*** and ***smarter*** than you.
Good luck.

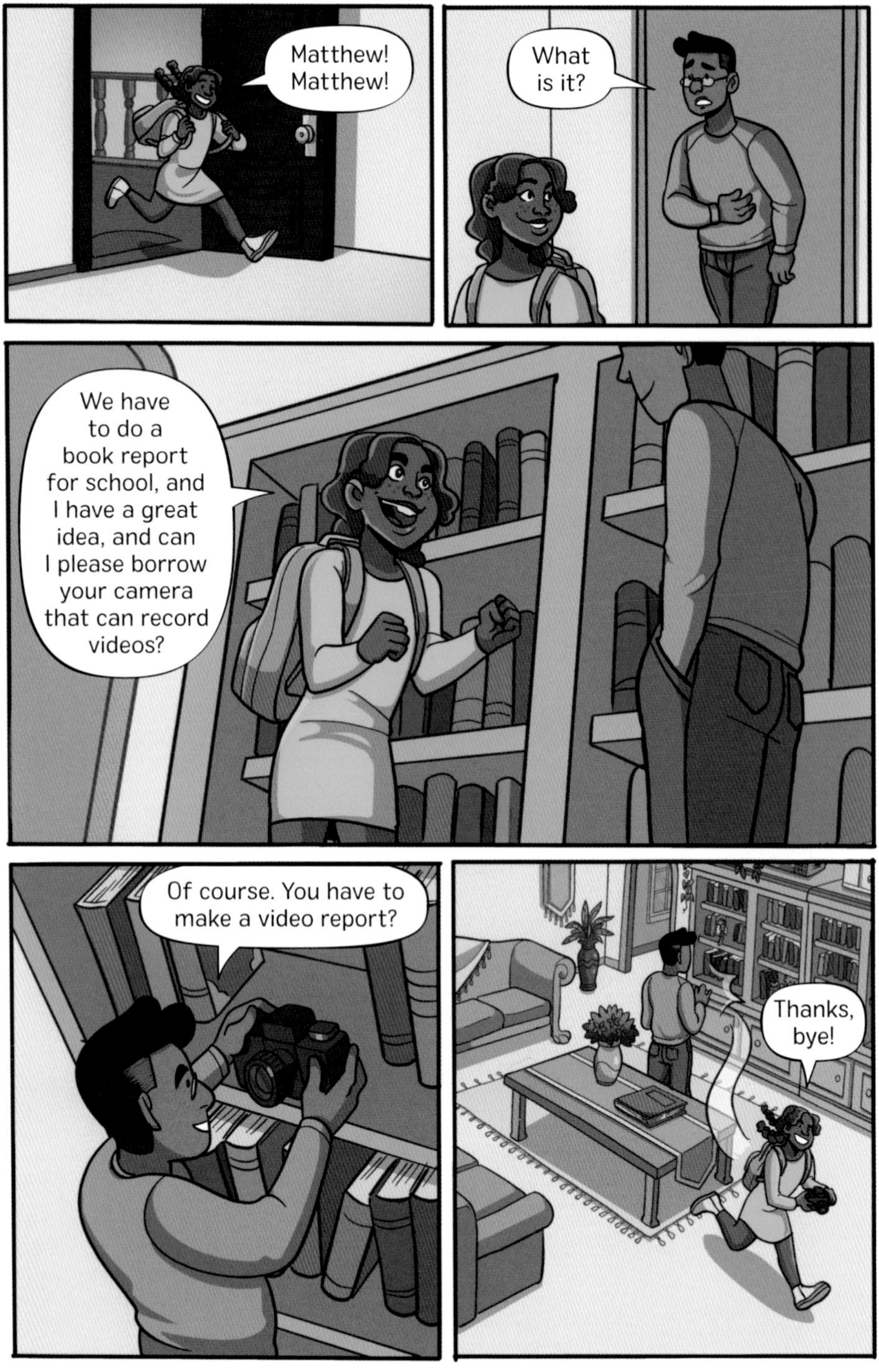
Matthew!
Matthew!
What is it?
We have to do a book report for school, and I have a great idea, and can I please borrow your camera that can record videos?
Of course. You have to make a video report?
Thanks, bye!

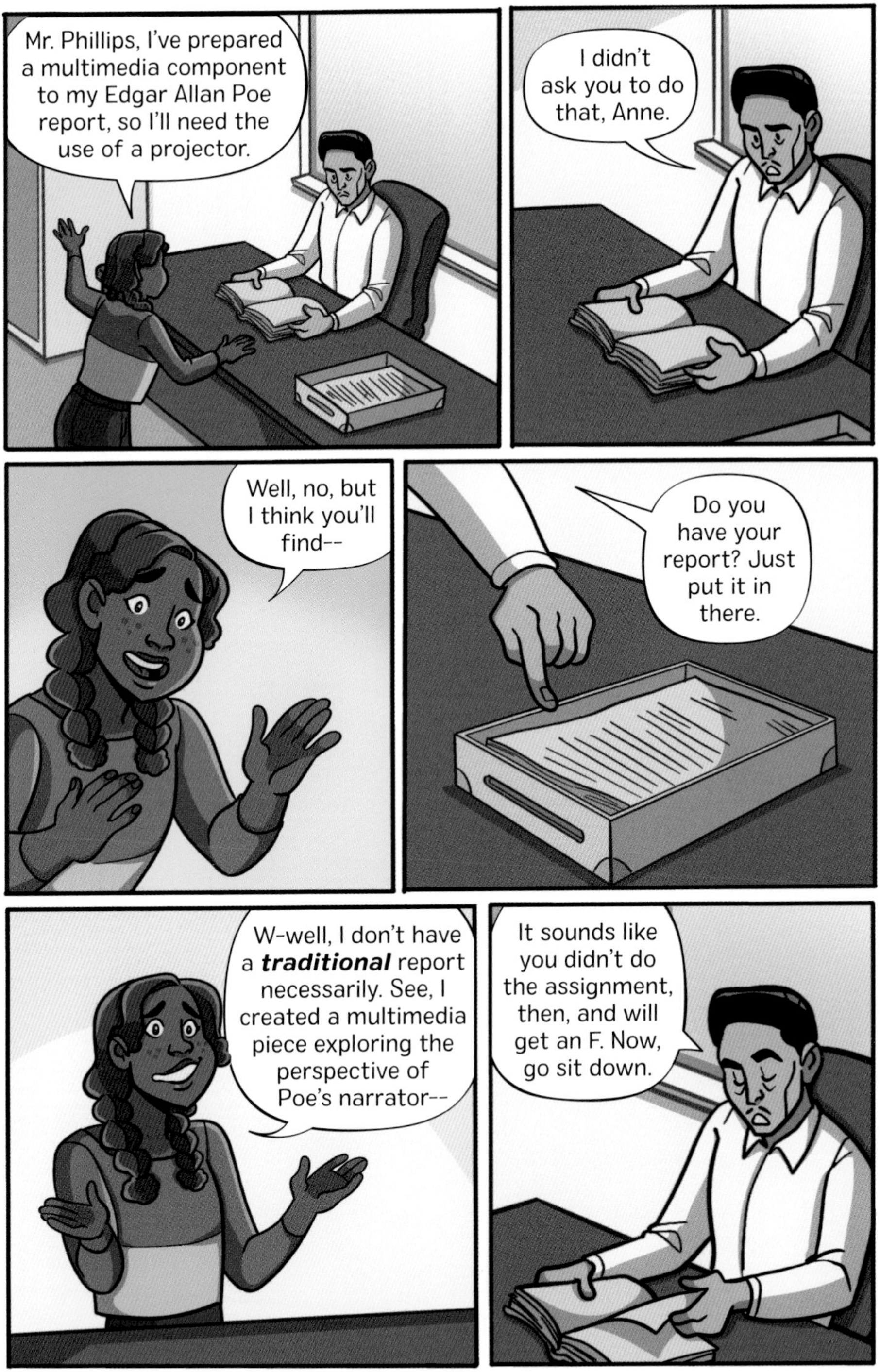
Mr. Phillips, I've prepared a multimedia component to my Edgar Allan Poe report, so I'll need the use of a projector.
I didn't ask you to do that, Anne.
Well, no, but I think you'll find--
Do you have your report? Just put it in there.
W-well, I don't have a ***traditional*** report necessarily. See, I created a multimedia piece exploring the perspective of Poe's narrator--
It sounds like you didn't do the assignment, then, and will get an F. Now, go sit down.

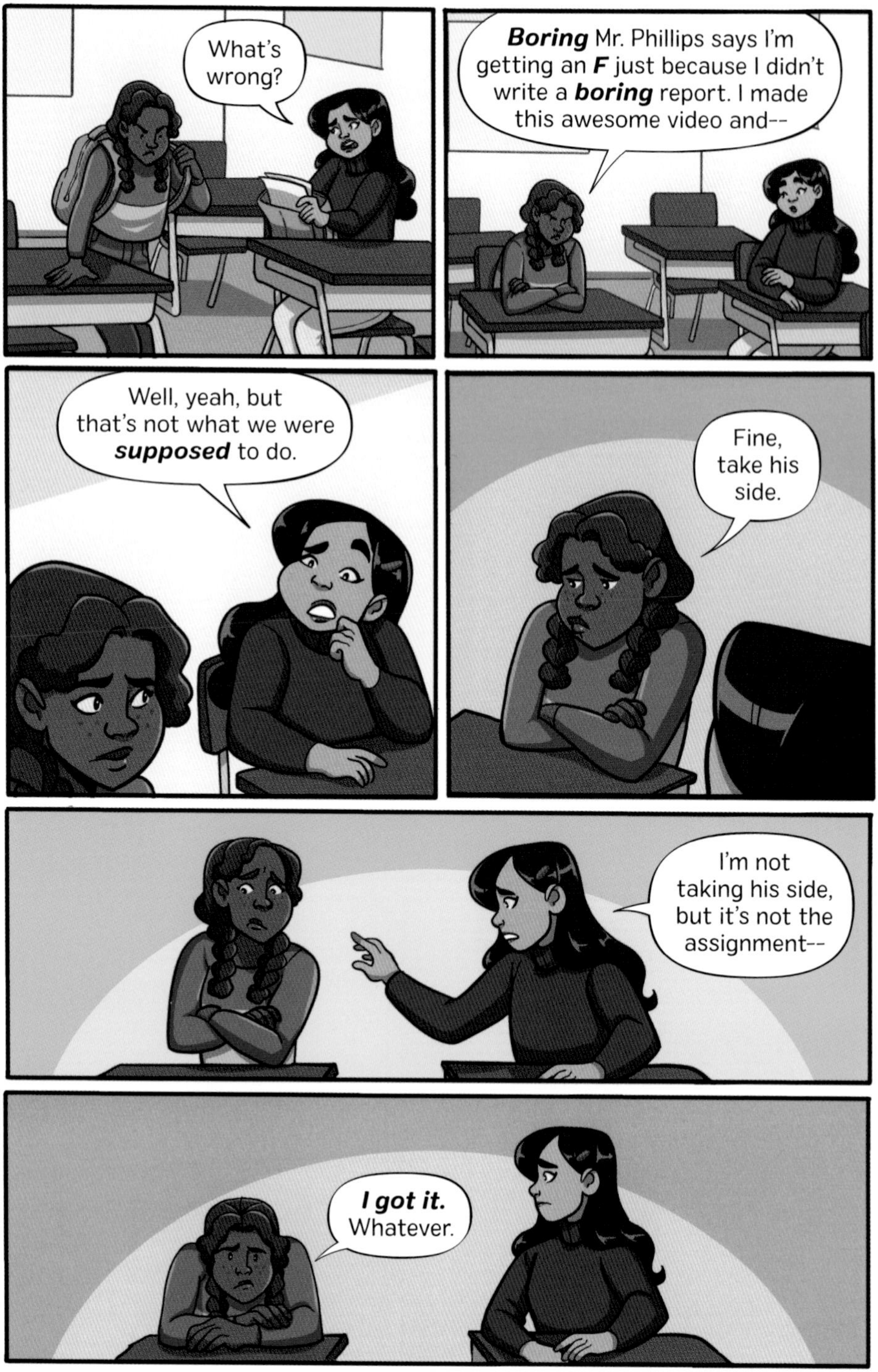
What's wrong?
Boring Mr. Phillips says I'm getting an ***F*** just because I didn't write a ***boring*** report. I made this awesome video and--
Well, yeah, but that's not what we were ***supposed*** to do.
Fine, take his side.
I'm not taking his side, but it's not the assignment--
I got it. Whatever.

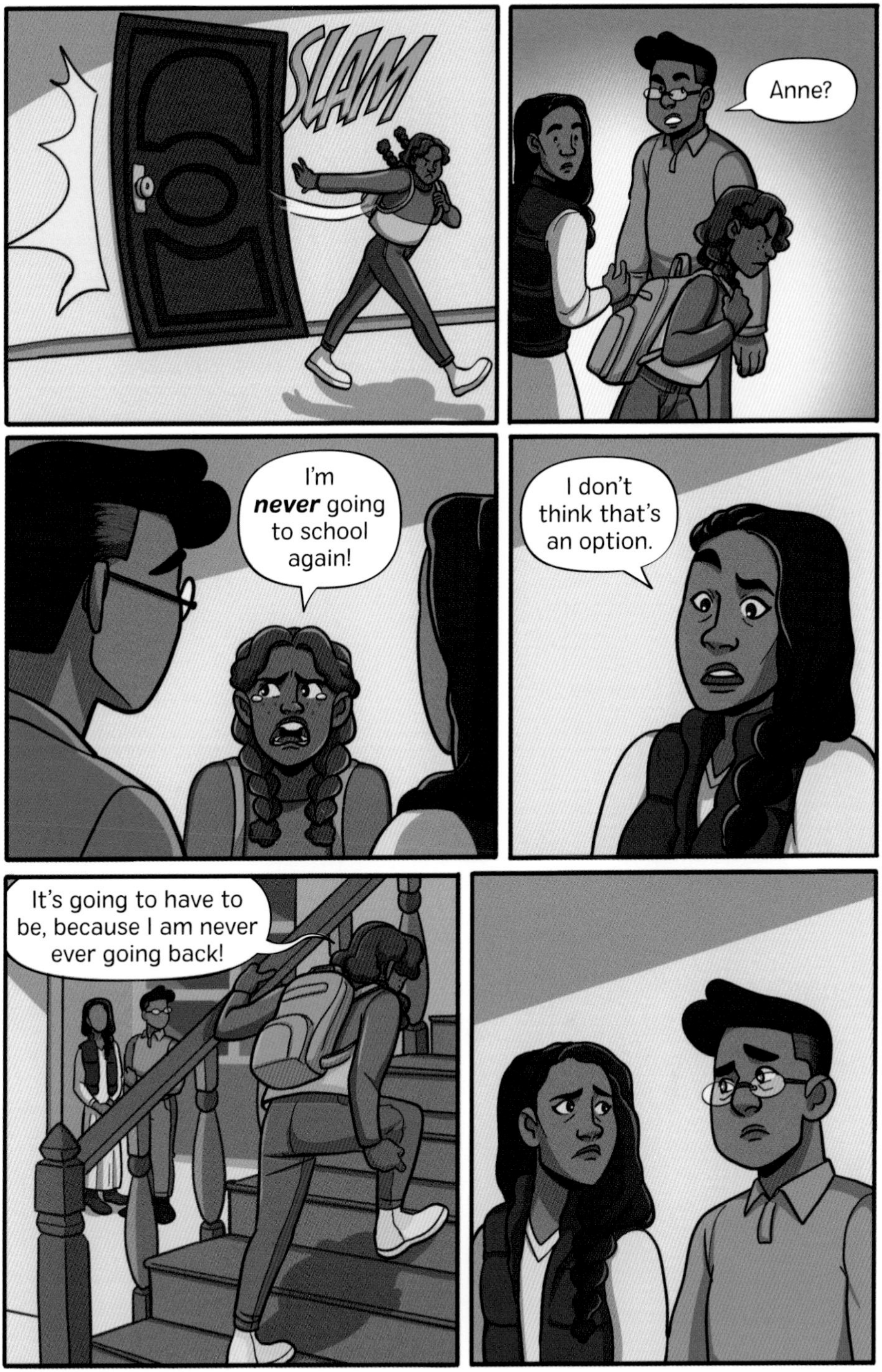
SLAM
Anne?
I'm ***never*** going to school again!
I don't think that's an option.
It's going to have to be, because I am never ever going back!

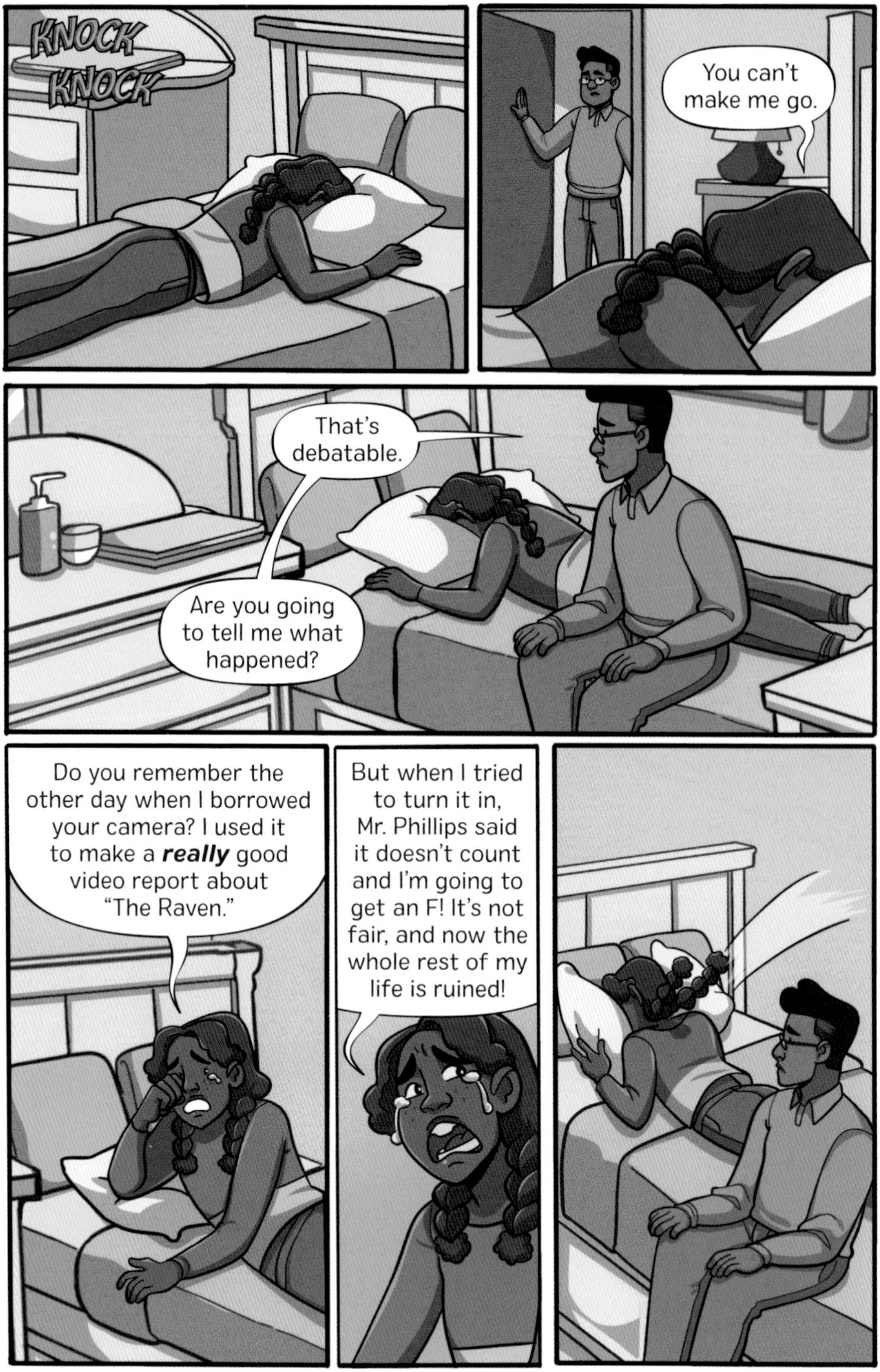
KNOCK KNOCK
You can't make me go.
That's debatable.
Are you going to tell me what happened?
Do you remember the other day when I borrowed your camera? I used it to make a ***really*** good video report about "The Raven."
But when I tried to turn it in, Mr. Phillips said it doesn't count and I'm going to get an F! It's not fair, and now the whole rest of my life is ruined!

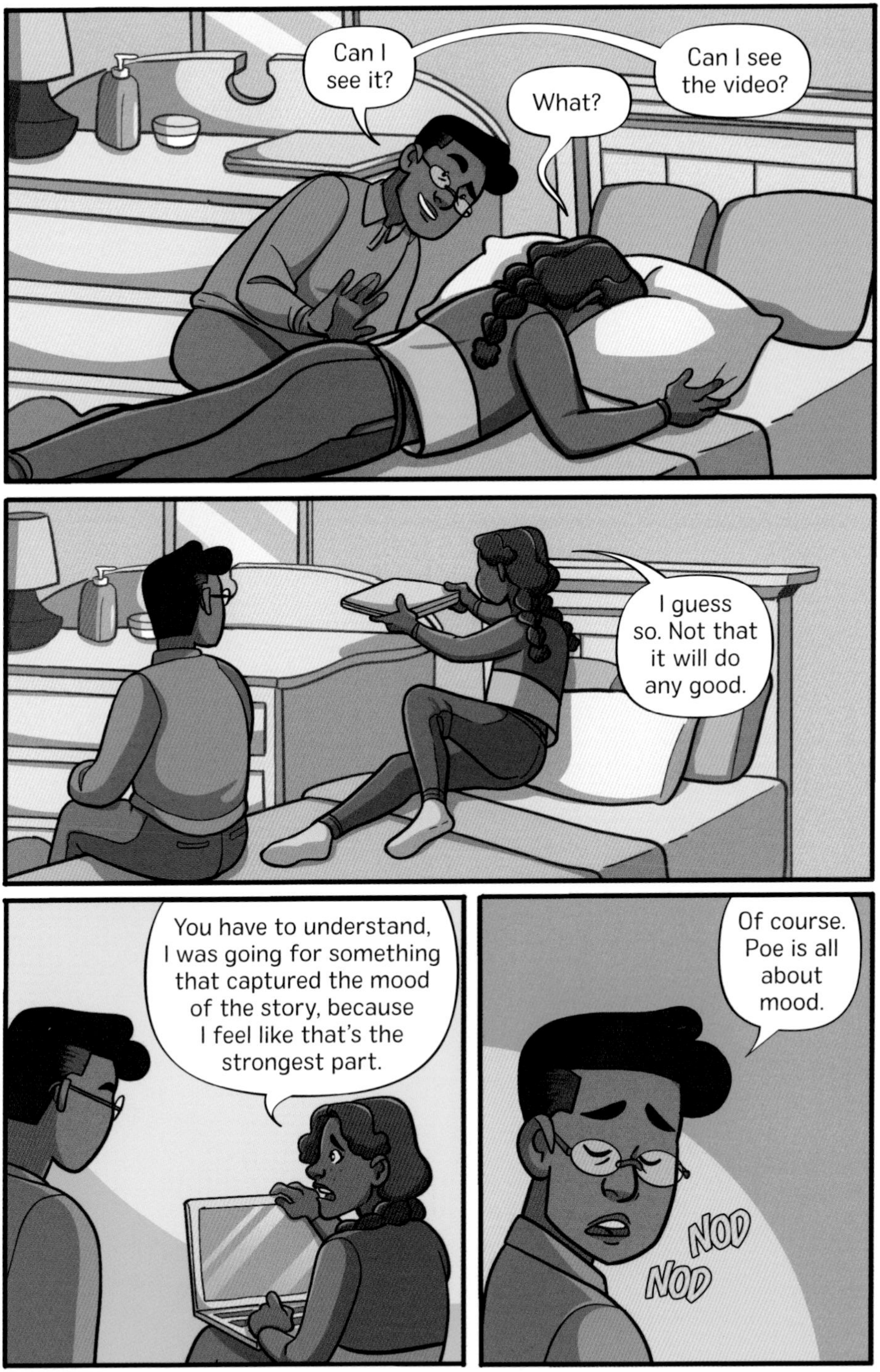
Can I see it?
What?
Can I see the video?
I guess so. Not that it will do any good.
You have to understand, I was going for something that captured the mood of the story, because I feel like that's the strongest part.
Of course. Poe is all about mood.
NOD NOD

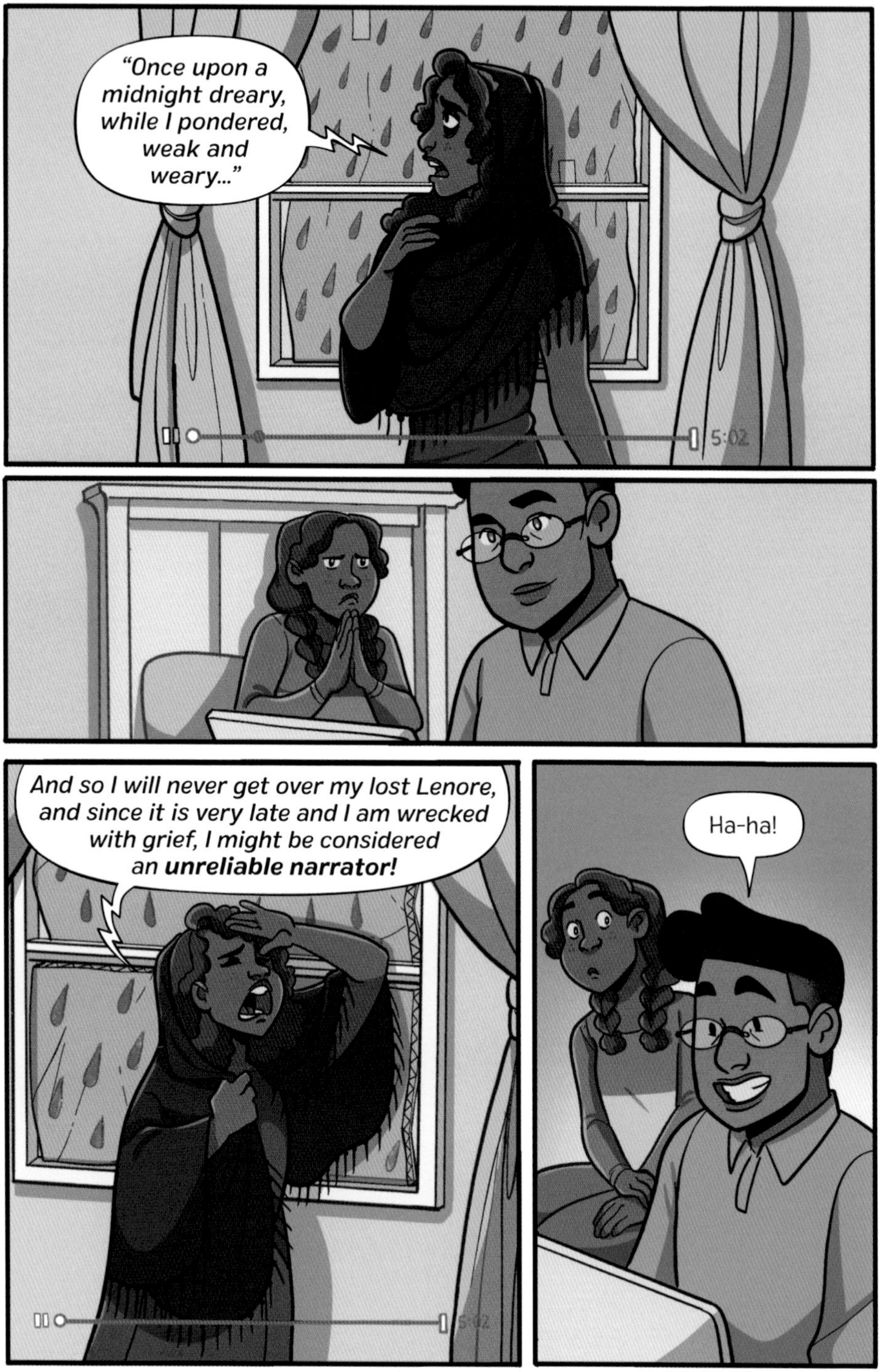
"Once upon a midnight dreary, while I pondered, weak and weary..."
5:02
And so I will never get over my lost Lenore, and since it is very late and I am wrecked with grief, I might be considered an **unreliable narrator!**
5:02
Ha-ha!

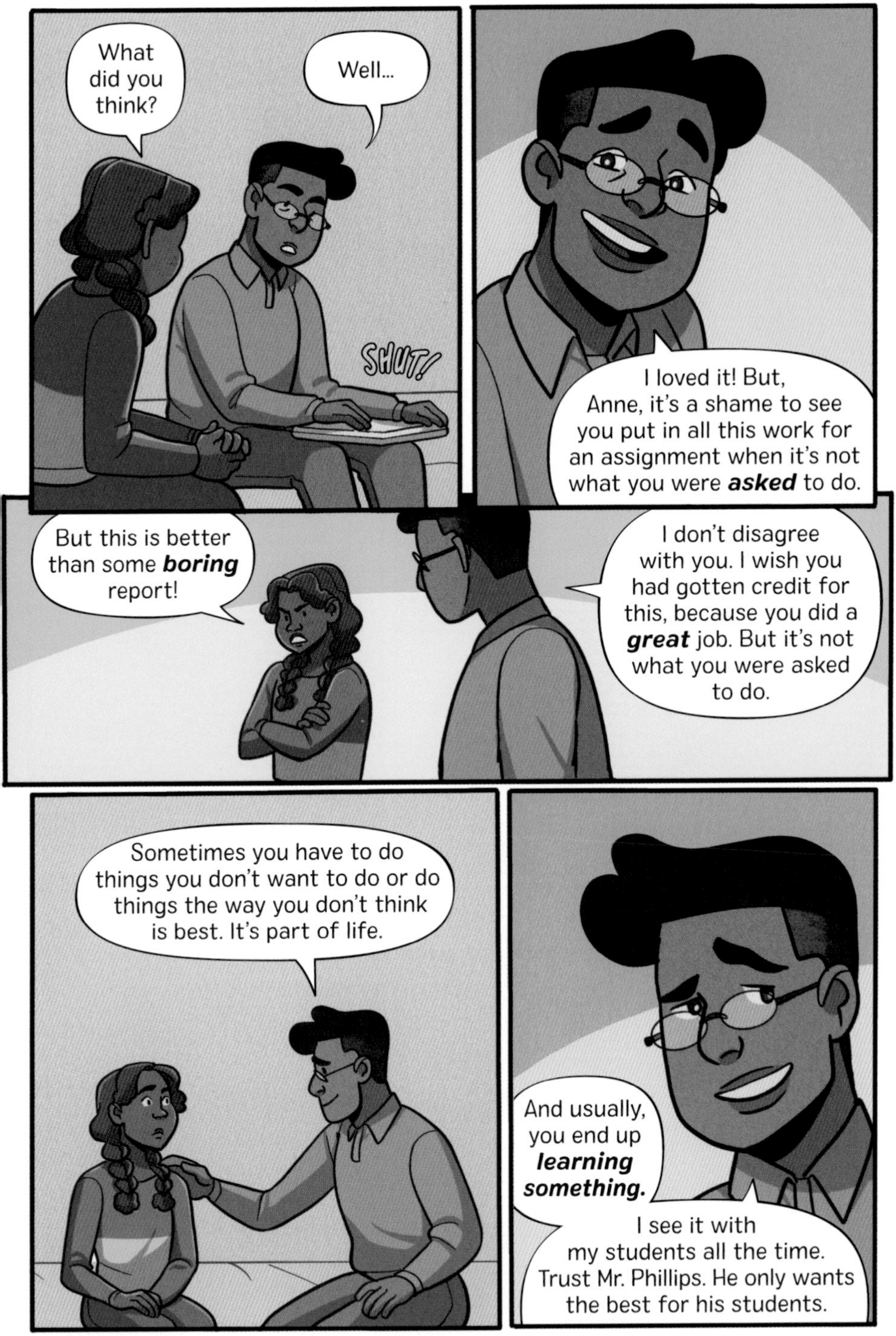
What did you think?
Well...
SHUT!
I loved it! But, Anne, it's a shame to see you put in all this work for an assignment when it's not what you were ***asked*** to do.
But this is better than some ***boring*** report!
I don't disagree with you. I wish you had gotten credit for this, because you did a ***great*** job. But it's not what you were asked to do.
Sometimes you have to do things you don't want to do or do things the way you don't think is best. It's part of life.
And usually, you end up ***learning something.***
I see it with my students all the time. Trust Mr. Phillips. He only wants the best for his students.

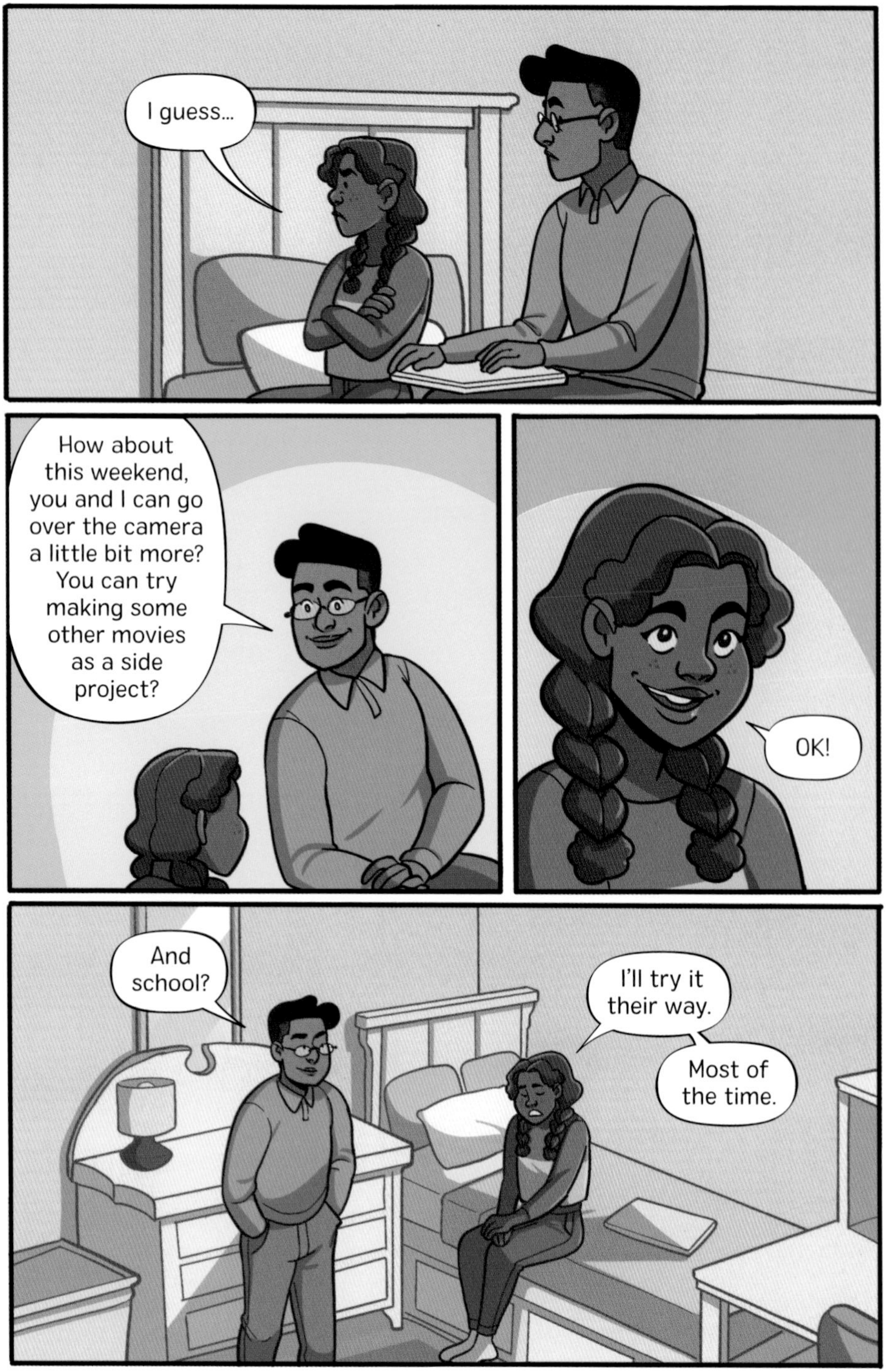
I guess...
How about this weekend, you and I can go over the camera a little bit more? You can try making some other movies as a side project?
OK!
And school?
I'll try it their way.
Most of the time.

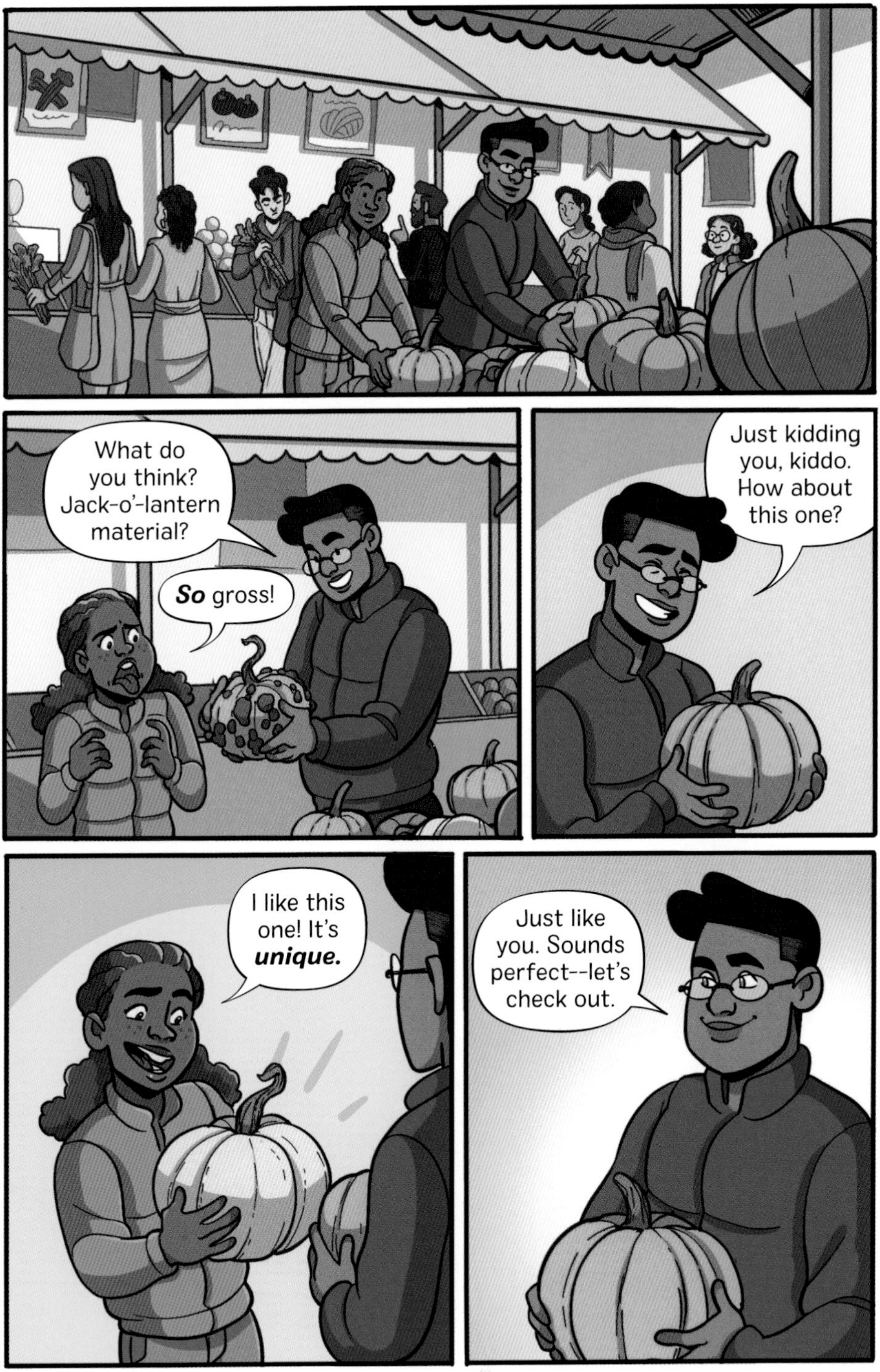
What do you think? Jack-o'-lantern material?
So gross!
Just kidding you, kiddo. How about this one?
I like this one! It's ***unique.***
Just like you. Sounds perfect--let's check out.

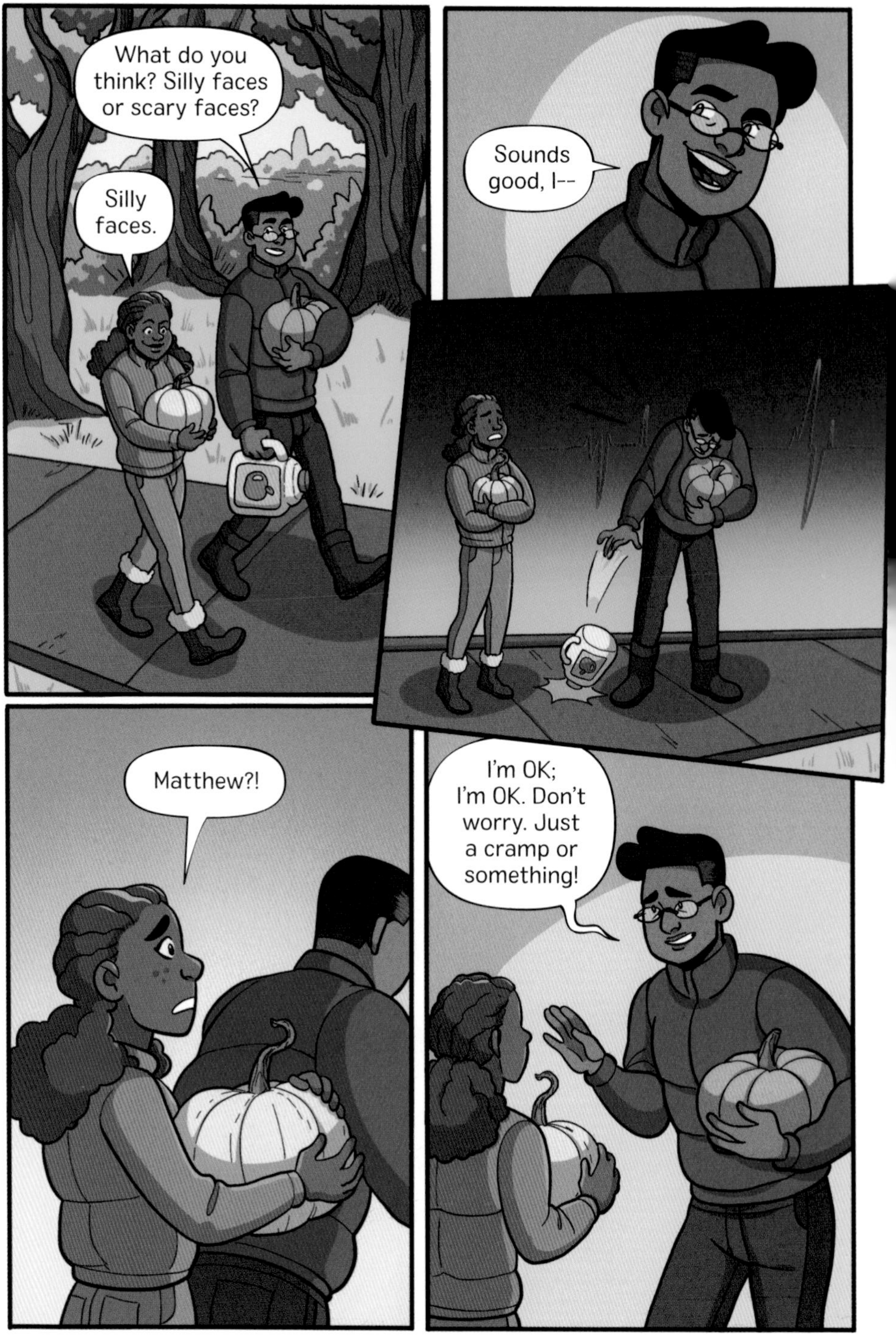

What do you think? Silly faces or scary faces?
Silly faces.
Sounds good, I--
Matthew?!
I'm OK; I'm OK. Don't worry. Just a cramp or something!

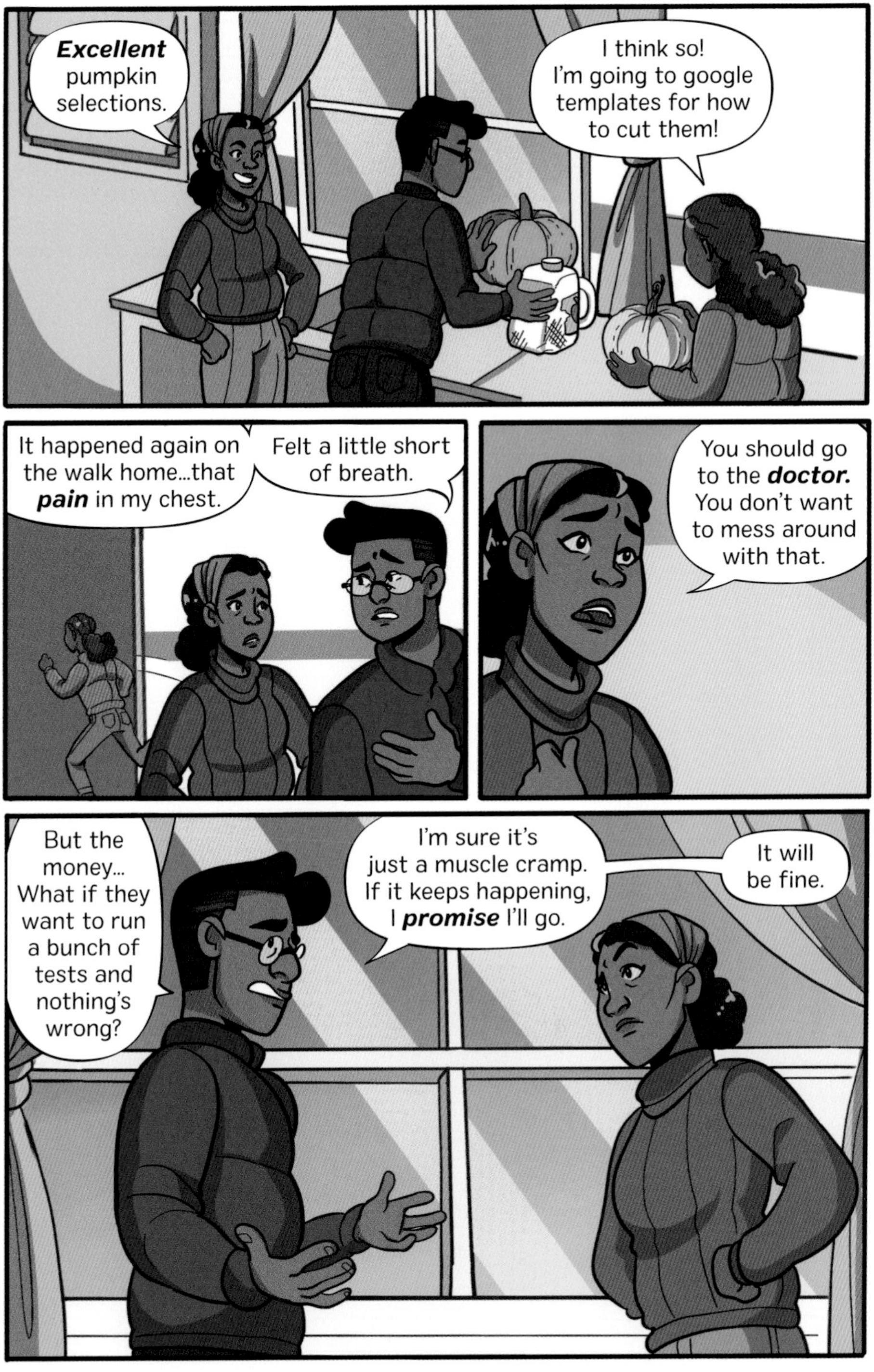
Excellent pumpkin selections.
I think so! I'm going to google templates for how to cut them!
It happened again on the walk home…that ***pain*** in my chest.
Felt a little short of breath.
You should go to the ***doctor.*** You don't want to mess around with that.
But the money… What if they want to run a bunch of tests and nothing's wrong?
I'm sure it's just a muscle cramp. If it keeps happening, I ***promise*** I'll go.
It will be fine.

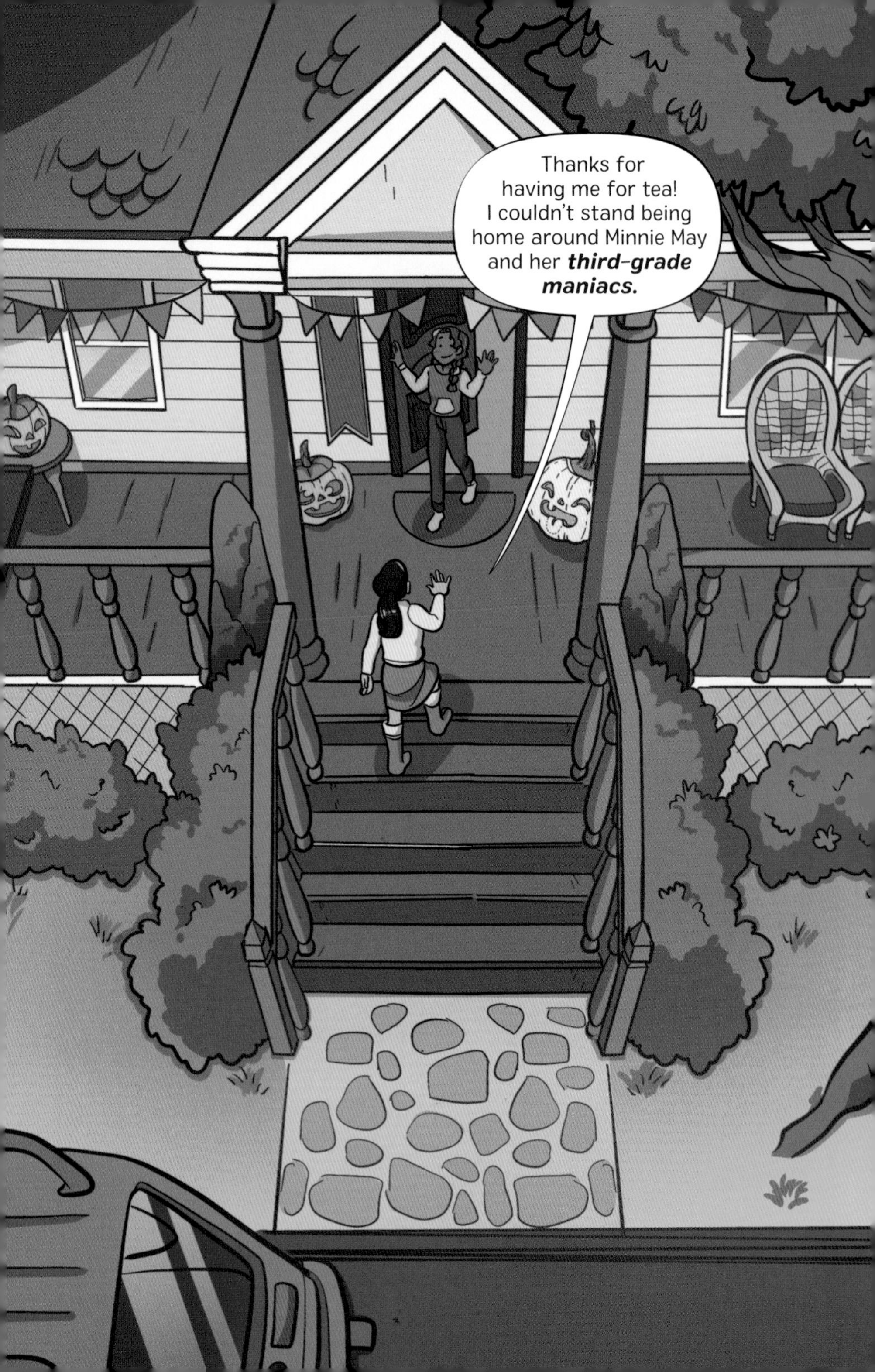
Thanks for having me for tea! I couldn't stand being home around Minnie May and her ***third-grade maniacs.***

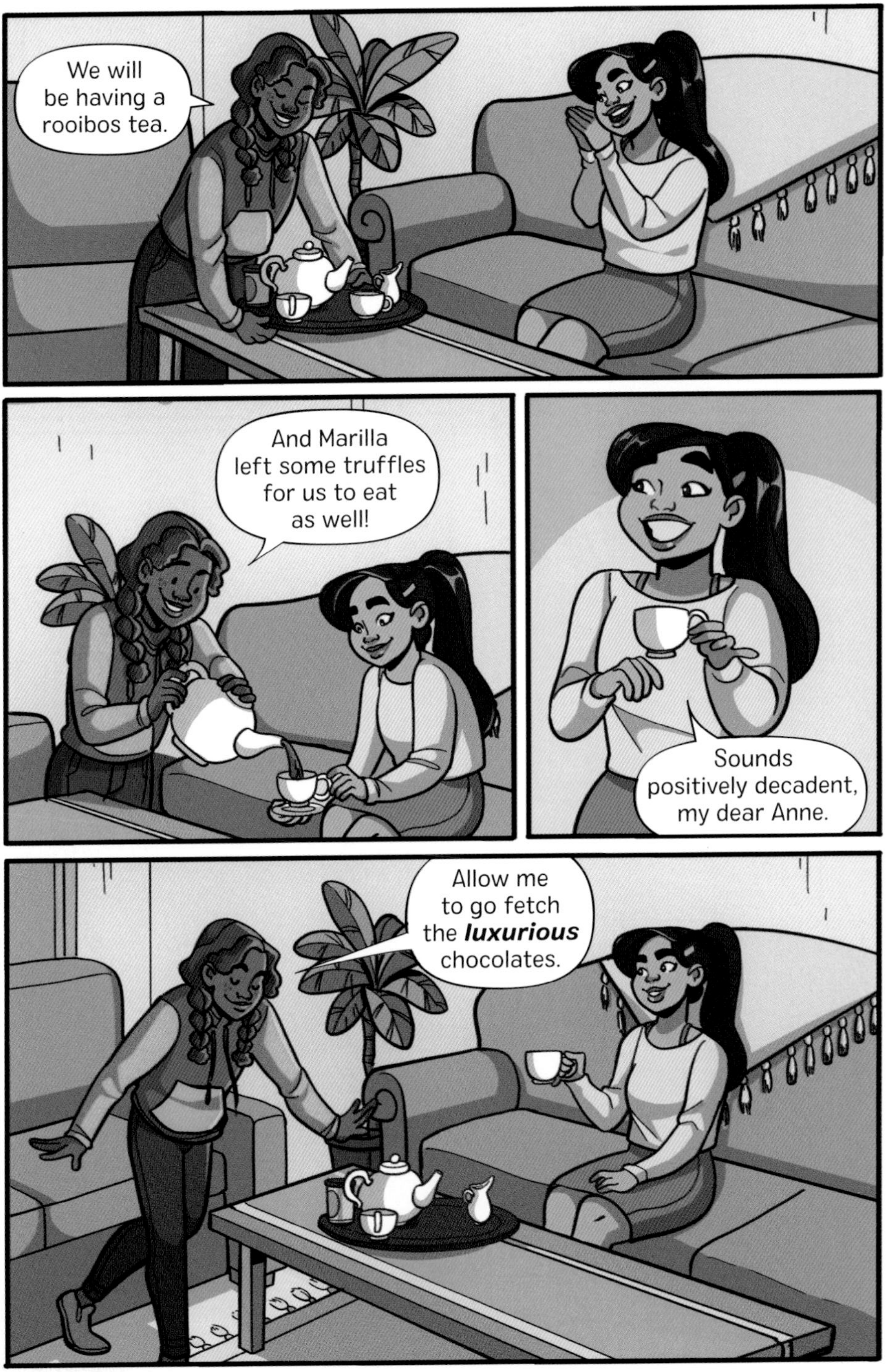
We will be having a rooibos tea.
And Marilla left some truffles for us to eat as well!
Sounds positively decadent, my dear Anne.
Allow me to go fetch the ***luxurious*** chocolates.

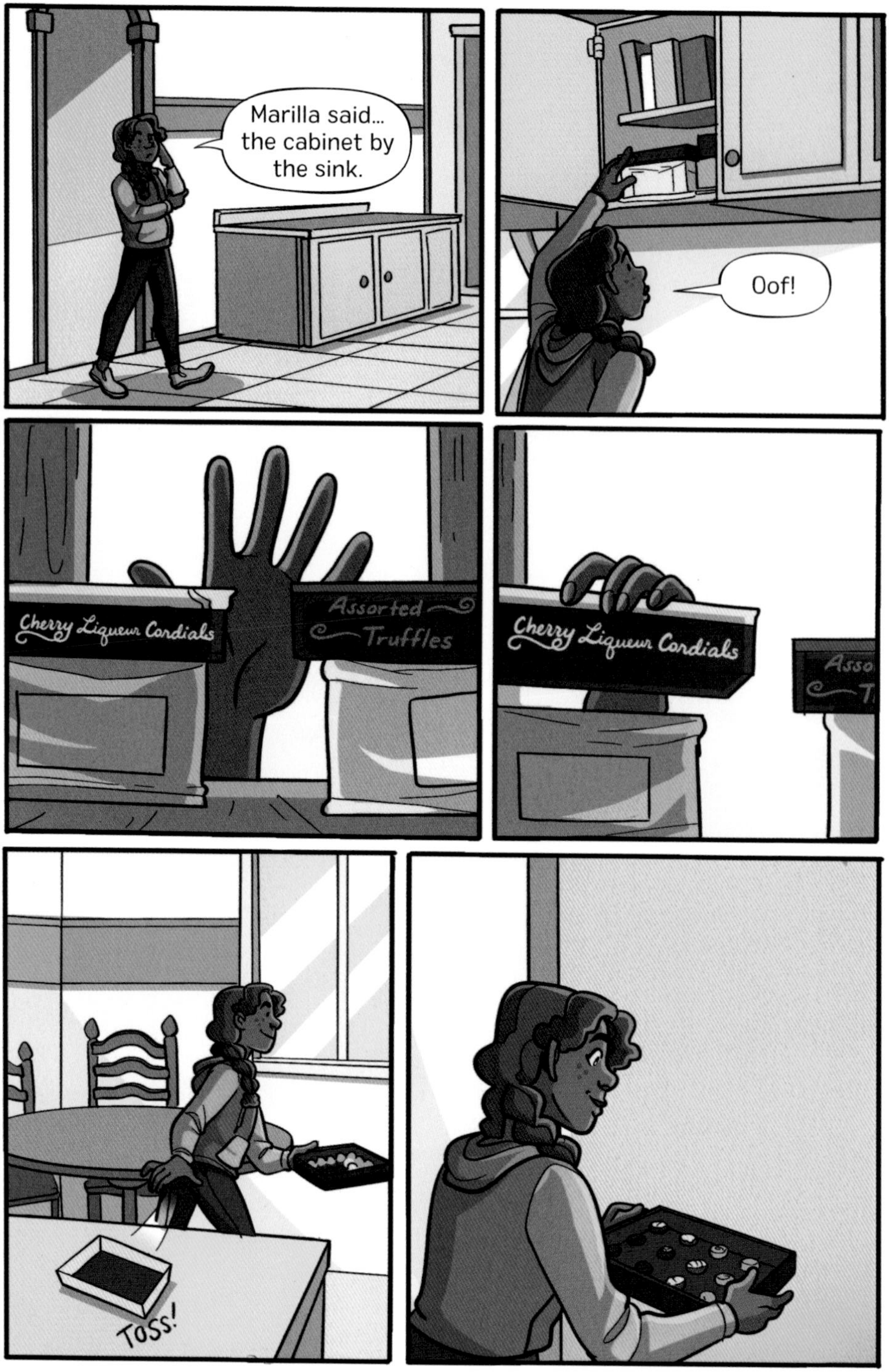
Marilla said... the cabinet by the sink.
Oof!
Cherry Liqueur Cordials
Assorted Truffles
Cherry Liqueur Cordials
TOSS!

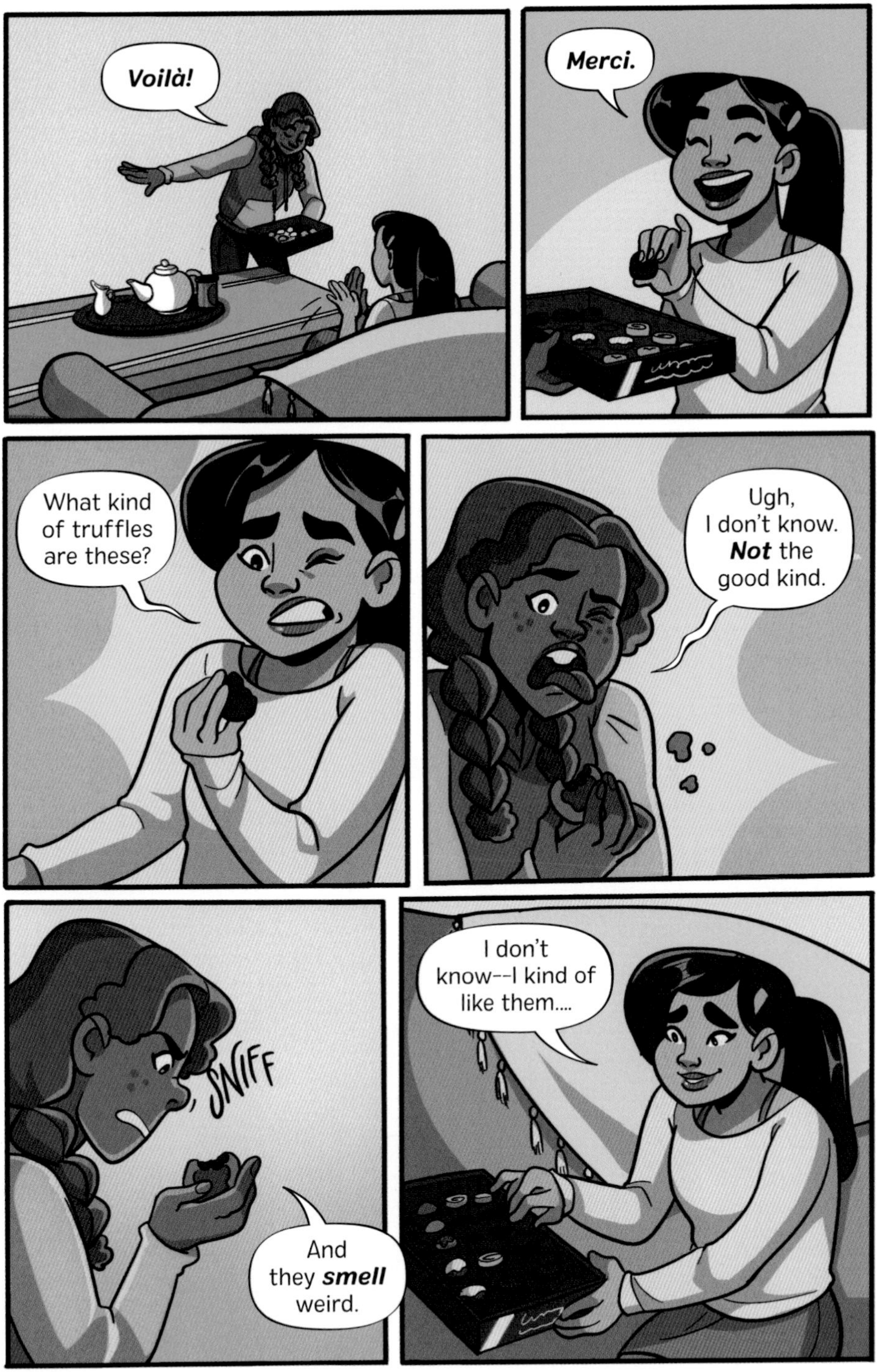
Voilà!
Merci.
What kind of truffles are these?
Ugh, I don't know. ***Not*** the good kind.
SNIFF
And they ***smell*** weird.
I don't know--I kind of like them....

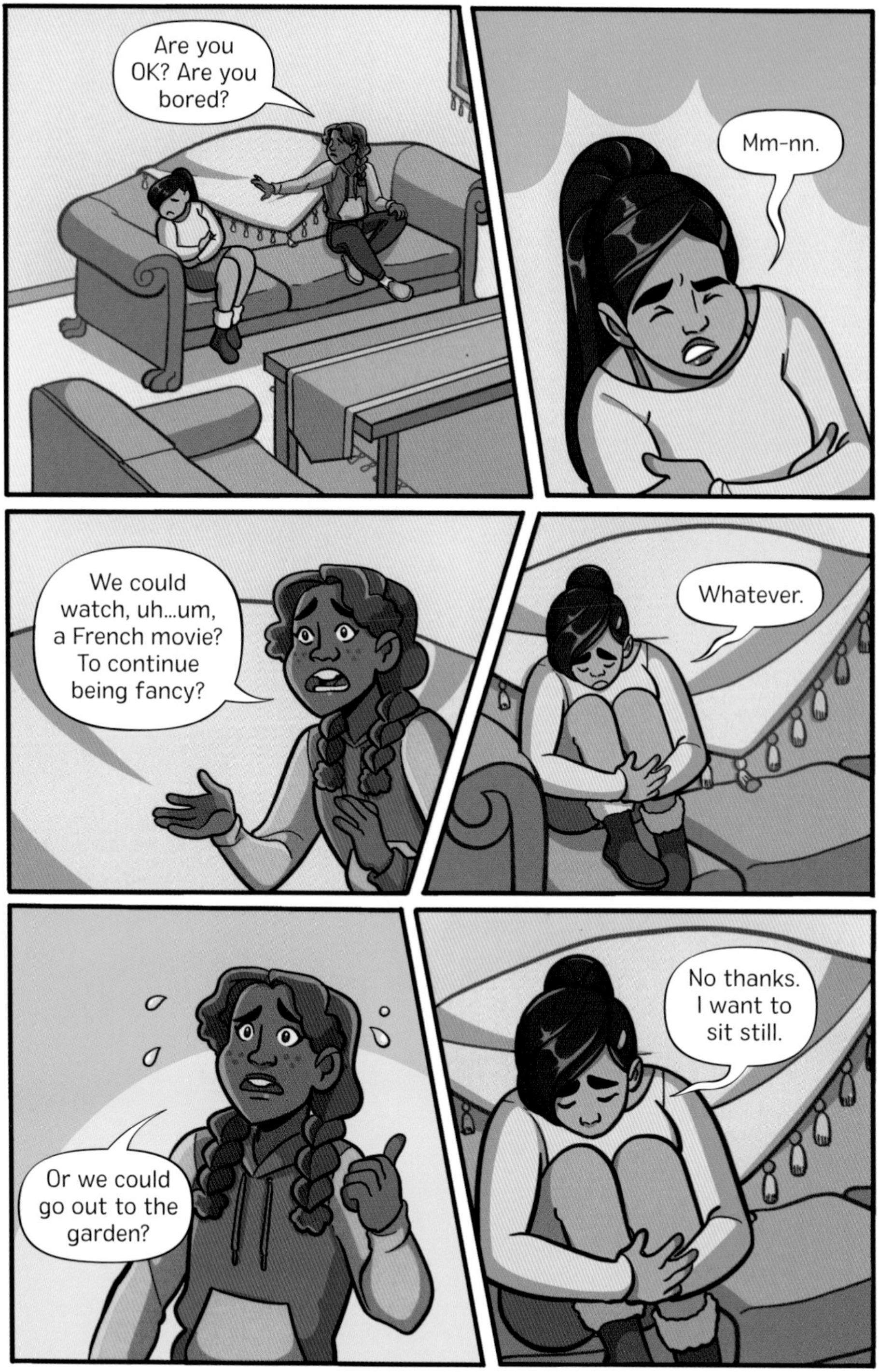
Are you OK? Are you bored?
Mm-nn.
We could watch, uh...um, a French movie? To continue being fancy?
Whatever.
Or we could go out to the garden?
No thanks. I want to sit still.

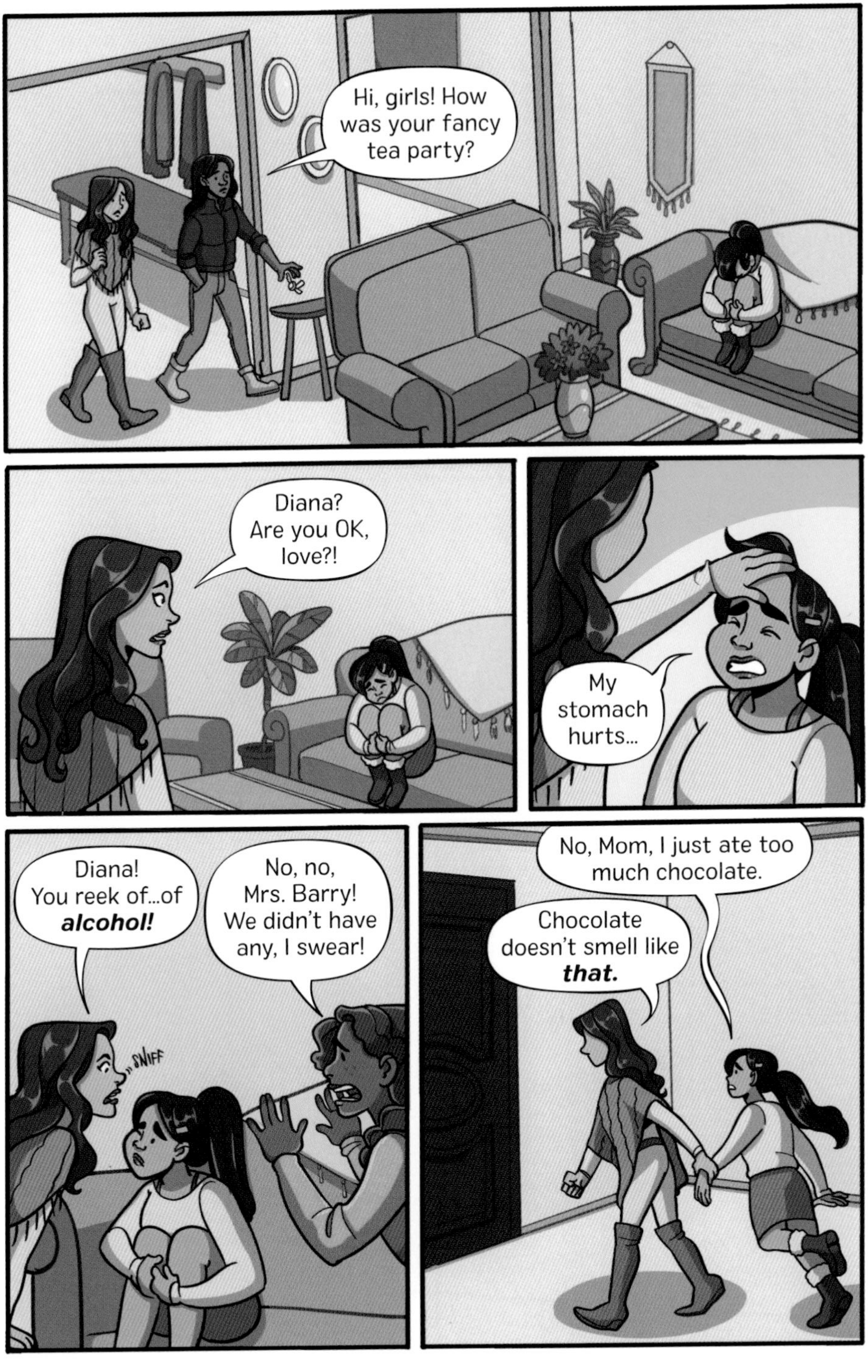
Hi, girls! How was your fancy tea party?
Diana? Are you OK, love?!
My stomach hurts...
Diana! You reek of...of ***alcohol!***
No, no, Mrs. Barry! We didn't have any, I swear!
SNIFF
No, Mom, I just ate too much chocolate.
Chocolate doesn't smell like ***that.***

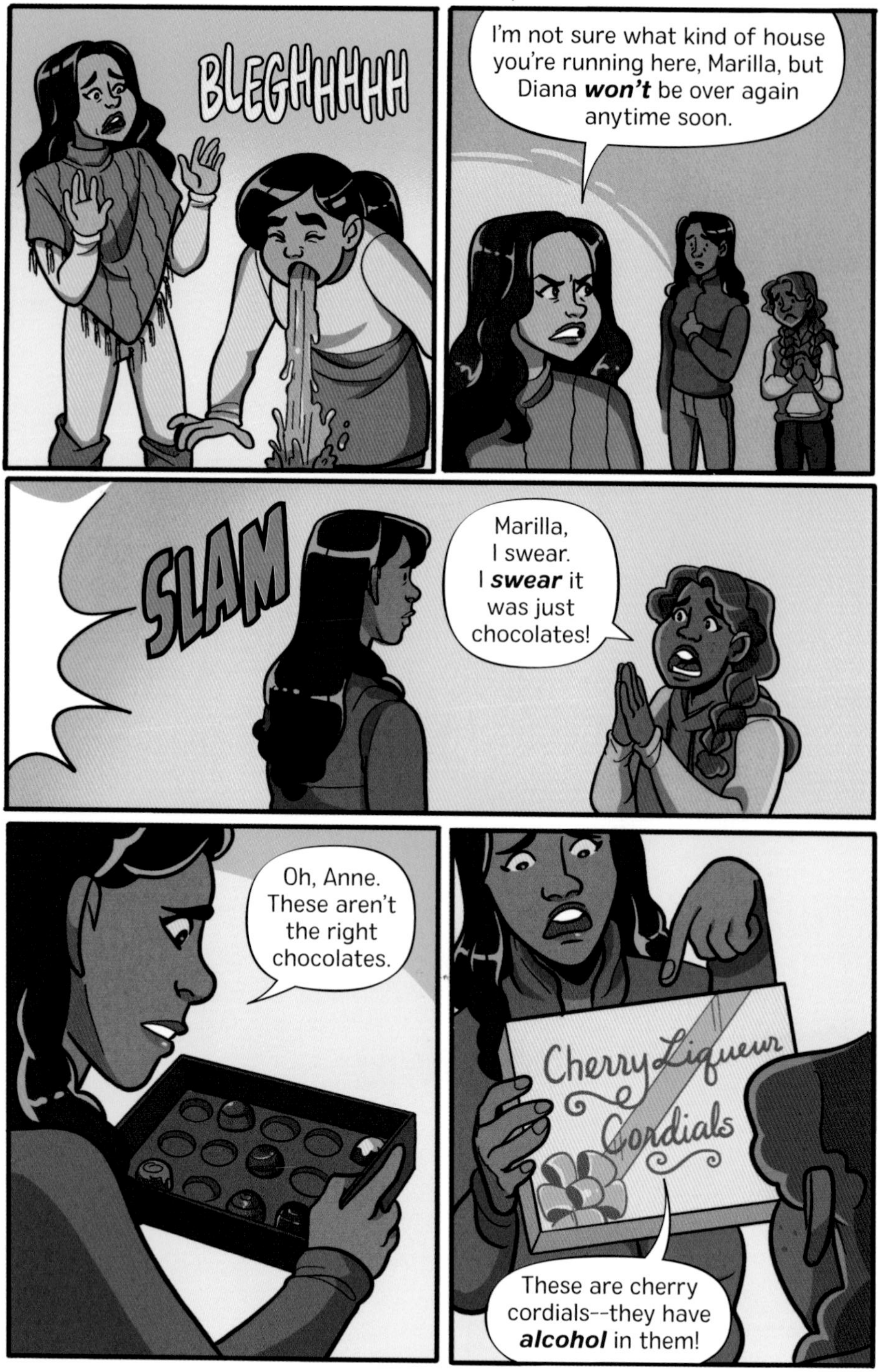

BLEGHHHHH
I'm not sure what kind of house you're running here, Marilla, but Diana ***won't*** be over again anytime soon.
SLAM
Marilla, I swear. I ***swear*** it was just chocolates!
Oh, Anne. These aren't the right chocolates.
Cherry Liqueur Cordials
These are cherry cordials--they have ***alcohol*** in them!

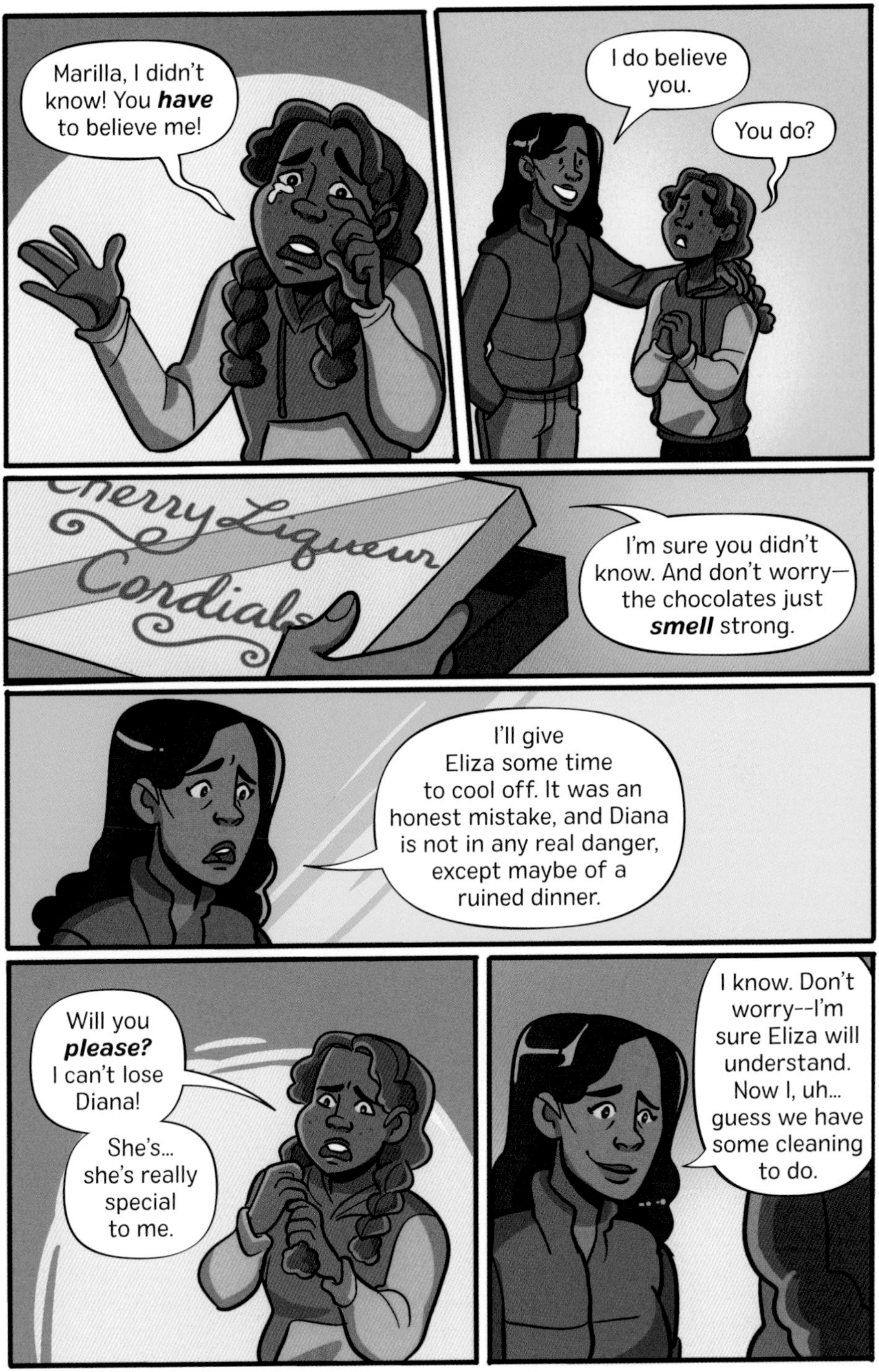
Marilla, I didn't know! You **have** to believe me!
I do believe you.
You do?
Cherry Liqueur Cordials
I'm sure you didn't know. And don't worry—the chocolates just **smell** strong.
I'll give Eliza some time to cool off. It was an honest mistake, and Diana is not in any real danger, except maybe of a ruined dinner.
Will you **please?** I can't lose Diana!
She's... she's really special to me.
I know. Don't worry--I'm sure Eliza will understand. Now I, uh... guess we have some cleaning to do.

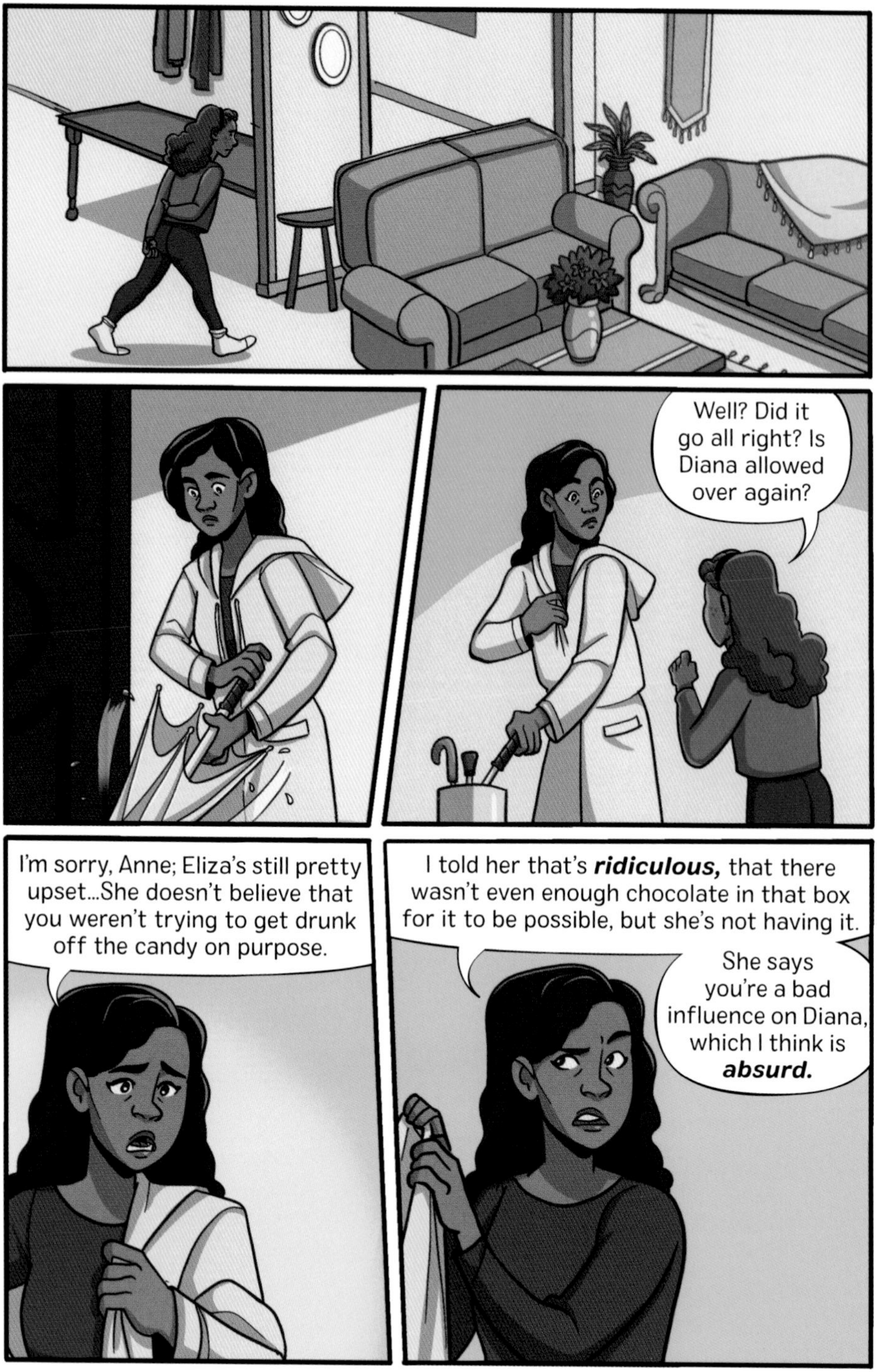
Well? Did it go all right? Is Diana allowed over again?
I'm sorry, Anne; Eliza's still pretty upset...She doesn't believe that you weren't trying to get drunk off the candy on purpose.
I told her that's ***ridiculous,*** that there wasn't even enough chocolate in that box for it to be possible, but she's not having it.
She says you're a bad influence on Diana, which I think is ***absurd.***

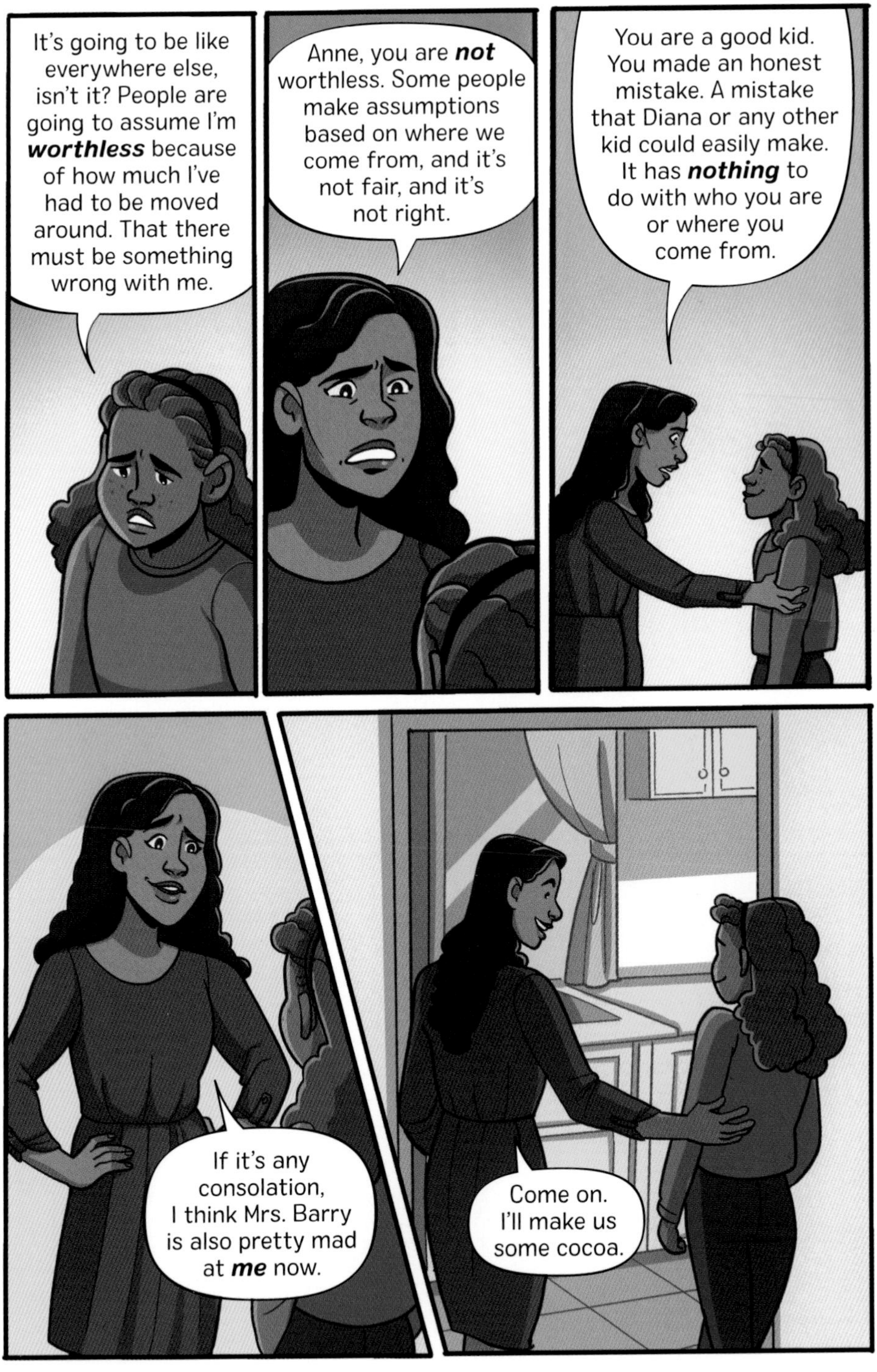
It's going to be like everywhere else, isn't it? People are going to assume I'm ***worthless*** because of how much I've had to be moved around. That there must be something wrong with me.
Anne, you are ***not*** worthless. Some people make assumptions based on where we come from, and it's not fair, and it's not right.
You are a good kid. You made an honest mistake. A mistake that Diana or any other kid could easily make. It has ***nothing*** to do with who you are or where you come from.
If it's any consolation, I think Mrs. Barry is also pretty mad at ***me*** now.
Come on. I'll make us some cocoa.

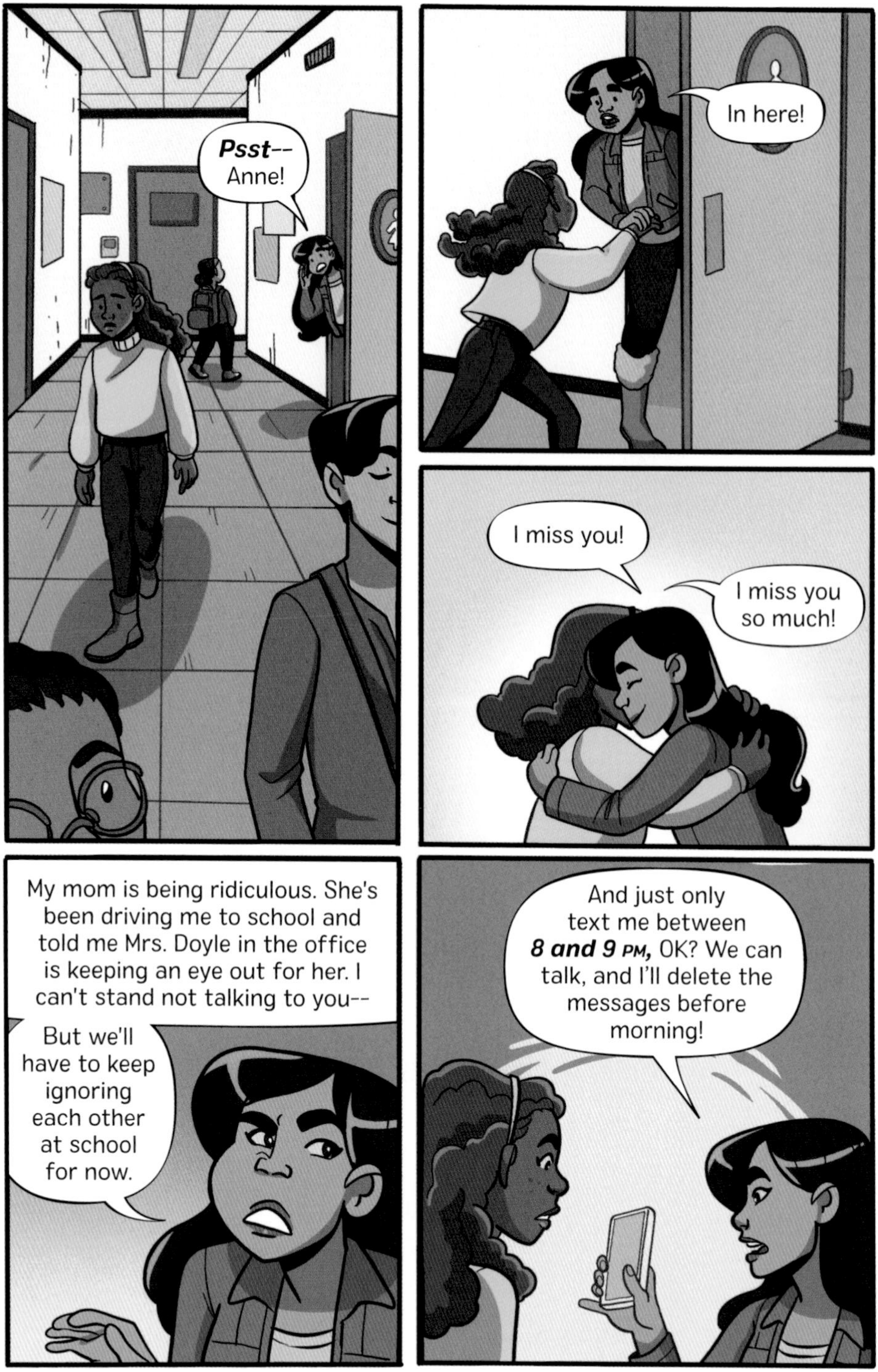
Psst--
Anne!
In here!
I miss you!
I miss you so much!
My mom is being ridiculous. She's been driving me to school and told me Mrs. Doyle in the office is keeping an eye out for her. I can't stand not talking to you--
But we'll have to keep ignoring each other at school for now.
And just only text me between ***8 and 9 PM,*** OK? We can talk, and I'll delete the messages before morning!

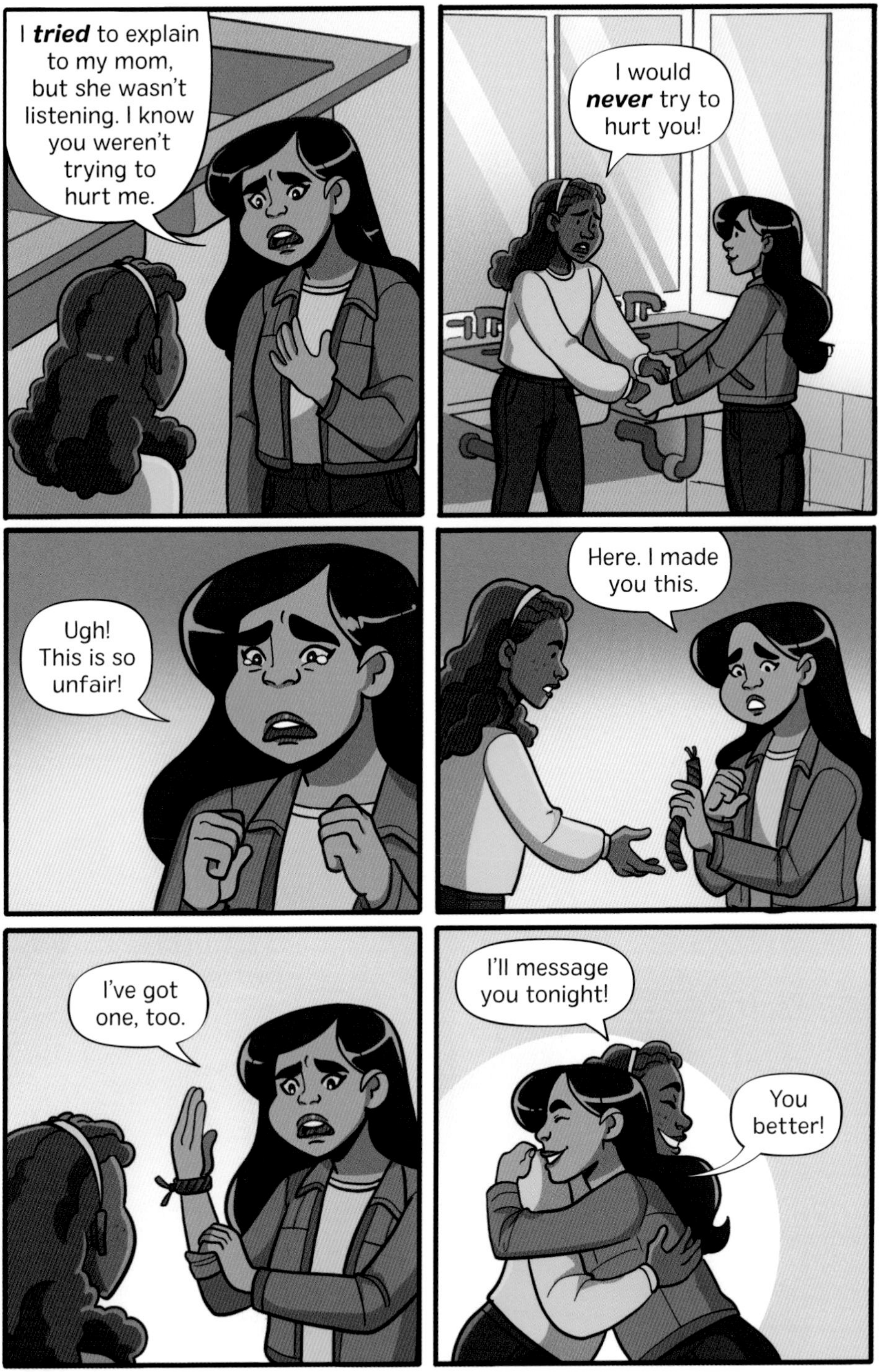
I *tried* to explain to my mom, but she wasn't listening. I know you weren't trying to hurt me.
I would *never* try to hurt you!
Ugh! This is so unfair!
Here. I made you this.
I've got one, too.
I'll message you tonight!
You better!

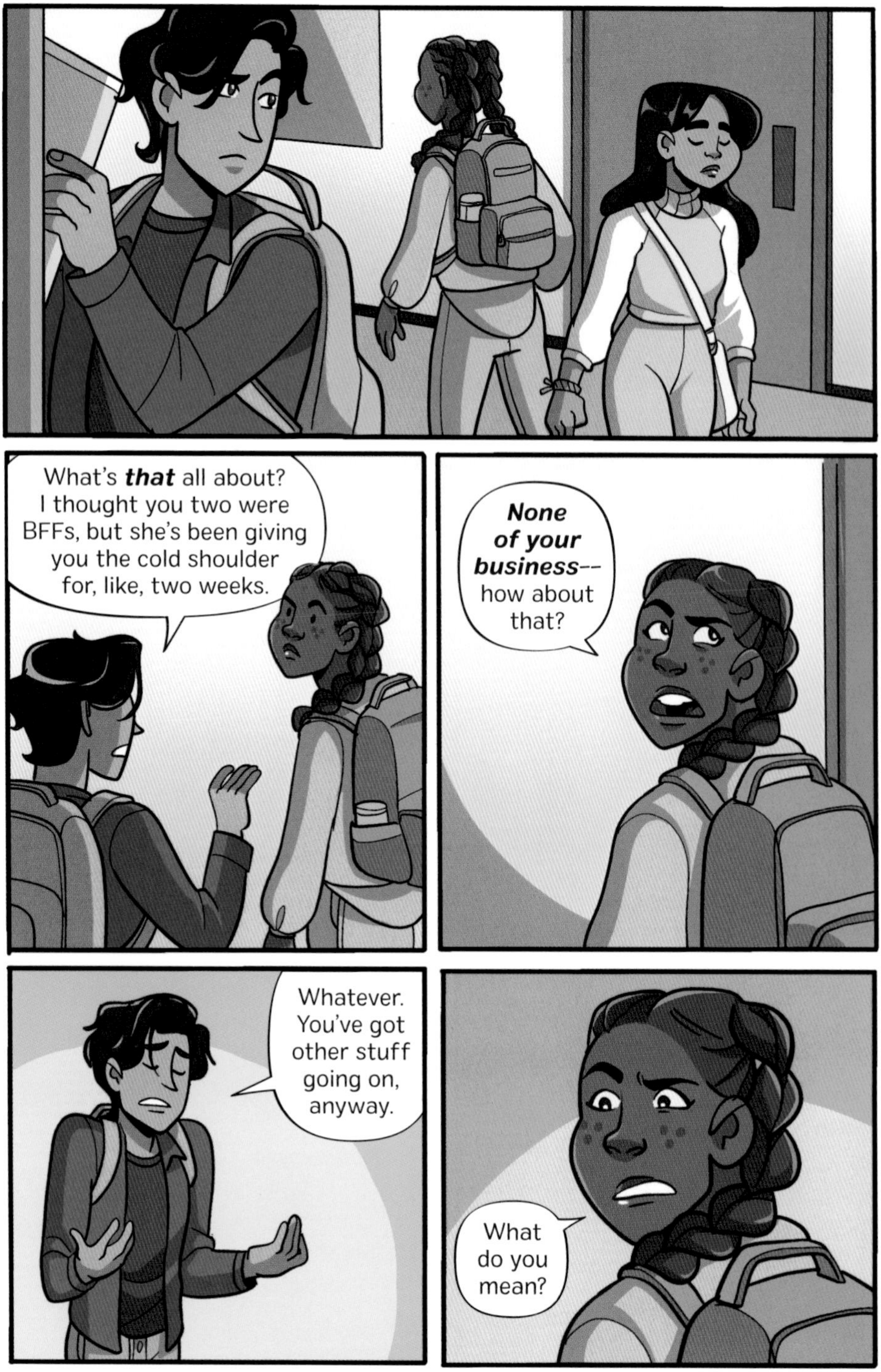
What's ***that*** all about? I thought you two were BFFs, but she's been giving you the cold shoulder for, like, two weeks.
None of your business--how about that?
Whatever. You've got other stuff going on, anyway.
What do you mean?

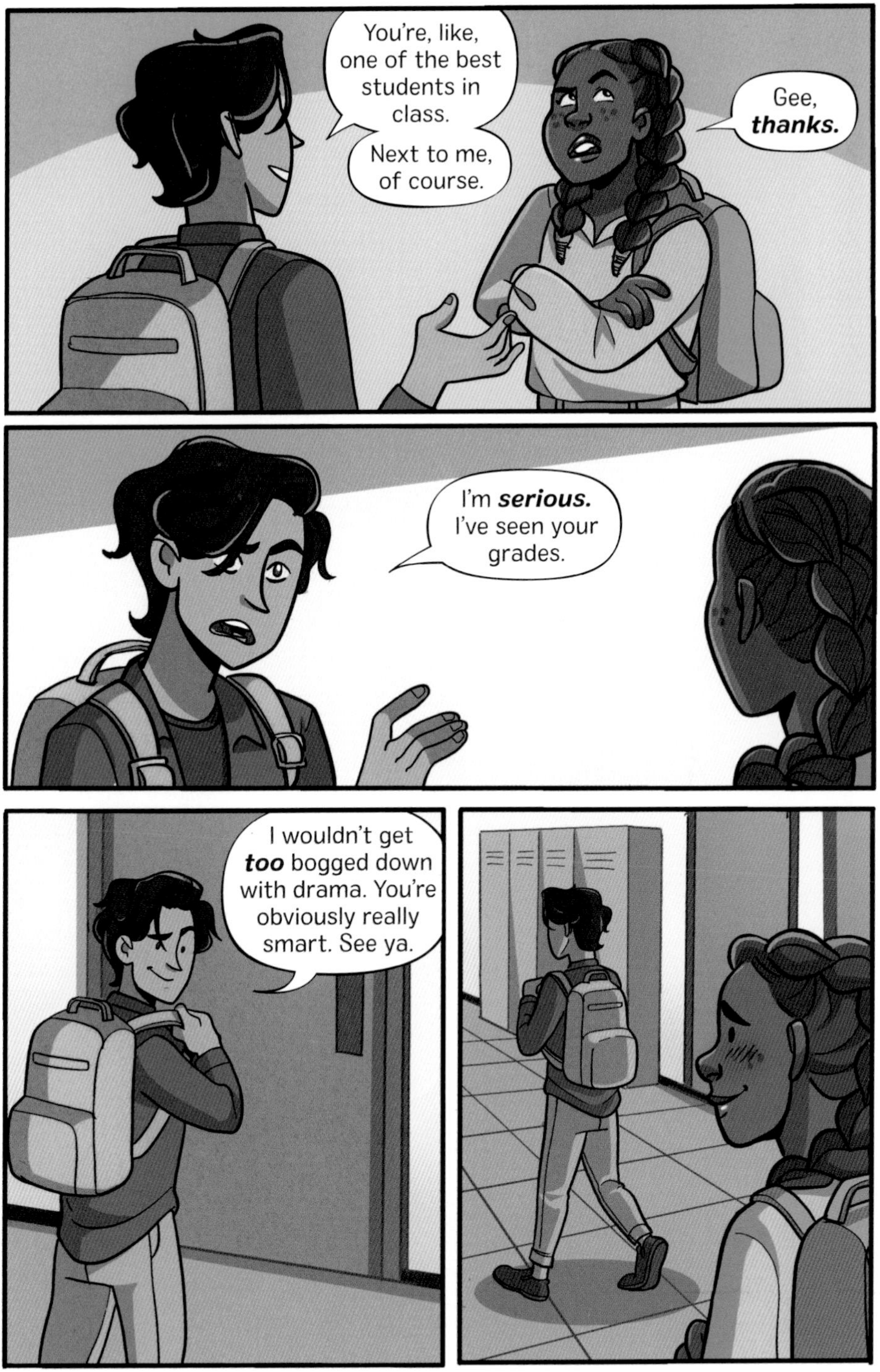
You're, like, one of the best students in class.
Next to me, of course.
Gee, **thanks.**
I'm **serious.** I've seen your grades.
I wouldn't get **too** bogged down with drama. You're obviously really smart. See ya.

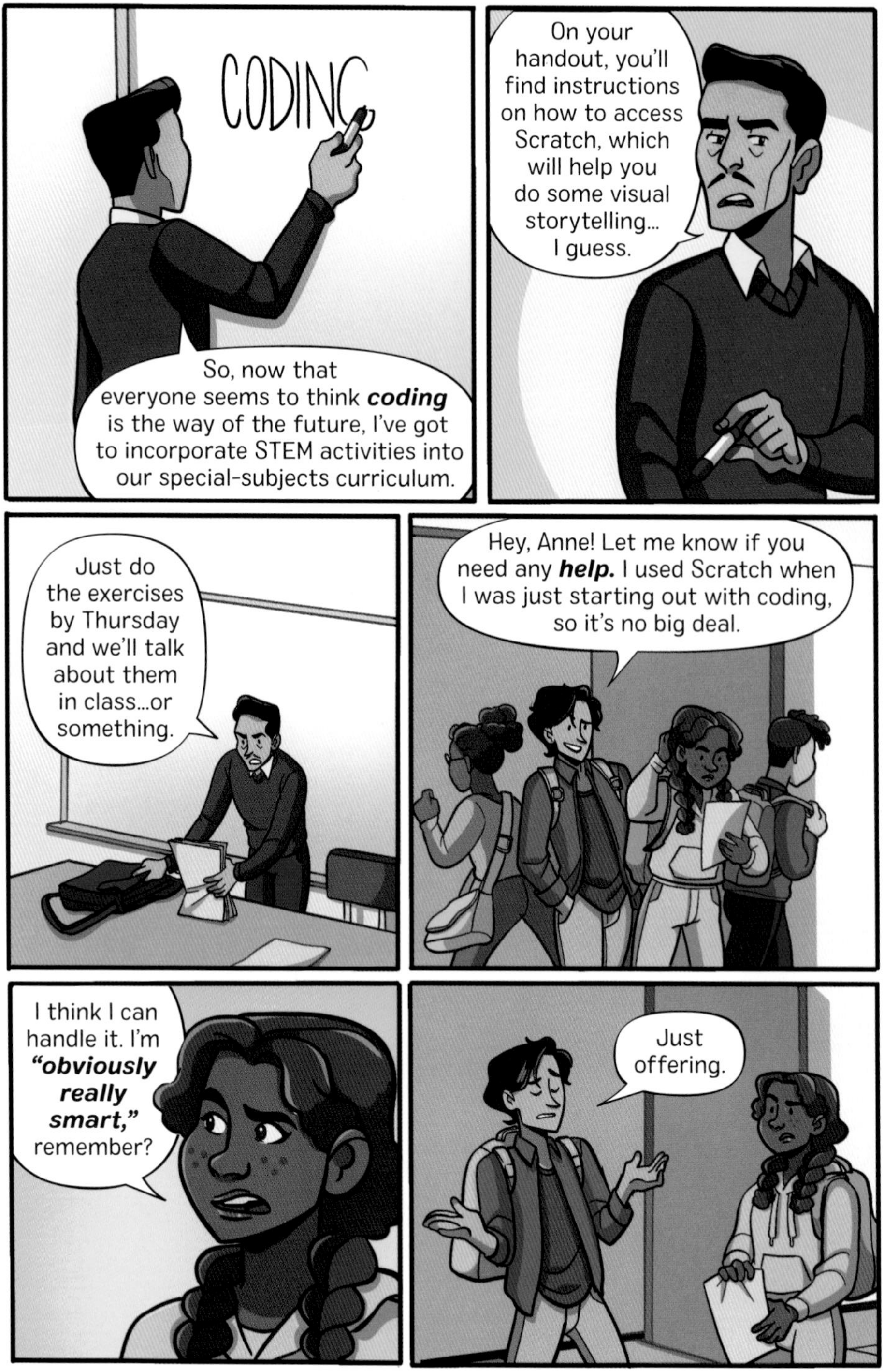
CODING
So, now that everyone seems to think ***coding*** is the way of the future, I've got to incorporate STEM activities into our special-subjects curriculum.
On your handout, you'll find instructions on how to access Scratch, which will help you do some visual storytelling... I guess.
Just do the exercises by Thursday and we'll talk about them in class...or something.
Hey, Anne! Let me know if you need any ***help.*** I used Scratch when I was just starting out with coding, so it's no big deal.
I think I can handle it. I'm ***"obviously really smart,"*** remember?
Just offering.

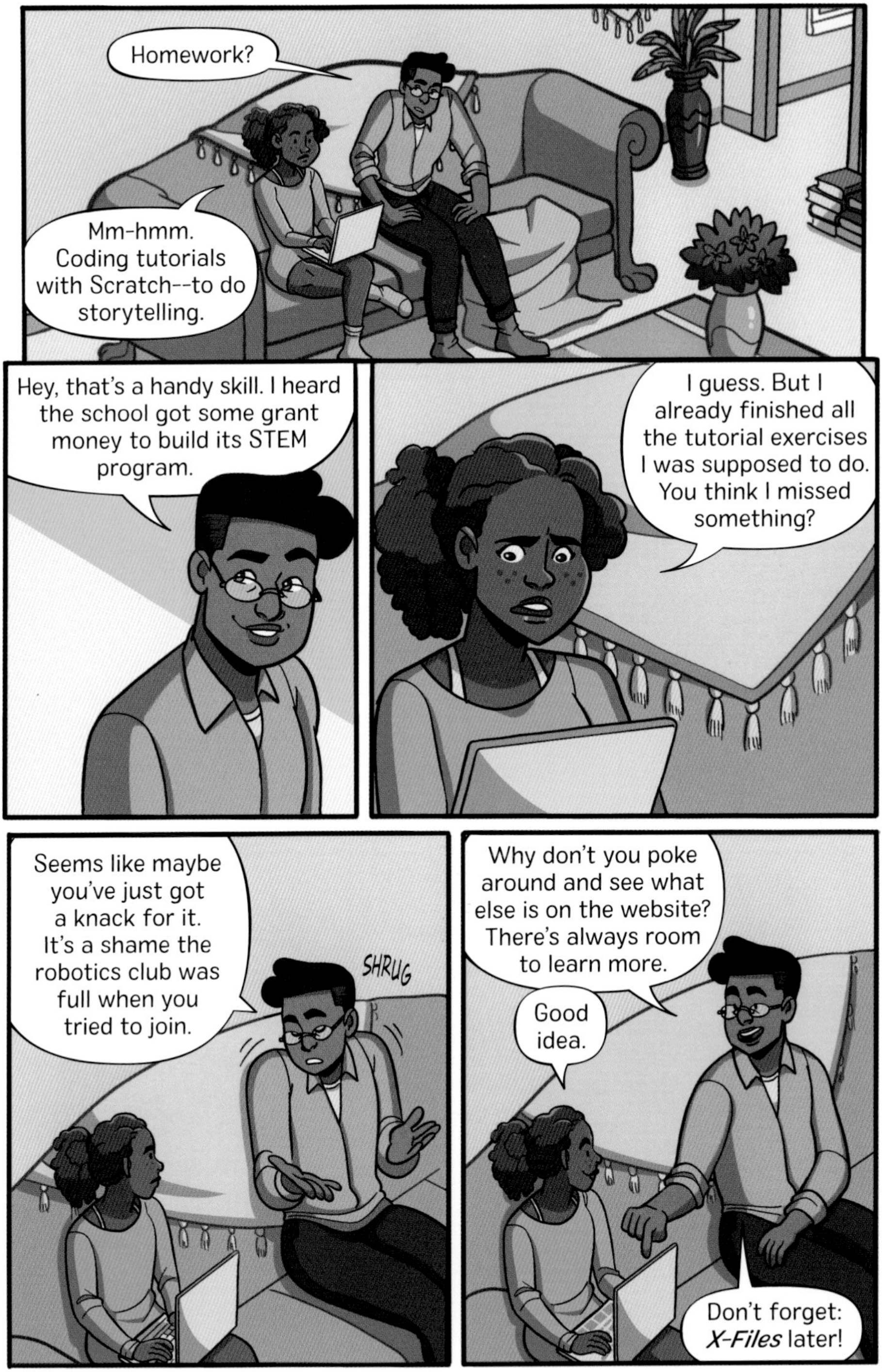
Homework?
Mm-hmm. Coding tutorials with Scratch--to do storytelling.
Hey, that's a handy skill. I heard the school got some grant money to build its STEM program.
I guess. But I already finished all the tutorial exercises I was supposed to do. You think I missed something?
Seems like maybe you've just got a knack for it. It's a shame the robotics club was full when you tried to join.
SHRUG
Why don't you poke around and see what else is on the website? There's always room to learn more.
Good idea.
Don't forget: *X-Files* later!

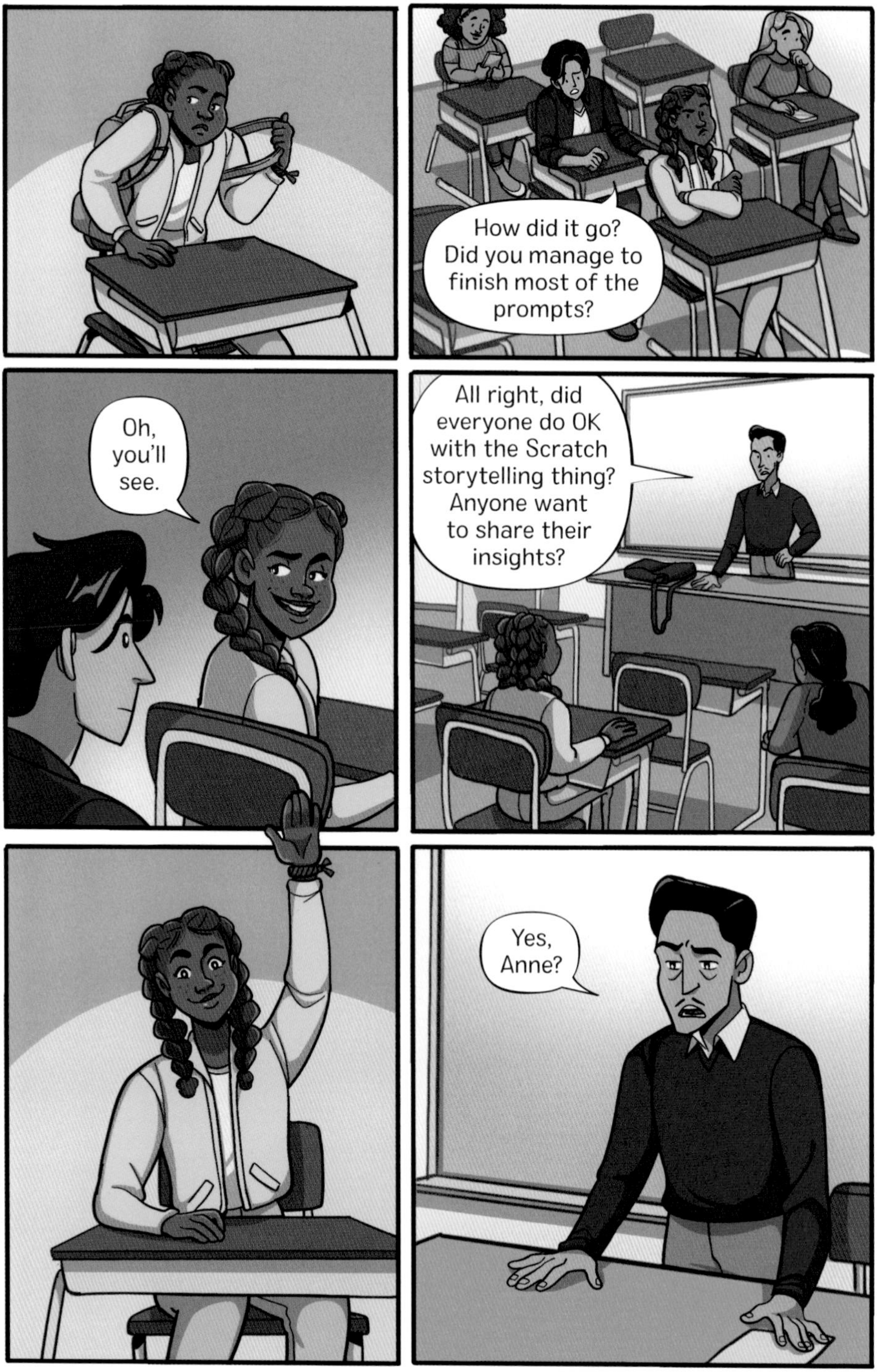
How did it go? Did you manage to finish most of the prompts?
Oh, you'll see.
All right, did everyone do OK with the Scratch storytelling thing? Anyone want to share their insights?
Yes, Anne?

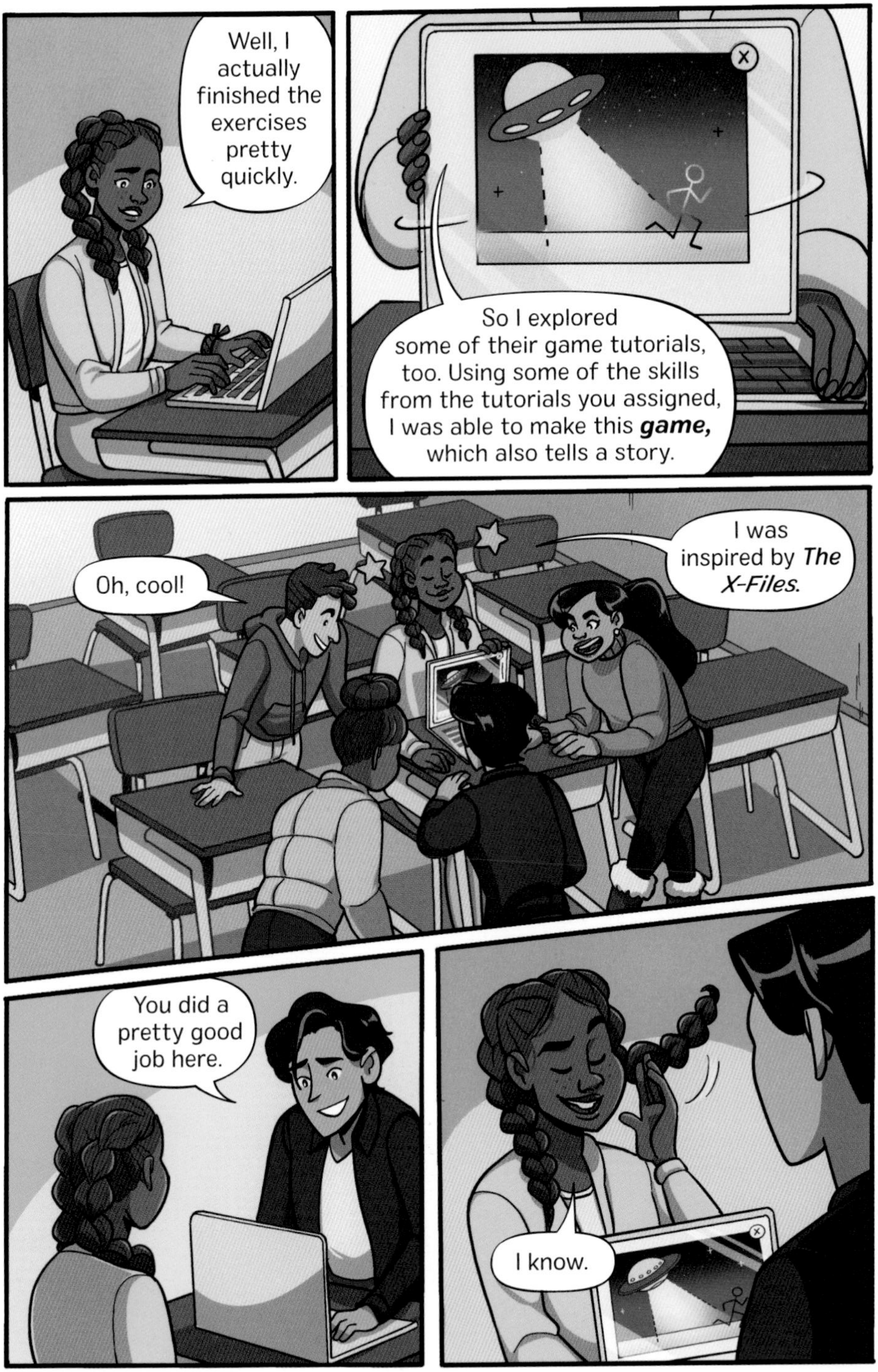
Well, I actually finished the exercises pretty quickly.
So I explored some of their game tutorials, too. Using some of the skills from the tutorials you assigned, I was able to make this ***game,*** which also tells a story.
Oh, cool!
I was inspired by ***The X-Files.***
You did a pretty good job here.
I know.

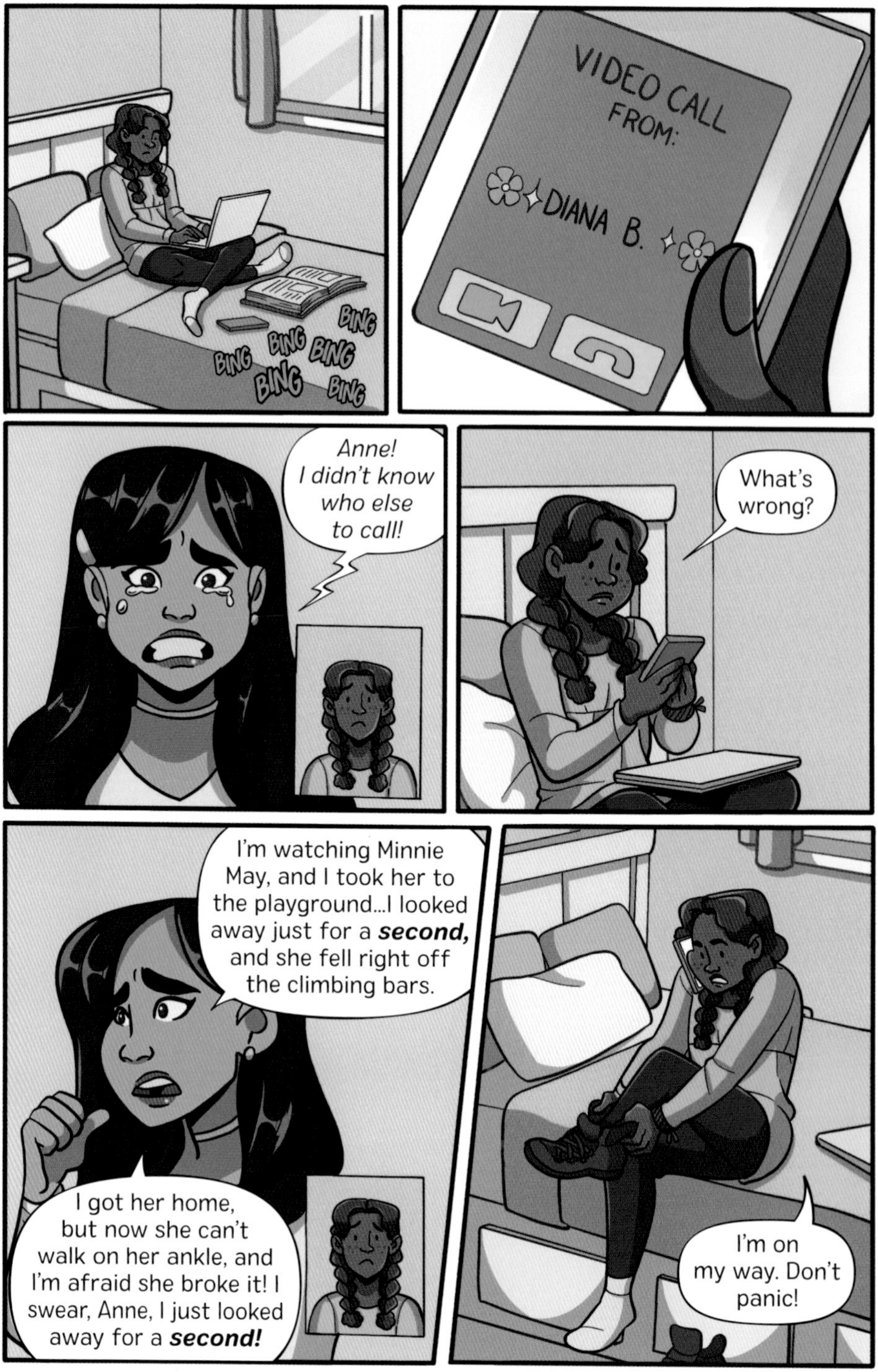
BING
BING BING
BING BING
BING
VIDEO CALL
FROM:
DIANA B.
Anne!
I didn't know
who else
to call!
What's wrong?
I'm watching Minnie May, and I took her to the playground...I looked away just for a ***second,*** and she fell right off the climbing bars.
I got her home, but now she can't walk on her ankle, and I'm afraid she broke it! I swear, Anne, I just looked away for a ***second!***
I'm on my way. Don't panic!

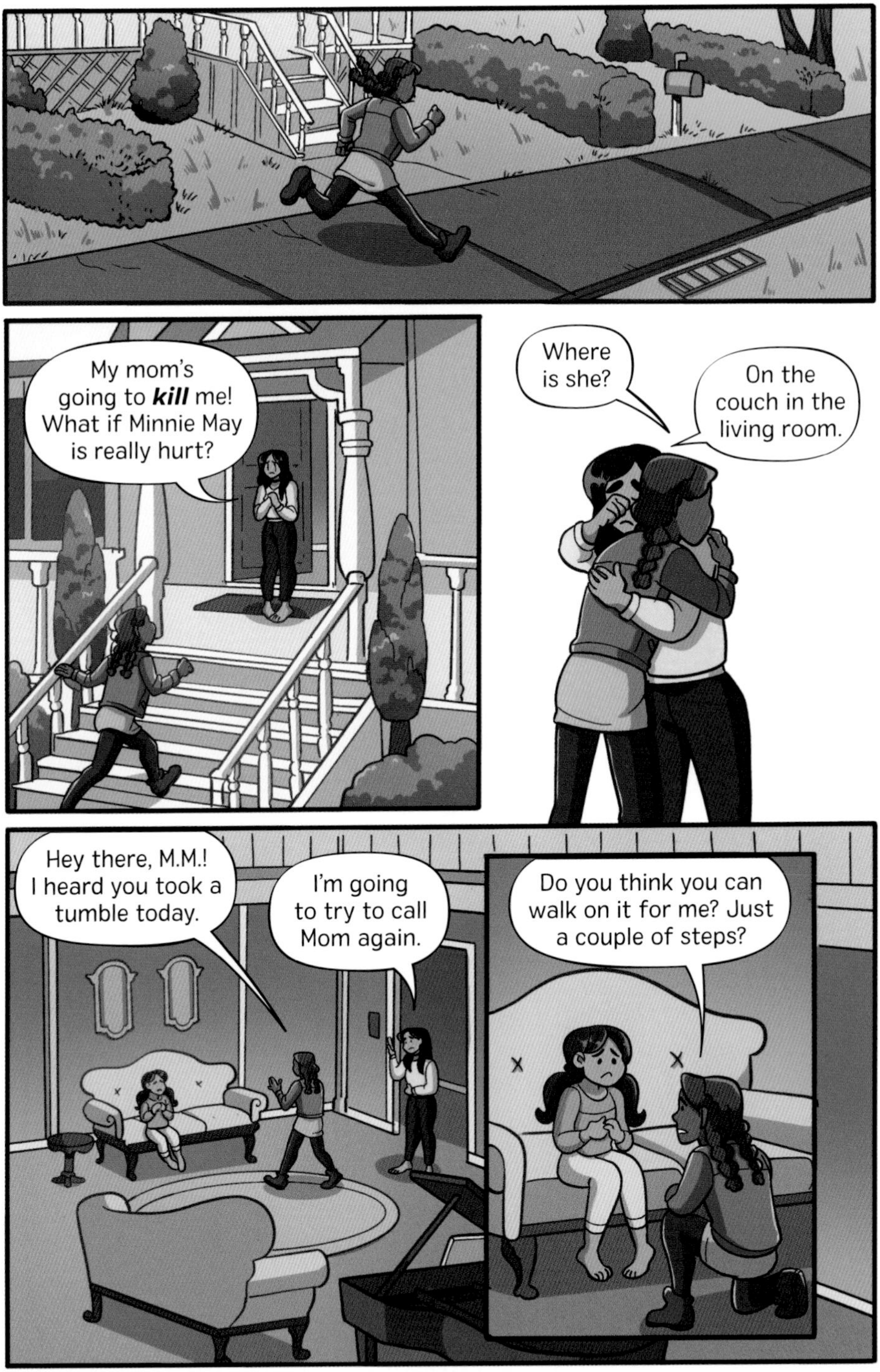
My mom's going to ***kill*** me! What if Minnie May is really hurt?
Where is she?
On the couch in the living room.
Hey there, M.M.! I heard you took a tumble today.
I'm going to try to call Mom again.
Do you think you can walk on it for me? Just a couple of steps?

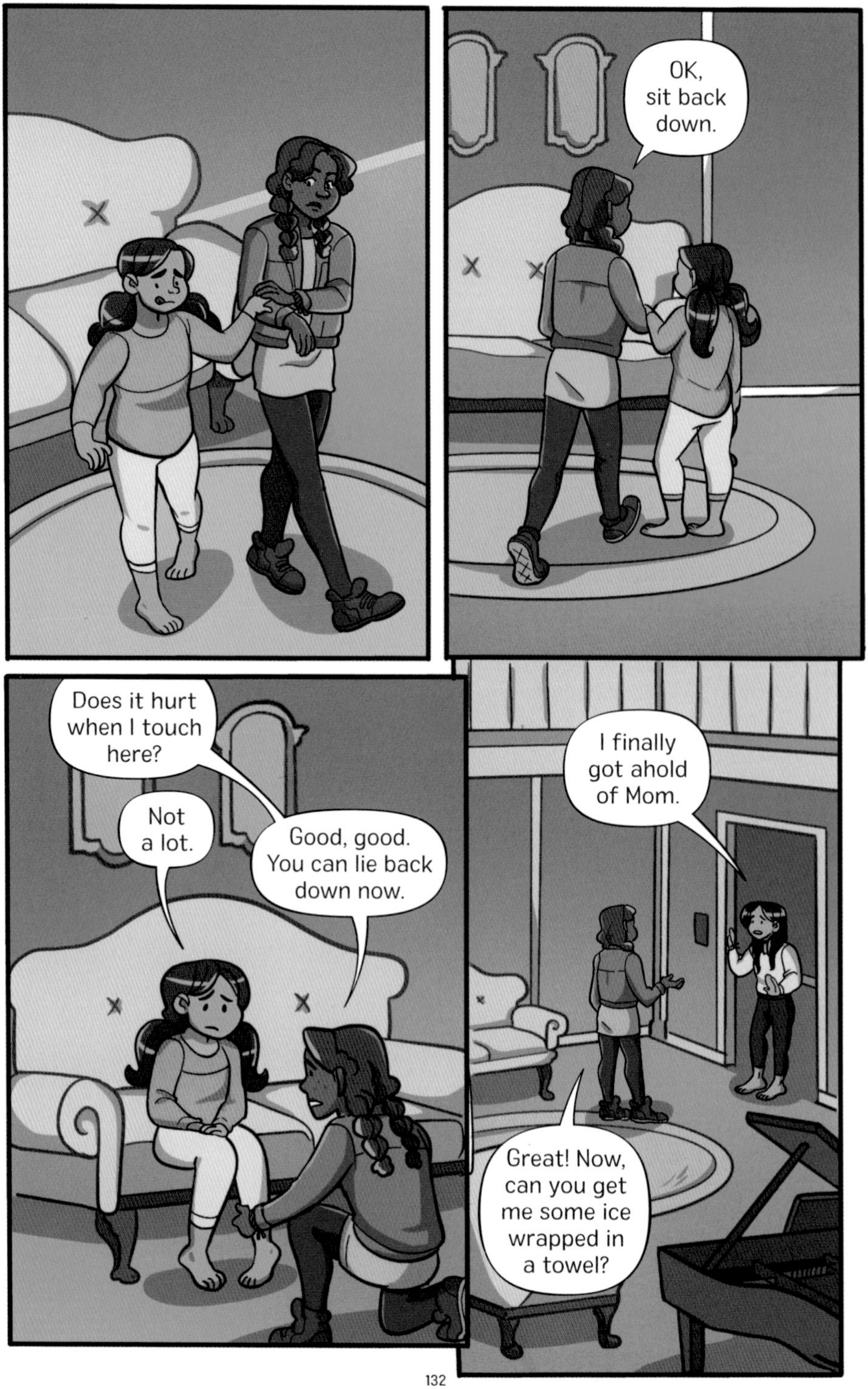
OK, sit back down.
Does it hurt when I touch here?
Not a lot.
Good, good. You can lie back down now.
I finally got ahold of Mom.
Great! Now, can you get me some ice wrapped in a towel?

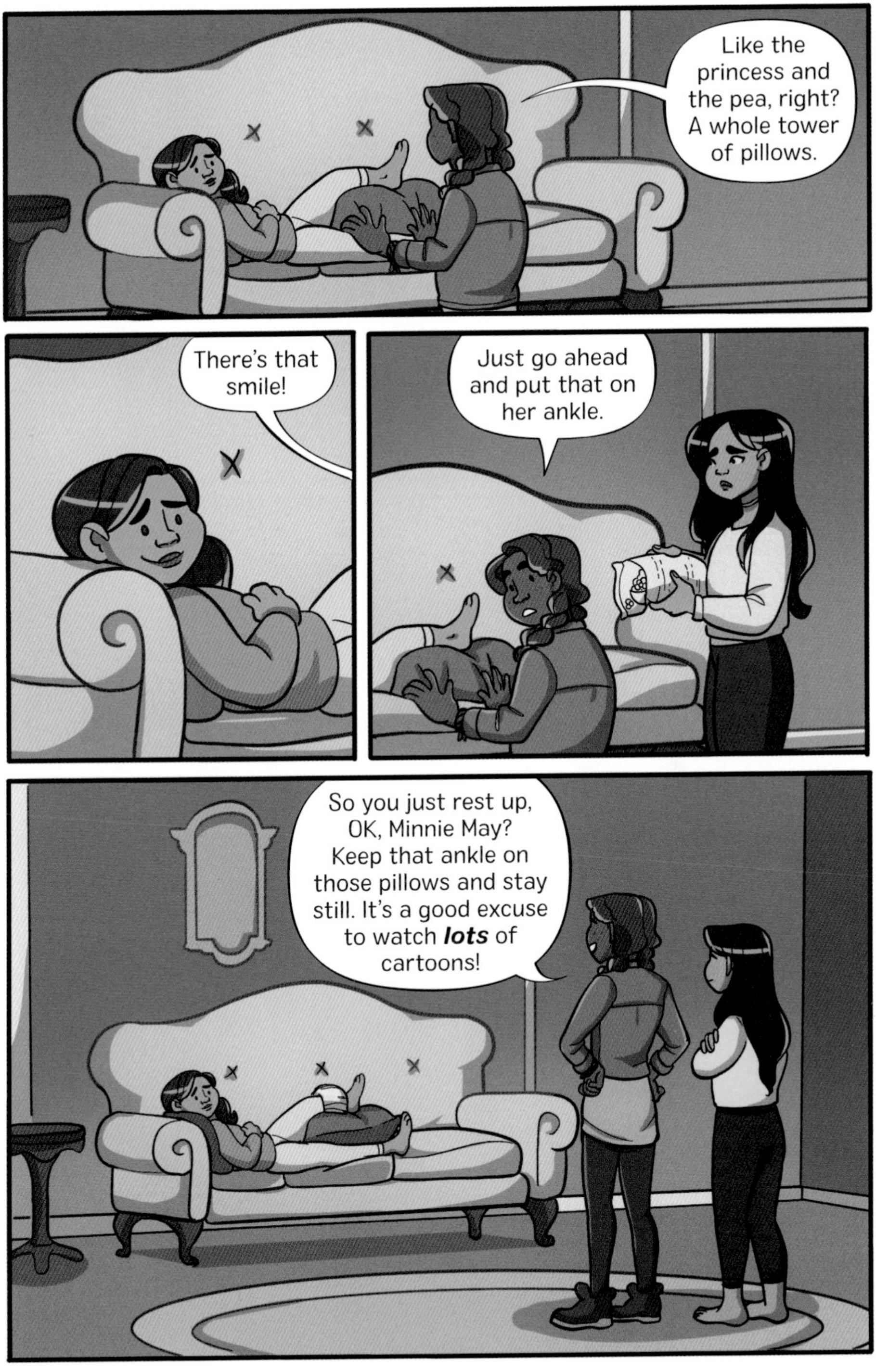
Like the princess and the pea, right? A whole tower of pillows.
There's that smile!
Just go ahead and put that on her ankle.
So you just rest up, OK, Minnie May? Keep that ankle on those pillows and stay still. It's a good excuse to watch ***lots*** of cartoons!

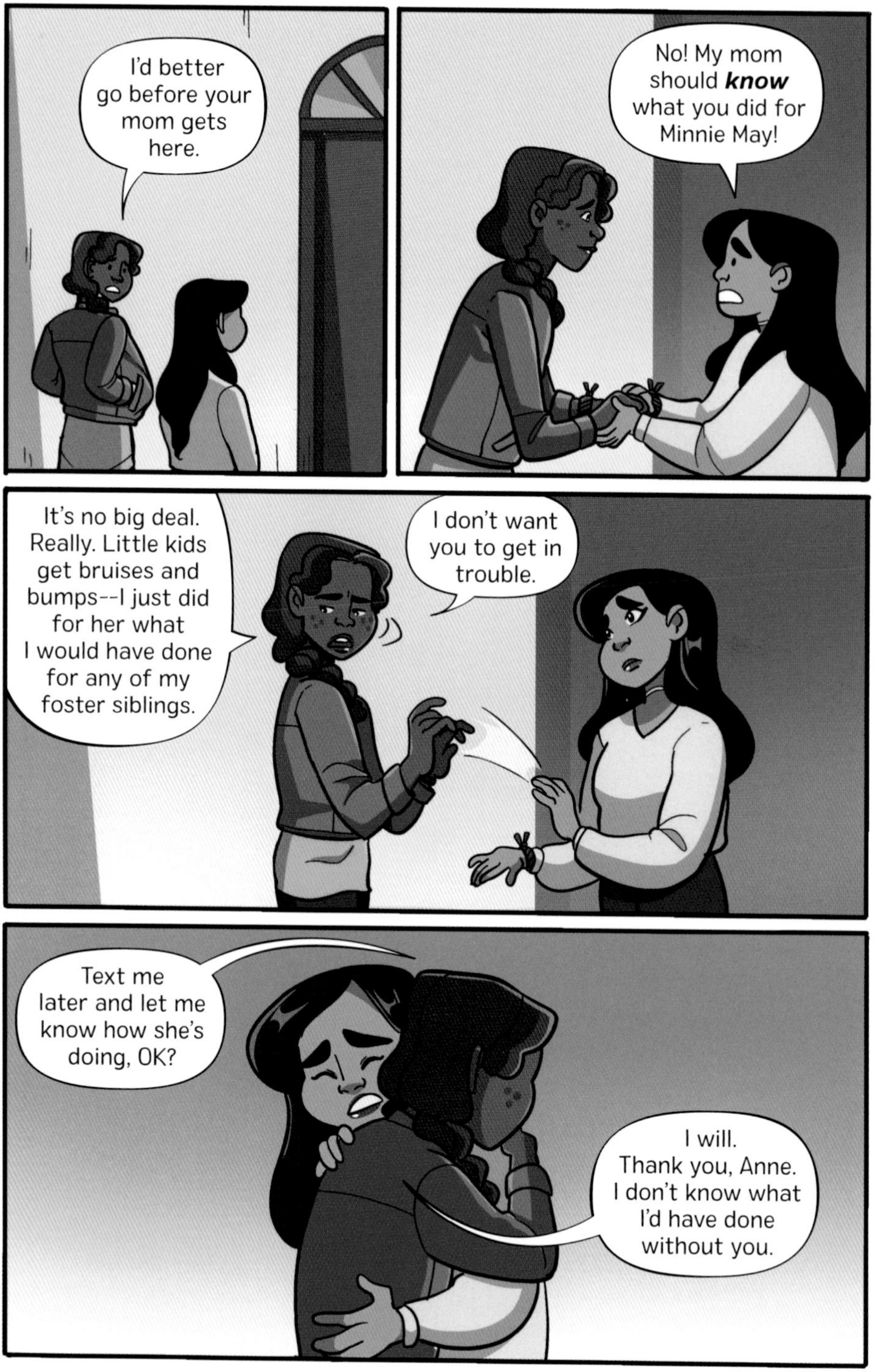
I'd better go before your mom gets here.
No! My mom should ***know*** what you did for Minnie May!
It's no big deal. Really. Little kids get bruises and bumps--I just did for her what I would have done for any of my foster siblings.
I don't want you to get in trouble.
Text me later and let me know how she's doing, OK?
I will. Thank you, Anne. I don't know what I'd have done without you.

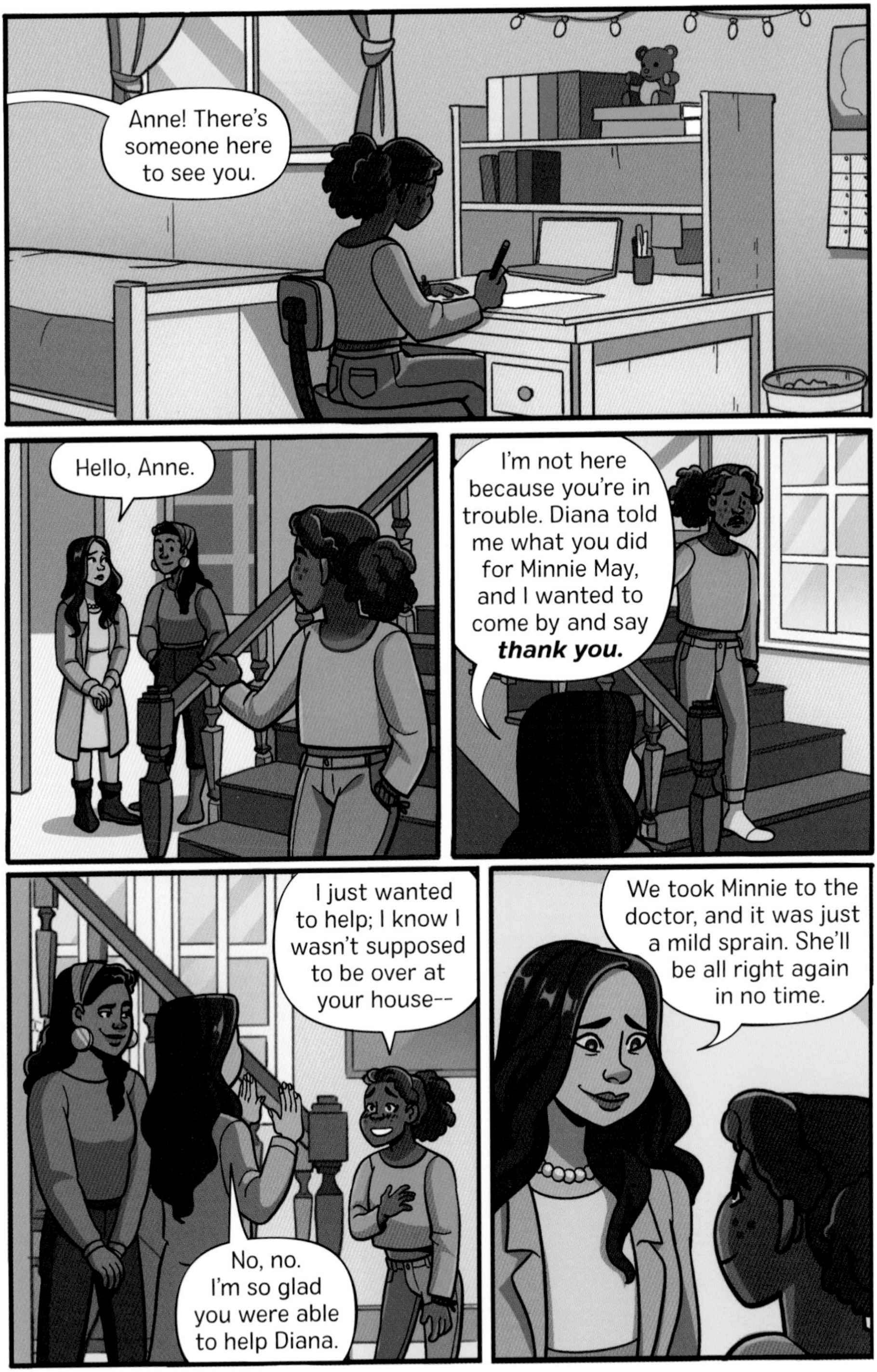
Anne! There's someone here to see you.
Hello, Anne.
I'm not here because you're in trouble. Diana told me what you did for Minnie May, and I wanted to come by and say **thank you.**
I just wanted to help; I know I wasn't supposed to be over at your house--
No, no. I'm so glad you were able to help Diana.
We took Minnie to the doctor, and it was just a mild sprain. She'll be all right again in no time.

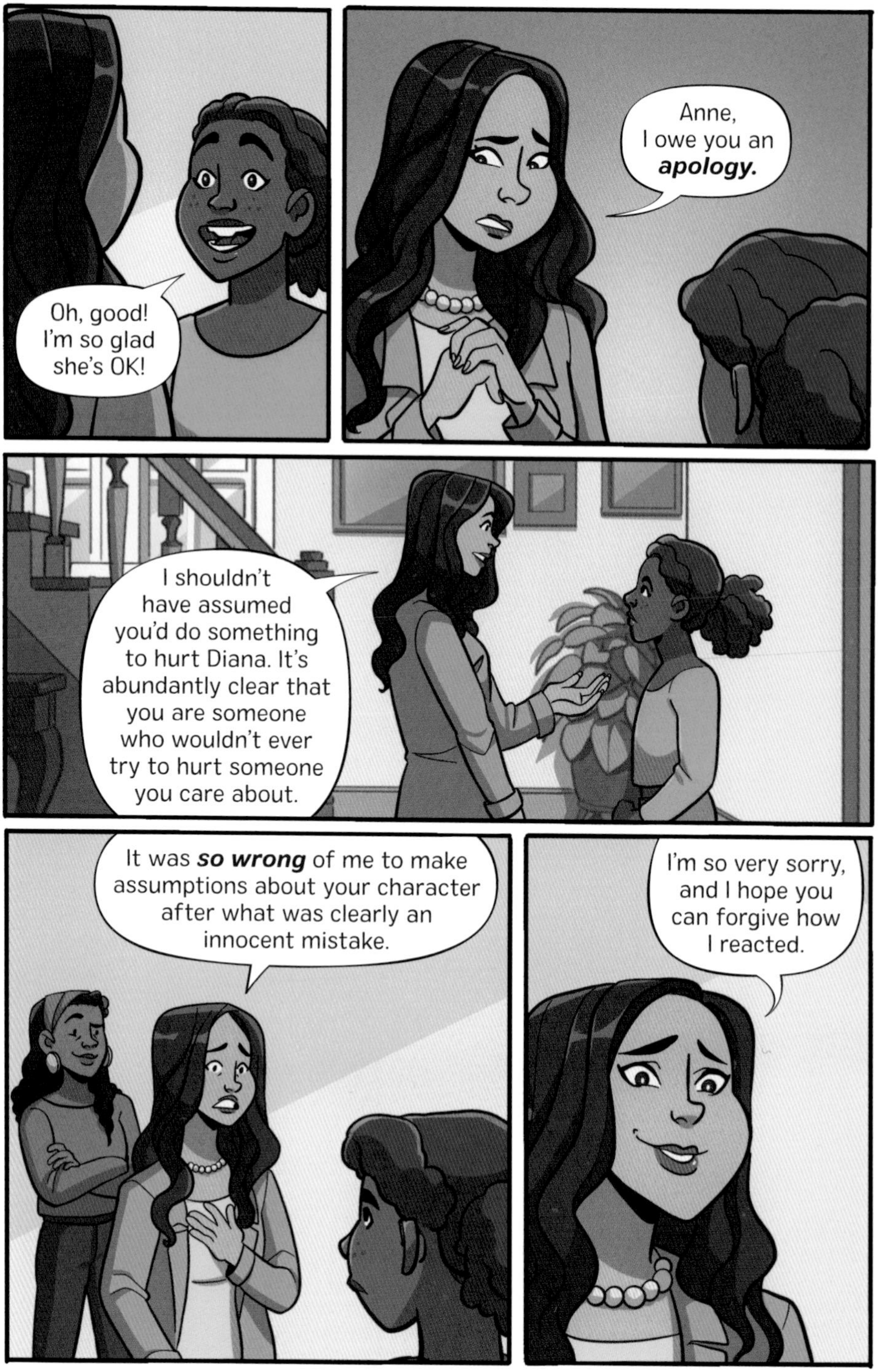
Oh, good! I'm so glad she's OK!
Anne, I owe you an ***apology.***
I shouldn't have assumed you'd do something to hurt Diana. It's abundantly clear that you are someone who wouldn't ever try to hurt someone you care about.
It was ***so wrong*** of me to make assumptions about your character after what was clearly an innocent mistake.
I'm so very sorry, and I hope you can forgive how I reacted.

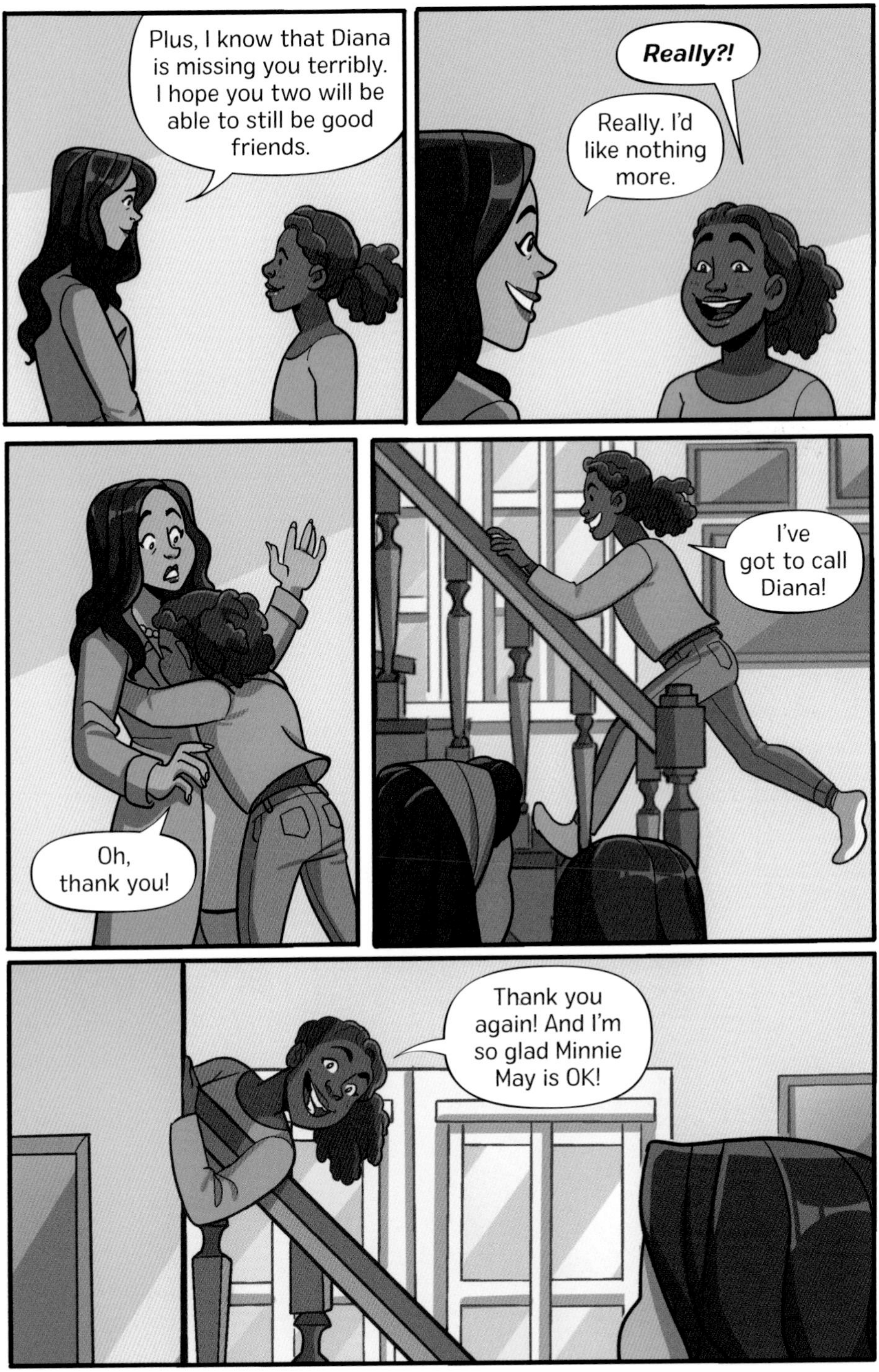
Plus, I know that Diana is missing you terribly. I hope you two will be able to still be good friends.
Really?!
Really. I'd like nothing more.
Oh, thank you!
I've got to call Diana!
Thank you again! And I'm so glad Minnie May is OK!

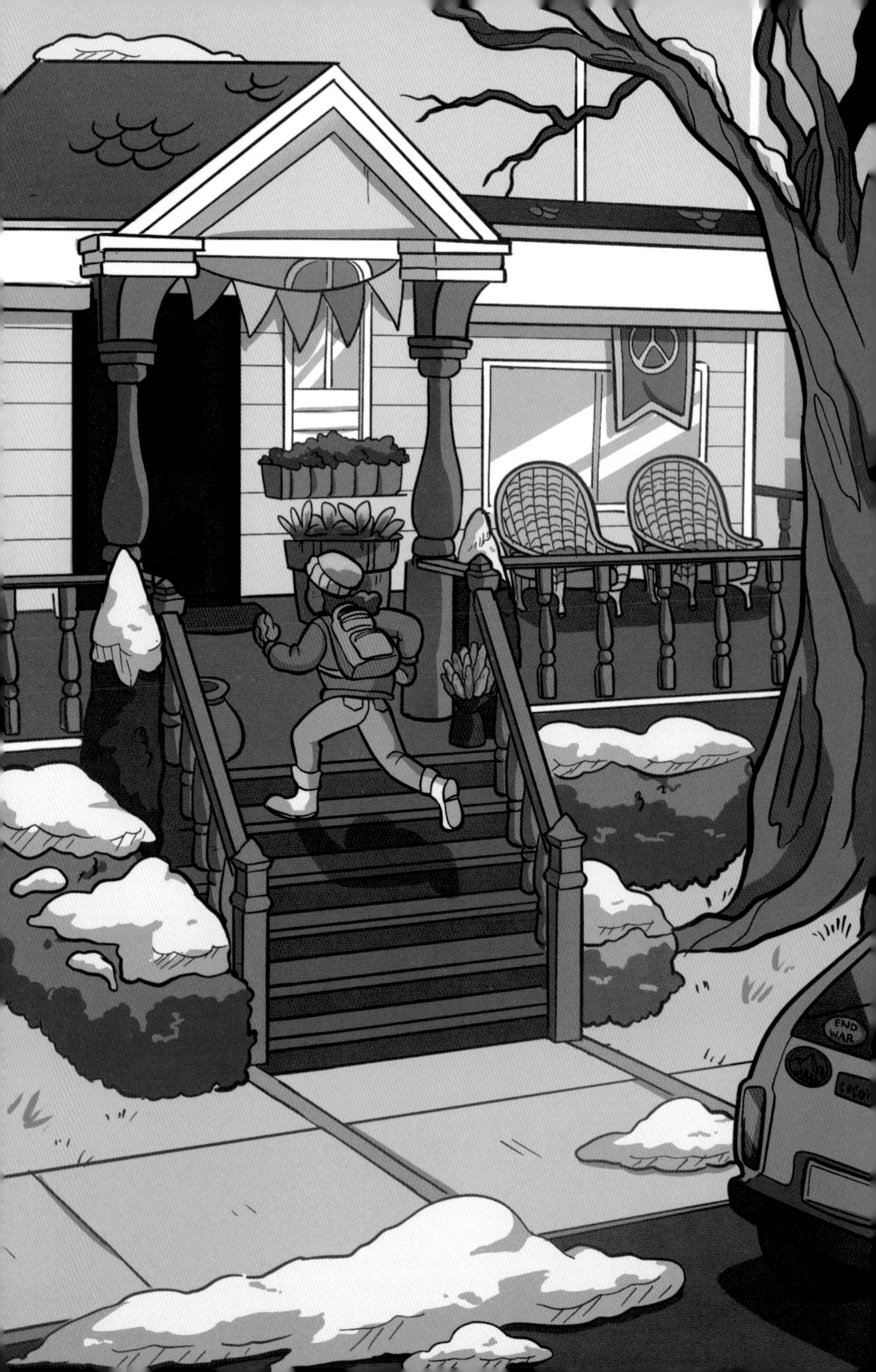
END WAR

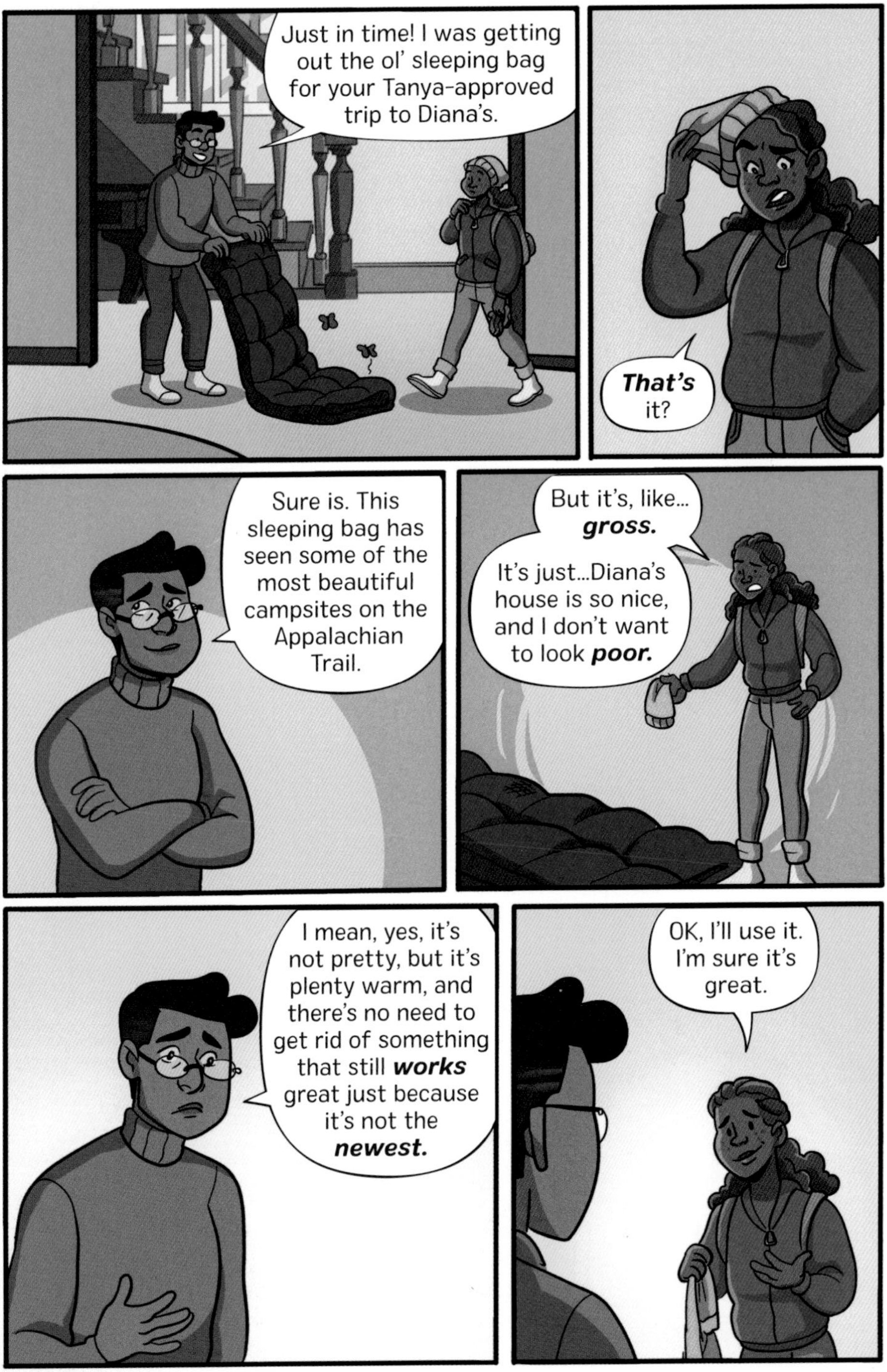
Just in time! I was getting out the ol' sleeping bag for your Tanya-approved trip to Diana's.
That's it?
Sure is. This sleeping bag has seen some of the most beautiful campsites on the Appalachian Trail.
But it's, like... ***gross.***
It's just...Diana's house is so nice, and I don't want to look ***poor.***
I mean, yes, it's not pretty, but it's plenty warm, and there's no need to get rid of something that still ***works*** great just because it's not the ***newest.***
OK, I'll use it. I'm sure it's great.

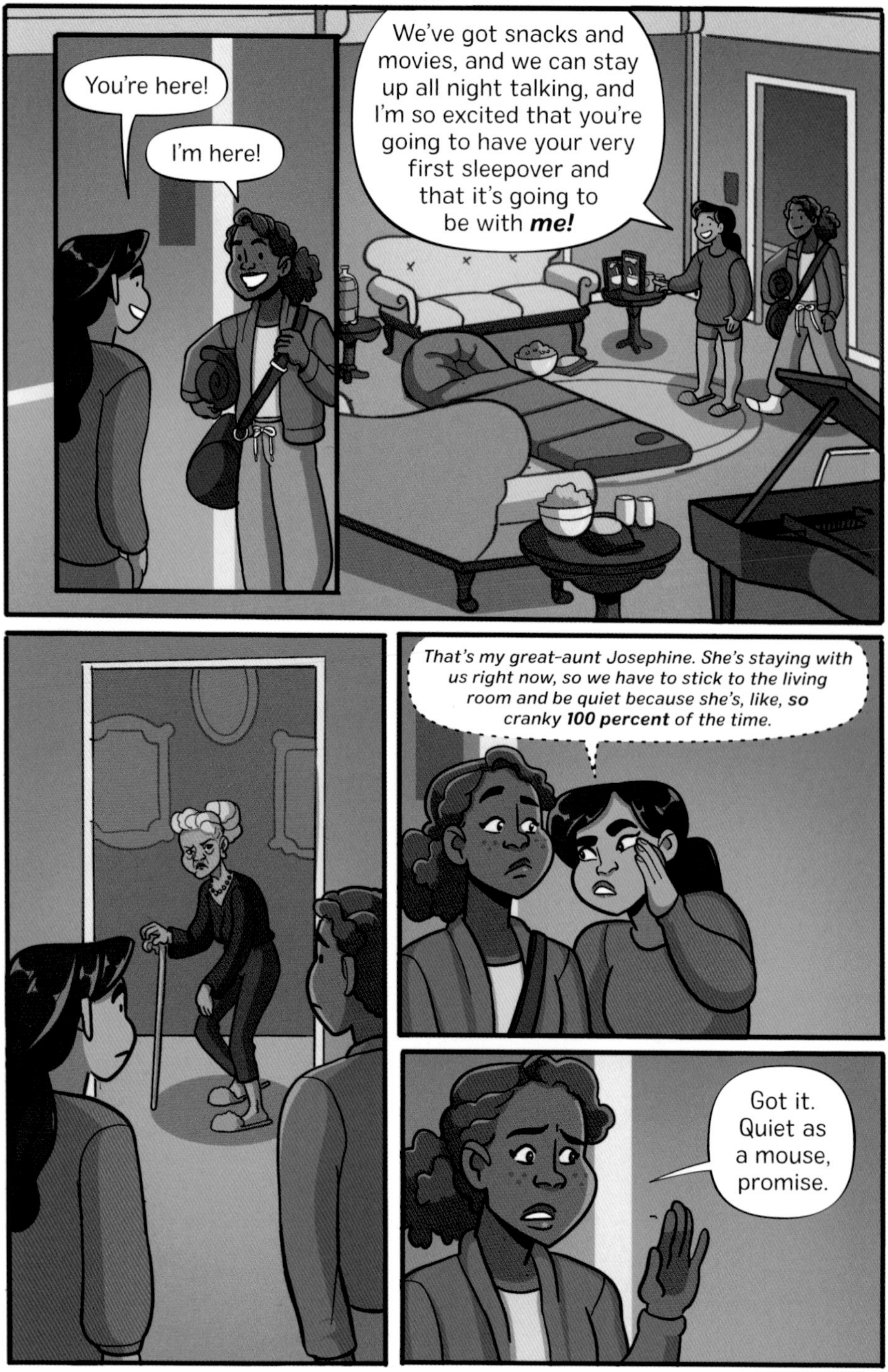
You're here!
I'm here!
We've got snacks and movies, and we can stay up all night talking, and I'm so excited that you're going to have your very first sleepover and that it's going to be with ***me!***
That's my great-aunt Josephine. She's staying with us right now, so we have to stick to the living room and be quiet because she's, like, ***so*** *cranky* ***100 percent*** *of the time.*
Got it. Quiet as a mouse, promise.

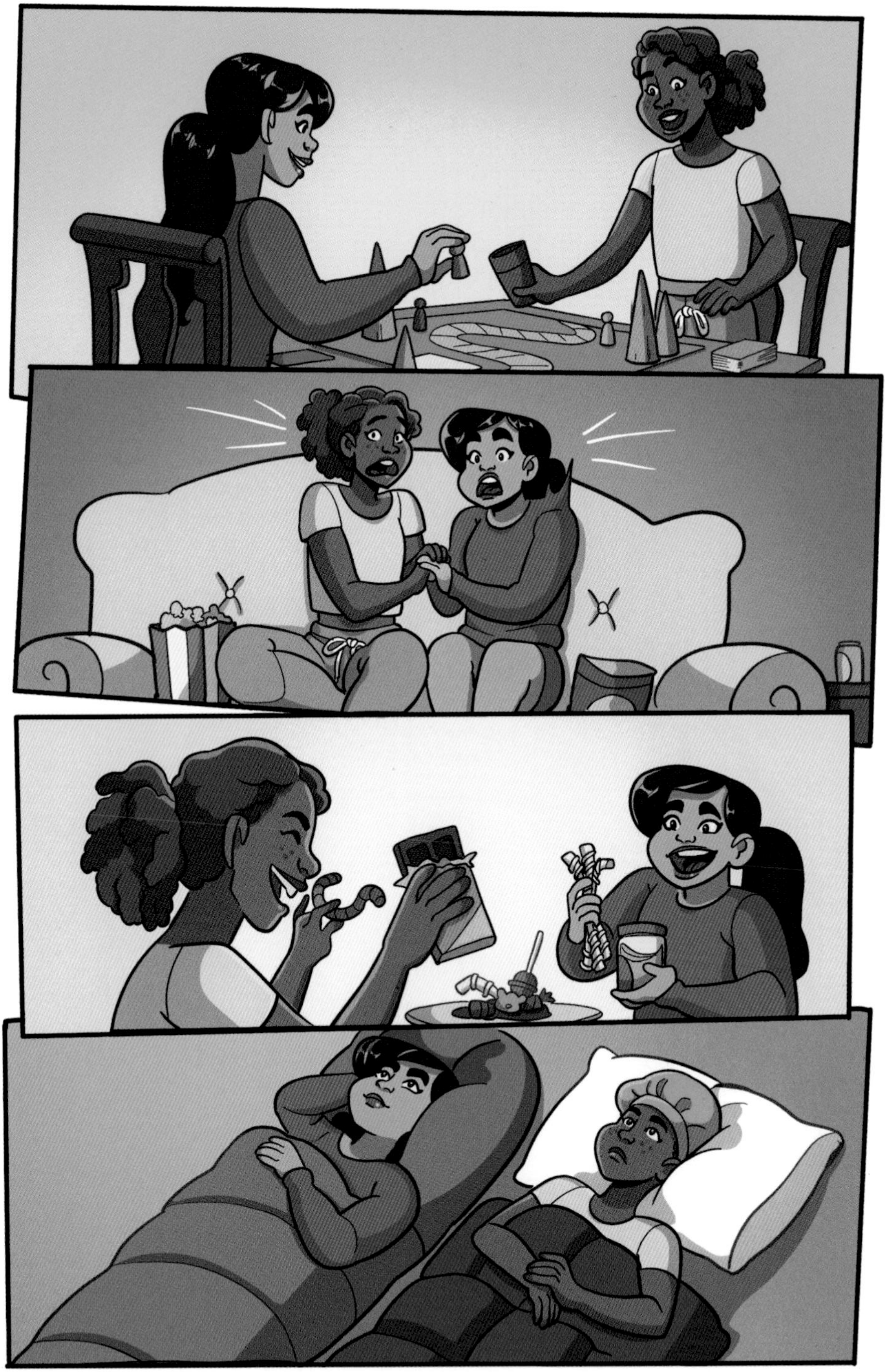

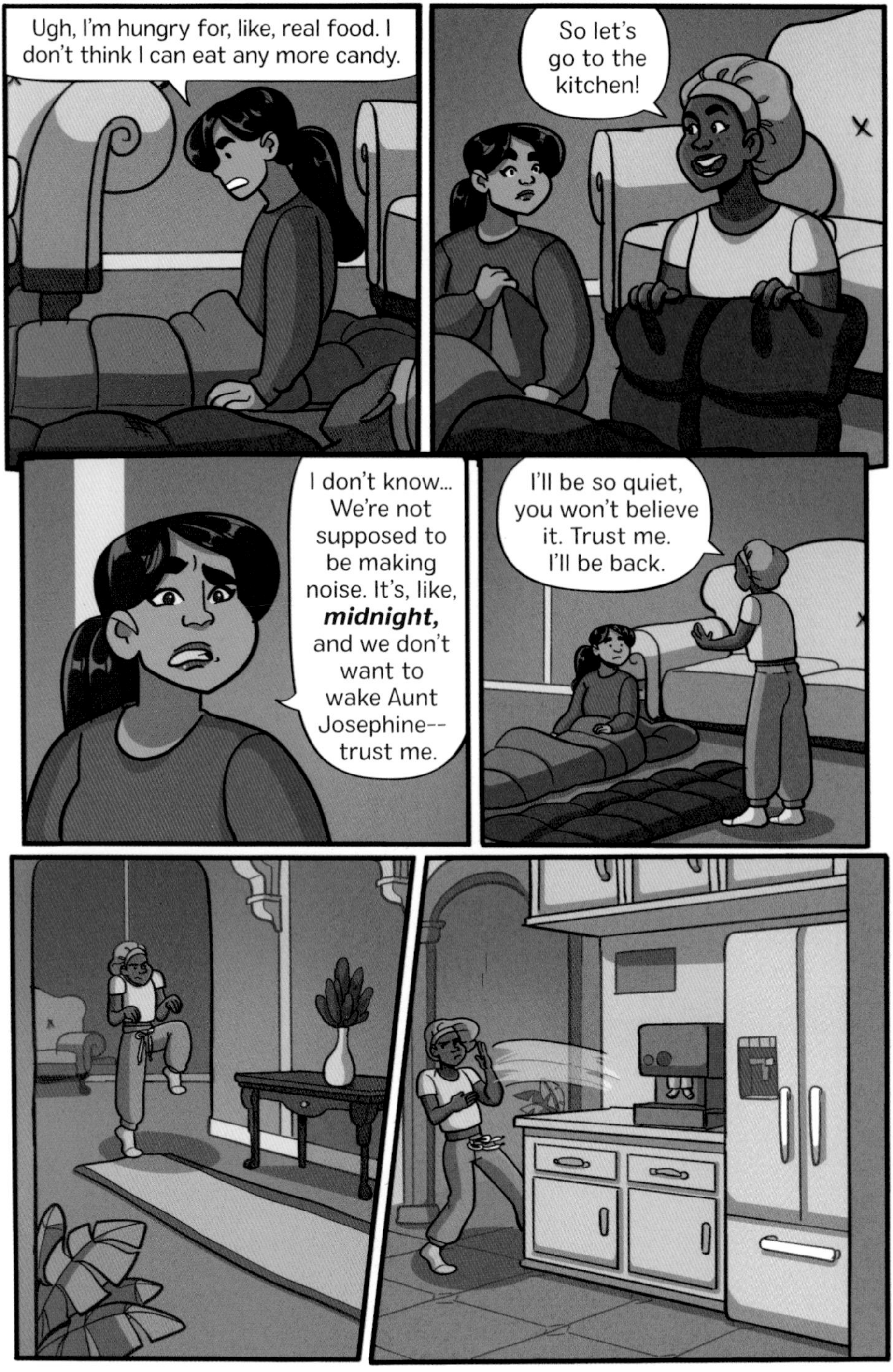
Ugh, I'm hungry for, like, real food. I don't think I can eat any more candy.
So let's go to the kitchen!
I don't know... We're not supposed to be making noise. It's, like, ***midnight,*** and we don't want to wake Aunt Josephine-- trust me.
I'll be so quiet, you won't believe it. Trust me. I'll be back.

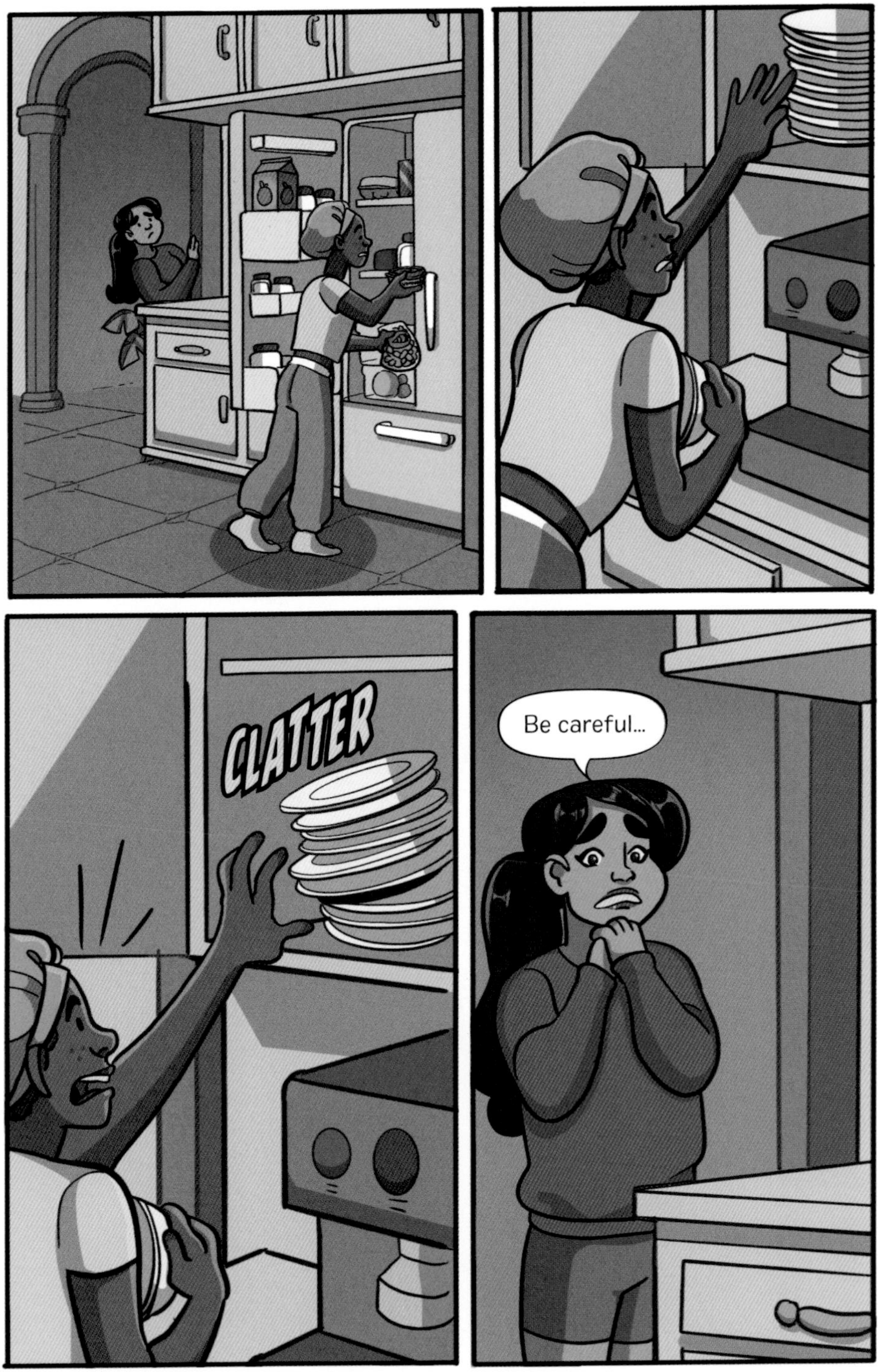
CLATTER
Be careful...

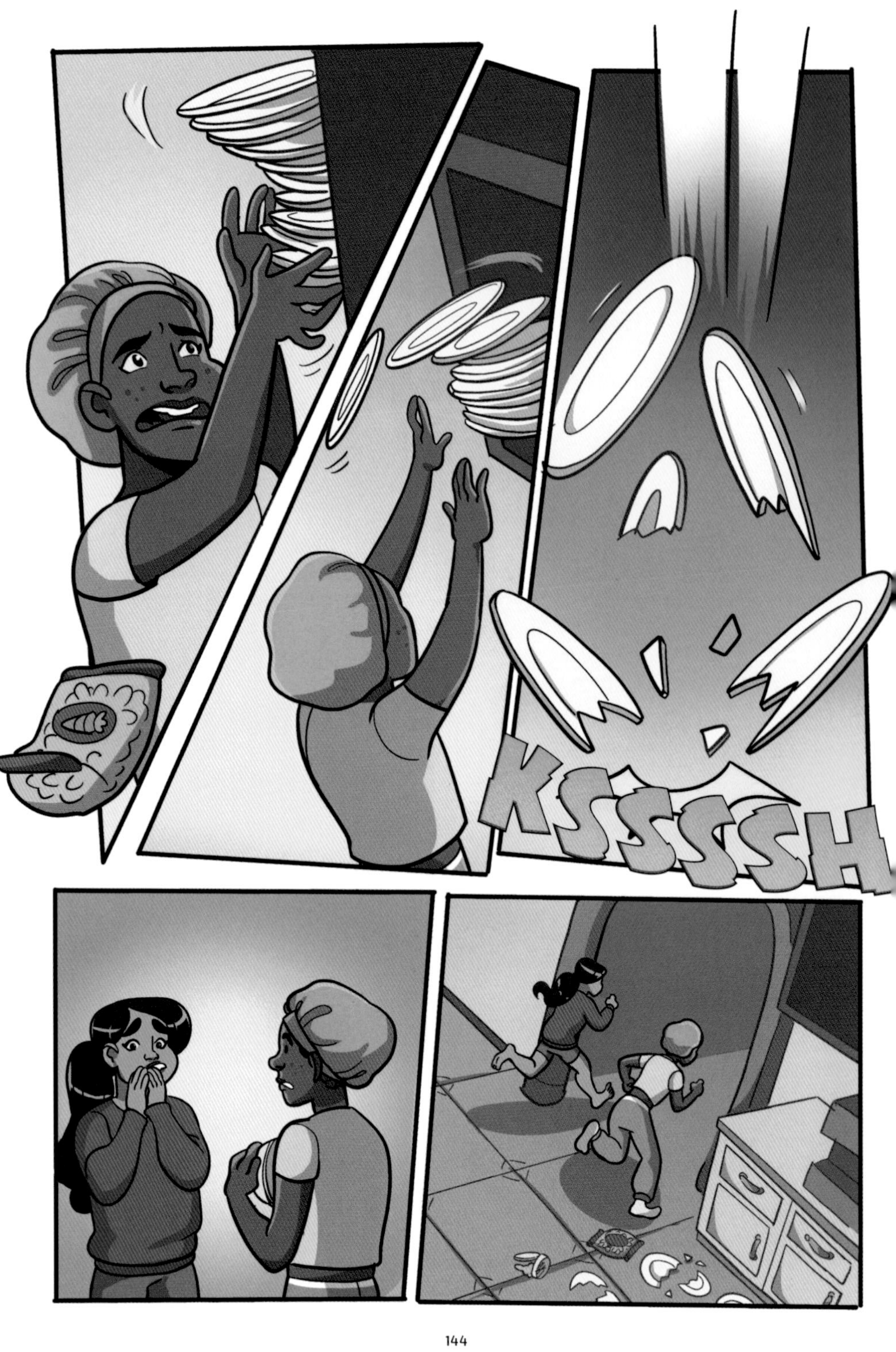
KSSSSH

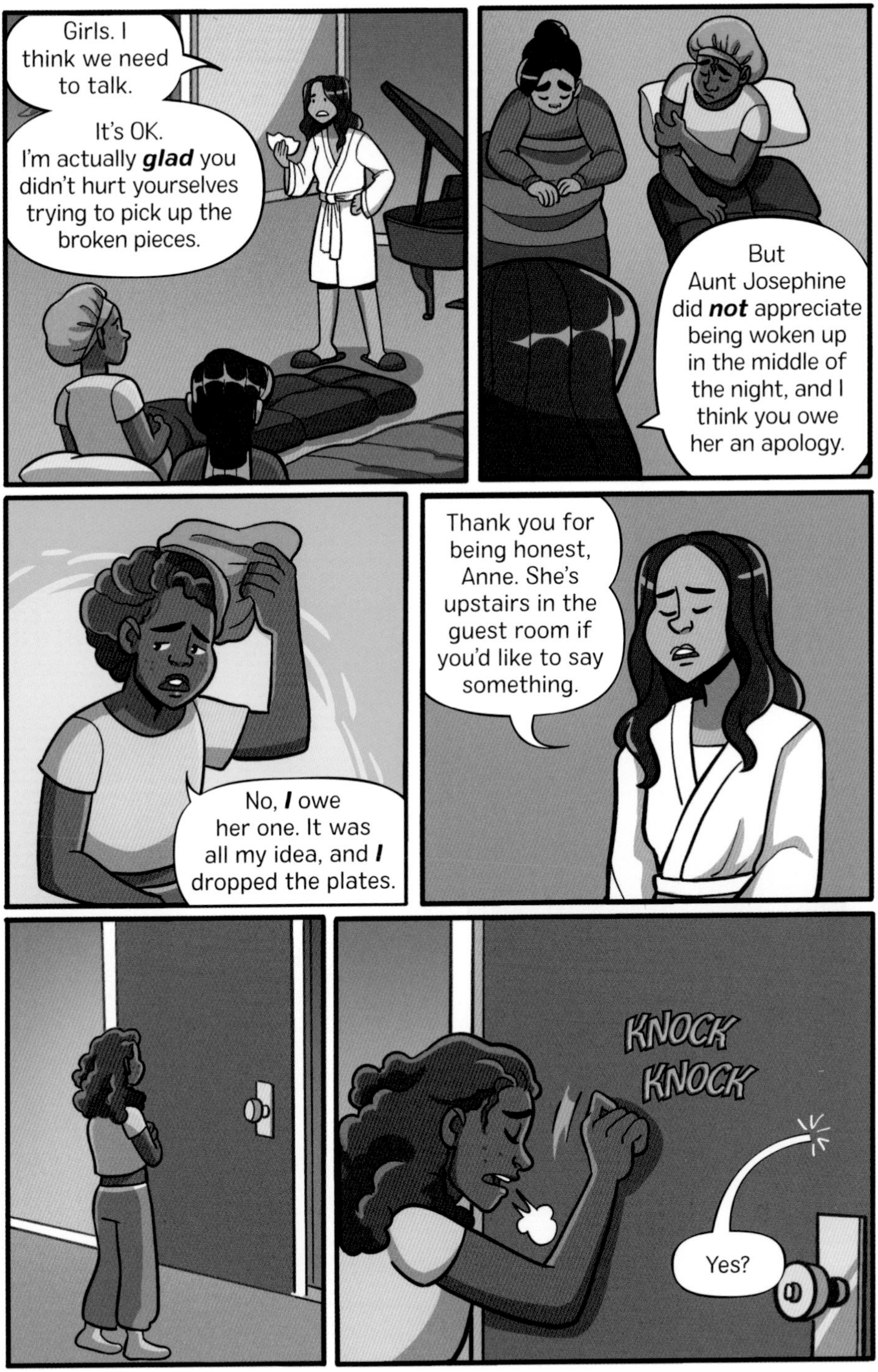
Girls. I think we need to talk.
It's OK. I'm actually ***glad*** you didn't hurt yourselves trying to pick up the broken pieces.
But Aunt Josephine did ***not*** appreciate being woken up in the middle of the night, and I think you owe her an apology.
No, ***I*** owe her one. It was all my idea, and ***I*** dropped the plates.
Thank you for being honest, Anne. She's upstairs in the guest room if you'd like to say something.
KNOCK KNOCK
Yes?

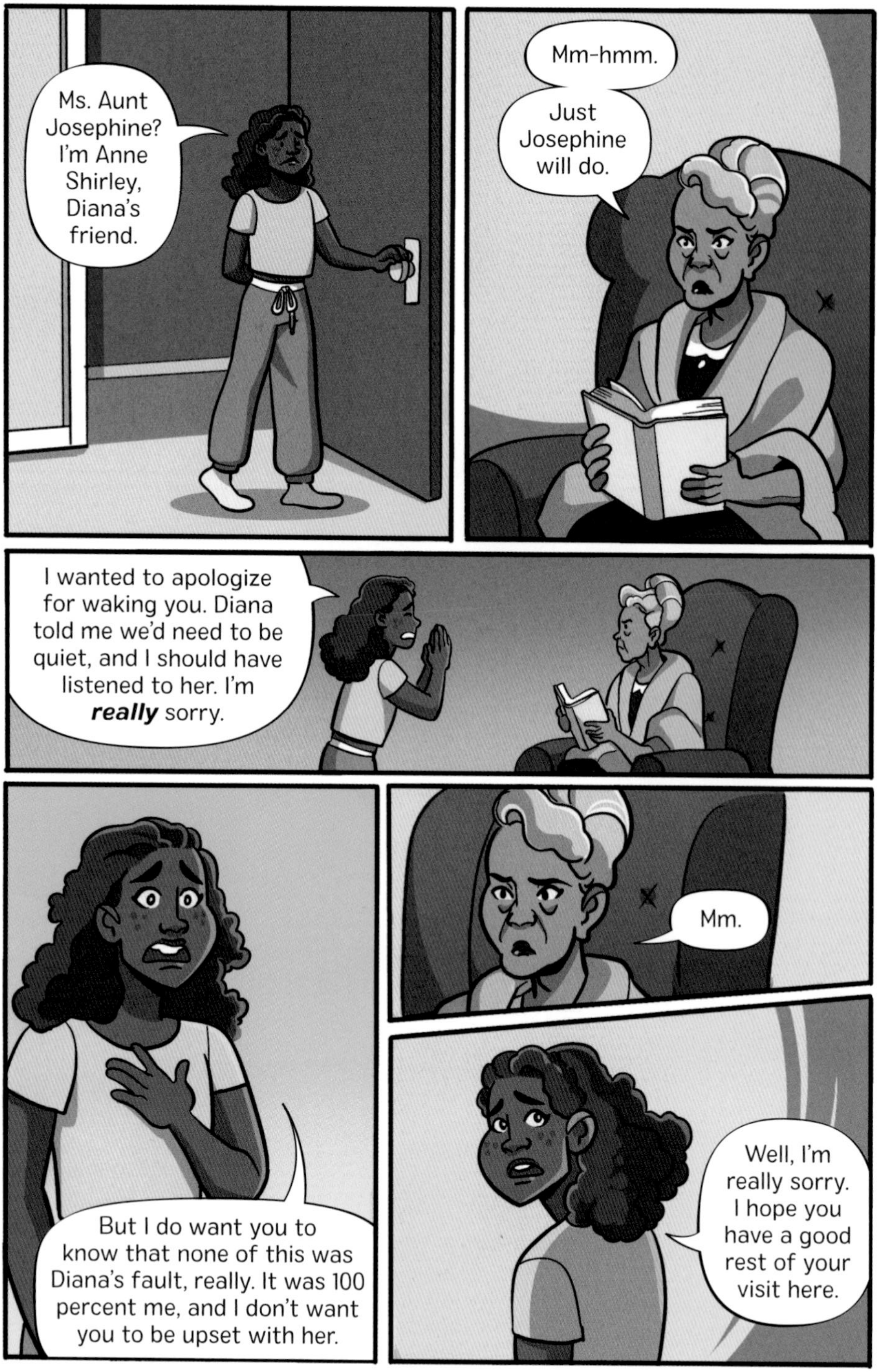
Ms. Aunt Josephine? I'm Anne Shirley, Diana's friend.
Mm-hmm.
Just Josephine will do.
I wanted to apologize for waking you. Diana told me we'd need to be quiet, and I should have listened to her. I'm ***really*** sorry.
But I do want you to know that none of this was Diana's fault, really. It was 100 percent me, and I don't want you to be upset with her.
Mm.
Well, I'm really sorry. I hope you have a good rest of your visit here.

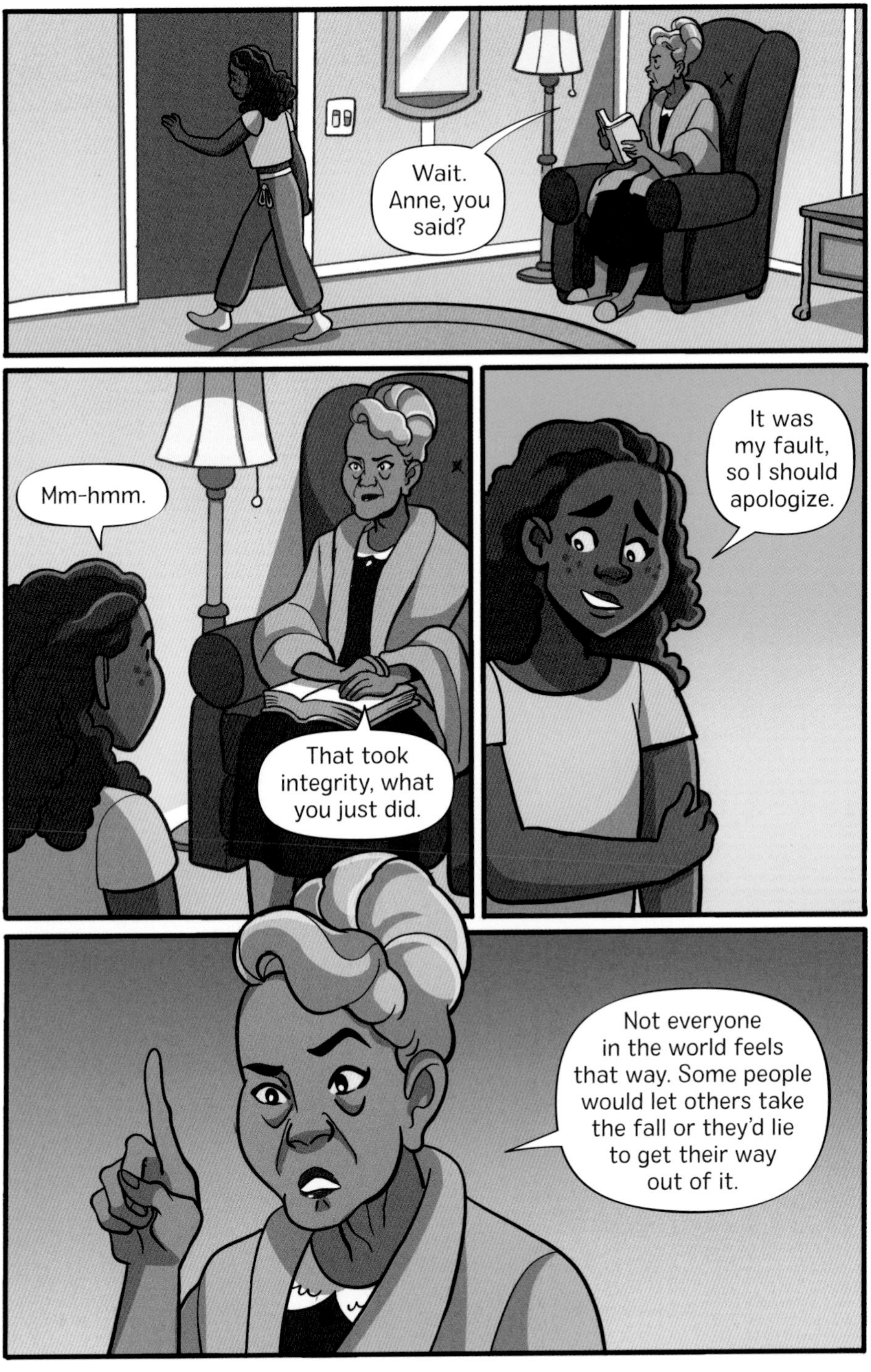
Wait. Anne, you said?
Mm-hmm.
That took integrity, what you just did.
It was my fault, so I should apologize.
Not everyone in the world feels that way. Some people would let others take the fall or they'd lie to get their way out of it.

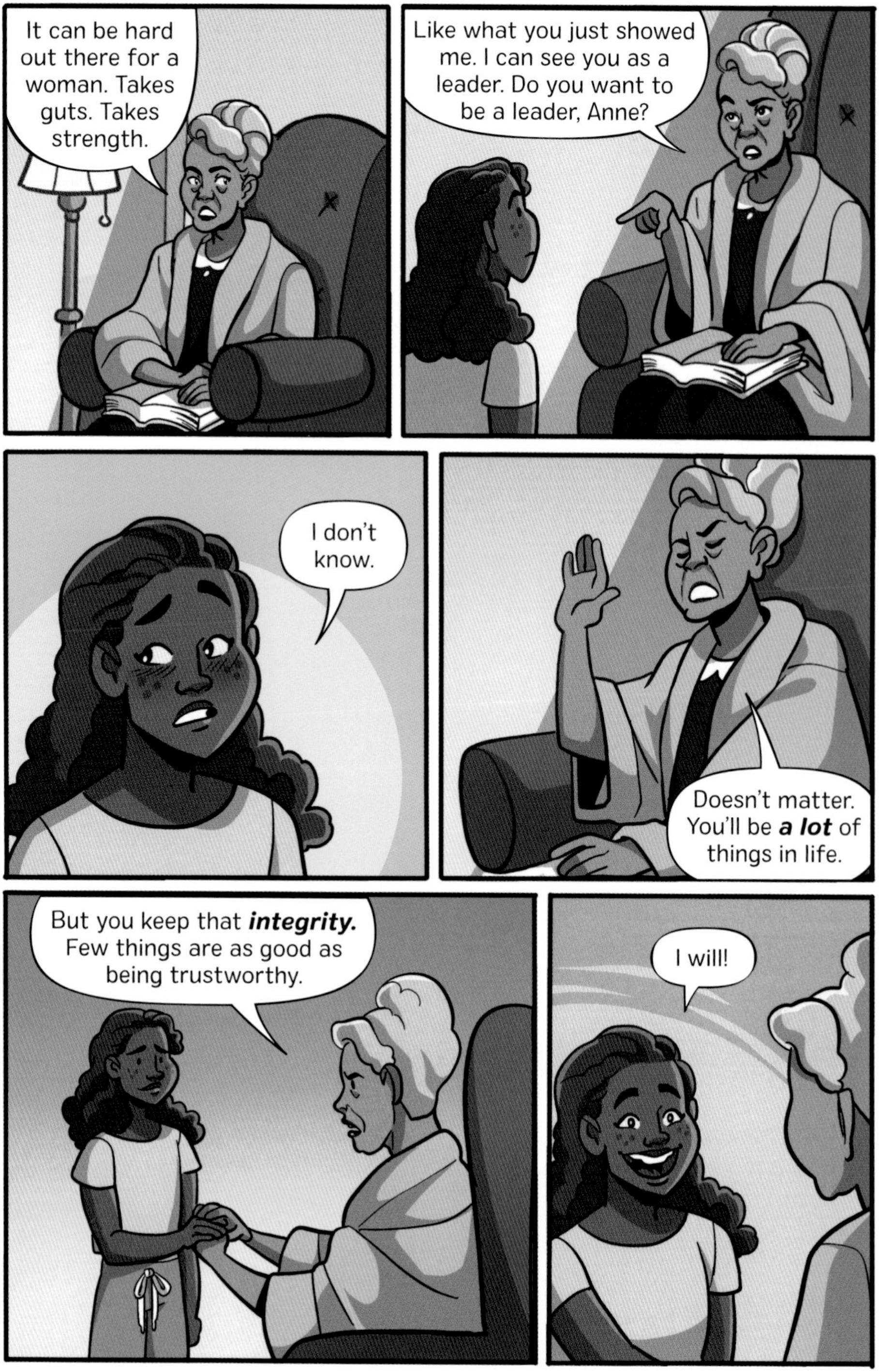
It can be hard out there for a woman. Takes guts. Takes strength.
Like what you just showed me. I can see you as a leader. Do you want to be a leader, Anne?
I don't know.
Doesn't matter. You'll be ***a lot*** of things in life.
But you keep that ***integrity.*** Few things are as good as being trustworthy.
I will!

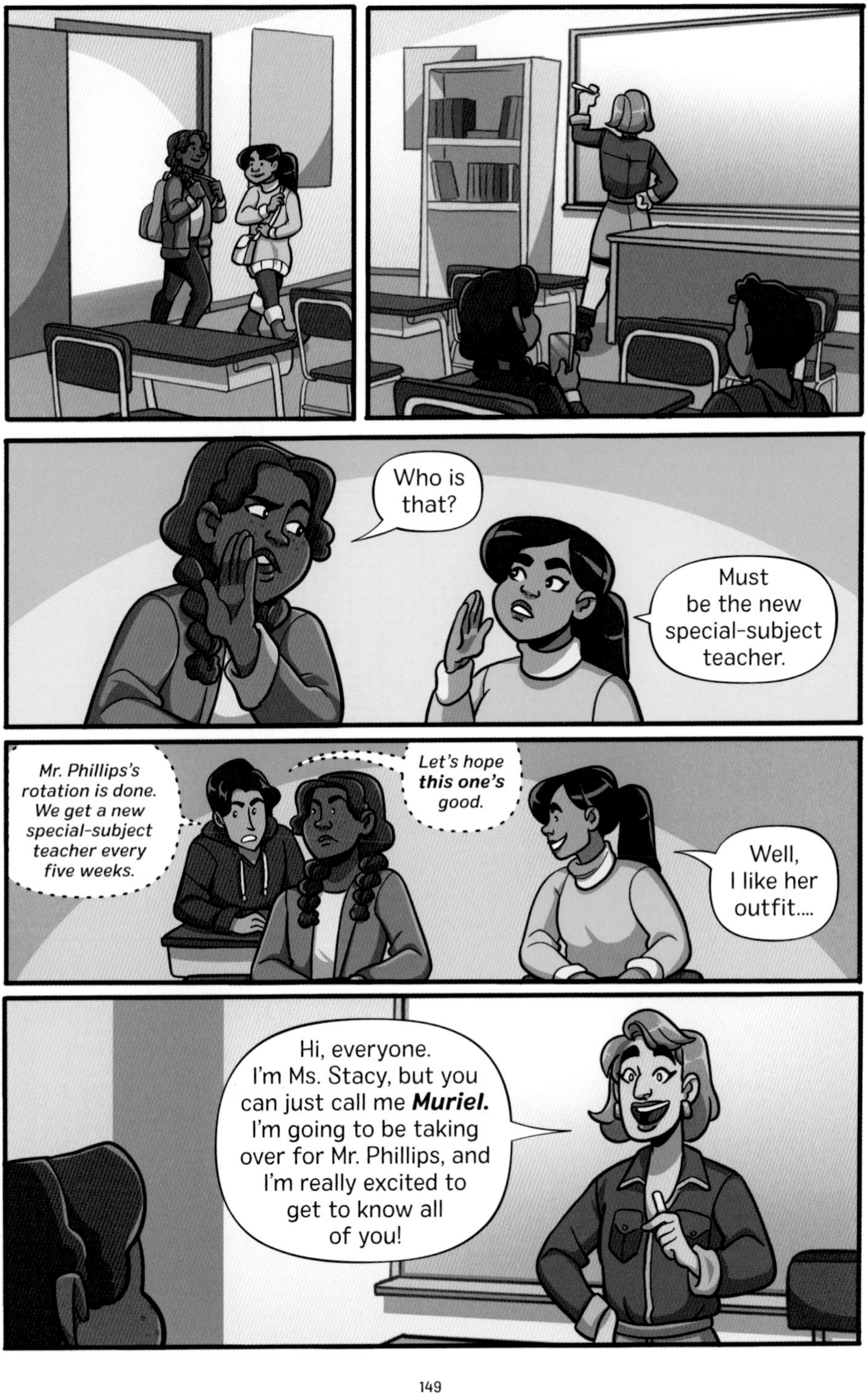
Who is that?
Must be the new special-subject teacher.
Mr. Phillips's rotation is done. We get a new special-subject teacher every five weeks.
Let's hope **this one's** good.
Well, I like her outfit....
Hi, everyone. I'm Ms. Stacy, but you can just call me ***Muriel.*** I'm going to be taking over for Mr. Phillips, and I'm really excited to get to know all of you!

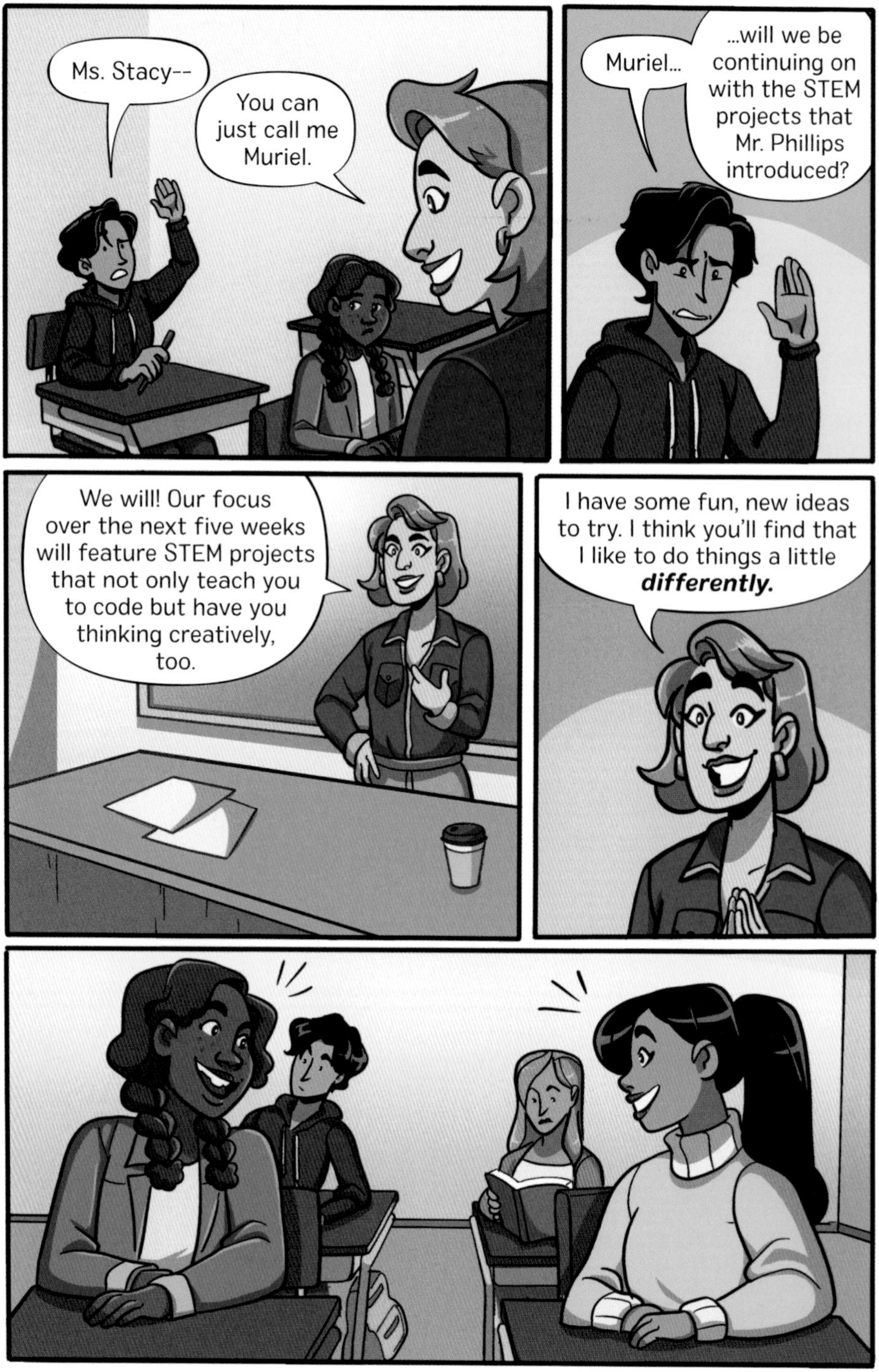
Ms. Stacy--
You can just call me Muriel.
Muriel...
...will we be continuing on with the STEM projects that Mr. Phillips introduced?
We will! Our focus over the next five weeks will feature STEM projects that not only teach you to code but have you thinking creatively, too.
I have some fun, new ideas to try. I think you'll find that I like to do things a little ***differently.***

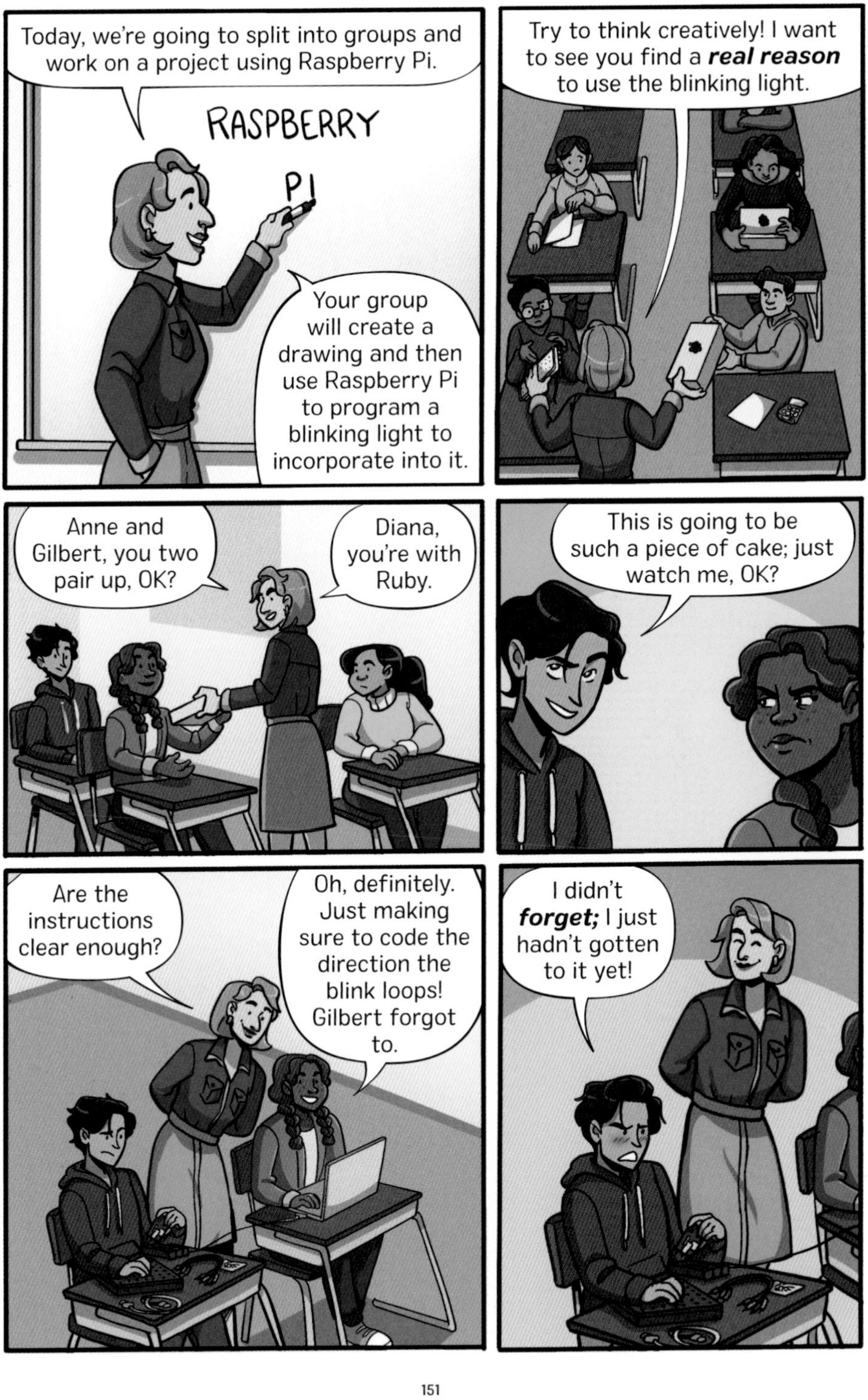
Today, we're going to split into groups and work on a project using Raspberry Pi.
RASPBERRY PI
Your group will create a drawing and then use Raspberry Pi to program a blinking light to incorporate into it.
Try to think creatively! I want to see you find a ***real reason*** to use the blinking light.
Anne and Gilbert, you two pair up, OK?
Diana, you're with Ruby.
This is going to be such a piece of cake; just watch me, OK?
Are the instructions clear enough?
Oh, definitely. Just making sure to code the direction the blink loops! Gilbert forgot to.
I didn't ***forget;*** I just hadn't gotten to it yet!

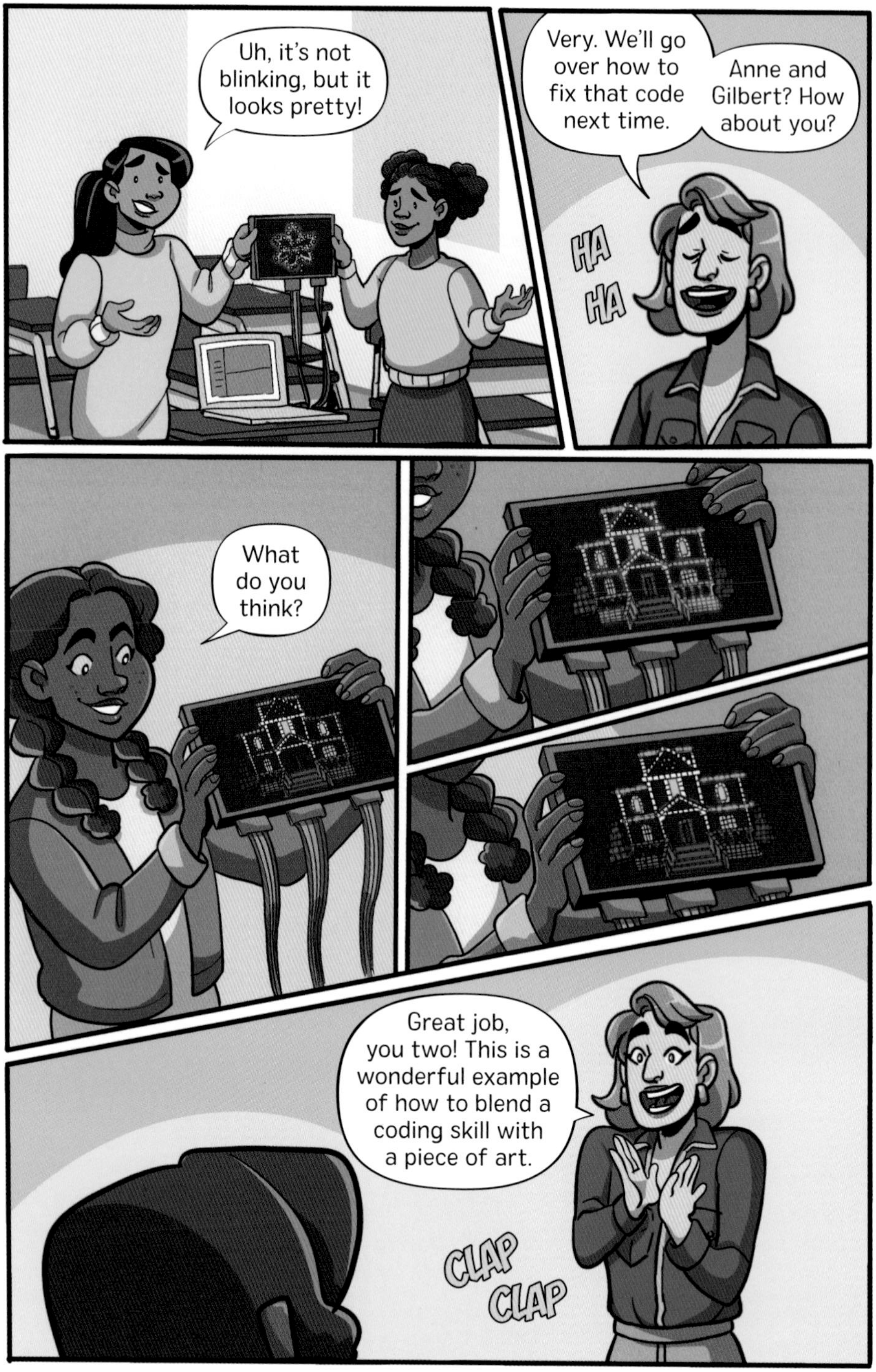
Uh, it's not blinking, but it looks pretty!
Very. We'll go over how to fix that code next time.
Anne and Gilbert? How about you?
HA HA
What do you think?
Great job, you two! This is a wonderful example of how to blend a coding skill with a piece of art.
CLAP CLAP

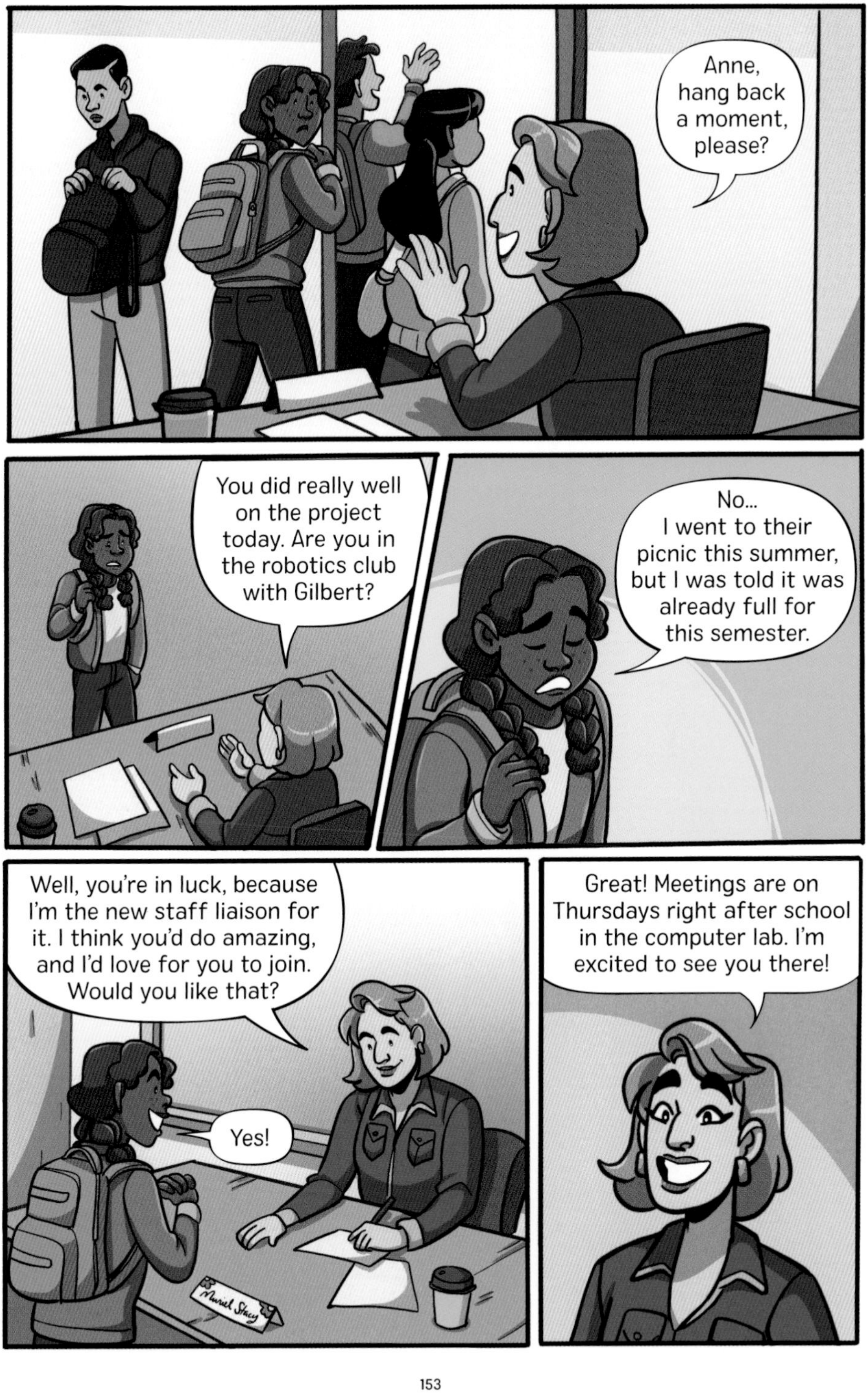
Anne, hang back a moment, please?
You did really well on the project today. Are you in the robotics club with Gilbert?
No... I went to their picnic this summer, but I was told it was already full for this semester.
Well, you're in luck, because I'm the new staff liaison for it. I think you'd do amazing, and I'd love for you to join. Would you like that?
Yes!
Muriel Stacy
Great! Meetings are on Thursdays right after school in the computer lab. I'm excited to see you there!

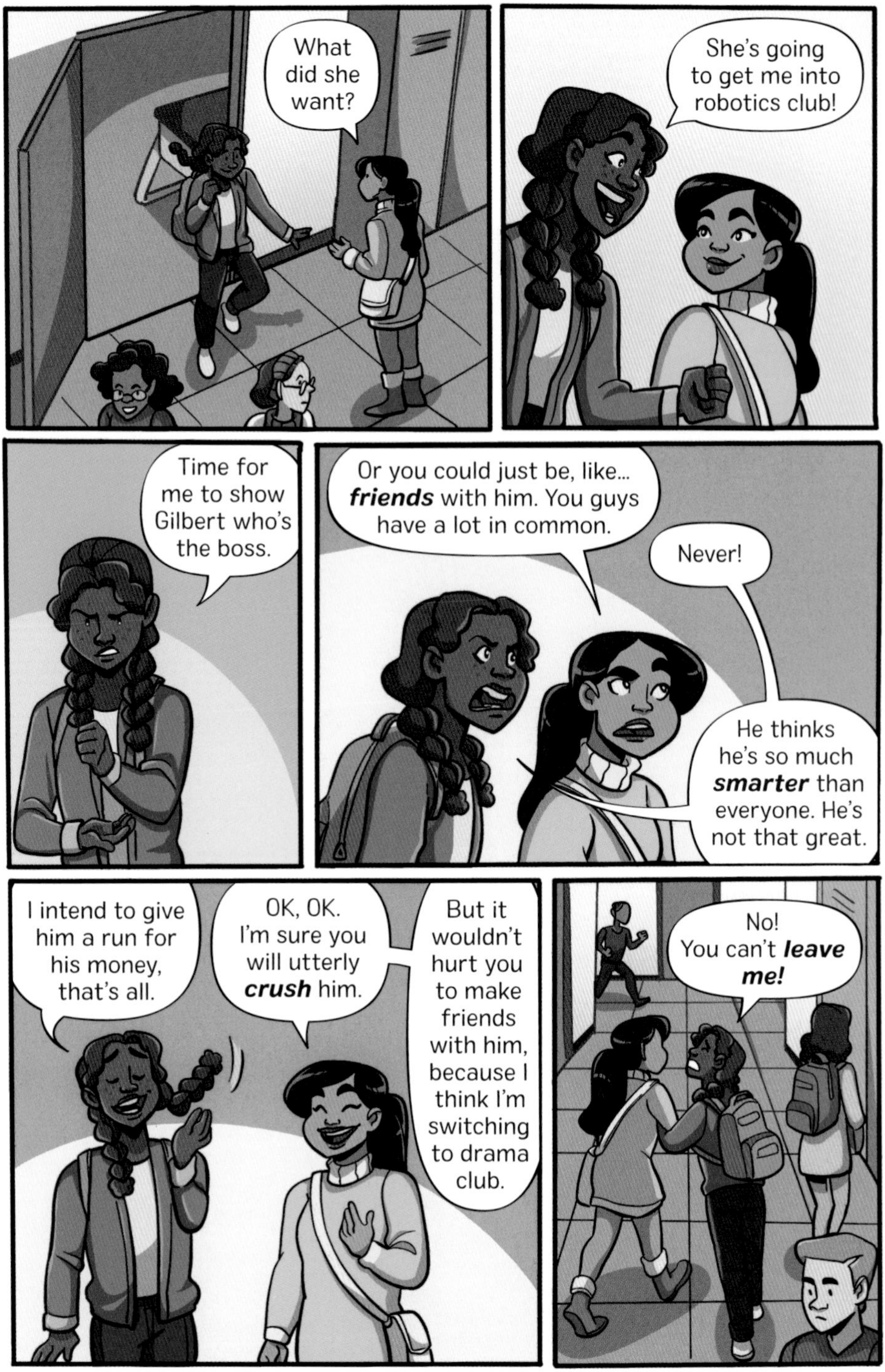
What did she want?
She's going to get me into robotics club!
Time for me to show Gilbert who's the boss.
Or you could just be, like... ***friends*** with him. You guys have a lot in common.
Never!
He thinks he's so much ***smarter*** than everyone. He's not that great.
I intend to give him a run for his money, that's all.
OK, OK. I'm sure you will utterly ***crush*** him.
But it wouldn't hurt you to make friends with him, because I think I'm switching to drama club.
No! You can't ***leave me!***

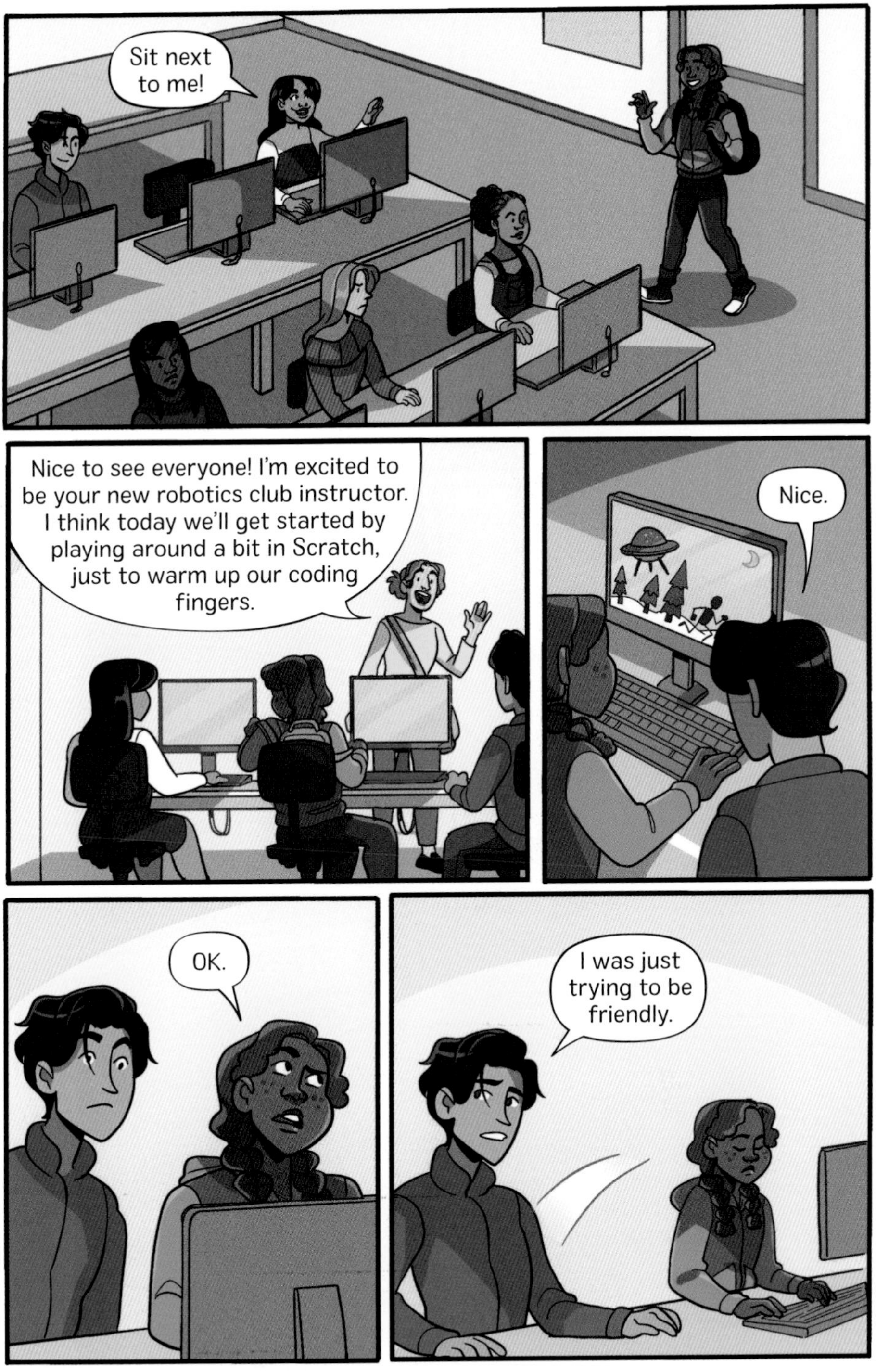
Sit next to me!
Nice to see everyone! I'm excited to be your new robotics club instructor. I think today we'll get started by playing around a bit in Scratch, just to warm up our coding fingers.
Nice.
OK.
I was just trying to be friendly.

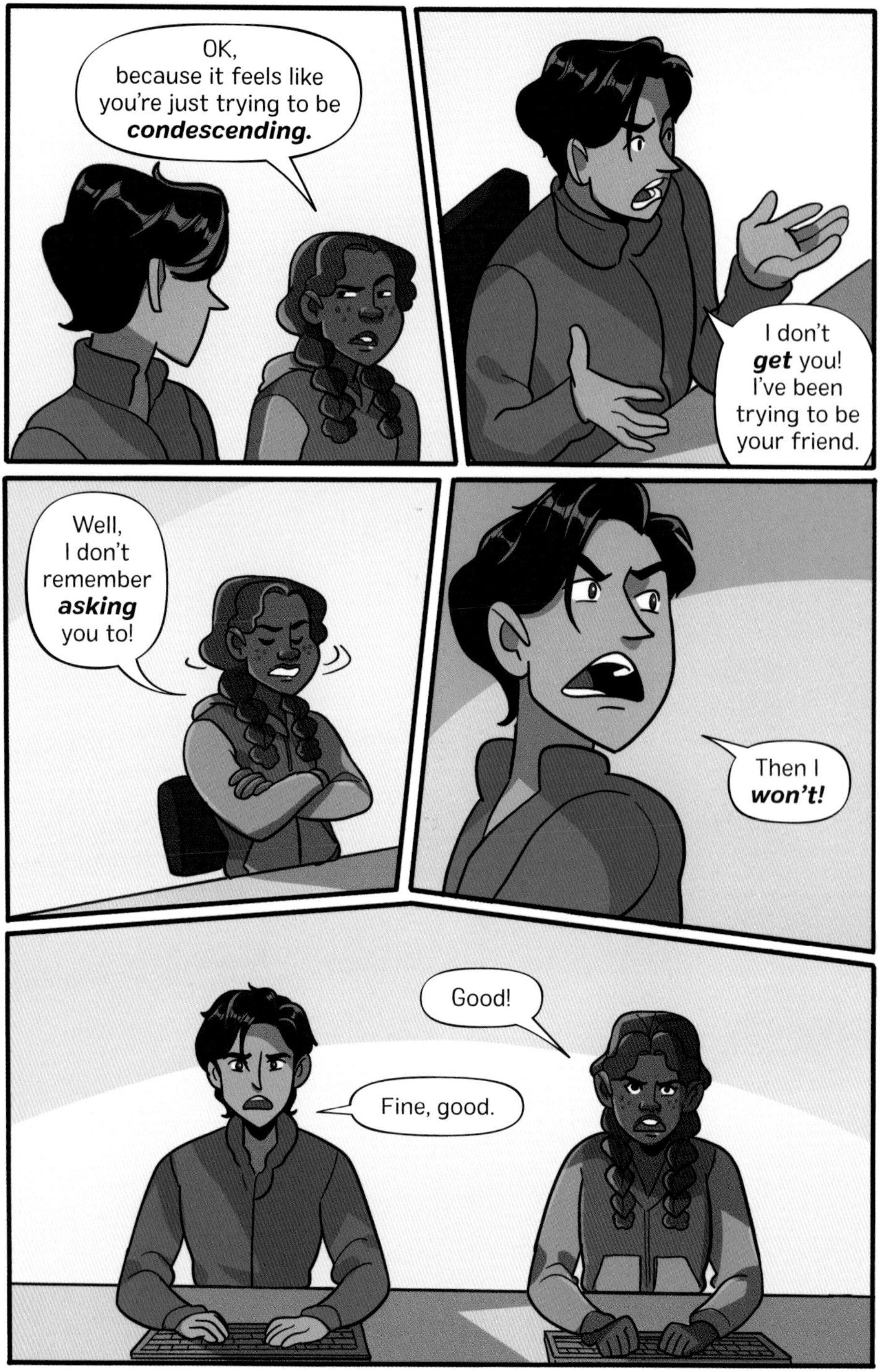
OK, because it feels like you're just trying to be ***condescending.***
I don't ***get*** you! I've been trying to be your friend.
Well, I don't remember ***asking*** you to!
Then I ***won't!***
Good!
Fine, good.

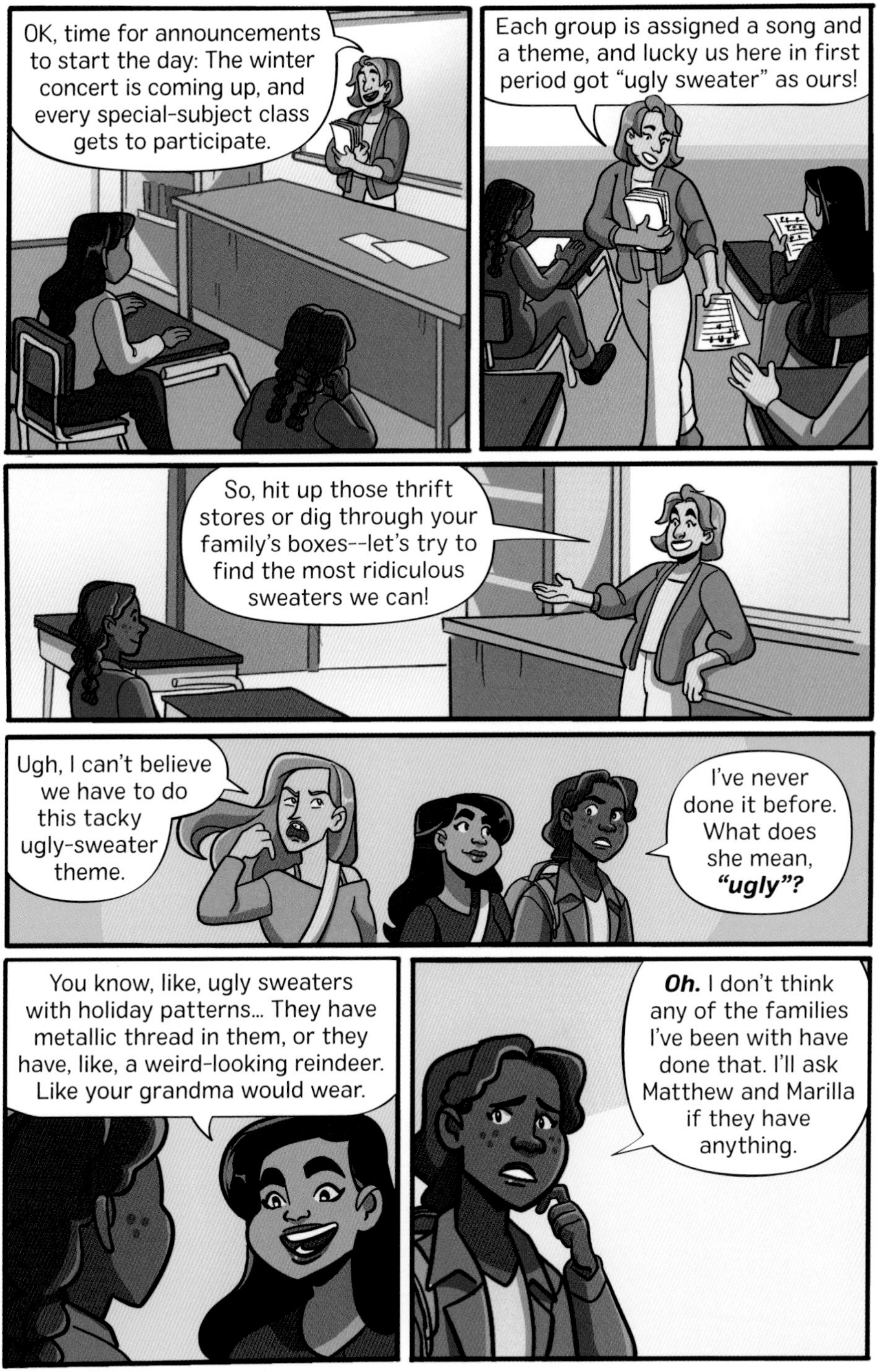
OK, time for announcements to start the day: The winter concert is coming up, and every special-subject class gets to participate.
Each group is assigned a song and a theme, and lucky us here in first period got "ugly sweater" as ours!
So, hit up those thrift stores or dig through your family's boxes--let's try to find the most ridiculous sweaters we can!
Ugh, I can't believe we have to do this tacky ugly-sweater theme.
I've never done it before. What does she mean, ***"ugly"?***
You know, like, ugly sweaters with holiday patterns... They have metallic thread in them, or they have, like, a weird-looking reindeer. Like your grandma would wear.
Oh. I don't think any of the families I've been with have done that. I'll ask Matthew and Marilla if they have anything.

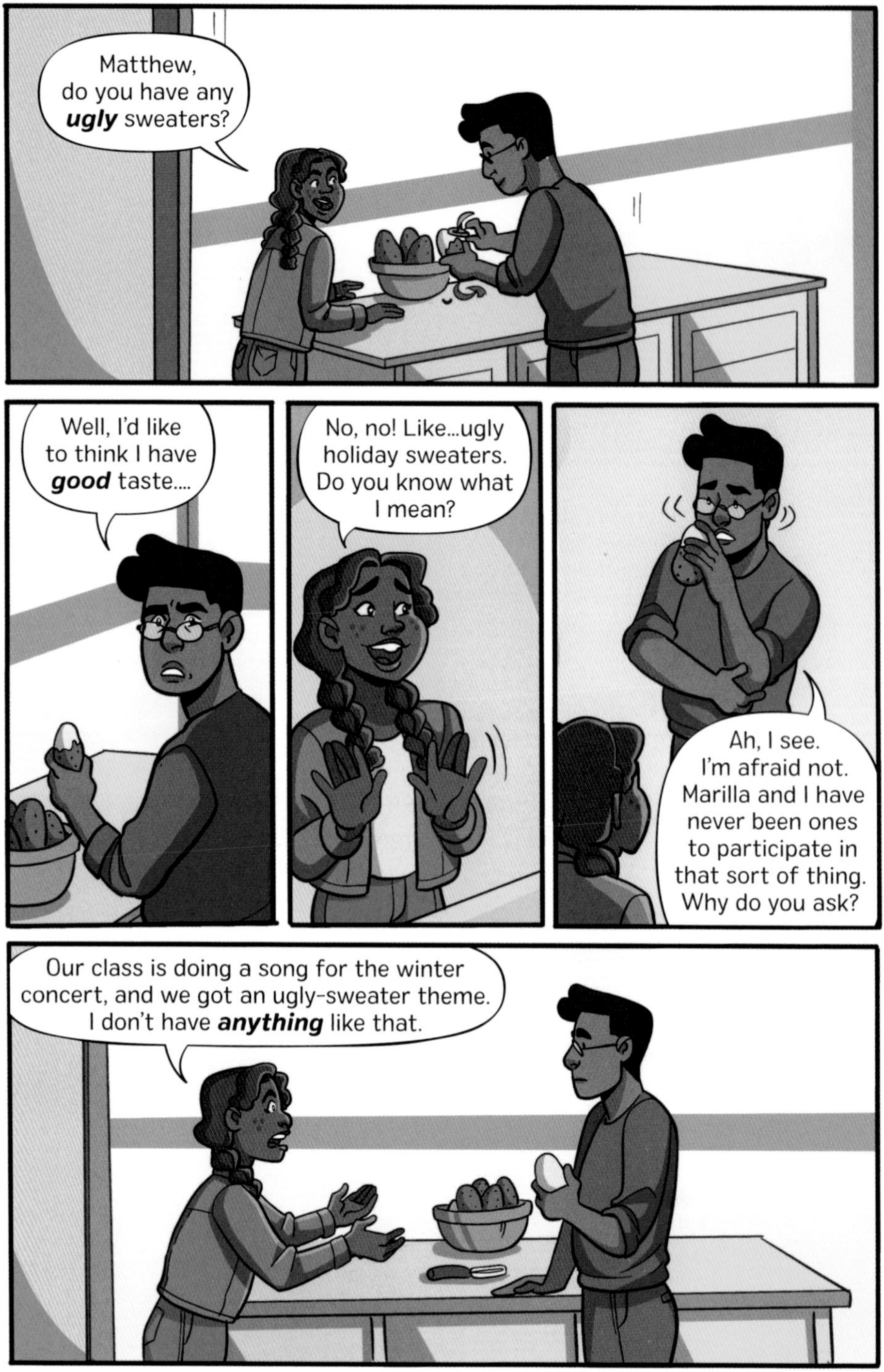
Matthew, do you have any **ugly** sweaters?
Well, I'd like to think I have **good** taste....
No, no! Like...ugly holiday sweaters. Do you know what I mean?
Ah, I see. I'm afraid not. Marilla and I have never been ones to participate in that sort of thing. Why do you ask?
Our class is doing a song for the winter concert, and we got an ugly-sweater theme. I don't have **anything** like that.

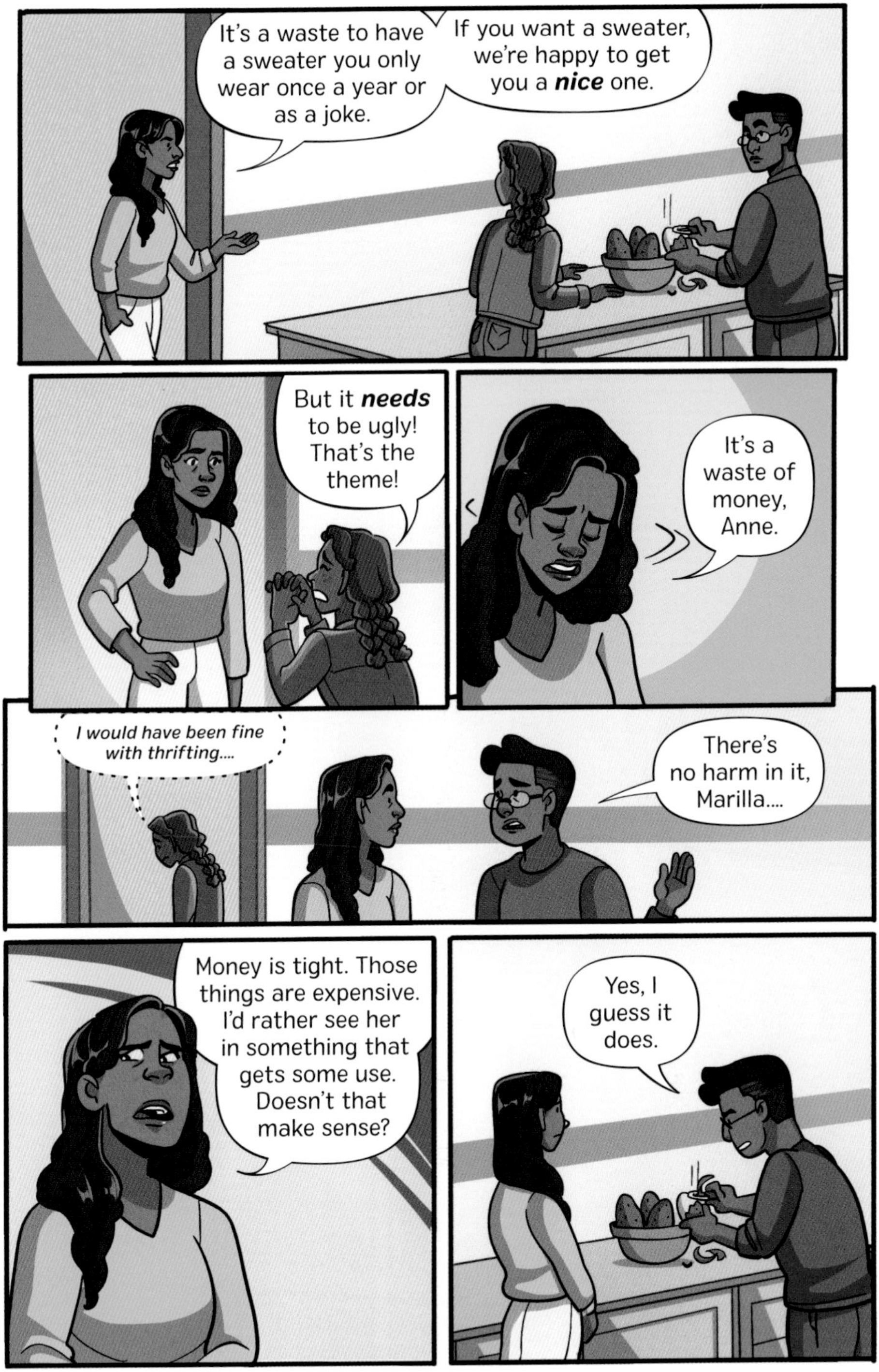

It's a waste to have a sweater you only wear once a year or as a joke.
If you want a sweater, we're happy to get you a ***nice*** one.
But it ***needs*** to be ugly! That's the theme!
It's a waste of money, Anne.
I would have been fine with thrifting....
There's no harm in it, Marilla....
Money is tight. Those things are expensive. I'd rather see her in something that gets some use. Doesn't that make sense?
Yes, I guess it does.

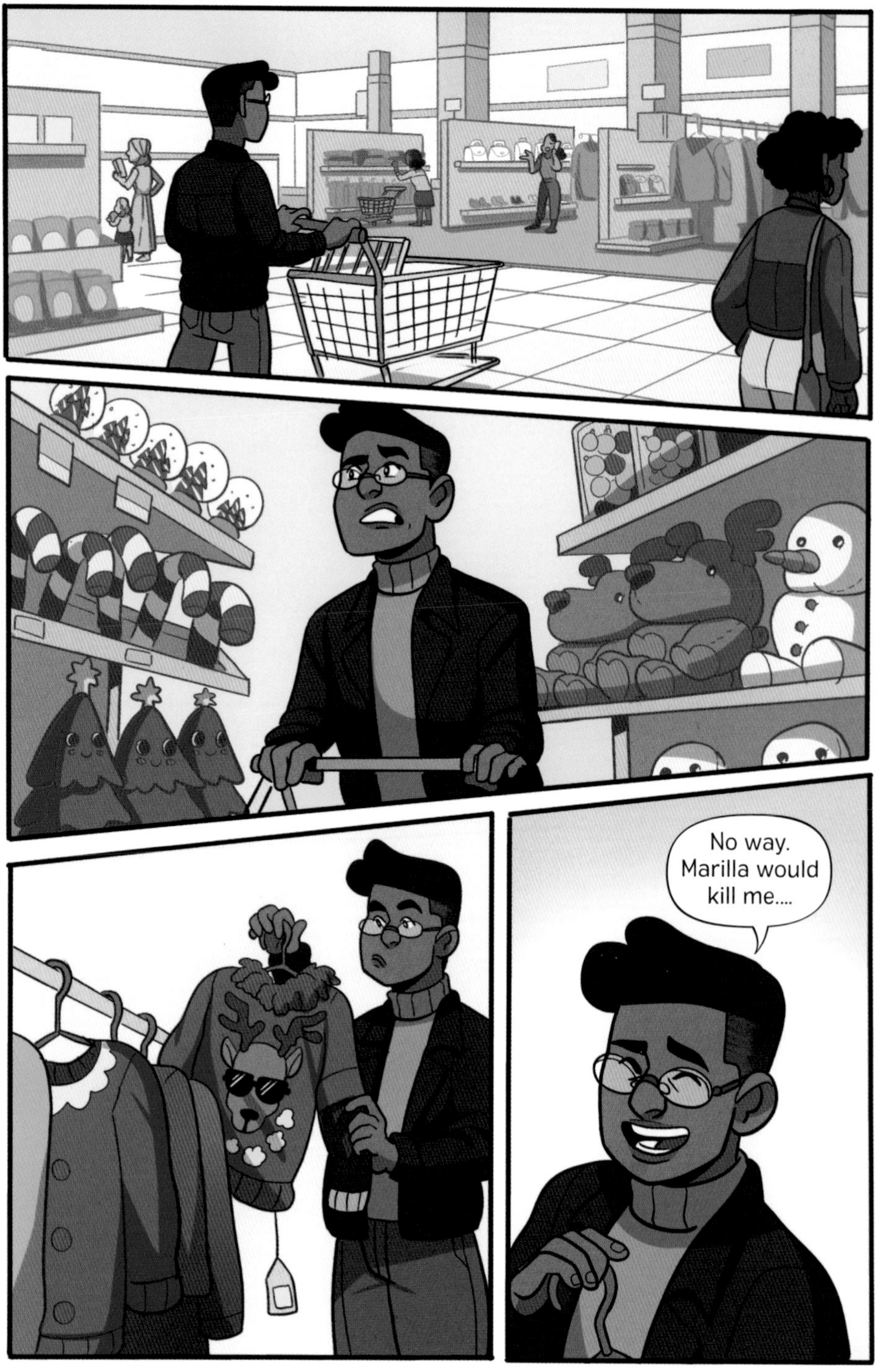
No way. Marilla would kill me....

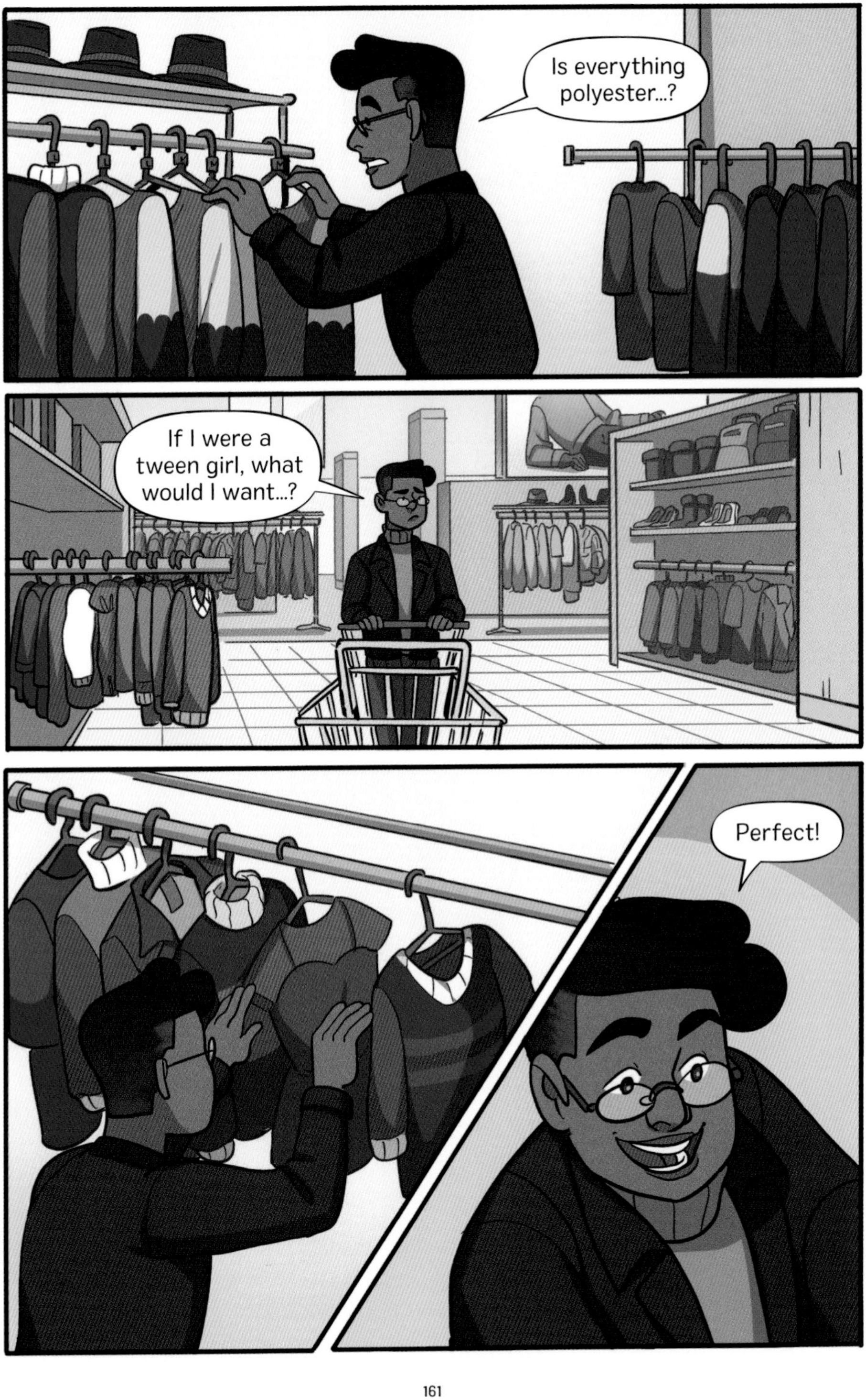
Is everything polyester...?
If I were a tween girl, what would I want...?
Perfect!

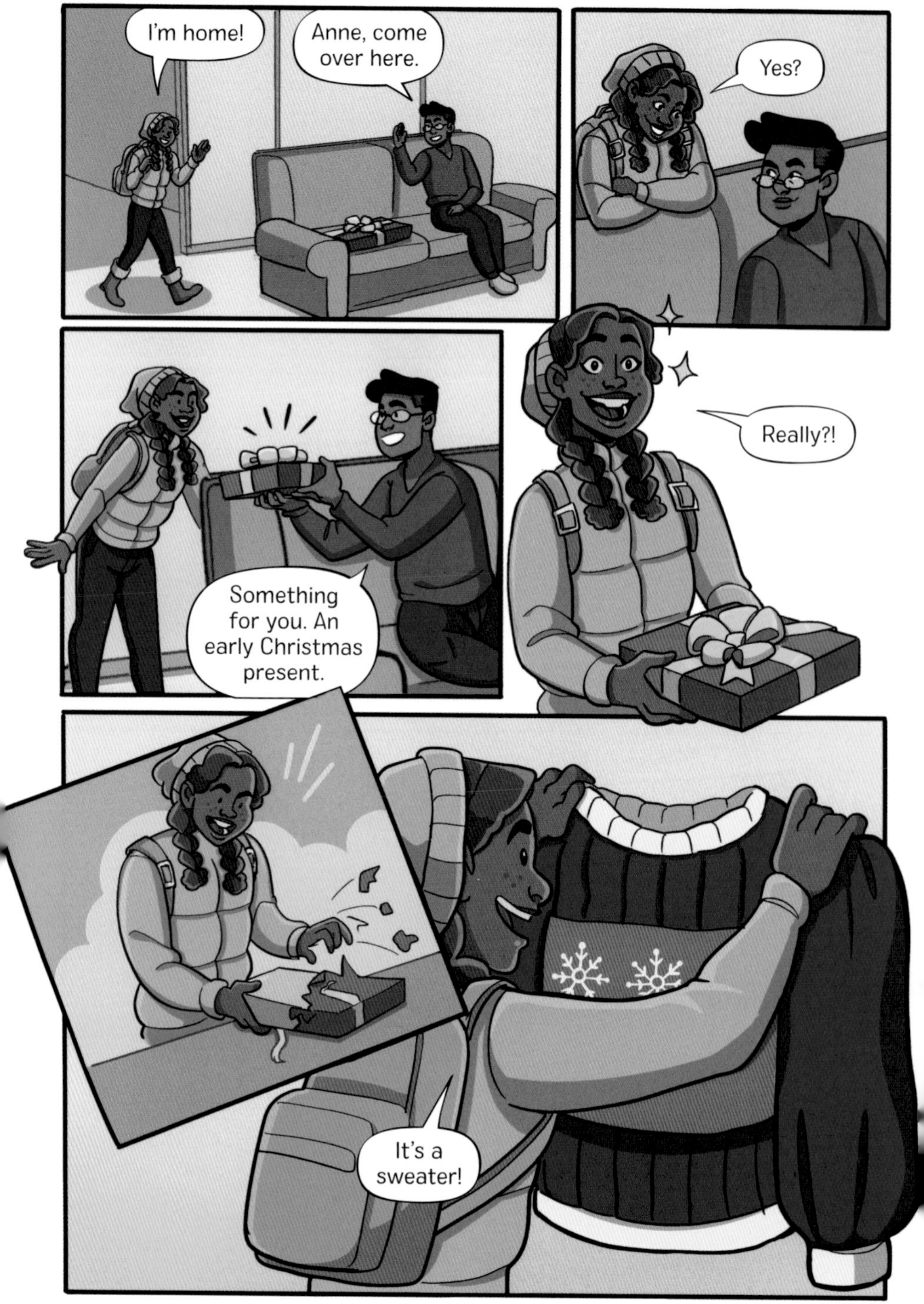
I'm home!
Anne, come over here.
Yes?
Something for you. An early Christmas present.
Really?!
It's a sweater!

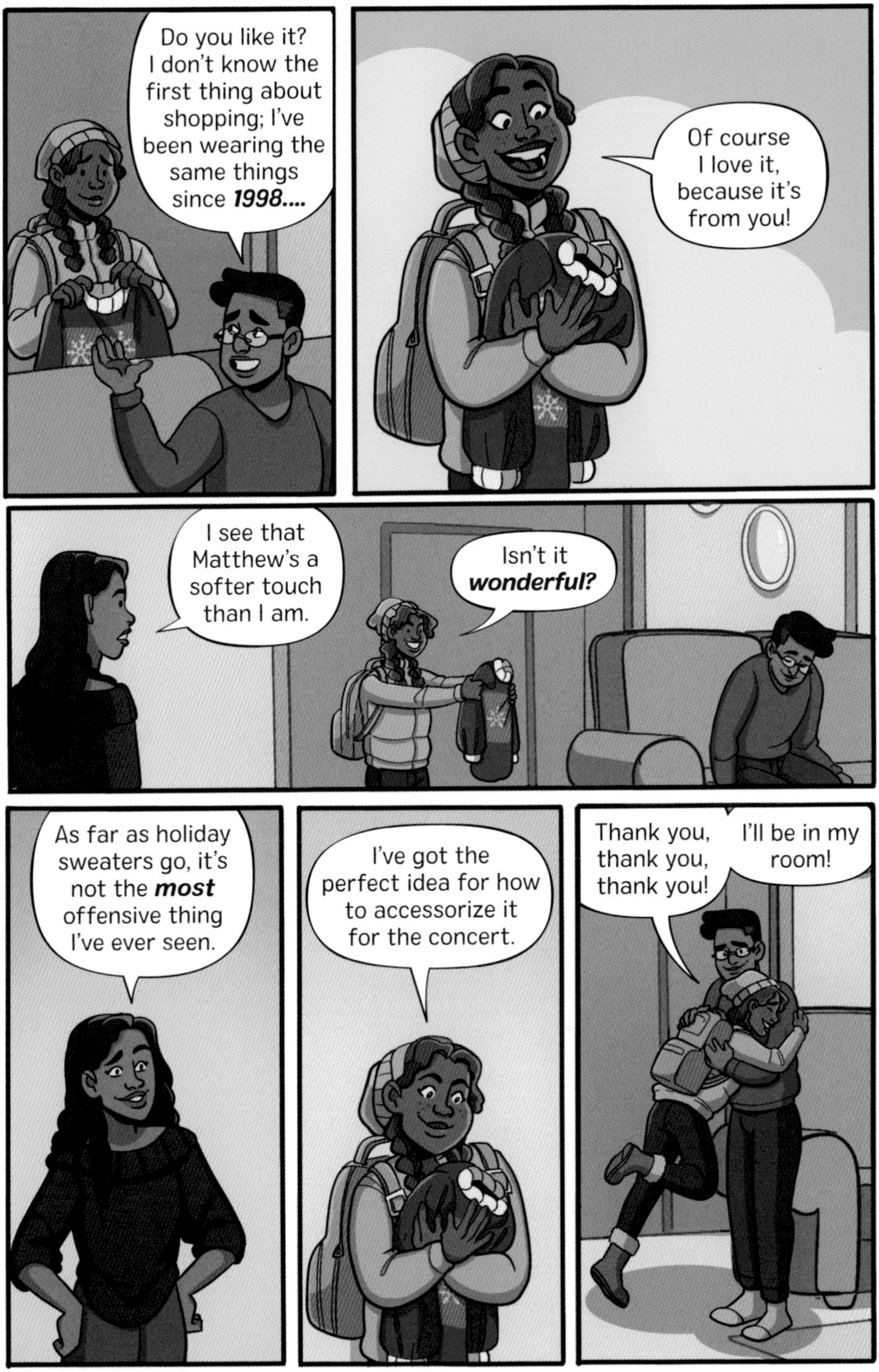
Do you like it? I don't know the first thing about shopping; I've been wearing the same things since *1998....*
Of course I love it, because it's from you!
I see that Matthew's a softer touch than I am.
Isn't it *wonderful?*
As far as holiday sweaters go, it's not the *most* offensive thing I've ever seen.
I've got the perfect idea for how to accessorize it for the concert.
Thank you, thank you, thank you!
I'll be in my room!

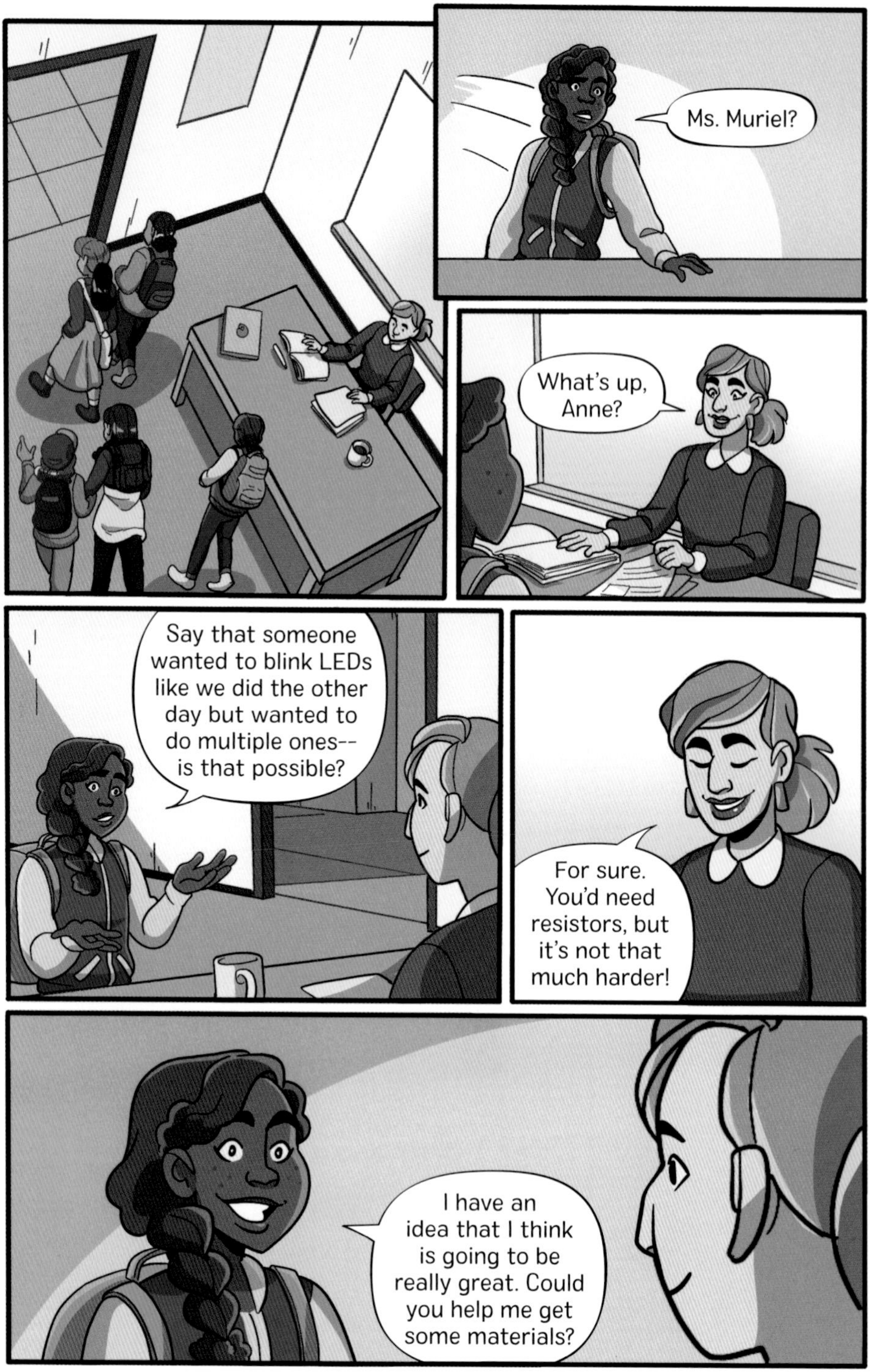
Ms. Muriel?
What's up, Anne?
Say that someone wanted to blink LEDs like we did the other day but wanted to do multiple ones-- is that possible?
For sure. You'd need resistors, but it's not that much harder!
I have an idea that I think is going to be really great. Could you help me get some materials?

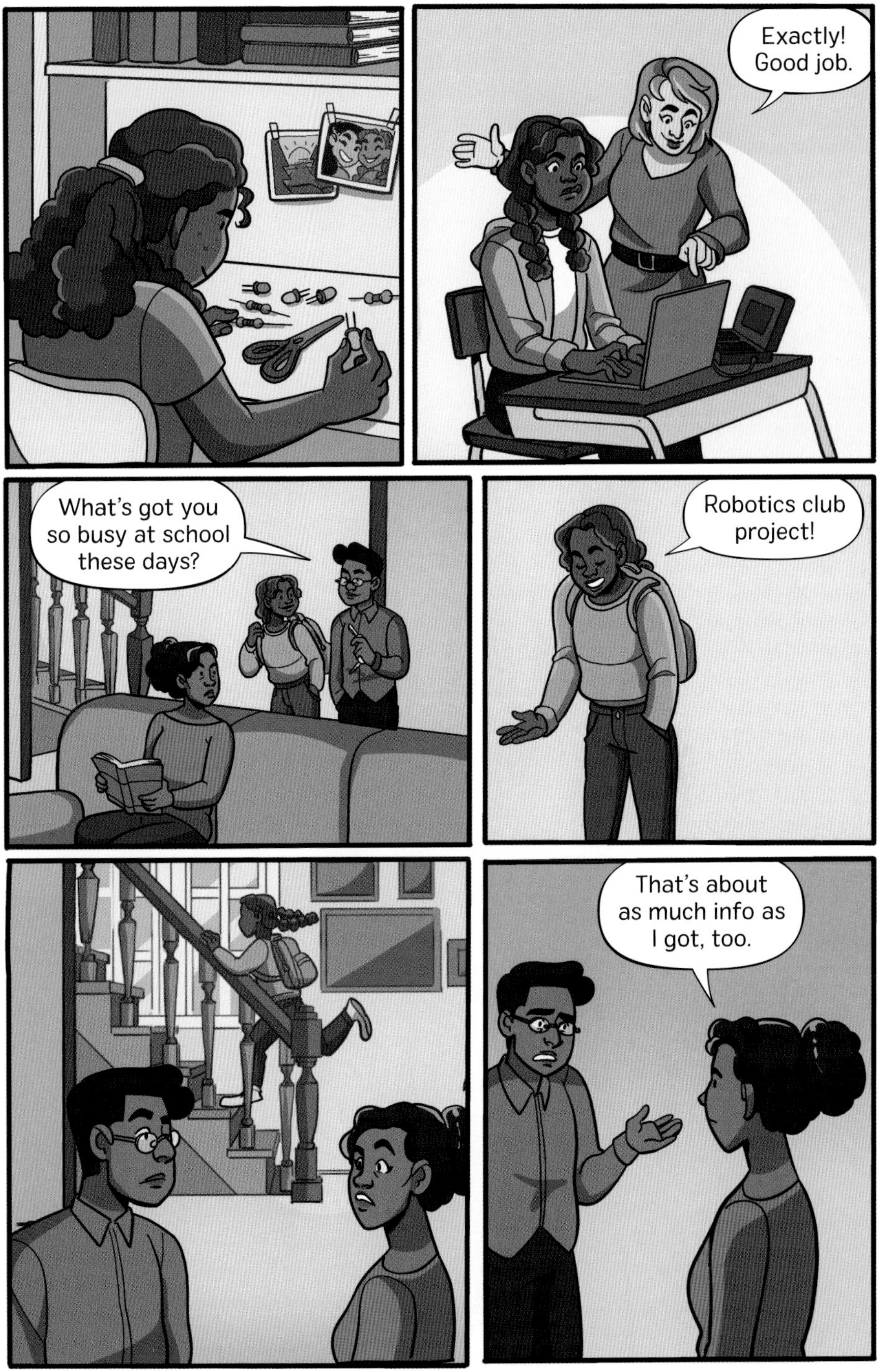
Exactly! Good job.
What's got you so busy at school these days?
Robotics club project!
That's about as much info as I got, too.

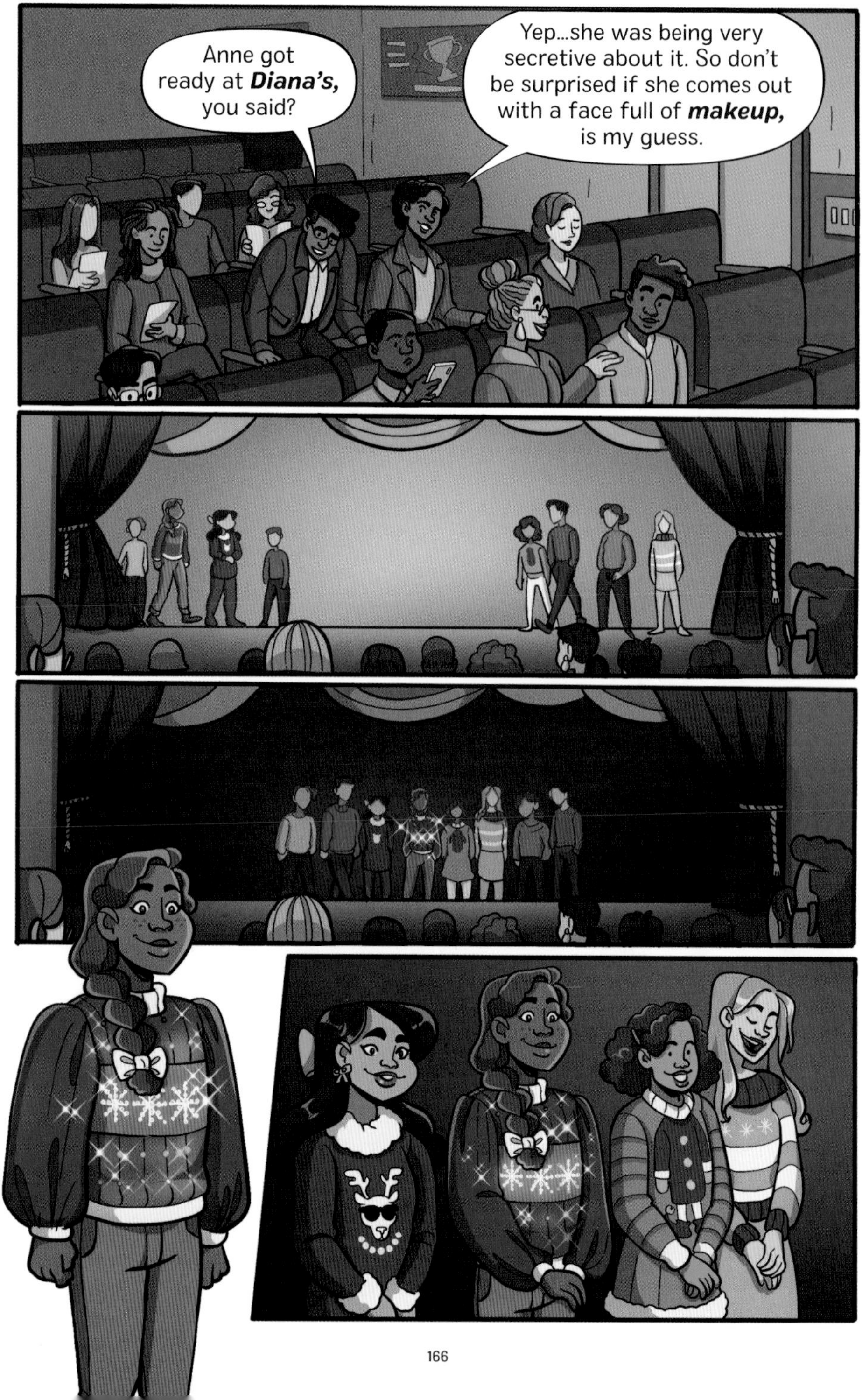
Anne got ready at ***Diana's,*** you said?
Yep...she was being very secretive about it. So don't be surprised if she comes out with a face full of ***makeup,*** is my guess.

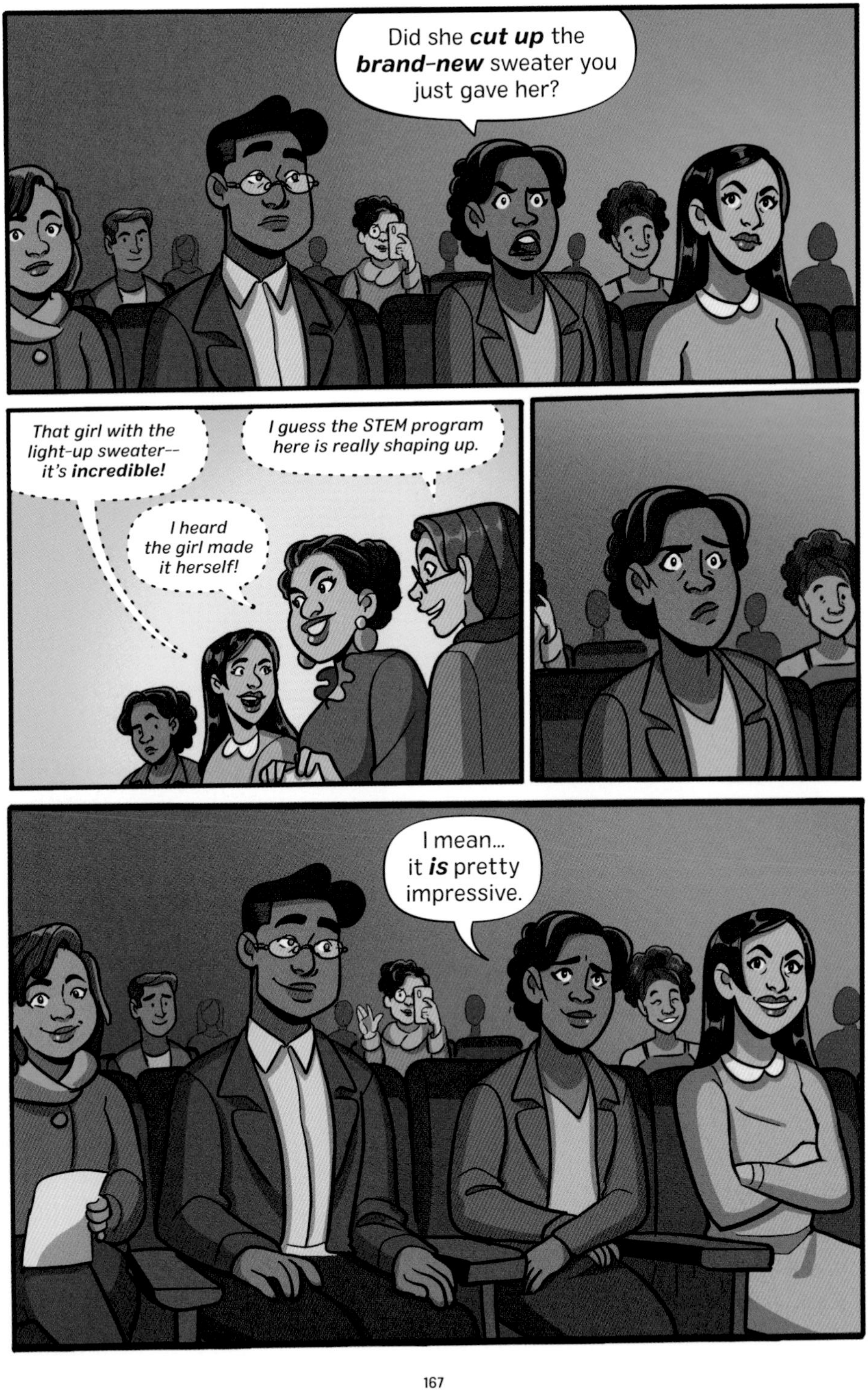
Did she **cut up** the **brand-new** sweater you just gave her?
That girl with the light-up sweater-- it's **incredible!**
I guess the STEM program here is really shaping up.
I heard the girl made it herself!
I mean... it **is** pretty impressive.

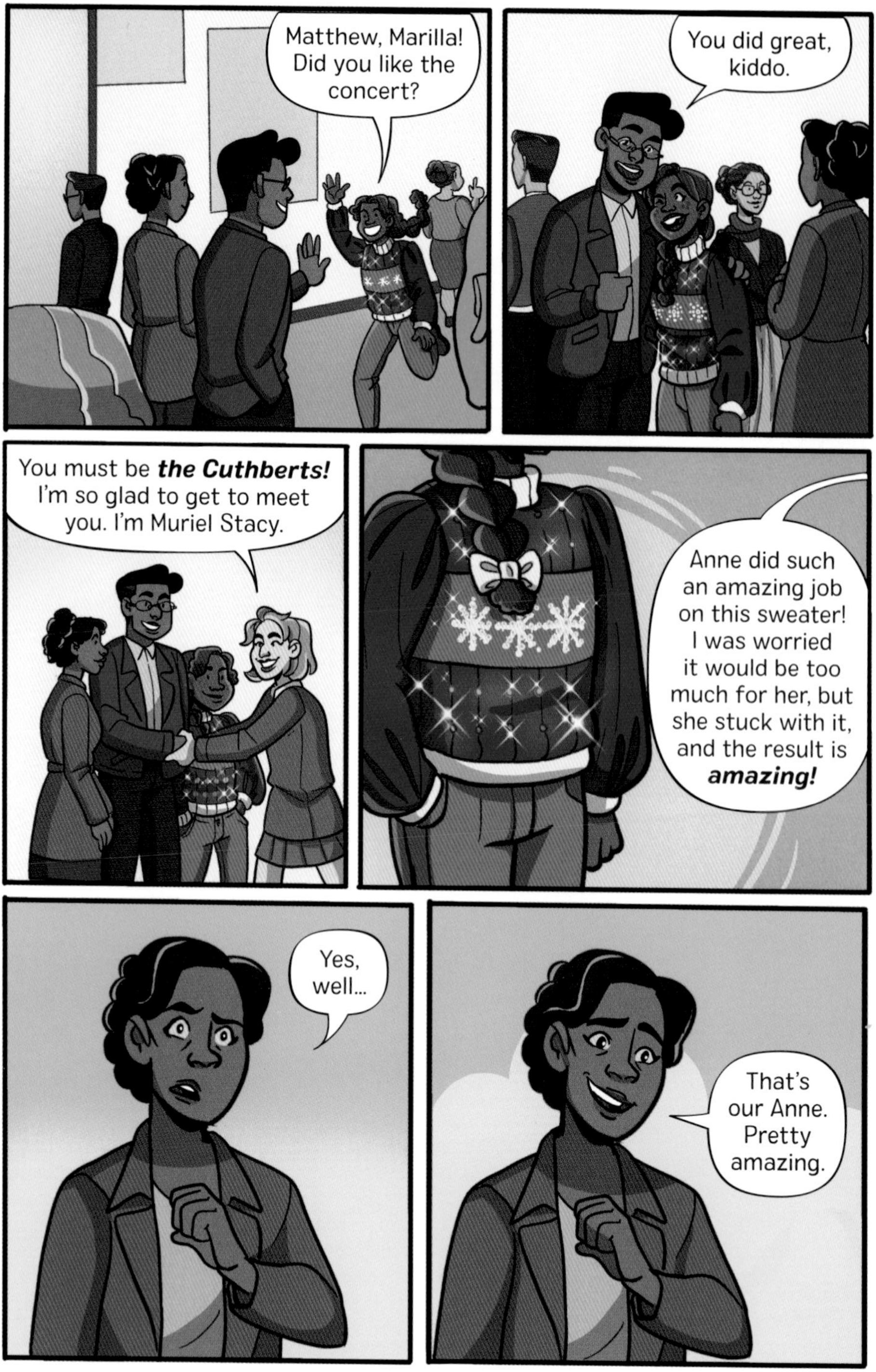
Matthew, Marilla! Did you like the concert?
You did great, kiddo.
You must be ***the Cuthberts!*** I'm so glad to get to meet you. I'm Muriel Stacy.
Anne did such an amazing job on this sweater! I was worried it would be too much for her, but she stuck with it, and the result is ***amazing!***
Yes, well...
That's our Anne. Pretty amazing.

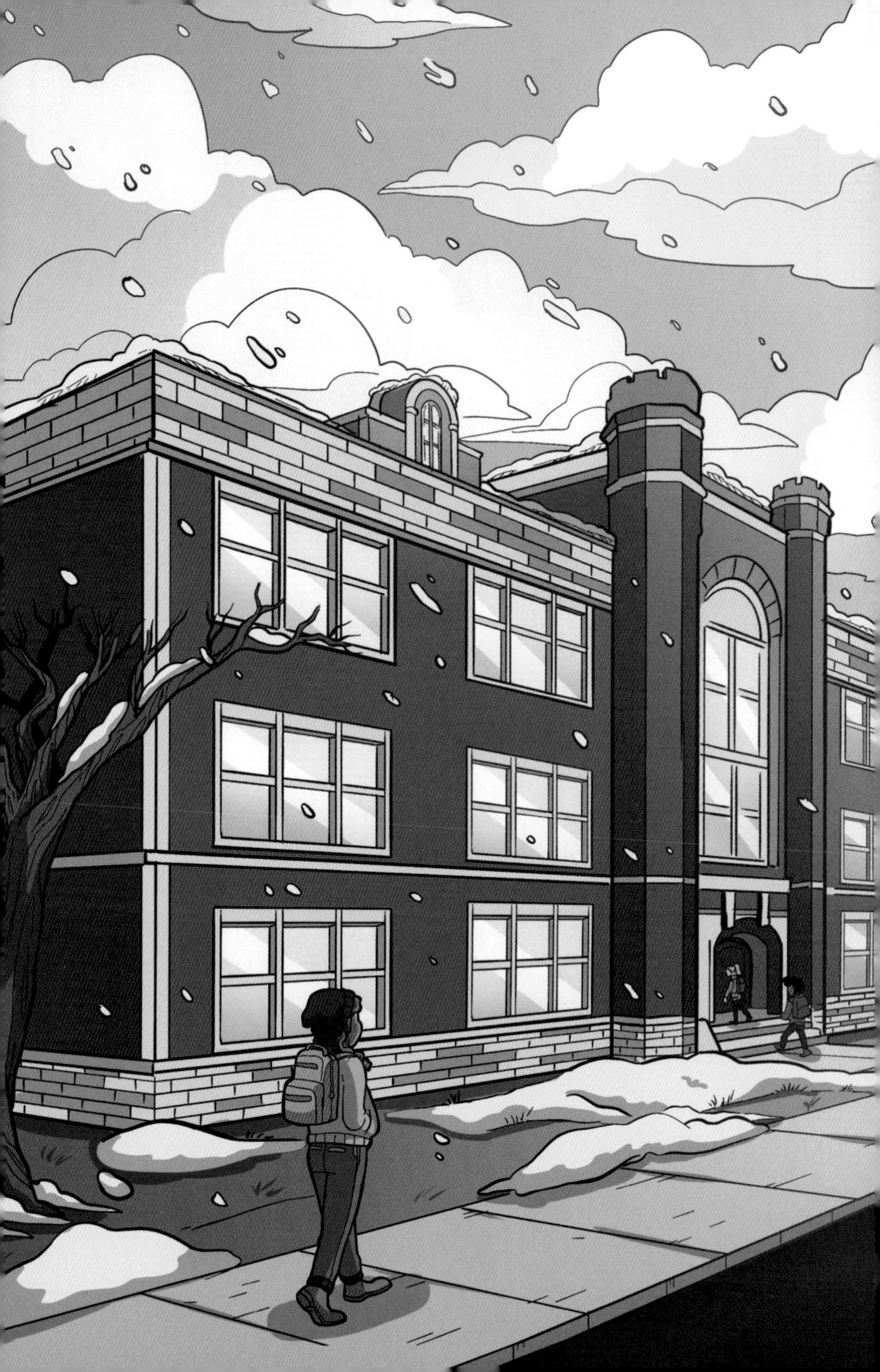

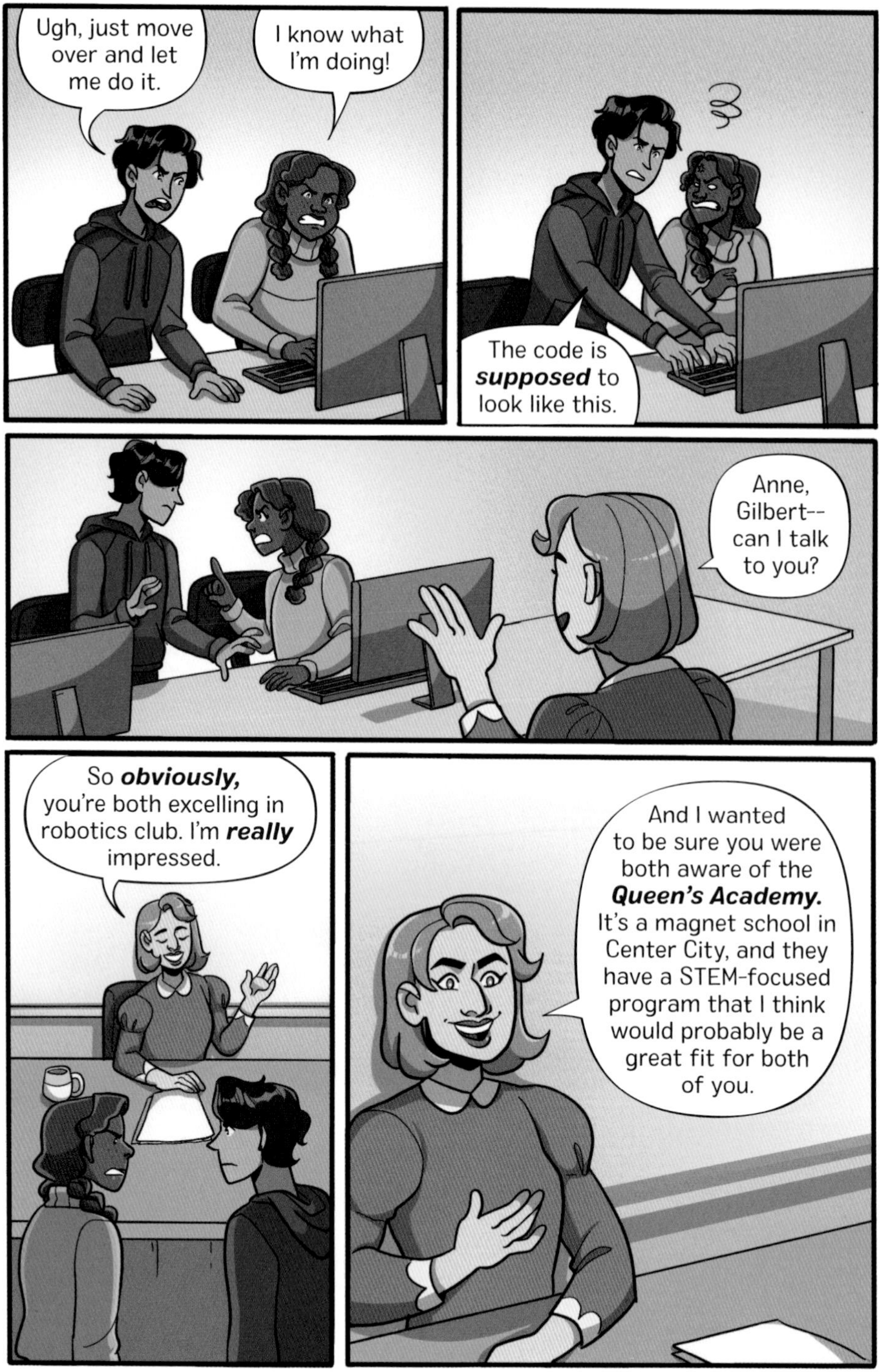
Ugh, just move over and let me do it.
I know what I'm doing!
The code is ***supposed*** to look like this.
Anne, Gilbert-- can I talk to you?
So ***obviously,*** you're both excelling in robotics club. I'm ***really*** impressed.
And I wanted to be sure you were both aware of the ***Queen's Academy.*** It's a magnet school in Center City, and they have a STEM-focused program that I think would probably be a great fit for both of you.

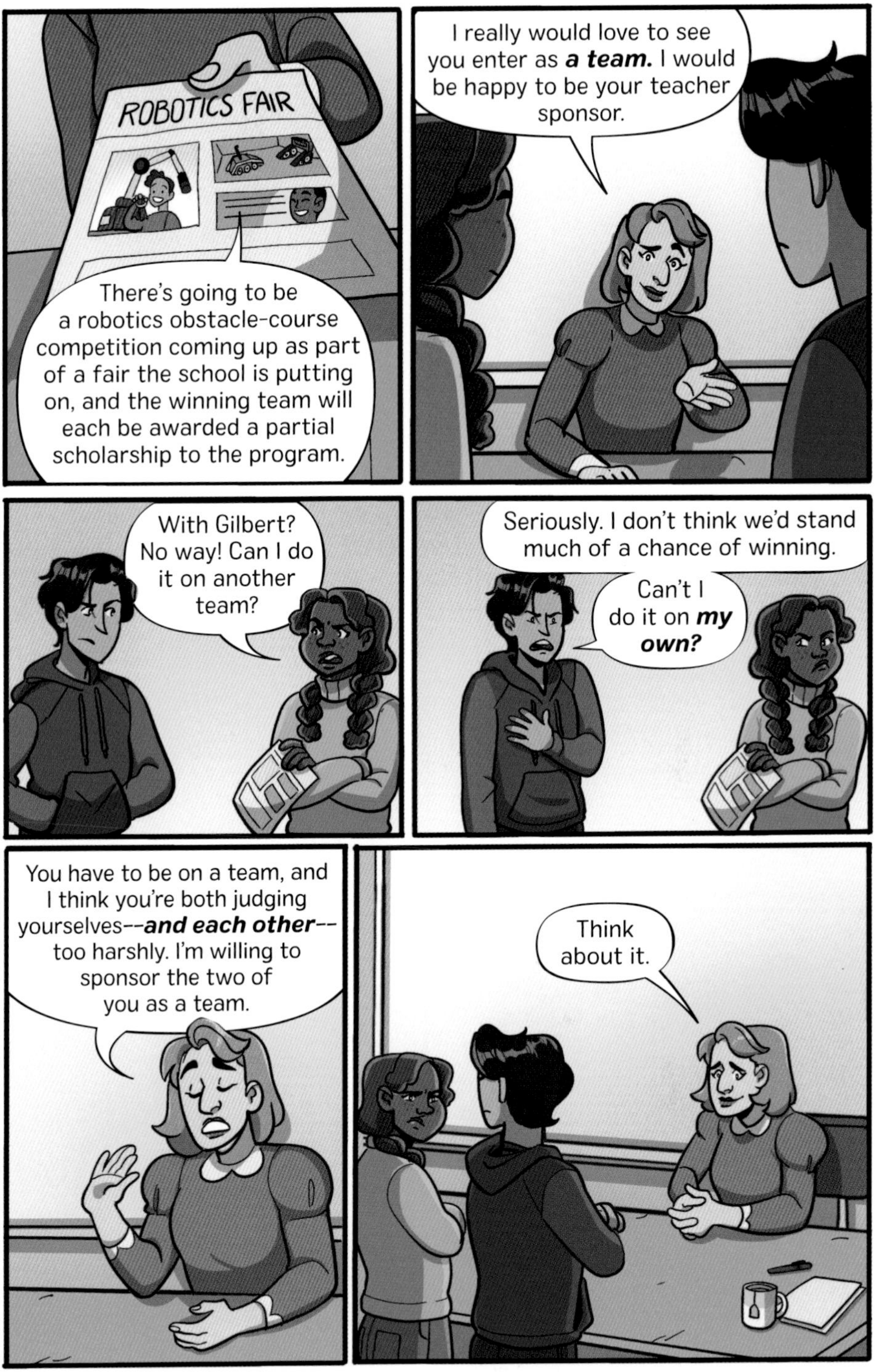
ROBOTICS FAIR
There's going to be a robotics obstacle-course competition coming up as part of a fair the school is putting on, and the winning team will each be awarded a partial scholarship to the program.
I really would love to see you enter as ***a team.*** I would be happy to be your teacher sponsor.
With Gilbert? No way! Can I do it on another team?
Seriously. I don't think we'd stand much of a chance of winning.
Can't I do it on ***my own?***
You have to be on a team, and I think you're both judging yourselves--***and each other***--too harshly. I'm willing to sponsor the two of you as a team.
Think about it.

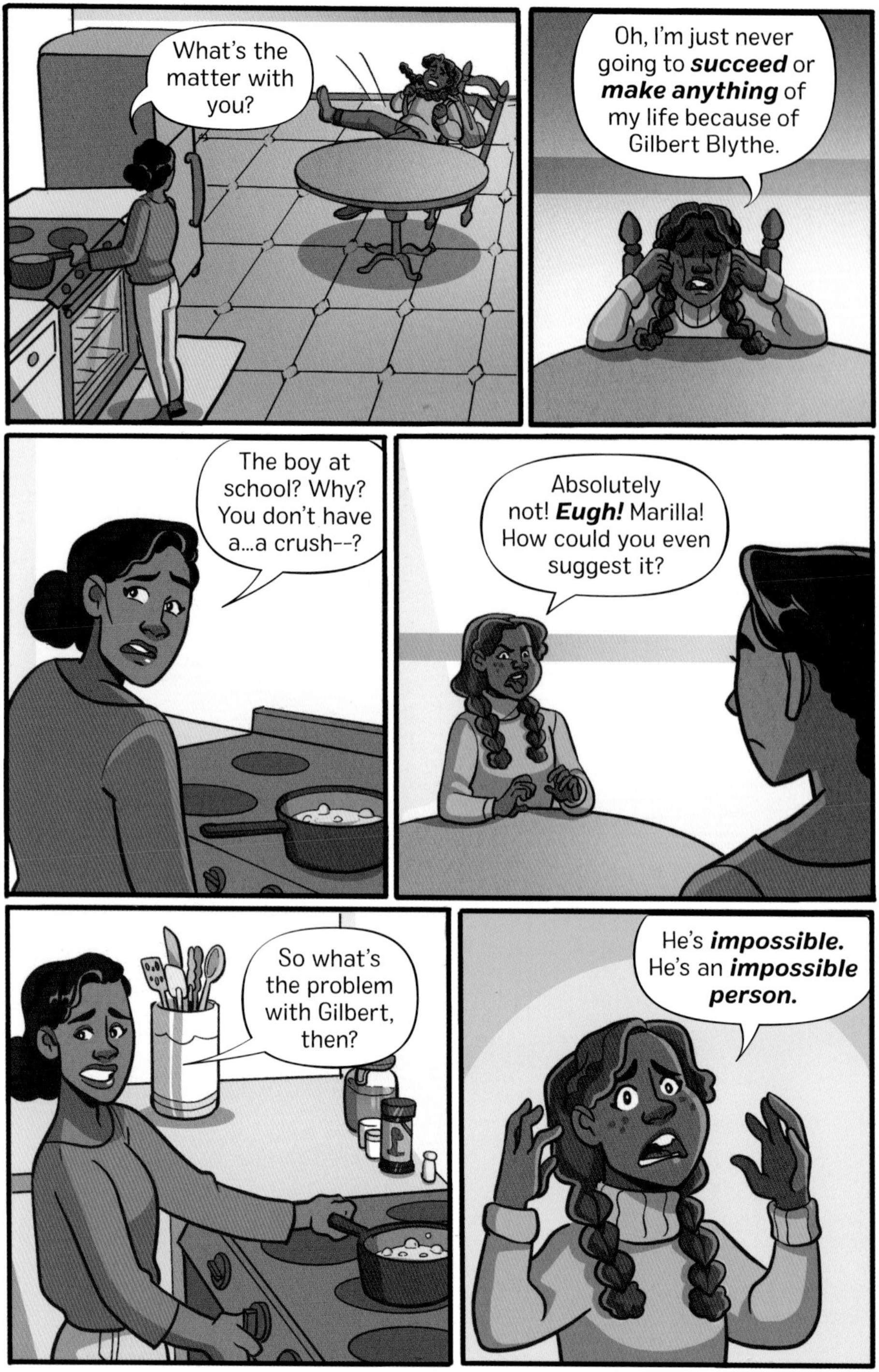
What's the matter with you?
Oh, I'm just never going to ***succeed*** or ***make anything*** of my life because of Gilbert Blythe.
The boy at school? Why? You don't have a...a crush--?
Absolutely not! ***Eugh!*** Marilla! How could you even suggest it?
So what's the problem with Gilbert, then?
He's ***impossible.*** He's an ***impossible person.***

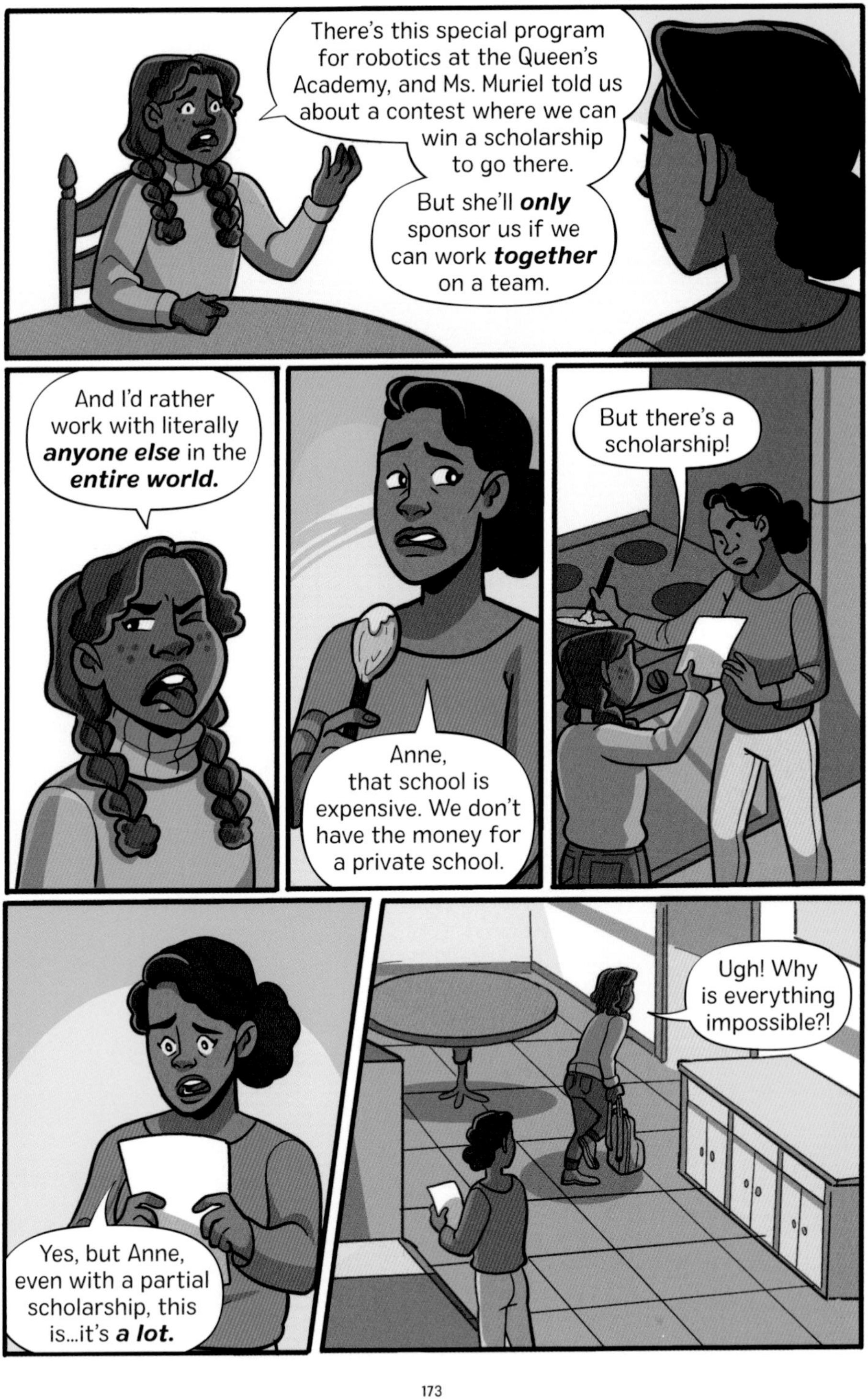
There's this special program for robotics at the Queen's Academy, and Ms. Muriel told us about a contest where we can win a scholarship to go there.
But she'll *only* sponsor us if we can work *together* on a team.
And I'd rather work with literally *anyone else* in the *entire world.*
Anne, that school is expensive. We don't have the money for a private school.
But there's a scholarship!
Yes, but Anne, even with a partial scholarship, this is...it's *a lot.*
Ugh! Why is everything impossible?!

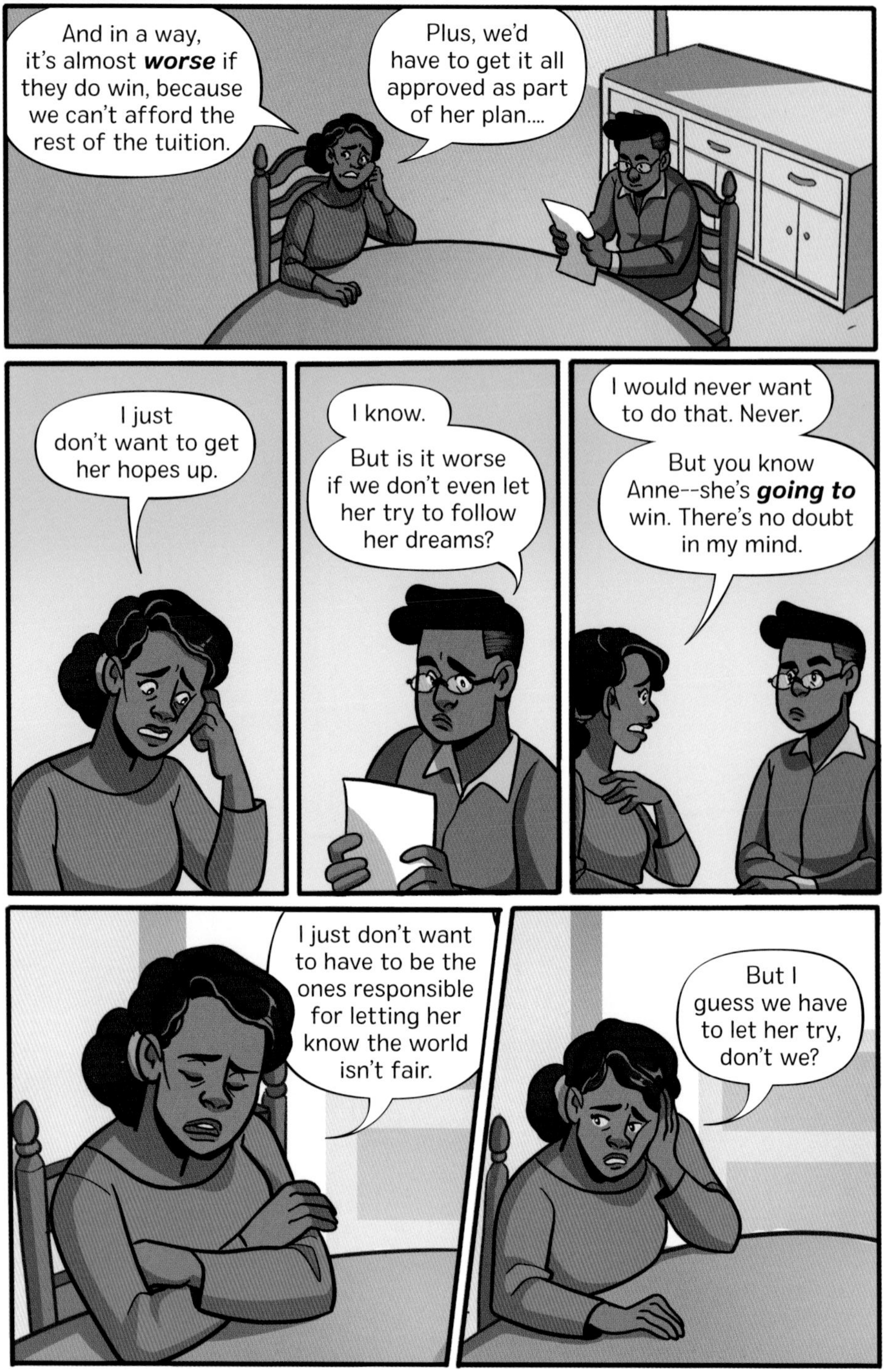
And in a way, it's almost ***worse*** if they do win, because we can't afford the rest of the tuition.
Plus, we'd have to get it all approved as part of her plan....
I just don't want to get her hopes up.
I know.
But is it worse if we don't even let her try to follow her dreams?
I would never want to do that. Never.
But you know Anne--she's ***going to*** win. There's no doubt in my mind.
I just don't want to have to be the ones responsible for letting her know the world isn't fair.
But I guess we have to let her try, don't we?

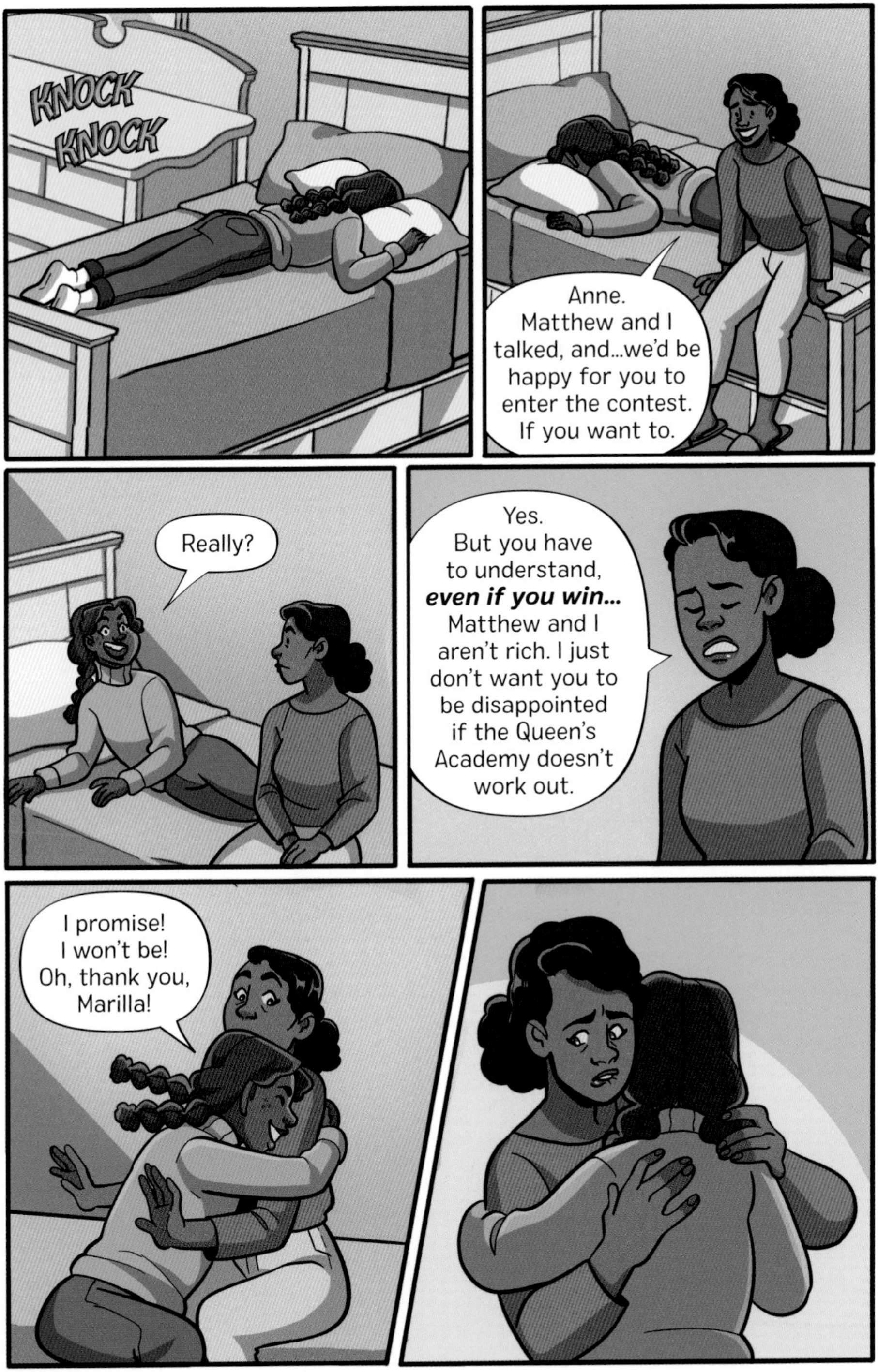
KNOCK KNOCK
Anne. Matthew and I talked, and...we'd be happy for you to enter the contest. If you want to.
Really?
Yes. But you have to understand, ***even if you win...*** Matthew and I aren't rich. I just don't want you to be disappointed if the Queen's Academy doesn't work out.
I promise! I won't be! Oh, thank you, Marilla!

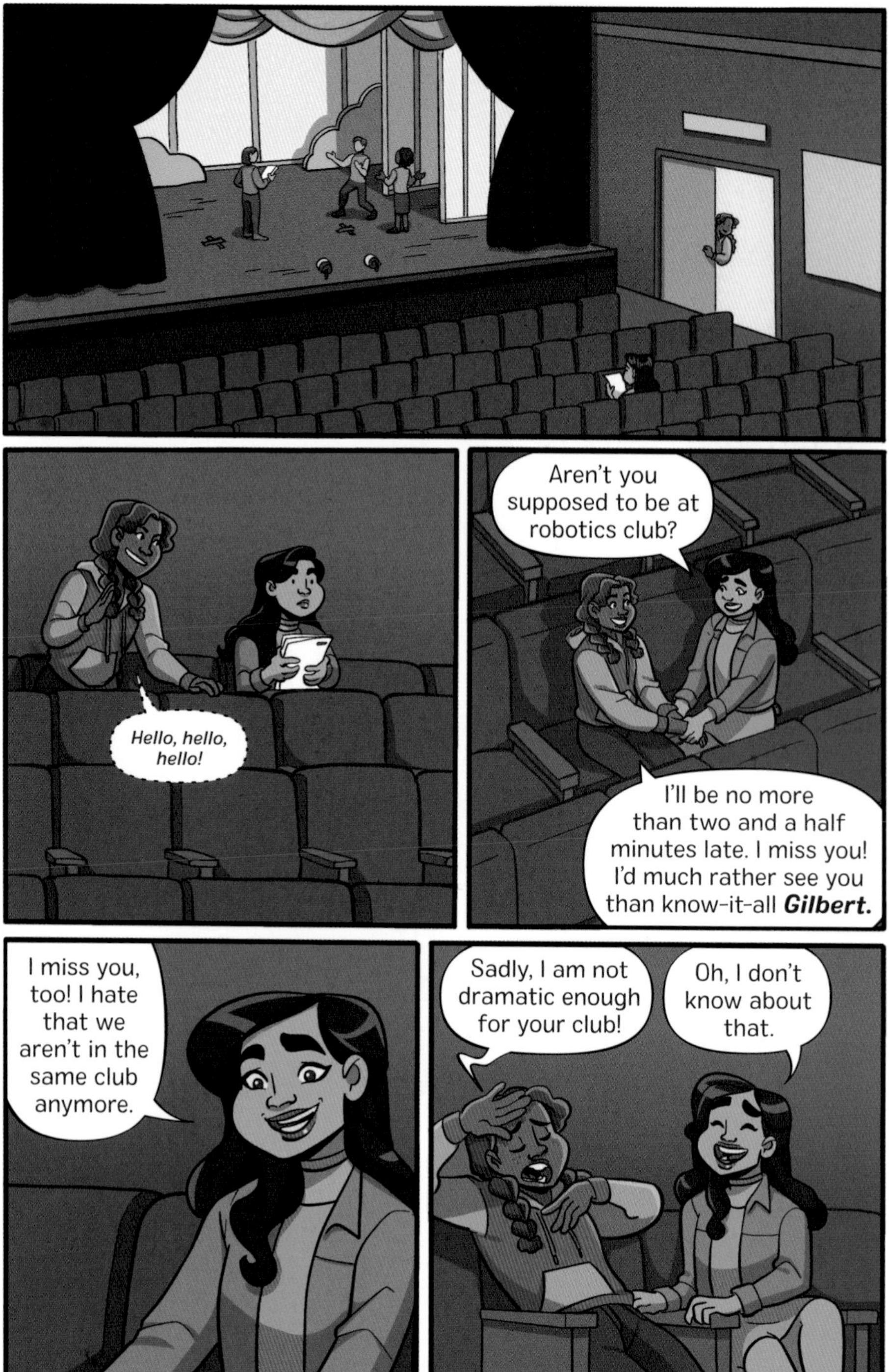

Hello, hello, hello!
Aren't you supposed to be at robotics club?
I'll be no more than two and a half minutes late. I miss you! I'd much rather see you than know-it-all ***Gilbert.***
I miss you, too! I hate that we aren't in the same club anymore.
Sadly, I am not dramatic enough for your club!
Oh, I don't know about that.

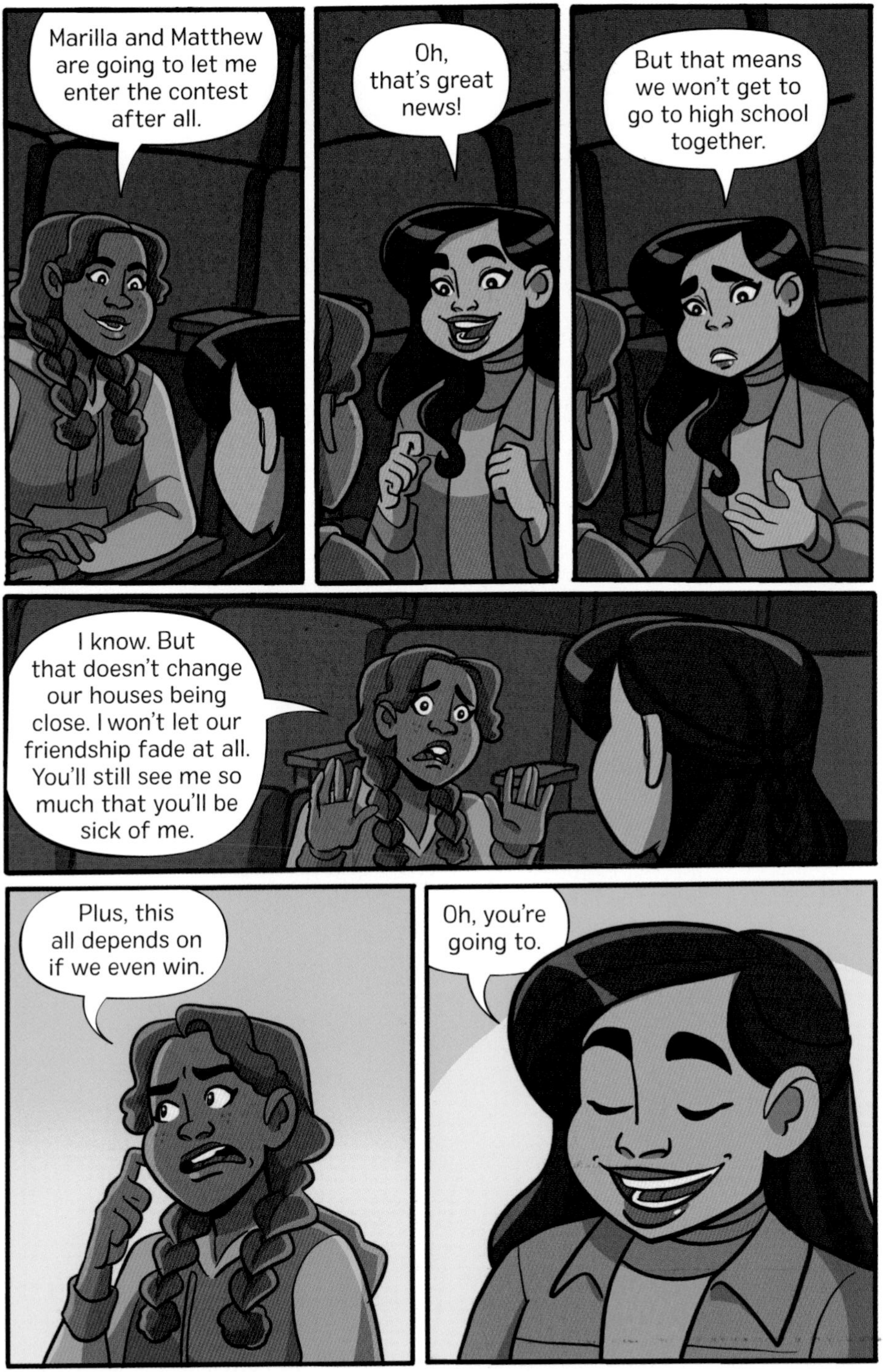
Marilla and Matthew are going to let me enter the contest after all.
Oh, that's great news!
But that means we won't get to go to high school together.
I know. But that doesn't change our houses being close. I won't let our friendship fade at all. You'll still see me so much that you'll be sick of me.
Plus, this all depends on if we even win.
Oh, you're going to.

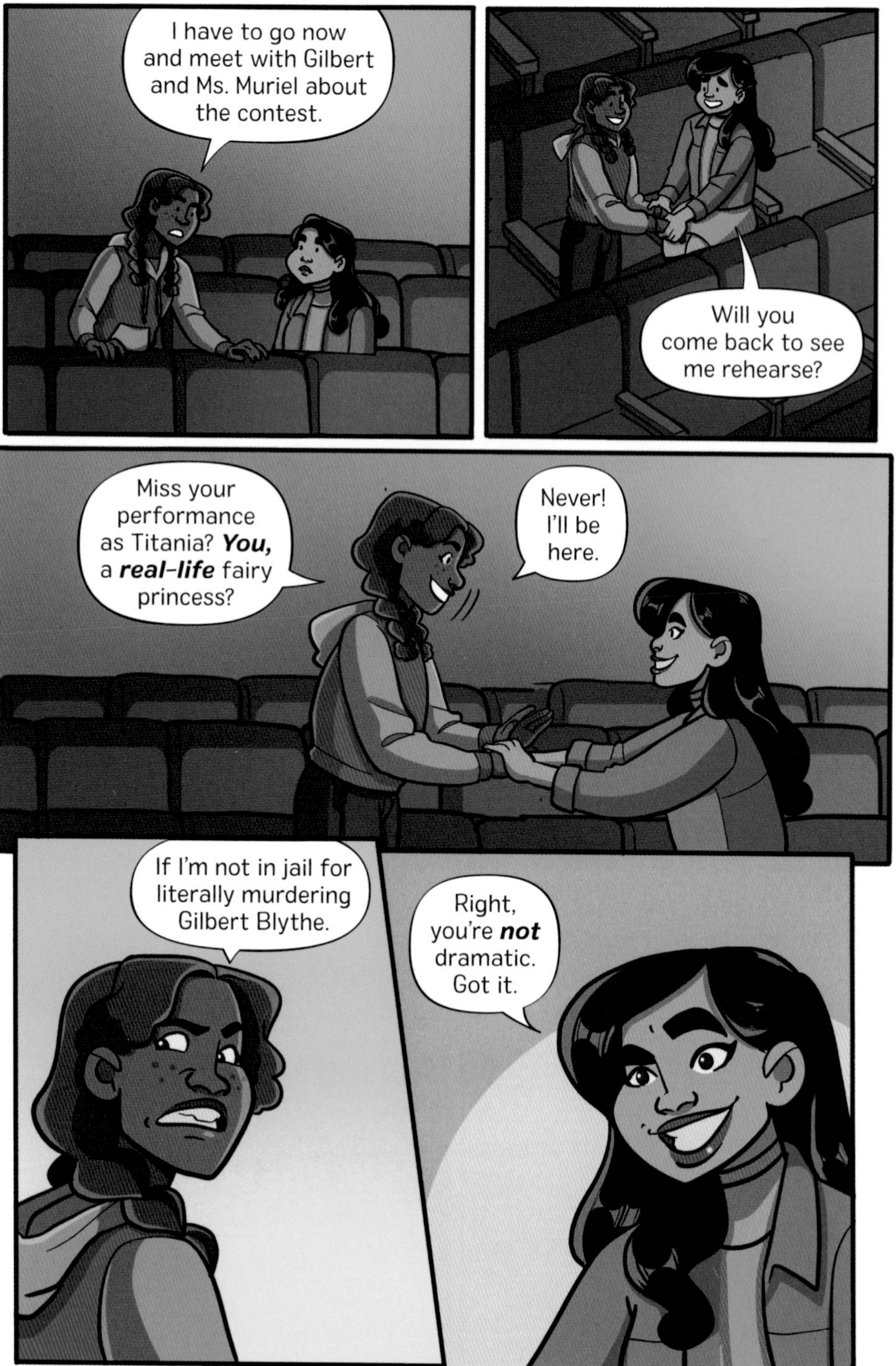
I have to go now and meet with Gilbert and Ms. Muriel about the contest.
Will you come back to see me rehearse?
Miss your performance as Titania? ***You,*** a ***real-life*** fairy princess?
Never! I'll be here.
If I'm not in jail for literally murdering Gilbert Blythe.
Right, you're ***not*** dramatic. Got it.

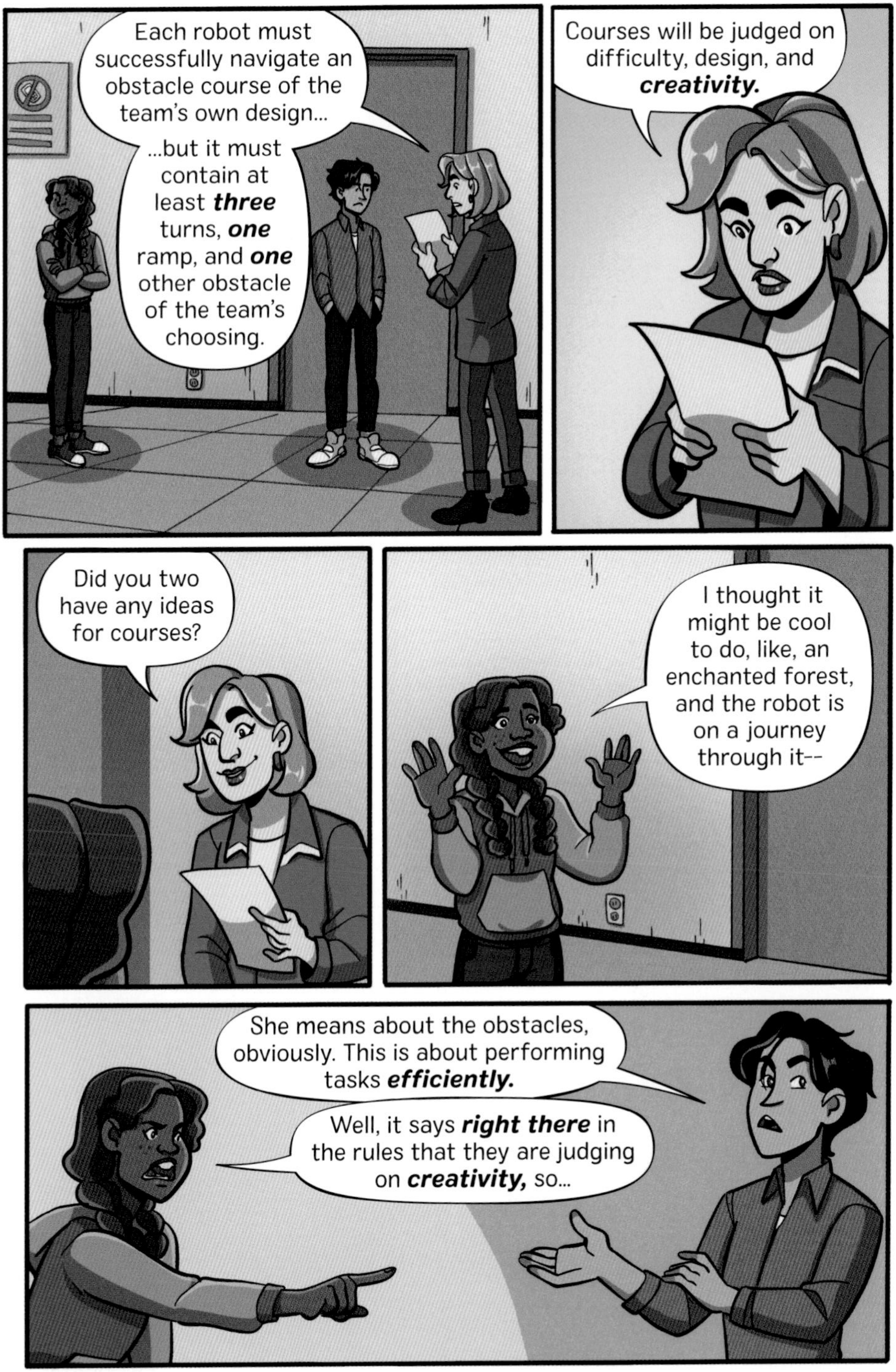
Each robot must successfully navigate an obstacle course of the team's own design...
...but it must contain at least ***three*** turns, ***one*** ramp, and ***one*** other obstacle of the team's choosing.
Courses will be judged on difficulty, design, and ***creativity.***
Did you two have any ideas for courses?
I thought it might be cool to do, like, an enchanted forest, and the robot is on a journey through it--
She means about the obstacles, obviously. This is about performing tasks ***efficiently.***
Well, it says ***right there*** in the rules that they are judging on ***creativity,*** so...

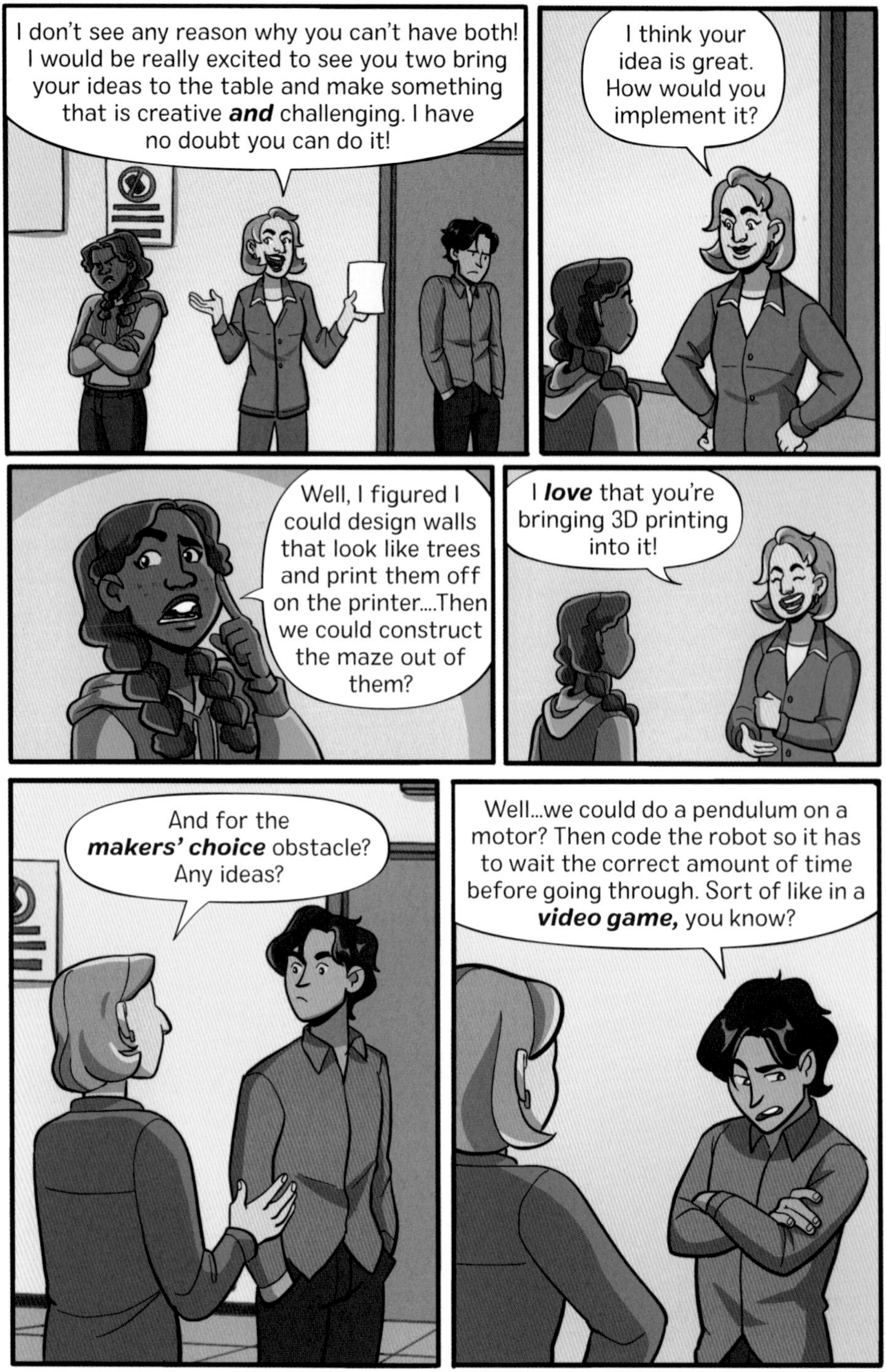
I don't see any reason why you can't have both! I would be really excited to see you two bring your ideas to the table and make something that is creative ***and*** challenging. I have no doubt you can do it!
I think your idea is great. How would you implement it?
Well, I figured I could design walls that look like trees and print them off on the printer....Then we could construct the maze out of them?
I ***love*** that you're bringing 3D printing into it!
And for the ***makers' choice*** obstacle? Any ideas?
Well...we could do a pendulum on a motor? Then code the robot so it has to wait the correct amount of time before going through. Sort of like in a ***video game,*** you know?

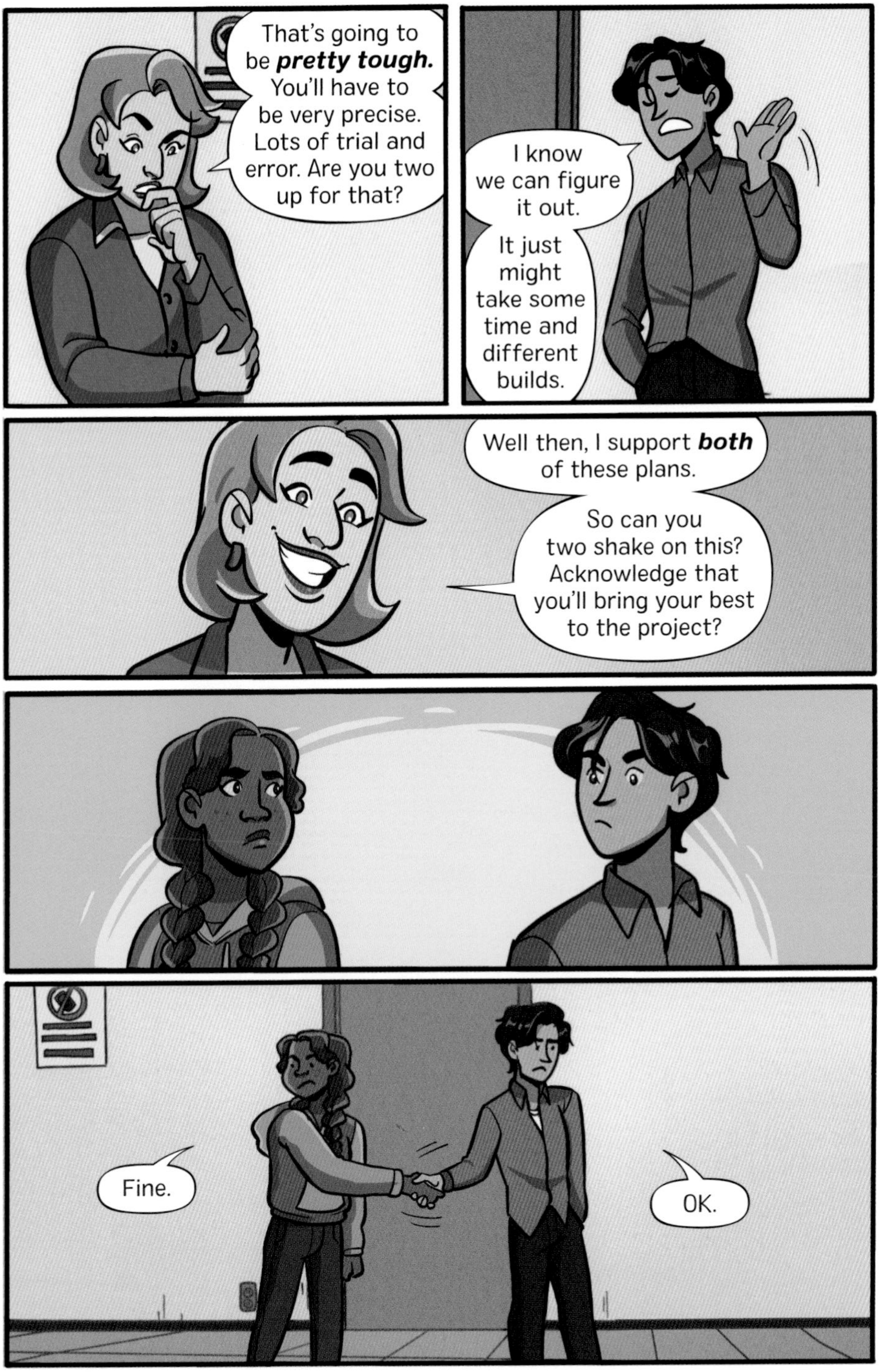
That's going to be **pretty tough.** You'll have to be very precise. Lots of trial and error. Are you two up for that?
I know we can figure it out.
It just might take some time and different builds.
Well then, I support **both** of these plans.
So can you two shake on this? Acknowledge that you'll bring your best to the project?
Fine.
OK.

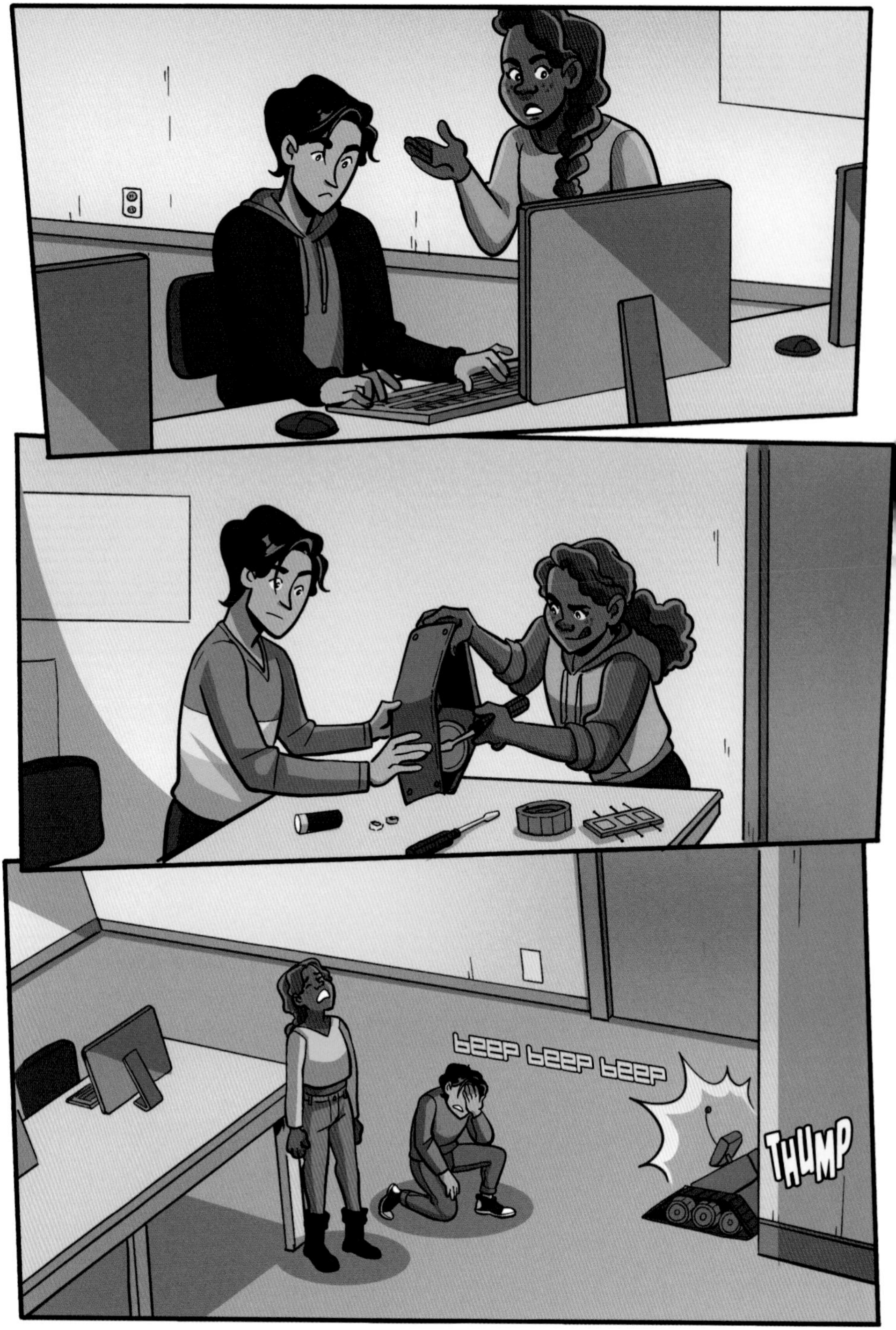
BEEP BEEP BEEP
THUMP

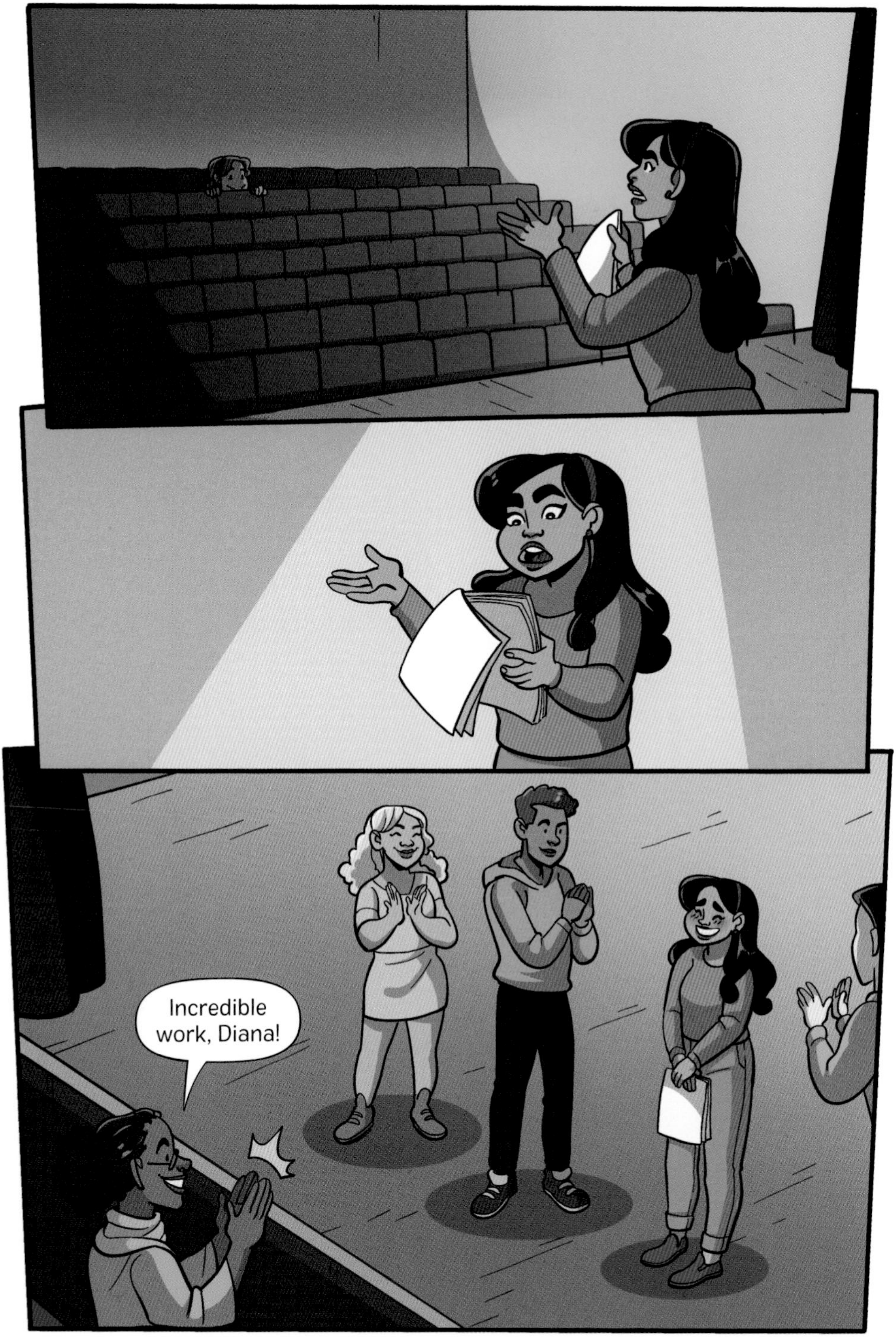
Incredible work, Diana!

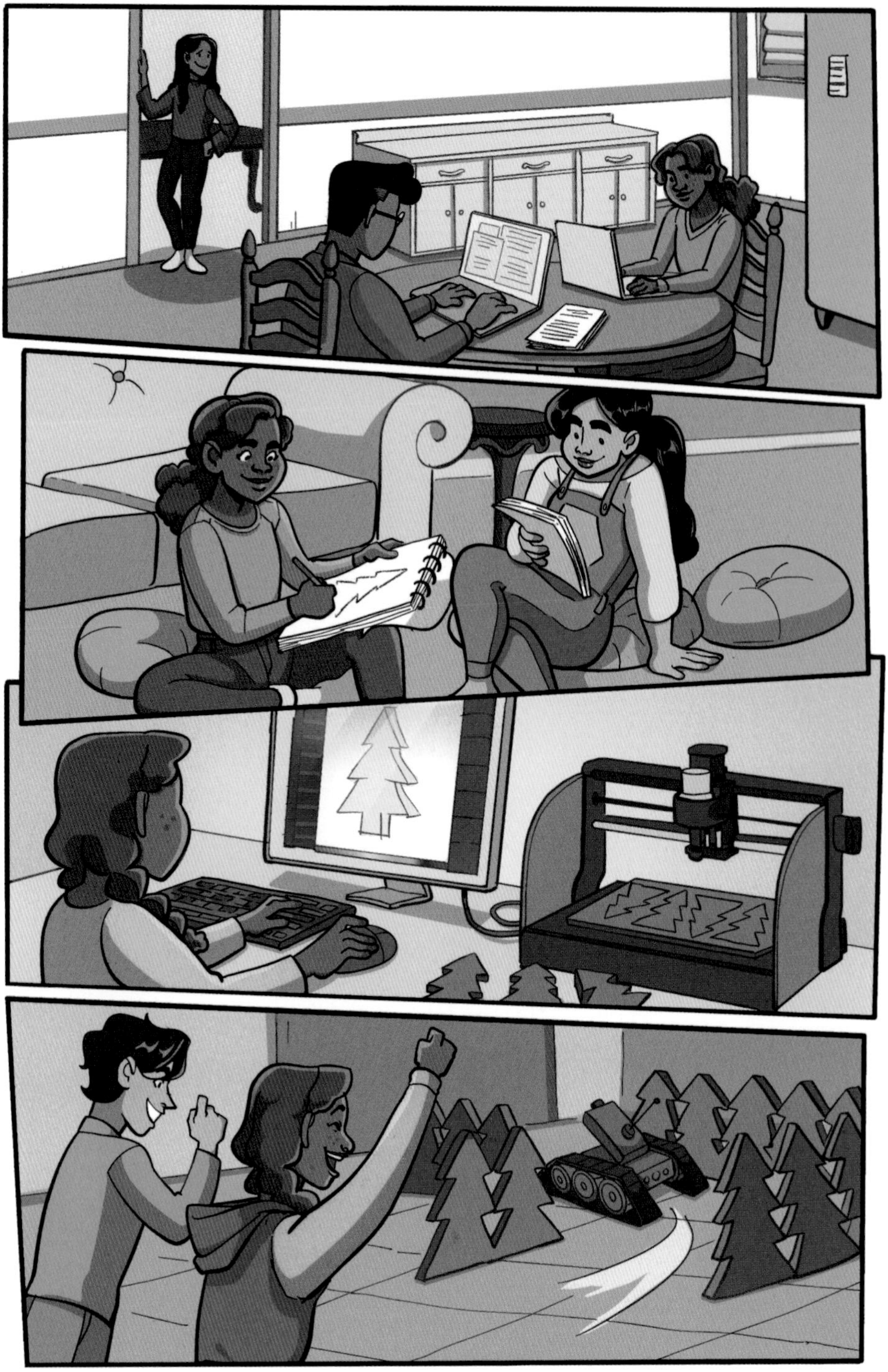

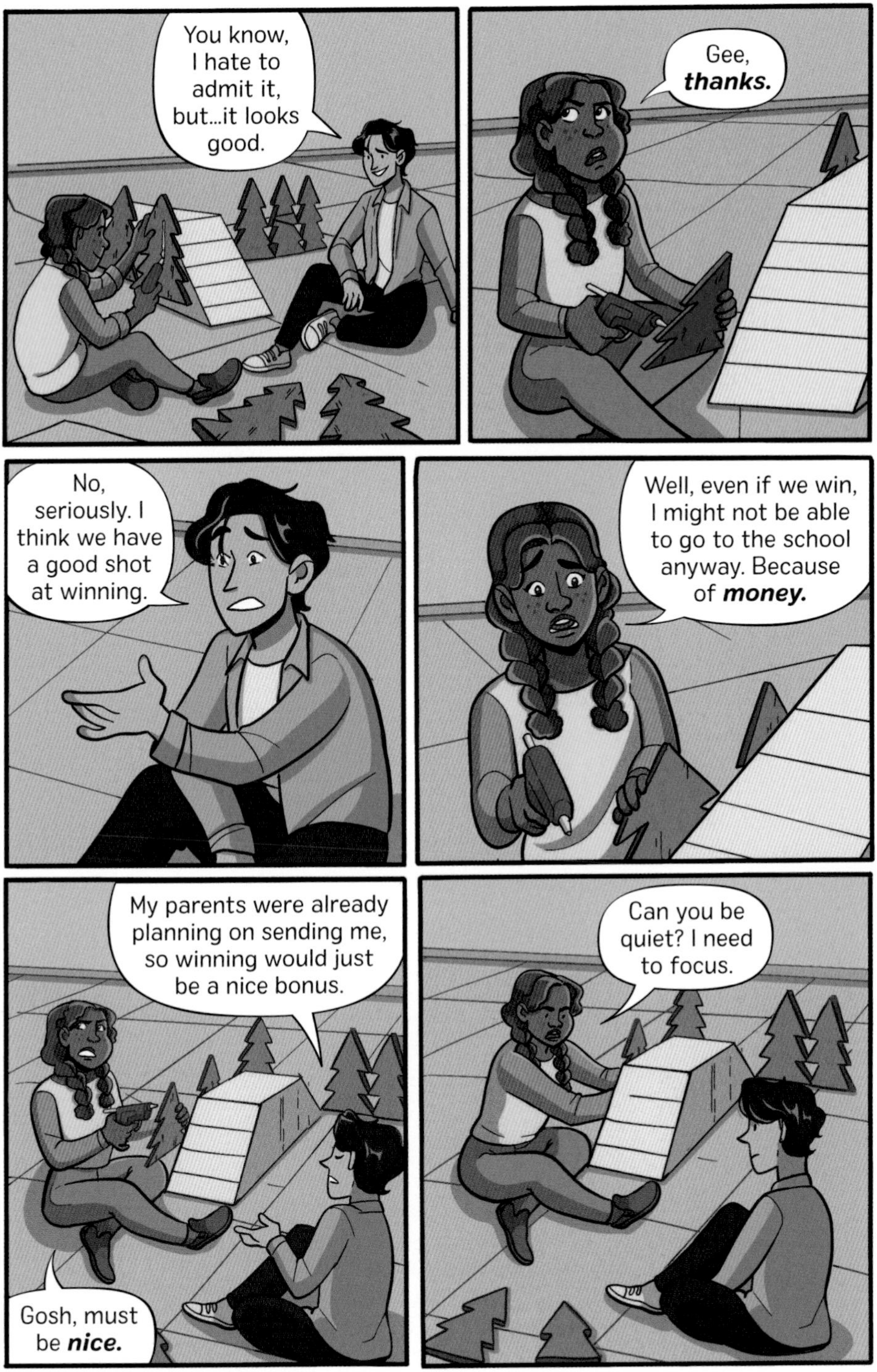
You know, I hate to admit it, but...it looks good.
Gee, ***thanks.***
No, seriously. I think we have a good shot at winning.
Well, even if we win, I might not be able to go to the school anyway. Because of ***money.***
My parents were already planning on sending me, so winning would just be a nice bonus.
Gosh, must be ***nice.***
Can you be quiet? I need to focus.

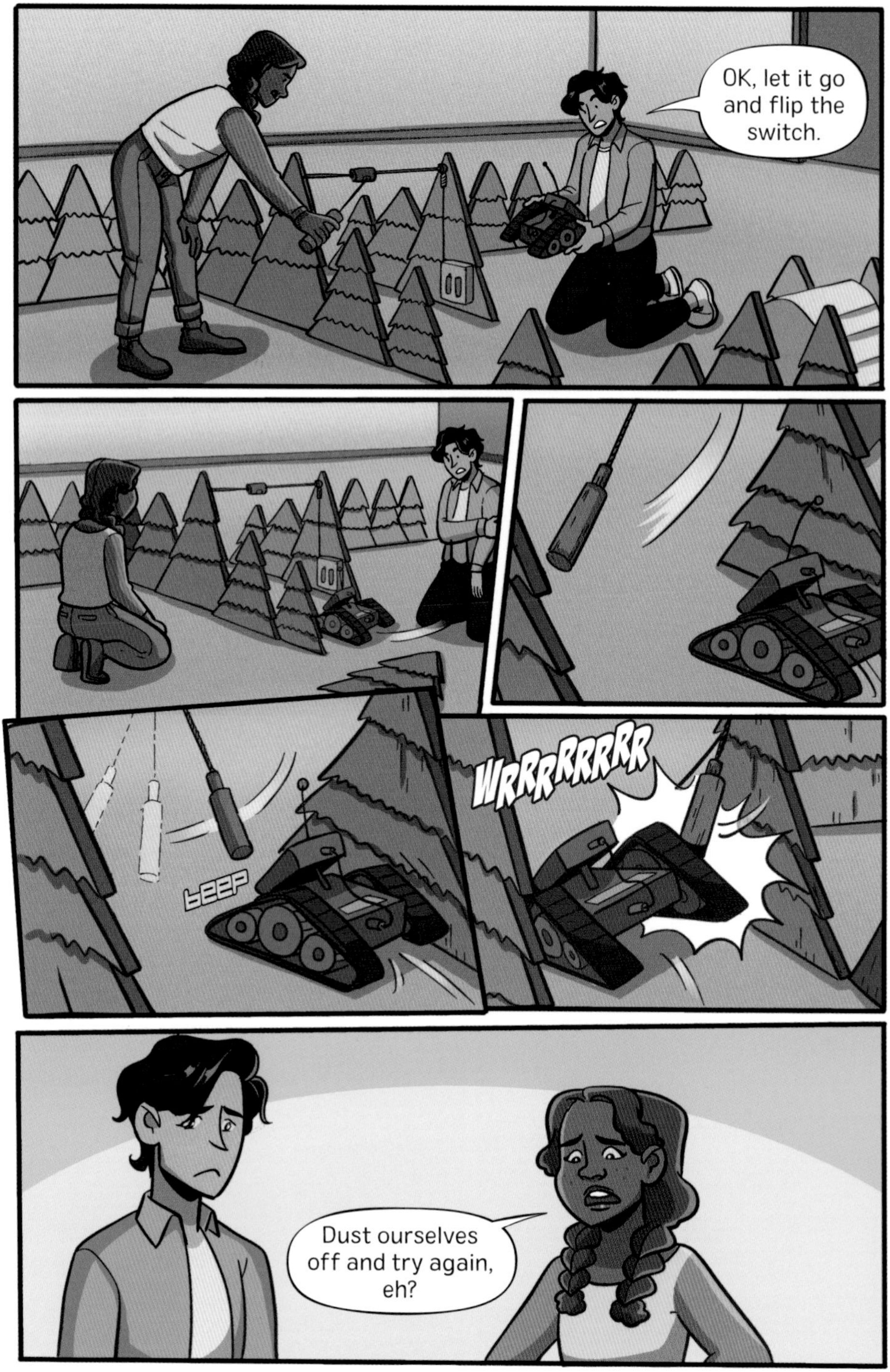
OK, let it go and flip the switch.
BEEP
WRRRRRRRR
Dust ourselves off and try again, eh?

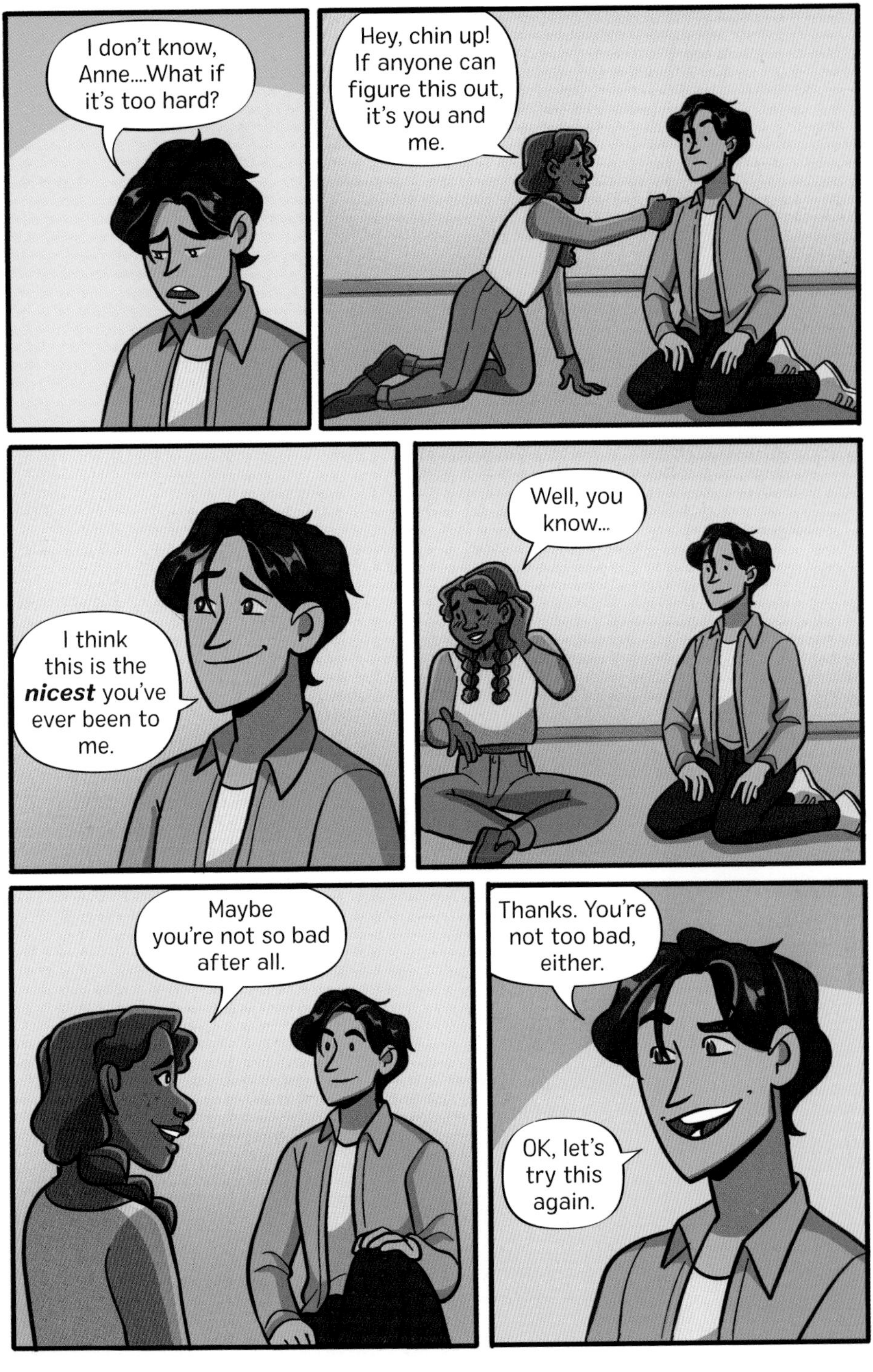
I don't know, Anne....What if it's too hard?
Hey, chin up! If anyone can figure this out, it's you and me.
I think this is the ***nicest*** you've ever been to me.
Well, you know...
Maybe you're not so bad after all.
Thanks. You're not too bad, either.
OK, let's try this again.

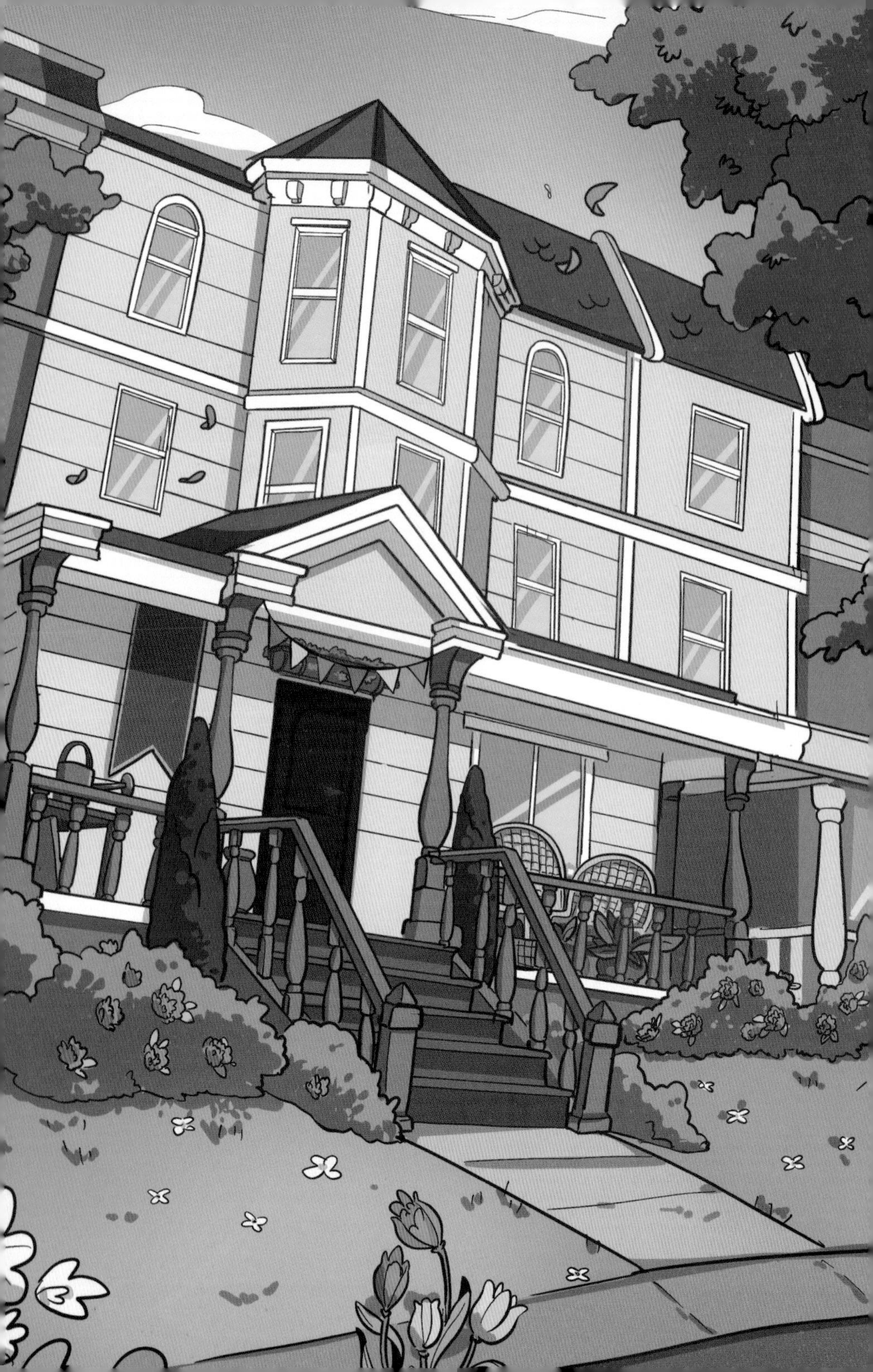

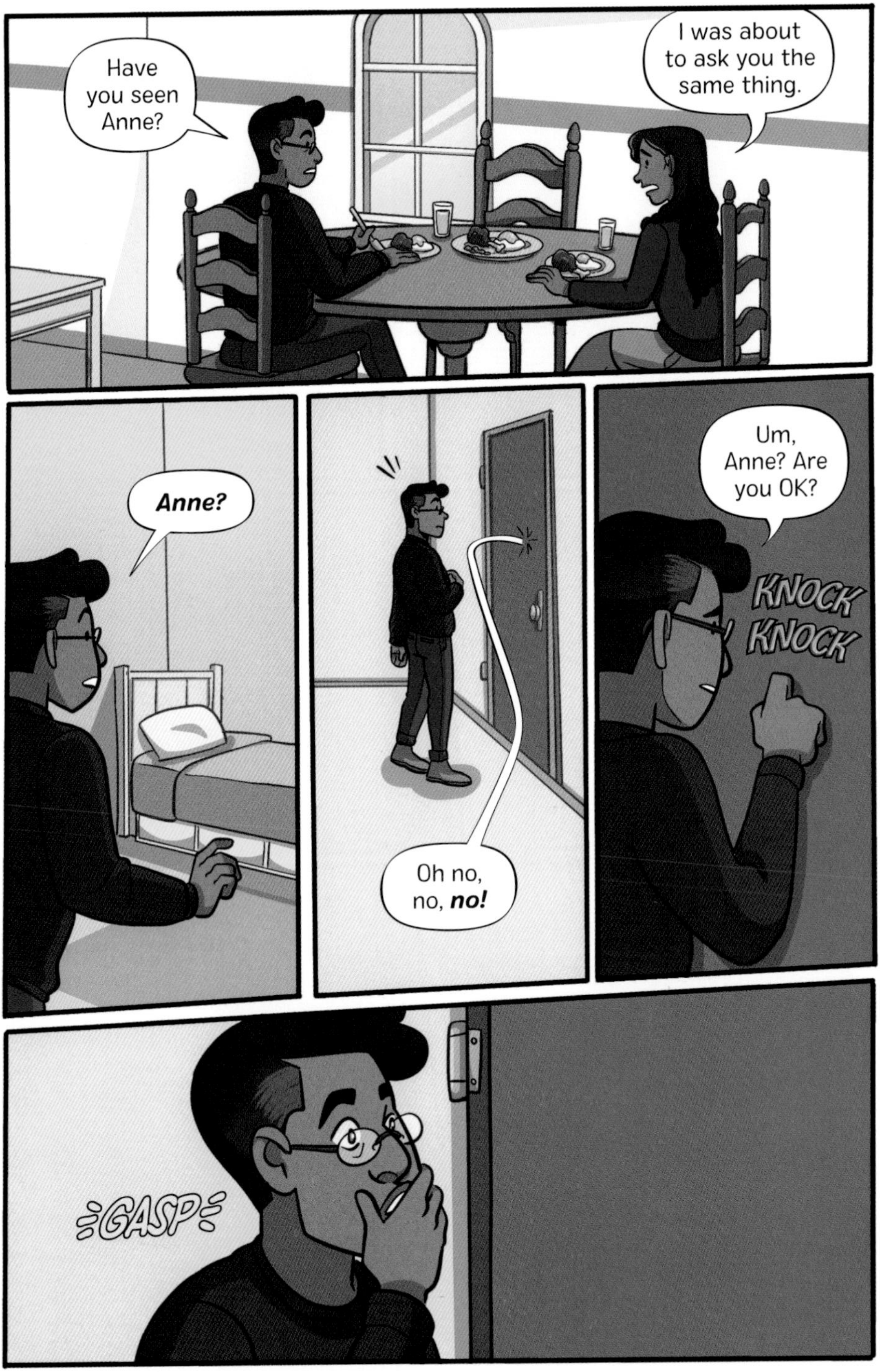
Have you seen Anne?
I was about to ask you the same thing.
Anne?
Oh no, no, no!
Um, Anne? Are you OK?
KNOCK KNOCK
GASP

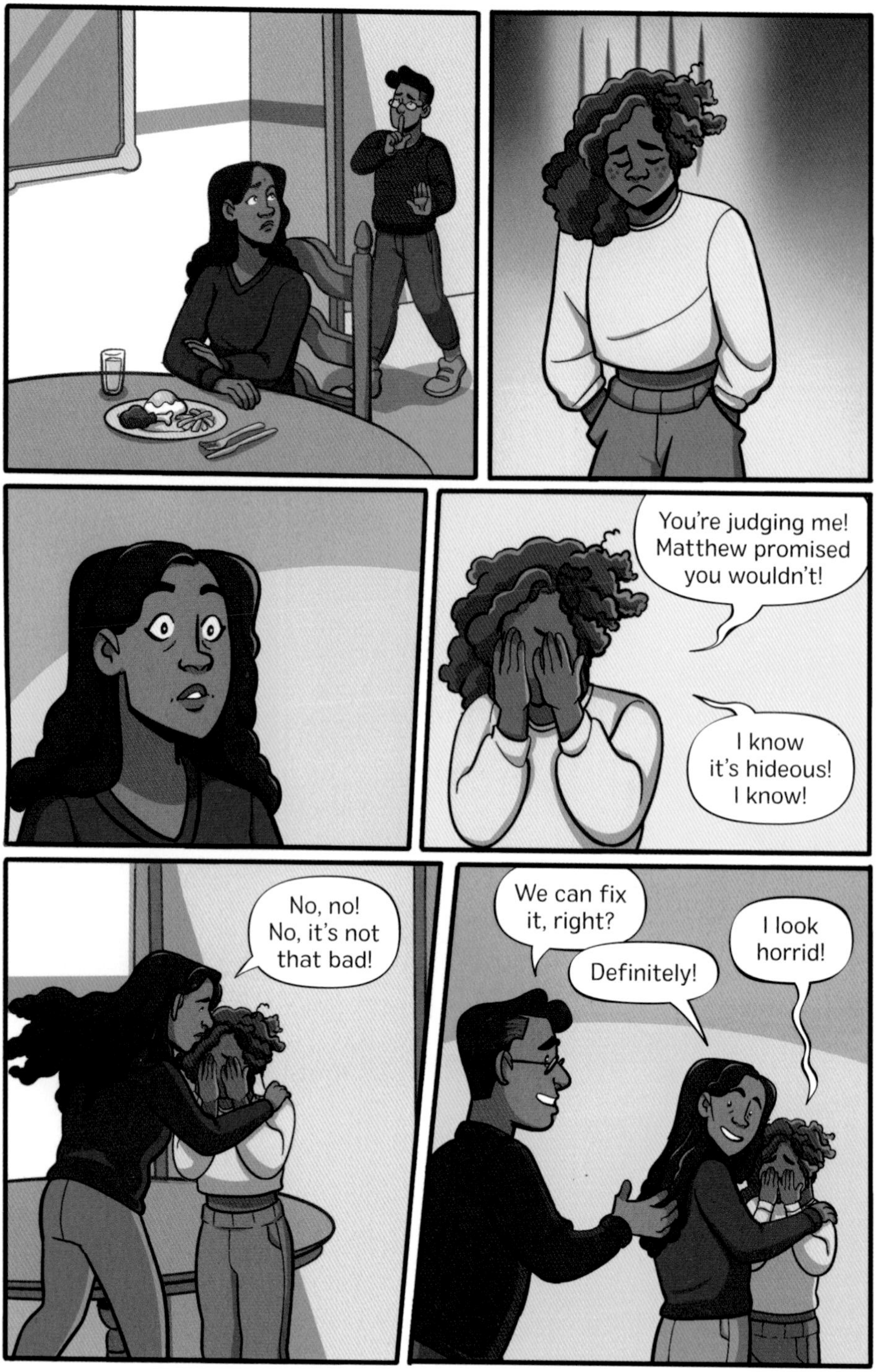
You're judging me! Matthew promised you wouldn't!
I know it's hideous! I know!
No, no! No, it's not that bad!
We can fix it, right?
Definitely!
I look horrid!

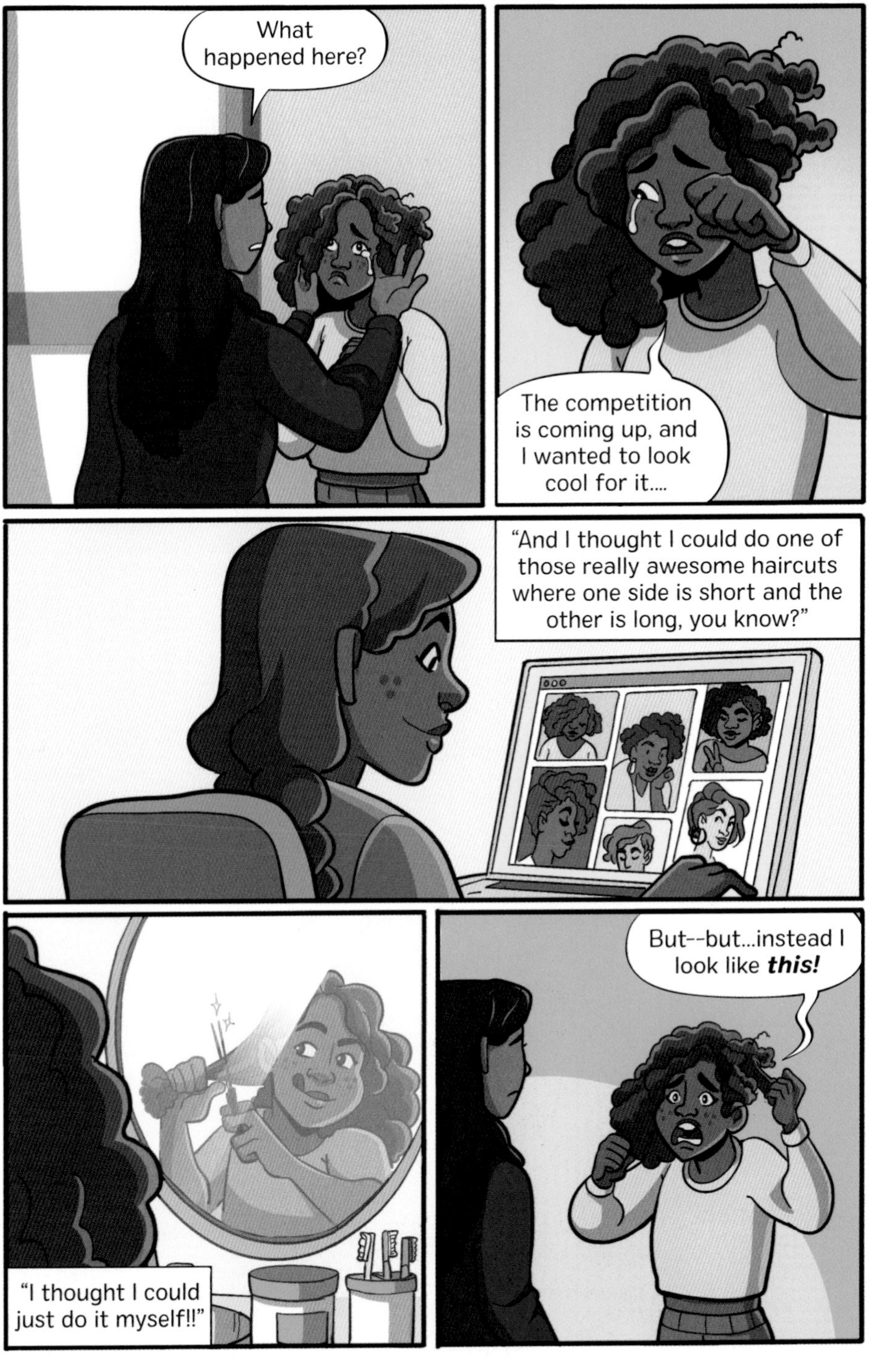
What happened here?
The competition is coming up, and I wanted to look cool for it....
"And I thought I could do one of those really awesome haircuts where one side is short and the other is long, you know?"
"I thought I could just do it myself!!"
But--but...instead I look like ***this!***

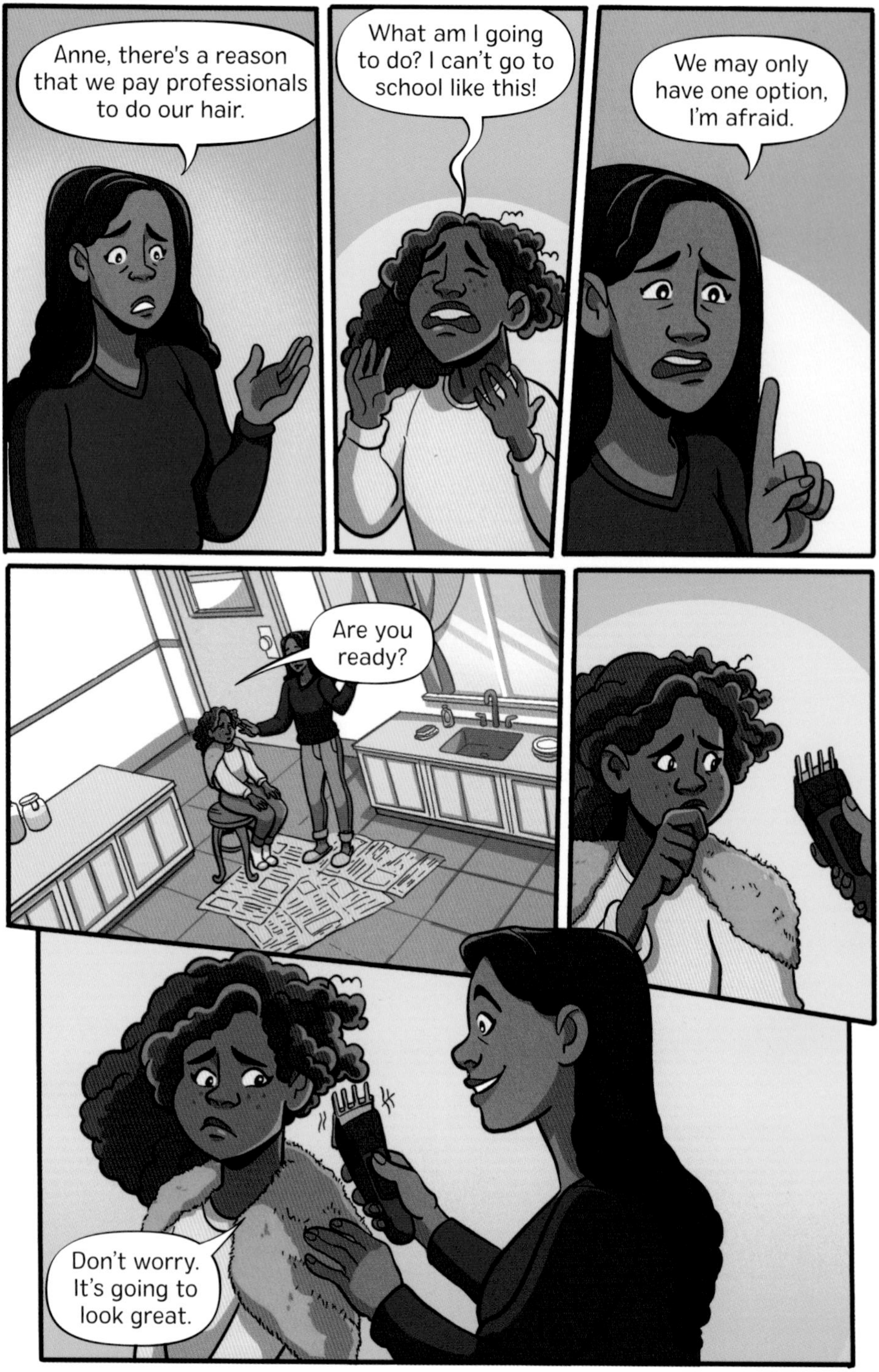
Anne, there's a reason that we pay professionals to do our hair.
What am I going to do? I can't go to school like this!
We may only have one option, I'm afraid.
Are you ready?
Don't worry. It's going to look great.

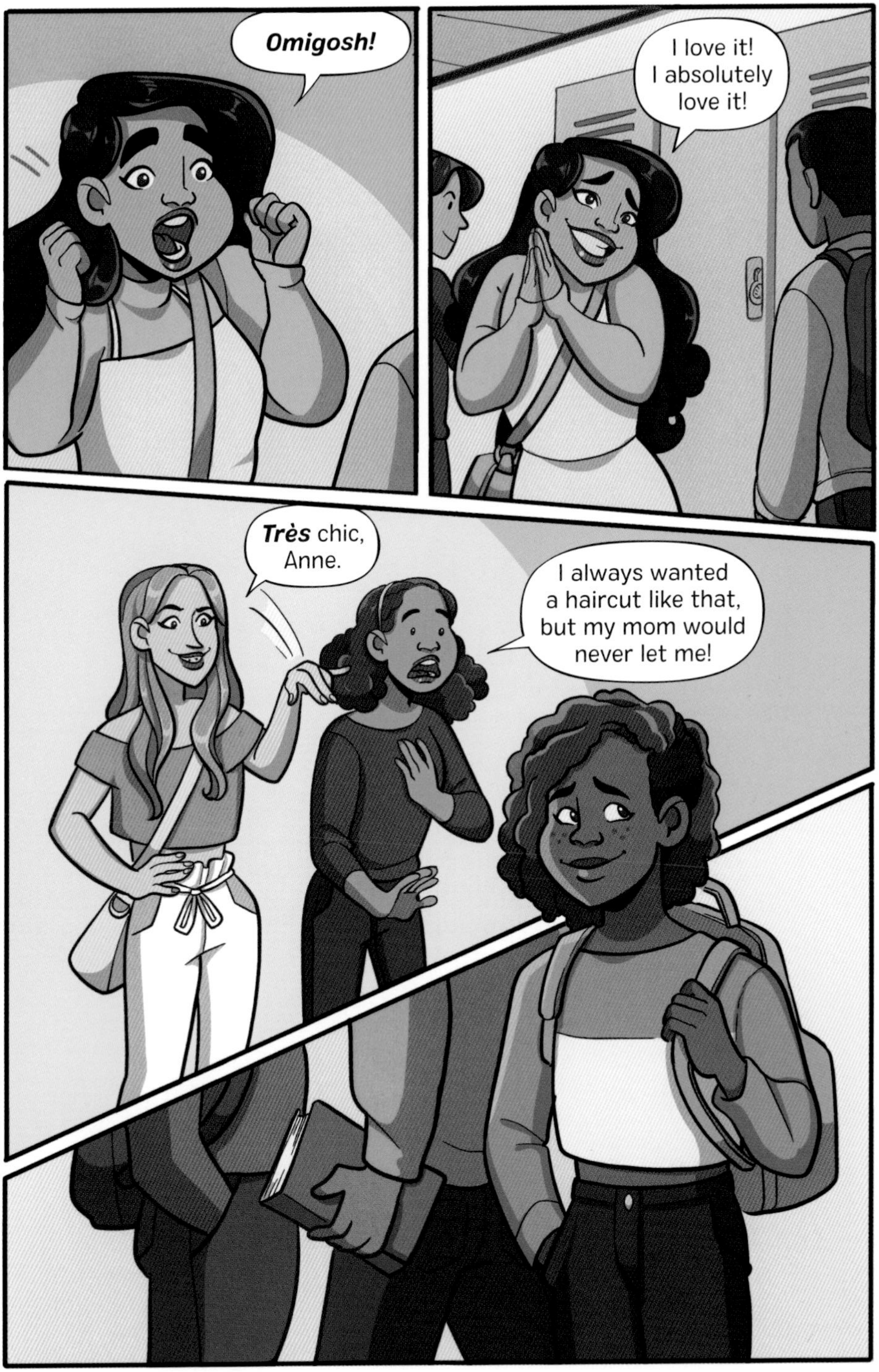
Omigosh!
I love it! I absolutely love it!
Très chic, Anne.
I always wanted a haircut like that, but my mom would never let me!

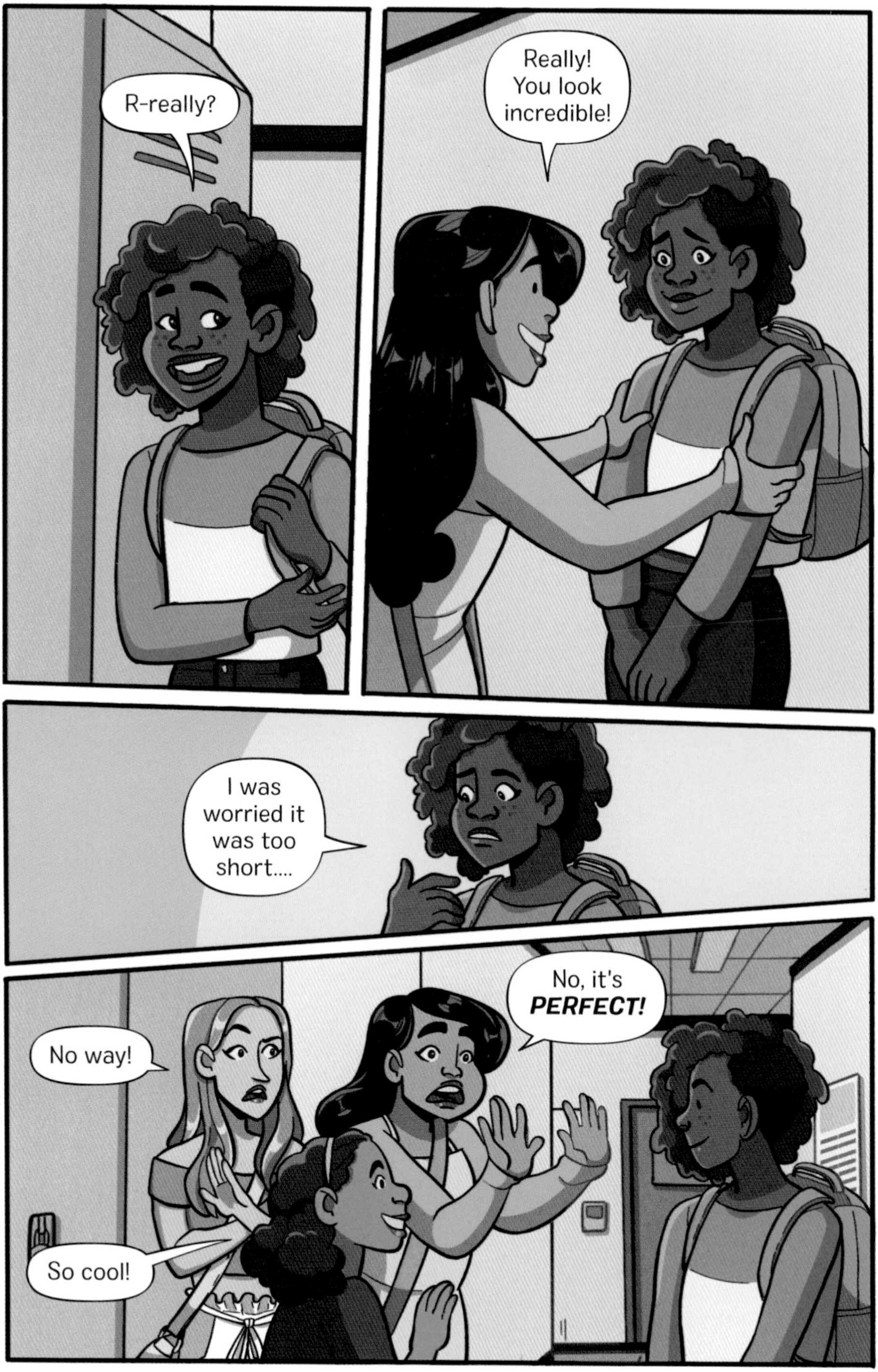
R-really?
Really! You look incredible!
I was worried it was too short....
No way!
No, it's ***PERFECT!***
So cool!

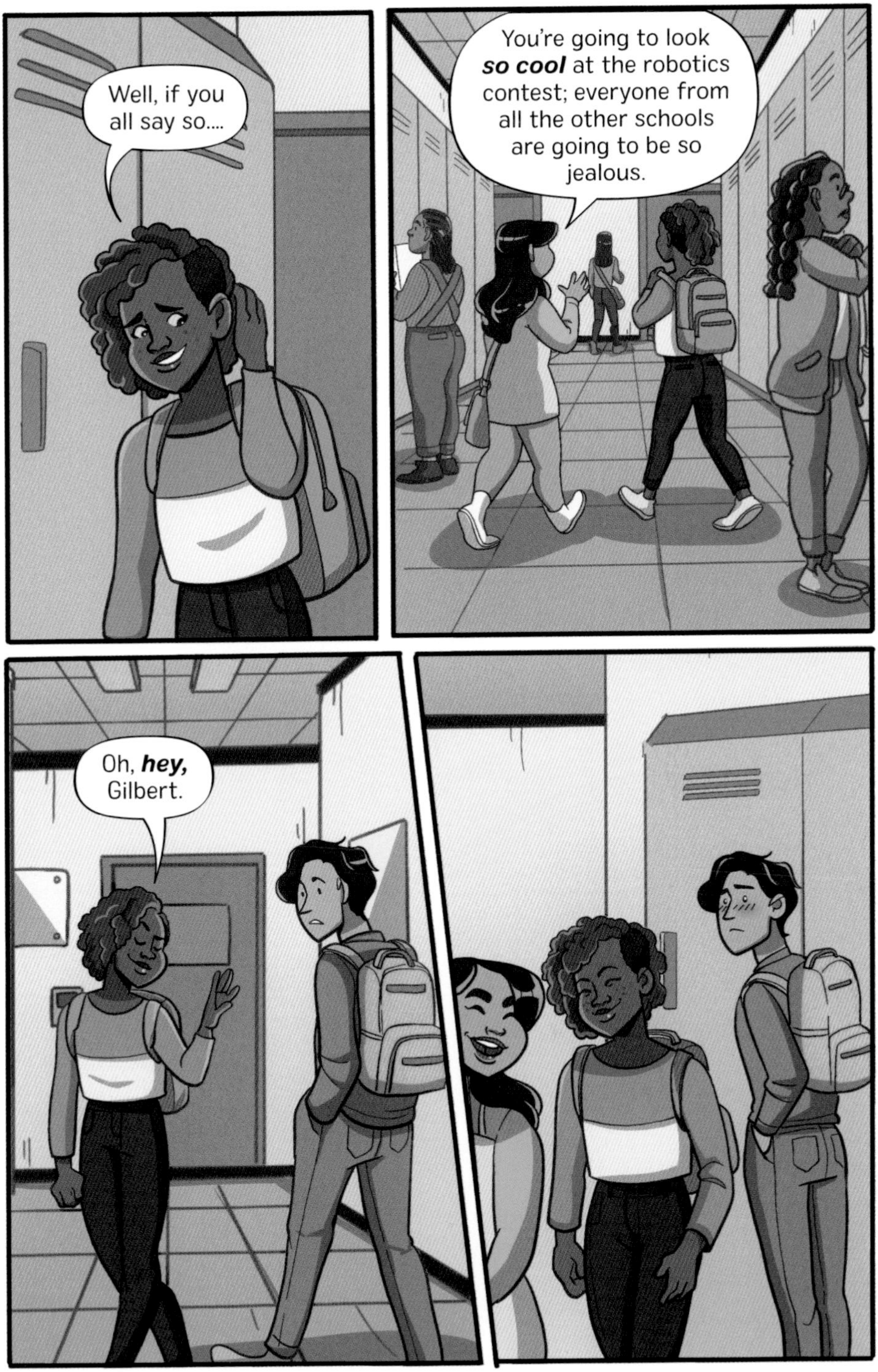
Well, if you all say so....
You're going to look **so cool** at the robotics contest; everyone from all the other schools are going to be so jealous.
Oh, **hey,** Gilbert.

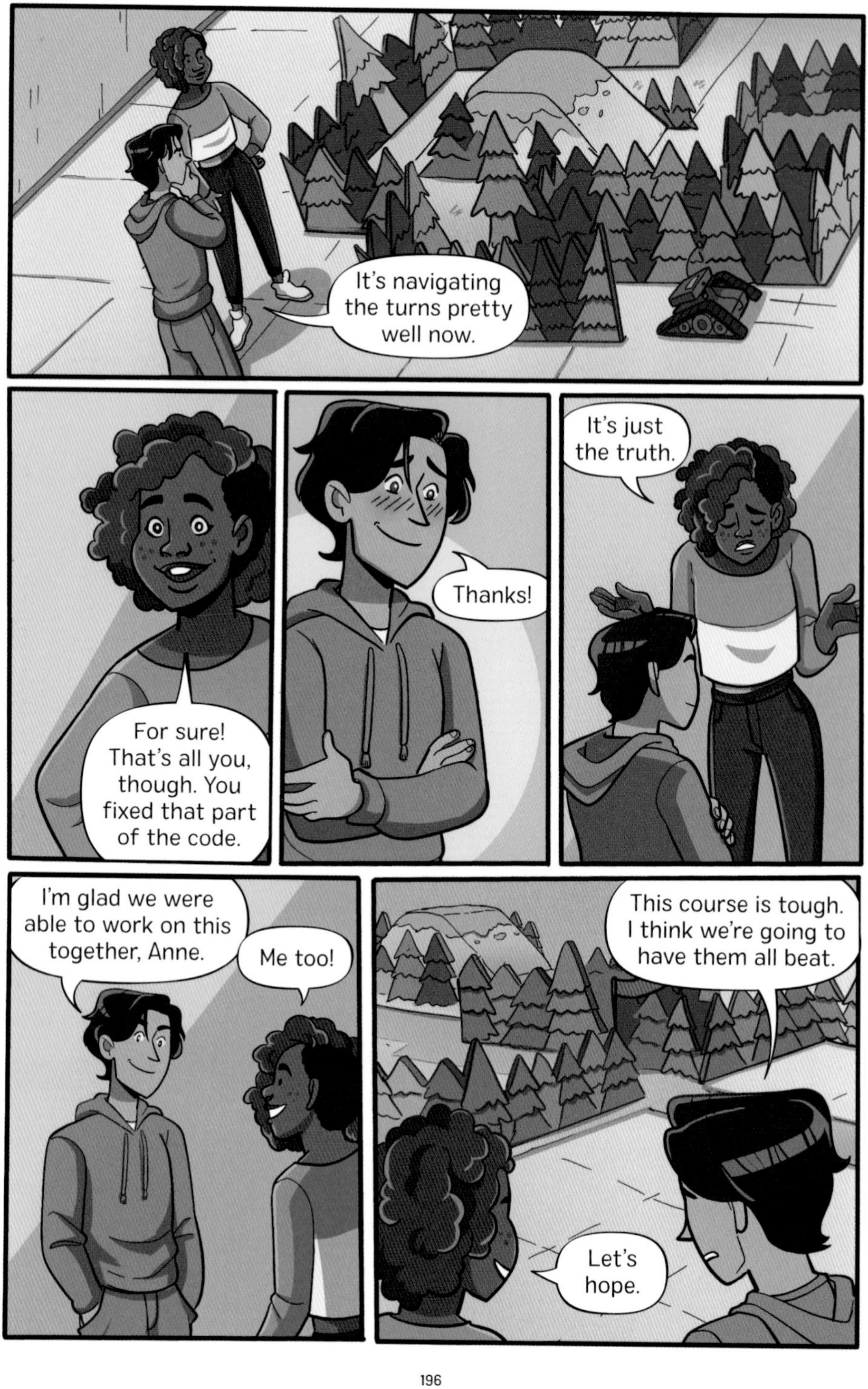
It's navigating the turns pretty well now.
For sure! That's all you, though. You fixed that part of the code.
Thanks!
It's just the truth.
I'm glad we were able to work on this together, Anne.
Me too!
This course is tough. I think we're going to have them all beat.
Let's hope.

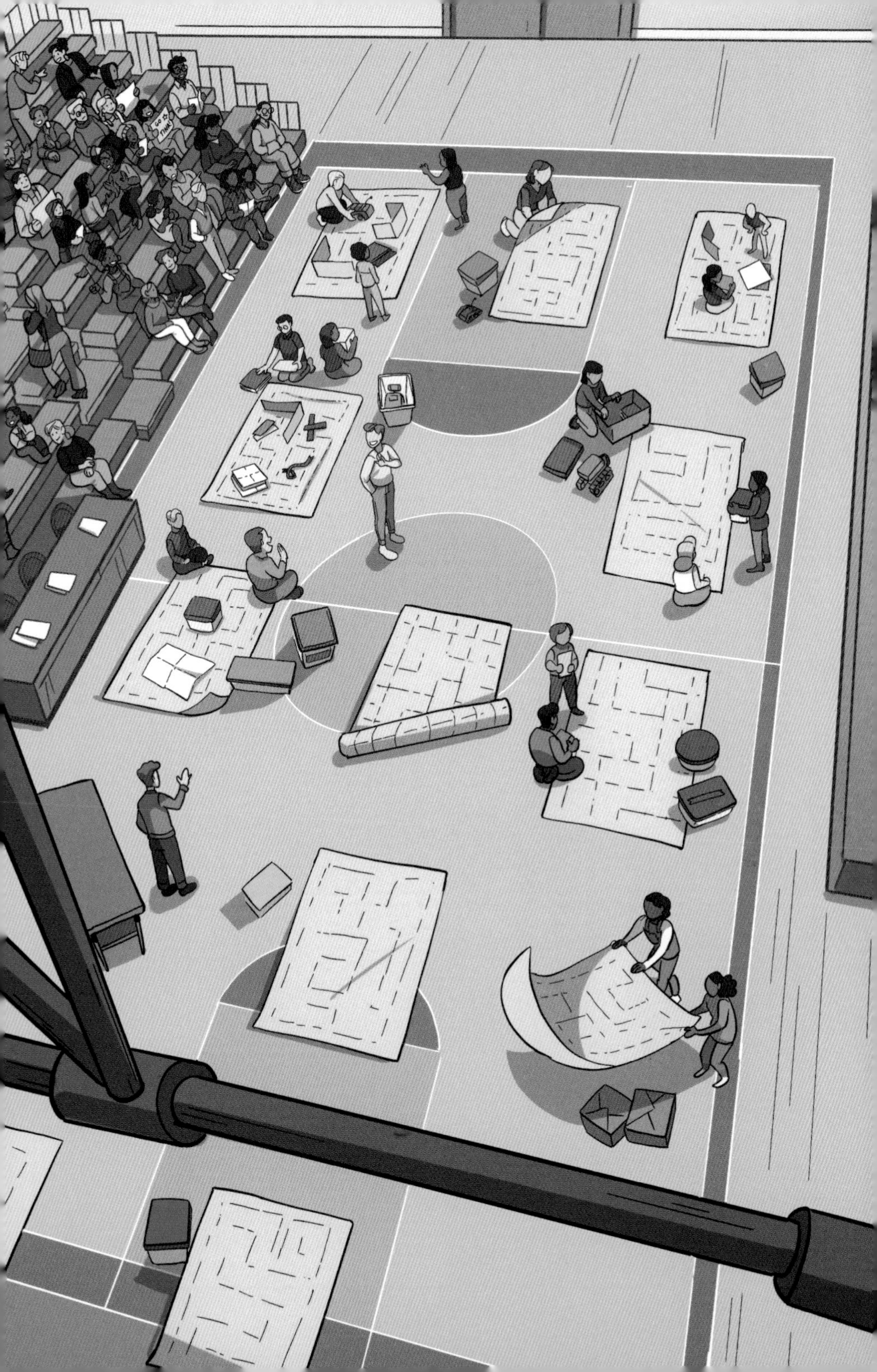
GO ☆ TINA!

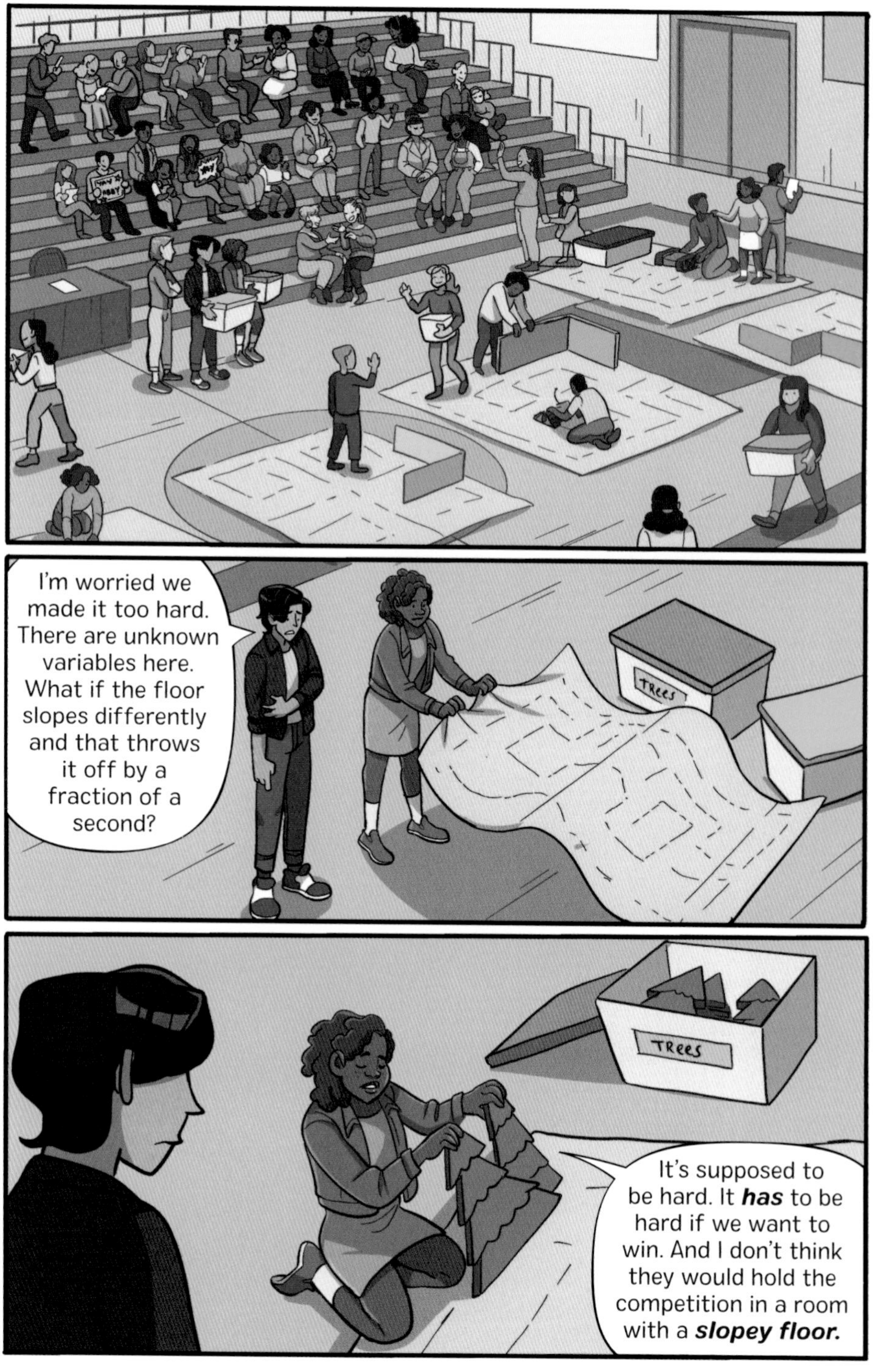
I'm worried we made it too hard. There are unknown variables here. What if the floor slopes differently and that throws it off by a fraction of a second?
TREES
TREES
It's supposed to be hard. It ***has*** to be hard if we want to win. And I don't think they would hold the competition in a room with a ***slopey floor.***

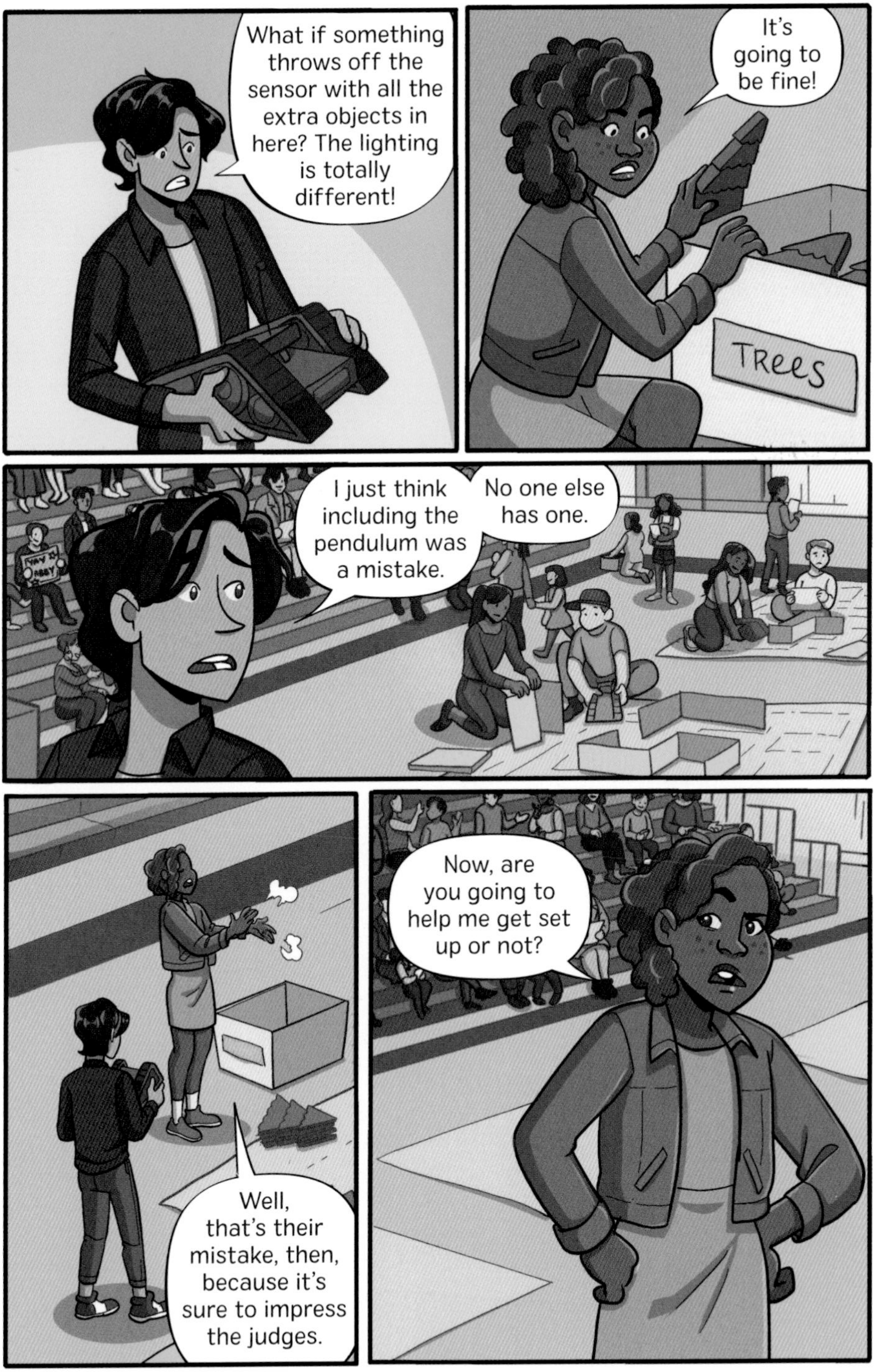
What if something throws off the sensor with all the extra objects in here? The lighting is totally different!
It's going to be fine!
TREES
I just think including the pendulum was a mistake.
No one else has one.
Well, that's their mistake, then, because it's sure to impress the judges.
Now, are you going to help me get set up or not?

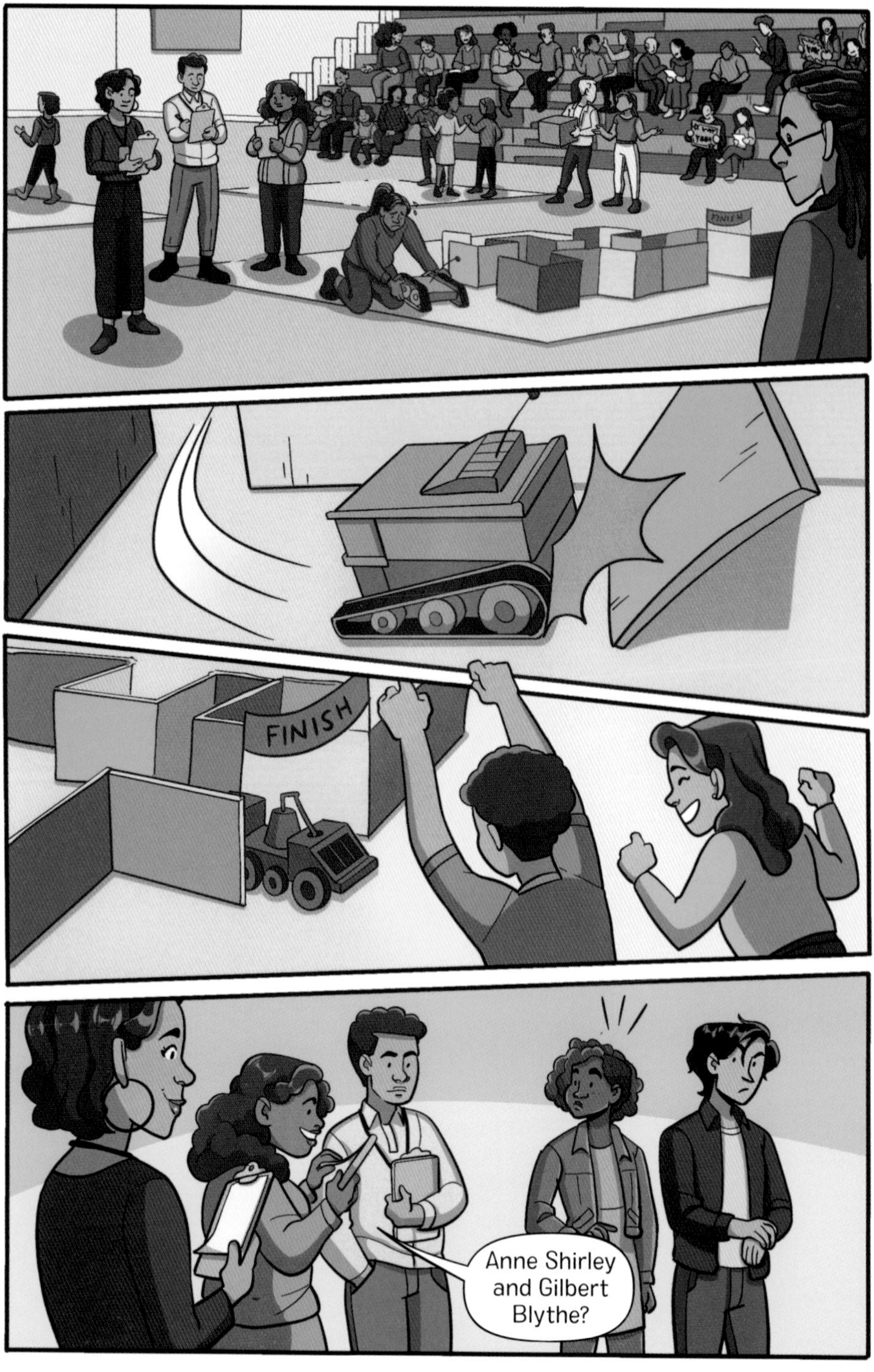
FINISH
Anne Shirley and Gilbert Blythe?

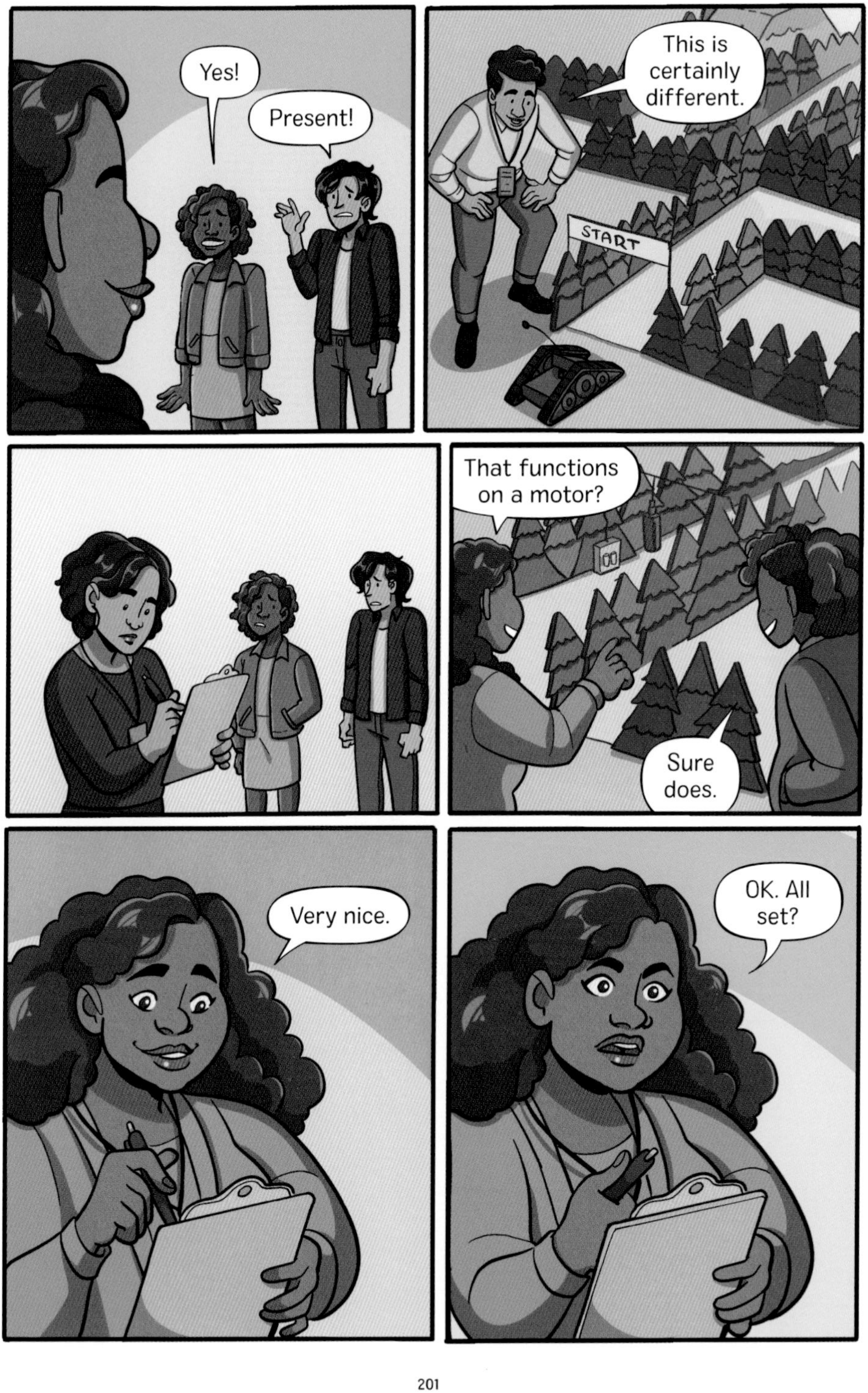
Yes!
Present!
This is certainly different.
START
That functions on a motor?
Sure does.
Very nice.
OK. All set?

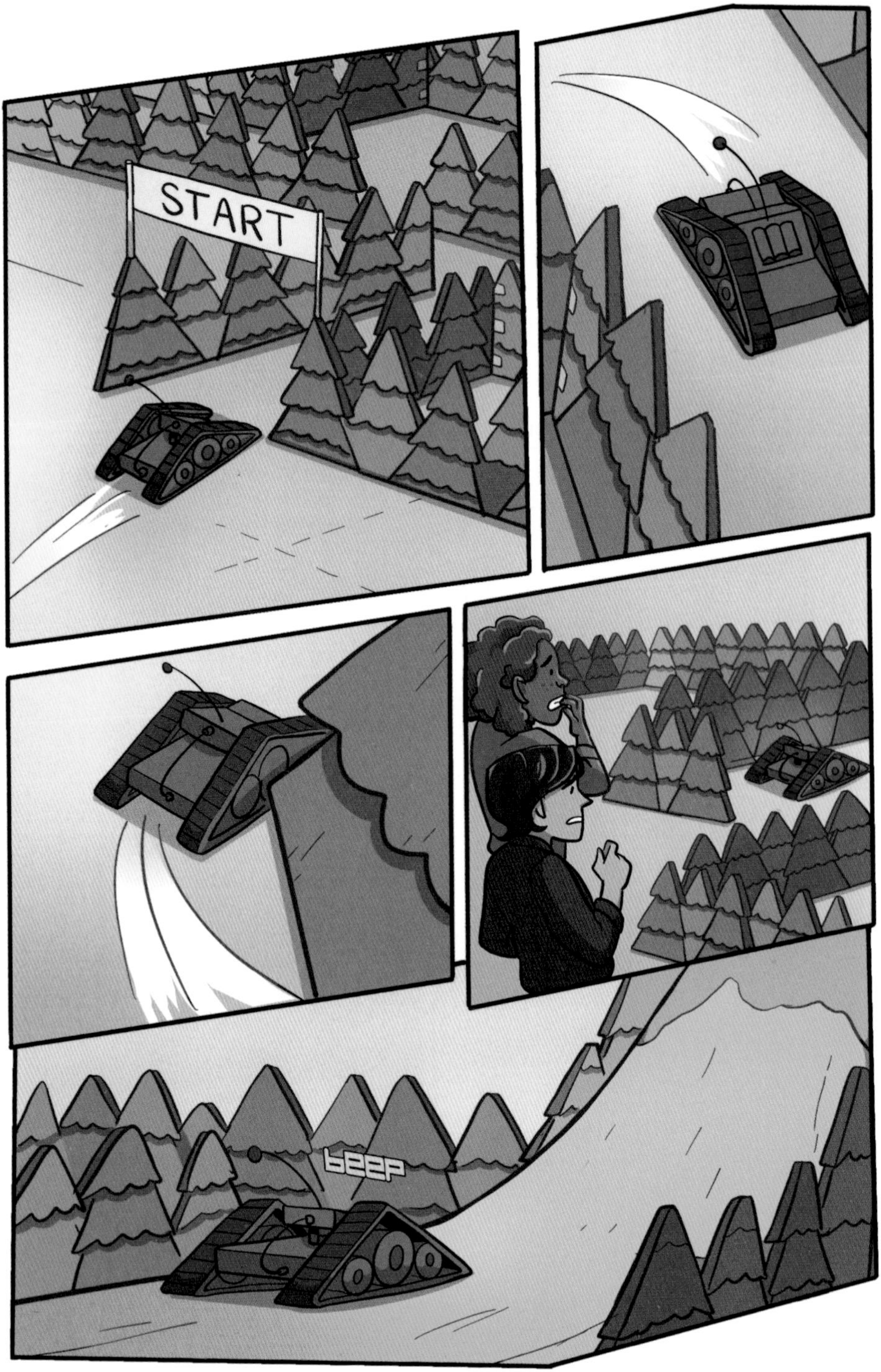
START
BEEP

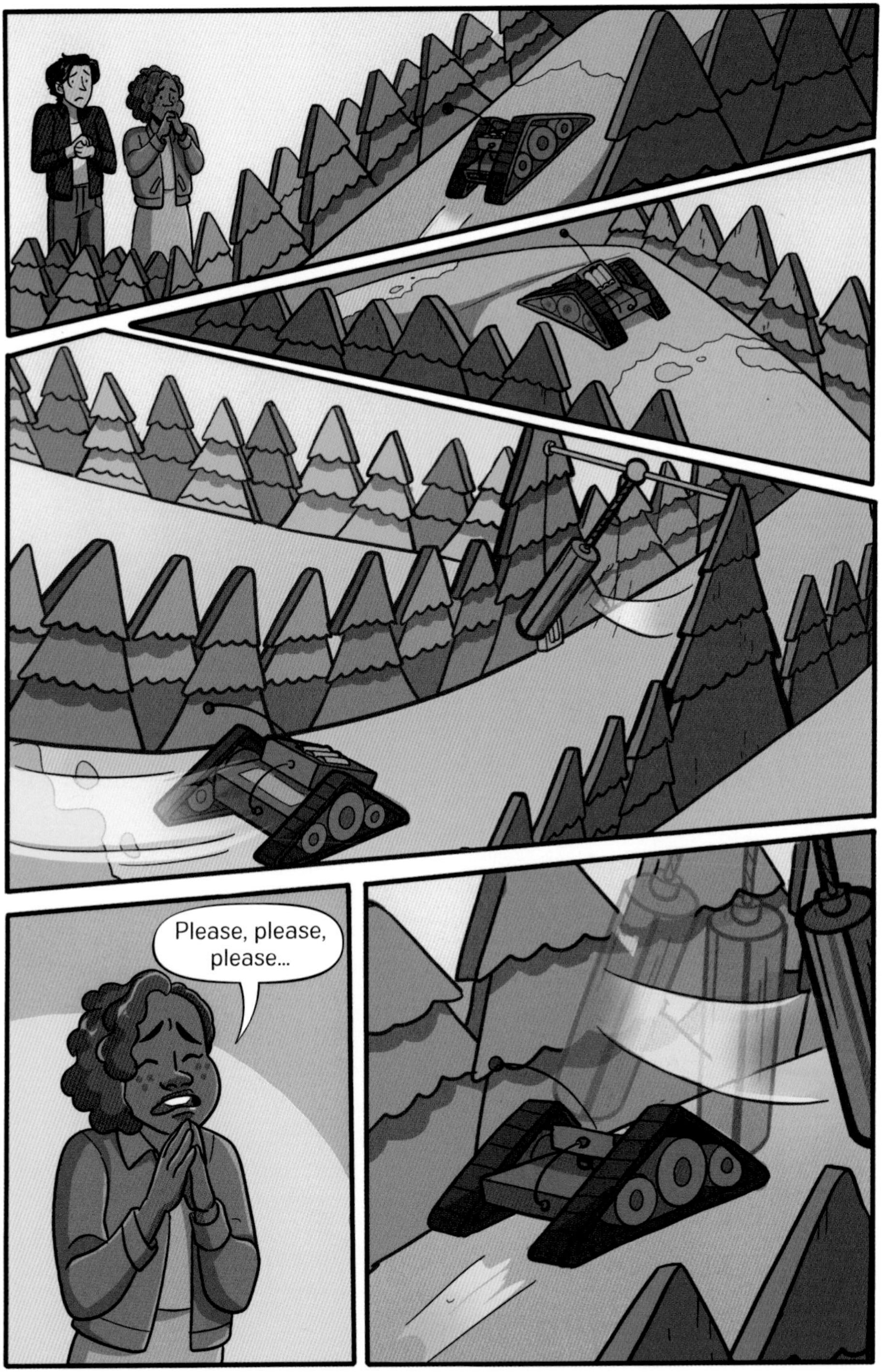
Please, please, please...

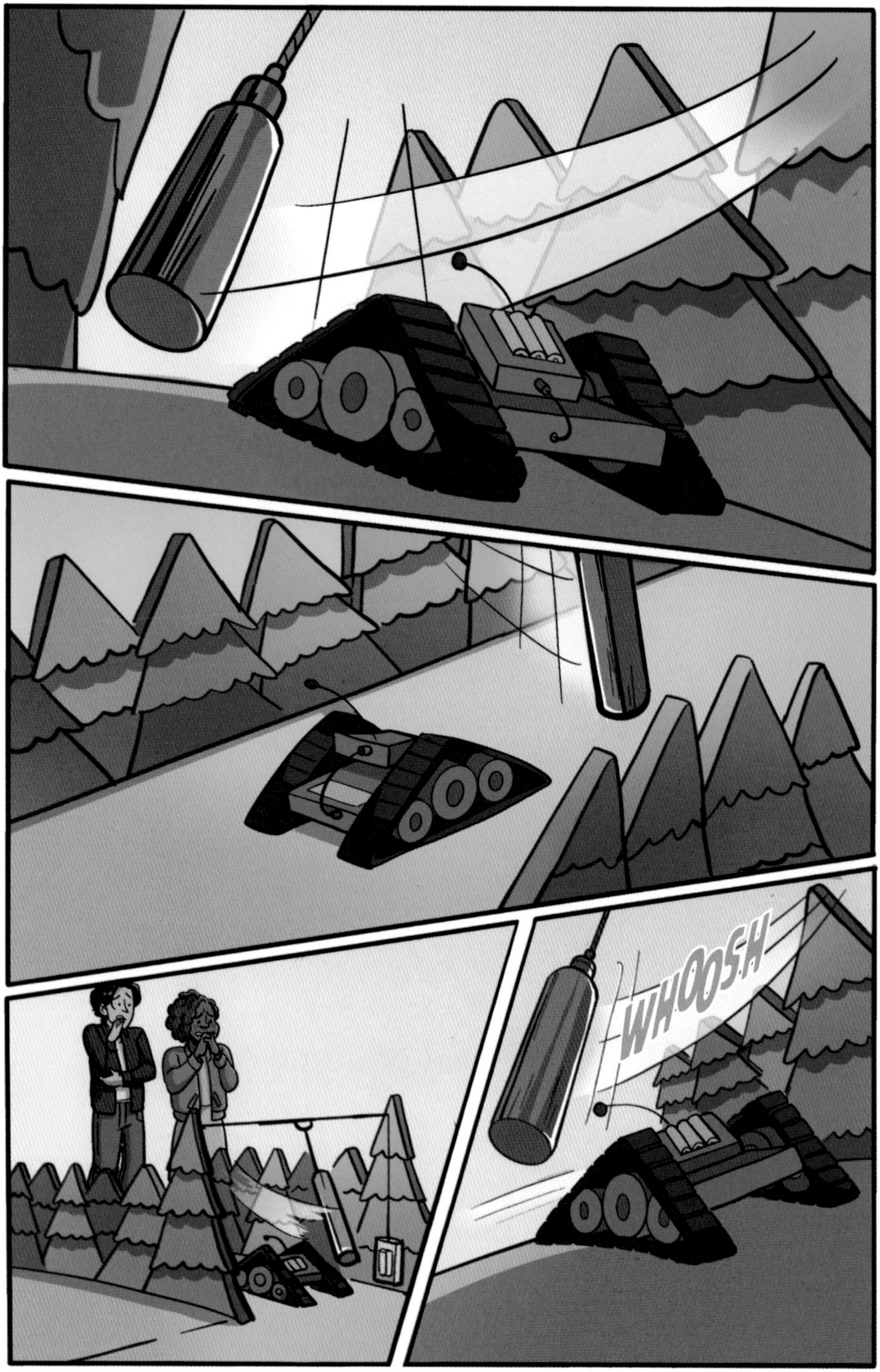
WHOOSH

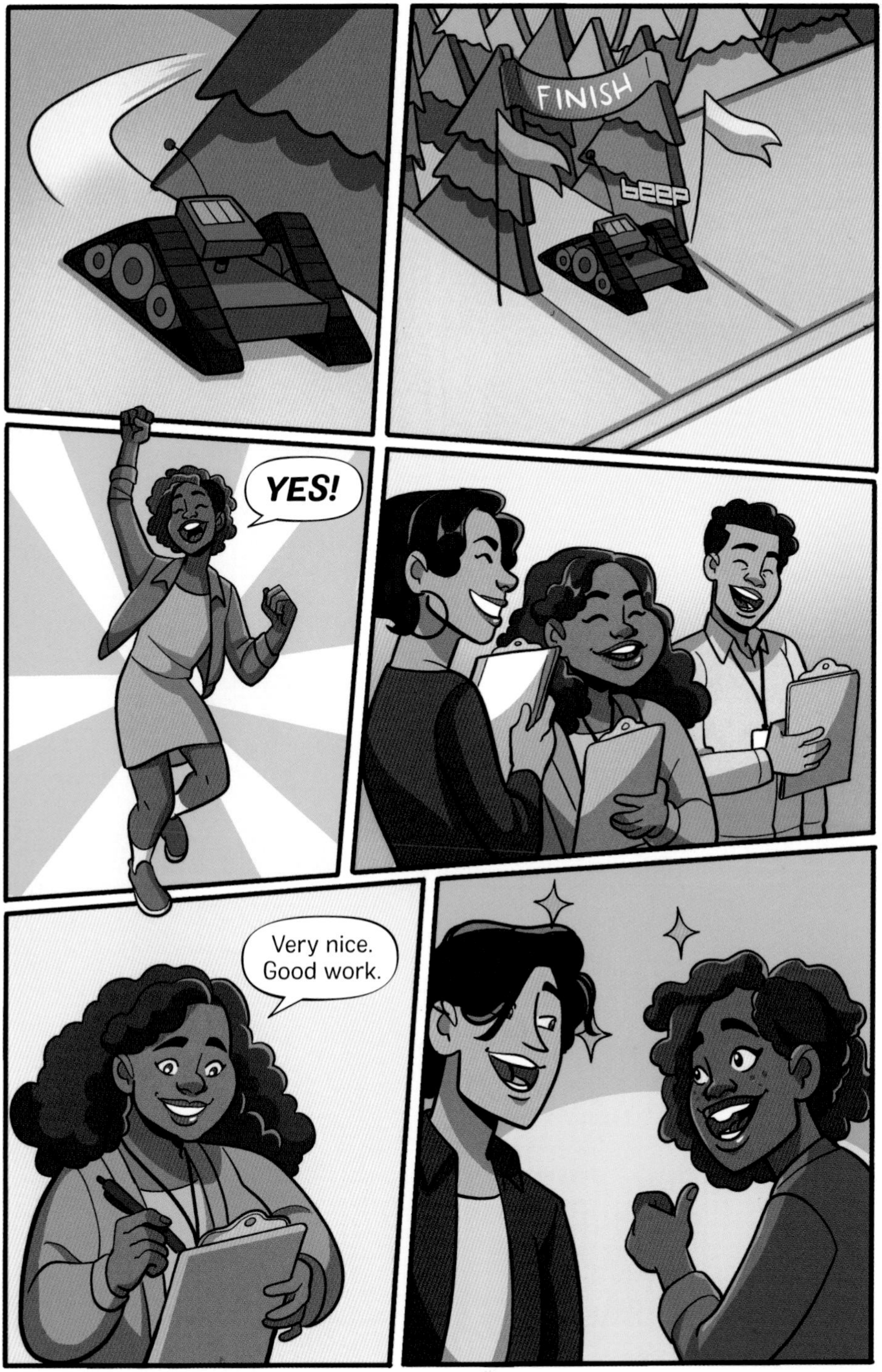
FINISH
BEEP
YES!
Very nice.
Good work.

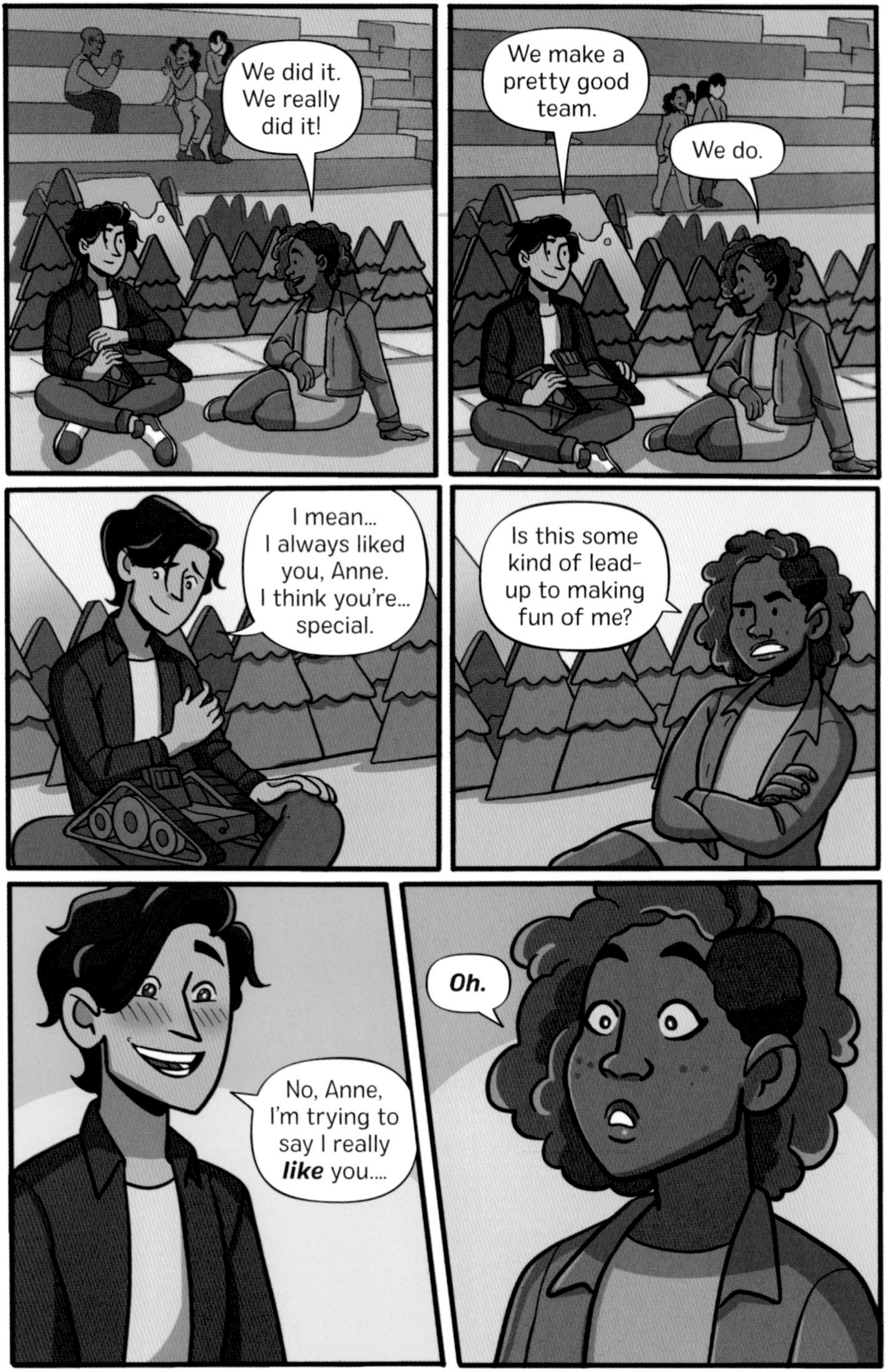
We did it. We really did it!
We make a pretty good team.
We do.
I mean... I always liked you, Anne. I think you're... special.
Is this some kind of lead-up to making fun of me?
No, Anne, I'm trying to say I really **like** you....
Oh.

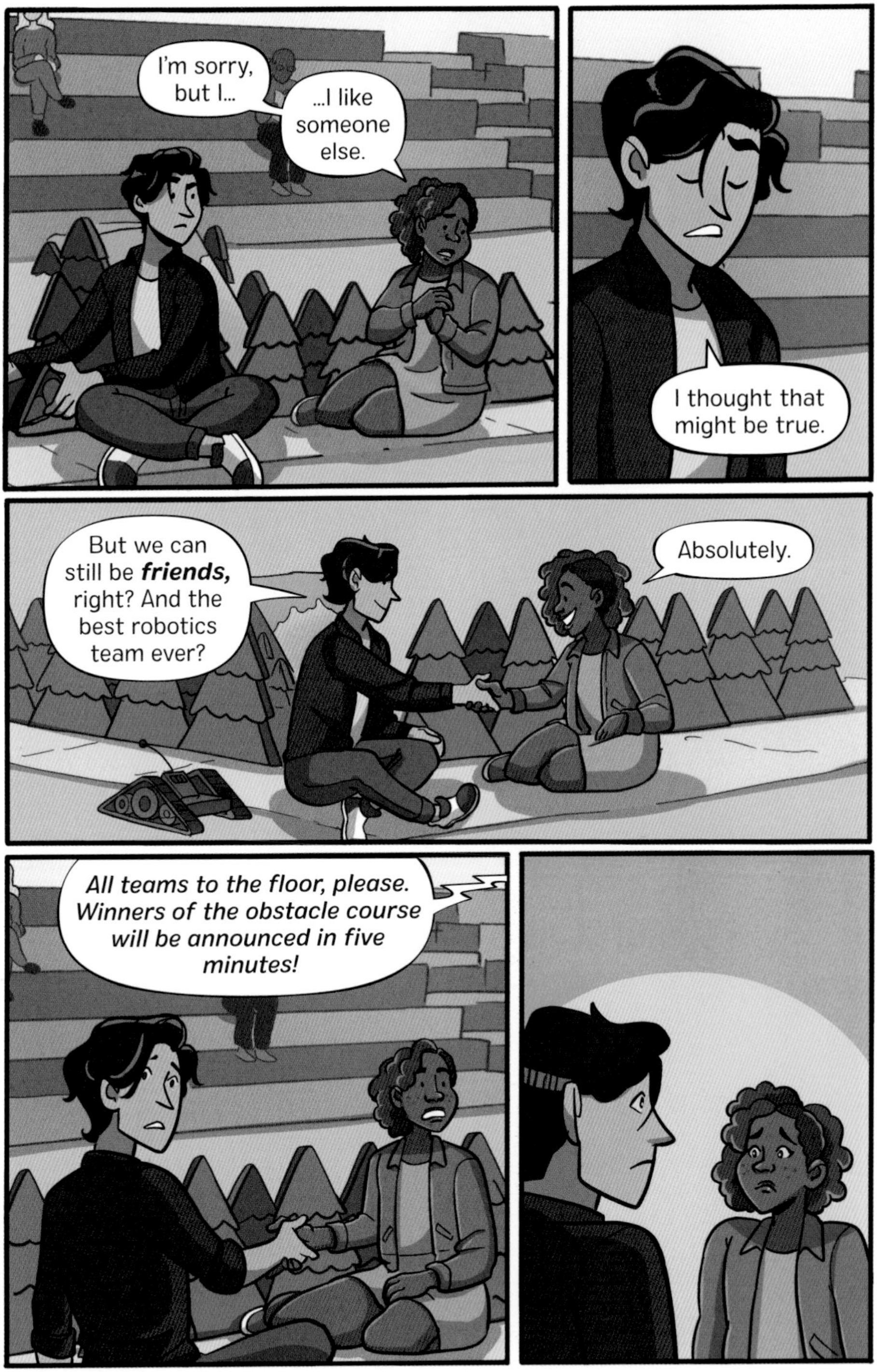
I'm sorry, but I...
...I like someone else.
I thought that might be true.
But we can still be ***friends,*** right? And the best robotics team ever?
Absolutely.
All teams to the floor, please. Winners of the obstacle course will be announced in five minutes!

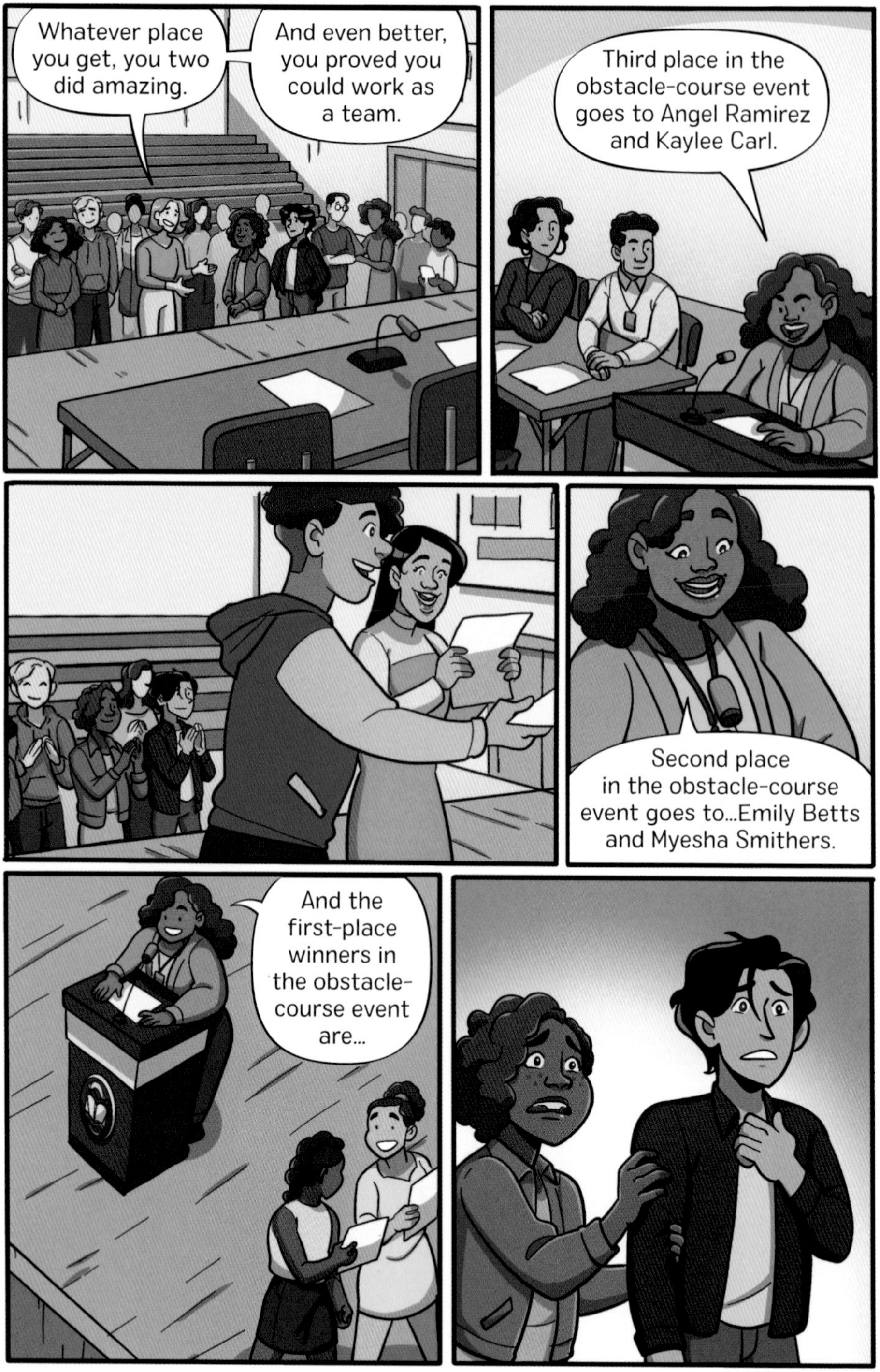
Whatever place you get, you two did amazing.
And even better, you proved you could work as a team.
Third place in the obstacle-course event goes to Angel Ramirez and Kaylee Carl.
Second place in the obstacle-course event goes to...Emily Betts and Myesha Smithers.
And the first-place winners in the obstacle-course event are...

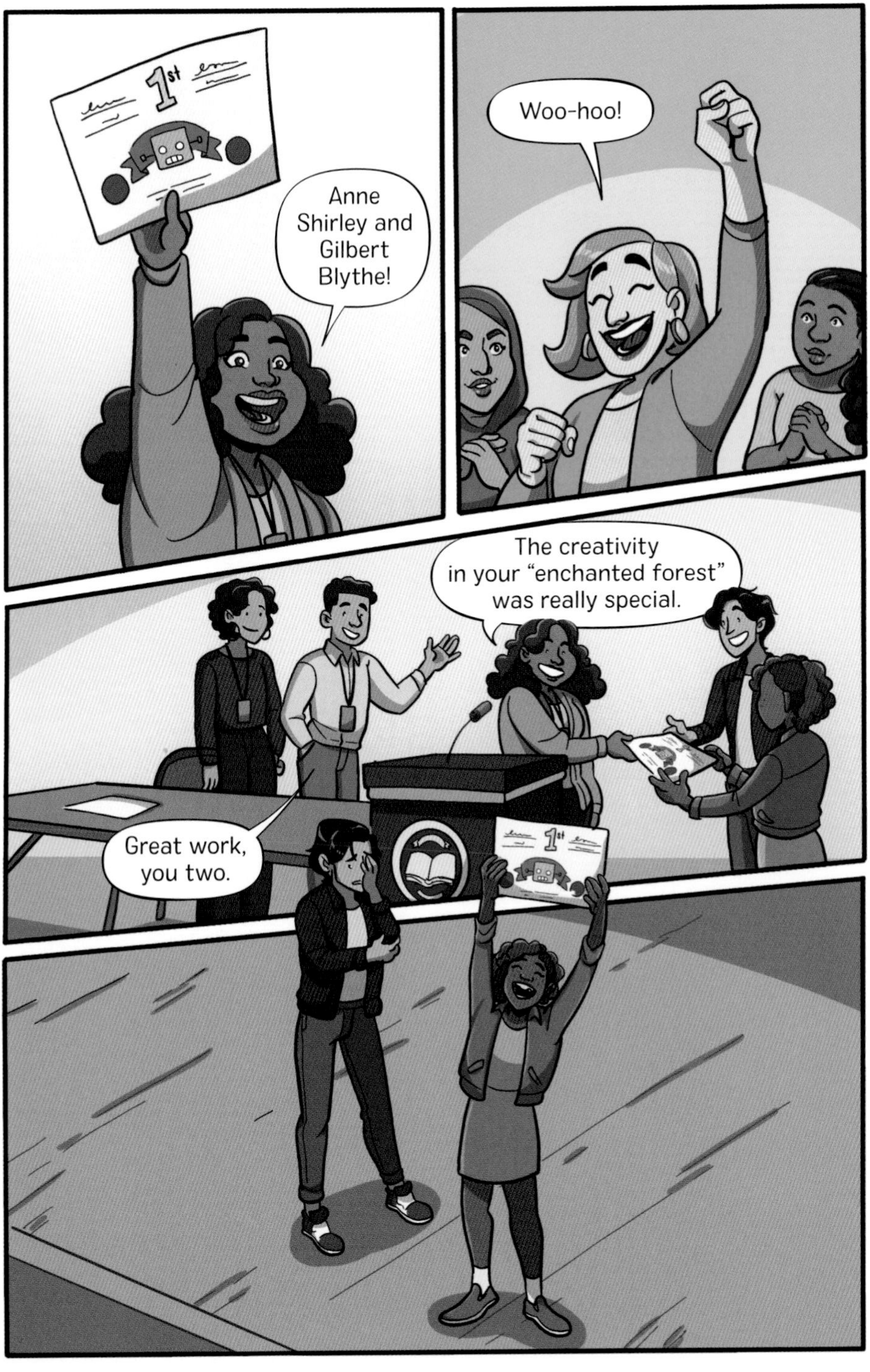
1st
Anne Shirley and Gilbert Blythe!
Woo-hoo!
The creativity in your "enchanted forest" was really special.
Great work, you two.
1st

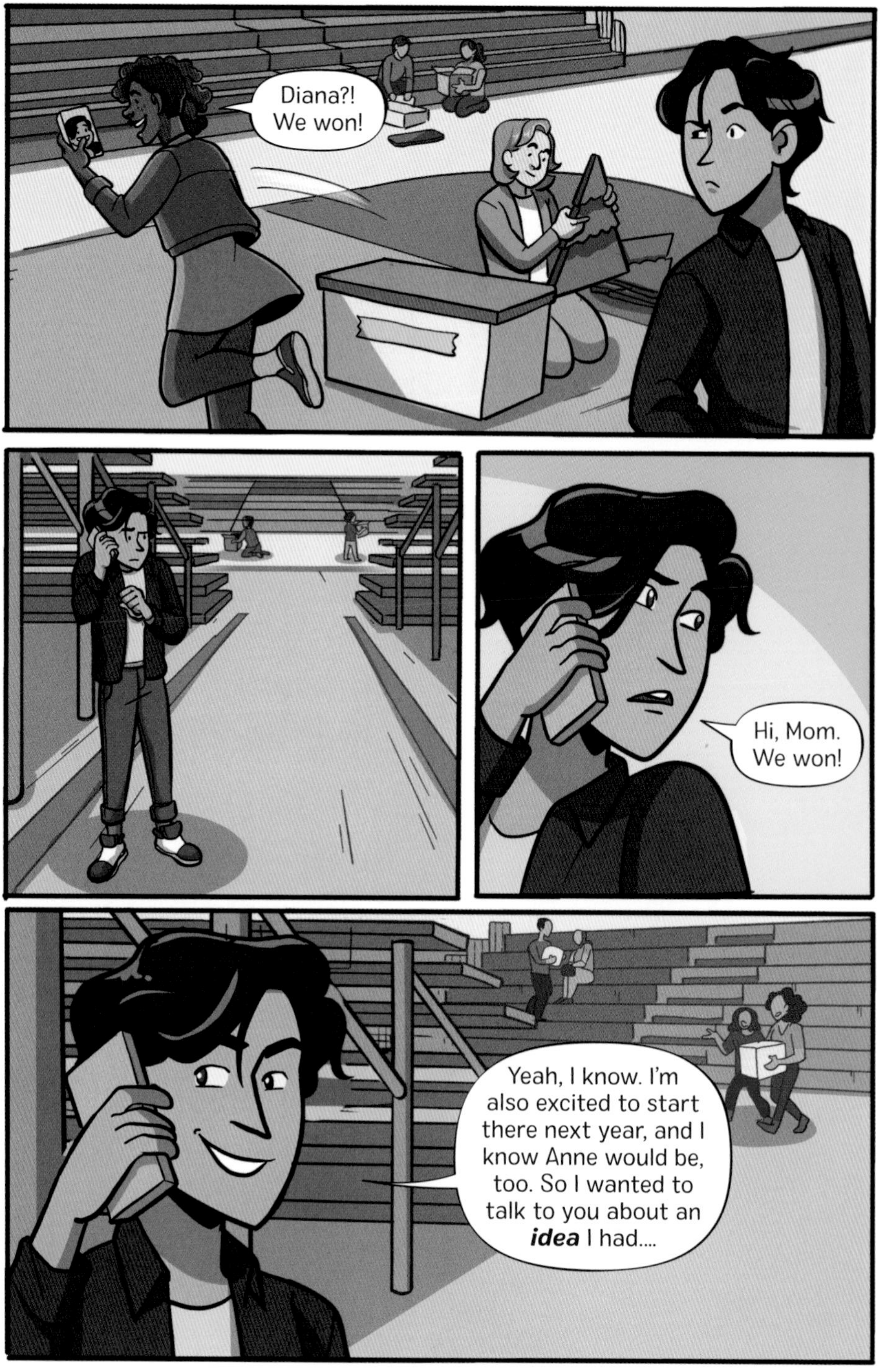
Diana?! We won!
Hi, Mom. We won!
Yeah, I know. I'm also excited to start there next year, and I know Anne would be, too. So I wanted to talk to you about an ***idea*** I had....

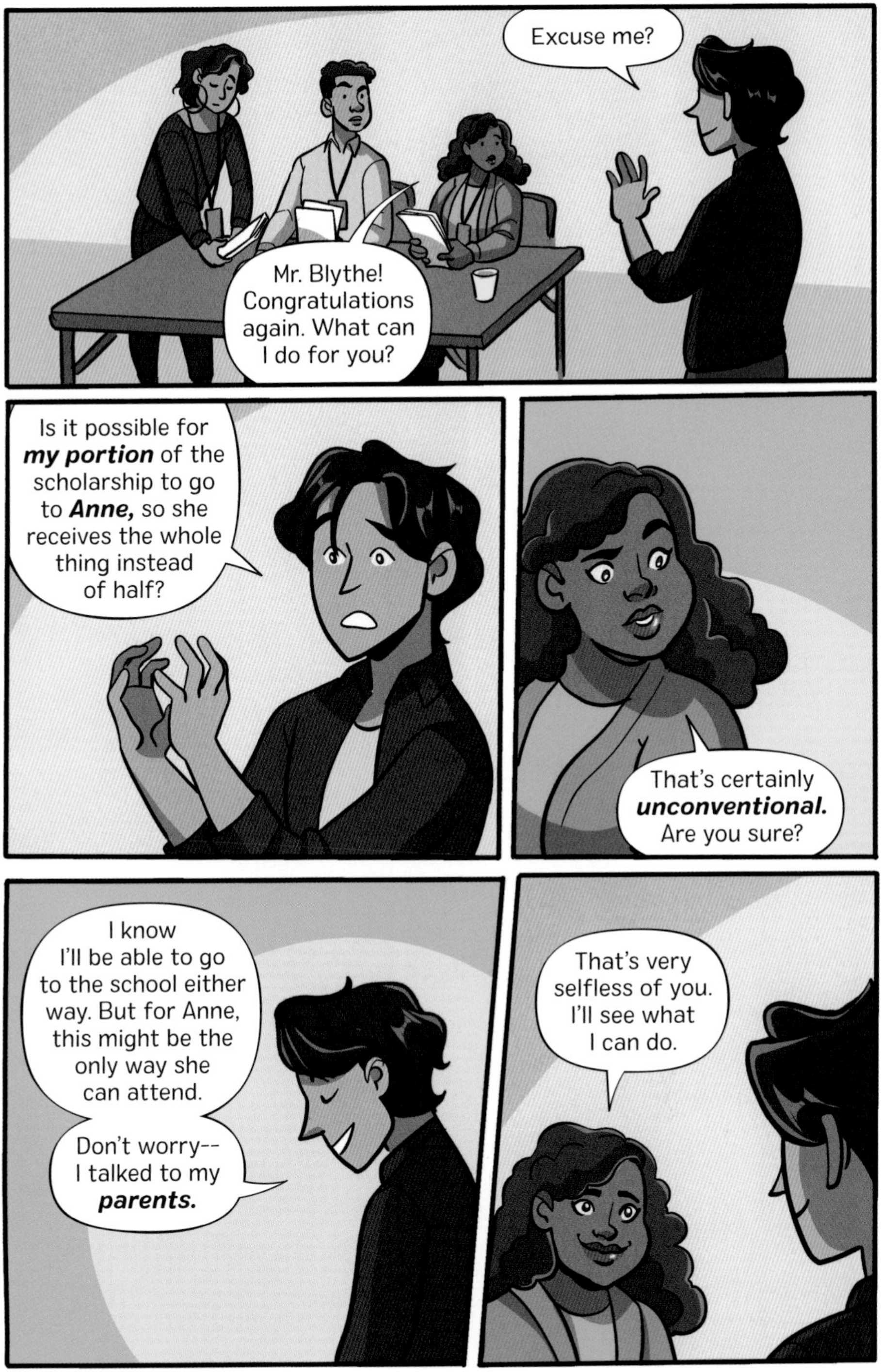
Excuse me?
Mr. Blythe! Congratulations again. What can I do for you?
Is it possible for *my portion* of the scholarship to go to *Anne,* so she receives the whole thing instead of half?
That's certainly *unconventional.* Are you sure?
I know I'll be able to go to the school either way. But for Anne, this might be the only way she can attend.
Don't worry-- I talked to my *parents.*
That's very selfless of you. I'll see what I can do.

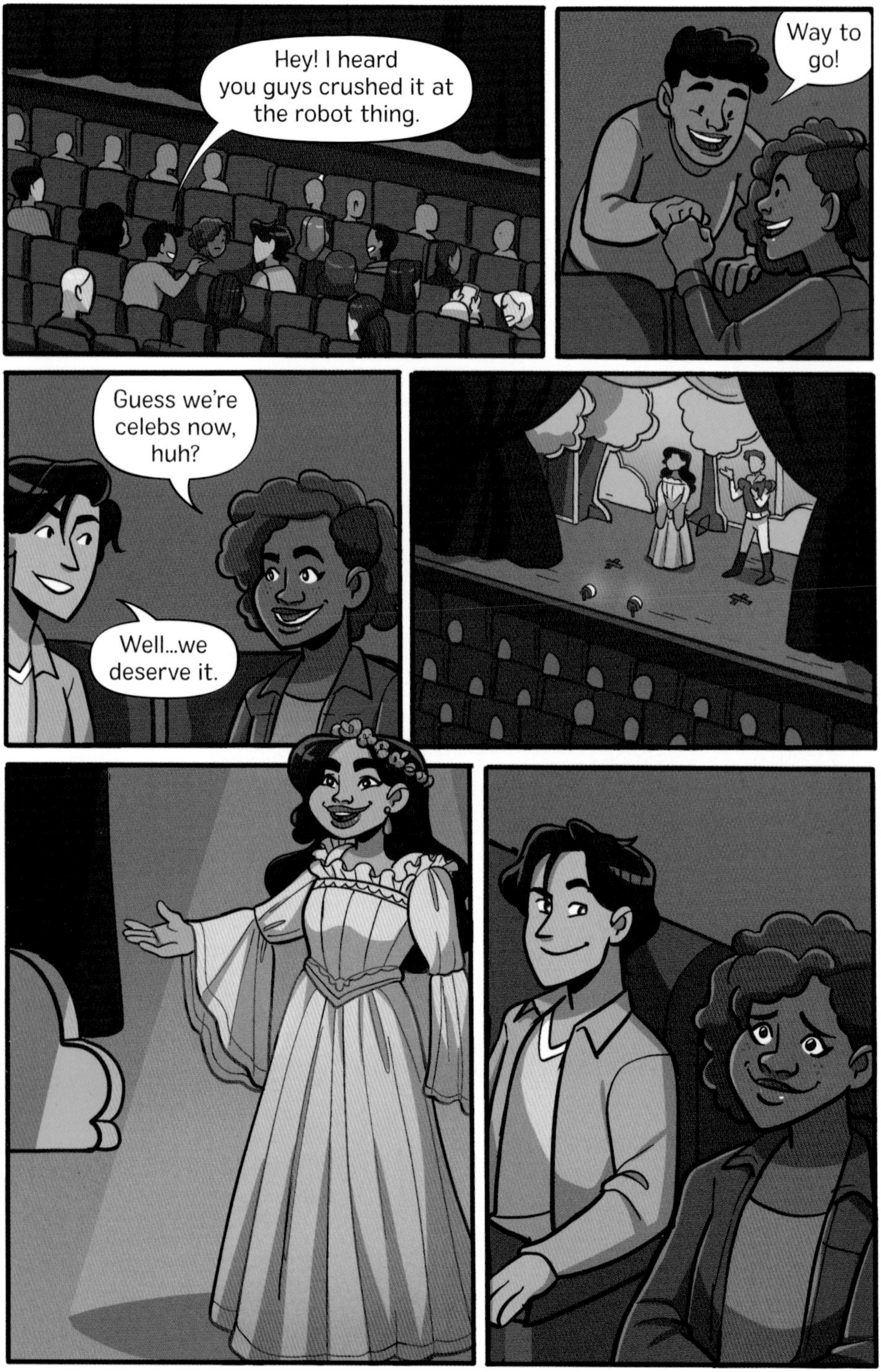
Hey! I heard you guys crushed it at the robot thing.
Way to go!
Guess we're celebs now, huh?
Well...we deserve it.

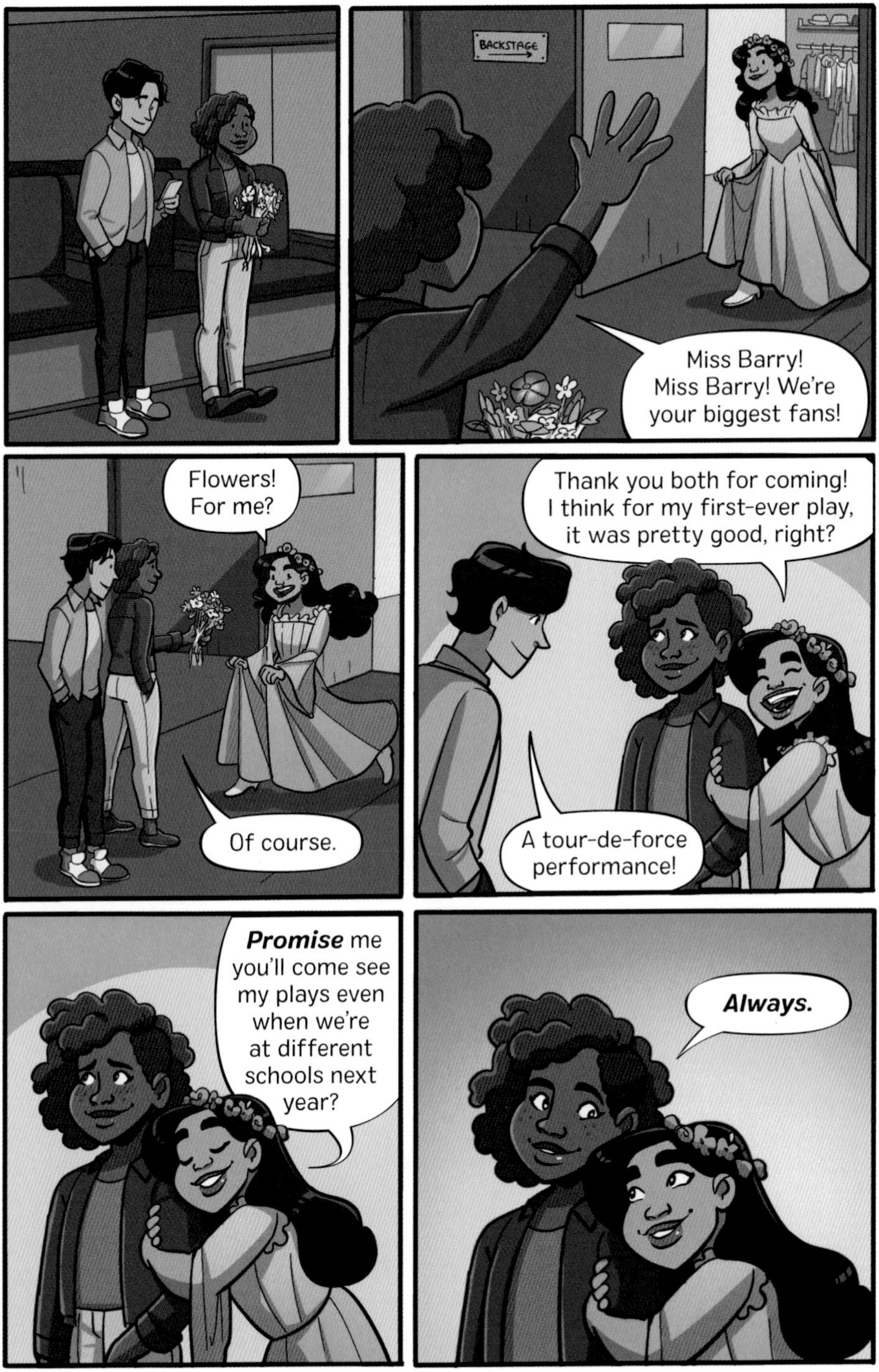
BACKSTAGE
Miss Barry! Miss Barry! We're your biggest fans!
Flowers! For me?
Of course.
Thank you both for coming! I think for my first-ever play, it was pretty good, right?
A tour-de-force performance!
Promise me you'll come see my plays even when we're at different schools next year?
Always.

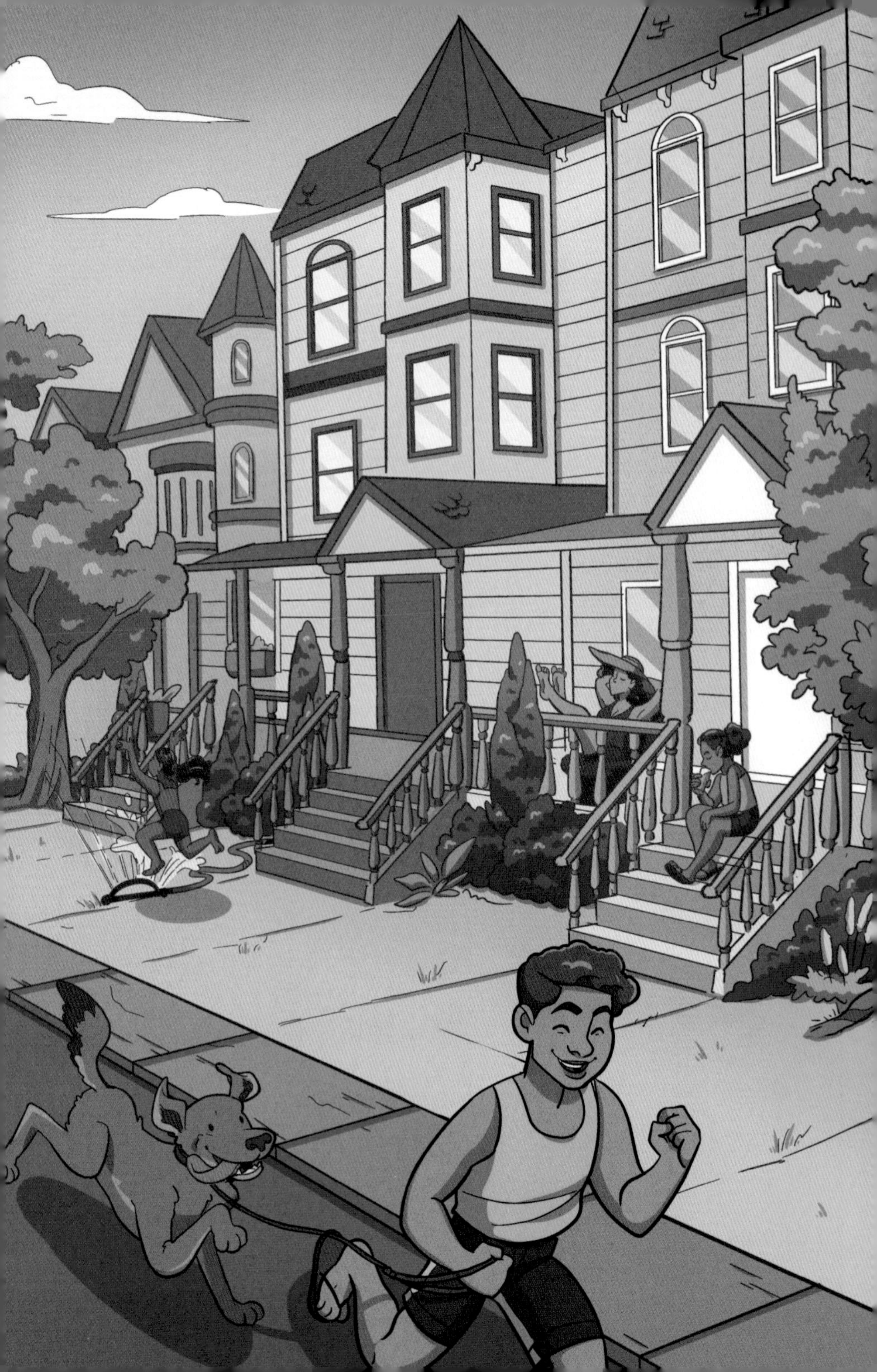

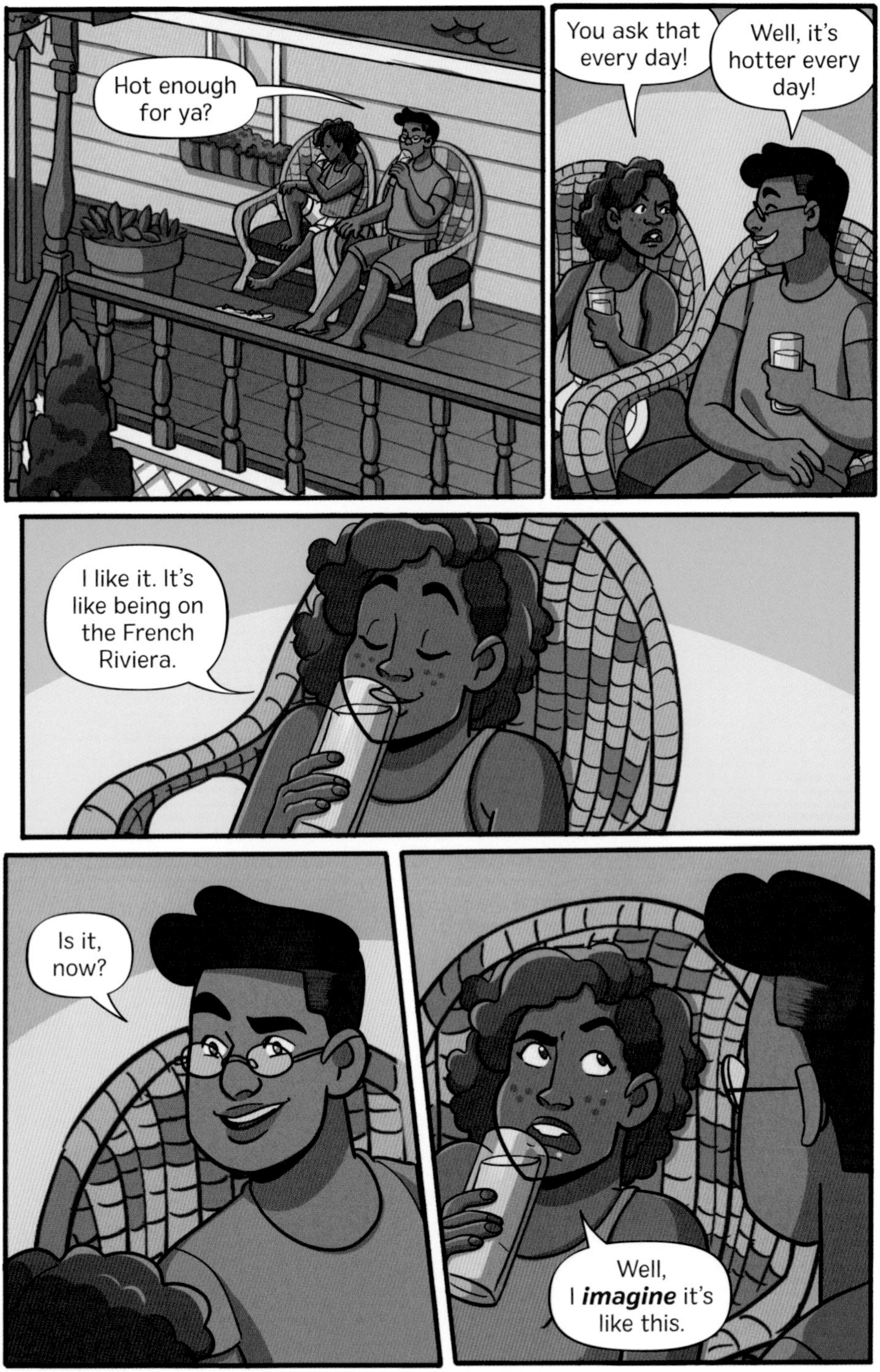
Hot enough for ya?
You ask that every day!
Well, it's hotter every day!
I like it. It's like being on the French Riviera.
Is it, now?
Well, I *imagine* it's like this.

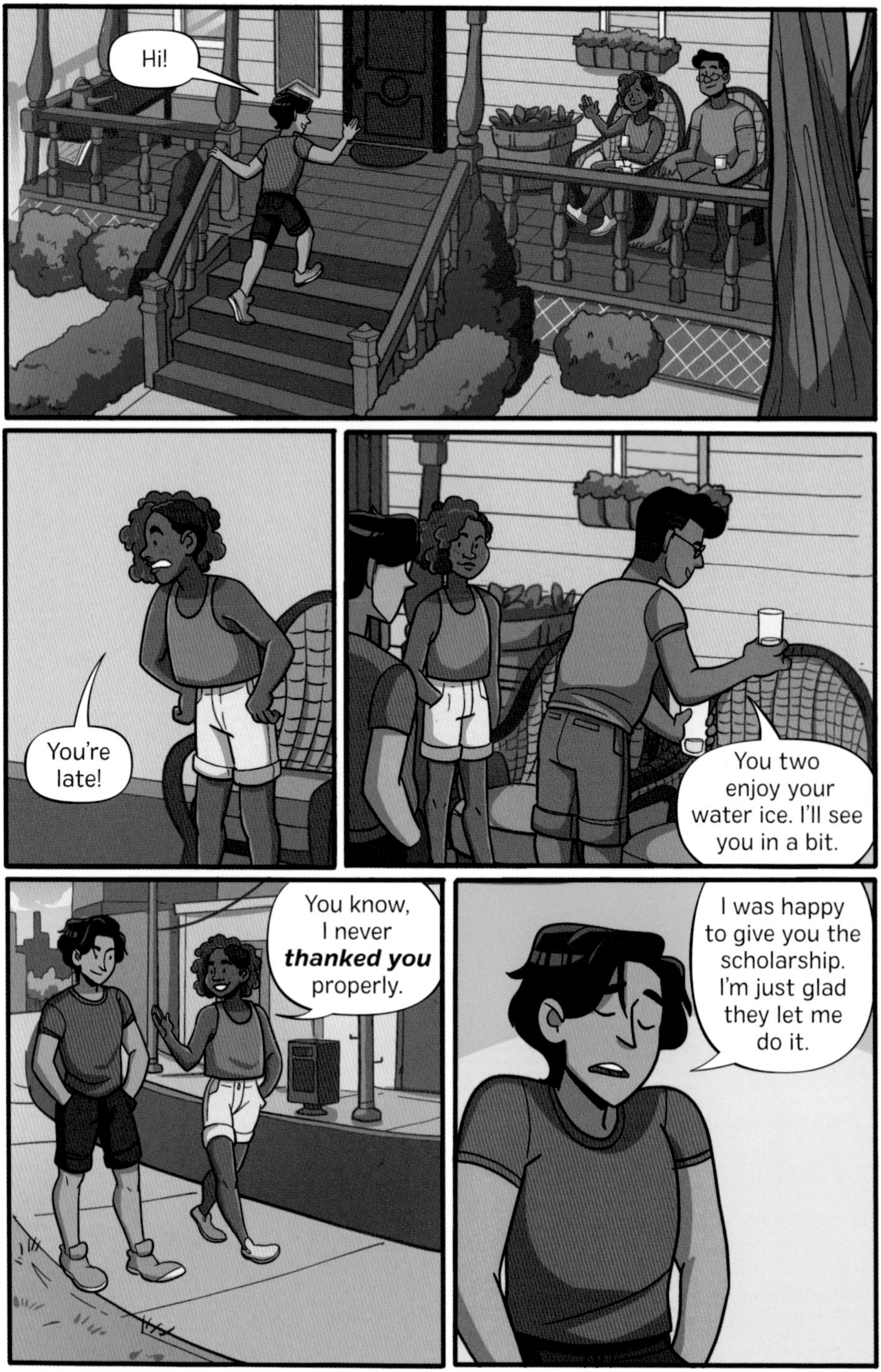
Hi!
You're late!
You two enjoy your water ice. I'll see you in a bit.
You know, I never ***thanked you*** properly.
I was happy to give you the scholarship. I'm just glad they let me do it.

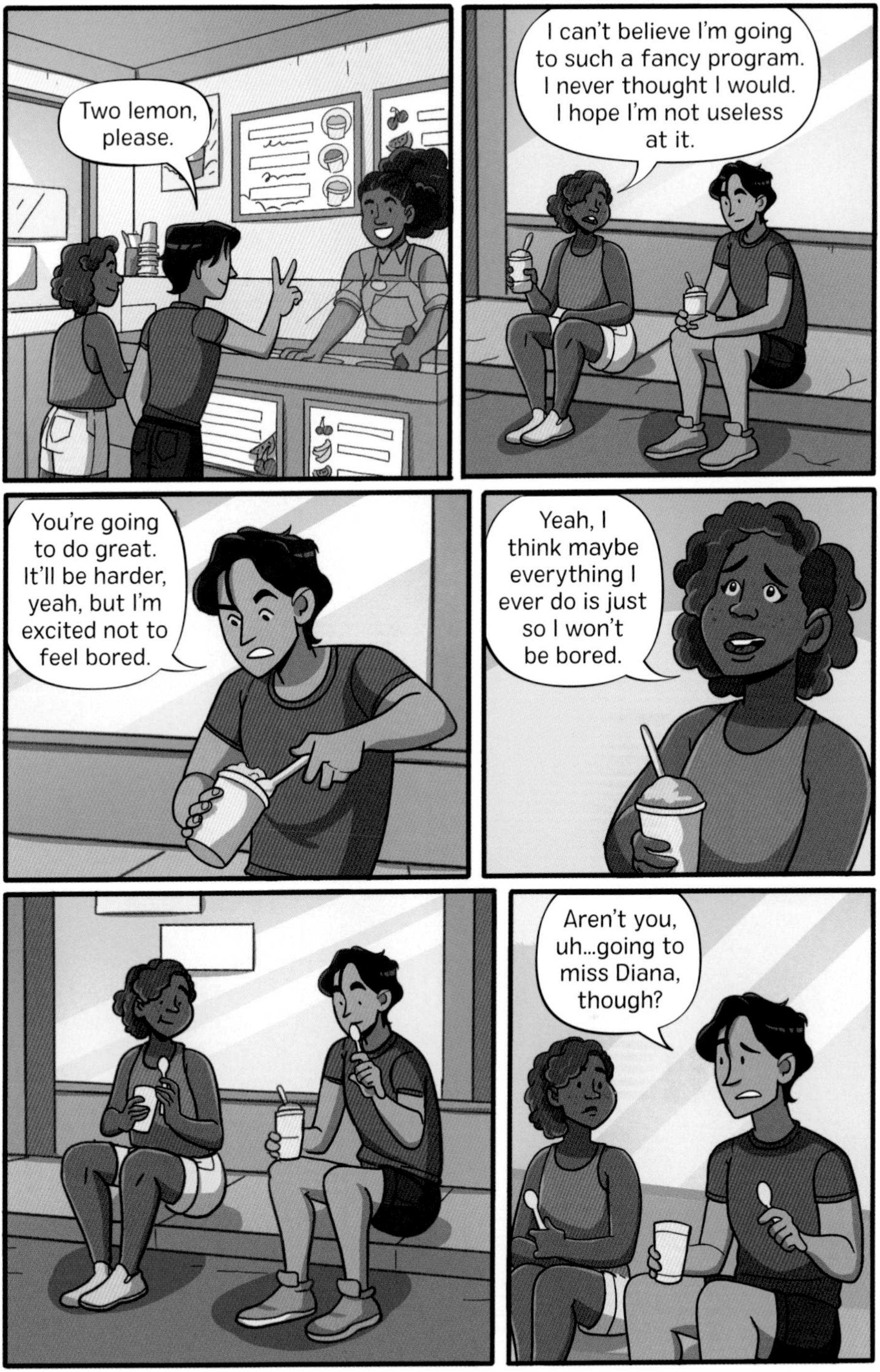
Two lemon, please.
I can't believe I'm going to such a fancy program. I never thought I would. I hope I'm not useless at it.
You're going to do great. It'll be harder, yeah, but I'm excited not to feel bored.
Yeah, I think maybe everything I ever do is just so I won't be bored.
Aren't you, uh...going to miss Diana, though?

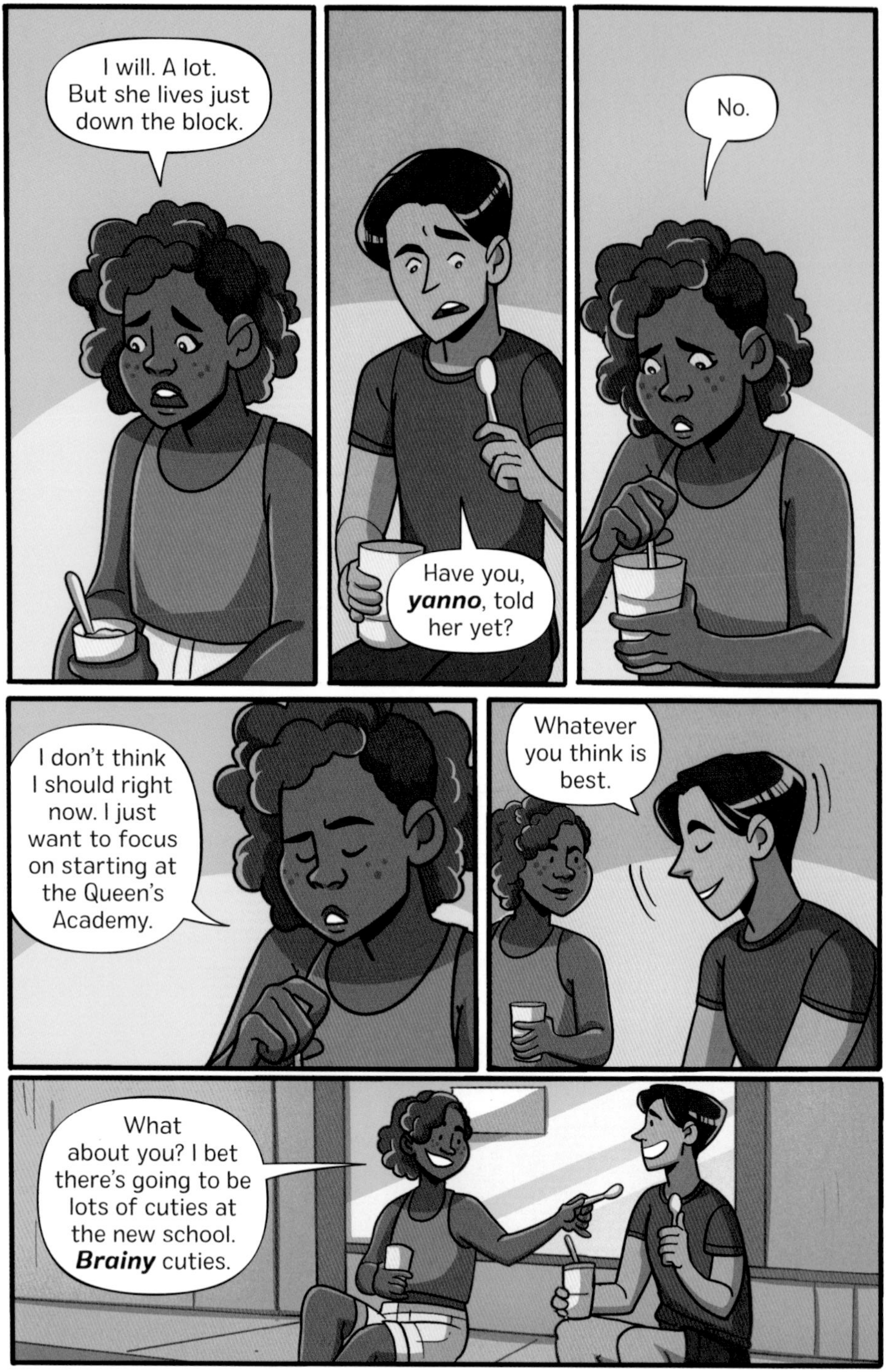
I will. A lot.
But she lives just
down the block.
Have you,
yanno, told
her yet?
No.
I don't think
I should right
now. I just
want to focus
on starting at
the Queen's
Academy.
Whatever
you think is
best.
What
about you? I bet
there's going to be
lots of cuties at
the new school.
Brainy cuties.

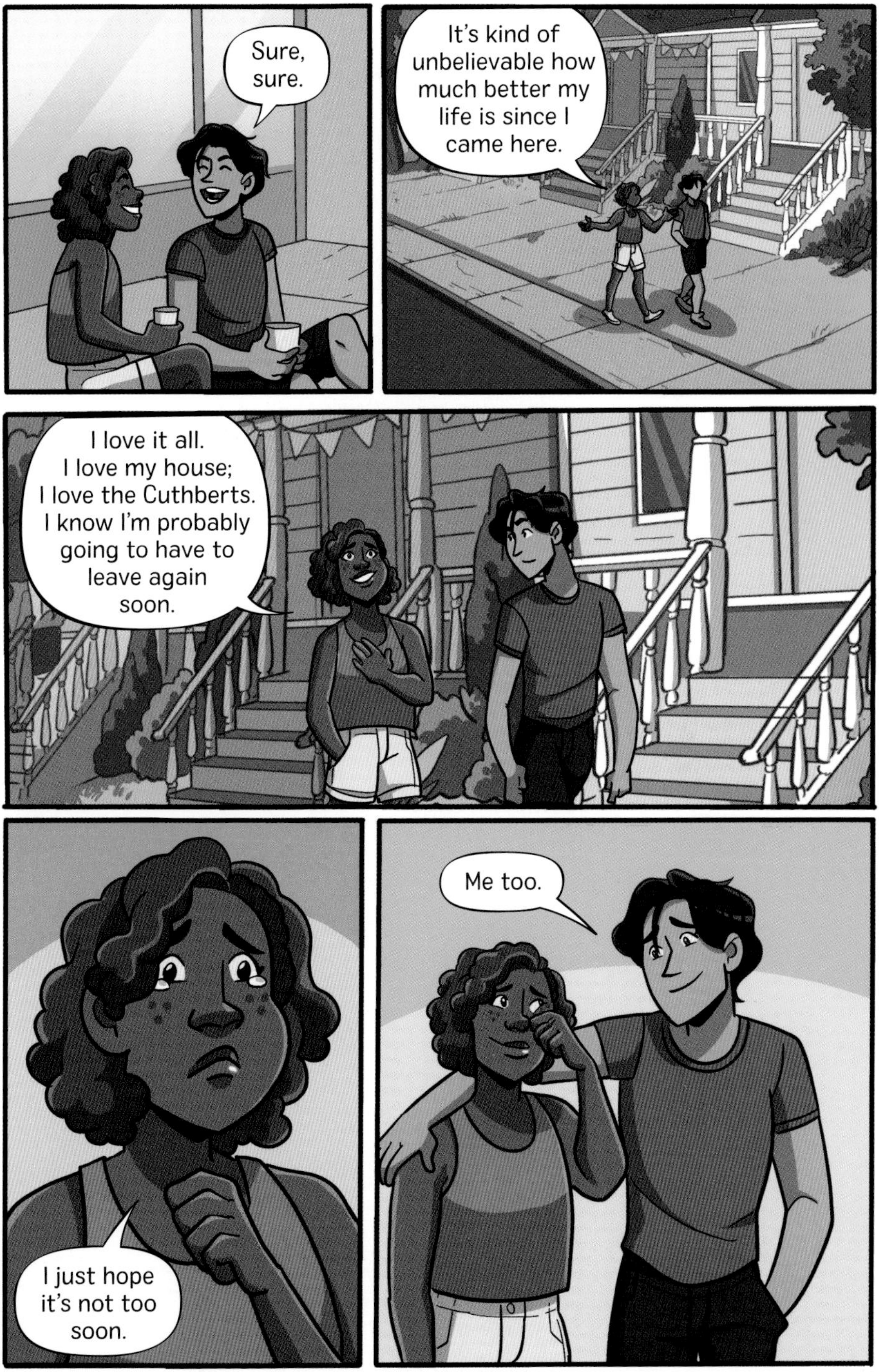
Sure, sure.
It's kind of unbelievable how much better my life is since I came here.
I love it all. I love my house; I love the Cuthberts. I know I'm probably going to have to leave again soon.
I just hope it's not too soon.
Me too.

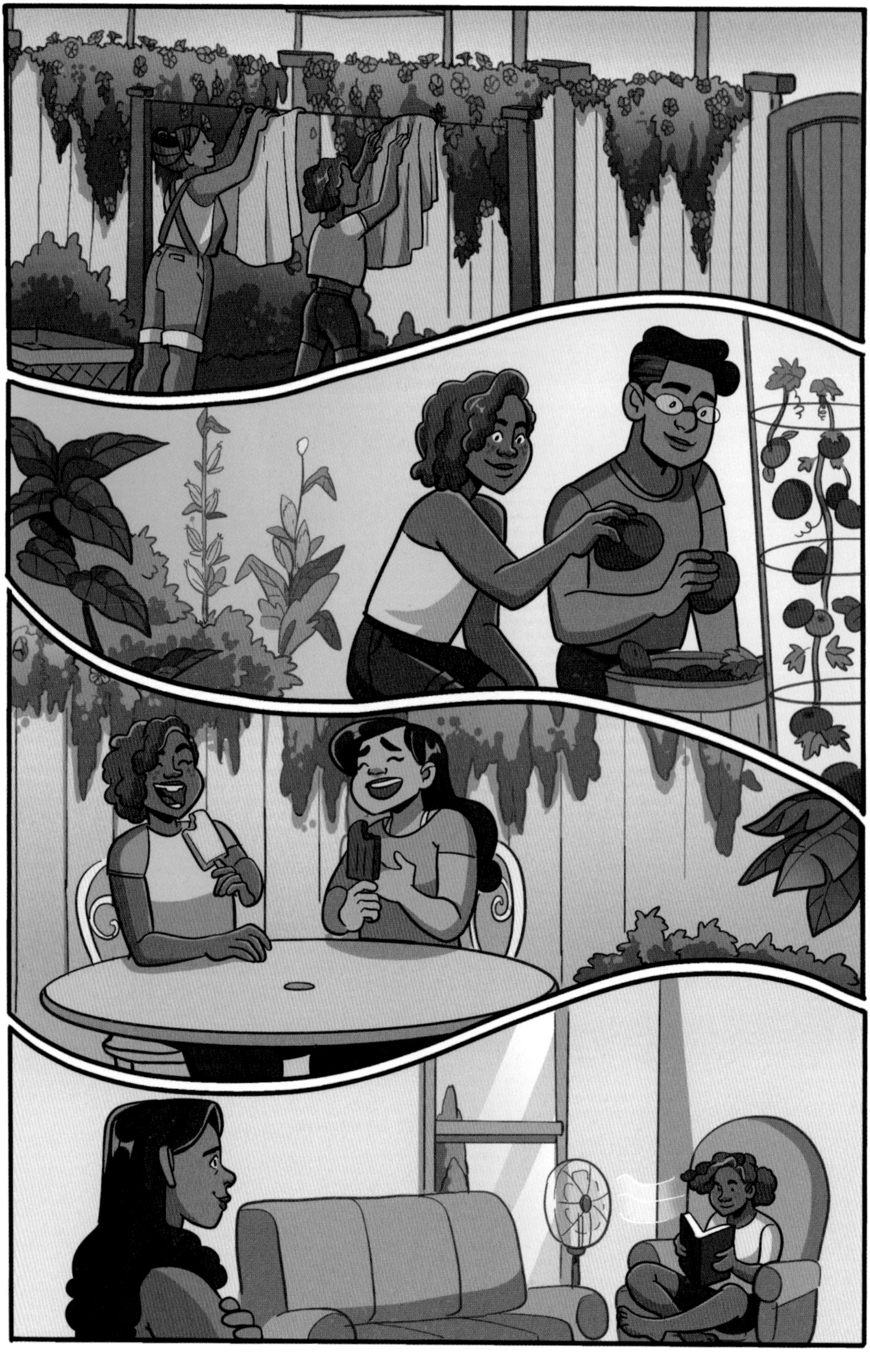

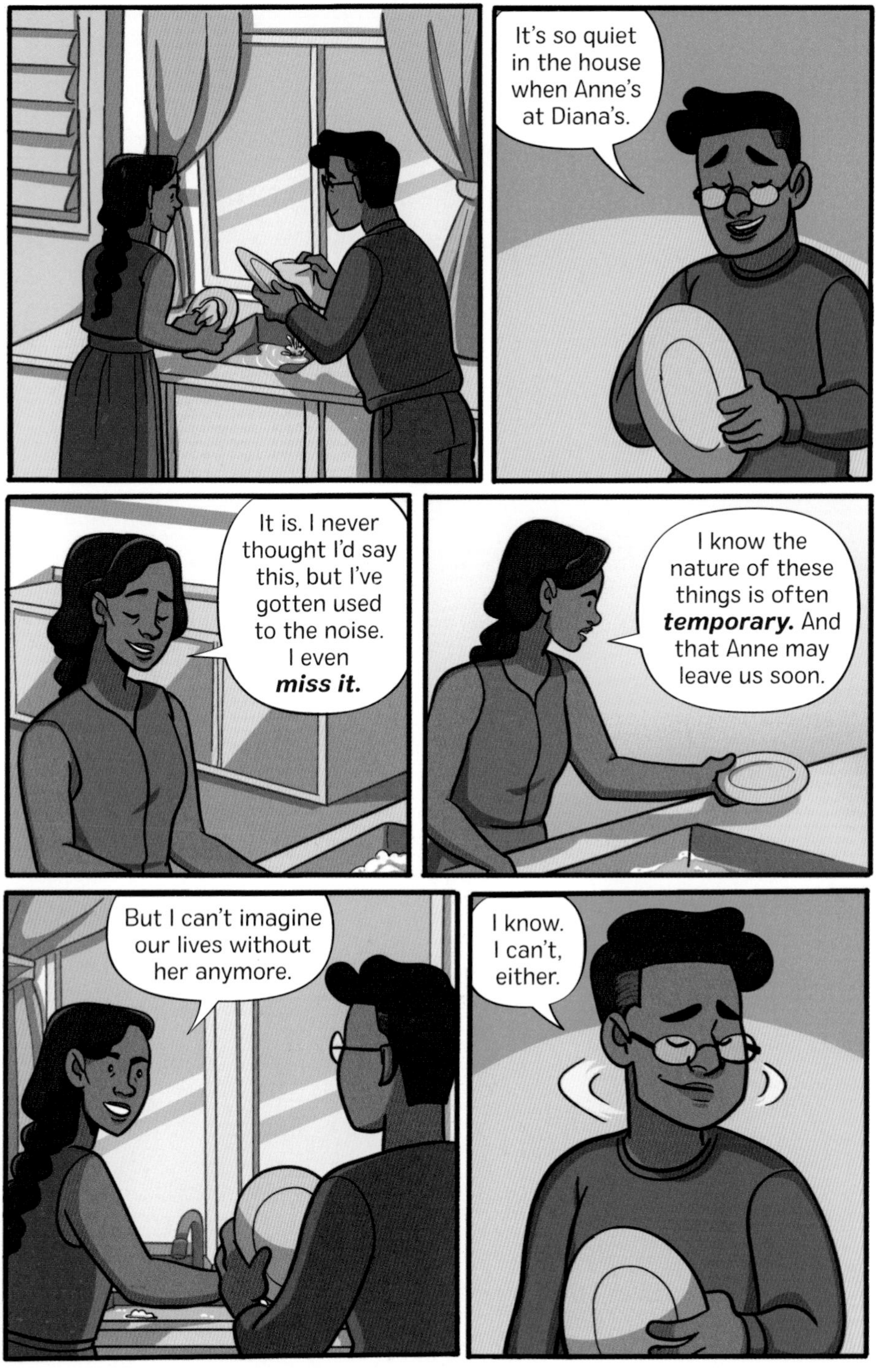
It's so quiet in the house when Anne's at Diana's.
It is. I never thought I'd say this, but I've gotten used to the noise. I even **miss it.**
I know the nature of these things is often ***temporary.*** And that Anne may leave us soon.
But I can't imagine our lives without her anymore.
I know. I can't, either.

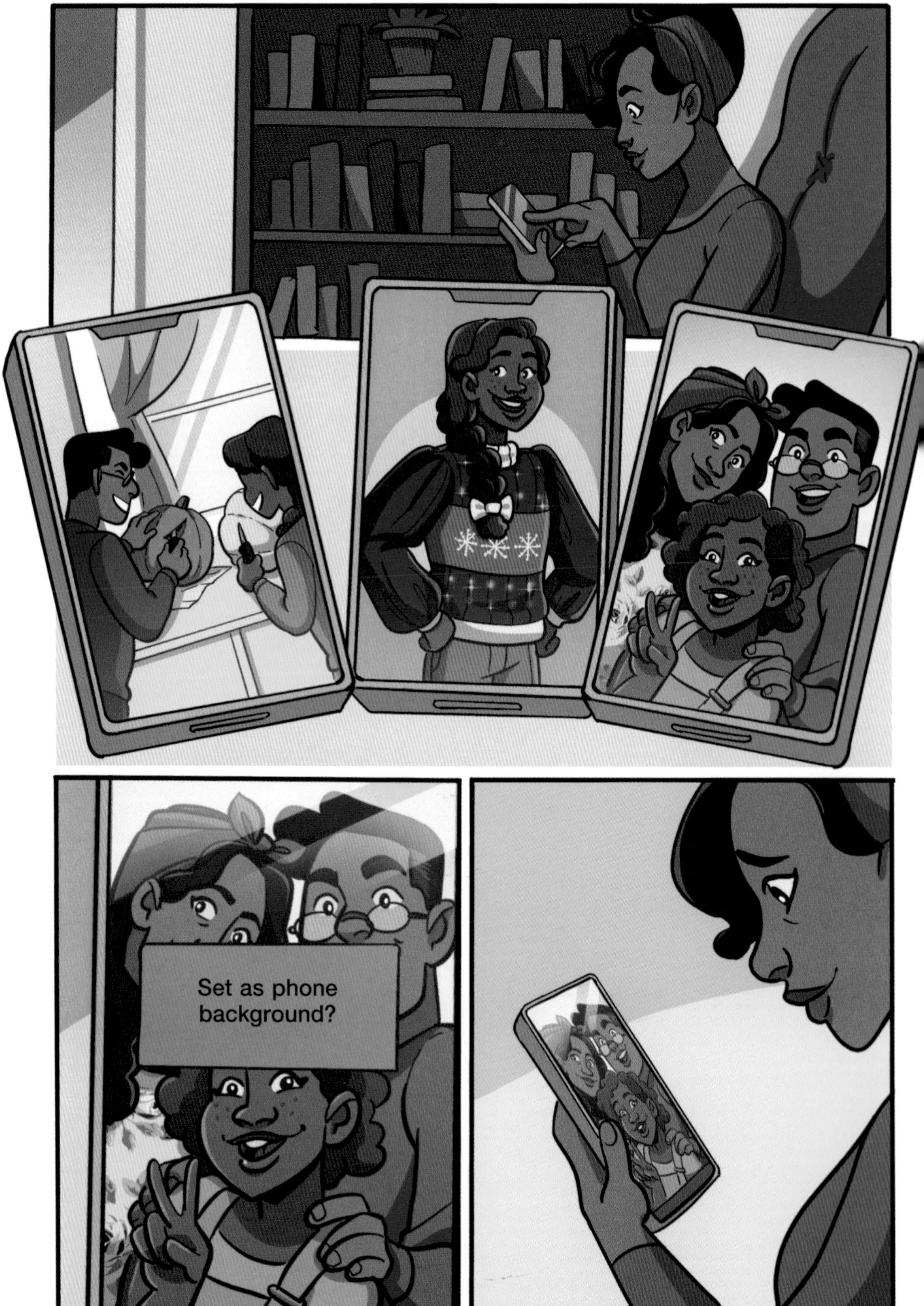
Set as phone background?

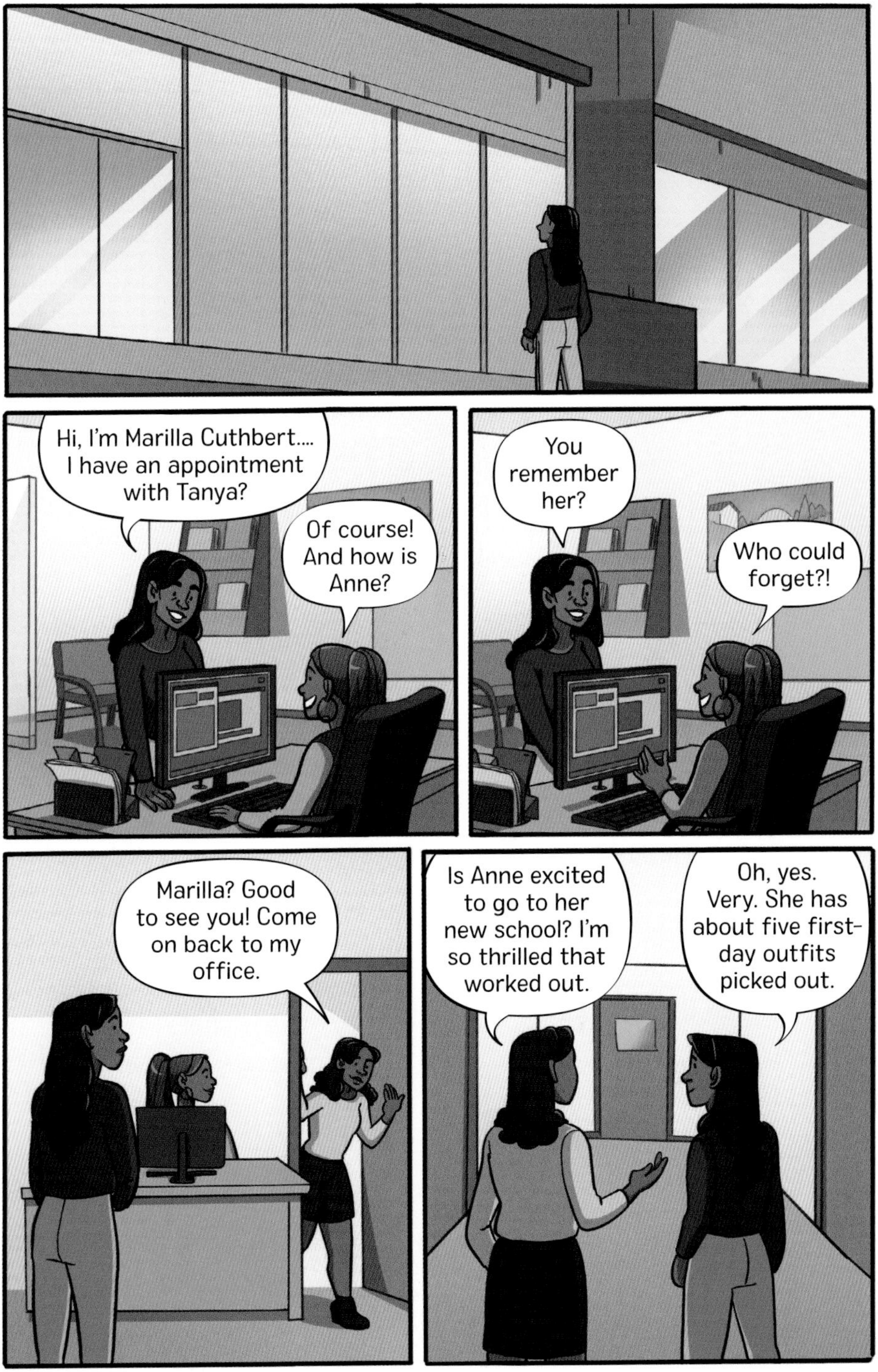
Hi, I'm Marilla Cuthbert.... I have an appointment with Tanya?
Of course! And how is Anne?
You remember her?
Who could forget?!
Marilla? Good to see you! Come on back to my office.
Is Anne excited to go to her new school? I'm so thrilled that worked out.
Oh, yes. Very. She has about five first-day outfits picked out.

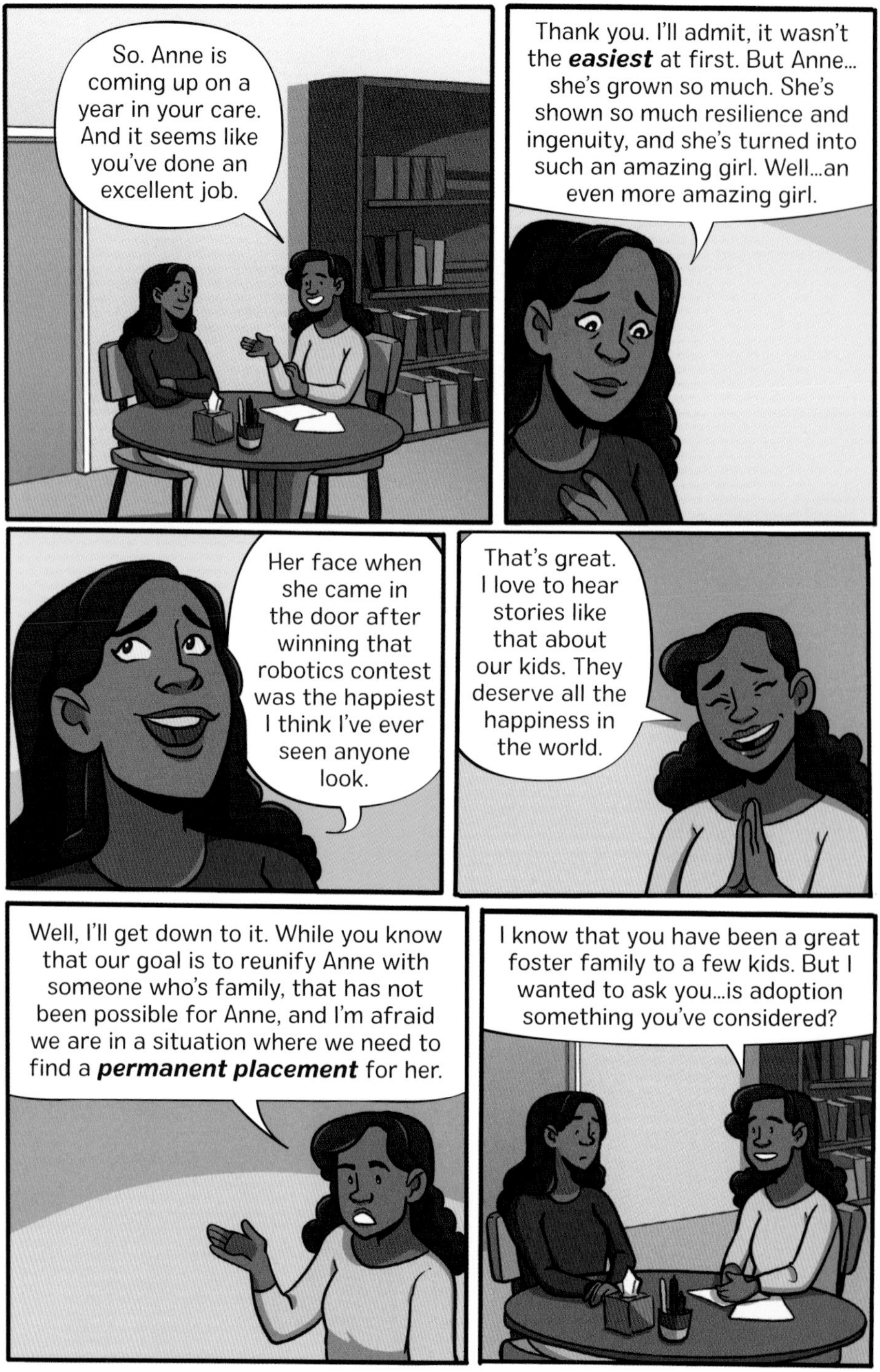

So. Anne is coming up on a year in your care. And it seems like you've done an excellent job.
Thank you. I'll admit, it wasn't the ***easiest*** at first. But Anne... she's grown so much. She's shown so much resilience and ingenuity, and she's turned into such an amazing girl. Well...an even more amazing girl.
Her face when she came in the door after winning that robotics contest was the happiest I think I've ever seen anyone look.
That's great. I love to hear stories like that about our kids. They deserve all the happiness in the world.
Well, I'll get down to it. While you know that our goal is to reunify Anne with someone who's family, that has not been possible for Anne, and I'm afraid we are in a situation where we need to find a ***permanent placement*** for her.
I know that you have been a great foster family to a few kids. But I wanted to ask you...is adoption something you've considered?

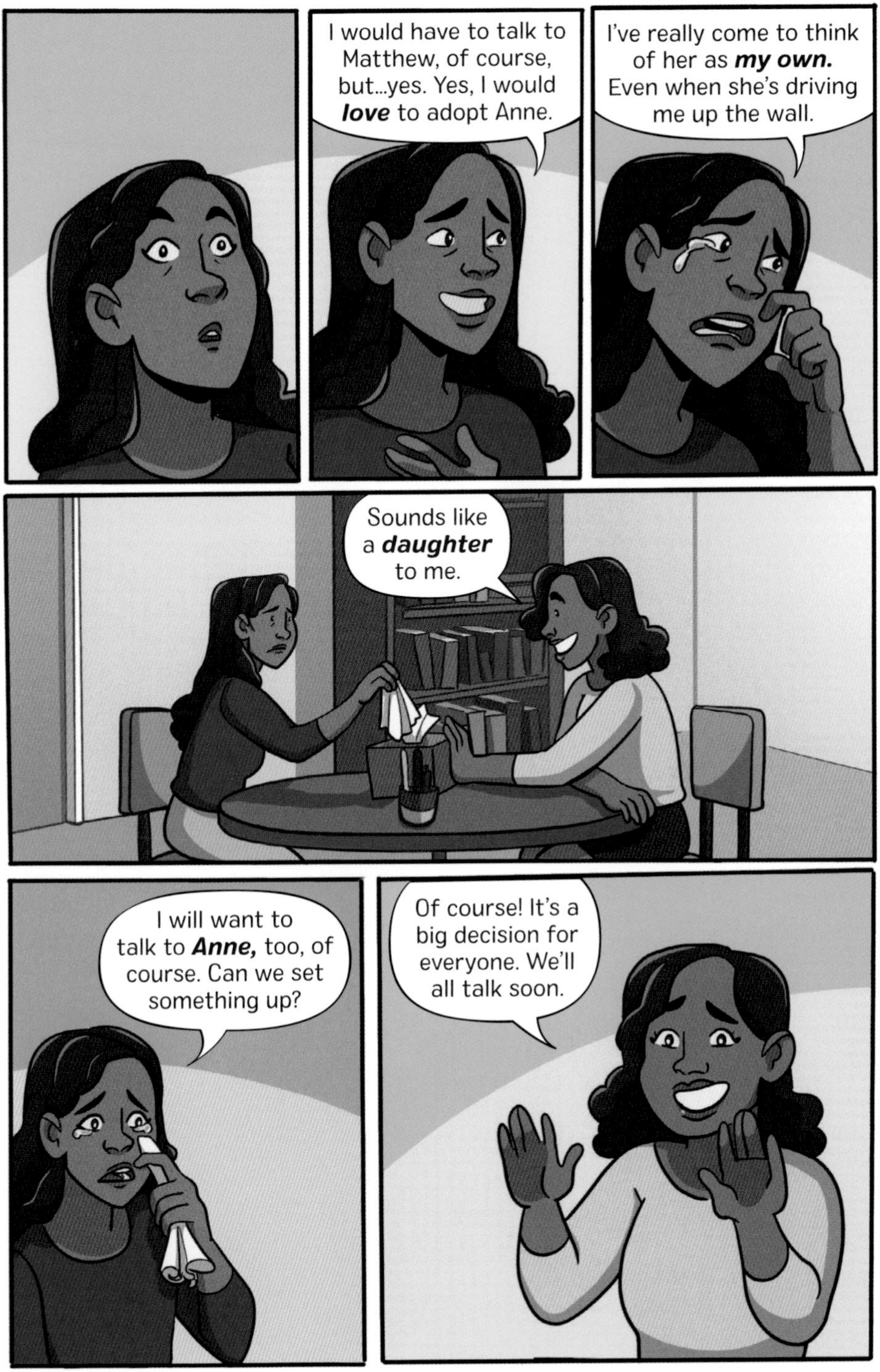
I would have to talk to Matthew, of course, but...yes. Yes, I would **love** to adopt Anne.
I've really come to think of her as **my own.** Even when she's driving me up the wall.
Sounds like a **daughter** to me.
I will want to talk to **Anne,** too, of course. Can we set something up?
Of course! It's a big decision for everyone. We'll all talk soon.

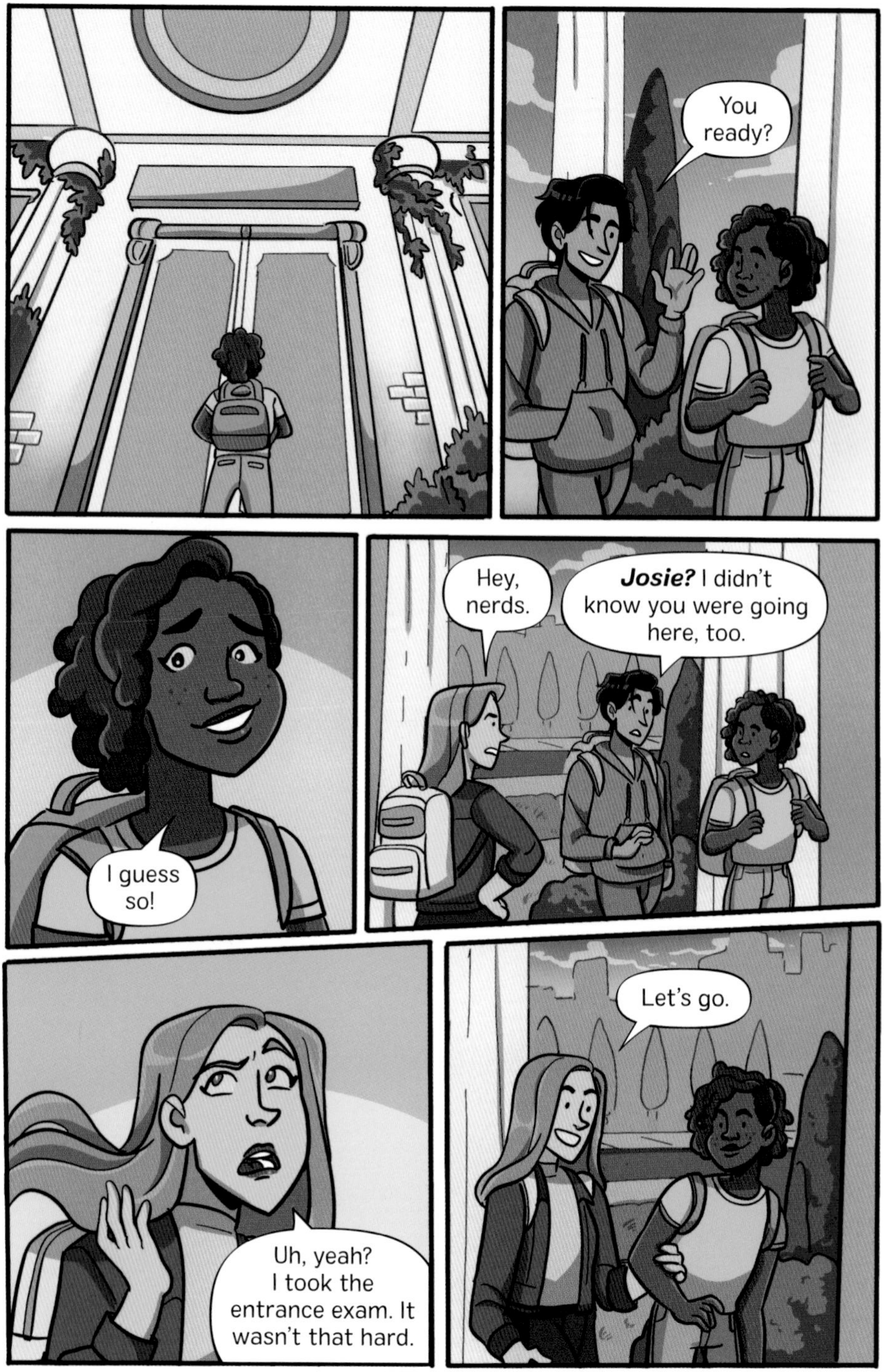
You ready?
I guess so!
Hey, nerds.
Josie? I didn't know you were going here, too.
Uh, yeah? I took the entrance exam. It wasn't that hard.
Let's go.

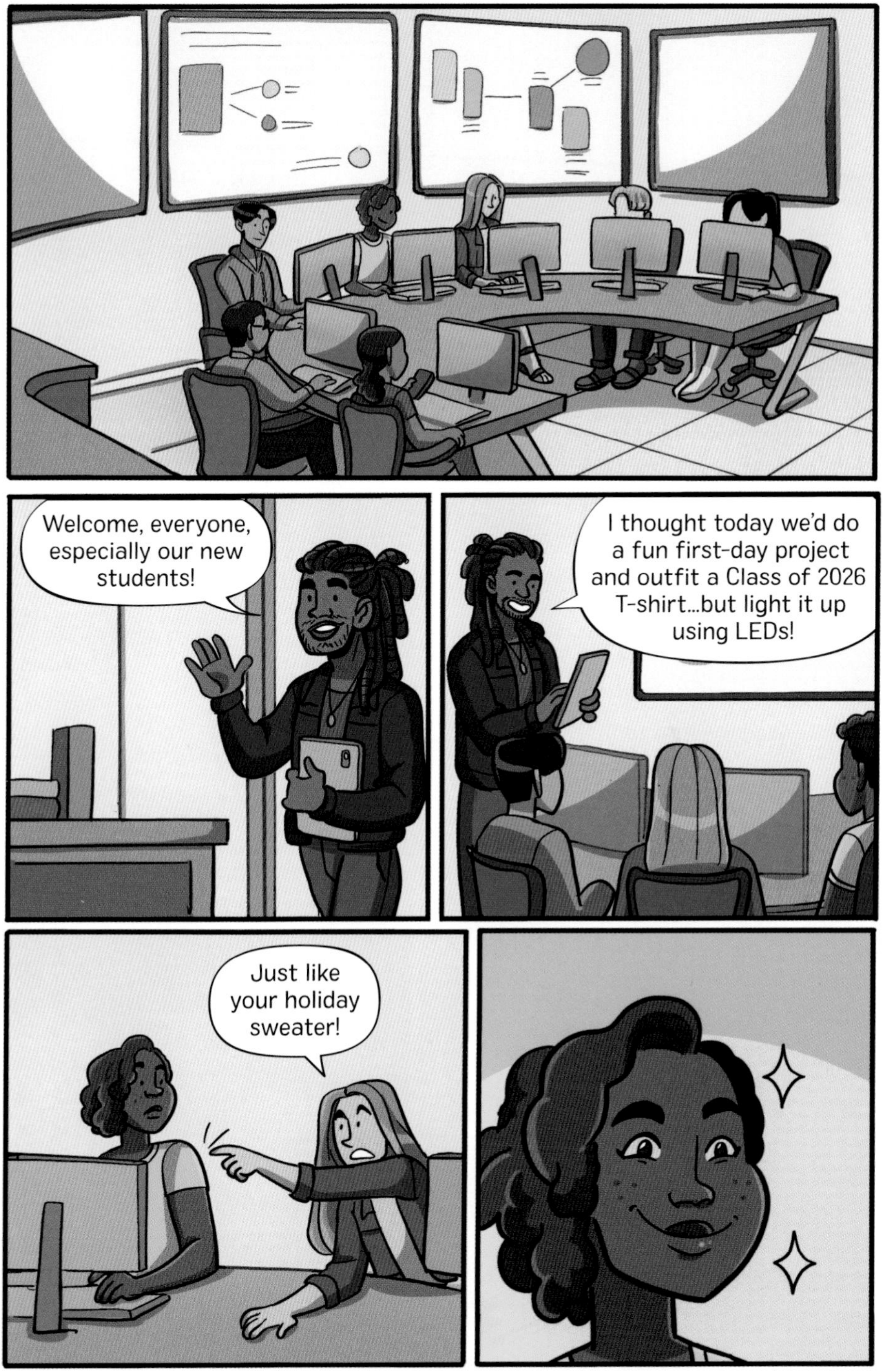
Welcome, everyone, especially our new students!
I thought today we'd do a fun first-day project and outfit a Class of 2026 T-shirt...but light it up using LEDs!
Just like your holiday sweater!

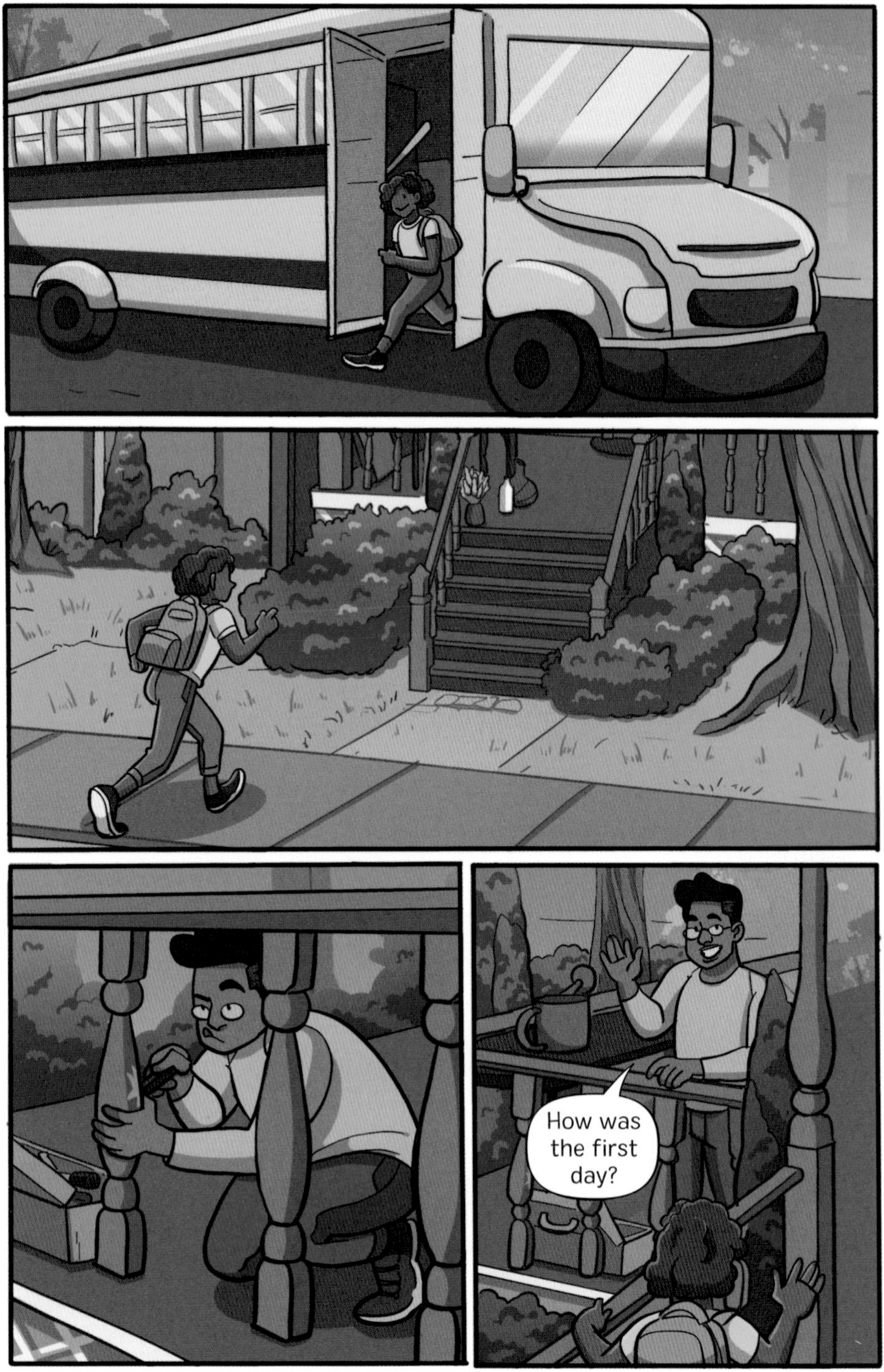
How was the first day?

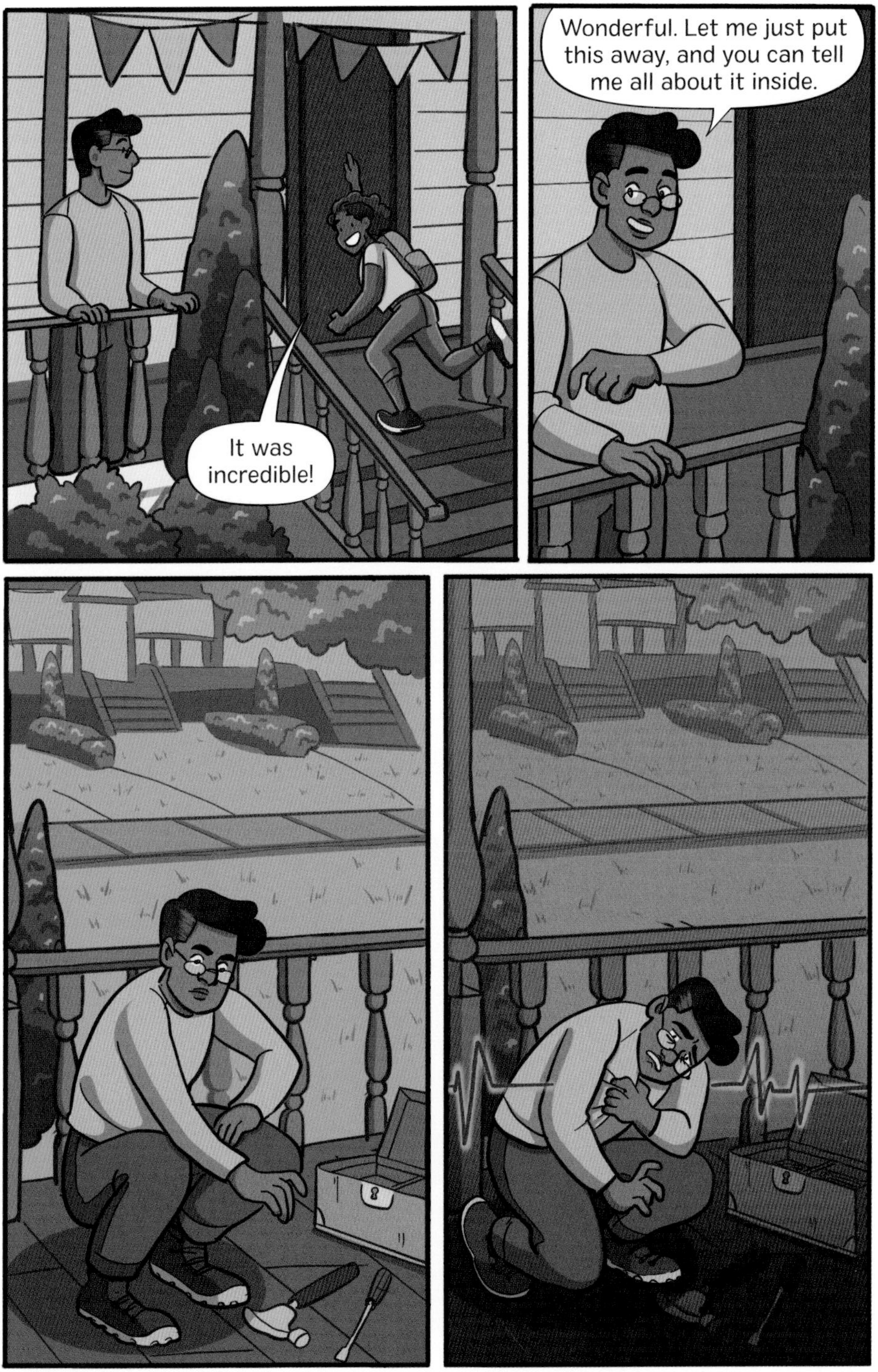
It was incredible!
Wonderful. Let me just put this away, and you can tell me all about it inside.

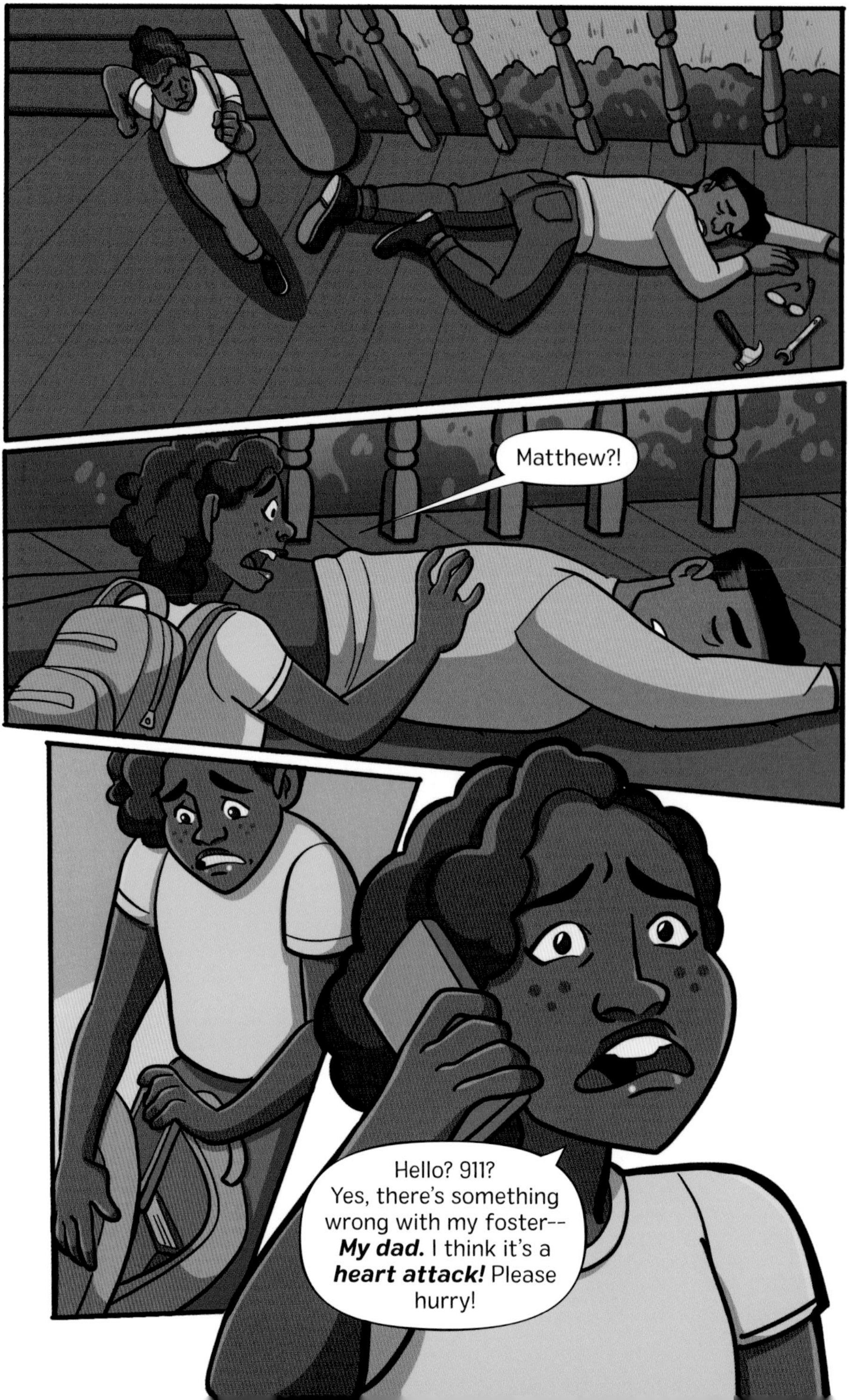
Matthew?!
Hello? 911? Yes, there's something wrong with my foster-- **My dad.** I think it's a ***heart attack!*** Please hurry!

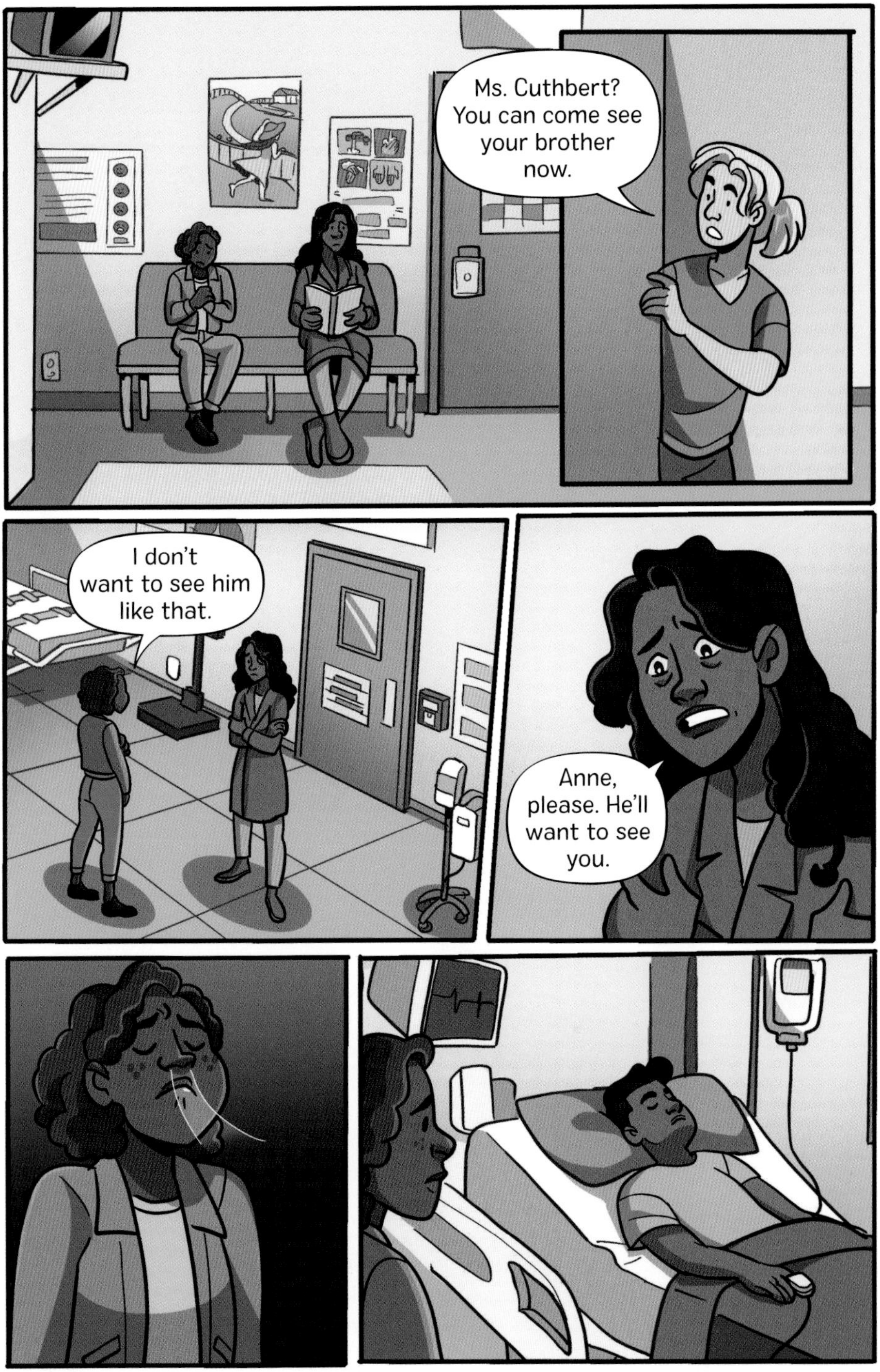
Ms. Cuthbert? You can come see your brother now.
I don't want to see him like that.
Anne, please. He'll want to see you.

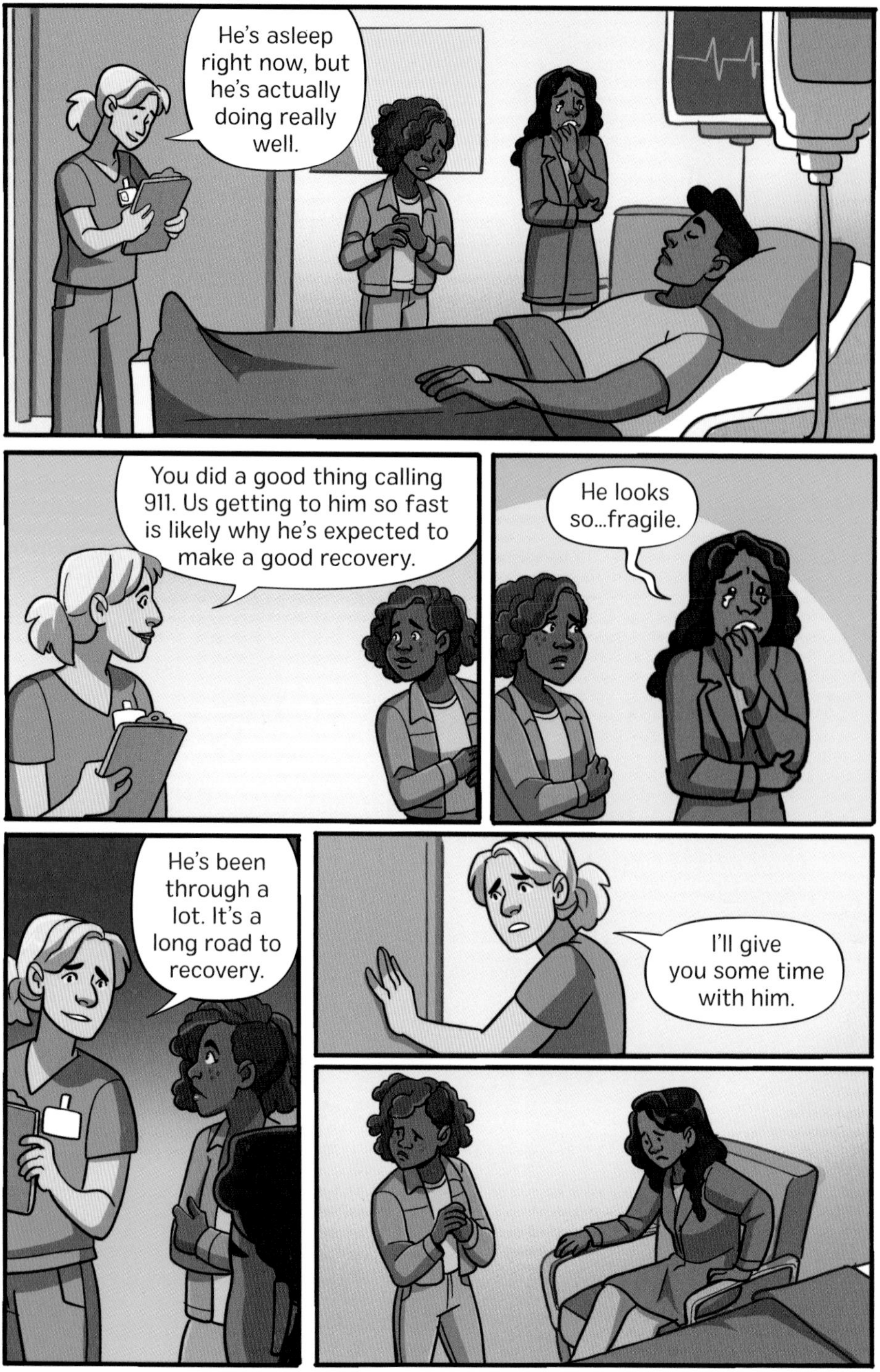
He's asleep right now, but he's actually doing really well.
You did a good thing calling 911. Us getting to him so fast is likely why he's expected to make a good recovery.
He looks so...fragile.
He's been through a lot. It's a long road to recovery.
I'll give you some time with him.

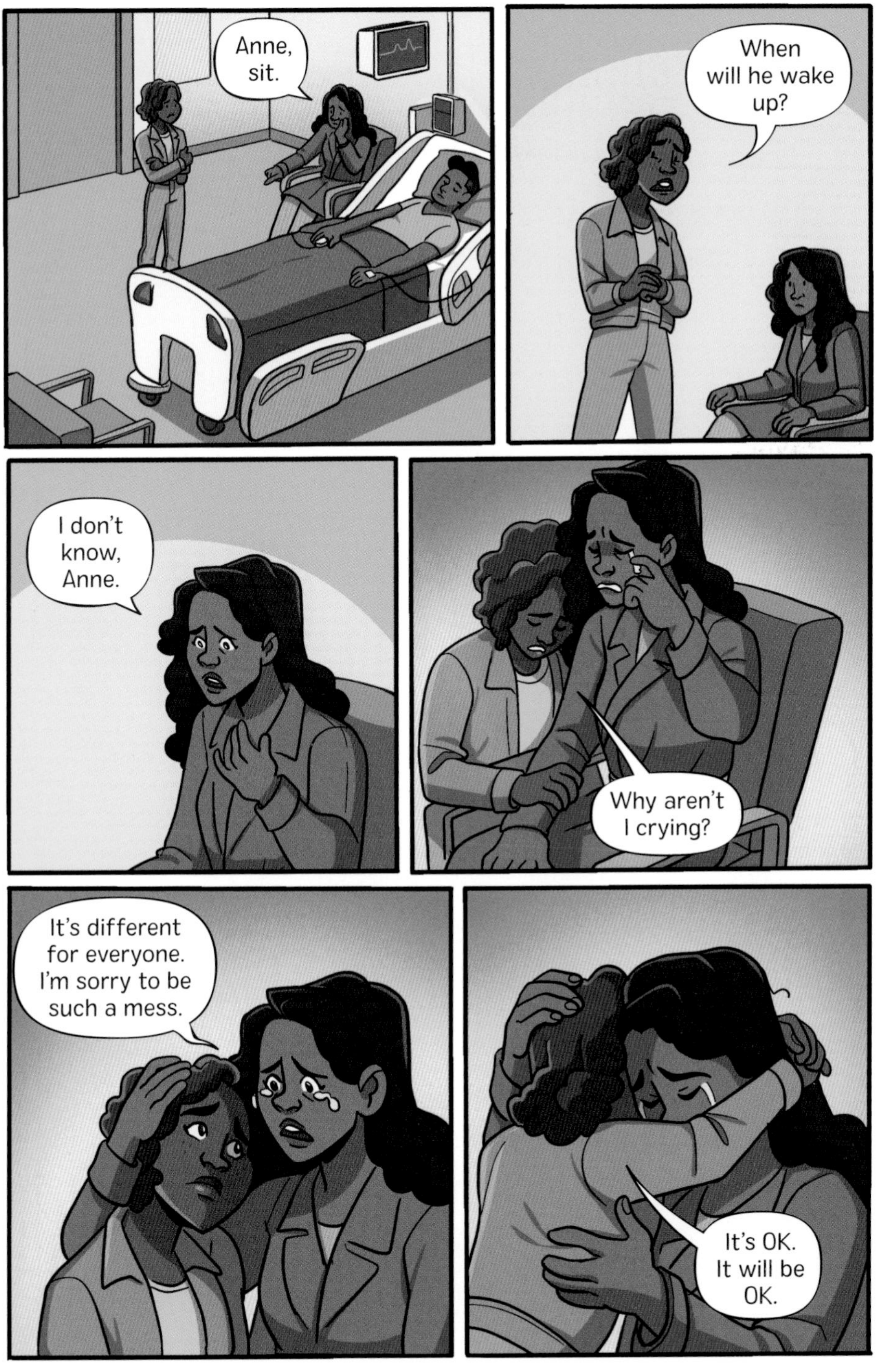
Anne, sit.
When will he wake up?
I don't know, Anne.
Why aren't I crying?
It's different for everyone. I'm sorry to be such a mess.
It's OK. It will be OK.

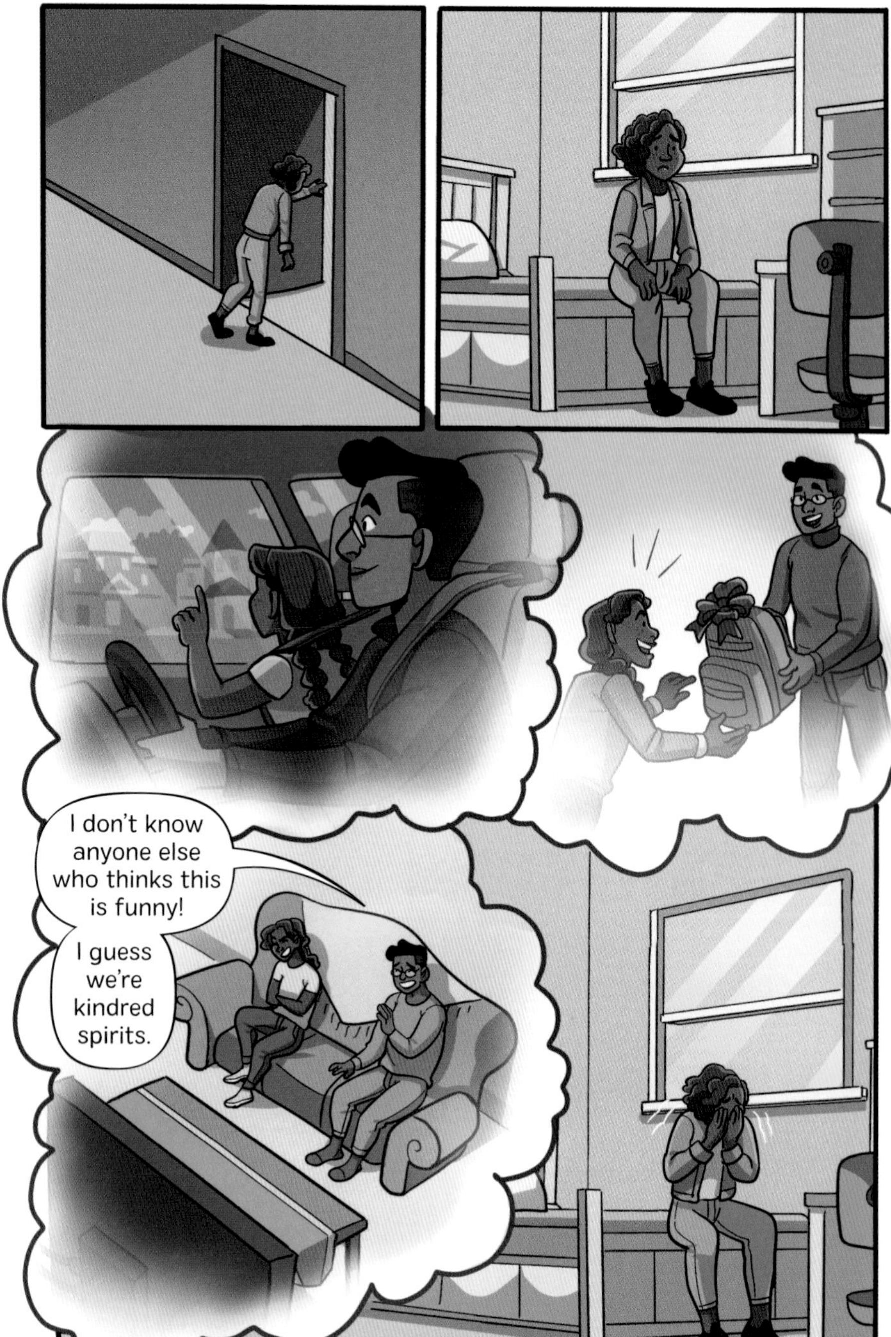
I don't know anyone else who thinks this is funny!
I guess we're kindred spirits.

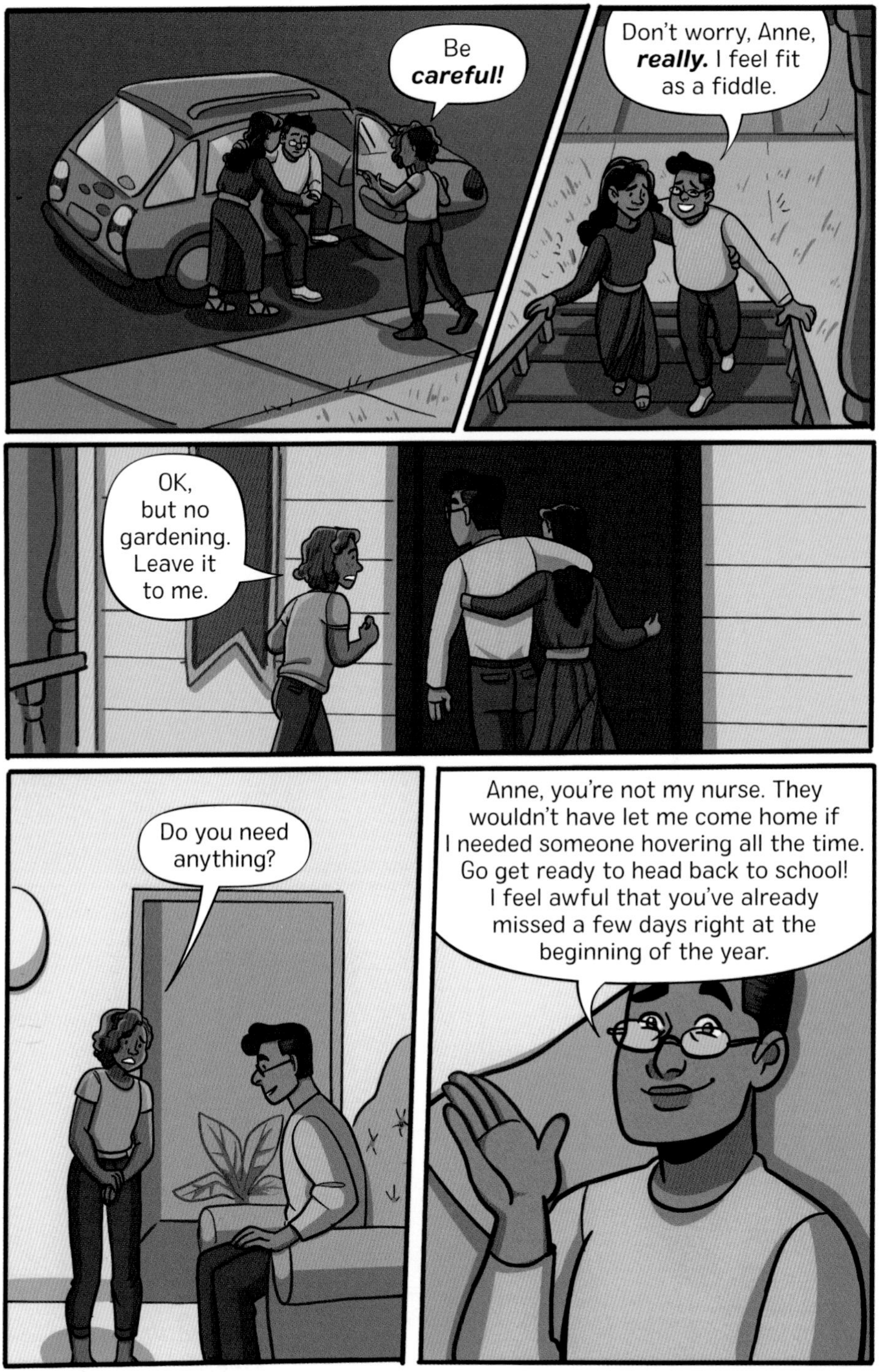
Be *careful!*
Don't worry, Anne, ***really.*** I feel fit as a fiddle.
OK, but no gardening. Leave it to me.
Do you need anything?
Anne, you're not my nurse. They wouldn't have let me come home if I needed someone hovering all the time. Go get ready to head back to school! I feel awful that you've already missed a few days right at the beginning of the year.

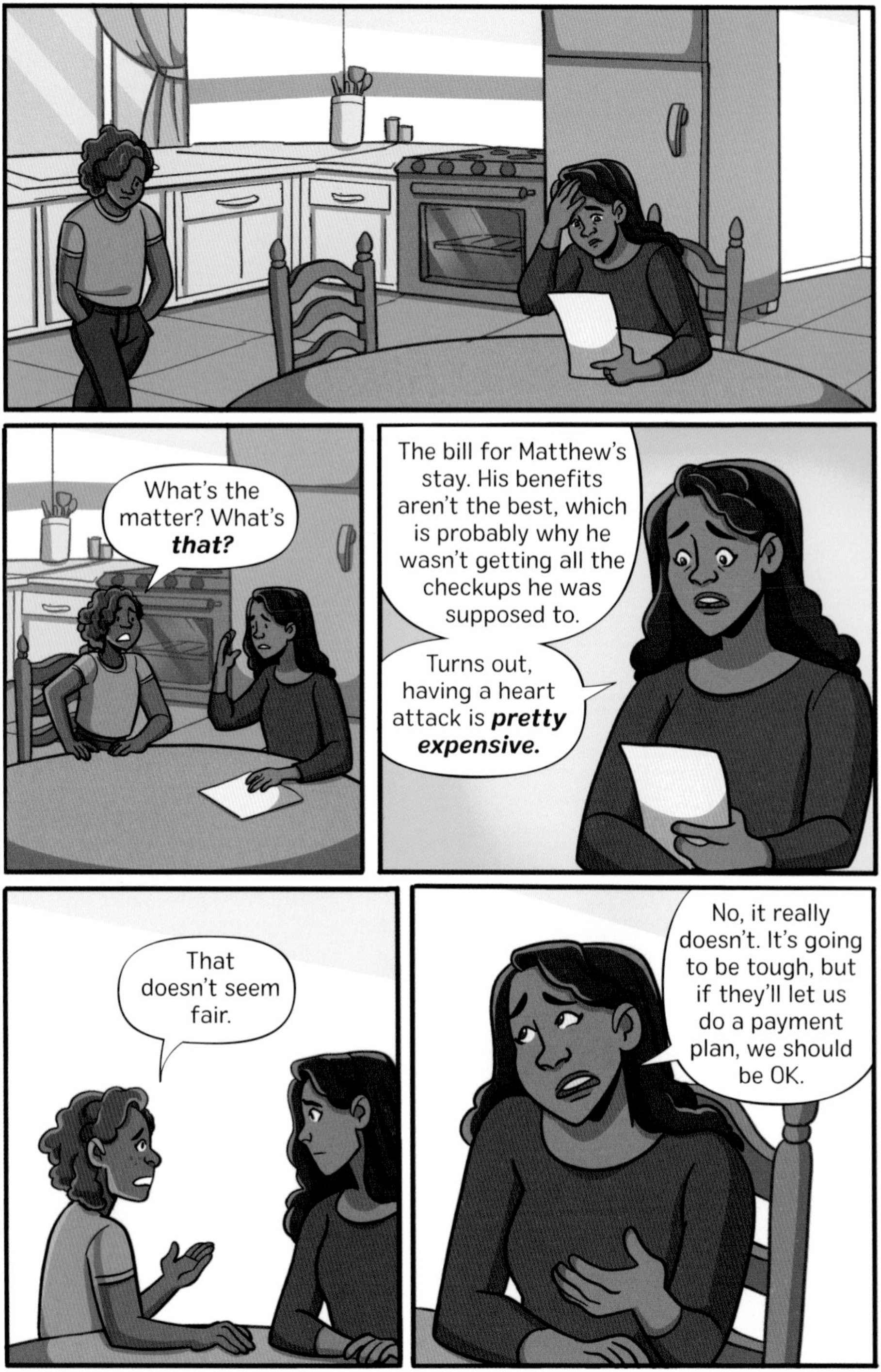

What's the matter? What's ***that?***
The bill for Matthew's stay. His benefits aren't the best, which is probably why he wasn't getting all the checkups he was supposed to.
Turns out, having a heart attack is ***pretty expensive.***
That doesn't seem fair.
No, it really doesn't. It's going to be tough, but if they'll let us do a payment plan, we should be OK.

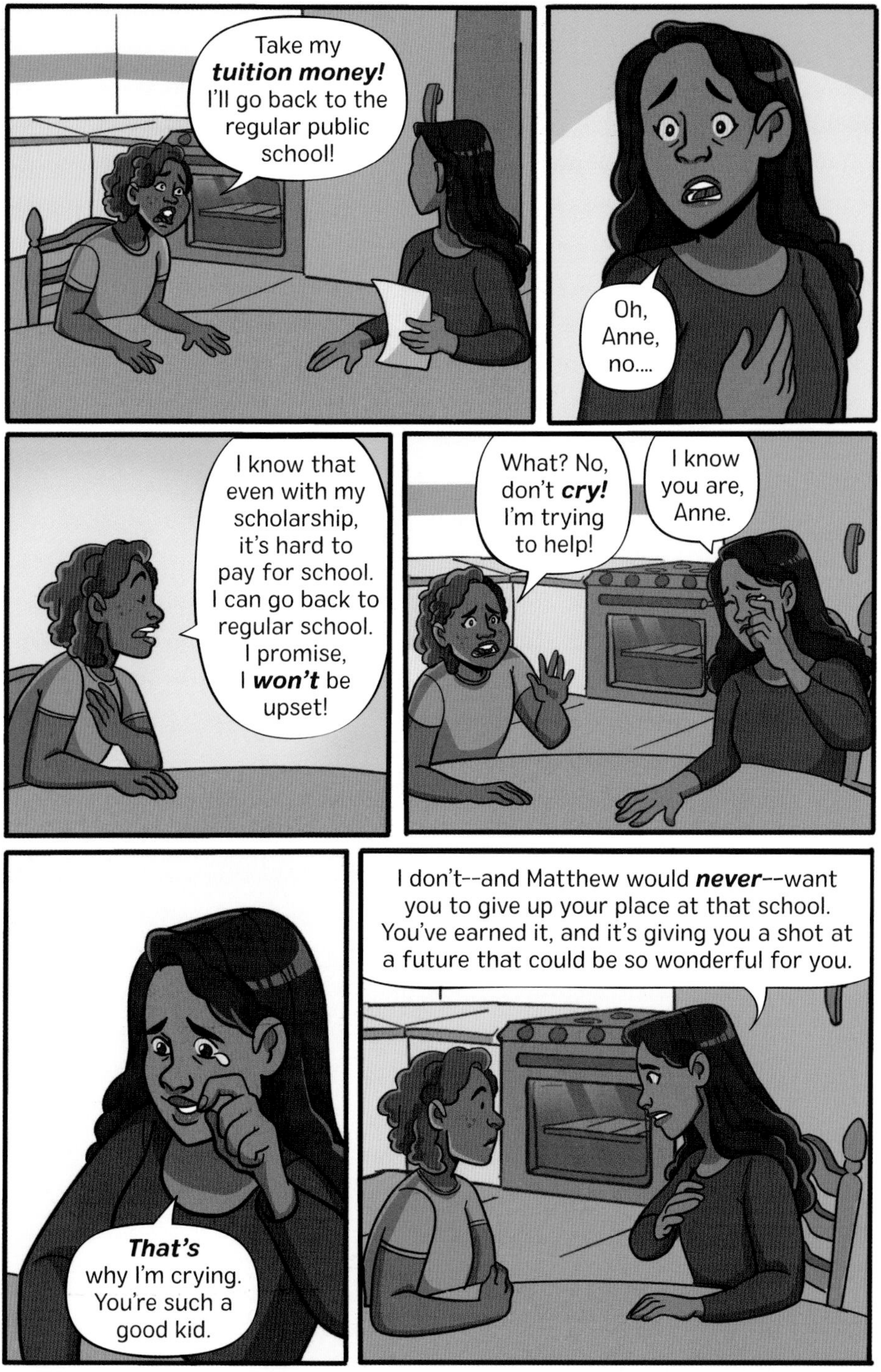
Take my ***tuition money!*** I'll go back to the regular public school!
Oh, Anne, no....
I know that even with my scholarship, it's hard to pay for school. I can go back to regular school. I promise, I ***won't*** be upset!
What? No, don't ***cry!*** I'm trying to help!
I know you are, Anne.
That's why I'm crying. You're such a good kid.
I don't--and Matthew would ***never***--want you to give up your place at that school. You've earned it, and it's giving you a shot at a future that could be so wonderful for you.

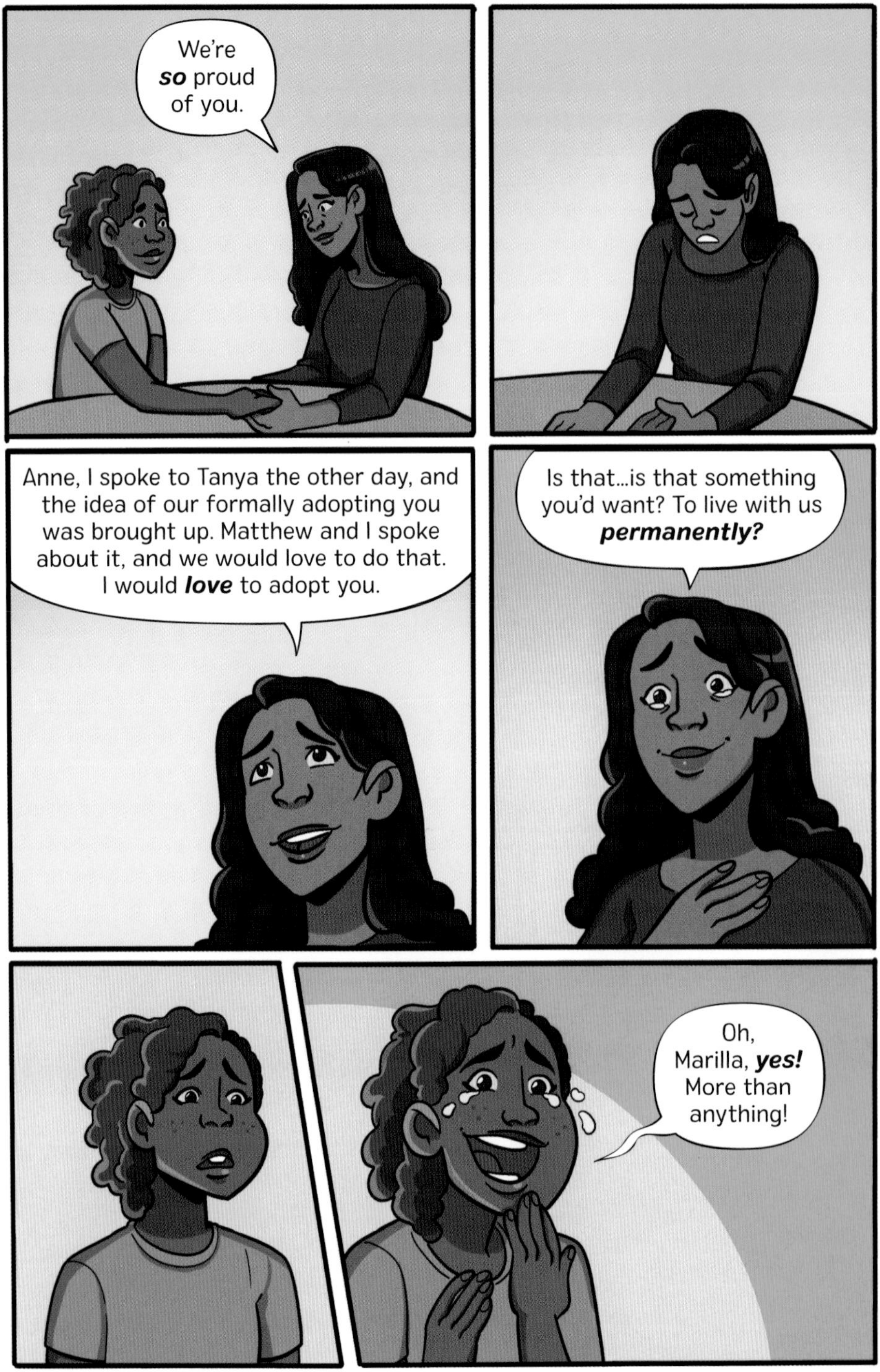
We're **so** proud of you.
Anne, I spoke to Tanya the other day, and the idea of our formally adopting you was brought up. Matthew and I spoke about it, and we would love to do that. I would **love** to adopt you.
Is that...is that something you'd want? To live with us **permanently?**
Oh, Marilla, **yes!** More than anything!

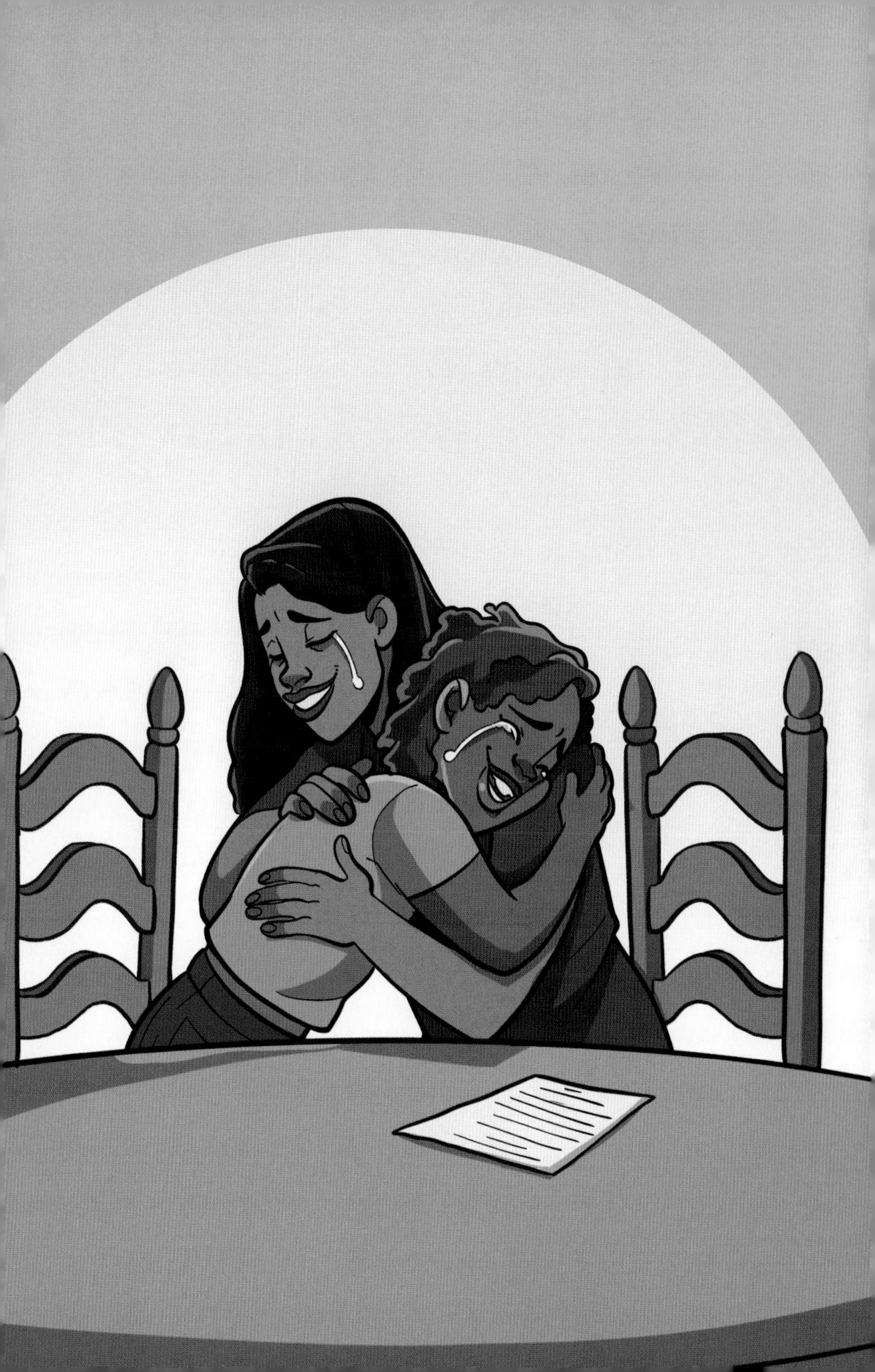

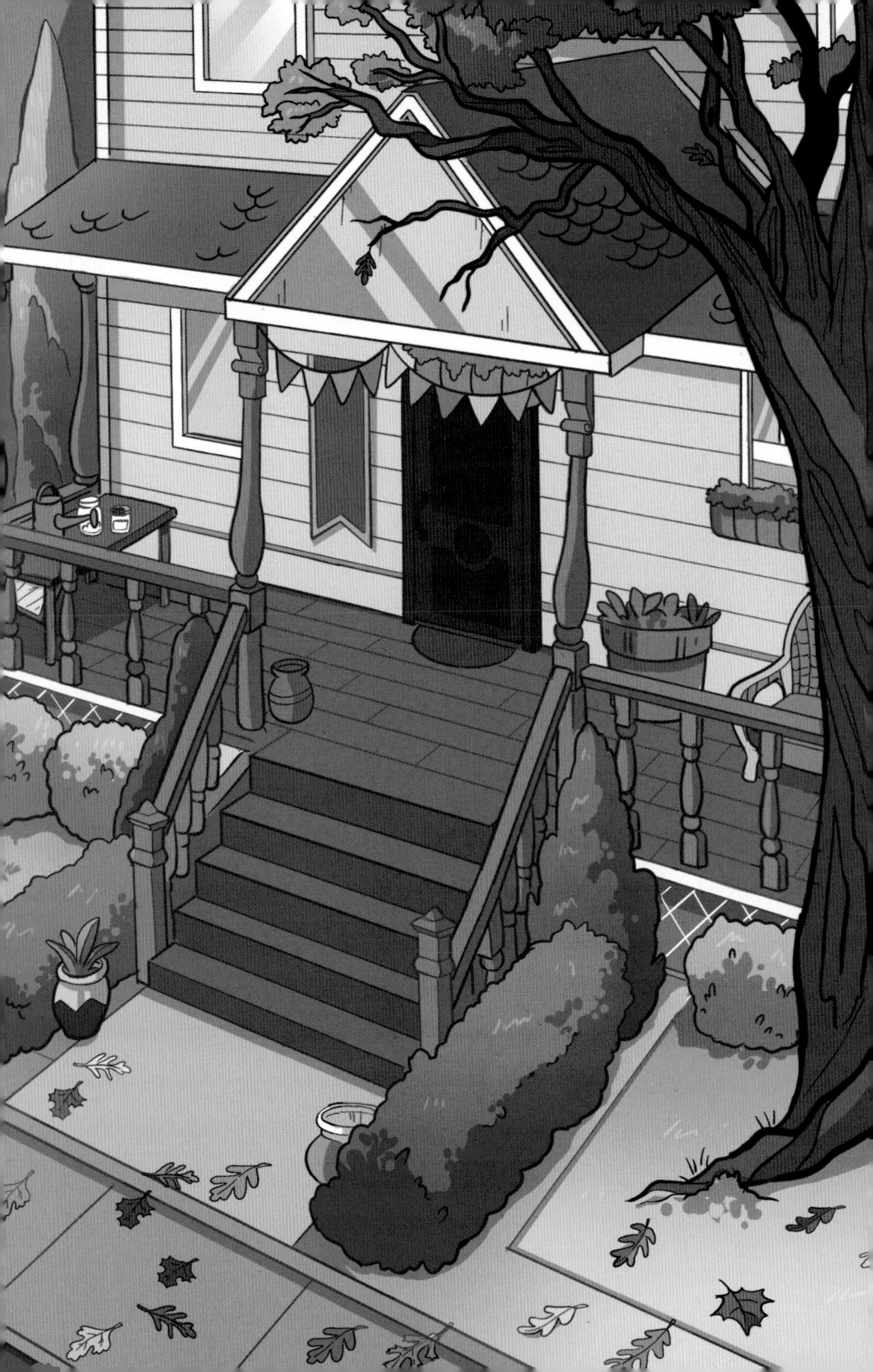

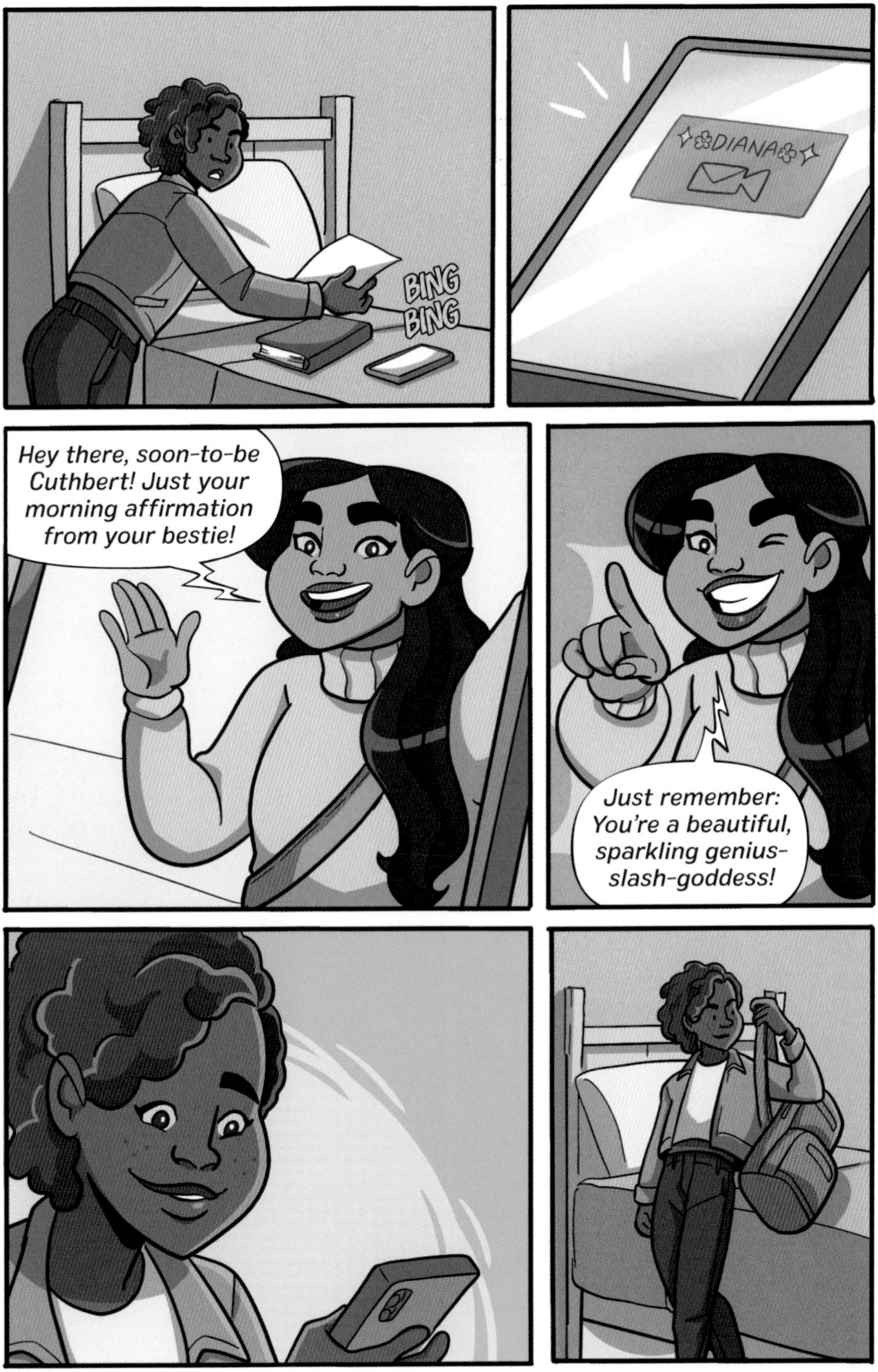
BING BING
DIANA
Hey there, soon-to-be Cuthbert! Just your morning affirmation from your bestie!
Just remember: You're a beautiful, sparkling genius-slash-goddess!

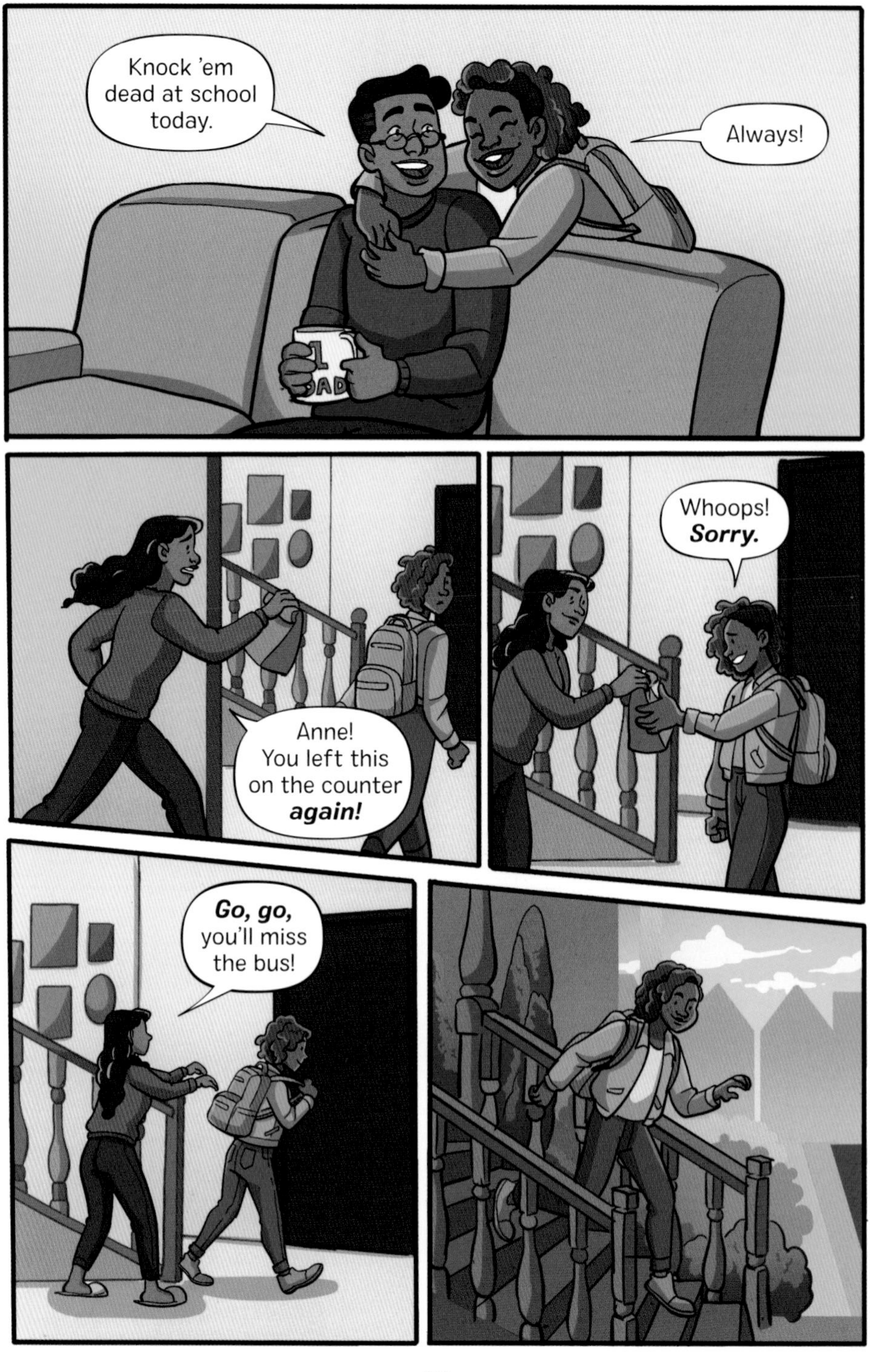
Knock 'em dead at school today.
Always!
Anne! You left this on the counter ***again!***
Whoops! ***Sorry.***
Go, go, you'll miss the bus!

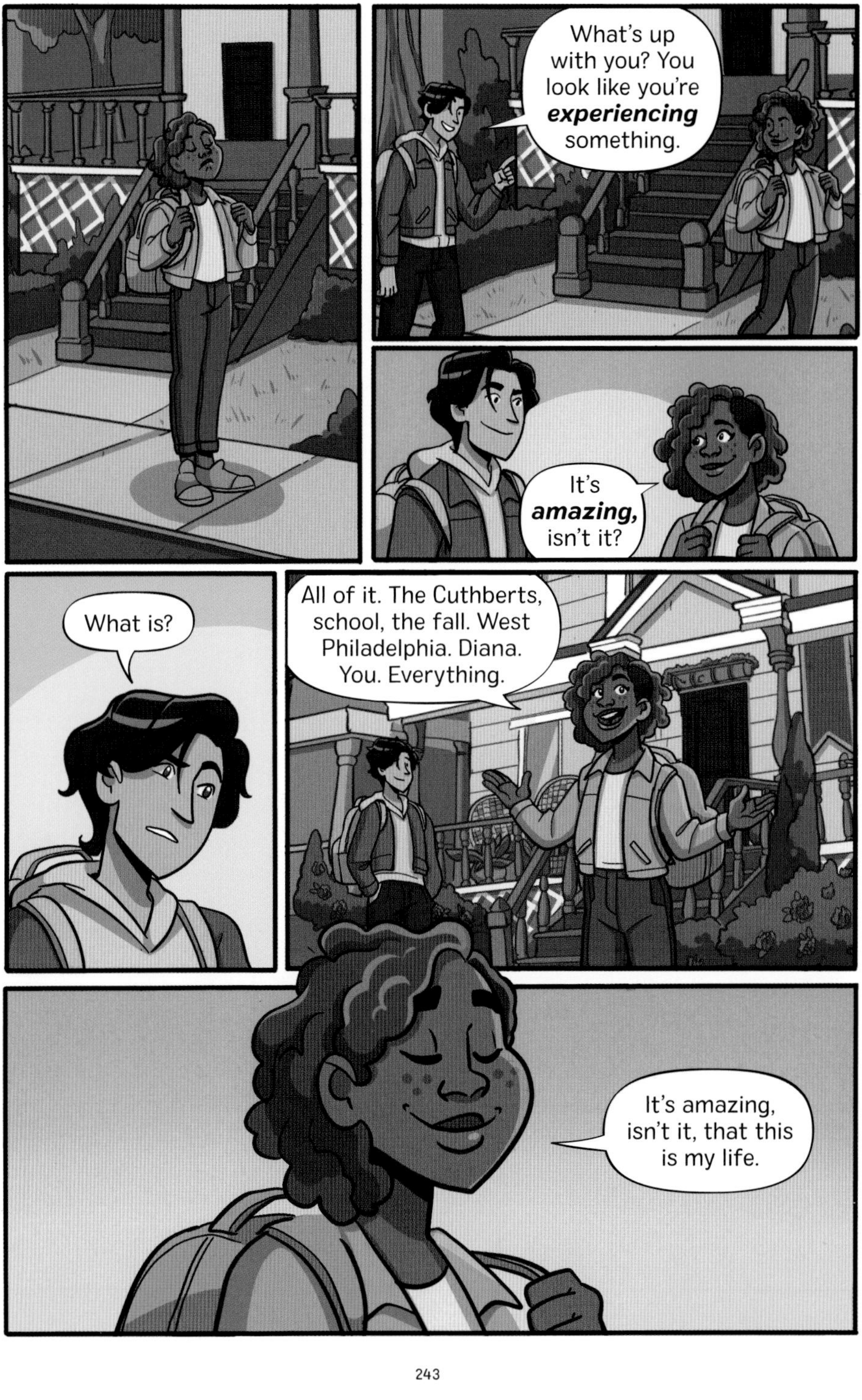
What's up with you? You look like you're ***experiencing*** something.
It's ***amazing,*** isn't it?
What is?
All of it. The Cuthberts, school, the fall. West Philadelphia. Diana. You. Everything.
It's amazing, isn't it, that this is my life.

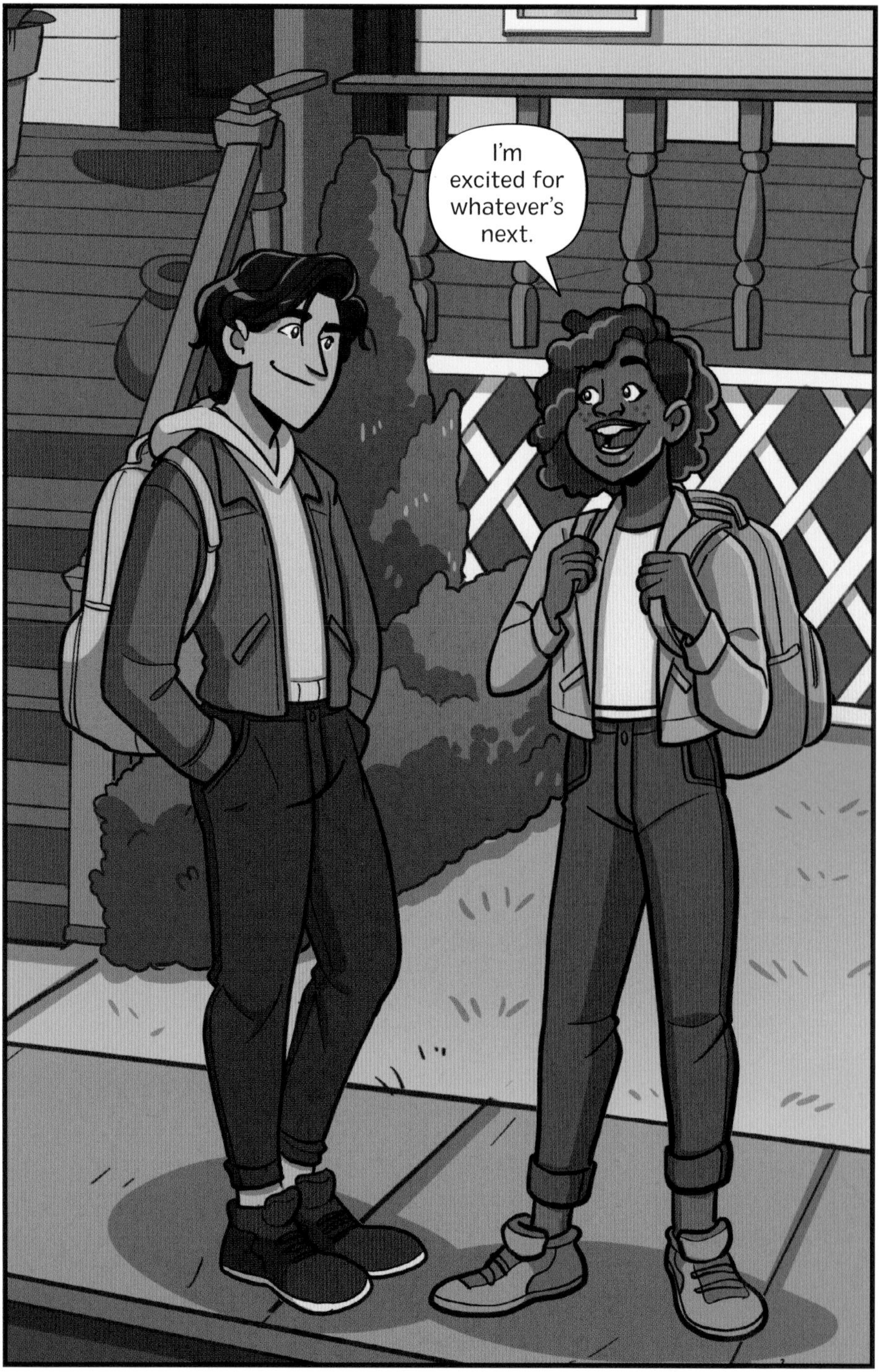
I'm excited for whatever's next.

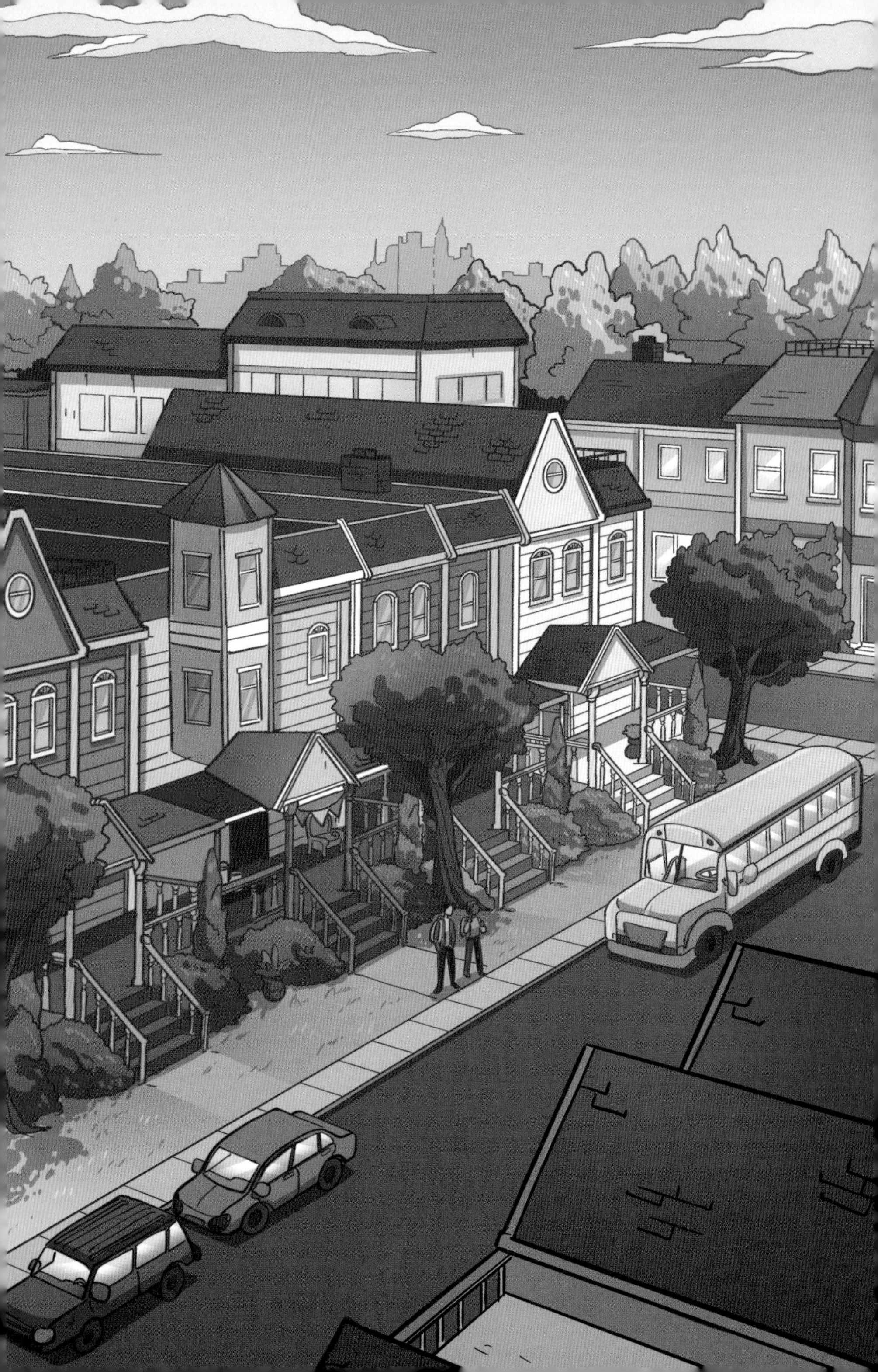

Eugene K. Ahn

Ivy Noelle Weir

is a writer of comics and prose. She is the
author of *The Secret Garden on 81st Street*
and the cocreator of the Dwayne McDuffie
Award–winning graphic novel *Archival Quality*.
Her writing has also appeared in anthologies
such as *Princeless: Girls Rock* and *Dead Beats*.
She lives in the greater Boston area with her
husband and their two tiny, weird dogs.

Myisha Haynes

is a Sacramento-based comic creator who loves creating BIPOC-focused stories about friendships, adventure, and self-discovery. Besides her modern fantasy webcomic, *The Substitutes*, her work can also be seen in the award-winning anthology *Elements: Fire*; *Rolled & Tolled*; *Power & Magic: Volume 2*; and Marvel's *The Unbelievable Gwenpool*. *Anne of West Philly* is her first graphic novel.

Author Acknowledgments

Huge thanks to my agent, Anjali Singh, for her wisdom and guidance, and my editor, Rachel Poloski, for her insightful notes and enthusiasm. All the love to my husband, Eugene, for his endless support and encouraging me to take a break when I need it. Love to my mom for always encouraging my writing (and for all the coffee drop-offs). Huge thanks to Steenz for hyping me up and letting me try out my dad jokes on her first, and to Randy Trang for the rides home from work so I could get to writing faster.